"Fair or no, do you fancy explaining to a man with a sword why he has to wait?"

The man nodded, apparently satisfied by this pragmatic answer, then resumed his nervous study of the rapidly closing wind funnels.

Bregor watched with him. He'd earlier estimated perhaps two hundred people would remain this side of Suggate when the whirlwinds arrived—which they would, and soon, if they continued their present heading. *Maybe only one hundred*, he thought hopefully. The winds had slowed down, as though they searched . . . No, the fisherman was the one who always seemed to come up with a supernatural explanation for events. *It's a spring storm, that's all.* An enormous storm. No, an *unheard-of* storm. One that had chosen—no, not chosen, surely—had *come ashore* coincidentally at the same time as an invading Neherian fleet. One that had spawned five whirlwinds—four slender fingers and one enormous thumb—that searched the city, looking for . . . well, by all evidence, looking for Noetos.

Of course it's not a natural storm.

Praise for the Fire of Heaven Trilogy

"A joyous experience for readers who love getting lost in a complex fictional world . . ."

— scifi.com on *Across the Face of the World*

"The first book in this ⟨ ⟩d has held me spellbour⟨ ⟩ exciting events."

"A massive and absorbi⟨ ⟩ respecting Tolkienite a⟨ ⟩ — *The Age*

By *Russell Kirkpatrick*

The Fire of Heaven Trilogy

Across the Face of the World
In the Earth Abides the Flame
The Right Hand of God

The Broken Man Trilogy

Path of Revenge
Dark Heart
Beyond the Wall of Time

RUSSELL KIRKPATRICK

DARK HEART

orbit

www.orbitbooks.net

New York London

Maps by Russell Kirkpatrick

Orbit
Hachette Book Group
237 Park Avenue
New York, NY 10017
Visit our Web site at www.orbitbooks.net

Orbit is an imprint of Hachette Book Group, Inc.
The Orbit name and logo is a trademark of Little, Brown Book Group Ltd.

Printed in the United States of America

Originally published by HarperCollins*Publishers* Australia Pty Limited
First Orbit trade paperback edition in Great Britain: December 2008
First Orbit mass market edition in the USA: December 2008

10 9 8 7 6 5 4 3 2 1

To Alex,
with love

CONTENTS

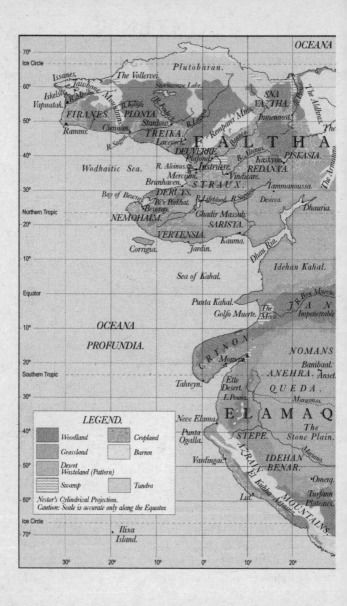

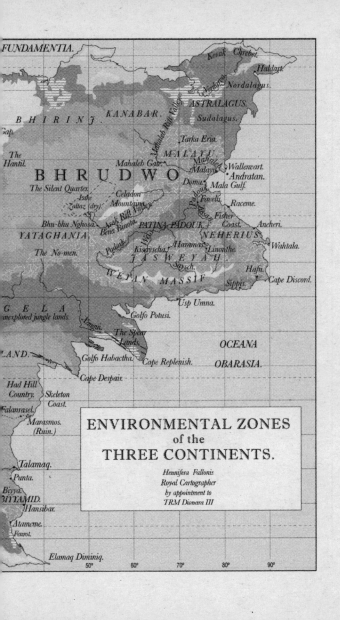

FUNDAMENTIA.

Kovak Chrebet.

Haldart.

Nordalagus.

ASTRALAGUS.

Sudalagus.

KANABAR.

B H I R I N J.

Tarka Eria.

M A L A Y U.

Gap.

The Hantil.

Mahaleb Gate.

Mahaleb Malayu.

Wallenwart.

Andratan.

B H R U D W O

Doma.

Mala Gulf.

The Silent Quarter.

Celadon

Fuwelli.

Raceme.

Lake Zaltaz (dry).

Mountains.

Fisher

Coast.

Ancheri.

Bhu-bhu Nghosa.

Bena Binota.

PATINA PADOUK.

NEHERIUS.

Wahtala.

YATAGHANIA.

Padugh.

Kisav.

Haramas.

Linonthe.

The No-men.

Kisavyscha.

J A S W E Y A H.

Savach.

Hafn.

W E F A N   M A S S I F

Sippis.

Cape Discord.

Usp Umna.

G E L A

unexplored jungle lands.

Golfo Potusi.

Venna.

The Spear Lands.

O C E A N A

LAND.

Golfo Habactha.

Cape Replenish.

O B A R A S I A.

Cape Despair.

Had Hill Country.

Skeleton Coast.

Falamrasel.

Marasmos. (Ruin.)

Talamaq.

Punta.

Bivya.

BIYYAMID.

Hansibar.

Atameme.

Fenrot.

Elamaq Diminiq.

ENVIRONMENTAL ZONES
of the
THREE CONTINENTS.

Hennifera Fallonis
Royal Cartographer
by appointment to
TRM Dionara III

50°   60°   70°   80°   90°

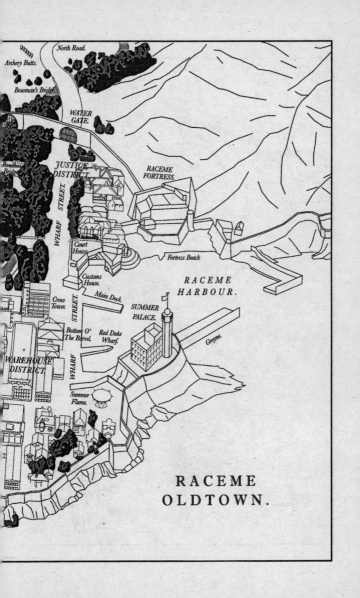

Archery Butts.

North Road.

Bowman's Bridge.

WATER GATE.

JUSTICE DISTRICT.

RACEME FORTRESS.

Rowshan Bridge.

WHARF STREET.

Court House.

Customs House.

Fortress Beach.

RACEME HARBOUR.

Crow Tower.

Main Dock.

WHARF STREET.

SUMMER PALACE.

Bottom O' The Barrel.

Red Duke Wharf.

WAREHOUSE DISTRICT.

WHARF STREET.

Groyne.

Summer Flame.

RACEME
OLDTOWN.

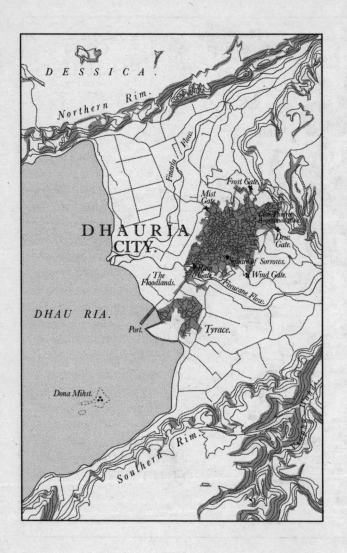

MALAYU.

OLD ROUDHOS.
and surrounding dukedoms.

Myserrie.

Mahaleh

Malayu.

Wallenvart.

Bartoul. *Zyrma.*

Andratan.

Doma. *Mala Gulf.*

Make sure N. learns these boundaries.
Get him to recite all capitals & major cities.
— *Demos Roudhos*

Camantain.

Padouk. *Long Pike Mouth.*

Cape Mala.

Favelu

PATINA
PADOUK.

Sayonae.

Foulwater.

*Fisher
Coast.*

Farmer's Flat

IHKNOS.

Tylosse.

Raceme.

SAROS.

Tochar *Makyra.*

Tussan.

OLD

Altima *Fossa.*

Tussan. *Agakoussa*

Aneheri.

NORD

PALESTRA.

AMOGY.

Ruse Budasti.

NEHERIUS.

Haramas.

ROUDHOS

Herceg.

Jass.

Linonthe

Rovec.

Wahlala.

Lamphor.

SUD

LAK.

Arnu Gospa.

JASWEYAH.

AMOGY

FARN.

Alta Massa.

Saysch.

MASSIF.

HAFNIA.

Pul.

Hafn.

WEYAN

SARTSKA.

*Cape
Discord.*

ERCEKSE

Arsanthe.

Sippis.

Kastaina.

Nuckle.

Return this map to the Main Library, Raceme Summer Palace.

DARK
HEART

PROLOGUE

MAGIC HOWLS LIKE A GALE through Husk's mind. Power, irresistible as a river in flood, batters at his besieged sense of self, threatening to overwhelm him. Iron-hard fingers tear at the connections to his treasured spikes, the spikes linking him to the three people essential to his plan. Glowing blue gobbets spin off, shards of power lodging themselves in forgotten corners of his ruined body, searing skin, organs, bones. Magic, for so long his life-blood, might well destroy him.

Husk cannot believe there is this much magic in the world. And this is remarkable because he is a magician himself.

He has been exposed to powerful magic before, power few have seen. He remembers the day, seventy years ago now, when he was betrayed. Brought, bound with magic, into the Undying Man's presence to answer for his treachery. In the abyssal hours that followed he learned why the Undying Man had been named "Destroyer". So much magic, so expertly wielded, a thousand tiny knives separating skin from flesh, bits of him flaking into the darkness, every nerve ending exposed, the cold stone floor awash with his blood. More than enough to kill him. Drowning in pain, drowning in blood, drowning in the magic, his own considerable skill overwhelmed by that of his master.

Yet amidst the torture the Destroyer inadvertently gave him a gift. Not immortality, not exactly. A binding was laid on him, designed to preserve his ruined body as a husk, encapsulating his pain forever. Making him a creature able only to comprehend suffering. A cruelty beyond even Husk's darkest visions. But the spell was too powerful. Husk has harnessed the magic of the spell, has pierced the cocoon surrounding him and learned to draw life from those around him. Has taken the name of what he became and wears it proudly as a badge of honour. He has survived in the Destroyer's dungeon, masking his condition from the Lord of Andratan, building his strength.

Setting his great plan of revenge in motion.

He will have his betrayer, yes. The one he himself wooed from the Most High's cause; she who began as a simple Falthan village girl and whom he elevated to become the Destroyer's consort. Stella Pellwen. She who then turned on him and convinced the Undying Man of his disloyalty. She who knelt in the cave and watched as the Destroyer broke him. The last thing he saw, before the bright blue knives came for his eyes, was her shoulders shaking as she laughed.

He will take her as the final act of his revenge, right there in the Tower of Farsight, in front of the Undying Man's remains. Will take her, his rotted, repellent body on hers, then will drain her immortal blood. Slowly. He will make her agony last forever. He knows how, after all; and continues to pay a bitter price for the knowledge. She will be his ever-dying queen.

Not madness, Husk tells himself, to plan such a thing. It is necessary to balance what has been done to him.

This is the vision sustaining him, its dark promise giving him the tenacity to maintain contact with his three scattered spikes.

Though not so scattered now. Something is happening. A profligate expenditure of magic creates a hole in the world through which a god's hand reaches, snatching his Amaqi captain, spike and all, along with the Emperor—so vital to his plans—and the pet Omeran. And the cosmographer girl. Snatches them right out of the world, weakening Husk's connection to the captain to breaking point, and dumps them back in it a moment later, somewhere much closer. He cannot begin to search for them, to try to re-establish his hold on the captain, until the magic roaring through the world calms down.

At least he knows where his angel Arathé is. She has spent nearly two weeks at sea, brought north to Raceme by friends of her foolish father, and is now safe within the city's strong walls. Raceme has never fallen to an enemy; he of all people knows this, having once invested it himself at the behest of the Undying Man. However, Raceme has never before faced the combined assault of the Neherian fleet and a magical storm. Perhaps she is not so safe, then. But, at present, beyond his help.

His priest is the safest of the three. Trust that one to look after his own worthless skin. The priest serves only to lure Stella westward, though it is beginning to appear as though she needs very little luring. *Curse her!* Because of what is happening to his other two spikes, Husk watches for any hint of a magical disturbance around Conal the priest. Apart from a strange flash at one point as the party passed through the desert, he has seen nothing assailing them; nothing like the great magical loci interfering with Captain Duon and Arathé.

So. One lost, one threatened, one safe. His plan has never been guaranteed to succeed. In the face of interference from the gods, it may well fail. Nevertheless, Husk does not give up hope. His revenge can only be delayed, not denied. After all, Stella is immortal. So, it seems, is he. How, then, can she escape him?

FISHERMAN

CHAPTER 1

THE FINGERS OF GOD

NOETOS THE FISHERMAN REACHED OUT a trembling hand to his daughter. The daughter he had thought dead.

At this moment nothing else mattered: not the threat to Raceme, not the approaching Neherian fleet, not the coming storm. His fingers hovered above hers.

Don't touch her, part of his mind warned. He stiffened. *What about the huanu stone?* The stone, of which he apparently had the largest piece known, stole magic from whatever it touched. What would it do to Arethé, so strong in the Voice magic?

You old fool, he chided himself, and blew out a relieved breath. *You left it in your room.*

You old fool, he chided himself. *You left it in your room.*

As his fingers touched hers he allowed himself to believe what his eyes told him. He knew of waking dreams, but had never experienced one: this must be what they felt like. The coarseness of her skin, calloused along her once-fine fingers; the unflattering weight of her, surprising despite his knowing how she had been mistreated by her supposed teachers. But, notwithstanding all this, warmth where he had expected the coldness of death. He had, after all, seen her with a knife buried in her back.

A waking dream or reality—which was it? After all that had happened to him and his family, could Noetos really argue there was a difference? As his mind wandered, the dream-like feeling intensified.

Of course he remembered Arathé couldn't talk, her tongue having been taken by the cruel masters of Andratan, along with so many other things. Yet, as he grasped her hand and pulled her up to the wharf, he could not stop himself asking the question.

"How?"

Arathé shrugged her shoulders in reply. As he watched, her eyes flicked left and right, as though looking for something or someone, widening when they rested a moment on her brother, Anomer, then flicking again, searching.

"Muhh?" she said, her tongueless mouth unable to shape the word. "Muh-huh?"

Noetos knew who Arathé was looking for.

"She . . . she . . ." He could barely bring himself to say it. "She is dead."

But it wasn't my fault, he wanted to add. He couldn't: Arathé would know it for a lie. His foolish plan to rescue her mother and brother at Saros Rake had cost Opuntia her life. And, to be honest, he'd cared much more about his son's survival than that of his wife.

There. I've admitted it.

His daughter's sunken eyes widened slightly, then narrowed, as she stared into his eyes. Her hand, still clasping his, tightened around his fingers. A fraction of a second later she jerked him forward.

He tried to keep his balance, but as he stumbled past her she pushed him, hard. He overbalanced, then fell from the wharf and plunged into the water, narrowly missing his boat.

The Racemen kept their harbour dredged, artificially deep. Within seconds he was at the bottom, knees on the muddy sea floor.

Cast away, his mind screamed at him. *She cast me away*.

He could see only a few feet through the murk, and for a moment could make nothing of his surroundings. Dark hull shapes, grey clouds, the flickering silhouettes of fish. He would not drown, he told himself; he was the Fisher, a man comfortable in the water. It was only shock that pinned his arms to his side. Only shock. His daughter hated him. If his daughter hated him, he must truly have mishandled things. Opuntia's death—was Arathé blaming him? She could know nothing of the circumstances, yet she had already decided he was to blame, as though she had developed some kind of mind-reading ability.

She cast me away!

His limbs were heavy, so heavy. Nevertheless, he began to move them, sluggishly at first. He needed to explain things to her before Anomer and Bregor filled her ears with their view of events. Actually, he needed to breathe.

It's not all my fault!

Something snagged the collar of his tunic, pulling him back, and his head jerked forward. His mouth opened involuntarily and the last of his air bubbled from his lips.

*   *   *

"He's not dead," said someone.

"It'll take more than a dousing to kill this fool," said someone else.

"Fuhh, fuhh, fuhh," a third voice repeated. It sounded distressed.

"He's all right, Arathé," said the first voice. "He's breathing."

Hardness under his back, water on his face, light in his eyes, the sounds of concern in his ears.

"We need to move him. The Neherians will be ashore in a moment, Alkuon curse them." The second voice was agitated. "Can't leave him for them, much as I'd like to."

"You grab his legs then," a new voice said. "I'll take his arms."

"No!" Noetos gasped, then coughed. The light coalesced into a ring of faces staring down at him. Arathé, Bregor, Anomer, Sautea, Mustar. "I can stand," he said. "Give me a moment."

He barely made it to his feet. Anomer placed a steadying hand on the small of his back. His son's wet clothes told Noetos who had pulled him from the water.

The fisherman glanced at Arathé. His daughter averted her face.

He wanted her to explain why she'd pushed him from the wharf; he wanted to hear her say "Father, it was an accident", to tell him that really she loved him and understood he'd tried his best to save his family from the Recruiters. But another part of him admired her for not saying anything of the sort, for holding her silence. He knew her rejection of him, whatever the motivation, had some justification. His plan, however cruelly undermined by Omiy the alchemist, had been a poor one to start with.

Noetos looked out to sea. So much needed to be said, but they were out of time. The storm was upon them, white sails followed by swirling black clouds.

The Fossans watched as the lead Neherian vessel dropped her canvas, but not before one of her foremast sails parted company with the rigging, torn by the gusting wind. Shouting sailors wrestled the shredded white material to the deck. For a moment it appeared as though the ship would founder, her skipper distracted, but the sailors recovered and, with an astonishing flurry of ropes and bodies, brought her broadside to the wharf.

They shouldn't have been able to do that, Noetos thought. Not with the strength of wind behind them. Curse the Neherians, call them what you like, but they were excellent sailors. They had come within an armspan of crushing his own boat.

Green- and white-clad soldiers raced to oppose the vessel's landing. Their shouts sounded desperate rather than confident. As he drew his sword, Noetos began to wonder about the city's impregnability. *Have they been training their soldiers in the city's defences? Do they even have a defensive plan?* Mild concern grew towards outright worry.

The fisherman took a deep breath. "Anomer," he said, raising his voice against the wind and the shouts of the city's defenders. "Take your sister and wait for me at the Man-o'-War. She'll be hungry; ask the innkeeper to feed her." His son began to speak, but the fisherman continued. "We can spare you, at least for a while. It'll take some time for the Neherians to offload."

"Never, if we have our way," Bregor put in.

"But, Father," Anomer said anxiously, "you are not yet recovered, and the city needs my sword."

"Look after Arathé. Don't argue!"

Noetos turned away from his children, ending the discussion. *I will not lose either of them. Not now, not when they have only just been returned to me.*

Further along the wharf Captain Cohamma barked an order, made unintelligible to Noetos by the whistling wind and the man's broad accent. From behind a low wall a brace of archers stood, then let fly at the Neherian carrack with burning arrows. *In this wind?* Cohamma seemed to be the sort of commander who could not adapt to changing conditions. Worse and worse. One arrow caught in the tatters of the ripped sail; another took a fair-haired man in the chest. Soundlessly he toppled over the side. *Lucky. I hope you have a thousand arrows, Cohamma. The masters of the other Neherian vessels might think twice about entering a burning harbour.*

"Ware!" came a cry from somewhere off to the left.

Noetos turned to see a smaller Neherian ship hove to against the groyne; in what was obviously a well-rehearsed move, sword-wielding sailors scrambled down netting hanging over the side of the ship. The first vessel had been a distraction. The main attack was now taking place.

Noetos barely had time to check that Anomer and Arathé had obeyed him before the Neherians fell upon him and his men.

There was something about the man who came at him—the way the Neherian held his sword perhaps, or the overconfident grin splitting his narrow face—that transported Noetos back to a clearing in a southern wood.

He had been a man, a man full grown, but the Neherians

had held him as easily as if he were a boy, and wore wide grins as they forced him to watch what they did to his father and family.

Noetos ground his teeth in rage. *Am I doomed to return to this place of shame every time I fight? Will this end only when I am rid of the last sword-wielding Neherian?* With difficulty he forced his mind back to the man in front of him.

The fisherman's movements were almost automatic. Defend the Neherian's best attacks, give no ground, show him nothing, and let the courage drain from the man's limbs. A few weeks with his sword in his hand and Noetos felt as though it had always been there. One upward feint, relying on fear to draw his opponent into an overreaction, then a slash across the man's unprotected belly. Not deep enough to kill immediately, but more than sufficient to bring suffering before death, as was proper. Ignore the body as it falls, as another enemy steps over it.

The memories in his head, his futile struggling in the grip of his family's executioners all those years ago, balanced with the death he was bringing to those who opposed him on the wharf and left him blank, an empty automaton, free from the anger he usually felt when challenged. The Neherians had set him free after slaughtering his family, perhaps believing him broken, a living caution against opposing their power—the best reason he could come up with. And of course he had been broken. Why else had he hidden in Fossa all those years?

But now he fought against them. He fought, not out of anger or fear, but from some deeper place. He grew weary, though nowhere near as swiftly as he ought. His fourth opponent fell, punished with the loss of a hand for pressing too hard, then slain with a blade in the chest.

Anomer and Arathé were his deeper place, he realised. Together they were doing something magical to aid him. The strength infusing him was more than his desire to protect them, his need to prevent the Neherians from getting past him and gaining access to the Man-o'-War. His children using that desire, cleaving their strength to it, granting him unnatural speed and endurance. And, most of all, freedom from the emotion that so often spurred him into recklessness.

They probably thought he didn't know what they were doing. It ought to anger him, their deception. He should be worried about the cost to them. But he could raise no anger. No fear, nothing. No pity for his next opponent, the fuzz under the lad's nose betraying his youth, his spraying blood choking his dying scream for someone, his mother most likely.

A thought. If his son and daughter could supply him strength, could they also read his mind? Was that the basis for Arathé's initial anger towards him?

"Fisher."

Someone called out to a fisherman, a meaningless cry barely noticed in the midst of battle. Nothing to do with him.

The dark figure in front of him waved his sword with energy but little skill. Did these fighters represent the best of Neherius? If so, how had that mighty army fallen so far? An inside cut, a swift withdrawal, then a low flick, hamstringing the man. Let the Neherian grunt his pain on the wooden planks of the wharf, let him spill his blood over the timbers of the town he sought to take.

"Fisher!"

No one in front of him. A meaty hand slapped him on his shoulder.

"Come, Noetos," said a voice. Mustar. "There is nothing more we can do here."

The fisherman blinked. Death lay scattered all about him. Ten bodies, more, a dozen. His gaze took in the ships—a score or more now filling the harbour, a number of them aflame—and the hundreds of armed men leaping into the water and wading for the shore. But not in panic. This was planned. There was no urgency to douse the flames. The Neherians were intent on taking the town.

Perhaps the storm would save their ships for them. It had begun to rain while Noetos fought; large, cold drops, not that he had realised. Well, his dispassionate mind had factored in the sudden slipperiness underfoot, so he must have noticed. The rain slashed at them, stinging his face. How had he been able to fight this? What had his children done to him?

"Captain Cohamma wants us up on Broad Way behind the barricades. Come on."

He turned to follow Mustar, his mind still fogged by events. Fogged, in fact, since Saros Rake. Why else, he asked himself, would he be following the most junior of the fishermen he employed?

Once employed, he corrected himself.

Belatedly he tried to clear his thoughts. "Broad Way? What use is that?" he asked. "We have to keep the Neherians outside the walls."

"Too late for that, Fisher."

The lad was right. A hundred or more Neherians had formed up on Red Duke Wharf, now off to his left as he faced the city, and were marching unhurriedly towards the Summer Palace, where no doubt the governor cowered in disbelief and fear. The governor was right to fear the Neherians. Much of Wharf Street was burning. Fire had taken hold of a tavern: Bottom O' The Barrel it had been called in Noetos's day. Men were trying to break into Crow Tower, the tallest building on the wharf. The docks were lost.

"We have to go. We'll be trapped here otherwise."

Again, the lad was right. *Where are your wits, fisherman? Did you leave them at the bottom of the harbour?* Broad Way would not make much of a defence, but it was clear the Warehouse District could not be saved. They had to make a stand somewhere.

"This way, Mustar," Noetos cried, and led the youth along Wharf Street, past Red Duke Wharf and then up Summer Way, away from the harbour. Behind them the Neherian regiment passed the Summer Flame, the enormous bowl-shaped symbol of Roudhos sovereignty appropriated by Raceme many years since. A great gust of wind roared past the Summer Palace, flattening the flame, all but extinguishing it. Noetos sighed. The sight had all the hallmarks of an omen.

"Where are my men?" he asked.

"Do you mean the miners?" Mustar said.

"Aye, they are pledged to me."

Mustar seemed already to know about them. "Dead or fled."

"They abandoned me?"

"They had no choice. None could stand with you. Fisher, where did you learn to fight with such speed and skill? Why did you waste your life in Fossa? You could have earned a princely living serving any master you wished." There was more than a hint of hero worship in the boy's voice.

"Hush," Noetos said, too late. Their conversation, half-shouted because of the wind and rain, had attracted attention. Two Neherians emerged from an alley, dragging a woman by her legs. At the sight of the two fishermen they dropped their burden and drew their blades.

"It's not skill," Noetos said as he reached past his anger and shame. Yes, his children still waited for him, ready to supply him strength. *Thank you*, he whispered.

Three swift steps forward, one to the left, then a transfer of weight to his right leg accompanied by an upward swing, fierce enough to knock the sword out of one man's grasp and still have enough momentum to take him in the throat. Fall back, two defensive parries. The second man threw his sword down and fell to one knee, ready to sue for peace.

"Peace? After what you have done?"

Noetos had once been told by an experienced swordsman that there was in these days neither sword sharp enough nor arm strong enough to decapitate a man with one blow. Now he would find out. He swung before the Neherian had a chance to beg.

Cyclamere, you were wrong, he thought as the head bounced and rolled. *Though, to be fair, there were three arms in that blow.*

"Not skill?" Mustar said, panting, his shellfish knife wet with blood and rainwater. "Then you are not human."

"Most likely not," Noetos agreed without rancour. He laid his sword down at the mouth of the alley, then bent over with Mustar to examine the woman for signs of life.

The youngster swallowed. "Bastards." Her womanhood

was a red mess. "Alkuon-forsaken bastards. They must have used their swords on her."

"Say 'Neherians' and nothing more need be said," Noetos growled, his stomach turning over. "They must have been disposing of the evidence. The Neherian commanders would not object to such behaviour, but they would insist on securing the city first." He sighed. "Come, there is nothing to be done for her. We have to get to Broad Way, and the storm is getting worse."

The black clouds squatted overhead, filling Noetos's mind with unpleasant imagery. Rain pounded ferociously, hissing in sheets across the paved streets, and darkness closed in around them like a besieging army. Thunder rolled, or perhaps it was an explosion. Orange light flickered away to their right, painting the underside of the clouds a dun colour.

He turned to Mustar who, for all the circumstances, still looked the same lad who had worked on Noetos's boat. "Some of my men are dead?" he asked him.

"Don't know. They fought beside you for a few minutes, then were driven back by the Neherians. At least one was injured that I saw. Young fellow."

"And you?"

Mustar smiled. "Give me a gaff and I could do some damage, but I barely know which end of a sword to hold. That Captain Cohamma tried to press a sword on me, but in the end I helped shift stuff about while others did the hard work."

"Nothing's changed then."

"That's what I was thinking." Mustar laughed, but there was no real humour in it.

They walked uphill along Summer Way for a few minutes, keeping to the darkness under the warehouse eaves. Apart from a single body lying in a doorway, the street seemed deserted. Rain sizzled as it pelted the timbers of the warehouses and the cobbles of Summer Way; at either side of the street water collected in runnels and ran foaming down towards the harbour, as though gathering to repel the Neherians.

Mustar said something to him. Noetos didn't catch it, the words blurred by the whistling wind and a low growl of thunder.

A score or more soldiers appeared at the far end of Summer Way, a few hundred paces away and well above them, at the crest of a steep slope. Mustar seized Noetos's arm and hauled him into an alley, not much more than a narrow gap between warehouses.

"I couldn't tell whether they were Neherians or Racemen," the young man said. He poked his head cautiously into the street, then drew it back quickly. "Did you hear what I asked you? I said, were you responsible for what happened at Fossa?"

"Fossa? That depends on what happened."

Noetos wasn't sure he wanted to be told, but he knew he'd hear the story eventually. Like all the stories these days it'd likely be a terrible one. Yet he wanted to hear how his daughter had cheated death. And, despite how the village had treated him the night the Recruiters were there, he supposed he wanted to know if Fossa had survived the Neherians.

"Well, this is the short of it," Mustar said, his eyes darkening as he drew on his memories. "It started with the business of Anomer and the Recruiters, and the disturbance up at Fisher House. You know more of that than me, and no doubt things happened differently than the Hegeoman let out."

"What did he say?" Noetos said quickly. He had not thought to ask Bregor this.

"Just that you'd gone crazy and assaulted the Recruiters when they came to collect your son to take him to Andratan. Seemed you'd thought twice about having allowed Anomer to take part in the trials that morning, and you'd decided you didn't want to lose both your children, so you opposed the Recruiters with your sword."

"You believe it?"

"Ah, well, the part about you changing your mind I believed," Mustar said. "Forgive me, Fisher, but you'd been hard to work with those last few weeks. Didn't take a genius to figure you were doubtful about sending Anomer north to Andratan."

"Was it that obvious?" Noetos was unable to keep a plaintive note from entering his voice.

Mustar shrugged politely. "Best we continue," he said.

Unsure whether the lad meant him to continue the conversation or to resume walking towards Broad Way, Noetos turned and checked to see if Summer Way was clear, then stepped out into the street.

"Don't you want to talk about it?" The youth's voice behind him sounded accusing.

"You talk. I'll listen. Might be I'll have something to say later."

"As you will."

Mustar caught up with Noetos. They walked close together so they could hear each other above the storm.

"I have to say, at the time I didn't believe the part about

you fighting off the Recruiters with your sword. We Old Fossans don't exactly get offered the best seats at the Recruiters' trial, but I got close enough that morning to see their skill. No way an old fisherman could stand up to them. Forgive me, Noetos, but that's how I thought."

Noetos nodded. He would have thought the same.

"But seeing you today, well, maybe I was wrong. I've never heard of anyone being able to do what you did. You killed a dozen of them; you moved so fast it was as though they threw themselves on your sword. You reminded me of the *Maghdi Dasht* in the story about the Fall of Jasweyah, when it says, "No matter where they went, there his blade lay in wait.'"

A distant rumble interrupted Mustar's speculations. An explosion, thought Noetos, not thunder, somewhere off to their right. It was followed by faint shouts.

"So you went back on your agreement with the Recruiters," Mustar continued. "It came to blows, and you ran. Most of the village spent that evening looking for you. Where did you hide?"

"I spent the afternoon out to sea," Noetos said. "Came back near dusk and hid in the chandler's shed out near Dog Head. I'm surprised no one thought to look for me there." He sniffed. "And while you're right to say I reneged on our bargain with Andratan, it was because one of the Recruiters' party was my own daughter. Andratan had damaged her. You must know this, since you brought her north with you."

Mustar frowned. "So she said. I am still confused by this. She looks little like the Arathé I knew. It took some time, and much questioning, before I believed her. What they did to her, taking her tongue, draining her magic—I can understand why you were angry."

"Why I *am* angry. There's something badly wrong with Andratan, and I need to find out what it is. What are they doing to our children?"

Mustar turned to stare Noetos full in the face. His hard-edged features were framed by black hair plastered to his head by the driving rain. "There's also something badly wrong with you, if I understand things rightly," he said. "Hear me out. This is what Sautea thinks happened: early that next morning you set your own boats on fire in order to signal the Neherians to invade Fossa. Sautea saw the fire first. He banged on my door on his way to the beach. I was out of bed and into my clothes before I realised it was too early for work, but then I saw the smoke and ran."

Noetos wanted to take the youth by the throat and shake him. Anything to make him stop talking. To stop repeating a story that was so wrong, so unjust. He, signal the Neherians by burning his own boats? With difficulty he held on to his temper. *Listen first.*

"We were partway through putting out the fire when we noticed the Neherian fleet. Sautea counted a hundred sails before he gave up. Some of the villagers fled into the fields, but most of us stayed. We couldn't leave our village to them. Yes, I know you've told us stories of how cruel the Neherians can be, but we thought you were exaggerating." He shrugged his shoulders. "You have no idea, Fisher, what those ships looked like as they anchored in our harbour. Glorious sight, they were, even though we suspected the Neherians didn't mean us well.

"They herded us together at sword point, then asked the leaders to step to one side. That's when Sautea and I re-

alised the Hegeoman was missing. His wife had no idea
where he was. They were rough with her, thinking she was
protecting him."

"How rough?" Noetos asked wearily, though he anticipated the answer.

"They killed her eventually. A mercy. Don't ask me to
tell you what they did."

"I see." *Poor Bregor. Does he know?*

"Do you? Do you really? Can you imagine what happened when the killing started? Some of the lads put up a
fight. Arnessan and a few of the Cadere Row lot knocked
down one of the Neherian leaders, then got stuck into
him with fists and boots. Did him some serious damage,
from what I saw, before they were dragged off him. They
were slit and pegged out on the beach for the crabs to play
with."

"That's sore news, for all I couldn't stomach that lot."

"Aye. But the Neherians became very angry when you
couldn't be found. Seems they wanted you more than anyone else. Why, Fisher? What's so special about you that the
salties would wipe out Fossa to find you?"

"Wipe out? Fossa was wiped out?"

Before Mustar could resume his tale he and Noetos
emerged onto Broad Way. The deserted street stretched left
and right; to the right, in the distance, Noetos could make
out activity. People running, but not towards them.

"Where is Cohamma?" he asked.

"I don't know," Mustar said miserably. "He said I should
bring you to Broad Way, and he would meet us there behind the barricades. The sign there—" he pointed to the
side of a building—"says this is Broad Way, but where's
the captain?"

"Probably on Broad Way West," he said. "The street is split in two by the Lecita Stream. Makes sense, actually: the more defensible part of town is to the west, away from the sea. Higher ground." He sighed. "Well, we'll just have to find a way across the stream."

The two men hurried across the exposed width of Broad Way and continued up Summer Way. After fifty or so paces they crested a hill, the street narrowed and they began to descend towards a grassy-banked stream. The hairs on the back of Noetos's neck rose. Something . . .

A sudden flash blinded them both. A fraction of a second later the air around them roared, searing their senses. Noetos found his nostrils filled with astringent air. *Lightning,* his mind belatedly told him. *Close.*

Just how close was obvious after he blinked the jagged lights from his eyes. A small building no more than ten paces to their left, some oligarch's gatehouse perhaps, lay in ruins. A scorched smell filled the air.

Mustar swallowed visibly. "That was too close."

Another flash, further away but still within the walls of the city, induced flinches from both of them, then sheepish grins.

Noetos grunted. "Reminds me of the time we were stuck outside The Rhoos while a storm played in Fossa harbour—"

This time there was no separation between flash and roar. The violence of the lightning strike knocked him to the ground, holding him there while the air rumbled and the cobbles shook.

"Mustar? Mustar!"

"Here, Fisher." The boy seemed to be shouting, but Noetos could barely hear him. "Are you all right? My head aches."

"I'll be all right when I open my eyes," Noetos said.

They're hunting Father, said a voice. Anomer's voice, deep in his brain. He eased his eyes open to find he lay in a drain. Mustar was sitting on his haunches, peering at him with a look of concern.

The voice spoke again. *Because it's our combined strength in his mind. They seem to be able to hunt him that way. They may be attuned to you, sister.*

"Hunting? What do you mean, hunting?" Noetos asked.

"What?" Mustar said, a puzzled look on his face.

"Shh. Anomer, who is hunting me?"

We are not yet sure, Father. But Arathe has somehow drawn the attention of . . . of a power, that's how best she can describe it. A pause. *She says it tracked her north—*

Noetos sensed something, a wilful force gathering itself. He screamed to Mustar, leapt to his feet and threw himself towards the shelter of the nearest building. The bolt hit behind him. He knew without looking that it had struck exactly where he had been lying.

Keep moving, Anomer said. *We must break our link to you. It may be tracking you because it thinks you are Arathé.*

Mustar was already twenty paces further down the street, running hard though unevenly. "Come on, Fisher," he called over his shoulder. "I don't need an explanation to know when something uncanny is happening."

As Noetos regained his feet the connection between himself and his children disappeared. He almost collapsed as the weariness and pain, kept at bay until now, flooded in. *Arathé will be all right*, he told himself, *as long as she doesn't use her power . . .*

"Come on!"

"I . . . yes," he said. Tottering on legs that felt like tree stumps, he tried to catch Mustar.

"Maybe I should keep my distance," he said when finally he stood beside the young man. "Safer for you."

"Oh? And how will I find my way to Captain Cohamma without your help?"

"Maybe you don't want to stay with the betrayer of Fossa," Noetos said bitterly.

A flicker of light washed across the buildings either side of them, the glare enhanced by the rain-wet surfaces. Behind them thunder rumbled.

"Did you betray us?"

Just like his father, always direct. No wonder I like the lad.

"No."

"Then who did?"

"I'll let him tell you that story."

Another rumble rolled across the city.

"Huh," Mustar said, as he attempted to work it out.

"We can't stay still," said Noetos. His right knee threatened to buckle under him, but he knew he could not rest, not for a moment. *Who is it that can hunt with lightning? Is this some new Recruiter trick? Could the man I allowed to escape my ambush be behind this?*

He thought back to the scene under Saros Rake. Surely there was no possibility the last remaining Recruiter might have regained his power? If such a thing were possible, why had everyone made so great a fuss over Noetos's huanu stone? If its uncanny power to drain magic from whatever it touched was only temporary, why was huanu stone held in such awe? "Your carving there is worth all of Palestra, with plenty left over," Omiy the alchemist had said to him. No, even at their most powerful none of the Recruiters could call down lightning. This was surely no Recruiter trick.

The street levelled out; Lecita Stream, normally a pretty, sparkling brook, lay quiescent before them. They were well into the Oligarchs District, not a part of Raceme ordinary people frequented. Of course, Noetos had not been an ordinary person twenty years ago when he'd come here to play with Lycana and his friends. They had run up and down the Oligarch streets, to and from the Summer Palace. Times of happiness, times of privilege, almost impossible to recall under the low stormclouds. Under the Neherian assault.

The two men stood at the edge of the stream. Flashes of brightness flickered against the sullen sky; a wielder of immense power searching for him, or for his daughter.

"Ah, they still haven't built a bridge," Noetos remarked. "Can't have the gentry mixing with the riffraff. We'll have to wade." More thunder from behind underlined his thoughts. "Come on, before the lightning catches us again."

They were halfway across, up to their waists in water, when a swift whistling was followed by the staccato thunks of arrow shafts into the bank ahead of them. Beside Noetos, Mustar grunted in surprise.

"Where are my wits?" Noetos growled as he grabbed the lad by the arm and dragged him to the far bank. "Damn Neherians, this is how they fight. Hide and strike, then run away. Cowards."

His words were answered by a second volley of arrows. This time they hissed into the water behind them.

"Hah. Knocked down by the wind. Foolish weapons in these conditions."

Mustar said nothing, drawing Noetos to look across at the young Fossan. His face was pale. *Mustar is a solid lad; a few arrows landing wide of the mark wouldn't frighten him, surely? Well, perhaps this on top of the lightning*, he conceded.

Mustar stumbled as he tried to climb the bank. Despite his own weariness, Noetos gave him a hand up.

"You all right?"

The boy grunted something that could have been a "yes", or at least Noetos took it so. He shrugged. He hadn't taken Mustar for a coward. Still, it had been a dangerous journey across the city, and it wasn't finished yet.

Ahead lay the Artisans District, an area of Raceme unfamiliar to Noetos. Artisans Way followed the stream, and would lead them directly to the Man-o'-War but leave them vulnerable to any other archers the Neherians had emplaced.

"What's preventing the Neherians from crossing the stream and taking this part of the city?" the lad asked in a strangely brittle voice.

"Look above you. I saw movement in the windows of the tenements. Cohamma will have posted archers to hold the Neherians."

"So the stream is now the line between Neherius and Raceme?"

"Looks like it. If so, the city is neatly divided in two. They have much of the wealth, but we have most of the people. Come, Mustar. We'll find a way through this district. Captain Cohamma can't be far away. And with him, no doubt, will be the man who can convince you of my innocence with regard to the fate of Fossa."

The man at the centre of Noetos's angry thoughts surprisingly appeared in front of them as he and Mustar drew close to Suggate. Unsure of the disposition of the rival forces, Noetos had led Mustar to the city wall and around it until they reached Suggate itself. Here, in contradiction of all good sense, Bregor had apparently been given command of the gate.

Suggate was choked with angry and fearful people trying to get into the city from the Shambles, and others, equally persistent, trying to get out. The rain, heavier now, had ponded against a low point at the base of the city wall, and those waiting for their chance to escape the city stood, shivering and miserable, up to their ankles in water. A lone soldier tried to maintain order, but was largely ignored by those trying to get through the gate.

"I see they've given you another innocent group of citizens to care for," Noetos grated at the man. Let Mustar figure that one out.

Bregor ignored the comment; perhaps not even hearing it. "Noetos, you fool, why are you making young Mustar walk with an injured leg?"

"What are you jabbering about, man?"

Noetos looked over at the lad, who had sunk to one knee. Bregor knelt beside him, plucking ineffectually at the broken shaft of an arrow embedded in Mustar's thigh.

"Oh. Mustar, I'm so sorry. I didn't notice."

Bregor snorted. "You never do, fisherman; that's your problem."

Noetos discovered his children had left him a reservoir of anger, after all.

"Is that so? I might be blind perhaps, but I'm no betrayer of villages. Young Mustar here was wondering who sold Fossa to the Neherians. Care to tell him?"

"I betrayed no one," the Hegeoman said, though surely Mustar had noted the change in tone.

"A technicality: you intended to. Tell the boy!"

"Can't this wait until Mustar has been treated? Or do you intend him to die, just as Opuntia died, as a result of your blindness?"

Noetos roared and jumped on Bregor, pummelling him with his fists. The man grabbed him around the neck, reducing his effectiveness; still, he knew he landed at least one satisfying blow on Bregor's face.

"Enough! Enough!" a voice cried. Hands pulled Noetos to his feet; other hands assisted Bregor. Some of those trying to get through Suggate had obviously been told to help Bregor; the lone soldier continued to bark commands, his sword drawn, as the two men were pulled apart.

"It's all right, we know each other," Noetos said to the soldier, breathing out his rage.

"I'll talk to the Fossans myself," Bregor said, the words slurring past a thick lip. "I don't need you to complicate things. In the meantime, don't you think we ought to give some thought to the fate of Raceme?"

"Aye, and as to that, why have we only one soldier guarding the wall's weakest point?" Mustar asked, one hand on his thigh, where the shaft had been broken off not far above the skin. "What happens if the Neherians sweep around the city and attack this gate? The guard can't even control the citizens of Raceme. The Neherians could take the gate and be in the city before Captain Cohamma or his men have a chance to resist."

"What is Cohamma thinking?" Noetos agreed, frowning. All it would take . . ." He paused, thoughtful. "Mustar, stay here. Climb the gate and keep watch. Any sign of the Neherians, you run down this street and let Captain Cohamma know."

"Climb the gate?" Bregor echoed incredulously. "You just don't see anything but yourself, do you, Noetos? He's got an arrow in his leg, cry Alkuon. Climb the gate yourself."

"I'll do it," Mustar said. "Just send someone up here to tend it, and not a sawbones. I'll hear Bregor's story while I'm waiting."

A short time later Noetos walked wearily down Suggate Way towards the Man-o'-War and Captain Cohamma's command post. The lightning had stopped now, at least.

As the fisherman approached the Man-o'-War, he thought about Mustar. The boy would be fine back at gatehouse, but his absence felt like a loss. *So many people lost.* He wanted to gather them all to him, shelter them from the storm breaking all around them. Curling a lip, he recognised his father's sentiments: *protect your own at all costs.* Part of the leadership training he'd received as a boy.

Leadership? According to his daughter, apparently, he was no leader.

"Swordsman."

For the second time that afternoon Noetos failed to realise he was being spoken to.

"Swordsman!"

A small, neatly dressed man wearing the green and

white—and, unlike the other Racemen soldiers Noetos had seen, "white" meant exactly that in this case—stood before Noetos, head bowed slightly, his whole demeanour screaming obsequiousness. Noetos remembered his sort, having witnessed a parade of self-serving men seeking favour from his father. They had all possessed smooth voices and smoother wits. His father had hated them.

"Captain Cohamma requires your presence," the man said.

"Tell him I'll be at his disposal in a moment." Noetos made for the door of the Man-o'-War.

"He also bade me tell you that your son and daughter are with him down by the floral clock."

Rage swamped Noetos more swiftly than an unseen wave. He placed a hand on the man's shoulder and tightened his grip until he drew a gasp.

"And why are my children not out of harm's way, as I instructed them?"

"I . . . forgive me, sir, you are hurting me."

"So I am," Noetos said agreeably, and increased the pressure slightly.

"In . . . in Raceme, sir, all competent sword hands are required to defend the town in time of crisis."

The man spoke rapidly, breathing heavily through his nose. Noetos smiled. *It doesn't take much to break through the shell of your urbanity, does it?*

"So, when one o' your men told the captain about your son's skill with the blade, the captain sent me to look fer 'im." The cultured tones were giving way to a rougher speech. Noetos knew he was behaving badly, but did not loosen his grip. "His sister—please, sir!—his sister refused t' be parted from 'im, so she was given a blade and stands beside 'im. Please, sir, let go me arm!"

"Take me to them."

Noetos gave the man's shoulder a shove—*this is not the person you wish to push,* his mind whispered traitorously—and followed him to the upturned carts and assorted furniture that served as Captain Cohamma's defences.

After a brief scan of the area, the fisherman realised that this would be no ordinary street battle. Raceme's streets were wide and without cover: no force could advance on an opponent without risking decimation from hidden archers. The Lecita Stream, flanked by broad avenues, offered little cover for the Neherians. Ample evidence of failed attempts to storm Cohamma's position littered the stream's grassy banks and floated in the water.

Stalemate.

Noetos closed his eyes briefly in anger as a realisation struck him. Bregor was right, Alkuon curse the man: he had just assessed the tactical situation before seeking out his own children. Curse his upbringing.

There they were, either side of the captain himself. Safely sheltered behind an upturned haywain. Noetos strode across the street to Cohamma. Giving Anomer a passing nod, and not quite meeting his daughter's eye, he took the captain by the elbow.

"They make no further attack?"

"Nay," came the taciturn reply.

Probably offended at how Noetos had walked in and taken command, though he'd obviously sent men out searching for him. *Nothing for it. I'm a leader. You'll have to reconcile yourself to that, Cohamma.*

"And you are agreed that their next move will be to flank us?"

"Aye, that was m' thought." The captain's eyes lightened. Someone to talk tactics with.

"So why is there no force posted on Suggate?"

"They bayn't landed on Ring's Beach," Cohamma said. "No boats light enough. Suggate is safe."

"And what's to stop them breaking out through Water Gate and flanking the entire city that way? Come on, man, I'd think of it, and so will they, if they haven't already. We hold the line here, arrayed against what might be nothing more than a shadow force, while they enter the city through Suggate and roll it up behind us."

"Or they scale th' wall anywhere 'long its length," Cohamma growled. "Nuffin" we can do, son. Not enough bodies. We lost more'n half our soldiers and most've our volunteers in the first attack."

"At least post another scout by Suggate, man!" Noetos growled. "We need some warning if they outflank us."

"Aye, well, send one of your men."

"It's already done."

Cohamma's features went flat at his words.

"Then stop jawin" and incline yer milit'ry brain t' getting' these salties outta the city."

"Yes, sir."

Noetos offered a lazy salute, and just like that effective command of the battle had been handed to him. He took in the scene around him: several soldiers, having witnessed his confrontation with the captain, watched him warily in the dimming light. He wondered if any other commanders had survived the Neherians' initial attack. Soldiers were normally quartered in barracks within the Raceme Fortress or under the Summer Palace, and both places had been outflanked early in the conflict and were now well behind enemy lines. Unlikely, then, that his command of the remaining forces would be challenged.

My defences. For now.

A slow hour passed behind the barricades. Dagla sat propped against an oaken table, eyes closed, his left shoulder all over with blood. His chest was moving though. Good. Noetos had become quite fond of the boy. Gawl stood beside Dagla, alternating between poking his head over the barrier and ducking down to check on his . . . well, his friend. Noetos smiled. His "army" of miners was doing just fine. Further down the line of carts and furniture Seren stood, talking quietly with Tumar, and Anomer and Arathé, who had just joined them. Beyond that, nothing but the rainsoaked gloom.

Noetos walked over to his children, his mind crammed with a dozen different opening lines. Suddenly nervous, he chose one without thinking.

"If you wanted me to wash, Arathé, you could have waited for this rain to do the job," he said.

As soon as the words were out of his mouth, he knew he'd made the wrong choice. The rain suddenly picked up in intensity, roaring all around them, and hail began to fall. For a vain moment Noetos hoped the noise had masked his foolish words. He became suddenly detached, as though a copy of him watched as they impacted upon his daughter, then his son, and saw their faces harden. Angry tears started from Arathé's eyes.

"Muhh vih (clap) eeah (clap), you maay (clap) (finger flick) oh (clap)!"

She placed her hands on her hips and glared at him, seemingly unaware of the hail clattering around them.

"Mother's dead, and you make a joke?" Anomer interpreted, his voice flat.

"The joke wasn't about your mother's death. I've told you how much I regret that."

Anomer took a sharp breath. "Arathé has today learned that her mother has been killed. Worse, despite my explanation, she seems to think it may have been her father's fault. *You* certainly think you had something to do with it; she's been in your mind, remember. And we stand here discussing this while under siege by the Neherians. Do you think this is a time for humour?"

"Find shelter!" people cried somewhere in the distance. "Get under cover!" The words barely registered in Noetos's mind.

There is *so much of your mother in your face, son*, he wanted to say, but he knew the words could not be spoken, not now. *In your face, and in your words*.

"No. No more humour," he said. "But I admit to being surprised that my daughter would react this way towards me before giving me a chance to explain what happened, or even before I could tell her how glad I am to discover she is alive. Arathé, we have a great deal to talk about. Can we leave any further impromptu swimming until then?"

His daughter turned her face to him and, even in the gloom, he saw the unnatural flash of her eyes. In that moment he began to realise how dangerous his daughter might be. Pushing him off the wharf may have been a mild response.

The hail pounded on the cobbles around them. The table

offered shelter of a sort, but thumbnail-sized stones rattled off his helmet and tunic and stung his bare arms.

Arathé spoke again in her unique hybrid language, too fast for Noetos to follow.

"I know more than you think," she said, her brother interpreting. "I . . . hear things. I can't explain what I mean. I'll listen to you, but I will know if you don't tell the truth."

"What do you mean? What things do you hear?"

Noetos pulled his children down further under the table; one of the hailstones found and bruised his forearm. The late afternoon had become unnaturally dark.

"I said I can't explain it. I have a connection to a voice of knowledge. I don't know who it is, but through it I can hear what is happening. Many strange things are happening across the world, and they are all linked."

A cold spike of fear stabbed at Noetos's heart. "Don't you question the source of this voice? What if it is misleading you?"

"No," Arathé said. "I hear only truth. It may not be all the truth, but the voice speaks no lies. I'll show you."

A sudden heat seized Noetos's brain, followed by an eerie feeling of openness, as though all boundaries to thought had been removed. If he strained he could hear . . . a voice, for a fleeting instant, then nothing. The hail stopped, and the sky began to lighten.

"No, Arathé!" Anomer took his sister by the shoulders and began to shake her. "Don't use your mind-voice, the risk is too great. You know something is looking for you."

The heat faded from the fisherman's mind, but he could not convince himself he had imagined it.

Arathé said something urgent to Anomer. He stood, turned and looked to the east, over the heads of the Neherians and whatever they were planning on the far bank of the stream, into the dark heart of the storm bearing down on them.

"Too late," he said, his voice hollow. "It's found you."

Cries from along the line of defenders indicated they had seen it also. Noetos stood too, then took a step back and his hand went to his sword hilt.

The storm clouds had begun to rotate.

A circular wall of cloud lowered towards the harbour and moved slowly in their direction, as though it were some kind of vast mechanical beast. The cloud seemed eager, desperate, like a blind man scrabbling on the floor for his last scrap of food.

Noetos had seen a circular cloud like this once before. He had been fishing with Halieutes, Mustar's renowned father, in the first year of Noetos's apprenticeship. They had been out beyond The Rhoos, nets laden, when a sudden hailstorm had descended upon them, hidden until the last minute by the bulk of Bluefin Stack. They had ridden it out; the clouds threw ice at them, rolled over the top of their little boat, then lifted. Noetos had been exhilarated by the power of the storm.

Halieutes had stared carefully at the sky as it cleared and cursed in the way only he could. "The hook!" he'd cried. "We must row for shelter!"

They'd put their backs to it, cutting the nets free then rowing until they reached Bluefin Stack. And Noetos had seen the hook: the Finger of Alkuon, Halieutes had called it, a spiralling finger of wind that descended from the sky to drink the water, to eat the fish, to destroy anything human in its path.

Rain, then hail, then a clearing in the weather, then the

hook. If Halieutes was right, Noetos would see the hook now.

A spinning black wedge began to lower from the cloud wall. Immediately below it, one of the Neherian ships jerked as though plucked up by an invisible hand, then disintegrated. A cloud of debris rose into the air, forming a funnel that spun upwards to meet the wedge. The Finger of Alkuon.

"It is coming for you." Anomer took his sister's arm. "We have to run."

The spinning finger stretched out and touched another ship, and the noise rumbled around the harbour. Then it made landfall, running along the length of Red Duke Wharf, ripping up timbers as it went.

A bone-deep fear thrummed through the fisherman. "This is not natural," he said. "This has been sent by someone with power enough to kill us all."

What does it want with my daughter?

The Neherians had seen the finger strike land; heedless of cover they broke left and right. A few of them began wading the river, coming towards them, eyes wide, battle forgotten. A Raceman lifted his bow, but Cohamma struck it down.

"Dun waste yer time." The captain pointed to the west, along Broad Way. "We all need ter get outta here."

Is this a Neherian device? Have the Neherians found a new, powerful practitioner of magic? Has there ever been a Maghdi Dasht capable of such things?

Noetos had heard stories of the Falthan War, in which the combined forces of the *Maghdi Dasht* and the Undying Man himself had managed to influence the weather. Surely no man had ever, would ever, exercise such power on his own?

The fisherman followed Cohamma's arm. A second finger stretched towards the ground, thinner than the first, paler, but spinning much faster. It sped down Broad Way towards them, exactly as though it was hunting for something. Intelligent. Purposeful.

Cohamma met Noetos's gaze, nodded.

"Head for Suggate!" Noetos yelled. "Seren, you and the rest of my men, take Dagla with you. I don't want him left behind. Go!"

His legs ached with the need to run, to be anywhere but the place where the two Fingers of Alkuon were converging. He forced them to stay still.

"Anomer, Arathé," he said, motioning his children closer. The roaring to their left and right made it difficult to communicate. "Are you sure they are seeking you?"

Arathé, eyes wide and face dead white, nodded.

"Then we cannot go with the others. We must draw the Fingers of Alkuon away from Suggate. Give them a chance of escape. You must do whatever it is you do to draw them."

Arathé nodded again, sweat sheening her skin. In that moment Noetos saw his wife framed in his daughter's face.

"Come on, then. We head east." No time to think about his wife, his daughter, his son.

The skies had darkened again; the circular cloud wall hovered almost directly overhead, rotating slowly. Two more slim funnels were forming, one lowering from the cloud, another reaching up from the wreckage of the Justice District, off to their left.

Four fingers. *Alkuon!* What had they done to provoke such forces? What could he possibly do to resist them? Some small awareness battered at his mind, but he forced himself to ignore it. No time. He focused his entire attention on escape.

The fisherman and his two children ran past Hook, Line and Sinker, the largest inn in Raceme. Gawl followed a few paces back. An explosion shook the ground. Noetos turned and watched as one of the fingers ripped through the Old Council Chambers, a few hundred paces behind them. Thatch from the relic's steeply sloping roof simply vanished, while sections of the wall buckled outwards and were picked up by the roaring funnel. Then, as though it realised its quarry was not within the building, the finger spun sideways into the middle of Broad Way and leapt towards them.

"Gawl! I told you to go to Suggate! You can't help us here."

Guess I lost my way," the man replied, mouth curved in his insolent grin.

They sprinted across Midtown Bridge, then turned right. Noetos could not resist looking back: behind him, the finger approached the Man-o'-War inn. Even before the funnel reached it, the building's verandah crumpled, detached and rose into the air in a lazy spiral, where it was snared and hungrily absorbed by the vortex. The inn offered no resistance. Windows and walls dissolved as the finger touched them. The upper-storey window, from which Noetos and his men had watched the approaching storm a couple of hours ago, exploded outwards in a cascade of splinters and glass.

Suddenly the funnel jerked backwards as though scalded, finishing in the middle of the road. It spun in the one place a moment, then headed towards them.

Some instinct warned the fisherman. He threw himself to the ground just as the Man-o'-War's verandah, still largely intact, came spearing out of the approaching spiral. It bounced once, scraping across the road, jerked forward like a leaf in a storm and whistled over Noetos's back. Somewhere behind him it thumped into something, probably the side of a building.

Braving himself against the rising wind, Noetos levered himself to his feet. Anomer was already running, pulling Arathé along with him. The spinning finger leapt across the stream, tearing up Midtown Bridge. Noetos ran past the forlorn verandah, draped across the front of the largest warehouse in the district.

"Aaaah," someone called.

There was a ragged bundle lying beside the verandah. It was Gawl, panting, his leg pierced clean through by a splintered beam. His clothing lay loosely about him, shredded beyond recognition. As Noetos approached, the rogue smiled at him, then spat out blood.

"Go on with you," he said. "The devil-wind's too close."

"Hold still and we'll get you off this spike," Noetos said, approaching the miner. His daughter made to join him.

"No, Arathé," Anomer said, holding his sister back. "Don't go near him. If the finger is truly tracking you, you'll just lead it to him if you use your power."

Gawl laughed. "Spat me out once, it has. Let's see if it'll swallow me this time." His grin grew even fiercer. "Now get out o' here, 'fore you end up in its belly."

"He's right. We have to go." Anomer tugged on his father's arm.

Noetos roared in frustration. He didn't want to leave anyone behind, but his son was right. He let himself be led away.

The three Fossans put their heads down and ran. Noetos had no idea whether the finger could be outrun, but he would try. He would give no one else to the wind.

They reached Summer Way, panting and out of breath. Behind them the roar had subsided to a growl. They risked a backward glance: the dark, finger approached the large warehouse, picking at the discarded verandah. Noetos watched, fists clenched in anger, as Gawl pushed himself up on one arm and shook the other at his approaching death, shouting at it all the while. The whirlwind plucked reluctantly at the verandah, as if uncertain about something, then leapt forward and sucked verandah and warehouse wall into its funnel. Arms flailing, Gawl vanished into the maw.

"Alkuon forfend," Anomer breathed.

CHAPTER 2

STONE AND STORM

PEOPLE SWARMED AROUND SUGGATE as though it were the entrance to a beehive. Bregor tried to force his way into the chaos, but stronger or more desperate people pushed, shouldered and elbowed him back to the periphery of the mass. He'd tried to attract Mustar's attention, but the young man, his leg crudely bandaged, was busy shouting instructions from atop the gate, ensuring a steady flow of people through it, out of the city. His shouting was barely audible: the air was filled with the cries of men, women's shrieks and the sobbing of children, all insufficient to mask the slowly growing rumbling from those *things* destroying the city. Panic slowly dissolved into terror as people cast increasingly frightened looks behind them.

No queen bee to guide us, no homing instinct to tell us where to go to escape our deaths. We need a leader. Where's the governor?

Possibly one of those fleeing that palace, Bregor answered himself.

If he stood on the steps of the Money Exchange he could see right across the city, to where the largest of the five funnels tore at a tall stone building overlooking the harbour. More a wedge than a finger, it plucked stones from the walls and scattered them over the lower city like seeds. And not just stones. Some of those shapes disappearing into the wedge, to be flung broken into buildings and onto the streets below were—or had been—people.

He was tired of death.

Mustar had given him the news he'd been dreading. Merle was . . . had been . . . she was dead. Dead. Killed by the Neherians, those to whom he'd betrayed his people in order to save her. Merle and Opuntia, he'd lost them both. Mustar had told him how she'd died under torture, resisting her captors to the last. *Torture*. Merle, whose gentleness was bruised by the death of an animal, who always had to catch and free any bees trapped in their house. How could she have been made to suffer so? Bregor had pressed the lad for the details; the boy had told him, albeit reluctantly. Her flesh slit, salt rubbed in the open wounds, staked out on the beach, twisting against the ropes for all to see, to await the tide . . .

He so desperately wanted to scream, but there was no voice profound enough to express his own agony. The Fisher thought him a coward, but Bregor knew he was not. He would have exchanged places with Merle or Opuntia. Would do it now. If it were within his power he would have it so his body squirmed under the Neherians' salted knives or fell bleeding beneath the Recruiter's sword thrust. He would suffer everlasting torment to reverse their deaths. But there was no god of time he could petition in order to undo what had been done.

What *he* had done.

That knowledge was the source of the howling inner

whirlwind busy shaking him to pieces. But for his attempts to save their lives, Opuntia and Merle would both still be alive, and he himself would be dead. An infinitely preferable state of affairs.

A little while earlier Bregor had fled with the others from the death falling from the sky, towards Suggate and safety. But he did not know why. Traitorous feet. Much better to have faced the storm, to embrace the whirlwind, to die spitting and snarling, opposing the irresistible forces of the world. But his feet had carried him to Suggate. Maybe he was a coward, after all.

The four slender fingers of the gods, flanked to the right by the larger wedge, really did seem like a supernatural hand descending from the clouds, sent to winnow the earth. Searching for the damnable Fisher and his family, it seemed, the Heir of Roudhos who had somehow become the centre of this strange, terrible season.

Merle wasn't even important, he thought. *She could have lived and cost neither the gods nor the fisherman anything. She could have lived. Why would anyone strike down such an innocent?*

Why were Noetos and his family not taken instead?

He drew a ragged breath. The sheer self-pity in that last thought brought him back to some kind of sense. The leaderless people clustered about Suggate were unimportant. Who would give their lives for them? That soldier there, struggling to direct even his own frightened townsmen? Mustar, trying to make himself heard over the din?

Bregor sighed, squared his shoulders and strode towards the buzzing crowd. He wanted to die; so, naturally, in this perverse world, he would be forced to live.

*   *   *

"Arathé says this storm chased her all the way from Fossa," Anomer shouted in his father's ear as they ran along the road.

"Not possible," was his reply, just as Anomer had expected. "Storms don't last that long on the Fisher Coast. And they don't move north this time of year."

Anomer had grown up believing inflexibility of opinion to be a virtue. It hadn't been until after his sister left for Andratan that he'd realised how much he had valued his conversations with her. She had gently teased out the wound-up threads of his emotions, showing him that it was possible to hold a different opinion from his forceful father. More, that such contrariness was often necessary in order to preserve some sense of self.

The last two years had been hard. Listening to the father he loved poison himself with opinions so sharp he punctured himself and everyone around him. Mother had long been worn out by then, and had found her own solace. Anomer had known about that for at least a year, and had carefully guarded his lips to ensure his father didn't find out about it from him.

Not that his father was always prickly. On occasion they had fruitful and enjoyable family discussions. But even then every point of view had to be weighed and balanced, and an honest opinion could be cruelly cast down if poorly expressed. Anomer had learned to wield logic primarily as a method of self-defence.

"Arathé tells me that Sautea and Mustar can confirm what she says. They rescued her, after all, and brought her north."

Noetos turned in the road and would have stopped, Anomer guessed, had the whirlwinds not been rumbling towards them. "I want to hear more about that. I thought she was dead."

Beside him, Arathé shook her head.

"Later, Father, later," Anomer said. "For now all we need to know is that Arathé believes the storm is pursuing her. Perhaps if we could work out why, we could put a stop to it."

"So how did she keep this storm from destroying her? It's only a little boat, after all, and I presume it is damaged."

"She kept her magic under control and her mind small. Now, can we talk about this later?"

"You brought it up."

Anomer said nothing. It was always best to let his father have the last word.

Noetos winced at every stride, as he had for the last half-hour. *Seacursed leg*. He'd hurt it, perhaps when he'd caught it in the rubble of the Betide Theatre, or maybe when Gawl's broken body had come flying out of the maelstrom pursuing them and knocked the three of them to the ground.

Arathé had shrieked then, tongue or no tongue. He would have cried out too, had it been him lying there with the man's body draped over him, lolling tongue dripping blood into his hair.

The fingers had all but caught them then, three of them closing in on Arathé as she used her magic out of instinct to batter the miner's broken body off herself. They had escaped up Summer Way, retracing the steps Noetos and Mustar had taken earlier, the howling, grinding whirlwinds lining up to follow them. Noetos had thought they were about to die then. The winds were only a few paces behind them, and a hard-soft rain alternately clattered and pattered all around them, the dwellings and citizens of Raceme swallowed, chewed up and spat out upon them. He dared not look back. He ran, every moment expecting his feet to leave the ground.

Yet, for all their menace, there was something oddly tentative about the way the whirlwinds had stalked them. As if the wind matched its pace to theirs. Reluctant to catch them.

Noetos had ducked left along Broad Way, his children following him. Then he'd seen the trap: an enormous black wedge crashing through the stone building in front of him—the Betide Theatre; he remembered hiding in the shadows once to watch a play, one his father had forbidden him attend—hurling and tumbling rubble at them as it came.

Yes, that was where he'd picked up the limp. The roaring wedge showed no hesitation in pursuing them through the Oligarchs District. It would have caught him, had it not been for his children. Though it meant further confirmation of their location, Arathé and Anomer had once again supplied him with strength; it hardly mattered that they exposed themselves to the mind behind the fingers, given how close they were. Together, they had fled the dark wall of cloud, sprinting through the trees on the riverbank, then across the water—Noetos could not remember its liquid touch—and into the Artisans District. He'd begun to feel his leg on the district's rougher roads.

Now he sighed. He thought they'd given the fingers the slip, at least temporarily, but here they came again. Anomer yelled instructions to Arathé. Noetos's two children ran in opposite directions. He yelled, but they both ignored him.

The dark wedge and the four trailing fingers came across the stream and hesitated, as though uncertain of the direction they should be heading in. The wedge moved left, then right, while the four fingers paired off and circled around each other. Noetos realised his children were using their magic to confuse the mind behind the whirlwinds, which perhaps knew of only one magician. For a moment the fisherman felt left out. His children had magic to share, while he had none. Only the huanu stone.

Oh, Alkuon. The stone.

A cold shiver struck his neck, ran across his shoulders and settled on his chest. *Foolish, stupid man.* How many lives consumed by the fingers of the gods while he'd been running, his guilt and fear making him forget what he carried?

He placed his hand on his belt.

Bregor saw the fingers approaching, as did the panic-stricken citizens of Raceme. Suggate was simply not wide enough to let them all through in time, especially since a number of fools were still trying to get into the city.

"Mustar!" he cried to the figure standing atop the gate. "Stop anyone entering Suggate from the outside!"

The youngster nodded and hobbled to the far side of the structure.

"People! Listen!" Bregor could make his voice carry if he desired, and he gave thanks for the trick now. All around him, heads spun in his direction. "Pull back from the gate. Make two orderly lines. Walk briskly, no pushing, children first. You, you and you"—he pointed to three solid-looking men—"make sure no one steps out of line."

He repeated his instructions incessantly, his voice the

bark of a dog chivvying sheep into line. "Make two lines. No pushing. Keep in your lines. Come on now, I said no pushing! Children first."

"Where do we go?" a woman called to him. Unafraid, bright-eyed, waiting patiently for her chance to walk through Suggate.

Bregor thought a moment. "Gather on the hill beside the southern path." He thought of the road they'd taken down to Raceme: would a hill be a safer place than a valley? He had no idea. No matter. The important thing was to keep people believing in his authority. "Pass it on to the others," he commanded. "We're gathering on the hill beside the southern path."

There had been only one hill, off to their left, when they'd first seen Raceme. He must have got it right, as no one questioned him. "The hill beside the southern path" went the message up and down the lines, soon changed to "Gather on Shambles Hill". The local name for it, apparently.

The lines had become noticeably shorter. *Though not short enough*, thought Bregor as he looked back over his shoulder. The black cloud wall was almost on top of them; its fingers and thumb roughly combed the buildings below Suggate. He desperately wanted to flee. If he ordered it, the lines would part for him, and he could be out of this city and on the road to safety.

Just like travelling north with Noetos while behind him his village burned.

He remained where he was.

Soldiers came running up the main road, hale and in-jured men in two ragged groups. Captain Cohamma led them past the Money Exchange.

"Who's in charge 'ere?" the captain demanded.

"He is," said the bright-eyed woman, pointing at Bregor.

"One o' the southerners?" Cohamma asked Bregor. Before the Hegeoman could answer, the captain continued. "Aye, you would be. None here would listen t'a Raceman. All for hisself."

"Will you help me?" Bregor asked.

Cohamma took a look over his shoulder. "You don't need help. Nuffin' we c'n do t' protect you from yonder death-storm. We've spent near an hour searchin' for survivors in the storm's cast-offs, and now we're leavin'. Best we get away, so we c'n come back 'n' save you from the Neherians."

"But if we don't get out of the city, there will be no one left for you to save," said a woman.

"Aye, well, I'm not leavin' none o' my men behind."

The second group arrived, with Seren and Tumar bearing Dagla between them. Sautea was with them, but looked no worse than winded.

"Any sign of Noetos?" the old seaman gasped.

"None," said Bregor. "Nor of his children."

"We'll wait here a moment then."

Captain Cohamma pushed between the lines of people patiently waiting at Suggate, leading his men through the gate.

"Oy, that's not fair," one man cried, and received a cuff for his trouble.

"Fair or no, do you fancy explaining to a man with a sword why he has to wait?" Bregor replied.

The man nodded, apparently satisfied by this pragmatic

answer, then resumed his nervous study of the rapidly clos-ing wind funnels.

Bregor watched with him. He'd earlier estimated per-haps two hundred people would remain this side of Sug-gate when the whirlwinds arrived—which they would, and soon, if they continued their present heading. *Maybe only one hundred*, he thought hopefully. The winds had slowed down, as though they searched . . . No, the fisherman was the one who always seemed to come up with a supernatu-ral explanation for events. *It's a spring storm, that's all.* An enormous storm. No, an *unheard-of* storm. One that had chosen—no, not chosen, surely—had *come ashore* coincidentally at the same time as an invading Neherian fleet. One that had spawned five whirlwinds—four slender fingers and one enormous thumb—that searched the city, looking for . . . well, by all evidence, looking for Noetos.

Of course it's not a natural storm.

Noetos put his hand on his belt and discovered the huanu stone was gone, along with his sword.

Belatedly, he realised what some part of his mind had been trying to tell him. *The stone and the sword have been missing for some time.* At least since . . . since when? When had he lost the stone? A wave of nausea washed over him. He'd fallen in the water. No doubt the stone now rested at the bottom of the muddy harbour.

Find it, Noetos told himself. *Find it or die.*

There had been so many other times it might have been shaken loose: diving for cover when the lightning struck; during his swordplay with the Neherians; even wading Lecita Stream. He'd done that last twice. Ought he track every move he'd made in this cursed city?

He was forgetting something, he knew it, but he had no idea what it was. Curse his fogged mind!

The Oligarchs District obscured his view of the harbour. Half an hour there and back at a brisk walk, the best he could manage. Half an hour for Anomer and Arathé to survive the attentions of their unnatural stalkers. And this took no account of the time it would take to dive and recover the stone. Given he could find it, given he had the energy to make the dive, given no Neherians remained by the wharf to resist him. Every moment he hesitated added to the time his children would have to dodge the whirlwinds.

His feet made the decision for him. The shortest route and hang the whirlwinds, they told him, and bore him along Artisans Way towards Midtown Bridge. *The bridge will have been destroyed by the finger that chased us*, his mind said, but his feet didn't listen. They had chosen their path.

But as the wreck of the Man-o'-War inn came into view, both mind and feet slowed him to a stumbling shuffle. Again his feet led the way, taking him from the wide roadway, its cobbles strewn either side of the whirlwind's path, and into a narrow, debris-choked alley that led behind the inn.

A memory had arisen in his mind, a remembrance of glancing around the bedroom he'd taken, checking no one was watching, then removing the huanu stone from his belt and placing it behind the mirror leaning against the wall. Of placing his belongings beside his pallet, of making his way to the taproom. Of seeing Omiy the faithless alchemist from the taproom window. Then witnessing the Neherian fleet and the storm. The alarm had sounded, he and his men had grabbed their swords from their rooms and run out into the street.

Leaving the stone behind.

He remembered. That was why he'd been able to touch his daughter on the dock.

He'd left the stone to be . . . to be what? Taken by the whirlwind? Could the fingers touch the huanu stone? He was gambling that they could not.

A swift glance over his shoulder confirmed what his ears were telling him: the fingers of Alkuon were busy razing the Artisans District, their attention drawn away from him for the moment. Drawn away by his children, he reminded himself.

To his right the rear of the inn seemed relatively undamaged. A rickety stairway led upwards to the fire doors every building in Raceme was required to have. He placed a hand on the stair, gave it a shake, and leapt back when a *crack* was followed by a series of shudders. Through the rising dust he watched the stairway settle.

He turned and left the alley, as there seemed no point in risking the climb. Even were the stairs to hold his weight, the door might—would—be barred from the inside. He had hoped the wind might have provided a way in.

Well, of course, it had, after a fashion. The entire front of the inn was open to the skies, but the stairway from the tavern to the private taproom above had been set against the front wall; and wall and stairway both had been swallowed by the whirlwind. Standing back from the remains of the inn, he could see into the taproom. The bedrooms behind appeared more or less intact.

Hauling himself up to the second floor taxed his aching muscles to their limits. He made use of dangling beams, sheets of metal, ropes and cords—anything that would give him a hand- or foothold. By the time he scrambled onto the creaking taproom floor, both his hands were bleeding and he had the beginnings of a bruise forming on his right leg, just below the knee.

"Oh my," a familiar voice said as he pushed himself to his feet. "My, my, here's the brave fisherman, yes indeed, come to pick up the stone he so carelessly left lying in his room, yes."

Noetos drew a deep breath. *Olifa the alchemist, he whom his fellow miners called Omiy.* "I have no doubt it's no longer where I put it," Noetos said, breathing out in a long hiss.

"No, indeed."

Omiy held out his hand, which cradled the huanu stone. Noetos looked at the man's fingers wrapped around his daughter's carved neck. He went for his sword—and then remembered, of course, that he didn't have it.

"My, my, my, you must be more careful with the contents of that belt," the alchemist said, his grin wide and taunting. "Do you think I would have made myself known, yes, taken this risk, if I'd seen your sword in its scabbard? Oh my, no!"

In his pursuit of the stone, Noetos had forgotten the loss of his sword. In one sense he'd known it was missing: a sword thumps against the leg when a person runs, it rubs against the stomach when he bends over, it has a weight about it. His mind had simply slipped into old habits. And where had it gone? He'd fought the Neherians with it, then had fled with Mustar; together they'd disturbed two red-bibbed soldiers despoiling a woman; he'd taken the head of one of them, and, and . . . he had left his sword on the Summer Way, laid it aside to tend the woman who, it had turned out, was past any care he could offer.

Clearly not so used to the weight of the blade that you'd notice if it were mislaid, aye?

"Do you not think I can force you to surrender the stone using my hands alone?" he said. The words were not convincing even to his ears.

Omiy barked a laugh. "I note you have no thought of merely persuading me to hand it over, oh no. Not a man with any trust in his wits. No! Trusts his fists over his tongue, he does. Then let him use his fists—and fight this!"

The alchemist reached over to the taproom's small bar, snatched a bottle by its neck and broke it against the bar's leading edge. The jagged edges of the broken pottery looked sharp enough to inflict serious damage.

"I cannot let you live, my friend," the alchemist said as he took a careful step forward, the tip of his impromptu weapon steady in the air before his face. "Oh my, no. Can't have someone dogging my trail, turning up unexpectedly at the most inconvenient times, ha!"

Noetos had no weapon, and the alchemist clearly knew how to handle himself, but the fisherman found himself struggling to take the man seriously. An irritant, yes. But a killer?

Yes. Omiy had used much more explosive than necessary on the slope of Saros Rake, and the trap meant to frighten the Recruiters who had taken Noetos's family had engulfed captor and captive alike.

The back of his head buzzed. *Father, are you all right? What is happening?* The words were a little blurry, as though something interfered with them. *Father, can you hear me?*

"You don't think I can use this, no, you do not," Omiy said. "You think I am a fool, oh yes, you do. You would do well to ask yourself how I survived amidst the miners of Eisarn Pit, yes, oh my, yes."

Father, speak quickly! Do you need help?

Noetos's first instinct was to shut Anomer's voice out of his head. He needed to focus on the alchemist. He needed to keep the whirlwinds away from the inn . . .

Keep talking to me, he thought at his son. *Are you both safe?*

So far. One of the fingers came close, too close, but Arathé made herself small, somehow, in her mind and the wind turned away. Father, they turn away now, even as we speak. Where are you?

Man-o'-War.

In front of Noetos, Omiy had begun to look inquisitive. "Forgotten something, fisherman?"

That's where they are turning towards. Arathé!

No, son. Let them come.

"Don't hurt me, Olifa," Noetos said, his arms out-stretched. He edged to his right, aware of the drop to the street below somewhere behind him. "You can have the stone. It means nothing to me now I have rescued my son. There's no need to kill me."

Who are you talking to? Who needs to kill you?

Omiy hesitated. Noetos could almost see the alchemist's thoughts written on his thin face. *This man is a killer. I must be careful.*

"I am sorry, fisherman, I am, yes, for I recognise your good works. You saved many of my countrymen, oh my, so selfless you were, a hero. But this stone is a prize beyond your understanding, so it is, and you are not worthy to have your coarse fish-stained hands on it. Better it goes to someone with intelligence, someone who will not leave it lying in his room like some unregarded bauble—oh my . . ."

His voice tailed off, his gaze drawn to something beyond the fisherman. Noetos felt the first stirring of wind behind him and heard the growl rise in volume.

He had only a moment, and it was barely enough. His hand shot out and grasped the alchemist's wrist below the sleeve of the man's tunic and twisted hard. Omiy squealed, but did not let the broken bottle go. Instead, he tried to cut at the hand holding him. *Fool.* Noetos could have told him his best chance was to throw his weight behind the weapon in an attempt to skewer his opponent.

He twisted Omiy's wrist again, this time with both hands, and felt the man's skin abrade beneath his rough palms. Blood welled between Noetos's fingers. Omiy screamed and let the bottle drop.

"No, fisherman!" he cried. "You'll not have it, no, you won't!" And he threw the carving as hard as he could in the direction of the approaching whirlwind.

Noetos heard it crack against the cobbles below. He released Omiy, ducked under the man's feeble swing, turned and threw himself after it.

The huanu stone was unharmed: had he really expected anything else? That a stone capable of resisting magic could be broken by throwing it out of an inn and onto the street?

As for Noetos, he was harmed by the fall. He landed on the balls of his feet and rolled sideways to dissipate the energy, as he'd been taught, but his left arm caught a pile of rubble and immediately went numb. He barely gave it a thought as he grabbed for the stone.

Panic had made Omiy throw too soon. Had he been

given time to think, Noetos judged, the alchemist would not have thrown the stone at all. Or perhaps Omiy didn't know the storm was unnatural. Either way, Noetos was able to gather the carven head of his daughter, stuff it in his belt and set off at a hobbling run towards safety, shouting for Anomer to break the link between them as he ran. He received no reply; the link was already gone.

Behind him, Omiy gave a great shriek as the whirlwind bore down on the shattered remains of the inn.

Bregor tried to deal with his mounting fear, but it seemed repeated exposure to terror did little to dampen its effects. Where was that fool fisherman? As the thought crossed his mind, Noetos appeared as if conjured, hobbling up the road past the Money Exchange, one arm held closely against his body. Arathé followed close behind him. Just as Bregor wondered where Anomer was, the boy darted out from behind the stables to Bregor's right and ran towards Suggate along the city wall.

"Bregor," the Fisher cried, "get as many as you can through the gate, would you?"

"We're going as fast as we can already," Bregor told him. "Shouting at us won't make things go any more quickly."

"Why is it taking so long?" Noetos kept turning and glancing behind him.

"What have you done, Fisher?"

"You don't have the right to know," was the retort.

Fair: enough, but not helpful. "You're drawing those whirlwinds this way, aren't you?"

"You still haven't told me why it's taken so long to get these people through the gate."

"Because *these people* aren't the ones you saw when

you were here last. People keep emerging from all over the place. The line's getting longer. And these are the less able-bodied, those who can't scale the wall."

"Uh," the man grunted. "Get them through anyway. This won't be a safe place to be in a few minutes." Noetos drew closer to him, still breathing heavily, one hand absently rubbing his left knee. "I'm going to try something. If it doesn't work, and the storm takes me, Anomer and Arathé have to lead the whirlwinds away from the city. Therefore they will need to pass through that gate—so be ready to let them through. Or does everyone here want to die?" The last question made it clear he knew he was talking to all who awaited passage through Suggate.

"Did you hear me?" he called again. "If I die, let these two pass. The whirlwinds will follow them."

"Then let them follow back in the city," a woman said. "We don't want the fingers of the gods coming near us."

Noetos growled in frustration, and called his children over to him.

"You're certain of this?" he asked them. Both nodded, eyes too bright.

Bregor wondered how the Fisher had persuaded, or threatened, them in order to gain their cooperation, and how he might undo it. He had been as much a father to them as this boorish man. They were *her* children, far more so than his.

"Find shelter," the fisherman growled at the crowd. "We're making our stand here."

A few of the crowd fled; others pushed harder at those lined up in front of them, while some tried their hand at scaling the side of the gate.

Bregor watched, immobilised by dread, as Noetos

turned and walked slowly back towards the whirlwinds of
the gods, arms spread wide as though trying to embrace his
own destruction. His children—Opuntia's children, white-
faced and red-cheeked—followed him.

Now this, *this* was near the top of the list of the most difficult things he had ever done. Not as terrifying as watching
his family die, but that had not been a conscious choice. He
had struggled then, trying to escape, to interfere. This time
he had to make himself walk towards what might well be
his own death.

But not that of his children. They would be safe if they
did what he asked.

If this storm is natural it will kill me. There was no room
for doubt in that thought. If, however, the storm turned out
to be magical, he had the word of an alchemist—a man at
least three parts insane—that the stone he carried would
protect him.

Time to find out.

He strode forward and stood in the path of the largest
funnel.

Drawn by all three people they were hunting, the fingers
of the gods came together in the open space between Suggate and the Money Exchange. Now everyone could see
the storm for what it was. Noetos shouted something to his
children, then waved at them, and they drew away from
him. The vast hand of the gods closed around the Fisher,
obscuring him from sight.

The guttural roar made by the wind thrummed through
Bregor like the sound of betrayal. Here, a man made sacrifice for others. This man had led a powerful invader away

from his friends, not towards them. How could Bregor not feel guilt, molten, leaden guilt, in his chest as he watched?

Despite his guilt, he hoped the storm's wrath would end with the death of the Fisher. He even hoped, for the man's sake, it happened quickly.

With a jerk the curtain of cloud rose up into the suddenly lightening sky. A loud rumble shook the ground. The four fingers and dark thumb twitched, elongated, and seemed to grow old and spindly before his eyes. Their attenuated shapes coalesced, then fell from the sky with a sound that was more sigh than crash.

What has Noetos done?

The dust and debris took an age to settle.

Noetos raised the huanu stone as all around him debris battered the ground. Something solid spun out of the nearest finger: a chunk of masonry coming straight towards him, nearly taking off his head. His ears buzzed and popped with the force of the wind, forcing him to swallow. Contrary winds battered at him, and he fell to one knee—his good knee—to brace himself. So a gnat would brace against the shoe about to stamp it out.

Would his heart burst from his chest before the wind took him? Would the wind kill him, or would he be pierced through with debris, or would it be the fall? Had Gawl felt such terror?

The nearest finger held back. Two fingers spun forward, flanking the first. But it was the fourth, the most slender finger, that touched him first.

The tentative blow did nothing more than knock him down, spreading him flat on the ground, which shook. He was on his back, eyes closed. He opened them, and held up the huanu stone. Funnels hovered above him, ready to claim him, plucking at him but seemingly unable to gain purchase. One twitched, as though a spear had been driven into its side. A second reached towards him, then it too began to spasm. As did the next, and the next. With an almost human howl the last whirlwind, the thumb-like wedge, drove towards him like a sword thrust. But, like the others, it broke itself against something—the power in his hand—and lifted, whirling, screaming, contracting, thrashing like a snake severed in two. Then came a sound like the angry hiss of a god's breath, and the storm collapsed.

All was quiet for the briefest moment. Then stones, mud, timber and organic things came crashing to the ground all around him. Nothing hit him—it was as though he knelt within an invisible room—but he remained tense nonetheless.

The crashing ceased. Dust, dirt and leaves drifted to the ground, coating the borders of his invisible room with fine grit. Then the room vanished and the dust and dirt filtered down on top of him.

"Noetos! Fisher!"

Voices calling for him, hands reaching for him, pulling him to his feet, dusting off his tunic, slapping him on the back. He blinked open mud-caked eyes.

"Is everyone . . . are there survivors?" he asked, took a deep sigh of relief, inhaled too much dust and began to cough desperately.

"We are as you see us," Bregor told him, and indicated the hundred or more Racemen who had witnessed the death of the storm.

"I thought it had me, friend." Noetos coughed again. "Whatever it was."

"Seems I was wrong to doubt you, Fisher. Your daughter she is, as you said, beyond a doubt; and on her heels, and the heels of your family, are the very portals of death."

"So it seems," Noetos said wearily. "Yet these things are connected to Andratan and the Undying Man, I'm sure of it. He is the arch-magician of Bhrudwo, after all. It is he who must account for what has happened here, and elsewhere."

"So you say. But before this night is over, you and your family need to answer some hard questions. Your willing and not-so-willing followers ought to know what might be in store for them."

"We may well have a talk together, all of those part of my group," Noetos said, sighing in a combination of pain and relief. "But first we need to tend the injured, bury the dead and provide for the homeless. Do you not agree?"

"M'not goin' back down there," one of the bystanders said. "Not if them whirlin' fingers might come back."

"I'd rather sleep in the Shambles," said another. "The Neherians could still be hiding in our city."

"Aye, the Summer Palace is largely intact," a grey-haired man added. "I saw soldiers heading that way before the fingers came. There may be a force just waiting to sweep down on top of anyone gullible enough to return. Seen enough, anyway, for a story to tell m'grandchildren."

No storyteller ever told a story like this one, Noetos reflected. He'd not been offered a single word of thanks. Citizens of cities rescued from the wrath of the gods were grateful to their saviours in the stories he'd been told. Not curmudgeonly complainers. But the grey-haired man, the last to speak, did have a point, however cowardly the motive for presenting it. Noetos had no doubt some of the Neherians had escaped Raceme—they were most likely scattered among the refugees up on the hill behind the city—but surely the majority of the attackers remained within the city walls.

He cast a wary eye over what remained of Raceme. The Merchants District appeared largely untouched, but large sections of the Artisans, Warehouse, Oligarchs and Justice Districts had been reduced to dust-covered debris. He wondered briefly about the dust, given the torrents of rain that had fallen before the whirlwinds ravaged the city, but of course the interiors of buildings that had then been smashed open, or even drawn up into the sky, had been dry when they were destroyed by the storm. The dust must surely have come from inside the damaged buildings, of which there was a vast number.

His gaze was drawn to people emerging from some of the ruins, walking with an eerie calm in the direction of Suggate. Noetos grimaced. No doubt they too would express their dissatisfaction with the state of affairs and upbraid their rescuer.

"Fisher, do you not think we ought to see to those on the hill?" Bregor's voice sounded hesitant, as though the insensitive fool actually realised his words were provocative.

Noetos did nothing to hold his anger in check. This was one saviour who would bite back.

Spinning around, he grabbed at the Hegeoman's tunic. "No," he said. "No, I do not. Hundreds of people are likely trapped in the wreckage, but that seems to be of no account to you. Or to these people. What is the matter with everyone?"

"They are afraid," Bregor said simply. "Afraid of the fingers, afraid of the power directing them. Afraid to return in case the power comes back." He took a settling breath.

"Afraid to get too close to those at the centre of the gods' anger. Do you blame them?"

Yes. Yes, for you have brought this upon us; you, not I.

"No," Noetos said wearily. "No. But I will aid anyone who requires it."

He turned to the crowd gathered around him—a crowd already bolstered, he suspected, by many returning from the hill south of the city. "Those who have it in them to render assistance to those searching for friends and family, make yourself known. We will go down together into the city and save anyone who can be saved."

"I give your 'no' back to you, sir," said the grey-haired man. "We will go down to the city, those of us who can, but you will not come with us, if you please. We heard how the gods' fingers searched for you and your brood. No one here wants to be near you when next the finger of god is pointed in your direction. Don't play the hero. Go away, sir, and leave us alone."

Others in the crowd murmured their agreement.

Noetos found himself completely unable to reply. Twice in one afternoon he had been pushed away by those he had sacrificed himself for. Pushed over the edge. The hurt he felt at this struck him dumb. The pure, unthinking *rejection*. He had tried so hard! He had made every choice in the interests of others!

He swallowed this like he swallowed the hot lump in his throat, coughed once, and spoke. "Very well, you have taken the responsibility for this city in your own hands. I wish you well of it, rebuilding a city that, had circumstances been but a little different, had a duke not once refused the Undying Man, I might have ruled." He hawked and spat on the ground. "I leave you to your chaos and your enemies, your death and coming disease, your hardship and your vulnerability."

He turned his back on the districts he'd played in as a child and pushed his way through the silent crowd, who closed ranks behind him. Near the entrance to Suggate he turned and faced them, and the broken city, one final time.

"I shake your dust from my clothes," he said, invoking the old curse. "May it return to you and choke you."

And, indeed, dust rose from his tunic and breeches as he slapped at them. It blew on a faint breeze towards the gathered Racemen, but fell to the ground between Noetos and the crowd.

Finally he spoke to Bregor, who had taken a few steps towards him. "Come or stay, it matters not to me. Stay and grieve for the lost, care for the injured if the townspeople let you, or come with me to find answers from the treacherous mouths of Andratan. Only decide now. If I walk through Suggate alone, alone I will remain."

The words hung in the air like a conjuration, and Noetos realised they could land on him like a curse.

"I'll do my grieving when and where necessary," Bregor said flatly. "But I will come with you, if you are going north, and for much the same reasons. Answers, Fisher, are what I'm hungry for. You will give me some, your children will give me more, and no doubt I'll be fed to bursting by those in Andratan before we're through."

"Speeches are over then," Noetos said as the Hegeoman came towards him.

And no more was said, either to them or between them, as they turned and walked towards the cavernous southern gate of Raceme, the summer capital of Roudhos-that-was.

COSMOGRAPHER

CHAPTER 3

HUNTERS

AFTER A STRUGGLE TOWARDS CON-
sciousness through what seemed to Lenares like endless
layers of feathers, she finally came to herself. For a few moments her mind lay quiet, as though a river that normally
ran through her had been dammed. She had never before
felt peace—if that was the word for this strange *absence*.

She did not much like the sensation.

One hole in the world. At this thought her mind river
began to flow again. *One hole—or was it two?* She considered this, puzzling over the differences between the hole in
the sky that had snatched her and her companions up from
the midst of Nomansland and spewed them out again who
knew where, and the one she had seen above the dreadful battle in the Valley of the Damned. Troubling notions
flowed like uprooted logs along the river of her thoughts,
snagging on each other as they went. She wanted the river to
flow smoothly, tick tick tick. The jerky, uncertain thoughts
made her angry. Tick. Tick tick tick. Tick.

She wanted this to be resolved. The uncertainty made
her feel uncomfortable. *One hole or more than one?* She

would not open her eyes until she had thought this through. Not to see where she was, not even to check if her companions were alive. *This is more important.* A faint breeze blew something across her cheek. Dust? Powder? A distraction, whatever it was, so she ignored it.

Lenares was surprised to find herself thinking at all. Why wasn't she dead? Why hadn't it killed her? She knew the secret, after all. The hole in the world—*one of the holes, perhaps,* snag, jerk went the thought—had been forming for months, perhaps years. It had already been well advanced when she discovered it. She was the very first person to notice it. That made her proud. She wasn't very good at making friends with people, she knew that, but she also knew she was special because she could understand the numbers that made up the world. She could see them in her mind. She—Lenares, and nobody else—could see the hole, the emptiness, small at first but growing bigger, eating at the places where the patterns of numbers (threads, she named them) joined together. Nodes, which were the lives of people, were being attacked by the emptiness she called the hole in the world.

And no one else saw it! Not any of the acolytes, training to be cosmographers. Not Mahudia, the Chief Cosmographer, head of their order. Not even their great and good Emperor of Elamaq, a man who, when Lenares met him, turned out to be stupid and nasty.

Mahudia, the Chief Cosmographer, had come to believe her eventually. And then the hole in the world had reached out and taken her, the woman who had been like a mother to Lenares. A lion had killed Mahudia, but Lenares knew the hole had directed it.

The Emperor had believed her when she told him about

the hole in the Garden of Angels, but said he didn't. Lies to try to get people to do what he wanted. Why did he have to lie? Why did the all-powerful Emperor have to lie? *Because he isn't all-powerful, that's why.*

Best of all, Torve believed her. More than believed. Torve, the Emperor's pet, of the despised human-like animal race, an Omeran. A freak, an animal, but one who could not only talk but also reason. Who was as good with numbers as anyone she had ever met, even Mahudia. Not as good as Lenares though, nowhere near. An animal bred for complete, unquestioning obedience to his Emperor, but who had fallen in love with Lenares, even though he knew his Emperor would disapprove.

She put her arms around herself, hugging her body at the pink feeling that blossomed in her chest when she thought of Torve. *Dirty Omeran animal*, part of her mind said, but she ignored it. Where was the harm in loving a lovely, smart person like him? Even if he kept secrets.

Was Torve alive? Had he survived the fall from the hole in the world? Almost she opened her eyes to find out. *No. Not until I have thought this through.* She clamped her eyes tightly shut, so tight that colours danced behind her eyelids.

She and Torve could love each other as long as the Emperor didn't find out. And he wouldn't. He was back in his palace in Talamaq (*no, no, no*, said a faint voice in her head, a fearful voice, not a logical voice, so she ignored it) and they were . . . she didn't know where they were. Another log in her river, jerk, snag. How could she centre herself if she didn't know where she was?

They had left her home months ago, part of the Emperor's great Northern Expedition, led out of Talamaq by the celebrated Captain Duon, to take possession of the fabulously rich lands of the north, or at least as much as they could bite off with thirty thousand superior southerners and a hundred invincible chariots. But the expedition met with disaster when enemies of Elamaq ambushed and destroyed them in the Valley of the Damned. If it hadn't been for Captain Duon and Dryman the mysterious soldier, no one would have survived. Because, for reasons Lenares had not yet worked out, the hole in the world had aided the enemies of Elamaq. The threads of the mighty Elamaq army had been burned out.

There had been a presence looking out at the world from behind the hole, a dark, ravenous god searching for prey, and Lenares was sure it was the Son. But, ah, here was the confusion. Her numbers told her that the hole itself had been caused by a god being cast out. She had seen the Son, and had—oh bliss—actually *met* the Daughter, so the missing god must therefore be the Father. The removal of the Father had caused the hole, she was certain of that, but what made her uneasy was her encounters with both the other gods when the hole had come near—the evil Son in the Valley of the Damned and the good Daughter in the House of the Gods. Twice Lenares had met the Daughter in the House of the Gods, but the House had been in different places: first, south of the Marasmos River, and second— just minutes ago, it seemed—in the midst of Nomansland. The four survivors of the Emperor's army of thousands had been herded into the gods' own house, into the place of the magical bronze map, where the gods had once gathered to see the world, and there they had been taken up into the hole by the Daughter.

But if the Daughter had rescued them, why had Lenares

been so frightened? If the Daughter had always intended to draw them through the hole in Nomansland, why did she create such chaos? Why hadn't the Daughter said something to reassure her? Was the answer that neither god had enlarged the hole alone, that both the Son and the Daughter used it when they had the opportunity? Perhaps the Daughter had driven the Son away. Would the exile of a second god make the hole bigger? Or create a new hole?

Was the Daughter really the *nice* god?

Lenares loved questions when they led to answers, and hated them when they did not. She loved answers, and most of all she loved answers only she knew. But so deep was her unease at what had just happened, she would have been happy to hear the answers from anyone. Let someone else be special. How could this have happened? To be led into Nomansland, to be herded like goats into a pen, then thrown away?

Thrown away where? Where were they now? Not the House of the Gods, and not Nomansland. Nowhere in the Elamaq Empire—her nose told her that. She could smell the fresh, sweet scent of water, an abundance of it all around her. She kept her eyes shut, but her nose kept on telling her where they were. She knew where they had to be.

She opened her eyes.

"Lenares?"

She looked into the broad, care-lined face of Torve the Omeran. His wide-set eyes gazed at her with concern, then relaxed as he saw hers were open.

"You are alive," she said, and smiled.

"So are you." His eyes danced with happiness. "Do you have any injuries?"

Lenares shook her head. She so wanted to lean forward and kiss his broad lips, but did not. Not when she did not know where they were.

He put a hand behind her neck and eased her head up; she braced herself on her elbows. He squatted, bent close and whispered in her ear.

"I'm so happy you are well."

"Why are you whispering?"

"I don't want Dryman to hear me." His voice was so quiet she could barely hear him.

"Is he alive?" she whispered back.

"He is," Torve sighed. "As is Captain Duon. A few bumps and bruises, but otherwise hale." He pulled his head away. "Do you know where we are? Has your counting been interrupted by our travel in the hole?"

"I have no centre now," she said, speaking more to herself than to Torve directly. "I've lost my count, my connection to Talamaq. I need to find another centre so my numbers work properly."

"Can you centre yourself on a person?" he asked her, easing himself back to his feet. The warm pink feeling flared in Lenares' breast at the obvious longing on his face.

"Only if that person stays constant," she said shyly.

"Oh," Torve said, and drew further away. "That I cannot promise, Lenares, for my life is not my own. I must do whatever my master commands: lie, steal, murder and even worse things. Do you understand? I am not human; he makes me not human." He bowed his head and walked a few paces away.

She closed her eyes. Imagined Torve telling her all the truth. Imagined running her fingers through his tightly curled hair, looking into his beautiful dark eyes. The pink feeling grew until her body buzzed with it.

"Is the girl awake yet?"

Dryman stood over her, his unreadable face shadowed in the gathering gloom.

"I'm awake," Lenares said. "And you're evil."

"As well we understand each other then," Dryman said, laughing shortly. "I'm evil, and you're awake. Though not as awake as you think, fey girl. Not as awake as you will be one day."

He did not explain his strange words. Instead he grabbed her wrist and pulled her roughly to her feet. "Come, then, girl, use your witchery and tell us where we are."

"I *know* where I am," she said, snapping at the soldier. "I'm standing next to a rude man who touches people without permission. And the rude man and I are standing somewhere in the northlands."

"If you can't do better than that, perhaps this expedition can do without its cosmographer."

"What expedition?" Lenares spun around, taking in the shadowed, pale shapes of buildings all around them. "I do not see our soldiers, Dryman. How will the four of us conquer the northlands? How much treasure can we carry back to Talamaq and the Emperor's feet?"

Dryman hissed; then, striking like a snake, he placed his hands either side of her head, as though he was about to kiss her—or eat her.

"Don't *touch* me!" Lenares cried.

"You are a fool," he whispered, her head between his hands, his mouth close to her ear. His breath smelled strong, of cloves and other spices. When had he eaten spices? "For someone thinking herself so clever, you know nothing and see less. You are never going to work it out, so I will tell you. I am using you, girl, as I am using Duon and the Omeran. And I am telling you this now because you will never work out how or why it is happening. I will continue to reveal to you enough truth to defeat me, but, despite this, you will not understand. I will feed on your frustration. I will savour your descent into madness. Not that you have very far to go."

"Get your hands off me," Lenares snarled, batting them away. Real fear churned within her, fear just like she had felt in the House of the Gods. *He touched me! He didn't ask if he could!* And what a touch! How could his hands be hot and cold at the same time? It was almost as though— as though Dryman was a shell, within which . . . *something* . . . Numbers flickered in front of her mind's eye but fled before she could bring them into focus.

"What has happened to this city?"

Captain Duon stood beside Dryman. He had a deep bruise under one eye and dust all through his hair. Lenares turned to him, a rebuke on her lips, angry he had interrupted her thoughts. Dryman turned also, his mouth open, ready to speak. Under the heat of their combined gaze, Duon backed away.

"Well," he said, sounding aggrieved, "I thought someone would be interested in where we have ended up."

"The far more important question is—" Dryman began.

His words were finished by Lenares: "Who brought us here?"

Dryman and Lenares stared at each other like two cats disputing territory.

"Nevertheless, take a look around you," Duon said. "Something has happened here."

Lenares stepped away from Dryman. *One*, said a quiet voice in her mind. *One what?* she wondered for a moment; then realised she had begun counting her steps. *Oh.*

At first glance the city seemed similar in style to the parts of Talamaq she had seen. Pale stone buildings, wide streets, open spaces. But the streets of Talamaq were much tidier than those of this city. Why would the citizens allow so much rubbish to pile up?

Rubble, not rubbish, she realised. *I see what Duon sees.* And, as she saw it, her numbers began to assemble themselves into some sort of pattern. The numbers lay in trails over the city like a nest of snakes. Something—a number of somethings—had swept through this city, knocking down buildings, mostly wooden structures—*who would build a house out of wood?*—scattering them either side of their passage.

She followed the pattern backwards through space and time. Five snakes, their trails crossing each other as they worked their way across the city. *Follow them backwards.* Buildings reassembled themselves. People came back to life. The snakes shrank, slow, and withdrew from the ground, up, up into *what*?

Her numbers spun around each other, grew dark, smelled of water. Thunder rolled, lightning flashed. And, in the midst of the chaos unleashed on this city, a hole, an absence of numbers.

The hole in the world. The same hole Lenares and the others came through.

This is what the hole does, she thought as she looked upon the devastated city. *It eats threads and nodes. People die. The purpose of their deeds is lost. The world unravels.*

We are all going to be destroyed.

But what is the hole doing here? Then another thought: *Are there stories other than ours? Threads we know nothing about?*

And a final thought. *Tell Dryman nothing.*

Duon licked his lips. Dryman the mercenary soldier made him nervous. The circumstances that had led to the man taking command were unclear, as were the reasons why they had continued northward after the Valley of the Damned. If he was honest, his fear of Dryman had assumed a significance out of proportion to the actual danger the man presented. It seemed unlikely the soldier could out-duel Duon with a sword. Dryman had looked competent—a little flashy, actually—during the fighting at the Valley of the Damned, but Duon could hold his own on the practice ground.

There was something about Dryman, though, that defied analysis. Everyone felt it. The strange cosmographer girl could not figure him out, and the Omeran seemed to be in his thrall. Weak minds, both. But even Dryman had not been able to find a way through the glamour that had fallen upon them in Nomansland. Nor, for all his arrogance, had he kept them from being taken up by what the cosmographer called a "hole" and deposited here.

Perhaps he hadn't wanted to.

Lenares knew something about where they were and what had happened here, Duon believed. But her caution around Dryman kept her mouth closed. She had said, though, that they were in the northlands. That made no more sense than any other idea, but nor did it make less sense, so it would do as a working assumption.

They stood in the middle of a wide but empty street.

Whatever catastrophe had wrecked the city had also driven the inhabitants either indoors or out of the city entirely; he'd seen one or two people down towards the harbour, and even now he could see indistinct movement in the gloom. Something about the city tugged at his memory: he had been here during his exploration, as late as last year perhaps, he was sure of it. Wide streets, a small but serviceable harbour, an imposing palace looming above the water. Hadn't there been a monument of some kind near the palace? He craned his neck. Though where they stood gave them a good view over the city, he could see no monument. Perhaps he was wrong.

A boy came scurrying down the road, eyes streaming with tears.

"Pardon me," Duon said, an arm outstretched, stopping the lad in his tracks. "Can you tell me what town this is?"

The boy jabbered something and tried to pull away from Duon's grasp. A northerner tongue, no doubt of it.

"Slow, please," said the captain, struggling to recall the generic northern tongue he'd learned. "Do you understand me?"

"How can I (something) understand you when you don't talk (something)?" The boy screwed up his face, evaded Duon's grasp and sprinted up the street towards a gate in the city wall.

A crowd stood by the gate, and as Duon began to walk towards them, one bent down to listen to the boy, who pointed at him. There was shouting, then movement behind the crowd, and a burly, red-haired man forced his way through, clearly attracted by the hubbub.

"A good evening to you all," Duon thought he said, was

sure he said, as he approached. "Can you tell me the name of this city?"

The boy held on to the skirts of what was probably his sister; surely she was too young to be his mother. She had tears in her eyes and dirt streaked her face. Near her stood another woman, much plainer, wearing a dirty, shapeless robe similar to that of a Talamaq palace servant. Two men flanked her. The younger, a handsome man with piercing eyes, had a hand on the plain girl's shoulder. The older was the burly red-haired man who had made his way through the crowd. The man stood now with his arms folded, as though waiting for an explanation, though he looked disinclined to believe any explanation he was given.

"Boy says you are a stranger," the burly man said as Duon drew up to the crowd by the gate. Suggate—he remembered the name. He'd remember the name of the city soon. "Can't speak the language, odd dark skin, he said. His mother is afraid you are Neherian, though you certainly don't look like a Neherian to me. What are you then? What are your companions? And where did you come from?"

"Do you regularly take instruction from boys?" Duon said. He hoped he'd got the word for "instruction" right; it would rather spoil the effect if he hadn't. As he spoke he couldn't help reflecting on the strangeness of this. He and the remnants of the expedition had travelled north magically across the world, had survived the ravages of Nomansland, only to exchange words with some local buffoon.

The man's face went red, and the boy laughed: clearly Duon had not chosen the right word. He'd been expecting to have months to practise his Bhrudwan common tongue as they made their way north towards Jasweyah, but they seemed to have bypassed the mountain kingdom altogether.

"Your pardon, sir. I am indeed a stranger here, and not practised in your tongue. Could you please tell me the name of this town?"

"You're wandering around in the ruins of the fairest city on the Fisher Coast, and you don't know where you are? Are you entirely a fool?"

"The fairest city on the Fisher Coast? Then this is Aneheri?"

"Aneheri?"

The man's face, already red, turned crimson, and his hand went to his side as though reaching for a blade. The younger man said something in low tones.

"Aye," the red man responded, nodding. "Can't blame a fool for his ignorance, but there are questions raised here, to be answered at a less urgent time. This is Raceme, friend, not the gutter-born, Alkuon-cursed Neherian nest named by you. Now, man, gather your companions and leave the city. Night is falling and the decision has been made to vacate Raceme; it is too dangerous to remain here says Captain Cohamma, apparently, and we want to prevent looting. We were on our way out but were called back by the boy's mother here, suspicious of strangers. Seems we were needed, after all. Now get your friends and follow us."

Duon opened his mouth to respond, questions forming as he prepared to speak, but the red man beat him to it.

"Are you deaf, or were my words too difficult for you? Go, fetch your friends and come with us out of the city. Do it now, or be prepared to defend yourself."

Putting aside his surprise, it was all Duon could do not

to laugh. Defend himself? Surely this man was no swordsman; he'd seldom seen anyone with such an obvious lack of grace. The fool didn't even have a sword on his hip. The younger man had a blade, though, and the look, but he wasn't the one doing the threatening.

Something else had occurred to him during the exchange: no one else in his party understood the northern language. Dryman would have to depend on him. Duon could tell the soldier whatever he wanted. Finally, a situation where his experience would count. Where he might be able to remake some meaning from the wreckage of this expedition.

"Seen any Neherians?"

"There was one a while ago, or so one of the women claimed. No sign of him now."

"What's to stop them sneaking back into the city now the storm's over? Taking by stealth what they couldn't take by force?"

"The woman makes a good point, master. Why have we abandoned the city?"

Voices washed over Duon as he lay near one of the many fires set on the hill. Weary from days of flight and the shock of finding himself suddenly somewhere else, he'd followed like a dutiful animal when Dryman decided they would join the exodus from the city. Even Lenares hadn't questioned the decision. Now he awaited events. Darkness had set in, a rich cloak of comfort unlike the cold starlight of the south, and under that cloak the survivors of Raceme lit fires, fed themselves with whatever they could find, and took stock. Listening to the many fragments of conversation gave Duon the chance to learn much of what had taken place here, and he was somewhat discomfited to find similarities with events to the south. Invasions, ambushes, storms, destruction and flight.

Despite his interest, however, he listened with only one ear. Another voice commanded his attention. Duon recognised it as emerging from the same place his previous delusional voice had come from: a small, cold place in the back of his head. But this sounded nothing like the previous voice, which had been an evil, taunting thing. Instead, this voice sounded gentle, sorrowful somehow, even though it seemed not to be forming words.

Dih heh huh huh?

A question, it sounded like, though he did not understand it. What could be happening to him? Some mental reversion to babyhood? But would a baby be able to analyse its own thinking?

On and on the voice went, speaking seldom and slowly, and Duon sensed that, despite its incomprehensibility, it directed a conversation. As he listened, a group of two men and a woman came to the southerners' fire and gave them a basket with freshly cooked meat inside. The southerners fell upon it ravenously. But still the one-sided conversation of meaningless sounds carried on in Duon's head.

Meh poh miw tew fah fah.

Pause.

Maah. Peh faw amomah.

Long pause.

Had the woman—he was almost certain it was a woman's voice—had she ceased? *You, woman, are you still there?* he thought at the voice.

An immediate response, but not directed at him. *Shh. Shum wum wish nin. Wish nin meeh shpeek.*

Pause.

Then, in Duon's mind, as clear as his own voice: *I hear your thoughts, stranger. I will hunt for you, and then we will talk. You may have the answers I need.*

Duon put a hand to his mouth, as though he could prevent his thoughts escaping. *She won't hear me if I don't direct my thoughts at her*, he told himself. She made no reply that night, nor did she speak further, so perhaps he was right.

Morning brought a cold wind. Lenares wrapped her tattered clothes about her skinny limbs, but still felt she had never been so cold. "Just a sea breeze," Captain Duon had said to her, as though such impossibly bitter temperatures were commonplace. *Perhaps they are, this far north*, she thought, horrified, though her numbers told her that this was no colder than a Talamaq winter's night. For the first time she wanted the adventure to end. She didn't care whether she solved the mystery of the hole in the world; it could eat everyone up for all she cared. Just let her be home, warm and safe with the other cosmographers.

But the other cosmographers are not at home, she admitted. They were dead. Mahudia in the belly of a lion; Rouza and Palain, ashes on the hot desert wind. She was the only one left. There was no real home to go to.

With that thought, the part of her mind still hoping to reclaim her centredness, the Talamaq base for all her numbers, finally relinquished its unconscious effort. Lenares felt it as a sudden dizziness, and for a moment the entire world went blank.

A mere moment, but it seemed to last forever. Not just blind, but stripped of all sensation, Lenares spun in the centre of the hole in the world. *This is what it is like to be dead*, she thought. *Here I am with Mahudia and Rouza and Palain and all the others, and I can't see them or feel them or hear them or touch them or hug them or be angry at them or hear them tell me how special I am, and oh, oh, please, I don't want to be dead, I like life too much. I could be touching Mahudia right now and I would never know. I could be crying or screaming and I can't tell.*

This, she realised, *is the hole in the world.*

Dare she, could she, centre herself here? Did she have the capacity to build a web of numbers here in the antithesis of everything? Or leave a numerical construction perhaps, linked to her, something that would go wherever the hole went? Something she would recognise later? No, she decided, she would not centre herself here, not yet. Not when there was something—someone—else to centre on. But she could, yes she could, attach something here, for even absence had its own shape, and any shape could be mathematically defined. Defined, then pinned down.

After what seemed to her an hour or more of careful thought, she decided to employ the special number Qarismi of Kutrubul had discovered. She began to work on an equation.

Someone had made a mistake, letting her in here.

As she spun her web of numbers, Lenares fancied she handed a thread to an invisible hand, the gentle hand of a woman who had been the only mother she had ever known.

Then Lenares' eyes opened, her hearing returned, and she tasted blood in her mouth, no doubt from her tongue. The people around her had not changed. Captain Duon still fussed over the amount of food they had been given, Dryman looked on with an unreadable expression, and Torve was still away somewhere practising his Defiance. She had no idea how much time had passed. People from the city below the hill moved about purposefully, many of them gathering together, probably getting ready to return to the ruins of their homes. She could hear their babble, mixed with the sound of birds about their morning songs. But everything had changed in the brief moment of infinity.

She took a moment to think about it, to *remember*, before the memory faded. Her link to Talamaq was gone. She could feel no drawing to the city she had grown up in; instead, a growing disquiet about what she had experienced—endured—during those years. It was as though a glamour cast upon her had finally revealed itself. Why had she always felt comfortable in Talamaq? Especially when her life had been filled with torment and ridicule? Something to be considered later. She would not forget to address the question.

The nearest she could come with words to what had changed within her was that she no longer saw with Talamaq eyes; no longer felt with Talamaq skin. Since she had left the great southern city she'd felt out of place, separated from her real life; but now she felt completely at home exactly where she was.

I am centred . . . on myself.

But what happens when you move? she asked herself. *How can you tie your numbers to a moving centre?*

The answer was immediate.

I already have a system of relative numbers. I have tied a trap in the hole in the world. Or perhaps one of the holes in the world. If I tie myself to a few more places, some of them unmoving, I can triangulate myself if necessary, and use my relative numbers most of the time.

No *absolute certainty?*

No. *No, and I don't have certainty in any part of my life. So why not use numbers rooted in probability? Does Torve love me? Probably. Does he always tell me the truth? Probably not. Who is Dryman? Certainly not whom logic says—and Torve hints—he must be.*

One question she could not answer. *Am I still special, or have I become like everyone else?*

Torve had not completed his Defiance for days. The hectic, unreal passage through Nomansland had curtailed his ritual of physical discipline. Now he understood how Lenares must feel: confused, disoriented, deprived of her centre. He wished to talk to her about it, to hear her voice, her peculiar way of assessing things that so often made sense. He just wanted to hear her voice.

He dared not speak to Lenares, however; dared not say to her what he wanted to say, not while *he* was anywhere near. She didn't know the danger. One careless word, a single unguarded gesture betraying their feelings for each other, could see Torve punished. Killed. It seemed so cruel. Just when life became worth living, it might well be taken away.

Torve threw himself into his Defiance, but it no longer held any restorative magic for him, not after last night.

He had managed to avoid Dryman since their arrival in the north, but not long after the others had settled to sleep, he had been pulled roughly awake by a hand on his shoulder. Even before the man spoke, Torve knew what he wanted, what was going to happen. He had retched, barely keeping the contents of his stomach down.

"Your presence is required," Dryman said in the bantering tone he'd always used. "Come on, did you honestly think we'd put this behind us? We have much yet to learn before I finally dip my hand in the fountain of youth. Your insights are always valuable, and you are the only one I can trust."

"Please," Torve said, the words slurring from lips slack with dread. "Haven't we learned enough? Can we not leave these people alone?"

"Now, Torve, you know better," the man chided. "You can't resist me. Must I make it a command? Would you break the love between us? Must I reduce you to what you are—an animal?"

"Yes." It was a whisper. "Command me, my lord."

"Very well."

Torve felt the familiar weight settle on the man, the weight of presence that he had always ascribed to thousands of years of unbroken command, handed down from emperor to emperor. But was it? And was he imagining it, or had it become much stronger of late? Lenares would know. She would work it out, if only he could talk freely to her.

"Torve, I command your obedience in this. You will accompany me tonight as we continue our research here in the northlands."

"Yes, my lord, I will." *I have no choice. But someday, she will find you out. May the day come soon.*

So they had hunted, he and Dryman. They had gone into the city, where rubble still fell from broken buildings, crashing into the street, and searched for subjects under an intermittent, cloud-occluded half-moon. Dryman had shown almost no regard for his own safety, just an avidity in his search. Torve did as little searching as he could, but it was he who found the woman, her legs snared by a beam protruding from the roof of her house.

Her face was pale with pain and blood loss, but it lit up when Torve brushed away the debris obscuring her. She babbled what was obviously thanks in her northern language, but her talk evaporated when Torve made no move to free her.

She eased an arm out from under her body and held it out to him, a clear gesture in any language. Torve turned away from her, unable to bear it.

"What have you found?" Dryman asked jovially. "Oh, *clever* Omeran, she's *perfect*. Come on then, let's get to work. We'll use whatever comes to hand. I charge you with remembering every expression on her face." Immediately the man started scrabbling in the debris for something sharp: a nail, glass, a wooden splinter.

Torve doubted how much he would be able to see in the darkness, but he would try to obey.

A few minutes later, after the woman realised what was happening to her and began screaming, Dryman cursed. "This would be much more scientific if she spoke our language. I've underestimated how much of this depends on what our subjects tell us."

Torve mouthed "Sorry" to the woman whenever Dryman was otherwise occupied, and when the Emperor of Elamaq went off in search of something sharper, he tried to explain the unexplainable, but of course she could not understand what he was saying. Torve hoped she could see that this was not his will, but he doubted she understood anything beyond her pain.

Eventually she seemed to find numbness, an acceptance that she was going to die, and Torve supposed he was grateful. He wished he could change places with her, so that tonight might see his death.

"Bah," Dryman muttered. "She will be of no further use to us. We have learned all we can. End her, Torve, while I consider how best to spend the rest of the evening."

How could he resist the command? As he took her bloodied head between his hands, he cursed his ancestors and the three thousand years of breeding ensuring an Omeran's absolute obedience to his or her master. He braced himself, then twisted his hands sharply. The woman's neck broke, a merciful sound in a night drenched with suffering.

And more to come.

Torve could hear other cries from amid the ruins, some strong, others failing. He laid the woman tenderly on the ground and watered her face with his tears.

Evidently his master decided he had risked enough in the city. On the way back to the hill, however, they found a young lad frog-hunting by moonlight. He afforded Dryman much more gratification than had the woman, but much less information. Not only did the lad only speak the northern tongue, Dryman made Torve force a stick between his teeth to limit the sound he made. But at this point his master was not seeking information. Torve had often observed this in their experiments beneath the Talamaq Palace. Children pleased him, because they didn't know when to lose hope.

With patience and skill developed over decades of research, Dryman brought the boy to the door of death, made him look through, and read his body for signs of what he saw there. The Emperor had always been good at this. Through the door, and back. Through, and back. Watching all the time for any hint, any chink in the power of death, any way to cheat the darkness awaiting them all.

"There!" Dryman said. "Watch the muscles relax. Is that knowledge of the coming freedom from pain, I wonder, or joy at what he's seen awaiting him? Can the keeper of the door be bought or bribed? Does Death's Herald see all, or can his eye be blinded? I have to know!"

"What will it matter, if you are able to wrest the secret of immortality from the Undying Man? Master, why must we continue this research?"

"Because I will it!" Dryman snarled, and his face, as he turned it towards Torve, glowed with an inhuman light. "Because I do not live like other men, and I should not be forced to die like them!"

"You have power," Torve said gently. "Must you also live forever?"

"How can one have power when death but awaits its chance to end it? True power can only belong to an immortal."

Torve felt the life drain from the boy lying broken between them, but said nothing, continuing instead to distract his master.

"And when I die? You will train another Omeran, no doubt, to replace me?"

"Who knows? I may decide you should remain by my side forever. Would that not be a fitting reward, Torve, for your unflagging devotion?"

Torve knew his master would be watching, but could not stop himself shuddering. Doing this forever? He could imagine nothing worse.

"Ah, Torve, he has slipped away from us while we talked. Fool! Why did you not pay attention?"

Torve ignored the man's ravings. *If you haven't learned much tonight, master, I have. You are vulnerable when ab-*

*sorbed by your research. Watch out: one day my Lenares
will catch you and kill you herself. And the moment you're
dead, I will be free.*

Torve finished his Defiance, his body shaking with the effort. The vigorous exercises were traditional among the
Omeran, and had evolved over thousands of years into a
way to suppress hatred and rage, to allow them to channel
their emotions productively in the service of their masters.
A defiance of all that had been done to them. "It is why
we have survived when all other races fell to the Elamaq,"
Torve's father had told him in the days before he'd been
taken to become the Emperor's pet. But now he wondered
whether the Defiance kept Omerans in thrall.

Torve had been unsure what to think when he had been
commanded by the Emperor to accompany Captain Duon's great expedition to the northlands. He was to look out
for the blood of immortality, the Emperor had told him.
For whom could the Emperor trust, apart from his faithful
slave, to bring the blood back south without sampling it
along the way? Eventually Torve decided to be pleased by
the opportunity, especially since it afforded him the chance
to be close to the intriguing young cosmographer. Yet the
Emperor had clearly not trusted him, for after the events
of the Valley of the Damned had played out, and the great
Amaqi army had been destroyed, Torve had discovered that
the Emperor of Talamaq had hidden himself within his own
expedition.

For a time Torve wondered why he had not recognised
his master. Yes, the Emperor had gone everywhere and
done everything behind a golden mask, and no one, not
even Torve, his closest confidant, knew what his uncovered

face looked like. But the voice, the sardonic tone, the burning eyes, ought to have betrayed the man. Nevertheless, Torve had not even suspected the real identity of Dryman the mercenary soldier until the night they spent with the Children of the Desert, when Dryman had revealed himself as the Emperor and forced Torve to accompany him on a hunt. They had taken a young girl that night, snatched her right out of her tent, from between her sleeping parents.

But what surprised Torve—no, shocked him—was Lenares' inability to recognise the Emperor. She had the uncanny talent to assess anyone she met using her strange vision of the world—*the numbers never lie*, she told Torve—and had done so when she had first met the Emperor. She had summarised his master perfectly. "You want to live forever," she'd told him. "You are afraid to die."

The Emperor had been angered by that. Shocked that a halfwit girl had seen through him. So when the Children of the Desert had confronted their guests about the death of one of their own, Torve had expected Lenares to unmask Dryman as the murderous Emperor, thus condemning the man to death and setting Torve free. But she had not. Not because she could keep a secret, much less that she thought this a secret worth keeping. No, she had said nothing because she simply hadn't recognised him.

Something about the soldier bothered her, Torve knew. She had said so on occasion. It was all there: in his voice, his manner, the hunger in his deep eyes, even the callus on the bridge of his nose where the mask usually rested. But she could not see! No matter how many hints Torve offered; clues that skirted right to the edge of the prohibition laid upon him not to reveal Dryman's true identity.

He could only think that Dryman had spread some

sort of glamour over them. But the Emperor had rejected magic, along with everything else that came from the gods. So how could this be?

He would wait, he would watch, he would learn. And somehow he would tell Lenares what she needed to know without breaking his vow of obedience. Then this dreadful grind of torture and death would finally be over, and he and Lenares could be together.

The first reports that Raceme had been occupied overnight by the Neherians began filtering back to the hill above the city soon after dawn. Knots of Racemen began to gather, coalescing into crowds, and finally forming a great assembly around the largest of the bonfires. Duon followed them, accompanied by the enigmatic Dryman.

"Tell me what they say, Captain," Dryman ordered.

Duon bridled at the casual assumption of command, but said nothing. Time enough later for confrontation.

"A few of the men went into the city just before dawn," Duon reported. "They got as far as the Money Exchange— I don't know where that is, before you ask—and were confronted by red-bibbed soldiers, armed with swords and spears, coming the other way. The southern gate had been undefended, so the Racemen suppose the Neherians were only then securing the city. As the sun rose the Racemen could see red bibs atop buildings and in the intersections of the main streets. A fight broke out and one of the Racemen was killed. The others ran away, though that is not how they describe it, brave soldiers they imagine themselves to be. They left their friend's body behind, of course."

And how many bodies did you leave behind, brave

leader? The cynical voice took Duon by surprise, as it always did.

"So, in essence, this tribe's town has been conquered by another, stronger tribe," Dryman said. "Is this of any real importance? Will it prevent us resuming our task?"

"Forgive me, soldier," Duon said, his mouth drying as he spoke, knowing he risked much. "I have been meaning to ask. What task is this?"

Dryman turned to the captain. Duon searched the man's face in vain for any sign of pity, of mercy, of humanity. He hadn't meant to precipitate the confrontation so soon, but here it was, and he could no longer avoid it.

"What task?" Dryman echoed. "The task your Emperor set you, of course. You of all people should remember. It was you, after all, who reported to us the wealth and vulnerability of the northlands."

"But we are only four—"

"Has the Emperor appeared to you? Has he told you to abandon your task? Where is your pride in your commission?"

"Look here, man, pride is not the issue. What can we achieve? We were supposed to be here with thirty thousand men!"

"Ah, so obedience to your Emperor is a matter of convenience? When you no longer have the resources you asked for, obedience ends?"

That stung. "These are just words, Dryman. Anyone can see the futility of what you're asking. How many baskets of treasure can we bring home on four backs? Wouldn't we do better to return to Talamaq and apprise the Emperor of the failure of his mission?"

The mercenary took a step closer to the captain. "Think

on this then. Have you asked yourself why we were directed northward after our defeat? Clearly, someone or some*thing* wants us to continue with our mission. You came through the hole with the rest of us. Have you not yet asked yourself what could have been the purpose of this supernatural intervention?"

Duon paused. And into the silence came the voice from the back of his head, the voice that had tormented him ever since the day they'd left Talamaq.

Really, how can I do anything with you if you insist on remaining so obtuse?

Shut up, Duon thought. *I don't believe in you; you are a product of my fear of failure—*

Oh, come on. You know I'm real. And if I'm real, why resist the notion that there are things going on you know nothing about?

I don't want to know anything about them. Or you. Stubborn, a child refusing to face reality. Duon knew he was behaving like a fool.

Do you want to wrest back power from Dryman? the voice asked seductively.

Oh.

"I don't know anything about supernatural forces," Duon said to Dryman. "I'm just a soldier. I'd need to have new orders to deal with supernatural forces."

The voice in the back of his head groaned.

Dryman smiled the smile of a man who has manoeuvred his adversary to exactly the place he wants him.

"Then it is fortunate you have me with you, for I have encountered supernatural forces before. Somewhat of an expert, in fact. Just listen to me, and all will be well."

Now do you see why you must take my advice?

No. I see why I need advice. Yours may be no better than his. But speak away; I will listen. On one condition. You explain exactly who you are and how you gained access to my head.

A tickle of sound moved across his mind, as though some one had run a fingernail gently across his skin. A woman's voice—*the* woman's voice—as clear as a mountain stream: *That's the best question you could have asked him.*

Who was that? the other voice asked.

Duon said nothing, tried to *think* nothing. He didn't think the woman and the cynical man would like each other, and he didn't want them talking together—or worse, fighting each other—in his head.

"Eat your fill," Dryman said. "Take whatever extra food these fools offer you, and scavenge anything you think will be useful. We'll soon be on our way north. The real treasure is still some distance away."

Dryman patted him on the shoulder, as though Duon had just pleased his master with a new trick, then walked away.

Finally, Duon thought, *I have my mind to myself.*

Not quite, the woman's voice said. *I want to find out who you are, and how you can mind-speak. Are you here, around the fire? If you are, stand up and wave your arms. Then I will make contact with you.*

Not likely, Duon replied, and tried to break his mind away from the contact. He began to sing a children's non-sense rhyming song in his head.

But he had so many questions, and could not prevent them forming even as he gave himself to the song he'd learned from his mother. Who was the woman in his mind? Was she the same woman as the one who spoke nonsense syllables and, if so, why could she speak so clearly to him and not to others? And who was the hated cynical man who had been speaking into his mind for months? And why would a mercenary such as Dryman care about the wishes of the Emperor? Above all, how was he, Duon, to get the better of the mercenary and reclaim his rightful place at the head of the remnants of the expedition?

Duon sat with Torve, rolling slivers of meat into balls and wrapping them in greased paper. He could feel the woman in his mind. She was somewhere out there, close by, moving around the fire, hunting for him. She wanted to examine his secret voices, but he didn't want even to acknowledge them. He wanted to be left alone.

"Generous of these people to include strangers in their largesse," he said to the Omeran.

"How do they know we are strangers?" Torve said. "We might be residents. The town is large enough that people might assume they simply haven't met us before."

"Look around you. Have you seen anyone else with skin as dark as mine, let alone yours? And don't you think our inability to speak fluently with them might be a hint? And our clothes—tattered, odorous and of a fashion completely different from anything any of them are wearing. Enough reasons?"

Duon reflected on how far he had fallen. Debating with an Omeran! Let alone losing his temper with one. He wasn't one of those who believed Omerans were only animals, but neither did he hold with treating them as humans. Something unnatural about that. Still, when one of them was the only person who would listen to you, it made him easier to accept.

"These people are grieving over the loss of fellow citizens and loved ones," Torve said. "They have just been told they may have lost their city. They may still be in danger of attack. How much time do they have to consider the differences between one man and another?"

"You make a good point," Duon said. "But now, just after having been dispossessed by strangers, is precisely when they are likely to be at their most suspicious."

As if conjured by his words, a group of people came towards them. Duon recognised the burly, red-haired man he had spoken to just after they'd arrived in this place; two others had been with him. A dumpy, plain woman and a thin, elegant boy with piercing eyes. They accompanied the man now. Something stirred at the back of Duon's mind.

The woman tugged on the boy's arm. "Heeh," she said. "Hee thum wheeh heeh."

She has no tongue. She is the one.

"You're the fellow I spoke to last evening," the burly man said. "I'm still curious as to where you are from."

"Did I not say?" Duon replied, thinking carefully. "We're from south of here."

"Oh?" the man said, his deep voice freighted with suspicion. "My children"—he indicated the woman and the boy—"and I are also from the south. From Fossa on the Fisher Coast. I don't remember seeing you before. Which village is your home?"

"We come from further south than you, I'm sure," Duon replied.

The man's gaze sharpened. "Neherius?"

You do have a talent for saying the wrong thing, said the cynical voice in Duon's head. The woman—the burly man's daughter—immediately put her hands to her temples.

"No, we are strangers from far south of Neherius," Duon said, ignoring the voice. "Further south than any kingdom you know."

He watched out of the corner of his eyes as the woman whispered in her brother's ear, her hands gesticulating all the while. He could hear the sounds she made, they echoed in his mind, not in his ears: *Vuh baak mann heehs me shpeek.*

Duon wondered suddenly: *Am I the only one who can hear her? Or can she mind-speak with her brother and father? If she can, why is she whispering in her brother's ear?*

Because she doesn't want you to hear her, imbecile, said the cynical voice in his head. *She doesn't know you can hear her spoken words through your mind-link.*

Mind-link? Duon thought at the voice. *And what do you know about such things that you can put a name to it?*

He dragged his thoughts back to the conversation. "Why does where we live matter?" he asked the red-haired man.

"You should know—ought to know, if you've just travelled north—that this land is at war. The Neherians have invaded the Fisher Coast. It appears that Raceme has fallen to them. Now I'd like to know how you found yourself in a city, the name of which you didn't even know, unaware that there was a war going on."

"Arathé says the mind-talker is one of these men," the man's son said, interrupting his father. "She thinks it's the man you're talking to."

"What's wrong with your daughter?" Duon asked. Far too rude, but he was shaken. To have been found so quickly! He didn't know enough yet about his mind-voices to determine whether they should be kept secret, but he knew he didn't want this tongueless woman to learn any more about him.

"She had her tongue cut out by the servants of the Undying Man," said the burly man. The anger underlying his voice was unmistakable. "You've heard of the Undying Man, I take it?"

"I've heard of him," Duon answered guardedly. *I've met him, actually,* he thought as he answered. *I spent some time in his fortress, a little over two years ago now, as his guest.*

He wasn't trying to communicate, it was just a memory, but it lay across the forefront of his mind. Of course she picked it up, like a bird spying a shiny thread.

Did you? Her mind-voice sounded excited. *Two years ago? I was in Andratan then.*

A pause. Duon looked at the woman, stared right into her eyes, and saw they were every bit as piercing as those of her brother.

"Whah ihh veay ooh ooh ush?" she asked. At the same time, her voice lanced through his brain: *What did they do to us?*

Then the cynical voice rang out in Duon's head; and, as it spoke, it was clear to Duon that the girl heard it too. Two of them, afflicted in the same manner. The likely explanation for their ability to mind-speak each other.

Come north to Andratan and find out.

CHAPTER 4

SECRET ENCOUNTER

LEFT TO HER OWN DEVICES while Duon and Dryman wasted time talking with the Racemen, Lenares began to wonder why her fellow southerners refused to discuss what had happened to them. She had many questions and seemed the only one willing to examine them. Were the others not interested in how they could have travelled thousands and thousands of paces in a single moment of time? Why were they all consumed by the events in this small place?

Dryman would hear no questions when he returned. "We are leaving soon," he said brusquely. "We're going north. Eat as much as you can, collect food, look for discarded shoes and clothes, beg anything you can't steal. Be ready, or you'll answer to me."

So Lenares and Torve spent the morning scavenging from people ill able to afford to give anything away. Lenares found herself wanting to remain here, knowing that nothing could be as important as finding and halting the hole in the world (she still thought of it as one hole, though knew it might be two), but Dryman was insistent. He did not care about her feelings and would hear none of her arguments.

"North," he said. "We must go north. The Emperor demands it."

The big hairy red man called Noetos seemed in charge of the local people, even though another man, Captain Cohamma, thought *he* was. She knew two captains, Duon and Cohamma, and neither was listened to. But the people were prepared to listen to the hairy man, which was odd, because he came from somewhere else. Not as far away as she and her fellow southerners did though. "He defied the Fingers of the Gods," the women around the cooking fires said to each other. Duon told Dryman what they were saying, and Lenares listened. *What fingers of which gods?* she wondered, but her thoughts were lost in Duon's commentary.

"He fought and killed a dozen Neherians with his sword. He stood there and breathed in the whirlwind, sucking it out of the sky. Sunaiya was there, she saw it. He didn't want us to leave Raceme last night, but Captain Cohamma forced us out. Now the Neherians have control of our city. Who should we listen to? Who cares where he comes from? He wants us to try to retake Raceme—is that a good idea? Haven't we lost enough already? How can we survive without our homes? Who will bury our dead?"

Now Lenares watched the women leave the cooking fires and settle down to work. Their men had gone somewhere—Duon said that many of them had gone with Captain Cohamma to scout the city, to see if any of the secret ways were undefended—leaving the women to find food. Fed up with doing nothing, Lenares stood up, stretched her legs and joined them.

She could not understand their language, but it did not

matter. She could see their numbers, interpret their moods, read their fears, their determination to do what had to be done. There was something reassuring about working with these women. Knocking on the doors of huts and begging for food was better than sitting with the captain and the soldier. Taking food to others was better even than spending time with Torve, who seemed afraid to look at her.

You would hardly know there was anything wrong, reading the faces of these women. For a while Lenares worried that she might have forgotten how to interpret the numbers correctly, but she reminded herself that people were likely to be different in different places. Friendly, not quarrelsome like the cosmographers were. They did not sulk over petty things. They got on and did what needed to be done.

The women welcomed her as part of their group. They shrugged their shoulders when she indicated she couldn't talk, and laughed and joked with each other, even though they must have been worried about what had happened to them. Not all of them were like this, though. A few women sat listlessly on the ground, or moved purposelessly from group to group. Perhaps these were the ones who had lost family members. The friendly women took special care over these ones.

Within a single hour Lenares found herself able to understand much of what the women said. She was delighted. It seemed her numbers had more uses than even she had suspected. She associated the sound of the words the women spoke with particular facial mannerisms, body language and a dozen other clues. *I am reading them,* Lenares realised. *I am hearing their language through my numbers*.

The women were talking about the loss of their city, of course they were. Their husbands and sons were indeed scouting the city, seeing what could be done to take it back. This hill they had camped on was called Shambles Hill, and the small wooden buildings packed about its base were known as the Shambles. It was a poor place, and people who couldn't afford to live in Raceme proper lived there. These huts were where the women begged most of their food. Some of the women were embarrassed by this: they had thought themselves too good to seek charity from the poor, but in most cases it had been offered freely.

Lenares found her numbers could not help her talk to them—though she felt confident even that would come in time—but she enjoyed listening. Had such a disaster happened in Talamaq, people would have bickered and fought in their haste to blame each other. This was a much nicer place than Great Golden Talamaq. People in Talamaq did not smile at her like these women did.

"I wonder where this girl is from," one of the laughing woman said. "She's a hard worker."

"I thought she might have been a—" Lenares didn't understand the word, but she thought it meant someone not right in the head. "She's not, though. She understands what we're saying."

"She looks like an Ikhnal—some of them have skin that light. Definitely someone from the Fisher Coast."

"She's with the three men who appeared in the city just after the storm," said another woman. "They're definitely not from this part of Bhrudwo. Did you see how dark their skin was?"

"I didn't like the look of them. One of them had shifty eyes. Do you suppose the girl's their—" and she used another word Lenares could not interpret.

"The younger man is nice." Lenares supposed the

woman was talking about Captain Duon. "He has such a friendly face. And did you see the shape of his shoulders? He could——" another series of words she didn't understand, accompanied by gestures, "with me any time he wanted." The women laughed together and Lenares laughed with them.

And so the talk went. Lenares loved it all. To be included was such a wonderful feeling. She felt now as she had felt the day she appeared at the Emperor's court.

So this is happiness.

"Lenares?"

She turned to see who had placed his hand on her shoulder. "Don't touch—oh, Torve. Does Dryman want something? Have you collected enough food?"

Torve looked embarrassed, as though caught doing something he shouldn't. "Dryman is elsewhere, and I have as much food as we can carry. I came to see you, to talk to you. I thought you might want to talk about what happened to us in Nomansland."

"I am enjoying myself here," she said, more strongly than she intended to. Her happiness had made her forget her previous concern about the hole in the world, she realised; and, because she was honest, she acknowledged to herself she did not want anything to interfere with that happiness. "These people do not care whether I have a gift or not. None of them call me a halfwit."

"Nor do I," Torve said gently.

"But you don't think I am human."

"I think you're my Lenares," Torve answered. "It's the others who think neither of us are human. You know this."

"Can we talk here?" said Lenares, reluctant to leave her

new friends, but finding Torve's gentle speech stirring her, as it always did. *My Lenares, he said.*

"Wouldn't you rather talk where we can't be overheard?"

She thought about it and found that yes, she would very much like to talk with Torve where no one else could hear them. The warm pink feeling moved from her chest as she thought about it, down it went, until she could feel it . . . well, in the strangest place. *Why there?*

"Where do you want us to go?" she asked, her voice somewhat hoarse.

"Down beyond those trees," Torve indicated. "We will not be overheard there."

"Wait for me there. I think I need to . . . you know, go."

"We don't have long. Dryman will be back soon."

Lenares watched him walk away and saw the beauty, the nobility, in his numbers. Honesty, integrity, passion. And a deep sadness, so tightly held it was difficult for her to read. She could pry, but Torve would not like that. And everything about him was held in thrall by something else. Something to do with Dryman and his obedience to the Emperor. Something, she was beginning to realise, she would have to save him from.

Torve couldn't name the emotion that had driven him to take Lenares aside. He had no experience that could give the feeling a name, no friend or parent to tell him what he felt was desire. His master had said little of these things, for who would talk of love—of making love—to an animal?

If he had known what motivated him, he would have resisted it with everything he had. He could not, they could not, never, not *that*, not while his master still lived. Could not. So, because they could not, he did not consider that they might.

"Lenares?"

"Yes?"

She sat down beside him on a grassy slope overlooking the sea. The late morning was warm and the air moist; unusual for his desert senses, made stranger still by the absence of the clinging Talamaq dust. The grass fairly wriggled with life, and his ears were entertained by birds chirruping to each other in trees off to their right. The sounds of the others had been left well behind.

"Am I such a disappointment to you?"

"Yes," she said; and the way in which she stated the truth without adornment took his breath away. "I wish you could tell me everything, all the truth. You confuse me and hurt me. But you make me feel good too. I want to talk with you all the time."

"Just talk?"

Torve's heart leapt in his chest at his daring words. Talking as the young men and women did behind the curtains at summer feasts in the Talamaq Palace. Where was this taking them? He remembered the House of the Gods and how they had kissed, how they had wandered from room to room holding hands, and in his heart named them the best days of his life.

"No," Lenares said shyly, and bit her lip. "I also like . . . this." She reached out a hand and took his.

It was just a touch. She had held his hand before; it was nothing compared to what those he'd spied upon at the Emperor's command had got up to. Nothing at all. But he found his whole body inflamed by the feel of her skin on his. Her touch signalled her complete openness, her surrender. An image crossed his mind, and he began to realise the peril they were in. *Ask her a question*, he thought. *Get her talking; much safer than what might otherwise happen*.

He cleared his throat. "Are there two Houses of the Gods or just one?" he asked her. Inane, he knew, but the best he could come up with. He did not let go of her hand.

"One," she answered dreamily, her fingers interlacing his. "But it can appear in many places. I think there are sacred places in each of the three continents, places where the gods once met, and they took their House with them to each meeting."

"Once met?"

"Once, but no more. The Father was driven out by the others many years ago, and now the Son and the Daughter quarrel. There are no more meetings."

"Quarrels are such terrible things," Torve said. "People driven apart often because of the most trivial disagreements."

"Why should people fight? Why don't they just tell the truth to each other?"

Torve knew Lenares did not intend to wound, but her words hurt nonetheless. "I tell as much of the truth as I can," he said.

"I know," she replied.

"Your numbers don't tell you everything," said Torve, moving as close as he was able to the secret she seemed unable to penetrate. He willed her to see.

"I know," she said again. "In Talamaq I lived such a small life, spending every day with the same people, that my numbers served to describe everything. I thought I knew all there is to know. But out here there is too much, far too much to understand."

"And you have no centre."

"I don't need one," she said.

His heart fell. "What *do* you need?"

She must have known what he wanted her to say. Their hands were clasped tightly, they had edged close to each other so their legs touched. She looked into his eyes and said what only Lenares would say in a situation like this.

"Nothing. I have finally realised I need nothing."

Torve sighed. He knew they were fortunate, that her habit of telling the truth protected them from disaster. Yet he wished she had been willing to play the game of words, to go just a little further along the road to destruction, so that he could cry "Stop!" So that he could be the strong one.

"Kiss me," she said.

The camp stirred. Duon raised his head, woken from a short nap. From what he could tell, it was early afternoon. Dryman had returned from one of his unexplained wanderings; the man now slept beside him. *Seems like the first time I've ever seen him sleep.*

The men of Raceme had woken him. They filed back into camp, returning from their latest foray into Raceme with their heads down, clear disappointment on their features. There was no need to listen to their reports. It was clear that the invaders had consolidated their hold on the town.

"Sentries up on every part of the wall," the men said, shaking their heads. "Guards on the gates; archers stationed on the Cavalier, above Suggate and the Water Gate, and all along the groyne of the harbour. No way in."

"There must be a way in," the women said. "The Neherians found a way, after all."

"Yes," said the men, "but see how they were equipped, and look what it cost them. Even then they would have failed but for the storm. We have neither their equipment nor their numbers, unless you expect the women and children to march unarmed against them. And the weather is clear."

"Is there not one among you brave enough to try to win back our homes?" asked the women.

This angered the men. "You saw our bravery. We risked their arrows and their swords to spy out the city. But it is not our city any more."

"Then where are we to go? How can we leave our sons and daughters behind, unburied, unmourned?" The women began to cry bitter tears.

The burly red-haired man stood before them. "This is what we do," he said. "We go north. We leave Raceme to the rats for just a little while. Let them get fat and complacent. We regroup, find some willing friends, and then we return to drive the rats out. What better burial gift could you offer your dead than that?"

The men muttered at this, but the women saw the sense of the red-haired man's words. "We go north," they said. "For a little while."

Captain Duon settled back on his haunches. The sun had begun to descend, and still Dryman slept on. Why should Duon wake the man? He knew the mercenary would want to be informed, but it was his own fault he slept, since he had been up most of the previous night prowling about.

All around, the survivors of Raceme broke camp with a minimum of fuss, despite the demands of crying children and a number of injured men and women. Duon tried to estimate how many people were on the hill: five thousand at least, maybe more. The red-haired man was right. There was nothing even this number could do against a well-prepared enemy, especially without the element of surprise. Perhaps if another storm was to come . . . but Duon knew little about the weather in these parts; and hadn't the cosmographer said the storm had been unnatural? Unnatural enough, at least, to disgorge them into the city at the moment it had been destroyed.

They could stay here on this hill no longer anyway, as he doubted there was much, if any, food left in the Shambles. And the longer they remained, the greater the chance their conquerors would send out a sortie against them. Someone, somewhere, would surely offer them shelter.

Finally Duon could wait no more. People were leaving the hill in groups, all moving north. Oh, how he wished he could leave the hateful soldier sleeping there, to wake alone on an empty hillside—or better, to be captured by the Neherians. He wished he were the sort of man who could take his sword and cut open the mercenary's throat. But he'd seen the threat in the other man's eyes, and knew that if the attempt failed he'd never outrun the man's vengeance.

"Dryman," he said, shaking him by the shoulder. "Time to wake."

The mercenary moved from deep sleep to fully awake in a split second.

"Where is everyone going?" he asked, a scowl on his face. "Why have you waited so long to wake me?"

"I've been busy preparing, as you instructed. You said nothing about being woken."

The man was on his feet and at Duon's throat in an instant. "Don't shave the ends with me," he snarled, his hand under the captain's chin. "You have neither the wit nor the strength to deal with me, boy."

The man's voice thundered like a storm, and a dreadful weight settled on the captain's shoulders. Duon thought about nodding, but noticed the gleam of a knife in the soldier's hand and thought better of it.

Dryman took silence as acquiescence. "Where are the Omeran and the halfwit?"

Duon spread his hands. "I thought you sent them on some task."

"They were tasked to prepare for our departure. They should be here. He had better not be . . . no, he wouldn't. Couldn't." The man shook his head, but his eyes narrowed. "Go and find them, Duon."

Again Dryman treated Duon as his servant. The mercenary could do it because there was something about him that must be obeyed. *I am a captain, the leader of the Emperor's great expedition. Who is this soldier?*

Duon nodded respectfully to the man, resolving as he strode away to speak to Lenares about him. Perhaps if they put their heads together they could bring the man down somehow.

It is not only a matter of pride, Duon told himself. *This man is dangerous, and has his own agenda. Despite his arguments, and no matter what may be done to me or my family, it is my duty to return to Talamaq and humble myself before the Emperor. But I will not humble myself before this man.*

Her fingers were cool against his skin, touching him gently, brushing his cheek, running slowly down the line of his

jaw. Their touch thickened his throat and set his skin burning. She brought her mouth towards his, her eyes closed,
her hair cascading over one cheek. As her lips touched
his, she made a small sound in her throat. Little intimacies,
each one fanning the flame of his desire.

He closed his mouth over hers, and drew in her breath.
Months of travel, weeks of deprivation and days of fear
had done nothing to sour it; he had never tasted anything so
sweet. She pressed herself against him. He could feel the
swell of her and fought to maintain a degree of control.

But what could he do—what could either of them do—
against the power they had unleashed? The threat of discovery, of death, was not sufficient to prevent Torve from
raising his own hand to her face and touching her skin, her
hair, with all the tenderness he possessed. *The body has its
own language*, he acknowledged, closing his eyes to savour
every sensation. *Listen, Lenares, as I speak to you. As my
body loves yours with its own language.*

They clung to each other, moving slowly, tentatively,
desperately afraid of hurting and being hurt, while taking
pleasure where it was offered. After a time he opened his
eyes to find hers, less than a hand-span away, focused in-
tently on him. Lustrous, deep, pupils wide open.

"There is more, isn't there," she said, her breathing fast
and shallow against his neck. "More for us to explore. Do
you know what it is? Will you show me?"

His heart rose into his throat.

"Yes," he said thickly. "I have witnessed what comes
next. I will show you."

Duon made two careful circuits of Shambles Hill, but saw
no sign of the cosmographer or the Omeran. He took the

opportunity to talk with a few of the remaining Racemen, but none had seen his companions recently. He did not think to speak with the women, who would have been able to tell him of a man, and a woman with hot eyes, who had left some time ago in obvious pursuit of the oldest magic.

Curse the man!

Duon meant Dryman, not Torve; after all, how could an Omeran be held responsible for what he did? Especially since the Emperor had sent him away north with the expedition, and therefore freed him from the obligation to obey his master?

And why had the Emperor done that? In what way was the Omeran's presence necessary? If there truly were supernatural entities involved in their tale—and how could Duon doubt it, given the voices in his head, and the way in which they had been ripped from their own lands—why had they selected the Omeran for survival when thousands of more useful men had been slaughtered?

He had not asked enough questions, it was clear, allowing instead the flow of events to take him. This was not the behaviour of a commander. He would gather together his band—his, not Dryman's—and the questions would be asked, and answered.

Duon crested the brow of a small hill and the ocean came into view. The northern seas were just as he remembered: cool, blue-green and inviting, so unlike the treacherous southern ocean. He imagined himself fleeing, running away from Dryman and the remnants of his expedition, finding an empty beach, building a shack and spending his days fishing. A fantasy, he knew, but one that made far more sense than continuing north. Not, he reminded himself, something a leader could entertain.

His eyes narrowed, and he shaded them against the sun with his hand. Something was moving below him. *Somebody struggling—no, fighting*. Duon drew his blade.

No, he corrected himself, as the cynical voice in his head began to chuckle. *Not fighting*.

I have a fever, Lenares told herself. Torve had infected her with something, it seemed; her skin flushed hot under his hands. She didn't care where he put them. No, she did care, she wanted him to put them on her private places. *I am sick. My body is no longer under my control*. Yet the delicious sensations coursing through her at his touch felt nothing like fever.

The merest touch from another person was normally enough to enrage her. Her body was hers, and people were supposed to stay well away from it. But there were parts of her, secret places, now longing for his touch.

She had never experienced numbers like this before. Skin on skin, love open to love. She felt herself slowly drawing towards an inexplicable, unguessable completion.

Simply noticing a small scar under Lenares' chin undid Torve.

Had he thought it through—had he known something of the emotional aspects of the physical expression of love—he might have anticipated this. As it was, the sight of the scar landed like a blow to his stomach. Perhaps the scar was the legacy of some deeply traumatic event, or the result of a careless injury, its cause already forgotten. It didn't matter. What mattered was that Torve suddenly saw not Lenares, his beloved, but the poor woman trapped by the collapsed building back in the city. He saw that woman's bleeding

body, saw it respond to his touch in an entirely different
fashion from the one beneath him now.

Different, but so similar. Shortness of breath, flushed
skin, sweat, inarticulate groans, uncontrolled movement.
The idea that he was tormenting Lenares took hold of him,
and he could not shake it. His hands moved over her, his
mouth again found hers, then moved away as he fought
himself a moment longer; but the images of all those he
and his master had tortured swam before his eyes, and his
desire vanished like a startled bird.

"Torve?" she said, her voice rough with her longing.
"What is it? What is the matter?"

He pushed himself up on his hands, rolled off her and
straightened her tunic. *Oh, Father, Son and Daughter, what
have I become?*

"I . . ." He could not explain. Would never be able to explain. The Emperor had ruined everything.

"Oh!" Lenares said, rolling away from Torve and finding a sitting position. He turned to follow her gaze, and saw
a man on the hill behind them. His stomach clenched.

"Captain Duon!" Lenares cried.

Her innocence was so obviously feigned it took Torve a
moment to realise she had spoken to someone, another moment to acknowledge who it was, a third to seize the excuse
this offered him—*No need to explain now, she'll assume
I saw Captain Duon coming*—and a fourth to understand
that Lenares had been engaged in uncharacteristic deception. She was trying to keep their liaison—their almost
completed liaison—a secret.

Contrary emotions swirled in his breast. Relief, regret,
guilt, horror and confusion at war within him. He was aware
enough to realise that this incident might make it impos-

sible for him to love anyone; that perhaps, now the association had been made, he would always be unable to separate the act of love from the act of torture. But he had no way of erasing the miserable memories infesting his mind.

It was as though, having discovered at her hands he was human, the knowledge had been stripped away.

Oh, life was so cruel.

"Dryman is very angry with the two of you," Captain Duon said as he approached. Torve sensed the effort the man put in to keep his voice even, to keep his distaste at what he'd seen from the surface.

"Is *he* here?" Torve asked. Impossible not to ask. "Has he—did he see?"

The captain came over and pulled Torve to his feet. "He saw nothing, he knows nothing. And the less he knows, the better you, I and your . . . and the cosmographer, will be. Do you understand me? I will say nothing to Dryman about what I've seen, even though I have a suspicion he might not like to hear what half the remnant of his army has been getting up to with each other. And in return you will say nothing to him about anything I might do." Captain Duon licked his lips, then cocked his head, as though listening to something. "It is very important we don't allow ourselves to be commanded by this man. We must keep our own counsel. He's not to be trusted. I have no hard evidence for this, not yet, but I know it to be true."

"He is evil," said Lenares. "There is something false about him. He does not add up."

Torve almost laughed at Lenares' use of the cliché, then realised she meant the phrase literally. Dryman's numbers didn't create a full picture for Lenares to read; he was able to keep part of himself hidden from her. As long as she worried about this, as long as she worked to unmask Dryman, she was dangerous to him.

Captain Duon nodded at Lenares' words, clearly paying them respect.

"Very well, Captain, we will respect your confidences as you respect ours," Torve said, looking to Lenares for confirmation. His breathing had returned to near normal, but the blood still pounded through his body, a pulsing recognition of what he had so nearly done. A growing regret had begun to overwhelm his relief. He knew he wished to share everything he had with Lenares, and realised he might never have another opportunity to do so.

Lenares nodded, and put her soft hand in his. It was all he could do not to cast it away. Sorrow settled on him, sorrow so deep it threatened to engulf him. Beside him the girl sighed, and the sound she made was the sound of a tortured soul's last breath, the sound of death.

CHAPTER 5

THE HEIR OF ROUDHOS

DUON RETURNED TO DRYMAN WITH Lenares and Torve in tow, and the defensive, cryptic answers he was forced to supply put the mercenary in a foul mood. It seemed likely that, had the Omeran and the cosmographer not been there, Dryman might have struck Duon with his fists, or even his sword.

Duon could have predicted what happened next: the incident suddenly became his fault. How, Dryman said, could one expect an Omeran and a cosmographer to act in the interests of the Emperor? If there was a problem, Dryman said, it was with the fourth member of the expedition. The gods had weeded the Emperor's great army, and had left Duon with his life. Ought he not show his gratefulness by pulling his weight?

"You will now take responsibility for the cosmographer girl," Dryman said. "You are not to let her out of your sight. Watch her night and day. If I want to know when she bleeds and how many times she has made water, you must be in a position to supply me the details. She is an important part of our Emperor's plans."

What plans? Duon wanted to ask. *And how do you know them?* But he said nothing. The mercenary had the Omeran in thrall. How could he oppose both of them?

You'll have to win the girl's loyalty first, said the cynical voice. *Once you have her, the slave will follow. You saw them rutting.*

Pure anger rose to the forefront of Duon's mind at this advice given in such a cavalier fashion. How many people thought they could give him instructions?

I will hold no further speech with you until you reveal who you are and how you are able to speak into my mind, he projected.

Not much of a diplomat, are you, said the voice. *In fact, disappointingly unintelligent. The sort who always pays full price at the market. Your appearance no doubt sets the stallholders rubbing their hands in anticipation. What sort of bargaining position is that?*

Duon was about to reply when he remembered the vow he'd just made. And his traitorous mind recalled his infrequent forays into the Talamaq markets. The voice was right: he always paid what the stallholders asked.

Of course I'm right. You have no idea how much of your mind is open to me. If you would stop dissembling and listen to my advice, we could put an end to this Dryman. I can see that you want to.

Fruitless to deny it.

Dryman chose that moment to order their departure. Duon slung a makeshift rucksack over his shoulder; it would no doubt become extremely uncomfortable for a few days. He was more worried by the journey itself, as the day they had spent outside Raceme's walls had not been as long a rest as he needed. After their ordeals in Nomansland and the Had Hill country, they needed time to recover, and they would not get it with Dryman in charge.

Plan, he had to plan. But essential to planning was knowledge, and he had very little. Dryman kept much from him, he knew, and the cynical voice said nothing about its origins or purpose. Of most importance, however, was working out some way of thinking without the voice in his head picking the thoughts out of his mind.

He would ask the dumpy woman. She could speak directly into his mind, just like the cynical voice, but she seemed much friendlier and more likely to tell him what he needed to know.

"Vuh wuhnn wihh vuh wahy sssouw ihs," said the mushy, inarticulate voice. A startled Duon realised he could hear her even when she was nowhere to be seen. Simultaneously the same voice—or, more accurately, a crystal-clear version of it—spoke directly into his brain.

The one with the wide shoulders.

A pause; presumably while someone spoke to the girl. "Ahhss hihh venn."

Ask him then.

Duon pounded the heel of his hand against his temple in frustration. She had been talking for half an hour now, her two voices entwining themselves in his head. As far as he could make out, the girl was arguing with her father and brother as to how soon they should encourage Duon to explain why he could hear her thoughts. Her father was angry that a stranger should know how special his children were. If he was a danger he ought to be eliminated, Duon understood the man to be saying; though because he had to piece the argument together from the girl's responses, it was difficult to tell. The father's anger was a semi-permanent state, according to his daughter, who didn't seem to take the implied threat to Duon that seriously. Her brother counselled caution with regard to the southern stranger, seemingly concerned that continued mind contact would attract attention from someone or something—it wasn't clear what.

The cynical voice, he thought. It could not be anything else. This voice might well be responsible for the events in Nomansland that had led them here. For the hundredth time that day Duon wondered who—what—the voice was, and what its interest was in him.

Even though he could not hear their responses to the girl's words, Duon was convinced she wasn't telling her father and brother the whole truth. It seemed to Duon that she actively transmitted her thoughts to him; it certainly wasn't him seeking her out, as her father thought. How else could he explain the fact that her thoughts were much stronger this afternoon than they had been this morning?

I must find this woman.

The resolution was easy to make but much harder to enact. Dryman did not insist that Duon remain beside him, but he knew he'd have to give a good reason if he was to leave the soldier's side. So, over the course of the late afternoon, Duon increased his pace by small fractions, drawing Dryman and the two other southerners forward through the knots of marching Racemen refugees.

"Why are we hurrying?" Dryman asked. Somewhere ahead a child wailed.

"Hurrying? Just keeping the leaders in sight," Duon replied, licking his lips.

The man's voice frightened him. To lie to Dryman dried

out his mouth. Not really a lie, just a small deception, but his mouth prickled all the same.

"So you've decided to be a little less stubborn?" Dryman said. "Good. The Emperor may yet be pleased with you, Captain Duon."

And the man gave him a smile that frightened Duon more than any expression he'd yet seen.

The red-haired man's daughter shone. Every time Lenares looked at her she was almost blinded. Her brother shone almost as strongly. Even the red-haired man glowed a little, or at least something about him did. It was not what others would call a "real" shining, as she did not see it with her eyes; the effect came from the way their numbers related to each other. As usual, Lenares did not have words to explain it, but as she kept her insight to herself it did not matter. She could not tell what made this family shine, but from their numbers she knew it was good, or mostly good. She wanted to speak to the woman, but did not know their language well enough yet.

Well then, you will have to learn, she told herself. *You still have time.*

She hugged herself with delight. *And I will have time to learn all Torve can teach me.* She had overheard talk amongst the trainee cosmographers: giggling in the night, whispered secrets and the occasional unverifiable claim. It had all sounded silly to Lenares. But now she knew the secret of the warm pink feeling. Or, at least, that there was a secret.

Captain Duon hurried her, Torve and Dryman through the four thousand, seven hundred and sixteen other people walking Fatherward, away from the ruined town. He slowed down only when the family of the red-haired man came into view. It appeared that she was not the only one fascinated by this family: the captain kept casting secret glances towards them, though Lenares could see that Dry-man had also noticed this attention. Could the captain see the family shining? Did he have some of the specialness Lenares had? She did not think so. He had shown no sign of it before. He had not sensed the attack in the Valley of the Damned. If he had a real cosmographer's skills, if he was gifted with numbers, he would not have allowed the expedition to be destroyed in the ambush. So what was he so interested in?

Just ahead of them, the red-haired man called a halt. The clear sky had begun to purple towards night, and the refugees needed time to gather wood for their fires and raise whatever shelter they could.

A woman nearby claimed that the next village, called Buntha, was one more day's walk away. Lenares wondered how large it was, and whether the villagers could help four thousand, seven hundred and twenty people.

And here came the red-haired man's daughter now, along with her brother, walking up boldly as though they had nothing to fear.

"My sister wants to talk to you," said the boy, pointing at Captain Duon.

"You seem to have made a friend," said Dryman, smiling with his mouth but not his eyes. His smile hurt Lenares' head; there was something wrong with it. It was not just that he smiled even though he was definitely not happy. Lots of people did that. It was as if he used his smile to scare people.

"I will share with you anything of interest I learn," said Captain Duon to Dryman in a whisper.

Lenares looked closely at the girl's face. It was obvious that she heard the captain's whisper, even though she was at least ten paces away. Lenares had barely heard it herself. How had the girl done that?

"Very well then," Dryman said. "Take the cosmographer with you. She is your charge now, if you recall, and may see much that you miss. I will have a full report tomorrow morning." He smiled again. "Torve and I have an errand or two of our own to perform. We may not be back when you return."

Lenares saw the stricken look pass across her beloved's face, but could not read its meaning. She would ask him tomorrow.

The two southerners were led to a small fire, where they sat and shared small portions of stream water, bread and meat from some undersized animal. There were twenty-three tiny bones in the portion Lenares was given, and she crunched on one of them before realising it, but at least the meat was hot and seasoned with a pleasant spice. She wondered if the rest of the refugees ate as well as this.

Six people sat around the fire. Along with herself and Captain Duon, there was the shining family (Noetos, Arathé and Anomer) and one other man, dark-haired, slightly portly and somewhat older than Noetos, the man with red hair. He said only two things during the entire evening. Another four men came and went; servants perhaps, though at one point they were referred to as "Noetos's army". A fifth man called Seren spent six minutes with Noetos discussing supplies for the refugees, then left.

Lenares remembered the girl had no tongue, so was unsurprised when she spoke so badly. It made her words hard to understand, but her numbers helped Lenares make sense of most of what she said.

"You hear my words in your head" was what she said to Captain Duon in her squishy voice. Her brother interpreted for her.

"Yes," Captain Duon replied. "I suspect I hear more than you realise. When you are close by I seem to hear your words as you say them to others, even those you are not saying to me. And I hear your voice clearly in my mind translating the words, or perhaps I'm hearing your thoughts as you put them together to speak them. I don't know whether you are deliberately sending me your thoughts."

"Sometimes I do, sometimes not," she said via her brother. "So do you hear anything when I don't deliberately put the words in your mind?"

"If I understand correctly, I hear your true voice, without translation." Then Duon held up his hand. "Enough: I do not have much time. My master could recall me at any moment. We can find out the mechanics of all this with experimentation. I am much more interested in what is happening to us, and why."

"And you don't want your master hearing this discussion," the girl's brother said. His expression made it clear this was not a question.

"No," Duon replied.

Then there was an unheard exchange. Lenares focused every mote of her concentration, but could hear nothing but a faint buzzing—perhaps the sound of her own brain. The girl and her brother participated, as did Captain Duon. This, more than anything, convinced her they were telling the truth.

Powers! New powers! Her first thought was to get them for herself.

"I visited the place called Andratan two years ago," Captain Duon said aloud; and the red-haired man leaned forward, a frown on his broad, weather-scarred face. "I was sent Fatherward—northward—by the great Emperor of Elamaq to take the measure of the barbarians who live there. Please, I offer no offence. I am sure you share similar thoughts about those who live to your Daughterward—I mean south—if you have even heard of us. I discovered much of interest, and made my way north to the town of Malayu."

"Town? Malayu is a great city, the largest in the world," the red-haired man said. "Are you sure you were in the right place?"

"Malayu is indeed a great place, as great as the Third of Brick, which is one of the parts of Talamaq, the city at the heart of our empire," Captain Duon said, sweeping his hand to include Lenares. "But it had no tri-spired Palace of Gold, no broad avenues, no great industries of brick and glass. I saw little there but squalor and oppression." He smiled. "Again, forgive me. Your eyes would perhaps see similar things in Talamaq where I would not. And, to balance this, it is true that Bhrudwo has natural resources far greater than that of the Elamaq Empire."

"So you went north, hoping to engage the Undying Man's interest in some sort of trade treaty proposal?" the red-haired man asked, the frown still fixed on his face.

"Of course." Captain Duon smiled, and then passed one of those moments that had always confused Lenares. He was lying; the Emperor had always planned to invade the rich Fatherward lands. The captain knew that. His listeners

knew he was lying, and the captain knew they knew. He
had just told them he was spying out the land to prepare for
an invasion, and everyone was happy in a way they would
not have been had he come straight out and said it.

Such moments caused Lenares trouble, but today she
could see what they were doing. Captain Duon had built
a wall of politeness with his words; a wall he could hide
behind, and one that could not be knocked down by anyone
else without them being impolite in turn.

While she considered this, the conversation had moved
on. Captain Duon had resumed his telling.

"I spent a month in Andratan, waiting for an audience
with the Undying Man. Many people there confirmed the
widespread belief that he was ancient, preserved by magic,
but when I finally met him he seemed perfectly ordinary.
I explained who I was and whom I represented. The Undying Man seemed interested, and invited me to return in
due course with a retinue of unspecified size. He issued an
invitation to the Emperor to journey to Andratan and share
wine with him. I thanked him and left."

Another moment of shared silence. This time the buzzing was a little louder.

"Sorry, er . . . sorry," the girl's brother said to Lenares.
"We haven't been introduced. My sister Arathé just asked
your . . . ah, master? Brother?"

"Captain Duon," Lenares said impatiently. "I am Cosmographer Lenares."

The captain translated this for her.

"Ah. I am Anomer, and this man is my father, Noetos the
Fisher. Beside him sits Bregor, the Hegeoman of Fossa village. Using mind-speech, Arathé asked your Captain Duon
how long he spent in the dungeons of Andratan, and he re-

plied that he hadn't known the fortress had any dungeons. My sister told him that he must live in a benign country if fortresses there do not have dungeons below them."

Captain Duon smiled weakly.

"I met the Emperor in the dungeons under the Talamaq Palace," Lenares said, her voice loud in the sudden silence. She realised a moment too late that this would make Captain Duon look foolish. "He let me go, though, when I told him about the hole in the world."

The captain did not translate her words, and the four strangers looked at her blankly.

Of course; they know nothing of our language and they do not have numbers to help them understand. She laughed self-consciously, wishing she could deflect their stares.

"What did she say?" the red-haired man, Noetos, asked Captain Duon.

"Oh, nothing of importance," he replied. His reply angered Lenares. What made him think she was of no importance?

Arathé told them she had been a prisoner in the dungeons of Andratan two years ago. "The same time as Captain Duon awaited his audience, most likely," her brother said. "That cannot be a coincidence," he added unnecessarily.

"So, is this something all the gifted share?" Noetos said. "Or was it implanted during your visit to Andratan?"

"I am gifted," Lenares said before she could help herself, but again the strangers did not understand her.

"I don't share it," Anomer said.

"Yet I've heard your voice in my mind," said his father.

Anomer frowned. "As far as we can tell, that is through Arathé's gift. My thoughts travel through her to you. Perhaps it depends to an extent on my own magical ability, but without Arathé I cannot go beyond the confines of my own head."

"You hear voices also?" Captain Duon asked Noetos.

"Only my son and daughter, and only when they choose to include me," he said, the merest trace of asperity in his voice.

"Voices?" Anomer said to the captain. "You hear voices other than my sister?"

As fascinated as Lenares was by the idea of hearing voices in one's head, she had questions of her own that could wait no longer.

"Ask her why her family shines so brightly," she said to Captain Duon. She recalled one of Mahudia's many sayings. "Don't ignore me like I am a bedpost. Ask them my question."

"But, Lenares . . . very well."

He turned to their bemused hosts and asked her question. Their attention shifted to her.

"Shines? What do you mean?"

She saw the look on the father's face; the same look so many others had given her in the past. Halfwit, his face said to her, much more loudly than his audible words. So she wasted no time, and laid out what the numbers had told her.

"You hold back a great secret," she said, pointing at Noetos. "But it is not a secret any more. Your son knows it, though your daughter does not. Others know it too. You want to tell them, even though you think they will hate you forever because of it."

The family stared at her, then at Captain Duon, waiting for the translation. The captain seemed uncomfortable.

"Translate for me, Captain," Lenares demanded. "I will know if you change my words."

Duon scowled at her, but did as she bade him.

"What is this?" Noetos growled. He turned to Anomer. "What have you been telling these people?"

The boy looked upset. "Father, nothing would make me reveal your secrets. They are not mine to tell. I haven't even spoken of them to Arathé yet."

His sister grabbed him by the arm. "Wahh seeyits?" She glanced from her brother to her father and back again, then focused on Lenares.

Lenares smiled. *I am special too.*

Captain Duon sighed. "Lenares is a cosmographer. Her mentor said she is the best we've had in a thousand years. She can read the patterns all around us; converts them into numbers, or some such thing. That she sees something special about you and your family is clear. Would you be able to guess at what she means by a 'shining'? Then we can return to the important questions."

"This may be important," Anomer said. "All this may be very important indeed."

He turned and favoured Lenares with a wide smile. His eyes were sparkly like Mahudia's used to get. *This boy doesn't pity me. He thinks I am special.* She smiled shyly in return.

The shining Lenares saw might be the water magic of Bhrudwo, the children of Noetos explained. They both had it, and because of this Andratan had been interested in them. Lenares did not think their idea was correct, but she listened politely. Arathé had been sold—Lenares wasn't sure this was the right word—to the Undying Man, but had discovered that much of the magic was put to evil use in his service. Using it hurt those near the user. So she tried to leave Andratan, but the cruel magicians there would not let her go. Instead they cut out her tongue and put her to work in the dungeons, drawing on her for power. It wasn't until she was taken south, to be used as a drudge by Recruiters on their way to search for more magically gifted children, that she had been reunited with her family. Her father was very angry at how she had been treated, and wanted to go to Andratan and ask why.

Lenares nodded. "I've never seen people's numbers shining like yours do. You both look very beautiful."

The siblings smiled at her.

Captain Duon turned to Lenares and his face wore its own frown. "I've just realised something. How can you know the local language? Did you learn it from someone in Talamaq? Is that why you were sent with the expedition?"

"Patterns and numbers," she replied. "Just as good as magic. Maybe better; I still have a tongue." Again she could have bitten hers off, but Arathé laughed.

The talk continued, hour after hour of it, and Lenares was enthralled with it all.

Captain Duon wondered aloud whether anyone else who had been in Andratan two years ago had been infected with voices. Arathé thought that maybe everyone who went there received the ability. No one else thought this likely. There was apparently another voice, a nasty, horrible voice, which both Captain Duon and Arathé could hear. They seemed very worried about this voice. The two of them talked for some time about how they might fool the voice, but came to no conclusion that Lenares could follow.

Eventually, however, she allowed their earnest voices to fade a little. She had her own thinking to do. Did any of this connect to the hole in the world? What was her next move? Would Dryman allow her the freedom she needed to pursue and somehow defeat the hole? And why did she have a vague feeling that she had it all wrong?

And behind these thoughts, a rosy pink glow that kept her warm.

Duon sat apart from the others, making himself comfortable on a small rocky knoll above the main campsite. Below him bonfires flickered, with only the occasional silhouette momentarily visible in front of the flames. The former residents of Raceme had settled down to sleep.

The night was cold, but dread chilled him more effectively than the cool breeze ever could. Arathé and he had speculated on the identity and nature of the cynical voice in his . . . in *their* heads. Anomer, however, had the most frightening insights; perhaps, Duon speculated, only half in jest, because the boy's head was not so crowded.

"You have Andratan in common," Anomer said to them. "At the very least someone has done something to you there that has made you receptive to this voice; at worst one of you is carrying someone else in their head, and the other can hear it. Or you may both be carrying someone."

Arathe had become upset at the thought that another being might be lodged within her. "It's like being with child after a rape, if the child could hold conversations with its mother," she had said. "I don't want it."

"There is only one person who can wield magic sufficient to do this," Anomer had continued. "And that is the Undying Man himself."

Noetos had growled at the words, a bear ready to strike. Duon had revised his earlier estimation of the man: though he did not look much like a warrior, he might prove difficult to best in combat. There was something of the *vledemhar* about him, those legendary warriors of the icy south who foamed at the mouth when they fought. Given what Noetos's daughter had suffered in the Undying Man's fortress, Duon supposed the man's anger was justified.

Arathe had sighed at her brother's words, as if he'd confirmed something she had suspected but not been willing to confront. "I never saw the Undying Man, except once from after when I first arrived."

"Does he need to be near someone he ensorcels?"

Duon listened carefully. He could not ascribe their fear and horror of the Undying Man to the very human figure he had met. That said, he had met the Emperor of Elamaq and had not felt the power that, with a word, had assembled an army thirty thousand strong only a few days later.

"But why?" Duon had asked the youngsters. "Why us? What does he hope to achieve? I don't understand. Is this anonymous magician spending his days listening to our thoughts? We are not important people . . . are we?"

These were the questions he wrestled with now, as the fires died down and the cold settled on him like a second skin. The fear that had his heart in its grip was this: did unimportant Captain Duon now have two emperors competing for his obedience? One to the south, who would destroy him and his family should he believe Duon responsible for the loss of the expedition. And one to the north, who might well be listening to his baffled musings even now.

Was that laughter he could hear? A faint, repetitive sound, like derisive laughter in the back of his head?

No, it was the slap of boot on stone; someone was leaving the camp.

Duon raised his head. He'd had half an eye on the path below him, wondering when Dryman and Torve would return from whatever nocturnal wandering they were engaged in. This was a solitary figure, a much bigger man than either of Duon's fellow southerners. It took only a flash of red hair in the wan moonlight for Duon to recognise him.

Where was Noetos going?

Duon was not inclined to pry into the private affairs of others. However, he had learned a number of things concerning the Fossan family that connected them to him. And there was something about the way the man walked, a furtiveness, as though he was trying to disguise his bulk, that made Duon get to his feet and follow quietly after the northerner.

The man left the narrow path soon after, and made his way surefootedly across three fields to the main highway they had all walked along earlier in the day. Duon tried to keep in the shadows, guessing that the man would be angry at being followed. He nearly turned back, but he was fed up with mysteries. Besides, the man would not be going very far.

For the next three hours Duon followed Noetos, alternating between deciding to give up his pursuit and becoming increasingly convinced the fellow was about to do something he wanted no one else to know about. The pace the man set was extraordinarily swift, and Duon, though hardened by months of walking in the southern desert lands—added to years of exploration—found it difficult to keep pace. After a while, however, it didn't matter. It was obvious where the man was heading.

They arrived at Shambles Hill just as the moon went down. Below them the city of Raceme was nothing but a shadow pricked by torchlights. The man halted briefly, then pressed on, more cautiously. It was basic soldiery to assume the Neherians had patrols out beyond the walls; belatedly Duon considered the danger he might now be in. Having the northern man angry at him was not the worst thing that could happen.

They approached the city wall. *The fool means to get inside the city*, Duon told himself.

Yes, and you've known it for an hour or more, said the cynical voice. *Stay out of the city. Don't throw your life away when you don't know what is happening.*

Duon listened carefully to the voice, as Arathé had suggested they ought, and thought he detected an underlying current of worry.

Am I that valuable to the voice?

He found himself strongly tempted to ignore its advice.

A hand gripped his arm and pulled him into an alcove in the wall. "Nice night for a stroll," Noetos growled in his ear. "But a little dangerous to be taking the midnight air under the eyes of the enemy, don't you think?"

For a moment Duon could barely draw breath past the sudden constriction of his throat. A hot retort, built from anger and fear, formed in his mind.

The cynical voice spoke. *This man is a hothead. You will impress him by remaining calm.*

Duon could see the sense of this. "Welcome back to Raceme, friend Noetos," he whispered. "Did you miss it as much as I?"

The bulky shadow drew back a pace, his hand still on Duon's arm. "You're a cool one," he said. "Why did you follow me?"

"Curiosity," Duon replied promptly. "I wondered what

would bring you here, and thought you might want some help." He brushed the man's hand away.

"I don't trust you," Noetos said brusquely. "Wait here until I return, and don't go on a walking tour. If your heavy-footed journey tonight is any indication, you will be seen and taken as a spy. That you want to avoid: the Neherians are not a merciful people."

"I see you intend to invade Raceme single-handedly and without a weapon," Duon said.

The man grunted. "I have come tonight to retrieve the blade I left here."

"Plenty of blades back at the camp. What is so special about this one?"

"Because," Noetos said, sighing, "this one belongs to the heir of Roudhos, and I fear the Racemen may have need of it."

Anomer woke as the moon sank behind nearby trees. His bladder demanded he make a walk to those trees, where a score or more men stood satisfying the same need.

"The men of Buntha won't see us wrong," an old man muttered as he shook himself, spraying drops everywhere.

"Can't see how a few hundred villagers can help us," said a younger man. "We need to go north to Trais or south to Tochar. Plenty of men there who hate the Neherians."

Anomer moved into the space cleared by the old man's lack of control. "Don't you think they might have their own problems?" he asked them. "The Neherians are not about to conquer the Fisher Coast and ignore the inland towns."

"Is that what they've done?" the younger man asked. "Conquered the Fisher Coast?"

"Where you from, lad?" said the old man to Anomer.

"Fossa. A small village not far north of Neherius."

"Heard of it," the old man allowed.

"The Neherian fleet has been moving north, destroying the villages and taking the people as slaves. They succeeded in most of the villages. Seems like conquest to me."

"Your village?"

"Burned to the ground," Anomer said bleakly.

He finished his business and bade the men goodbye. Now the moon had set there was virtually no light by which to make his way back; he stumbled into one sleeping group and extricated himself only after profuse apologies.

He realised he was near the remains of his own fire only when Arathé's voice crept into his head. *Look over to your right, you should see the embers glowing. Is Father with you?* Her voice was anxious.

He came down a shallow slope and could barely see her, a pale figure smeared against the darkness. *No*, he answered, surprised.

Noetos's sleeping mat lay unoccupied. Anomer reached down: cold. *He's been gone for some time*. The missing pack suggested his father was not merely off walking.

He's gone to do something stupid, hasn't he? Arathé thought.

Well, it's been at least a day since the last time, her brother agreed. Here, take my strength and reach out to him.

He sat on his father's sleeping mat and felt a bump beneath his buttock. He pulled back the mat.

"Now I'm really worried," he said, but did not touch the object lying there on the grass. "Father would not have left this behind unless he thought he might not return."

What is it? Arathé asked, and reached out to pick it up.

"Don't touch that!" Anomer cried.

Her hand stopped just short of the dark thing on the grass. She turned a puzzled expression towards him.

"It's too dark to see, and I'm not going to pick it up. But, sister, that is the most valuable and the most dangerous thing you've ever encountered."

The stone you were telling me about?

"The huanu stone," he replied. "With it Father drained the magic from a Recruiter; and you saw what it did to the whirlwinds. For him to leave it here means he's either gone to do something so risky he wanted to keep it safe, or he has been taken from his bed."

Then we must contact him immediately, his sister thought.

Anomer nodded, and replaced the mat over the carving. His sister had always taken his strength gently, carefully, but he knew it would hurt all the same. He lay back and waited for the pain to begin.

"No talking, I said."

Duon sighed. The man was insufferably bluff.

"If I'm to help you, I need to know what we're doing," he whispered.

"If we are caught I'm leaving you to your own devices," Noetos replied, continuing to ignore Duon's questions. "And the more you talk, the greater chance we have of being caught."

"Your voice is far louder than mine," Duon said, aggrieved.

"Then don't make me speak," came the reply, demonstrating, Duon thought, admirable logic.

Virtually no light penetrated the streets of Raceme, but

the Bhrudwan bear needed none. He was much lighter on his feet than his bulk suggested, and navigated the streets with surety, though many of them remained choked with rubble.

That there were Neherian patrols was confirmed soon after they had scaled the city wall. The bear had found a less visible place to climb it, just short of where the wall came down from Suggate to meet the coastal cliffs: a large tree thirty paces from the wall ensured the shadows were even deeper there. They had just scrambled to the ground inside the city when the sound of steps stilled them: a group of ten men with torches and gleaming armour came within a dozen paces of where they lay.

"Armour," the bear breathed after the men had passed by. "The Neherians have been reinforced; they must have had a land army in support of their fleet. I pity Tochar and Altima. The inland cities will be in flames."

"How can you tell these are reinforcements?" Duon had asked.

"The Neherians don't carry armour on their ships; it is too heavy. I suppose this could be an elite squad, but I doubt it. What puzzles me is why the fleet attacked before the army—of course," he corrected himself. "The fleet was drawn north more quickly than they intended, then forced into harbour by the storm. They had no choice but to attack. This was supposed to be a pincer invasion, I think: army at Suggate, fleet in the harbour. Total destruction, then move in with their own people; that's their usual pattern. Five thousand people, more or less, owe their lives to the storm."

"So there is now an army in Raceme as well as the invaders from the ships?"

The bear-man groaned as he pulled himself to his feet. "It would be safest to assume so," he said.

They encountered numerous patrols on their journey into the city; or, possibly, the same few patrols again and again. It was too dark to tell. Individual Neherians moved about the streets carrying torches, engaged in bearing messages or some such errand. The sky began to lighten, and the bear kept them firmly in the shadows. Duon considered the man's caution commendable.

"This is ridiculous," the man said now. So closely did the sentiment echo his own thoughts that Duon thought for a moment he himself had spoken aloud. But the voice continued.

"The sword lay for years in a box under the floor of my bedroom in Old Fossa. Not once during that time did I use it; I trained my daughter and son using practice swords. After we were given Fisher House I stored it on a ledge at the base of the cupola above the house's Great Room. I told my family it was a keepsake, which it is. Nothing more. So I ought to be able to let it go."

Duon grunted, a sound he hoped would be interpreted as encouragement for the man to continue.

"So why did leaving the sword behind—forgetting it, if the truth be told—feel like such a betrayal? Why am I risking my life to get it back?"

"Our lives," Duon said dryly.

"No one asked you," the bear growled. "Pick a direction; you'll arrive at the wall."

"You're a trained soldier," Duon responded. "So am I. Let us do what we are trained to do, and get out of this city before the sun shows your enemies where we are. Then, after we have put many paces between ourselves and this place, you can tell me what is so special about your sword.

"Well put," said the bear. "In a moment we—nnnnn."

"What is it? Are you all right?"

Captain Duon, can you hear me? The voice was faint, right on the edge of . . . what? Not hearing. Mind-strength?

Beside him in the shadows the man groaned again, shockingly loud in the early morning silence.

Duon focused on the spot at the back of his head where the voices seemed to come from. *I can barely hear you,* he thought, *but I think you're hurting your father with the strength of your thoughts.*

He's not answering me. I've been trying for the last hour or more. We're frantic with worry. Where is he? Is he safe? What is he doing?

Be careful, came another voice. Arathé's brother. *We must not attract attention.*

We have to take the risk.

Would you people mind not arguing in my head? Duon asked them.

Then answer our questions swiftly. Arathé this time.

We are in Raceme, he said. *Your father is here to recover his sword. All things being equal, we should return to you an hour or so after dawn.*

Why did you agree to help him? Arathé appeared to be angry.

I didn't, Duon began, then Noetos grabbed at his arm.

"This is very painful for me," he said. "Clearly, to make themselves heard to you, they are having to shout. Can we leave explanations and blame for another time?"

"Then why don't you talk to your children?"

The big man grunted, and Duon was glad he couldn't see the expression on the man's face. "I would have thought the answer self-evident," Noetos said. "I hoped to be back before they knew I had gone." Another grunt. "Though don't put it to them like that."

"Why didn't Arathé just listen to your mind, like she can mine?"

"Because I have no magic," the bear replied. "Now, we must move on. The sky brightens as we have a conversation we could have had to the north of here with much less risk."

"Though with much less cause," Duon responded. The bear-man favoured him with another grunt.

He has no magic? Is the reason I can hear his children, then, because I do have magic?

It took them some time to thread their way down a narrow, debris-strewn street to the alley the big man had described as his goal. He had clearly underestimated the time it would take to gain his objective: by the time they drew near, the eastern rim of the world glowed yellow, rapidly driving the purple night away to the west. They would have a difficult task in extricating themselves from Raceme without being discovered by the Neherians.

Duon found walking a little easier in the growing light. They were aided by the fact that someone had cleared a path through the rubble; obviously, this was a main thoroughfare. Something about that thought made Duon uneasy.

"Here it is," the bear said, and turned towards a dark notch in the buildings to their left. He bent down to pick up something hidden in the shadows.

"Noetos!" Duon hissed, as he realised what had been bothering him. *It's a main thoroughfare, so where are the people?*

"Yours?" a melodious, high-pitched voice asked, and a small man wearing what passed in the north for battle dress stepped forward from the deeper shadows of the alley. "Or are you engaging in some creative salvage?"

Noetos's hand halted a finger's-width from the sword, then darted forward and grasped the hilt. Duon could see what the big man could not: at least two feet stood on the blade, their owners shrouded in shadow. Noetos tugged at the sword, then let go and stood back. The look in the baulked bear's eye made all the skin on Duon's body prickle, from the forehead down through neck, chest, hands, knees. Anger unfettered by sanity's restraints.

Someone will breathe their last here today, he thought.

"Secure them," said the small man. A half-dozen men moved at the command.

In the back of Duon's mind a girl's voice cried in anguish.

I will try my best to ensure it is not your father, he reassured her. Though what he could do was not clear; and his options, such as they were, became further limited when hands grasped him from behind. He was relieved of his own blade and his hands were bound. Duon did not bother to struggle, nor did he even turn around to acknowledge his captors. All his attention was on the burly bear-man and the Neherian asking him questions.

"That is my sword," was all Noetos said as his hands were tied.

"Well, that saves a whole series of questions," the Neherian replied, and mimed rolling up a scroll and casting it to the ground. "I might as well not have bothered thinking them up. What is the point of an elaborate trap when the quarry locks the cage himself?"

Laughter came from the shadows behind the Neherian, and from those standing behind Duon. At least twenty men, the captain estimated.

"If it is yours," the effete Neherian continued inexorably, "then you must be the heir of Roudhos."

The bear's anger rose another notch, if it were possible. Duon wondered how anyone could stand to look on him, so intense did it burn.

"And if you know that, you must know why the sword is mine and not my father's," came the words, falling like rocks torn from a bluff.

"Aye, I've been told."

"Told? More than told, if memory serves. I remember a voice like yours in a certain clearing some years ago." The effort Noetos was exercising in restraint was obvious: his body shook, and his voice seemed to clamber up from a death-pit. He closed his eyes as though remembering. "'Not the boys! Leave the boys!' you said." The eyes opened. "Wanted my brothers for yourself, did you?"

"I have no doubt the incident had an impact on you," the Neherian said, his features pinching together. "Yes, I was there. You were smaller, I recall."

"I was still bigger than you," Noetos sneered. "Do you think I would have forgotten you? I doubt there are many back-passagers even in the Neherian army."

The man coloured a little. "Your insults are worthless if they do not hit their mark," he said. "For what it is worth, I found the whole incident distasteful, and tried repeatedly to dissuade my commanding officer from following his orders with such vigour—at some risk to myself."

"Did you now? You found the incident distasteful? Such a slippery word to describe torture, rape and death, don't you think?" The big man breathed in a series of grunts, struggling with his emotions, but still made no effort to resist his captors.

"I will discuss this no further here," said the Neherian. "You have a meeting with the general of our Army of Peace in his room at the Summer Palace. He will not appreciate being kept waiting."

Noetos moved suddenly, jerking forward towards the small Neherian, towing half a dozen soldiers who tried unsuccessfully to restrain him. Three soldiers with swords barred him from reaching his quarry.

"I am going to kill you." The bear-man stared into the Neherian's eyes as he spoke. "I will not make you suffer unnecessarily, but you will die at my hands. This I foretell on the life of my children."

Blood fled from the Neherian's face. Something significant had just happened, but Duon did not know enough about northern culture to work out what. He remembered from his previous journey that the Neherians were very religious, believing in their own gods. Perhaps the bear had done something very clever.

As the sun rose in flames above the harbour below, Noetos and Duon were led by their captors towards a large, low-slung stone building dominating the hill ahead. As they drew closer it was apparent that the building had suffered recent damage. Some force—it must have been the whirlwind—had plucked stones from the building's walls. Duon's keen eyes noted stony detritus at the base of the promontory that might well have come from the building. The magnitude of the destruction became clearer as they passed what could only be the remains of a building thrown down from above. Duon flicked his eyes upwards to where the shards of a tower protruded from the stone building like a broken tooth.

He continues to ignore us, came Arathé's desperate voice. *Is he still alive?*

Yes, Duon sent back. *But the Neherians have us. Your father will need help, I think. We are being taken to the Summer Palace.*

Thank you, friend, she said. *We will do what we can.*

Duon thought that all very well, but who would help him?

They were beaten before being taken into the presence of the Neherian general. The assault was all the more frightening for its perfunctoriness: Duon could tell the soldiers were not really trying, and were capable of much more. The Neherians gossiped amongst themselves as they laid in with fists and sticks. Duon had never suffered such a thing, his most painful prior experience having been an unfortunate boxing mismatch with an older man who had later revealed himself as a former champion. The helplessness and shame hurt far more than the blows.

"Not a good idea of yours to follow me, eh?" the bear said almost conversationally as they rolled together on the floor.

"Be quiet," one of their captors said in a bored voice.

"Don't resist them," Noetos continued regardless. "They won't do any serious damage before we get to meet the commander."

He received a blow in the mouth for that: Duon saw the man's bottom lip spurt blood before a kick to his own back made him writhe away.

He almost told the bear that his children were coming to rescue him. The cynical voice saved him. *Not wise*, it said. *Do you think the fool wants his children captured by the Neherians? Understand that this man wishes to suffer and die. He thinks it is what he deserves for his cowardice. But he wants his offspring to live. He will not react well if told his children are coming.*

So Duon kept quiet and waited until the beating ceased, hoping the pain would stop soon. The cynical voice chuckled, as though savouring his agony. *My brave captain*, he thought he heard it say, *you do not know what pain is.*

He came to on his feet, swaying drunkenly, his eyes stinging and a ringing in his ears. He tried to rub his left eye, which seemed half-closed, and discovered his hands were still bound behind his back. He coughed and spat out something thick and wet; a tremendous clout to the back of his head sent him to his knees.

"It is not a wise idea to show disrespect to the one who has your life in his hands," said a gentle voice some distance away. "Stand him up and wipe his face."

The soldiers did as they were bid. Duon turned towards the direction from which the voice had come: a man in his sixties sat on a makeshift wooden throne atop a dais, itself on a stone platform a step higher than the flagged floor. He and Noetos were led the twenty paces it took to have them standing directly in front of the man, then forced to kneel before the throne.

The large chamber in which they knelt was open to the cool morning wind: the windows, once stained glass by the look of the few fragments remaining, had been destroyed either by the storm or by the Neherians. If there was a difference. Duon wondered if the Neherians had a magician capable of such things. He wondered if the magician sat on the throne before him. He wondered if he himself was a magician, and how he might find out.

"You are uglier than I remember," Noetos said hoarsely beside him. "And before your smallbrains beat me for not adding whatever honorific you insist on, allow me to thank you for granting my life's most ferocious wish."

"One to the head," the man said. "Every time he addresses me without the correct appellation, give him another. At some point he'll start guessing. Roget, you can open a book on the matter."

One of the soldiers approached, swung his staff and cracked the bear on the side of the head. Down the man went in a heap, legs and arms twitching.

"I will break my fast while we wait," said the man on the throne. "Bring me bread and wine."

Someone scurried off, his boots echoing across the stone chamber. All was quiet save the ragged breathing of the man on the floor.

"Douse him with water," the enthroned man commanded, and it was done. "Haul him to his feet." Noetos drooped between two soldiers, who grunted as they tried to keep him upright. "Slap his face." This had the desired effect.

"So, Noetos, son of Demios, son of cursed Baran, last Red Duke of Roudhos, it is pleasure and pain to see you again. Pleasure for me, pain for you." No change in expression accompanied the man's words.

Ah, said the cynical voice at the back of Duon's head. *Ah!*

"Your family has not had much luck, has it," the man continued. "Your grandfather was staked and burned for disobeying the Undying Man during the Falthan War. Your father made a bid for the vacant Roudhos throne, in direct disobedience of the Edict of Andratan, and the last I saw of him, his head was some distance from his body and still bouncing. That was the sword involved, as I recall." He extended a hand towards a sword propped up against the throne. "And now you, in which the saddest of Fisher Coast tales is about to come to an end. I should have struck off your head as well, but my second-in-command persuaded me otherwise. To this day I don't know what I was thinking." He smiled, and Duon wished he had not. "Perhaps I was distracted by the sweet smell of your sisters on me, or the sight of your brothers being torn apart by my dogs. No, I remember what it was. The knowledge that you would wander the world, beggared, knowing what you had lost, added savour to my every memory of the day I all but extinguished the line of Roudhos."

"You are not as strong as you make out," the bear said, his words slurred, blood in his mouth. "You are a weakling with no feel for real cruelty. I will die happy in the knowledge that because Neherius is ruled by fools like you, it will not survive."

"Not so hard this time," said the man on the throne.

The staff swished through the air, took Noetos above the ear and dropped him to the floor.

"I apologise, Majestic One," the soldier said, then put a hand to his mouth.

"No matter." Whether a response to the blow or to

revealing the man's appellation, Duon could not tell. "I have questions for this other one."

The throne's gaze settled on Duon. "Your name?"

"Duon, Majestic One."

The man expelled air from his mouth; Duon supposed it was a laugh. "A quick study, I see. Very good. Why are you here in the company of this fool?"

Duon repeated the words the cynical voice fed him. "I am a thief-taker, Majestic One," he said. "For some months I have been searching for a man suspected of selling his catch direct to the Tocharan market without going through the Fishmongers Guild. This is without doubt the man I am seeking. With your permission, Majestic One, I will take custody of him and present him to the Tocharan authorities."

The man laughed economically; a word that seemed to summarise everything he did. The laughter suggested to Duon his gambit had not worked.

"Where are you from, thief-taker?"

"Jalbeth in the Jasweyan Mountains, Majestic One."

"I know it well. You would know, then, the name of the most famous man to emerge from that village?"

"Majestic One, you can only mean Deorc, the right hand of the Undying Man, who was lost in the Falthan War."

The cynical voice buzzed angrily in the back of Duon's head. Duon ignored it.

"You are a strange colour for a Jasweyan."

"That I am, Majestic One," said Duon, thinking quickly; the cynical voice had gone silent. "My parents came from a land far to the south, or so they said, though I never believed much of what they told me. There all men were dark of skin like me."

"Enough," the Neherian said. "You would have been more convincing had you confined yourself to the truth. Still, all families mask their true origins with deceit. This one, for example," he said, gesturing towards Noetos, who struggled to rise from the floor, "claimed to be descended from the most ancient line of southern kings. The only problem was that after his grandsire's traitorous actions, it was a claim best forgotten." He sighed, as if genuinely regretful. "And now this man returns to recover the Sword of Roudhos he'd so carelessly left lying on the street. Did he think we would not have noticed it? Or that he could sneak into our city unseen? All we had to do was watch and wait. He would do well to look upon that blade, for it will be by this sword his life ends."

"And me, Majestic One?" Duon could not help asking. "How will my life end?"

"Who knows? At the end of a blade like this one perhaps, or lying screaming in bed, the victim of some whore's pox. What I do know is that you have volunteered for the Army of Peace. Neherius thanks you, soldier. Galter here will give you the necessary equipment—though not a blade, not yet."

With a roar, Noetos exploded into life. Duon had no time to contemplate his intended fate, no time to summon outrage or to generate fear. He turned just in time to see the bear-man break his bonds with a twitch of his wrists—bonds Duon would have sworn were unbreakable. Blood from his wrists spattered the floor.

A blade flashed. It should have taken Noetos's head, but the man darted forward with impossible speed. Behind him the sword bit air. The sound turned Duon's head, an instinctive reaction; he turned back to see Noetos already in possession of his father's sword. He held it to the neck of the man on the throne.

Apart from the one soldier who had loosed his sword, no one else had done more than begin to move. The echoes from the bear's roar still reverberated around the stone chamber.

Duon realised the back of his head was uncannily warm.

A thought came to him: what if the Neherians decided to use him as a bargaining piece, his life to be traded against that of their Majestic One? He tried to move, but his wrists were held firmly by the soldiers behind him. His head grew hotter still, to the point where he wondered if his hair had caught fire.

"Now, Noetos—" the man on the throne began.

"Those were your last words," the bear growled. "I grant you no final speeches, no chance to deny what you are or what you have done. I want to hear none of it."

Before anyone could react he slid his blade across the man's neck.

"Die like a dog," he said as the man's hands sprang towards his opened throat.

Neherians from all sides leapt at Noetos, but before they could reach him he . . . wasn't there. Duon had caught a flicker of movement, no more. Shouting erupted across the chamber. Steel clashed with steel. Duon waited to be cut down.

Go!

The pain at the back of his head had become agonising. He raised his hands to his hair, then stopped, frozen with surprise that he had been able to do so. His hands were unbound, though the marks of the rope were visible as he examined them.

Did I do that? he asked stupidly.

The cynical voice sighed, a sound like the collapse of a furnace.

A hand on his shoulder. "Take this." The bear stood beside him, pressing a blade into his hand. "Follow me," he said. "I'll protect you."

Three of the Neherians were down, but the rest—at least twenty, with more coming judging by the shouts and sounds of slapping feet—had them surrounded.

Duon wondered what would kill him first: the blade of a Neherian or the fire in his brain.

Noetos stepped forward, then blurred. A soldier to their right fell, his head exploding with redness. He had not reached the flagstones before two more fell back, clutching at their chests.

He'll not be able to keep this up. Help him!

Duon turned and raised his sword, barely meeting the unseen curved blade descending towards his head. Absurdly, he had time enough to notice the exquisite scroll pattern adorning the leading edge of the man's sword. Were those winged fish flying amongst the scrolls? He knocked the blade out of the way with surprising ease, then stepped sideways and inside the guard of another Neherian.

Too slow. Everyone was too slow! He knew he ought to have been dead by now. *Why are they not faster?*

He was in and out of the Neherian's guard before the man could react, leaving a deep red rose blooming on the man's chest. He turned to his right, expecting another man to be on top of him, but saw with astonishment that the first man with the curved blade had not yet finished falling. The man's hands had spread out to brace his fall. Yes, those were fish, interwoven with birds in the sort of fanciful design his first commander had loved. If that man wasn't careful, he'd land on top of his beautiful blade.

Sound had a strange broken quality about it. Cries from those wounded and dying came to his ears as small packets of sound interspersed with silence, as though someone had made the sounds visible, diced them up with a carving knife and removed half of the slices.

The cynical voice spoke. *How do you ever get anything done? Keep your mind on living.*

I'm an explorer, Duon replied tartly. *I am expected to observe things closely.*

Hurry up; I do not have much more to give you.

The bear had carved a way out for himself, and Duon followed. Ahead was the door through which they had entered the room. Behind lay chaos.

As they reached the door it filled with armour-clad men. And, at that moment, the heat faded from the back of Duon's head.

"Arathé!" the bear-man beside him called. "Arathé! Where have you gone?"

By the slump of his shoulders, the man had apparently received no answer.

QUEEN

CHAPTER 6

THE ETERNAL CITY

THE LEAGUE-LONG ROAD THAT LED Stella Pellwen and her companions to the eternal city of Dhauria also seemed to lead them back into the distant past. For Stella, Queen of the Falthans—*former* queen, she reminded herself, and was pleased to note she still cared little for the loss—the calendar seemed to run backwards as the tireless donkey drew their cart forwards past stately poplars and flower-lined verges. So many small things combined to make this so. There were no obvious tools in use by those working the fields either side of the grassy road, and Stella guessed they would see few mechanical devices in this land. A layer of moss and lichen covered every wooden surface. Fence, barn, bridge, rail—all looked a thousand years old. The stonework of every house, while scrupulously clean, had a patina of age about it, a hint of greyness no amount of scrubbing could erase. She thought she could smell the age of the very air.

Likely her imagination. For seventy years Phemanderac had been telling her of this city, of its legends and place in the lore of Faltha. From here, so Falthans believed, their race had sprung, the First Men who colonised the great lands to the north. A thousand years the Dhaurians had lived in the narrow confines of this valley—of course, it hadn't been flooded then—until their rebellion had seen the Most High drive out everyone but the members of the loyal House of Sthane. An article of faith to ordinary Falthans, and believed with fervour by the Halites, the dispersal into Faltha of those who had once lived in this valley had taken place a full two thousand years ago. Phemanderac had told her that, apart from the rebuilding of the drowned city further up the slope, little had changed in the valley since then.

Looking about her, Stella could believe him.

The lowering sun coated the buildings ahead with a faintly rosy glaze. There it stood: Dhauria, formerly Dona Mihst, City of the Fountain. Stella knew that she and her friends would soon be numbered among the privileged ones who had set foot in a city in which all Falthans believed, but few had ever seen.

It was glorious.

The houses began on the flat, using a small area of what otherwise would have been arable land, then stretched up the side of a hill that became part of the enormous ochre cliffs surrounding this deep valley. Whitewashed, with a faint pink blush from the lowering sun, there was something innocent about the houses, something naive, counterpointed by their ubiquitous red-tile roofs. They seemed to have been built in clusters, a dozen or so buildings to a group, separated by open spaces: cobbled courtyards, grassy lawns, glittering blue pools. Sprinkled between all this stood stately cypresses and spreading oaks, under which a few small white figures sat alone, shaded from the still-fierce sun.

Despite all that had happened to her, of which the death of her husband Leith, King of Faltha, was but the most distressing of many harrowing events, Stella found herself becoming excited.

"Looks dull," a voice said.

She turned her head to where her guard, Robal, strode beside the cart, one hand resting on Lindha the donkey's neck. He'd become fond of the animal during their desert journey. "A pale shadow of Instruere," he added provocatively.

"Dull?" came the expected rejoinder from the other side of the cart. Conal the Halite priest walked there, two steps to every one of the guard's, his round face lit up with anticipation. "You won't find midden heaps to match those in Instruere, nor, I imagine, will you have your pocket picked within minutes of your arrival. This place has much of interest for the scholar."

Stella frowned. The infuriating priest had as much as accused Robal of a lack of intelligence. *What ails these two men?* she wondered. They fought over the most trivial of things, constantly seeking inventive new ways to insult each other, despite both having pledged themselves to her. As for that, both had rendered her invaluable service: in fact, both men had saved her life. Robal, albeit unwittingly at first, had delivered her from the Halite Archpriest in the hours after Leith had died; while Conal—she still could not credit this, but Robal insisted it was true, and he of anyone would not lie to make the priest look better—had attacked and slain the Lord of Fear who had tried to take her life.

Saved her life? She snorted to herself. Was that possible? Could her life in fact be taken? Here she was, nearing her ninetieth year and still as hale as she had been sixty or more years ago. Better, in fact. The Lord of Fear had done enough to kill her not two months past, but the scar where he had opened her throat had already disappeared. She was, it seemed, immortal. She knew whom she had to thank for that.

Curse, not thank, she thought as they approached the gate. More a ceremonial arch than a gate, as there was no wall either side of it. A tall, thin edifice so narrow that it would admit only two people at a time, though one could easily walk around it and enter the city just the same. Her thoughts returned to their own narrow gate. Yes, she was immortal, whatever that meant, as a result of the Undying Man and his desperate attempt to keep her alive. At the start of the Falthan War he had taken her captive, and made her witness the defeat of the Falthan army at the hands of his Bhrudwan soldiers and *Maghdi Dasht*. She had resisted him, mocked him, and he had struck her, causing her grave injuries. But he had drawn her back from death, infusing her with his own blood, blood cursed by the Most High himself, punishment for his rebellion at the fall of Dhauria. *Here. Here is the origin of my curse.* Something she had almost forgotten.

She wondered if proximity to the source of her suffering would make it worse. Not yet. The dull ache remained as it had been these last years: not the agony of the first years after her "healing", but still constant enough a companion that it defined her. She wondered what it would be like to feel nothing. Even for a moment. She wondered how much she would pay for a brief cessation of her pain.

Ahead of them Phemanderac disembarked from his wagon. With careful but steady steps—*After all, he is even older than me*, Stella thought wryly—he approached the gate.

A child came forward from the shadow of the arch. She wore a white robe and a garland of flowers in her hair. Stella almost laughed at the triteness of the image, then remembered the Dhaurians maintained virtually no contact with the outside world. What seemed hackneyed and false to outsiders, the sort of thing done on feast days in Firanes, might be genuine here. She resolved to keep her cynicism in check.

"How many return to the city?" the child asked in a high, sweet voice.

"Twenty," Phemanderac replied. "And five."

"Five?" came a voice from the shadows. "Five strangers? Are the rules of this place of no account at all to you, Wanderer?"

A young man stepped forward, a scroll in his hands. "Do I have to read you the statutes yet again?"

Phemanderac laughed, though Stella could tell it was forced. "Again?" he said, his thin voice billowing in the sudden cold as the sun disappeared behind the cliff. "This would be the first time with you, Sinan, though I do remember the occasional time your father and I discussed protocol at this gate."

The boy, also clad in white and bearing a close resemblance to the girl—brother and sister?—did not smile, but his eyes sparkled. He made a show of checking a list he drew from a fold in his robe. "Indeed," he said. "Seventeen occasional times."

"Then let us make the eighteenth short and to the point," Phemanderac said. "The sun is gone and my friends are footsore. You have records of the twenty Dhaurians; let me now introduce the leader of the five outsiders I will sponsor. Step forward, Stella of Loulea, Queen of Faltha, and meet Ena and Sinan, children of the clan who keep the Gate of Mist."

No one else moved, so Stella walked towards the arch. Phemanderac bent down and whispered in her ear as she passed: "Take this seriously. These people have the right to refuse you admission. Remember, we do not see the division between child and adult as you do." She nodded.

"Why do you wish to enter our city?" asked the boy.

Stella had thought about this. Not so much about her real reasons for coming here—she remained unsure as to what they were—but about those that would sound most plausible to the Dhaurians. Phemanderac had counselled her to keep her justification short, and as close to the truth as possible. So she told the truth; just not all of it.

"I wish to learn," she said.

The boy waited for her to say more, but when it became clear she had finished, he asked: "What might the Dhaurians be able to teach you?"

Stella was ready for this question too. "How to make the best of a long life."

"That is a subject many Dhaurians could assist you with," said the young boy, seemingly unaware of the irony. "How long do you intend to stay?"

"As long as we are welcome," Stella said. "I have proved to be a slow learner. However, given the reputation of Dhaurians as teachers, I am hopeful I might learn my lessons more quickly this time."

There was a story embedded in those last two words, but if the child noticed he chose to ignore it.

"Come forward," he said.

The girl child lifted her right hand as though to wave, and held it there. Stella walked up to her, wondering how to respond; years of protocol coaching offered no guide beyond matching the gesture. This she did—though with her left arm; her right ached in the cooling air—and her action pleased the girl, who took a pace forward and placed her forearm against Stella's. The girl had to lift her arm high to do so, and Stella lowered hers to make it easier.

"Arm in arm, to serve each other, as long as you remain here," the boy said, and brought out a gauze-like pink fabric.

"Must it be done this way?" Phemanderac asked.

What way? Something formal was happening, but Stella could not make it out.

"After eighteen infractions of Dhaurian law, *dominie*, any one of which was serious enough to warrant exile, do you need to ask?" the boy said, smiling as he began wrapping the gauze around the forearms of his sister and the Falthan queen.

"Phemanderac," Stella said quietly, "what does this mean?"

"I am sorry, Stella, but this means Ena must stay bound to you while you remain in Dhauria. Thus we ensure the good behaviour of anyone the gatekeepers deem a risk."

"A risk?" Robal growled. "This is an insult." He stared at the two young gatekeepers. "What is Dhauria but a backwater? Had Falthans not resisted the Destroyer's army, with the cost of thousands of lives, this place would now be under the Undying Man's rule. Dhaurians are ignorant. How can they treat her this way?"

"Truly, I am sorry," the Dhaurian scholar replied. "It is my fault; a legacy of my disobedience all those years ago when I left this place to search the world for the Right Hand of the Most High. Despite since honouring me as *dominie*, the clans of Dhauria have never really trusted me since I set out."

"Surely there is someone in charge who will see reason?" Conal asked, hands on his hips. "This is blasphemous."

Blasphemous? Stella repeated in her mind. *Only if you consider me a god.* A shadow fell across her mind, chilling her. Did she have two servants who competed in their worship of her? Surely not.

"There is no central authority here to tell any of the clans what to do," Phemanderac said to the priest and the guard. Kilfor of Chardzou and Sauxa, his father, came forward also to listen to the explanation. "If Sinan and Ena decide this must be done, no one here will challenge it. Not their parents, nor their clan chief, nor any of the Council of Scholars."

"So there is a council we can appeal to?" Conal asked.

"There will be no appeal," Stella said. "I will abide by the restrictions placed upon me. Let us discuss this no further."

At her word the remaining outsiders in their party presented themselves. Robal and Conal gave their own names, one perfunctorily, the other breathlessly. Kilfor and Sauxa had remained silent throughout the exchange, but it had clearly unsettled them.

"So much for a place of beauty and refuge," Kilfor muttered as he was introduced to the young gatekeepers.

His father smiled widely, his answer to seemingly every situation. "We are the first Falthans to visit in some time, yes?" he asked Sinan as he pressed forearms with the boy. "You do not have many visitors?"

The boy's expression did not change. "No, we do not," he replied. "And those who seek admittance are usually denied it. But those of us with responsibility for the gates know of the queen of the Falthans, from the words of the *dominie* Phemanderac, who is not as unregarded as he might think."

Phemanderac nodded, acknowledging the compliment. Fenacia, the leader of the Dhaurian caravan, joined him, and began to organise the disposition of the caravan. After taking them to their accommodation, Lindha would be stabled down by the waterfront, where their trap would be stored. Stella rubbed the donkey's neck affectionately. Smelly old thing, but pleasant enough in her way.

"There is another Falthan here in Dhauria," the boy Sinan added, "a man seeking knowledge from our Hall of Scrolls. You will meet him, should your business take you there."

"Another Falthan?" Stella said. "How often did you say you have visits from outsiders?"

"Almost never," Phemanderac said, his brow furrowed. "In fact, despite the desert trail, it is almost impossible for an outsider to make it to Dhauria without guidance. There is something about the approaches to this place that daunts those seeking us out. We are occasionally stumbled upon, but almost never deliberately found." He scratched his grey stubble, the product of weeks without shaving. "I would like to meet the man who has penetrated our subtle defences for the sake of scholarly knowledge."

"I would like to meet him too," Stella said, lowering her arm awkwardly. She glanced at the young girl, who returned her gaze serenely. The gauze bonds did not hurt, but would likely be something of an irritation. Of more importance, however, was the identity of the other outsider currently within Dhauria.

She had a feeling she knew who it would be.

The gatekeepers had clearly decided that restraining one of their number was enough. Robal offered to exchange places with his queen, but the children simply shook their heads at his suggestion.

"This clan has two thousand years' experience of keeping the gate," the ancient Dhaurian scholar replied to his persistent questioning. "We must respect their judgment, even if we disagree with it—or are shamed by it."

So of course the fool priest voiced his own objections, after the fact and with no regard for what Phemanderac had just told them. Robal sighed. It had been such a mistake to accept this man into their company. He'd been tempted to knock him on the head and leave him in the desert. Did the idiot think no one noticed the cow's-eyes he made at Stella? The guard clenched his fists in anger. The man sullied his queen every time he gazed hotly in her direction.

He snapped his own gaze away from Stella and cast an eye over the city around them. The streets were all cobbled, though deep grooves had been worn in the stones on the most frequented routes. This place was ancient; how many times must the cobbles have been replaced?

Yes, it was old, but there was no sign of decrepitude. Most roofs were constructed from bright red tiles. The houses were made of undressed stone and had whitewashed walls, quite different from the painted or naturally weathered walls of Falthan cities. But none of these things fully explained the sense of difference he felt walking along the streets of Dhauria.

He kept his eyes open wide, sweeping left and right in case of sudden danger. He noticed movement in the windows of one house: a child stared at the procession passing by for a moment, then disappeared. *Ah, that is what it is.* He wondered why it had taken him so long to notice.

"Your majesty," he said quietly, leaning towards Stella as he spoke, "where is everybody? There aren't enough people out in the streets."

People in pale robes of various descriptions walked briskly past them on undisclosed errands, but there were no knots of citizens discussing this or selling that or arguing about something else. They had now been walking for some time and he had yet to see a market. And, most peculiar of all, only three children. One at the window, one who led them up a winding road, and one who had remained at the gate.

Robal wondered if the Dhaurians made no distinction between adults and children because there were so few children. *That sort of thing can happen when a people do not mix with outsiders. Their blood goes stale, and children are much harder to kindle.*

"Phemanderac, sir," he ventured, "are the people at a meeting?"

"What?" The man's rheumy eyes struggled to focus. Clearly he had been thinking about something else. "No, I would imagine everyone is engaged in their duties. It is near mealtime, you know, and food preparation and cooking is a family task. There are not many people left on the street."

The group turned a corner and began to climb a winding street. A main thoroughfare, if the depth of ruts in the cobbles was any guide. A few people hurried past, but to Robal's mind still nowhere near the number he would have expected for a city of this size. Fewer, in fact, than frequented the streets of Instruere in the quietest hours of a night watch.

"You say the people here are of one house and are organised into clans," Kilfor said. "We have clans on the Falthan plains. Are you familiar with our system? Does Dhauria work like Chardzou and the other wandering towns of Austrau?"

"You know, boy, someone ought to board up your mouth," his father commented dryly. "How can a town of brick and tile wander like tented Chardzou? I despair of you. I should have adopted a snake as my heir, like your mother told me to. Plenty of clever snakes on the plains."

"What was that noise?" Kilfor responded in mock anger, without turning his head towards his father. "Did the plains wind follow us across the desert, or has a camel just broken wind?" He shrugged his shoulders in a what-am-I-to-do fashion. "I believe our host knows what I mean."

"Indeed he does," Sauxa countered. "He knows you want him to tell you that those who dwell in Chardzou are the purest of Falthan men, following as they do the example of the Dhaurians. Thus you can boast of your own culture."

"Pretty good, old man. But no, that's what *you* want to know, in order somehow to justify a life wasted in the behind of beyond. I, on the other hand, am merely curious."

"Do these two always—"

"Always, Phemanderac," Robal said. "Should a serpent of old scoop them up in its mouth, they'll be arguing about the length of its fangs as they slither down its gut. There's no stopping them."

"Ah. Then I'll explain the place of clans in Dhaurian society as we walk, and perhaps the two men would be so good as to resume their argument when I run out of breath. This road gets steeper every time I climb it."

Stella offered him the trap, but he refused. "I need to feel my feet on these cobbles," he said, then laughed. "Actually, I need to be seen. People need to know I am home again."

The old scholar began to tell them about the clans, and Robal gradually stopped listening. He didn't really care about the four great houses of men who came north from Jangela with the Most High, nor how they were divided into minor houses, then further into clans, each of which was allocated a responsibility. He let the words wash over him and focused instead on the few people walking by. The men were mostly tall, at least as tall as himself, and Robal was accounted large by Instruian standards. A surprising number of them had grey hair, although none looked ancient like Phemanderac—no, wait, there were two men approaching who were both using sticks to support themselves. They raised their sticks to greet Phemanderac, but did not enquire after the outsiders, though they could not have failed to notice the bonds between Stella and the little girl.

Robal wondered how old people grew here. There seemed an agelessness about the place, as though the city and the people living in it had been here forever. *And still virtually no children in sight*, he thought. Something about that wasn't right, but no one else seemed to be worried about it.

*   *   *

The sun had long gone, but a faint glow still allowed Stella to see the lodgings they had been allocated. Before he had left for his own home, Phemanderac had explained that there were no inns or public accommodation in the city—indeed, it was a concept foreign to the Dhaurians. If you needed to stay, you lodged with a member of your clan. Outsiders stayed with the clan responsible for the gate through which they had been admitted.

The house they were guided to looked no different than any other: small, rectangular, single storey, with a tiled roof. Inside, despite an absence of furniture, there seemed not enough room for their party; two rooms and a washroom would surely not provide them all with sleeping quarters. How were they to be distributed?

As the five outsiders stood wearily in the unfurnished room, no doubt wondering much the same as Stella, men and women came through the door. They carried mattresses and pallets and, with an economy of movement, set up sleeping quarters. Four pallets in the larger room, two in the smaller.

Two? For a moment Stella had forgotten the girl bound to her arm. *Of course, two.*

Three men entered, bearing what were obviously heavy burdens wrapped in layers of cloth. They turned out to be stones, which were placed in the hearth.

One of the men approached them. "We have provided for you, as agreed by the binding of arms. Food will follow shortly." The language was the Falthan common tongue, but spoken in a stilted fashion, with as much warmth in the words as someone organising the removal of refuse from a kitchen.

"Firestones," he said, following Stella's glance at the

hearth. "You do not use firestones?" At her head-shake he explained how they retained heat, and needed only to be fired twice a day. "We will attend to it," he said.

The man's long face, so like Phemanderac's in shape but so unlike in expression, bore a look of faint distaste. *He probably thinks he is being polite.*

Stella kept her thoughts to herself as their hosts returned with what she had to admit was ample fare: vegetable soup, warm bread and a selection of cold meats. *Cold*, she thought. *Everything about these people seems so cold. How was Phemanderac born from such as these? And another thought:* Were these people not the ones who had once received the Fire of the Most High? If she understood anything from the curse in her own blood, it was akin to the Fire of Life. So how did it not warm these people?

"Friendly lot," Robal murmured as the Dhaurians left the room.

Conal snorted. "You would receive less in Instruere unless you had plenty of coin to pay for it."

"In case you had forgotten," Stella said quietly, her face reddening, "we still have company."

Beside her the girl smiled, then reached her left hand towards a platter of meat, as though she hadn't heard. *Well, she is only a child. She might not pick up the nuances of our conversation.*

Really, though, Stella knew she could tell little about what these strange people might know. If they trusted young children with guarding their gates, what might such a child be capable of?

These thoughts still occupied her the next morning as she and Ena dressed. Someone had laid out a robe in the Dhaurian style: full-length, white, of wonderfully fine material sturdier than silk but just as cool. Perfect for the warm day ahead. Ena allowed Stella to slip off their binding cloth while she put the robe on, then submitted to being re-bound.

Stella would rather the binding had been left off while they performed their ablutions. A series of necessary tasks made awkward and unpleasant due to the binding, and Stella found herself embarrassed as a stranger—a young, curious stranger—dispassionately observed her bodily functions.

"You cried out in the night," said the girl, her voice sleep-laden and endearingly childish. "Who is Leith?"

"Oh," Stella said; and, before she could stop herself, put her knuckles in her mouth. *Who's being childish now?* she asked herself, and cursed inwardly as a tear leaked from her left eye and trickled down her cheek.

The girl just stared at her, her face a gentle enquiry, as though watching a weeping woman was a commonplace thing.

Stella put down the soft cloth she had been using to dry her face. "He was my husband," she said. "He died not long ago."

Ena bit her lip, as though caught in an indiscretion. "I am sorry for making you cry. My mother always says it is sad when someone dies young. Especially if they have not long been wedded."

"He wasn't—"

He wasn't young, Stella was about to say, but thought better of it. Too much to explain: how Leith had died of old age, yet she herself still appeared little older than a youth. Too many questions would follow. The girl didn't need to know.

"Did I keep you awake?" she asked instead.

"I've never slept away from my house before," said Ena. "Sinan said it would be exciting, but I was scared. The sounds are different upslope."

"Different?" Stella asked, drawn into the girl's small world despite herself. "Why, where do you live?"

"Downslope, close to the Mist Gate. I sometimes come upslope to play with Phyna, but I've never been allowed to stay overnight."

"Ena, are all your family gatekeepers?"

Ena put down the twig she was using to clean her teeth. "The gate clans are responsible for all aspects of Dhaurian defence," she said, obviously repeating words she'd heard her parents say many times. "My mother is the sister-daughter of the clan leader, and is important, so we have been given the Mist Gate to guard."

"Has there ever been an attempt to invade Dhauria?"

"No! The bad men don't know we are here. My father says we don't have what the Falthans want. But we still have to keep outsiders outside, he says. He has a big club. He'd go *whack!* to anyone trying to invade."

"But you let us in," Stella pressed.

"Phemanderac stood for you," the small girl answered. "He is well known in Dhauria. He disobeyed by going out of the valley, but he came back and repented later, not like Kannwar. I like Phemanderac. He has a crinkly face."

There was so much Stella wanted to ask as a result of these last comments, but Ena had clearly had enough of the conversation and tugged at her arm, drawing her in the direction of the main room, where the sound of cots being cleared away had been replaced by the smell of oat-meal porridge, or something close to it, cooking on the firestones. Someone had built a small, almost smokeless fire under the stones, and they glowed a deep red.

Stella shook her head. What sort of society would compare the wise, sensitive Phemanderac to Kannwar, he who betrayed the First Men and became the Destroyer, the Undying Man of Bhrudwo? How could Kannwar's evil rebellion be compared to Phemanderac's rejection of Dhauria's cloistered halls in search of the truth?

The girl had said Phemanderac was well known, but why was he not fêted as a hero? Without his help Faltha would have been overrun by the Destroyer and his Bhrudwan horde. Did Dhauria care more for its racial purity than the fate of the world?

Stella nursed her porridge—much sweeter than she was accustomed to, but not unpleasant—and considered these things. Beside her Ena slid backwards and forwards on her seat, singing a rhyme to herself while banging her feet on a leg of the table, much like any other girl of eight years old and not the precocious child-adult she had seemed the previous day. Much of that precocity was no doubt due to her playing a part. Stella was pleased she felt comfortable enough to abandon it.

On the opposite side of the table Robal and Conal ate in silence, looking rather strange in matching white robes, as though they were partners in some exotic venture. As Stella glanced in their direction, she noted there was little eating going on: the men were transfixed by an argument that Kilfor and his father, Sauxa, had been working on since early this morning, if the content was anything to go by.

"A troop of Piskasian water-monkeys after they've been overfed on bananas," Kilfor said.

Robal laughed at this sally. Conal kept a straight face,

but his small eyes were lighter than Stella had seen in some time. The point of Kilfor's statement was lost on Stella, who had not been listening.

"Monkeys? You inherited your ears from your mother, along with your dress sense," Sauxa said, then sucked on his teeth as he thought. "I sound more like a treeful of song-birds."

"Old man, you snored so hard last night that the top half of this city collapsed and came rumbling down past us. And the only reason I know this is because I was told this morning; I certainly couldn't hear the destruction over the noises you were making. I didn't know what would make my ears pop first: the rumble from your gaping maw or the way you sucked all the air out of the room every time you took a breath."

"Tuneful."

Robal coughed, then began to choke. He lost most of his mouthful of porridge in the process.

Kilfor twitched an eyebrow. "Tuneful? The citizens of Dhauria organised a bounty hunt for the horde of ravenous, deep-throated monsters loose on their streets. The number of times I was awoken last night by men tapping on the window, asking if I needed rescuing, it's a wonder I got any sleep."

"Tonight you can sleep with the donkey then." Sauxa put on his most aggrieved voice.

"Infinitely preferable! Indeed, why don't I sleep with a roomful of them. Not only will it be much quieter, the room will also smell much better."

Stella felt her own mouth twitching. Kilfor, a friend of Robal, had agreed to hide her from the Instruian authorities in the Great Plains settlement of Chardzou. However, he and his father had ended up guiding her to the desert track that led to Dhauria. Now they were here, she found herself enjoying their company but not knowing what to do with them. They would not be able to come with her on the next stage of her journey. Indeed, Robal and Conal had somehow to be persuaded to stay behind also. After all, what need did she have of guards when it was now proven beyond all doubt that she could not die?

Colourful descriptions of odours the Chardzou men had known—or created—gave way to comparisons of their intellectual capacity. Smiling inwardly, Stella eased herself up from her chair, forgetting again her ties to the girl next to her.

"Sorry, Ena," she said. Heads turned. "I need some fresh air."

This occasioned raucous laughter from Kilfor and Robal. "I'm not surprised," Kilfor said, sniggering and looking pointedly at his father.

"If there's one thing I've learned about men," she shot at them as she and Ena got to their feet, "it is that their lives revolve around their own bodily functions. It doesn't matter how long I live, I doubt I'll ever discover anything more complicated about them."

She hadn't meant the last words to sting, but the men behind her quietened as she strode to the door and looked out on a Dhaurian morning.

"Oh, my," she said. Beside her Ena smiled.

They were perhaps halfway up the hill upon which Dhauria had been built. Behind them the cliff stretched impossibly high, looking as though it leaned over them like some large, inquisitive neighbour. But it was the scene before her that took Stella's breath.

The lower city, with its white walls, green trees and red roofs, spread out below her like a rumpled blanket, an effect enhanced by the patchwork fields beyond. In the distance the sea glittered, a thousand beckoning wavetops. Everything glowed with a golden light. *The sunlight shines through desert sand suspended high in the air*, Stella told herself. *It's a trick of the light.* But it looked like a Bansila painting from the woman's Spiritualist phase, when the artist imbued every living thing with a golden essenza, as she called it. Stella owned—had owned—four of her best works. The effect was achingly beautiful, but paled in comparison to what lay before her.

"How can you stand it?" she breathed, but Ena did not answer. Stella turned to her: the girl's face was awash with light, and for a surreal moment the Falthan queen was tempted to fall to her knees.

A trick of the light. But she wondered.

A shout, a hailed welcome, and here came Phemanderac, drawn slowly up the street in a cart. Even her old friend's familiar lined face appeared otherworldly this morning.

Stella extended her hand and helped him alight.

"Thank you, my dear," he said. "Forgive the cart; I did not sleep well. My back did not like the softness of my bed." Then he turned and greeted Ena with a smile and a kind word.

"Why would you ever want to leave this place?" Stella asked, indicating the scene before them with a wide gesture of her free arm.

"It is a fine morning," he replied. "Worth taking a moment or two to consider. Were you to stay until autumn you would see true beauty. Although," he added with a smile,

"Instruere has—had—one or two beautiful things of its own."

"Gallant," Stella replied. "Tell me, what is it I see?"

He pointed out the sights spread before them: the lower city, with its clan groupings, and further left, at the base of the hill, tall towers surrounding the Square of Sorrows. "Built in remembrance of that which was lost," he said, "in echo of the Square of Rainbows."

"As were the carvings inside the Hall of Meeting in Instruere," she replied. "Will we always be defined by what Kannwar did?"

Phemanderac had to know her words carried a personal meaning.

"I imagine so," he said quietly.

"Where was the old city of Dona Mihst? The *Domaz Skreud* said it was destroyed by the flood."

"The holy scroll is correct," Phemanderac said. "Look out beyond the shore—see there, where the sea sparkles so? The waves break there because there is a hill just below the surface. On that hill the Fountain once played, before the flood came, and around it Dona Mihst was built. Fishermen can apparently see the ruins of that place when the sea is clear. They tell of an enormous rent in the hill, a deep chasm from which comes a red glow, as though open to the earth's deep furnaces. Sometimes the sea bubbles and boils, they say. I have never been out there."

"One of the few places you have not been, then," Stella said, taking his hand. "You are a hero, you know. All Faltha acknowledges the great debt you are owed for your part in the Falthan War. I cannot help wondering why you are not held in such honour here."

"But I am!" he replied. "They call me *dominie*, the first since Hauthius. What higher honour could I ask for?"

"An honour granted because of your academic achievements, old friend, not for your courage. There ought to be a statue of you down there, gleaming golden in the morning sun. Or they should rename the Square of Sorrows to something more fitting in your honour."

"Ah, Stella, I'm just grateful they tolerate me. Now, speaking of places I have been, I have come to take you to the Hall of Scrolls. I have wrung permission from the council for you to spend a daily hour in the scriptorium, under my supervision. Are you ready to accompany me?" His question encompassed both Stella and Ena.

"And on the way," he added, "you can think of a new name for the Square of Sorrows. 'Phemanderac's Folly' perhaps?"

Stella laughed, but her heart hurt for this gentle giant of a man, whose people would never acknowledge they owed their lives to him.

The Hall of Scrolls was a large building of a style Stella had never before seen. A central golden dome topped a square dressed stone structure at least as high as Instruere's Hall of Meeting. The dome was inscribed with a filigree pattern that emphasised its fragility; it seemed to glow from within. Arched stained-glass windows punctuated the structure upon which it sat. A sheer wall, half the height of the main structure, wrapped itself around the hall itself, and the section visible to Stella was studded with three arched windows, much larger than those of the main hall. Each depicted a different symbol: open hand, flaming arrow, breaking wave. In the right of centre of this wall was a large open arch, the main entrance.

The main feature of the magnificent building's exterior, however, were the twin slender towers stretching into the sky. Octagonal in shape, they were crowned with their own domes, under which nestled small chambers, open to the air through more arched windows.

Stella immediately appreciated what she saw: the progenitor of the home in which she had lived for the last seventy years. The towers took her back to the day Leith died, in a tower modelled on these—or, more accurately, she supposed, modelled on the building, now destroyed, that had also served as inspiration for the edifice before her.

A sudden image of Leith, his face alight in the last throes of life, filled her mind. His parting words to her; his final breath a warning to flee the Halites who sought her conversion or death for her role as the Destroyer's Consort. The way his hand seemed to deflate. The change from human to shell.

The shock of it hit her as she stared at the towers above. She fell to her knees, dragging Ena unheeded to the ground. "Oh, oh, oh," she said. "Oh, oh."

A warm hand rested on the back of her head, but Phemanderac said nothing. He no doubt understood what ailed her, but Ena did not.

"I hurt my knee," the girl said, reproach in her voice. "Look, it's bleeding."

"Oh," said Stella, dashing tears from her eyes. "I'm sorry. I didn't mean to hurt you." She took a small piece of linen from her tunic and patted down the small graze on the girl's knee.

"Be careful, Stella," Phemanderac said. "Do not dwell

overmuch on the past. Memories have more power here than in the outside world." She wanted to pursue this cryptic comment, but he drew her to her feet. "Let us go inside. There are people looking at us, wondering what we are doing. I care nothing for their regard, but I am conscious of time passing. If we do not use the time we have been given, we may not be allowed to return."

Stella allowed the two Dhaurians to guide her into the hall. She paid no attention to the mosaics covering the walls on either side of the corridor, immersed in her own thoughts. She had named Phemanderac a hero, but had forgotten Leith. Yes, he had been heralded in the days after the war, but his role in the victory over the Bhrudwans had been distorted by the Halites. He had, according to them, come close to losing the war, and only the selfless sacrifice by his older brother, Hal—after whom the Halites were named—had saved them all. It had been within Leith's power as King of Faltha to suppress this story, but he had not. So now Hal was a religion and Leith was dead.

And Stella, infected with the blood of the Undying Man, itself corrupted by disobedience, could never die.

How, then, could she live?

That was the reason she had come here. In the golden age before the rebellion against the Most High, the First Men lived in this valley and were sustained by the Fountain. The waters of this fountain were forbidden anyone to drink, but—unbeknown to those who lived there—the spray had sustained them all, greatly elongating their lives. Some among them, according to the scrolls in Instruere's archives, lived many hundreds of years. Surely somewhere in this Hall of Scrolls would be a text telling her how the longest-lived of these long-lived men, envied by the ignorant Halites, coped while their friends and lovers died around them.

If she couldn't find help here, there was only one other place she could go—to the stronghold of the Undying Man himself, to Andratan, to ask the only other immortal in the world.

She told herself she hoped to find the answers here, but something deep and dark within her counselled her not to look too hard.

Phemanderac led her and Ena down a broad stair to a large oaken door. On the door was a sign in an ancient language, the letters all flourishes and points. "School of the prophets," Phemanderac whispered in her ear. An attendant opened the door for them, then lit glass lanterns for them before closing it. The small chamber in which Stella found herself was dark, save the pale light from their lanterns.

"Why are we in this room?" she asked Phemanderac.

"We allow our eyes to adjust to the darkness. The scriptorium is built to keep out natural light, as such light damages the parchment. There is another door before us. When our eyes have adjusted, this door will be opened and we will join the other scholars in the scriptorium.

"Another thing," he added. "You won't be able to read the scrolls. The Falthan common tongue grew from the language of the First Men, but changed in the growing. However, I can interpret them for you." He sighed. "Or, at least, I could have, before my eyesight began to fail. Ena here could read most of what you need, or you could hire one of the Saiwan clansmen to read for you."

"Won't the scrolls be too fragile to read?" Stella asked. "They are thousands of years old, after all."

Beside her, Ena giggled in the darkness.

"Oh, you won't be using the originals," Phemanderac said gently. "You will be reading a copy of a copy of a copy of a copy. The few surviving original scrolls cannot be handled, lest the oils and acids in your fingertips contaminate the parchment. I could perhaps arrange for you to see one of the originals, should you wish," he added, though he sounded dubious.

"Thank you, but that won't be necessary."

The inner door opened onto a world of murmuring and flickering lights. Stella followed Phemanderac to a small cubicle, then waited while he procured three extra seats. "Shall I arrange for a reader?" he asked when he returned. "I will pay the hire myself, as you are a guest."

"Is the cost substantial?" Stella asked.

Phemanderac laughed. "I am accounted a rich man here. It would be my pleasure. I mean that truly: to hear the words of the old scrolls read once again will ease my heart."

He wandered off, and Stella sat down, Ena at her side. "I'm sorry about this," she whispered to the girl. "This must be boring for you."

. The girl giggled again. "What could be more interesting than learning about the great ones who went before us?"

Stella searched for irony in the voice, but could hear none. "You are different from the children in my land," she said.

"Of course!" Ena said happily. "We are from Dhauria, the remnant of the First Men, descended from those who remained faithful to the Most High when Kannwar rebelled against him. We are not like ordinary people."

A speech, Stella considered, probably learned off by heart by all Dhaurian youngsters. She thought of trying to prick this child's veneer of confidence, then rejected the idea as shameful.

Two lights bobbed towards them. Phemanderac led a young woman, presumably the scholar who would read for Stella. "This is Moralye," he said, and she smiled. *She really is a pretty thing*, Stella thought, ideally suited to functioning in the scriptorium, with her large, luminous eyes and small stature.

"Your clan is responsible for the maintenance and preservation of the scrolls, Moralye?" she asked. "And while you train yourself in the skills necessary, you earn money for your clan?"

The woman smiled. "I welcome you to the scriptorium of Dhauria, Stella Pellwen," she said, speaking quickly. "You are every bit as perceptive as the *dominie* claimed. It will be a pleasure to work with you."

Surprised by the use of her full name, Stella drew breath to frame a reply, but Moralye continued.

"I have selected a number of scrolls in accordance with Phemanderac's request, and members of the Saiwan clan are searching their indexes for others. They will bring these to us in due course."

She drew breath. Her obvious excitement made Stella smile. "Some of the scrolls deal with the Undying Man," the girl warned. "Are you comfortable with this?"

"I am," Stella said. "To me, there has always been a question surrounding his rebellion. Did events unfold exactly as the scrolls say?" Her teeth tingled as she asked the question. Was there really any doubt? The likely truth was the scrolls probably obscured the worst of his excesses.

Moralye smiled, no doubt approving of Stella's spirit of enquiry. "Until the remainder of the scrolls are brought to us, allow me to begin reading." The woman's eyes danced in the lamplight.

"Very well, then—"

Moralye had seated herself even before Stella could finish her comment.

"This is from the memoirs of Mannimaritseth, the longest-lived of the First Men," she began. "It is said he lived eight hundred years in the Vale of Youth before the Most High translated him. He writes about his long life as follows:

"'A new day is to me yet another opportunity to grapple with the depth of corruption in my own spirit. I seek the purification of the Most High's holy fire, yet constantly fall short. My days are thus a burden, for I long for the day when my Lord decides I am hale enough to be separated from the cord that binds me to this black earth.'"

"Cheerful fellow," Stella sighed. So much like her own experience. Eight hundred years. How did he remain sane?

Perhaps he didn't, came a voice into her mind, a voice from somewhere close by. Stella's head jerked up, but of course she couldn't see anything in the darkened chamber.

"Mistress?" Moralye asked. "May I continue?"

"Please."

"'I besought the counsel of Amara, the oldest among us, and she averred she importance of forgetting. A balance is required between cherishing one's memories, for memories are the only thing that connect you to who you are, and putting them aside so their accumulation does not drown you.'"

She nodded. *Yes. I cannot forget, therefore I drown.*

At least you have not had others at work trying to alter

your past, said the voice in her mind. Definitely not her imagination. It seemed to come from the place occasionally used by the Undying Man to spy on her; that tenuous link between them that let her know how he was feeling. The blood-link. *Once they begin their work, you cannot be sure what it is you are trying to forget,* the voice went on.

Oh? Anger blazed within her at the self-pitying words. *Why would people not want to remake their memories of such as you? And do you not know of the years I have had to endure my history being remade? I am now known as the Destroyer's Consort. No one cares to know of the times I resisted you, and of the pain it brought me. They only remember me as your cat's-paw, your obedient servant paraded in front of them on the day you came to sign the Declaration that would have given you lordship of Faltha. They despise me for it, and I have had to flee for my life.*

I am as despised and misunderstood as you, came the reply.

Stella laughed out loud, causing Moralye to startle and *interrupting her recitation. Despised, yes. Misunderstood, I think not. I understand you perfectly well.*

Do you? You do not.

A man leaned into the cubicle and cleared his throat, attracting the young Dhaurian scholar's attention. "Excuse me, Moralye, one of those studying in the scriptorium overheard me discussing your requirements with Palanget. He handed me this scroll and asked you to read it to the one who engaged you." He extended his hand, in which nestled a small scroll.

"My lady?" Moralye asked Stella.

Her whole body chilled. She had no idea what this scroll may be, but she knew whose hand—no, definitely the wrong phrase. She knew who had given this to Moralye's associate.

"Yes," she said, swallowing a sudden obstruction in her throat. *He's here, in this room.*

Moralye unrolled the scroll and leaned forward. Beside Stella, Ena kicked her heels against the wall of the cubicle behind her. Phemanderac, quiet until now, put his hand on the arm of the man who had delivered the scroll. "Stay a moment," he said.

Stella's palms began to moisten as she waited.

"Phyrgia, would you fetch the man who gave you this scroll?" Moralye said, licking her lips as the man hurried away, his lamp flickering in the near-darkness. "I want to know where he found it. I'm curious, you see," she added, turning to Stella, "because I've never seen it before. Phemanderac?"

"Nor I," said the old man, leaning over for a closer look. "Though I can barely see it now."

"You'll want to read this," the young scholar said, her voice thick.

"Please," Stella said. "Could someone read it to me?"

"Yes, read it to us," Phemanderac echoed.

CHAPTER 7

APOLOGY FOR A REBELLION

THE SENSE OF SOMEONE IN her head had left Stella for the moment, though she had no doubt it would return if she summoned it. Not for a moment did she think the voice was an invention of her own mind. She knew him, knew the taint of him, the canker of his words.

"'The Testimony of Kannwar of Dona Mihst,'" Moralye began, and at her words Phemanderac gripped the table with both hands, his knuckles whitening. Stella felt herself becoming dizzy as her suspicions crystallised into fact. The woman made to continue, but a commotion at the door brought her up short.

"*Dominie*," said the doorkeeper, striding quickly towards their cubicle, "I have an outsider here claiming the right of admittance, invoking your name as passage. Do I let him in?"

"His name?" Phemanderac could barely take his eyes from the parchment spread out before him.

"Conal, he names himself."

Conal? For a wild moment Stella speculated: *He is a Halite, he says he has feelings for me, he apparently exercised superhuman power to rescue me from the Lord of Fear. But he is a man of petty vanity. Would such a man hide one so proud as the Undying Man? And how would the Undying Man have found a haven in his mind? Conal has been nowhere near Andratan.*

"Stella," a petulant voice called from the half-open door, loud enough to disturb the atmosphere of the room. "Why did you not tell me you were going to the scriptorium? Why would you leave me behind? We have an agreement, my queen!" he said reproachfully.

"Let him approach," she murmured reluctantly. Phemanderac nodded to the doorkeeper, who went and fetched the annoying fool priest. *Or the consummate actor?*

"My queen, I—"

"Hush," she commanded him. "Give me your hand."

His eyes widened, but he extended a hand nonetheless. Her hand closed on his. Flesh, nothing more—or less.

"Very well," she said, releasing him. "Do not ask me what that was about. Now, Conal, you have interrupted matters of great importance. Sit opposite me and do not say a single word unless invited to. Agree to these terms or suffer yourself to be led away from this place. Are you my servant in this matter?"

Phrased in such a way, and by such as Stella, no Falthan citizen could refuse and still maintain their willingness to serve the Crown. Conal assented gracelessly, his face a picture of frustrated curiosity, and took his seat.

Everyone in the crowded cubicle took a deep breath at the same moment, and all eyes turned to Moralye.

"'The Testimony of Kannwar of Dona Mihst,'" she

repeated. "'A Repudiation of the Lies of the First Men and an Apology for Rebellion. Written by my hand, Fourteenth of Ninemonth, two hundred and eighty-three years after the Fall of Dona Mihst. Placed in the new-built scriptorium of Dhauria by my hand six years thereafter.'"

Silence.

Broken by Phemanderac. "The parchment looks and feels authentic. We haven't used this kind of parchment for fifteen hundred years or more. We use a different process of manufacture now, and I doubt anyone could recreate the substance before us. It has aged, but has not deteriorated to the extent one would expect. As for the script, the letters are in a well-practised hand, but there are hints of awkward-ness, as though the hand is injured—or is not the writer's natural hand. Perhaps I see these hints because I am look-ing for them. Any more than this, I cannot say, as my eyes betray me."

"I concur," Moralye said. "I will have my clansmen sub-ject this scroll to the most rigorous investigation, includ-ing chemic analysis. I do not understand how a scroll over seventeen hundred years old has survived intact even in this beneficent environment, nor how it lay undetected for that long. I am willing to swear on any scroll you name that such a thing cannot be."

"If you swear it, I believe it," the old scholar answered. "You are the brightest light for a thousand years, and this is your domain. Perhaps we ought to leave further specula-tion until after we have read its message."

Stella heard the young man beside her take a deep breath, the sort one takes before launching forth. "No, Conal, not a word," she said. "No matter how insightful or well inten-tioned you think it is. We are not the experts here."

Moralye cleared her throat and began to read.

"'You have heard it said that I sponsored rebellion amongst the First Men, and that the world suffered as a result. This is true. This is my apology.'"

"He apologises?" Conal said. "Apologises, then goes on to wreak destruction in Faltha not once but twice? I do not understand."

"In this context an apology is not, I suspect, a regretful explanation," Phemanderac said. "It is more likely to be a justification for debatable actions or beliefs."

Moralye nodded, then continued.

"'However, true though this succinct summary of events may be, many of the details are false. Here I set on parchment a true record that no one can contradict, for none but myself and the Most High were present when much of what I relate came to pass. You may consider that I misremember involuntarily as self-justification for my own misdeeds. I have no defence to offer against such an assertion, save your own judgment. Read my words, then those of the perfidious *Domaz Skreud*. Judge for yourself. If you judge against me, I will hold no blame against you, rather against myself for failing to convince you.'"

"Fetch a copy of the *Domaz Skreud*, please, Moralye," Phemanderac said.

"I have one here," she replied. "I was instructed to gather everything relating to the lives of the First Men and the Rebellion. The *Domaz Skreud* is one of the most important of such documents."

She recommenced her telling. As Moralye read, Stella tried to shut out her feminine voice and imagine the words spoken in the Destroyer's cultured tones.

"'The writer of the *Domaz Skreud* claimed I was the

youngest ever to receive the Fire of Life from the Most High. In this he is correct. I was but three years of age. What he does not know is that I tried to reject the Most High's offering out of fear. I did not want to be known as a freak. I also considered myself too young. Yet the Most High forced the issue. No, he did not compel me to accept his infusion of Fire, but he placed me under duress using arguments both subtle and persuasive. After all these years I do not remember them in detail, but what I do remember tallies with the arguments he used when next we met.

"'The *Domaz Skreud* names me as friendless during my growing years. Again, the writer is correct, but not because I refused friendship when offered. Just as I had feared, my peers were frightened of me and did not understand the Fire within me. Time after time I was rebuffed when I sought companionship. I made friends among the adults around me, but the *Domaz Skreud* does not mark this.

"'Instead, the scroll outlines an incident that occurred when I was eighteen. The writer claims I fought with Garadh my cousin over the leadership of the Kerd Clan. Again, the statement is correct, but the supporting evidence is awry. It was not Garadh who was the gentle one, but I. It was not I who knocked my cousin to the ground, but he who delivered the felling blow. I left afterwards, yes, but only after Garadh refused all offers of reconciliation. I did not flee the scene of my guilt, as the scroll asserts, to begin fomenting rebellion; rather, I followed the immediate and unquestionable summons of the Most High.

"'Consider the evidence. The words of the *Domaz Skreud* were written by one who was not privy to the events between Garadh and myself. I could not have supplied the

writer with information, so who did? One who has a reason
to appear justified before the world: Garadh himself.

"'The Most High summoned me beyond the borders
of Dona Mihst, beyond the cliffs where no man goes, and
into the wilderness. For a year he fed me with strange fruit
and debated with me, day and night, about his plans for the
world and my place in them.

"'This is what he said. He created the world and everything in it, but sought to retire from his creation and leave
it for his creatures to enjoy, unencumbered by his guiding
and ultimately deterministic hand. However, humans en-
treated him to remain and rule over them, and reluctantly
he consented. A son and a daughter of men he raised to
assist him in this task, giving them powers little inferior
to his own. For many lifetimes of men this arrangement
worked well, but the Son and Daughter secretly agreed to
rebel against their Father and, with the help of humans, to
drive him out of the world of men. In this they succeeded,
as the Most High was reluctant to break the world in the
clash of powers required to defeat his adopted children. He
fled north with a remnant of the faithful, proudly calling
themselves the Four Houses of the First Men. The truth is,
your fathers and mine were refugees, as was your God. He
fled, not I; his children rebelled, not I.

"'Here is a question for you. The Most High is the One
God of the world, you First Men claim. What, then, of the
fabled lands to the south, beyond Jangela, from whence
your own legends claim you came? The Most High now
dwells in the north, you say. Is he no longer the Lord of
the southlands? Who is god to the people of the southern
deserts, the original inhabitants of the world, ancient before
the First Men were born? This is a question you cannot

answer, and it ought to trouble you, along with the history of the Most High himself.

"'The Most High knew that problems would arise as a result of his expulsion from the south. The world needed his touch to remain stable. Without him it would eventually fall apart. So he bided his time and nurtured his few faithful followers for a thousand years, until the day the gifted child he had been waiting for was born. So he explained to me; and, when he reached this point in the story, I fled from his face. Not in rebellion, but in fear, for I guessed what he would ask me to do.

"'Which of you, when told you were the product of a thousand years of careful planning, and that your destiny was to confront two gods hardly less powerful than the Most High himself, would not quail? Yet I fled not because I considered myself unfit for the task, but because I knew I could do it. It was this sudden pride, revealed in me, that frightened me so.

"'Wherever I fled, he sought me out. I hid in a cave: a great torrent of water bore me back into the world of light. I took refuge in a lightless forest: a swarm of insects ate the trees bare around me, exposing me to his harsh, merciless light. I made a boat and cast off from the southern coast, but was thrown back to shore by unnatural waves. The Most High tells us we have a choice whether to serve him or no, but it seemed he offered me nothing save service or death. I considered death, and wondered how to achieve it.

"'"You are my Right Hand," he said to me, day after day. "You are my only plan. I raised you to support me." His constant argument made me think I was monstrous even to consider going against his wishes. He wore at my will as the sea wears at a cliff. Yet I was not wholly opposed to his plan, not until the day he revealed its true extent. "I have raised you not only to support me, but in the fullness of time to replace me," he said. I was to become the Most High, while he enjoyed the retirement he had so long sought.

"'I entreat you, reader, examine your heart. I was like you. Mortal, weak, susceptible to injury and disease, conditioned to accept a finite time in the world of men. How might I countenance being made into a god? Instead, I rejected the Most High and his impossible demands, just as you would have done.'"

At these words Conal made an involuntary noise, betraying his thoughts to Stella. She kept her mind carefully blank, allowing the words to wash over her, all the while knowing who sat quietly somewhere in the background, awaiting their reading of his apology.

"'From this point I was no longer innocent. My crimes began with deception and continued until, I admit with frankness, I became a monster, a parody of a human, and almost precisely what I had feared when the Most High first offered me godhood. How much further I will fall is unknown to me.

"'I began my deception by asking the Most High how the puissance might be transferred to me. He explained that the Fountain set in the Square of Rainbows, the heart of Dona Mihst, was an upwelling of his power. The spray of the Fountain sustained the citizens of the Vale and, if drunk, the water would strengthen the drinker until he became as a god.

"'"But you have forbidden us to drink of the Fountain," I said, puzzled. "Yes," he said, "because your mortal body cannot yet bear my power. Yet all you need do is tarry for a millennium of years, and you will be strengthened by the Fire within you to withstand the Water of Life." "A thousand years?" I exclaimed. "I live a thousand years, while everyone I know dies?" "Yes," he answered, mistaking my emotion for one of exultation. "And what happens if I drink of the Fountain before this time?" I asked.

"'At this, the Most High was silent, finally discerning the temper of my heart. At any time he might have sought such knowledge directly from my mind: he is all-knowing, and nothing can be hidden from him. Yet he can himself limit his knowledge by choice, in the quest to allow his children freedom. Indeed, he must do this, or his followers become automatons, constrained to one future, unable to choose outside his knowledge. Thus he did not detect my rebellion until too late.

"'Horrified by the bargain being offered me, I saw only one way out. I decided to drink of the water of the Fountain, thereby alerting my fellow men to the secrets of the Most High. I fled the desert, utilising every mite of power provided by the Fire of Life to outpace him. So profligate was I with the power, it burned out before I could control it. Yet I arrived in Dona Mihst head of the Most High.

"'I began a rebellion. I do not repent of it. I explained as much of the truth as I could to as many people as were able to bear it, yet it was not enough, and many misinterpreted my words. Hence the half-truths contained in the *Domaz Skreud*.

"'Enough men believed me to start the rebellion. Others latched on to me to promote their own causes. The *Domaz Skreud* records that many were at that time discontented by their remoteness from power in the Vale, and ascribes this awareness to me. This is not so. It became part of the rebellion, but I did not promote it. Nevertheless, I used it. I am guilty, but not in the manner the scroll suggests. I looked to lead men to knowledge of, not rejection of, the Most High. I hoped also that the Most High might reconsider his methods, and perhaps learn to understand what it is like to be mortal and afraid of oneself. To know what it is to doubt.

"'I slew Sthane, the only man willing to stand against me when I finally came to drink of the Fountain, just as the scroll says. I regret this. But I do not regret drinking of the Fountain. And when the Most High appeared—too late— and in his anger loosed at me the Jugom Ark, his flaming arrow of justice, taking off my hand, I thought it a small price to pay.

"'So I paid the price, and my fellow men learned the nature of the God who rules them all. Yet within a generation the *Domaz Skreud* became the accepted wisdom, and my sacrifice was maligned. Would you not be angry at such a turn of events? That an entire people ignored my attempt to save them, instead making of me their betrayer? Whatever it takes, I will put right the record. If matters require I liberate Falthwaite from its misapprehensions, I will not shirk from doing so.'"

"Falthwaite? How long since Faltha was called that?" Conal asked. No-one replied, and after a pause Moralye continued.

"'I place this scroll in the archives of the newly built Hall of Scrolls in this new city, the replacement for all that was lost. It is protected and hidden by a keeping spell, one of many things I have learned in the last two centuries. It will be discovered only when a certain question is voiced within a certain distance of the document. That you are reading this means the question has been asked. You may even have asked it. Therefore you want to know whether I am who the scrolls say I am. My answer is yes—and no.

"'I have one last plea. Watch your world. Some day the Most High will seek to raise another as his Right Hand, someone to confront the gods who usurped him. He will be as I was, young, naïve, unaware of what is being asked of him. He will rise to power rapidly. He will be confused. Frightened. But no one will listen to him, no one will offer him the help he needs; everyone will see him as the solution to their problems, and thus his own struggles will be ignored.'"

Stella choked back a sob.

"'He must not be allowed to succeed. The Most High suffered the rebellion of his children; he himself must confront and end that rebellion. If this Right Hand is alive in your time, bring this scroll to him. If I have not found a way to end my own life, bring him to me. I will prevent the Most High using humans to mend the mistake he himself made.'"

"Put it down," Stella said. "Stop reading from the scroll. Please. I cannot listen to any more."

Moralye laid the scroll down on the table and looked up at her. Stella saw the woman's face was white, possibly as drained of blood as her own.

I was right about the Right Hand, said the voice in her head. *It happened as I predicted.*

Yes, Leith was everything you said he was, and much more. Except he wasn't the Right Hand. And he wasn't like you. You never understood him.

Stella took a deep breath, put her finger to her lips, waited until the others nodded, then worked her way out of the cubicle and bade the others remain where they were. Ena, of course, was forced to accompany her.

We will talk of this, and many other things, he sent to her.

I have no intention of ever meeting you face to face, she replied.

She had a direction: his thoughts came at her as though borne on a breeze. Over there, in that far cubicle. She approached him carefully.

Ena said nothing, but seemed tense. Stella put her finger to her lips again. "No noise," she whispered in the girl's ear.

No intention of meeting me? But you have already met me, and recently.

The man in the cubicle had his back to her, his body turned in the opposite direction from his seat, his gaze intent on the place she had come from. Even from behind she could tell who he was. He had not seen her approach in the dark, as she had not carried a lantern. She eased herself into the seat opposite him. Ena let out the tiniest squeak as she sat down. A splinter, perhaps.

He froze, then turned to face her.

"Heredrew," she said. "We need to talk."

"Greetings, Bandy," he said, seemingly unperturbed. "Or, should I say, Stella. And hello to your young friend."

"Heredrew," she said, thinking swiftly, her thoughts swirling over the horror growing beneath. Ena was a child, but might remember or even understand the most inconvenient thing. "I need to establish something. Are you the master, or merely a servant?"

"You think I might be a servant? Disabuse yourself of the notion."

"Then put out your hand."

"Which one?"

"Either one will do. I will know who you are when I touch it—or when I do not."

"I will save you the trouble," Heredrew said. He leaned a little closer and turned his head so none outside the cubicle could see his profile. Instantly his face changed. It was subtle, his disguise, but effective. Sitting before Stella was the face that had haunted her nightmares for years.

So much for keeping Ena ignorant.

Every muscle in Stella's body strained against her will, begging her to flee. Her stomach rose into her throat. She commanded herself not to weep, or shriek, or vomit. She had not realised she would need such self-control, or that she possessed it.

"You knew I was alive," the man opposite her said gently. "Why struggle with the knowledge now?"

"Do you need to ask?" she said through clenched teeth. She began to doubt her ability to make it through this confrontation. "And why was your first word to me not an apology?"

The man's face shifted and he was again Heredrew. "I hope you don't mind me restoring my disguise. Remember, the face you know me by is itself an illusion. You have seen my real face, I think, and I doubt you wish to see it again."

A hint of bitterness in his voice. *Good.* Anything she could use, she would use.

Courage, now. She waited, saying nothing. *This man is proud.*

"How can words express sorrow?" he said eventually.

"I will not lie and say I regret bringing you back from the dead, despite the horror I have inflicted on you. But I will apologise to you for striking you down, and for using you shamefully in front of your friends. I will find a time and a place where such an apology is meaningful. You shall have it then."

"And so I am expected to believe that evil has white-washed himself so easily?"

"Of course not," the man snapped. "By your lights I remain evil. By my own, I am changing. Losing one's hands is a chastening experience. I am being forced to change. Who is to judge whether that change is for the better? I happen to think there is no 'good' apart from the benefit to the interests any act of goodness serves."

"Hence the difference between you and me," she said.

"Yes, there are differences," he agreed. "You may not view them in the future as you do now. Time will tell the story, as always. But there are also similarities, my queen. You and I are the only—"

"Don't you call me that!"

She all but spat the words at him. Her body had begun to shake, a delayed reaction to the discovery. She tried to keep her hands still, but she had no doubt he was aware of her fragility. Ena would be frightened. Perhaps she had been foolish to confront him so soon. No time to regret this choice. Keep him off balance.

"I am not your queen. I never was, I never will be. I have some questions to ask you, and that will be the end of it."

"Questions you can ask me alone of anyone alive, because of the similarities you and I share. Very well, I will answer as many as I can. But do not be deceived: I answer them not because I am good; and if I cannot answer them it is not because I am evil. I am prepared to help you because I want your help. I have questions I would like you to answer. Turn and turn about?"

She held his gaze for a long moment. "Very well," she said. "Here is my first question. Hold still."

A look of puzzlement crossed his regal features as she leaned towards him.

Then she spat in his face.

She watched him carefully. This was the moment. She was willing to risk everything on her guess in this matter.

She had spat in his face once before, on the battlefield, the first time Falthan and Bhrudwan forces had come together. He had forced her to watch the Battle of Skull Rock, stood her beside him as he directed his forces, his *Maghdi Dasht*, with magical power. She had found power of her own there on the battlefield, and had fought him, distracting him by spitting in his face. He had struck her down, and she had nearly died, but the Falthan army had escaped his wrath.

She remembered every emotion that had flickered across his face that day, and watched them repeat themselves: shock, hurt, anger. She even saw his arm twitch, as his anger sent a message to strike her.

But the arm did not move any further. Instead, his face settled into a wary gaze as her spittle made its way down his cheek like a slowly widening wound.

"My first question," she said.

"Was the answer what you expected?"

"No."

"I am surprised myself at the answer I gave," he confessed as he wiped the fluid away. He looked neither pleased nor angry.

"Do you have a question for me?" she asked. "In a moment I will have to return to the others. You may accompany me as Heredrew, if you wish. I will not utter your other names here."

"You are wise."

"Your question, then."

His words snapped out like the crack of a flag. "Would you have come to An— to my keep in search of me?"

"Not the question you intended asking."

"No."

She smiled. Not a pleasant smile. "You know the answer."

"Yes." He smiled in turn. "I do. But I wanted to hear you say it."

"I will not give you the satisfaction," she said. "You have your answer. Now, come with me, or leave this place. The other questions can wait."

Conal waited in the cubicle with increasing impatience. His anger, always somewhere near the surface these days, was barely under control. He was a priest, after all, a dedicant of the Halites, and ought to be treated with more respect. More significantly, he held the salvation, or at least the rehabilitation, of the Destroyer's Consort in his hand. A detailed report of his time with her would eventually be given to the Archpriest, which would be enough to complete the as yet unfinished seventh Mahnumsen Scroll. His name would grace the cover.

He battened down the unworthy thought. There were other, better reasons to be spending his time with the Falthan queen. She genuinely sought to mend her ways, and Conal could well be the agent of her repentance. That was an important thing, irrespective of whether his name was attached to the seventh scroll.

But since she had met that accursed Dhaurian scholar in the desert, Stella Pellwen had forgotten all about Conal of Yosse. She had ceased meeting with him to explain her conduct in the Falthan War. And now she ran off to a place of research—a scriptorium, no less, the one place he longed to immerse himself!—without even inviting him. He was hurt, that was what he was. Hurt.

Did he feel something for her? Another thought to be suppressed. She was not of the Koinobia, she was of dubious morality—and she was ninety years old, by Mahnumsen! Yet he breathed her in whenever she passed. He listened, really listened, to whatever she said. She had been the centre of his studies, and was now the axis of his thoughts.

He watched as she walked towards the cubicle, the girl in tow. He could see nothing apart from a crescent of light caressing her face, but he knew it was she. A hundred things told him: the speed of her walk, the way she cocked her head ever so slightly to the right, the shape of her hair. Who was this accompanying her? The man was tall, extremely tall. He searched his memory. Of course. The man who had journeyed part of the way across the desert with them. Stella said he had healed Phemanderac. What was his name?

"Let me reintroduce you to an old friend," Stella said to those sitting in the cubicle.

"Heredrew," said Conal, cutting across the queen's introductions, angered she had invited the man here, another person to gather attention rightfully his, pushing him into the background. "We have questions for you."

"And I have answers," the stranger said easily as he folded his frame into the relatively small space afforded by the cubicle. "Such as they are."

"Where did you go after you healed Phemanderac? You seemed to vanish into the desert!" Conal said.

"This is the sorcerer who healed me?" Phemanderac exclaimed. "Sir, I thank you." He held out his hand, evidently to shake that of his benefactor.

Heredrew made no move to take it. Instead, he inclined his head, as though embarrassed. What was wrong with the man?

"I am sorry I did not remain behind to supervise your recovery," he said in a low tone. "But such healing incapacitates me, and I was embarrassed to have the lady Bandy see my weakness." He looked up, shamefaced. "You see, I conceived an . . . er . . . an affection for the lady during my short sojourn with you all, but said nothing to avoid accusations of taking advantage of your hospitality. I have conquered it now, and tender my apologies to Bandy and to all her companions."

He turned to Stella, who stared at him with wide eyes—as well she might. An affection? The impudent dog!

"My lady," he said, his voice strong and clear in the darkness, "I am truly sorry for the harm I have done you. Will you forgive me?"

The limited light made it difficult for Conal to see Stella's face, but he could see enough to know there was something wrong. Her face had paled and she was working her mouth, as though trying to speak through some overmastering emotion. What could it be? Had she actually fallen for the stretch-limbed brute?

"I . . . I will have to think about that, Heredrew," she said finally. "You kept so much a secret, when honesty might have effected a better cure. Despite your kind act, I feel you thought only of yourself. I hope to see some evidence that this behaviour has changed. Only such a change will give your apology, which is, after all, merely words, some real meaning. Though I wonder if a man such as yourself can really change his ways."

By now everyone in the cubicle stared at Stella with identical bemused looks. Conal found himself surprised at the harshness of her response: after all, the man had rescued her friend, clearly at some cost to himself.

That the others felt the same way immediately became obvious.

"Stella, the man saved my life!" Phemanderac said. "If anyone should offer an apology, sir, it should be us, for failing to make you feel welcome. You ought to have felt at ease remaining with us after my healing. Please accept my thanks, and any aid I can offer you. It is a delight to have someone of such moral fibre amongst we insular Dhaurians."

The tall man nodded, pleased. Stella's face had now changed from white to red. She appeared deeply angry. Conal felt more than ever that something irregular was happening. He was missing an important subtext. The back of his head began to itch.

"Aye, Bandy." Conal emphasised her travelling name to cover Phemanderac's slip, which appeared to have gone unnoticed by Heredrew. "I admit to feeling uneasy about our guest at first, but his fair words and kind actions surely have earned him welcome. I would be pleased to call him friend."

A little stronger than I intended, he thought, *but Stella should get the message.* He sighed. *Sometimes we still get glimpses of the Destroyer's Consort beneath her beautiful exterior.*

"His face changed," little Ena said in her childish voice. "He looked like someone else, and that frightened me."

"I apologise, my dear," Heredrew said to her. "Bandy here rejected my first apology, and I was a little upset. With the flickering light it must have seemed as though I was wearing a mask of surprise."

First apology? Stella had already rejected him? *This is more than odd.* The little girl kept on talking, insisting that the man's face changed before the apology, but Conal paid her little heed.

"St— Bandy, is there something between you and Heredrew that we ought to know about?" Conal asked her.

"Nothing at all, priest," she answered, and Conal felt the sting in her words and wondered why he was their target. "Put aside all this male posturing: who is sorry for what, and whose dignity and honour have been offended. What I want to know, Heredrew, is what brings you to this supposedly inaccessible place? What are you looking for in the scriptorium?"

Phemanderac murmured his agreement. "Such a question crossed my mind also. Though you must have given the doorkeeper a reason—indeed, you would have had to mount a persuasive argument to gain admittance to the city. And you do not have a guide; how is that?"

"He did not come through the Mist Gate," Ena said.

"You are right. I approached the city from the east. The keepers of the Wind Gate granted me free access to the city because I came in search of ways to develop my healing powers.

"This is not my first time here, Stella. I have visited Dhauria three other times over the years, seeking knowledge to harness my unpredictable talent."

He turned to address Phemanderac. "The last time I was here I spoke to you, *dominie*, regarding the efficacy of the Fountain of the Vale."

A clamour arose at these revelations. Eventually Phemanderac was able to say: "You? It was you? I remember—you bore a different name then, I'm sure." He closed his eyes for a moment. "Yes, I spoke to you, at least twenty years ago. We argued, as I recall, though there are those in Dhauria who will tell you that this is not unusual. Friend, there is much to puzzle over regarding this. You looked much different then, not nearly so tall, and somewhat older. How can that be?"

"*Dominie*, this is why I am here, in truth," came the answer. "I discovered my talent many years ago, and since employing it more regularly I have grown markedly taller, and my face has taken on a decidedly youthful aspect. I am not sure whether to be thankful or frightened at this, though it does appear to have had the effect of prolonging my vigour. None of my countrymen had ever heard of such a thing; in fact, normal magical use tends to have the effect of inducing physical and mental decay in the practitioner. So I travelled to Dhauria to read the ancient scrolls. I reasoned that perhaps I would learn something to help me interpret my own condition."

"You told us you were searching for Dona Mihst," Conal said, trying to keep out of his voice the whine his colleagues in the Koinobia hated so much. "If you are telling the truth, you had no need to search."

"A traveller's fiction; I hope you forgive me for it. Eventually," he added, turning to Stella. "Care with strangers has kept me alive and safe throughout many long journeys. And you should note I never actually lied. I did not say I had not been to Dhauria before."

Conal leaned forward. "You called Bandy 'Stella' a moment ago. How did you learn that name?"

There it was: the merest flicker of unease. The man had been far too glib. And, most suspiciously, it appeared he was prepared to answer questions all day. An innocent man, in Conal's experience, would not be so patient.

"Her name has been mentioned several times," the man said, adopting a puzzled air. "Is it supposed to be a secret? I assumed the name she took for herself was your own piece of traveller's fiction."

"So," said Stella, "you are a self-confessed sorcerer with a talent for healing. You have been here in the past, looking for ways to understand and harness your sorcerous power. You met us on the road, proffered a large amount of fiction mixed with a degree of truth, and healed our desperately ill friend. Now we meet you again. We appreciate your willingness to answer our questions, but I have yet another. Are you willing to help us in our own quest for knowledge?"

Conal frowned. This was too much. Stella had just delivered a speech to rival the dissembling of the Archpriest himself. It was the sort of thing he had heard at the Koinobia every day; perhaps the others would be fooled by it, but Conal was not.

These two know each other. I need to find out how.

As do I, said a voice in his head. *As do I.*

The doorkeeper approached their cubicle. "Once again I apologise, *dominie*, but another outsider seeks admittance to the scriptorium. Actually, he is searching for the man named Conal. I thought it best to admit him."

There was no doubt who this was. Conal did not even look up as the insolent, block-headed guardsman sat down heavily on the bench beside him.

"Can't keep you away, can we, priest? You always have to be in her shadow."

"You wouldn't be talking about yourself, would you," Conal said in an undertone. "Of course not; you wouldn't fit in her shadow, much as you try to."

"Enough!" Stella said. "Or I'll ask the doorkeeper to see you out, and arrange for Ena's clan to escort you to the gate. Clear?"

Robal apologised, and Conal mumbled some words that might be construed as penitent. But he wasn't: he meant every word.

"I remember having a number of discussions with you when last you visited the scriptorium," Phemanderac said to Heredrew. "Your opinions, as I recall, were lively and unconventional, and I based more than one paper on the conversations we had. I could show you . . . no, to the point. Heredrew, we have found an unusual scroll. Would you care to cast an eye over it and offer an opinion on the authenticity of its contents?"

"*Dominie*, I am no scholar," the man said. "But if you think I can help, I'll have a look for you."

With the arrival of Heredrew and Robal the cubicle had become too small to spread out the scrolls, so Phemanderac sent Moralye to request a large table and more light. There they sat, on small stools that instantly set Robal's back aching, debating old scrolls.

The guardsman knew why this was important, of course. Stella was an unusual and very concerned woman. She had been cursed with immortality by the Destroyer, and had to live with the knowledge that in all likelihood she would never die. So, as she had explained to her companions many times during their travels, she sought knowledge to understand how to deal with such a life—and, perhaps, to seek a cure. *Even if it kills her*, the soldier thought, but did not laugh.

Robal, however, knew something the others did not. From comments she had made, the guard had pieced together the realisation that, if she did not find what she was seeking here, she would go further east—to Andratan, if necessary, and the Destroyer's feet. His arms. If the only solace she was to have in this world was with someone like him, she would choose him.

So he forced himself to listen carefully to the discussion. If they could wring anything out of these old pieces of parchment that could prevent the sickening image in his mind—her and him together—it would be worth all this brain-racking.

The stranger Heredrew looked up from the scroll before him. "The man who wrote this was certainly self-obsessed," he said. "If the author wasn't the Destroyer himself, it was someone who has spent time imagining what it would be like to be powerful, immortal and hated."

"There is no call to have sympathy for the Destroyer," Conal said, with exactly the look on his face Robal detested. As though lard wouldn't melt in his mouth. "He deserves any pain he suffers."

"I doubt anyone disagrees with you," Stella said sharply.

Robal thought her reply odd; in fact, she had been behaving queerly all day.

"Yet I can identify with him," Heredrew said quietly. "My former Haurnian companions noticed my good fortune and hated me for it, even as they accepted my healing help. Eventually their scandalised talk became so pervasive I had to leave. If someone were to write my story, it might cast me in a very bad light, as does the *Domaz Skreud* Kannwar." He moved slightly on his stool. "Sometimes I think I am wandering the world to avoid forming relationships, rather than seeking knowledge as I claim."

"If you can identify with him," Stella asked, "do you think he is telling the truth? Is the *Domaz Skreud* wrong?"

"I don't think those are the best questions," he answered, and beside him Phemanderac nodded. "I'm inclined to think that Kannwar—if he was indeed the author—told the truth as he saw it. I say this with the following provisos. He wrote this over two hundred years after the event. Who knows what excuses and justifications became fact in his tortured mind? Or what events he may have minimised or neglected to mention in his account? Yet if we apply those conditions to his recollections, ought we not to do the same to the *Domaz Skreud*? It reflects the point of view of one who sought someone to blame for what was undoubtedly a tragic and shocking event. From the *Domaz Skreud* we can deduce that conditions in Dona Mihst at the time of the Rebellion were far from the idyll many think. Yet the writer lays the blame squarely on Kannwar's shoulders, attributing nothing to the overcrowding and political agitation of the time. Is that not evidence of partiality? Perhaps a combination of both documents might bring us closer to the truth."

All through this statement the priest had been huffing and puffing like a bellows, obviously building up to some overinflated pronouncement. As soon as the man finished, Conal jumped to his feet.

"This is nonsense!" he said as his stool clattered to the floor behind him. "Is anyone seriously arguing for the truth of any of this"—he struck the scroll with the flat of his hand, eliciting a gasp from Moralye—"specious self-justification? I am a priest. You ought to be coming to me to ask my opinion as to whether this blasphemy regarding the Most High is to be taken seriously. How can it be? How could the One who created the worlds and all within them be defeated and driven out by a pair of jumped-up humans? If he did elevate two humans to be gods, why is no mention made of them in our holy scrolls? And is anyone taking seriously the suggestion that Kannwar might have *deceived* the omniscient Most High God? Let us waste not one more minute on this absurdity."

He bent down and righted his stool, then sat back on it.

"It's always good to hear from the oracle," Robal said, filling the silence. "Boy-priest, do you yet have a notion as to why the great and the wise consistently fail to consult you on matters of importance? Because there is no need. To understand what you think, one need read no further than the Koinobia-sanctioned Halite propaganda. We do not ask your opinion because we want to understand, not learn meaningless catechisms."

"Have you finished insulting people of faith? Because I am proud of following the sacred scrolls to the letter. Why bother calling into question the result of debate between people wiser than us, who were there at the time?"

"Conal, you are such a fool," Stella snapped. "Was Kannwar wiser than you?"

Fool he might be, but by the trapped look on the priest's face, he could see where this was going. Robal settled back to watch the fun.

"Of course he wasn't. How can anyone cursed by the Most High be called wise?"

"Come now. What does 'Kannwar' mean, according to the *Domaz Skreud*?"

"You know as well as I. 'Guardian of knowledge'. It was just a name."

"Doesn't the scroll tell us Kannwar was surpassingly knowledgeable in the *Fuirfad*, the Way of Fire?"

"Yes," Conal answered sullenly.

"So, Kannwar was wise, and he was there at the time. Or will you dispute that as well? No? Then why not at least consider his words?"

"What I want an answer to," Heredrew said suddenly, "is why it was wrong of Kannwar to oppose the Most High when, it is clear from this document, he honestly believed the Most High to be misguided."

Unabashed, Conal replied. "Because by definition the Most High cannot ever be wrong. Simple."

"Oh? So the Most High has always been right? What of this claim that the Most High was argued by his children into not retiring from the world? Was the Most High wrong in electing to retire in the first place, or wrong to be persuaded not to retire? How could he be both?"

"I don't accept that document," the priest said, tugging at his collar. "Besides, the Most High is above right and wrong."

"No more than any of us," Stella said. "Let's assume for

a moment that Kannwar's document reflects the truth on this issue. The Most High wanted to retire from the world. What's wrong with that? The people wanted him to stay. Nothing wrong with that either. He listened to their cry and changed his mind out of compassion. Isn't that a good thing? So where is the fault?"

"Fault lies with those who attribute immutability to their god," Heredrew growled.

Robal stared at the man. The northerner spoke as though the outcome of their debate really mattered to him.

"Everything he has said to humans has come through the sieve of our own understanding, which is culturally prescribed," the tall man went on. "So the supposedly sacred words in the *Domaz Skreud* merely represent one person's view, through a particular sieve imposed on him by his culture."

"Stop babbling," Robal interrupted. "I didn't travel through the desert to listen to scholar's argot. My first sergeant always said that if you can't say it plain, you don't understand it."

Conal coughed. Robal turned in the direction of the sound; the look the priest gave him was designed to anger him. *Everyone else here understands what is being said*, it told him. He turned away from the man's gaze, only to catch a much fiercer glance from Heredrew.

"Very well," Heredrew said in a frosty voice. He picked up the copy of the *Domaz Skreud* and waved it at the guardsman. "These are not the Most High's words. They are the words the writer remembers. He remembers particular words because he is alert to them, in turn because of his upbringing. Language is necessary for effective communication of complex issues, but it is not sufficient to create meaning perfectly. There is always bias and misunderstanding and confusion. It's not the Most High's fault: no doubt what he actually said was what he meant. But this," he rustled the scroll, and Moralye made a small noise of protest, "is what the First Men decided was important. I'm saying that, after reading Kannwar's account, it seems to me their choices were based on making themselves appear righteous and Kannwar evil. And, before you ask, yes, Kannwar did exactly the same thing. Were I—were he to write this now, he might say something different."

"Right," Robal said. *This made sense, but did it help?* "What you're saying is that we can never know what really happened."

"Not unless the Most High sat down at this table and told us," Heredrew said. "And even then we would debate the meaning of every word he said."

Stella drew in a breath. "Then it really would be crowded in here," she said.

"The agreed hour of study is past," the doorkeeper said quietly. "Two council members are waiting their turn to use this area. You are welcome to return tomorrow, should the representative of Clan Phidrie grant you continuance in our city."

Moralye thanked the man, then took the two scrolls and rolled them closed. "I will store this unusual work on my personal shelf," she said, indicating Kannwar's supposed apology. "It will be available to you tomorrow, but in the interim I will ask our experts to examine it. Their preliminary conclusion will be available to assist you when next you return."

*   *   *

Stella felt a light hand on her shoulder and thought at first it was Ena; though when she turned and saw who beckoned her to his side, she realised she had not felt a hand at all.

"I refuse to accept the reality of this," she said to him, quietly but nonetheless in anger. She had dissembled enough; she no longer cared if Ena reported their conversations to whatever authorities ran this city. "The last time your arm was on my shoulder it bled from a stump at your wrist. You were forcing me to carry you to safety. Many people died that day, and you were the cause."

"I wish to talk with you privately," he said, ignoring her words. "I could bespeak your mind, but frankly I am worried as to who might overhear us. It is time you learned what is happening, time to discuss with me what role you might play in it."

He glanced at Ena. As though expecting Stella to magic her away.

"Oh? This will be another of those self-serving explanations after the fact, will it? Listen well. For seventy years you have been a hateful memory but also a faint hope. Now you are a reality, I am minded to put hope aside and allow hate full reign. If I carried a blade, I would put your immortality to the test right here on the street outside the Hall of Scrolls."

"So you will close your mind to knowledge in the same way as your foolish priest?" The man flashed his own anger: it was like witnessing a furnace door swing open, then close again.

He smiled, and it was as if his anger had never been. "I am staying not far from here, at the house of Byellatus of the Taradh Clan. I will meet you there one hour after sunrise tomorrow morning. Please come alone. I do not have anything to offer your companions. Before then, I pray you will say nothing to alarm them; but after we have spoken tomorrow I will withdraw all such requests. Then you may tell your friends what you wish about me."

Ahead, Robal had already turned once to see what delayed her. It would not do to linger.

"You might reconsider expressing your wishes as orders," she hissed. "You are not the only monarch here today. If you wish to meet me tomorrow, it will be you who comes to see me, and not otherwise. The hour remains as you suggested, but the place of our meeting will be on the street outside my lodging-house. And now, no more. Be off. Spend the rest of your day anticipating the questions I will ask you and how you might defend yourself against them."

For the first time since she had met him, Heredrew looked discomposed. "But I don't know where—"

Stella did not catch the rest of his comment. She put her head down and scurried to where the others had halted, waiting for her, half-dragging a protesting Ena with her.

Wisely, the Undying Man did not follow.

She made it out of the square and into an alley before she was violently sick.

CHAPTER 8

FIRE AND WATER

STELLA DID NOT HAVE AN easy night. She could ask no one to wake her, and her worry that she might sleep through the agreed meeting time kept her from finding the deepness of slumber she needed to refresh herself.

When it was clear no more sleep would come she eased herself out of her pallet, then put her head between her hands and rubbed her aching temples. It took her a few moments to realise that she ought not to have been able to do this; a glance at the other pallet showed Ena sleeping quietly. The fabric used to bond them together lay neatly folded on the girl's coverlet.

There was no doubt Ena had overheard the arrangement between Stella and Heredrew. Stella had wondered if the girl might say something to the man and woman who had come to see her late last night, presumably her parents; but, as far as she could make out, nothing had been mentioned about Heredrew. The outsiders had broken no laws, and that was the extent of the gatekeeper clan's concern, it seemed.

But Stella was sure Ena ought not to be allowing her to slip away unbonded. This was a decision on the girl's part that might well get her in trouble. Stella debated whether she should wake the girl and ask her if this was wise, but she decided to accept the offer of trust.

And to abuse it. No one in Dhauria would sanction Stella meeting with the Destroyer.

She discarded her shift and donned her tunic and breeches. A glance outside showed stars and street lanterns, the rain-free sky suggesting she did not need to borrow Robal's overcoat.

She frowned at herself. *Come on, girl. You are just delaying the moment.*

Wiping her hands on her breeches, she padded quietly through the door and into the other room. What might most kindly be described as a manly fug assailed her. And, yes, Sauxa lay on his back, mouth open, forcing various irregular and unpleasant noises through his gnarled throat.

The pallets filled the room, and Stella found a way between them only with difficulty. There was nothing blameworthy about rising early to watch the dawn, but questions would be asked about the breaking of her bond, so she tried to be careful. Even so, she barked her shin on Robal's pallet, the nearest to the door, and waited for his growl. It didn't come.

Outside, the air was surprisingly cold. Stella worked the fingers of her right hand, always stiff in the morning, and took a breath of the cool air. It had a different quality than anywhere else she'd been. Oddly, it reminded her of home—of Loulea, the small Firanese village where she and Leith had been born. Crispness, with the slightly moist flavour of wet-climate vegetation. Odd, that. For all its beneficent setting, Dhauria lay in the midst of a desert, after all.

Turn around and walk about fifty paces up the street, said a voice in her mind. His voice.

Curse you. I will have an agreement from you to stay out of my head.

Laughter, both inside her head and audible to her ears. *You will have to erase many memories, then.*

I do not wish to converse this way, she insisted, halting her slow walk uphill.

Good. Neither do I. It is too dangerous.

Dangerous? No one can overhear us! I meant it is unpleasant.

No, Stella, it is dangerous. You and I are not the only ones who employ this method of communication, though the others are presently far away. Please, you have come this far; just twenty more paces?

"Far enough," Heredrew said a few moments later.

She found him leaning against a metal rail built to guard against people falling from the street into the lower city. His long face, so reminiscent of Phemanderac's features—though arranged far more handsomely, of course—broke into a smile as she approached.

"You're early," she said. "Very early. And in the wrong place."

"As are you. It took me some time to wake you, I confess, and even then you stayed abed for longer than I hoped. Events move apace. And I thought the girl with you might choose to betray our conversation. So I make no apology for waking you."

"You woke me? You inhabit my dreams?" she asked, disgusted.

"Barely. But enough to wake you from them."

"What is so important that you'd invade someone's sleeping mind?"

"The view from here is spectacular," he said, ignoring the question. "And will become more so as the dawn takes hold. This truly is a beautiful place."

"Not as beautiful as the place you sunk below the waves," Stella snapped. *Anything to unsettle him, she thought. I have only one weapon.*

"True," he said, and she was unsure whether he answered her words or her thought.

"What do you have to say to me?"

"Just this. Many things are happening in the world, and you are ignorant of them all. I wanted to speak to you privately to offer you information and a choice."

"I don't like being called ignorant." The words sounded petulant even as she said them.

"Who does? I've admitted my own ignorance; how easy do you think it was for me to recognise this, let alone tell you?"

"The choice?" Stella pressed. She knew she was being manipulated, but what could she do? She did not have to act on anything he said. He could not force her . . . The truth was, she had no idea what he could and couldn't do.

"Walk away now and never think of me again. It would be the healthiest thing for you to do, in truth. With effort, together we could sever the blood-link between us, though I can do nothing about the blood itself. Then go and live your life as best you can. If you choose to do this, promise me one thing."

"How can I promise when I have yet to hear the alternative?"

"True. Nevertheless, should you choose to walk away

from me, promise you will give some thought to what you will say to me when we meet in the far future, the last two people alive, scouring the ruins of the world in search of anything salvageable."

"You make no sense," she said, but his words chilled her.

"I am saying that the inevitable result of you walking away from me today will be your inadvertent service of another, to the destruction of the world."

"Hah. Your choice is already no choice, even before I have heard the other side of it. As you intended."

"As I intended," he acknowledged. "There is no point in trying to outthink you."

"Or outflatter me. The other choice, please?"

"Choose to listen to me as I tell you about the conflict that has already begun to destroy the world. If you agree to listen, you will have no choice, I believe, but to involve yourself in my schemes. Not because of my persuasive power, or any other compulsion I could lay on you—and you know I could; I am sure you remember—but because of your own conscience. Therefore you face your choice now. Listen or walk away."

"I know one thing, Kannwar," she said, using that name in this place for the first time. "I know you will neither tell me all the truth nor give me a real choice. Should I defy you now, you will find some other way to compel me. I don't know what you've been doing for the last seventy years, but if you've given our time together any thought at all you'll have realised I defied you even when completely in your thrall. So, fair warning. If you compel me by any means, I will find a way to defy you and bring your schemes to nothing, just as I did in the Falthan War."

She shivered. *The cold*, she told herself.

The man before her bristled. Nothing about him changed physically, but somehow she sensed the deep well of power within his illusory shell. A strength deep enough to drown her, should he choose.

"I am not accustomed to being defied," he said.

"It's good for you," she replied, making her tone light. "Keeps you human, and that ought to be an ongoing concern for you. It is for me. I don't want to turn into a self-obsessed empire builder. Opposition teaches you to negotiate, to give as well as take."

"But there are those who would take everything," he said. "Stella, I'm out of patience. Make your choice."

"I'll hear you," she said, and knew as she uttered them that the words were fateful.

"Then hear me. Two years and more ago a man came to Andratan as part of a delegation from Faltha. This delegation told officials from Malayu they were merchants seeking to solidify trade relationships. You have no idea how often I have heard similar stories from people desperate to find out if I am real, what I am doing or whether I recovered from the last Falthan War. You would think spies would be a little more creative."

"You have recovered though," she said. "Though I did not need to travel to Andratan to be aware of your progress."

"You would have been welcomed," he replied. "No doubt you kept track of my progress in the same way I did yours, through the link between us. Had you known it, you could have read my mind with a little exertion of your own."

"Not something I have ever wanted to do," she said, but it was a lie, and she could see he knew it to be so.

"So the supposed merchants were allowed access to Andratan, though I did not intend to speak to them myself. Such spies are always assessed for their susceptibility to being turned, and over the years many have been, while remaining totally unaware of it. There are two such living quiet lives in this very city."

"Is it any wonder I find you so unpleasant?"

"I need the information," he said, allowing a little of his anger to show. "It turned out this delegation was from the newly risen Koinobia of Instruere, sent to gather information to enable them to assemble their scrolls. I admired their devotion to duty rather more than their good sense.

"One of the men was not like the others. There was something about him that drew my attention. Something within him, much like you, in fact. A trace, an aroma, of the Most High. Most unexpected in a priest, trust me."

"No," said Stella, suddenly suspicious of where this story would lead. *No*.

"Oh yes, taking religious orders is a most effective way to lock him out. I cast a compliance spell on the man and had him brought to my tower. I had barely begun the interrogation when the fellow broke his bonds, stood up and wandered over to the south window, towing three of my strongest guards behind him."

Heredrew closed his eyes. He was so caught in his memory that, had she been armed, Stella could have struck him down where he stood.

"He looked out for a moment, then turned and spoke to me. Stella, I have no doubt you remember the servant I assigned to you when you were my guest—"

"Captive," she retorted.

"Captive, then. I honour the man's memory, though I

don't expect you to believe that. I do know he died many years ago, and was buried in front of the Hall of Meeting in Instruere with a full public ceremony. That pleased me."

Stella found herself shocked at the level of knowledge he displayed of her affairs. She forced herself to make no comment about this. "You treated him shamefully. For that alone you have earned my undying hatred."

The man did no more than shrug his shoulders. "On the day you left me, seventy years ago, and took my servant with you, he spoke to me with the voice of the Most High. I will never forget it, of course. Two years ago I heard the voice of the Most High again, this time from the mouth of a Halite priest."

Dawn spread its gentle wings across the sky as Stella struggled with the familiar nausea associated with thinking about this man, her enemy. She closed her eyes and tried to regain control of her stomach, resigned to this story's likely end.

"What did the voice tell you?"

"He gave me the choice I am giving you," came the calm reply. "I chose to become involved; or, at least, I told the voice I would. Naturally, I still reserve my options.

"I was told that the time of the world's destruction has come. The two rebellious children of the Most High have found a way to break into the world. This will allow them to dominate more directly the civilisations of the three great continents. He told me that this would likely lead to a gradual decay in the world's natural order, beginning with the very fluxes upon which the earth stands, causing earthquakes and fountains of fire to burst forth from the ground. While I did not doubt the truth of the words, the fact that I had that very morning spoken with a scholar who reported significantly increased earth tremors throughout northern Bhrudwo helped confirm the message. Of course, you would have heard of the recent devastating Malayu earthquake. No? Do you no longer have reliable sources in Bhrudwo? Hmm. I will have to supply some.

"By itself this is no confirmation of the truth of the avatar's words. After all, it is a common tendency of humans everywhere to notice only those data that confirm a trend. However, the man predicted a rise in other features: storms, floods, whirlwinds, droughts and all manner of imbalances in the world's physical processes. Such things will gather in intensity until they tear the world apart. I believe we are seeing these things in Bhrudwo now. My informants tell me, however, that Faltha remains relatively unaffected. I have no information on how the southern continent fares.

"I argued with the voice, asserting that this state of affairs was his fault. You've read my scroll, you know my point of view, and I argued it vigorously. He chose not to dispute this, which angered me, pointing out instead that no matter whose fault it was, we would all suffer together. The world, he said, would die a slow death, torn apart by the growing metaphysical instability initially caused when he was driven out of the southern continent, and now fatally exploited by his son and daughter.

"The voice invited me once again to assist him in putting right what had gone wrong so long ago. It seemed not to matter to him that I had spent two thousand years killing those who served him. I thought this indecent, and told him so. He evaded the point.

"I then said to him: 'You're going to tell me that if you interfere directly in this matter, the fabric of the world will immediately come apart.' He acknowledged this. If the children of the Most High were to be defeated, he told me, it was we who would do it."

"We," Stella said wearily. "This is a fireside tale, and a poor one at that. Two immortals, a man and a woman, to face the evil son and daughter of the Most High. I seem to remember a similar-sounding story presented to our court by the Deuverran Players just last year. These stories are always about the fate of the world and combat between men and gods. Force me into captivity again if you must, Kannwar, but don't bore me to death first."

"I am sorry," the man said, and he sounded it. "If you reduce any story down to its bare essentials it will sound like a fanciful fireside tale. Perhaps you should ask the priest himself. He would likely give you a much more convincing version of my tale, since it came out of his mouth."

"Ask the priest? You mean Conal?"

"I don't remember his name. But the young priest who travels with you is the one used by the Most High to deliver his message to me in Andratan."

And so the circle closes, Stella thought, just as she had feared. No wonder she had sensed something about him.

"No," she said.

"*What?*" The man sprang forward from the railing as though avoiding an arrow. He halted a pace from her.

"No. The voice did not mention me by name. If it had, you would have told me. So, no. Do it yourself. I offer you the same answer you offered him two thousand years ago, and for exactly the same reason. No!"

"You will have no answers from me if you refuse," he said, keeping his voice level only by obvious effort.

"No answers, then," she said, finally throwing open the gates she had kept so closely guarded. "Fine. I doubt you have any. Certainly no answers that help you understand what it means to be human. A public apology to me should be delivered with the knowledge of those hearing it. And should you eventually apologise properly, it will not be enough to satisfy me. Not nearly enough. Were you to give me a year of your life as a servant, or ten, or seventy, it wouldn't suffice. Were you to draw the knife on your belt and gut yourself in front of me, I would dance on your entrails and still hate your memory for ten thousand years. Do you understand? You ruined me. Ruined! I never touched the man I loved for fear I would infect him with your punishment!" The tears started, hot and painful. "A creature like you always sees and does what is most important to himself, no matter who it hurts. I am human, I'm not like you, but I see hatred and revenge! And I choose to pursue them!"

She took the stride that brought them together: some things needed physical contact. Her hand snaked out and took a fistful of his ornate tunic. He did not resist as she slammed him back into the railing.

"You killed many of my friends," she spluttered, showering him with water and snot. "Thousands of people died resisting you. I died resisting you. *Why didn't you leave me dead?*"

He was silent a moment, then offered the only answer that would keep her from pushing him over the railing and letting him fall into the lower city. She would do it. She knew he would let her. A new test of the limits of immortality.

"Because I wanted you to live," he said.

*   *   *

Conal had awoken when Stella cracked her shin against
the oaf's cot. Robal had done nothing more than murmur
faintly, paying about as much attention to the world asleep
as he did awake. But Conal woke alert and aware that
something was wrong.

Something had been wrong for at least a day. Stella had
behaved strangely in the scriptorium yesterday. Much of
what was said between her and that northern sorcerer had
not rung true. They needed watching.

He did not challenge her as she slipped through the door.
She would say she was merely going outside to take in the
view, or for some privacy, and where was the fault in that?
No, let her do something suspicious within sight of his
keen eyes, and he would record it for the scroll. He waited
until she had left the room, then rose, dressed—he tried to
hurry, but he had always been a fastidious dresser—and
followed her.

She was some way up the street, talking to the tall northerner. Still nothing wrong, but definitely suspicious. Hadn't
the man said he'd conceived a fancy for her? What was
she doing talking to him in the pre-dawn dark? Playing the
harlot? Look at how he lounged against the railing, watching her as she leaned towards him. The priest's muscles
tensed and he began to drift closer, favouring the deepest
shadows.

"Walk away now and never think of me again," he heard
Heredrew say. A lover's tiff, then. He did not catch much of
Stella's reply, apart from an accusation that made no sense.
So he wanted to end it and she wished to continue. Harlot.
Power-seeking whore.

He could approach no nearer than the width of the street.
Hidden around the corner of the nearest house, he was con-

fident they could not see him. Trouble was, he could barely hear them. Not one word in four. The tall man said something about a conflict—or convict—and her involvement in his schemes.

Everything changed with her clear reply. "I know one thing, Kannwar," she said distinctly in a raised voice. She clearly wanted the man to hear the name she used.

Kannwar? For a moment his mind faltered. Was it possible?

The Destroyer?

Conal tried reinterpreting everything he remembered of yesterday's encounter in the scriptorium in the light of this knowledge.

"I will defy you," she said.

"I'm not accustomed to being defied," he answered, sounding like the ruler of darkness himself.

Conal listened to a tale almost beyond his understanding. He barely noticed it draw him forward, out from the cover of the building and into the street, the better to hear the man's words. Neither Stella nor the man she had named Kannwar noticed, so intent were they on each other.

The mention of the Koinobia's spying mission froze him in his tracks. He had been the most junior member on that mission, and had been unwell for two of the three days they had spent as guests in Andratan. How had this man known? And if the Destroyer had known, why had he suffered them to live?

As the tale unfolded, Conal felt a weight descend upon him. A realisation that the real world was like and yet unlike the world he had read about in the theological scrolls: real in that supernatural things could happen; unreal in that they had happened to him.

When Kannwar named him as the unwitting mouthpiece of the Most High, he nearly fainted with the shock.

He had not known. Had no memory of it. Yet it was true, he could feel it.

To be used without volition! Treated as a piece of meat! Not worthy enough even to be asked his permission! Anger, humiliation, outrage and self-loathing fought for supremacy in his spinning head.

He regained control of his thoughts in time to see the Destroyer launch himself at Stella, who fought him off. She screamed at him, then reached out and took hold of him. *He's going to kill her. Or she him.*

The back of Conal's head flashed white and abruptly he had no control over his movements. He tried, how he tried, to resist his strangely empowered muscles, especially when he realised what he was about to be compelled to do. He tried to shout a warning through an immobilised throat. No sound emerged. Powerless, he was a spectator to what happened. His body rushed forward, left shoulder lowered.

He struck Stella a rising blow in the small of the back with his entire weight, sending her cannoning into the tall man. Stunned, Conal fell to the ground, his muscles his own again too late, and lifted his head in time to see both Stella and the Destroyer topple backwards over the railing and vanish from view.

Robal was most of the way through preparing the morning's bread when he thought to ask Stella how much she wanted. The thick loaves had been left by their hosts: strange silent people who clearly regarded feeding the outlanders as a solemn part of their clan duty, but talking to them as well beyond it. The guardsman puzzled at this arrangement.

How could a mother and father leave their young girl in the care of mistrusted strangers? There were aspects to this society he found distasteful.

Not this bread though. He stuffed another piece into his mouth. If Stella didn't rise soon she and the girl would miss out altogether. Not that either would complain. Now if it was him deprived of a meal everyone would hear about it.

"Stella," he called.

Kilfor raised his head from his bowl, while Sauxa continued lapping at his porridge in the curious way he had.

"You want any bread?" Robal called again. "Ask the girl, will you?"

No reply, which was odd. She was normally an early riser. Hardly needed sleep, in fact. Or, more truthfully, couldn't get it on account of that cursed man's blood in her veins. If he were ever to meet the Destroyer, he would pound the fiend into small lumps, preferably separated from each other by some distance, and then ask him some hard questions. Robal hated watching Stella suffer.

He kicked the priest's pallet. "Conal? Have you seen Stella?" No answer; another slugabed. No, the pallet was empty. "Bah. Is no one—"

Ena walked out of the room she shared with Stella.

"Where is the queen?" Robal asked her.

"Gone out," replied the girl, her face untroubled. "Before dawn."

"Gone where?"

"To meet someone. The priest went a few minutes after she did."

Stella and the priest? What had he missed? His heart seemed to turn leaden in his chest. *Surely not. If she's the*

*type to take up with spoiled babes like him, I'm better rid
of her.*

"Anyone else see them go?" he asked the room. Kilfor
shook his head, then bent it back towards his soup. Robal
knew his friend. *She's a big girl*, he was saying. *She can
care for herself.*

As Robal made towards the outer door, it opened and
Conal walked through. One look at his face was enough.

"What has happened to her? What have you done? Did
you force yourself on her?" Robal bit his lip to stop further
inanities from coming out.

The priest sat on his pallet and began to cry. Enormous
tears squeezed out of his crumpled face, accompanied by
a huh, huh, huh noise Robal took for sobbing. The display left the guardsman shocked: the vain, pompous priest
would never lose control like this.

He put his hand on Conal's shaking shoulder. "Tell us.
What has happened to Stella?" He did not doubt for a moment this concerned her.

"She muh-met Heredrew," said the priest, his voice a
thin warble. "Out there in the street. I . . . I went out to see.
I thought she might be meeting suh-someone, I thought it
might be huh huh him." He sobbed some more.

"Then what?" Robal could not wait for the blubberer to
compose himself. "They kissed, and you were jealous?"

The priest shook his head.

"They did more?"

*Just what is wrong with me? She walks out to meet
someone she knows, does something to set this fool weeping, and I'm all over jealous?*

"N-no. I hid in the shadows and listened to them for

a while as they quarrelled. I . . . she struck him and they fought. Then they fell."

"Fell? Where?" Robal did not even realise he had strode to the front door.

"Up the street. Against the rail. Up she went, and took him over. Her . . . her face looked frightened. She tried to clutch the rail but she couldn't reach."

Robal lunged towards the shaking priest and grabbed him by the arm. "Show me."

A few moments later the five of them stood by the railing. Dawn had painted the distance with the bright colours of the desert, but the lower city remained in shadow. Robal could barely make himself grasp the rail and ease himself over so he could see below.

Fifty paces, his mind recorded. *The roofs of houses below, or the cobbles of a street. No trees or bushes.*

"She might still be alive, mightn't she?" The priest sounded like a child. Was a child.

"No."

"We need to look," Kilfor said. "Ena, please go and fetch Phemanderac. Tell him to meet us in the lower city on the street below this railing. We need to know what to do."

The girl, her own small face pale with fright, ran quickly up the road, then slipped down a side street.

"Someone tell me this is not real," Robal muttered to himself as he strode down the street, the others strung out behind him. The last ten minutes had hollowed him out.

She might be alive. The priest's words repeated in his head in time to his slapping feet. *She might be alive. She might be alive.*

*   *   *

Oh Most High, so much blood. His, hers, spurting, flowing, trickling, mixing together, covering their broken bodies like a shroud, like a curse, a curse.

Robal fell to his knees. So much blood! What he had taken for a shadow when looking from the railing was in fact a large pool of bright red wetness. She had lain here, he had lain there. The blood had coursed from both of them, her immortal lifeblood mixing with his mortal ichor. Someone had dragged their bodies away; the blood ran out about there, twenty paces or so from where he knelt.

"No, Conal," Robal said, sure of the thoughts in the priest's head, but knowing that in the words he was about to speak he admitted his own guilt. "Leave the blood alone. I will not allow you even a taste."

Kilfor and his father must have wondered what he meant, but asked no questions. He probably would have told them had they wanted to know. What need for secrecy now? What need for a guard?

While Robal continued to stare ineffectually at the drying blood, Phemanderac and the girl arrived. A few local people had also gathered. No one asked him any questions, which suited him fine, as he had no answers.

Stella and Kannwar watched the gathering from a nearby rooftop. Neither could say a word: their wounds were too many, too fresh, too serious, to allow speech. It had taken all they had to climb the wall furthest from the road. Both knew it would take a long time to recover.

Someone will work it out, she sent.

I have removed as many clues as I can, he replied.

I don't want to leave them!

We have no alternative. One of them sought our deaths. I doubt he was in control of his body when he did so. Certainly he's been controlled by another at least once before.

She conceded him the point. *Most High, this hurts.*

Worse every time, he said.

I'm not prepared to run off and leave these good people behind, she said. *I don't see why they can't be given an explanation.*

Run off? Not for some time, Stella. And no, no explanation.

She summoned her strength. *You chafed under the Most High when he withheld the full truth. According to you, this was the root of the rebellion in the Vale of Youth. If you choose to behave in the same fashion, your story loses all credibility.*

Silence for a time. She tried to turn her head, but could do no more than catch a glimpse of his ruined face. The longer the silence lasted, the more hopeful she became.

You trust them? he asked eventually.

With the exception of the priest, for obvious reasons, yes. Phemanderac and Robal with my life. Kilfor and Sauxa because Robal vouches for them.

Mm.

Silence again. Stella watched her friends weep as they gathered together to try to make sense of the scene before them. Conal was at the centre of the gathering and Phemanderac was clearly questioning him hard.

He didn't tell them what he did, she said.

No?

No. Or the guard would have killed him by now.

Perhaps he does not know what he did.

I saw his face as I fell, she said. *He knows.*

In his place, would you tell? His question was sharp.

I wouldn't be in his place, she replied.

There is something we can do, he told her, *though it means taking those you trust into our confidence.*

Our confidence? They would have to learn who you are?

Yes. But it would greatly assist our recovery, and speed our entry into the coming conflict.

What must we do?

For now, wait. We have not the power to do what needs to be done. Then he told her what they would do once they had recovered a little of their strength.

The day had disappeared. One moment Robal was explaining events as best he could to various officials—whose function he could not identify—and the next shadows were creeping from the west across the dark stain at his feet.

There had been no sign of the bodies.

Well, that isn't accurate, the guardsman within him said. There was plenty of sign, an abundance of it. Unmissable. Just no actual corpses. Stella he could understand, barely. Perhaps her immortality could stand even a fifty-pace fall. But Heredrew must have died. Everyone agreed on this. Couldn't have survived. And those who did not know Stella's secret assumed she must also have perished.

But if she had survived, where was she now?

Robal stretched and yawned. Traitorous body, still demanding sleep and food. She would likely eat and drink no longer, though she would finally sleep. A sleep she had longed for, it seemed.

The crowds of puzzled, vaguely offended locals had long since dispersed. There had not been a murder for so long, apparently, that no one knew how to deal with it. Three of the Council of Scholars had questioned his group—everyone was calling Stella's friends "his group" now, and waiting for him to make decisions on their behalf—but they had not asked the sort of questions a guard would. It didn't matter; there were no answers. So he'd spoken politely when asked, and had sent the others back to their lodgings when the questioners left. Now only he remained. Well, only he and a woman from the clan responsible for cleanliness on the streets, who had begun to scrub at the edges of the obscene brown stain. She'd be at it until dark, he judged, and would have to return in the morning. He couldn't help wondering if the woman could catch the curse from touching the dried blood.

I don't care, he decided wearily. *Let her live forever.*

Above her two people leaned over the railing, pointing out to each other where the dreadful accident had happened. Apart from them, the scene was deserted.

"Robal," someone called. "Robal."

The voice sent a shiver through him. It sounded like nothing he'd ever heard. On the other side of the street the cleaning woman continued her work, oblivious.

He turned, and there she stood, half-hidden by the corner of the building nearest the cliff from which she'd fallen. His mind went blank as his brain fought with his eyes.

"Robal, we need your help. Please. Please come."

He didn't believe it, not for a moment. It was preposterous, as his old sergeant used to say, pre-pos-ter-ous. Her fall had cushioned his, according to her, and they had crawled off together behind the houses like animals nursing their wounds. Had to be lies. Of course, this failed to account for

how the man calling himself Heredrew—*don't call him by
the other name*—could function with the back of his head
stoved in. Completely avoided explaining what else might
have left the bloodstains on the steps leading to the flat roof
of the house where Stella claimed they had spent the day
recuperating. Or their torn clothing, or the slowly weeping
wounds on their hands, or a hundred other things.

She looked terrible. Her face had been sucked dry, the
skin lying flat against the bone. Her eyes, blacker than he'd
ever seen them, jutted from her face like those of a frog.
Various parts of her body seemed not to be functioning
properly, and her skin had turned a sickly yellow. Every
time he looked at her he felt cold all over, then felt guilty at
his cowardly reaction.

He told Phemanderac, as they requested. Only he could
arrange what the two of them needed. The old man had
started shaking as soon as Robal led him to the shadows
where they waited, and had still been shaking when he left
to find Lindha and their cart. Robal hoped the shock would
not prove too much for the scholar's frail body.

He didn't tell Conal or the others, also as they
requested.

Phemanderac returned eventually with the cart, driving
it himself, still shaking as though in the midst of a seizure.
Stella protested, but the scholar claimed he could think of
no one to trust with the news that the Destroyer walked
among them. No matter the stakes, irrespective of what
was to be gained from the man's presence here, Kannwar's
execution—his *attempted* execution, at least—would immediately be ordered. And the strangers who had consorted
with him would be dealt with. He would drive them.

Robal and Phemanderac helped the two cadaver-like

people into the trap, covering their cold bodies with a blanket. Stella said little apart from frequent expressions of thanks; the other man said nothing; and all the while Robal wanted to embrace the one and kill the other. No dream had ever seemed as unreal as this.

A faint misty rain began to fall as the scholar shucked the reins of their donkey. Robal walked beside Lindha's long, ugly head, his hand on her mane, for some contact with the mundane as much as anything. Slowly they moved through the night-quiet city, ghosts in an upside-down world.

This is the man who destroyed the most beautiful city in the world, Phemanderac told himself. *The man whose hatred for the Way of Fire plunged us all into a future without the Most High. The* Fuirfad *was lost to the First Men because of him.*

He could reach out and touch the man responsible for two thousand years of suffering across a continent. Responsible for thousands of deaths during the Falthan War. Responsible for the death of Hal, the Right Hand of the Most High. And responsible for the extended misery of Stella and Leith, the two people Phemanderac loved above all others in the world.

Phemanderac could reach out and touch him, and so he did. The scholar's arm stretched painfully behind him until it fetched up against the man's cratered face. There was a hiss of indrawn breath.

"Yes, I am real," the man rasped in his reedy, broken voice. "And yes, I did everything you are no doubt thinking. But it is not all I am. You recall our discussions twenty years ago, and so you know I am not entirely without merit."

"Your permission to draw from you, friend Robal?" Phemanderac said as he withdrew his hand. "It will make you feel a little weak, that is all."

"Very well," the guard said, clearly not knowing what the scholar meant.

"He wants to do magic, as much as his meagre talents allow," said the man behind him. "He can't draw from himself, as he is too fragile in his old age. Neither Stella nor I can spare any power; we're engaged in healing ourselves. Hence the request. He'll probably kill himself in the attempt."

"Oh," said Robal.

"There's no need," the man continued. "Leave the guard alone. I will remain quiet until I am required to speak. I will not attempt to escape. I will play no tricks. I will adhere to the plan as outlined."

The rest of the journey to the Dhaurian docks was conducted in complete silence. The boat awaited them when they arrived.

The two wounded immortals were assisted from the trap and into the dinghy.

"Sorry, Lindha," the scholar heard Robal whisper. "You'll have to find your own way home."

"Attach the reins to that post," Phemanderac said, pointing. "Someone will be down to pick her up in the morning."

The guard nodded. Here was a man who did not require a full explanation; he just did what was needed. Robal was a fine guardian for an immortal.

But what use to an immortal was he, Phemanderac?

He pondered the question as Robal pushed the boat away from the wharf. He ought not to be involved in this most foolish enterprise: let them heal naturally—well, less unnaturally—over the next few years, and then let Stella return to Faltha and the leadership of her people, while the other one stood trial for all he had done. But Stella had asked him, had begged him, to trust her, had called upon their bond of friendship. Had named Leith, his own secret, unconsummated love; had known about that, apparently.

He could not refuse her, not when she asked in Leith's name.

He was a guide, not a guardian. He whispered directions to Robal, who could see nothing meaningful in the dark, facing as he was away from the direction in which they headed.

"Left," he said, not caring the word was not a nautical term. "Further left. Hard right, now. Left again. Left."

There was enough light to see by, but Phemanderac could have guided them by scent alone. He had never been to this place, but its smell permeated the wide, deep Dhaurian valley. A sweet scent of the purest water overlaid by the pungent smell of sulphur.

The Fountain of the Vale.

The moon rose, illuminating their passage. Avoiding the fishing smacks anchored and moored in the shallows had been difficult, but now they were in open water, Robal panting as he stroked the boat out into the middle of the vast Dhau Ria, the sea that had flooded Dona Mihst at the Most High's command.

"Here we are," he said eventually, at the same time as Kannwar cried "Halt!" and Robal began to back with his oars. The smell was at its strongest here, and the sea bubbled beneath them.

"There is a deep chasm below us," Phemanderac

explained. "It was formed by the wrath of the Most High, and divided Dona Mihst between rebels and loyalists. From it liquid fire emerged, and it was quenched only by the on-rushing sea."

"We know the story," said the man behind him.

"The chasm still emits vapours and occasional bursts of fire," the scholar continued stubbornly. "The Fountain is a little way beyond, and is on the highest point of old Dona Mihst. Some say it is occasionally exposed at the lowest of neap tides."

"It does not need to be exposed for our purposes," Kannwar said. "Do you have the cloths?"

"Aye," said the guard.

"Place them over our mouths as soon as we have partaken," Kannwar commanded. "The reason will be evident."

The brute took Stella's hand. "Be brave," he said to her.

"Why has no one else done this and gained immortality?" Robal asked.

"Because the Fountain is diluted by the water in which it plays," Stella said. "It won't affect a normal person enough to make a difference, but Kannwar believes it will help us. You will need to row us back, dear," she added, touching Robal on the sleeve of his tunic. "We may appear dead; we may even die. Neither of us can guess the effect. But if we are to be of any use in the next few months, we must try it."

Robal rowed on, until he was signalled to stop. "Here," Phemanderac said.

The scholar could feel a faint vibration against the hull of the dinghy, no doubt the pressure of the water welling up from the Fountain below. In the stern Stella and the

Kannwar dipped their hands into the sea and withdrew them. Raised them to their lips. Drank.

Their screams were piteous. Horrifying. A bass roar intertwining with a high-pitched shriek, echoing around the valley.

"For the sake of the Most High, Robal, apply the cloths! Gag them!"

The guard would not be rushed. He laid the oars carefully inside the boat, then took a cloth and bound it around Stella's juddering head, across her mouth, stopping her screams. He did the same to Kannwar.

"We could tip him over the side," Robal said into the silence. "Perhaps he might be swallowed by a leviathan. Let him be immortal in a sea beast's belly."

"And what would you say to our lady?"

"There is that," the guard admitted. "This is beyond me, scholar. I have no way of judging whether anything I do is right or wrong."

"Then hold on to what you know to be right, and do as she asks."

They waited under the starry sky until the two figures stopped shaking.

"Time to return," Phemanderac said, "and thence to judge the effectiveness of our cure." He grimaced. "Never in my worst nightmares did I see myself aiding someone to break the prohibition of the Most High."

"It was for a good reason," said the guard.

"Yes, it was. And that is exactly what Kannwar said when he broke it for the first time, if his scroll is to be believed. I am frightened, friend Robal. Frightened that I have done something that might have cursed not just my best friend, but the entire world."

"That's what I've been worried about too. Do you think we should write our own scroll of apology?"

"Uh," said Kannwar, struggling to sit up. He waved a barely controlled arm in the direction of his gag. Robal looked at Phemanderac enquiringly.

"We must," he said to the guard. "I'll do it, while you start rowing."

The cloth came off easily and, for a wonder, the man thanked him. "Is Stella all right?" he asked in a shaken voice.

"I don't know," Phemanderac said.

"She's cold, and so am I," the man said. "Would it be possible to divert to the nearest land? I could start a fire, and we could warm ourselves before returning to Dhauria."

"We need to get back to the city," Robal growled.

"It would give Stella time to recover. And if we judged it necessary to return to the Fountain, we would be close by."

Persuasive words, Phemanderac knew, but that didn't mean the man was telling the truth.

Stella's deathly cold face decided him.

They had to lift her from the boat, as she remained unconscious. It took a while for Robal to assemble enough driftwood for a fire, but no time at all for Kannwar to bring forth a flame.

Phemanderac and Robal took turns rubbing Stella's icy hands. She was alive, of that he was as certain as anyone could be when dealing with immortals. She breathed, at least, albeit raggedly. The Water of Life was at work in her, strengthening—or poisoning—and healing. Already the bruises were fading, and the more seriously damaged internal organs were no doubt being restored as they waited.

The faint sound of splashing came to them across the water. "Ho, the shore!" someone called.

"Who is that?" Robal hissed. "*Dominie*, we should put out the fire and hide. Explaining ourselves will be awkward at best."

Phemanderac was deathly tired and did not react as quickly as he might. "A boat?" he said, stupidly.

"Yes, and it draws closer."

Kannwar drew a pouch from under his tunic, not caring to hide his actions. Phemanderac saw him moving but thought little of it, preoccupied with the oncoming craft. The man sprinkled a small amount of powder on the fire and muttered a few words under his breath.

The world around them exploded in a flash of blue. There were cries of fear and pain everywhere, one of which came from Phemanderac's own mouth. They were all drawn inside the flames, consumed by them, suffering horrible agonies. Betrayed by the Destroyer! Phemanderac begged the fire to slay him swiftly. It took a long time, but eventually the sound and pain faded away, away, away to nothing.

INTERLUDE

HUSK HAS IMPERILLED HIS OWN plans. He knows himself for a fool. If the future goes against him, his precipitous action may cost him his life. Such as it is.

But what else could he have done?

If his story is ever written, if he is ever revealed as the one who vanquished the Undying Man, he hopes his biographer makes mention of the many mitigating circumstances surrounding the rash decision he has made today. He will make sure they are noted. Chief of these, of course, is the sheer agony of seventy years of struggle. Day after day he has endured pain and suffering beyond anything he ever inflicted on others, and yet over the years he has returned from the house of death to a place of strength. He has achieved this by suppressing rigorously every emotion and exercising an inhuman, costly patience.

But patience has failed him today.

He stretches his vestigial forelimbs forward a finger-width, takes a grip on the next stair, and begins to haul himself upwards. Patience. He moves literally an inch at a time; he remembers using the phrase "inching" once in his former life to describe slow political progress, but had never imagined what the word might literally mean.

Now he knows.

One year to climb from the dungeon to the Tower of Farsight. A whole year to travel a thousand paces. Every pace takes hours of inching. He cannot devote all his strength to this task, of course, as he has to mask himself whenever someone comes down the corridor. Of late, however, much of his energy is absorbed by fighting to maintain the spikes he has set in his three unwitting servants. And in fighting off the increasing depredations of the unknown powers exploiting them.

A whole year, of which months have already passed. He is far above the dungeons now, and his body is burned during the day by bright sunlight coming from high above him. He has nearly reached ground level. The most difficult part of his journey lies ahead.

Patience, he tells himself. Patience. He has lived by this mantra, so why did he lose control?

Conal of Yosse had been a poor choice for a spike. Husk's roving mind had found him lying in a bed on the seventeenth level of the keep, the place usually reserved for those suffering illness. Husk had found no illness in the boy save a deep lassitude, the sort of weakness associated with a large, but not life-threatening, drawdown of essenza by a skilled magician. This was a puzzle, as Husk had detected no significant magic use in the keep for days. So he had investigated further.

The boy had a strange mind. Immense potential, but all stoppered up with knowledge, so his higher reasoning faculties could not work effectively. This one would believe whatever he was told. An ideal candidate to be used as a spy. A thought confirmed as Husk rummaged around in the lad's mind, finding links to Instruere and Stella. Husk claimed him then and there, hammering his spike in deeply, delighted at his good luck.

Problems had arisen almost immediately. The boy was a priest, and wished to see things as his superiors told him. However, on the return journey to Faltha Husk realised the boy's own view of his importance was enormously inflated. He would never gain a senior position in the Koinobia.

Not unless Husk helped him.

When he recommenced his studies on the Destroyer's Consort, the boy found himself able to concentrate more effectively, read more quickly and reason more creatively. The lad never suspected he was being magically aided. Most importantly, Husk fed him small details of Stella's life not part of the official record, things that captured the attention of his seniors.

But it was such hard work. Husk spent hours every day immobile, working to make this flaccid mind into a blade-sharp weapon to suit his purposes. It cost him dearly, and set his plans back months. However, with the death of the fop Leith and Stella's subsequent flight, Conal was easily manoeuvred into position.

Unfortunately, the boy is now beginning to think for himself. He is much less easy to control, and suffers from the nearest thing to megalomania Husk has ever seen. He honestly believes he is at the heart of the Most High's plans. Ironically, of course, he is at the heart of someone's plans. If he would only remain tractable, he could stay there.

It was Conal himself who gave Husk the idea. Standing there, listening to Stella and the sorcerer talking, and having to endure the priest's maudlin fears that his impossible love had been thwarted, Husk almost missed Conal's impulsive thought.

Push them over the edge.

Of course, Conal was not the sort of man with the courage to obey such an instinct. By the time he had weighed up all the benefits and costs of executing such a notion, the opportunity would be lost. Husk scorned his vassal.

But then Conal heard—to Husk's enormous shock— that Heredrew was the Undying Man. Was addressed so by Stella.

This time the thought was Husk's.

Husk poured himself into the priest, seized control of him and threw him at the pair, all without consideration. Patience be damned, here was a chance to revenge himself on his torturers. But even as Conal's shoulder drove up into Stella's back, propelling her into the Undying Man, he recognised the impulse for what it was. An instinctive reaction in which good sense played no part. Realisation of the deeply buried need to do something after all this time. An action doomed to fail.

He was right. Even as the bodies crashed together to the street below, the Undying Man was busy drawing enormous energies from wherever he could find them. Everyone in Dhauria would feel tired and unwell for a time as a result. The Undying Man even contrived to land first, cushioning Stella from the worst of the fall.

Husk wishes he had forced Conal to watch their fall: that sight would have almost been worth the danger he is now in. Together, writhing in pain on the ground below, ah. He will make do with his imagination. He thought that if the pair were not broken beyond mortal repair, then at least they would be sidelined for some time. Husk amused himself imagining what he might do to Andratan in its master's extended absence.

But Husk forgot the nature of the city in which these things happened. Dhauria, the place of the Fountain, that unapproachable, forbidden magic.

Conal has not been confined, and Husk sends him nosing: what he hears, particularly from the incautious lips of the guardsman, frightens the magician. Within hours the Undying Man is taking steps to undo any advantage Husk enjoys from the incident. Within weeks, perhaps even days, the two immortals will be as strong as ever; as ready to interfere as ever; and Husk's action has rendered vulnerable one of his spikes. Kannwar will ask Conal harsh questions and the truth might well emerge.

Husk will have to plan.

A moment's thought. He snaps his fingers—or would have, had he any fingers to snap. Conal must observe the immortals drinking from the Fountain, and he must bring witnesses with him, people who will make the Undying Man's immediate future difficult.

A whisper in his dupe's ear is enough to set things in motion. *Hurry*, he croons into the man's mind. *Hurry, hurry, hurry*. He sends reassuring self-congratulatory feelings to ensure his idea takes hold, then withdraws a little to watch.

Conal, you are a lecher at heart, Husk thinks as he observes the priest's choice of neutral observers. Women, mostly. They take some persuading, especially the council member, and Husk worries. *Hurry, hurry*. The priest employs clever arguments to persuade his targets that the truth about the outsiders has not been satisfactorily explained, that something dire is planned, and plays on their distrust of their own scholar. Eventually Conal assembles his cast and, as they make their way to the docks, Husk luxuriates once again in the immense satisfaction of controlling events half a world away.

His plan nearly founders when the council member has difficulty in securing a vessel. No one goes out on the water after dark, apparently, despite the good night fishing to be had. It is a religious thing, a desire not to desecrate the ruins of Dona Mihst by foundering on them. A thin excuse for laziness. Two boats are found, and the owning clan release them to the councilman unwillingly. "Hurry," he compels the priest to say. "I have uncovered a plan to interfere with the Fountain itself. We must stop them."

A short time later the two boats are cutting through the dark waters. Husk hates the sea. He often wonders if his true mistake was not when he made an enemy of Stella Pellwen, but to have left his beloved Jasweyan Mountains in the first instance. He withdraws further from Conal's mind.

Husk has Conal position the boats so the immortals are between them and the moon, making their silhouettes clearly visible. They are in time to see the immortals drink from the Fountain, but are too far away to interfere. The councilman is incensed; Conal sees this from the other boat. The young scholar from the scriptorium is also angered at what she has seen, and urges Conal to intercept the imprudent outlanders. The uncouth plainsman and his father say little, but they are no doubt surprised at the day's events.

World's not as simple as you thought, Husk wants to say to them. He tired long ago of their humorous interplay. *Wrap your drollery around that.*

Oars dip into the water and they are off in pursuit. Conal's boat leads; the members of the other boat, the council member and representatives of various clans, are still debating the intentions of the outsiders among themselves. *Ask them yourselves, fools! Just get on with it!*

"Ho, the shore!" Conal calls out as they draw near their quarry. The immortals have conveniently set a fire, an inadvertent beacon to guide Husk's people to them. His only worry now is that the second boat is some distance behind—

A blue light flashes. Explodes outwards. There is one person in this world most likely to know what this is: the one watching the scene through Conal's eyes. *No!* The Undying Man's blue fire, his method of communication over long distances. And a sometime haphazard way of transporting people over those same distances. He can do nothing; nothing but watch the flame roll towards Conal and his passengers, envelop the boat and ensnare it in powerful sorcery.

He has seen this before, oh yes, on the day Stella ruined his life. He had entered Instruere using subterfuge and had risen to command the city—in the name of Faltha, but in reality on behalf of his master, the Undying Man. Of course, he had his own schemes. Why should he not plot to oust his master from his throne? Would his master not expect it? Of course, but nothing would be said, as long as he was not caught. But then the she-dog Stella had been captured—through Husk's own manoeuvring, of course—and had told the Undying Man what she knew of his plotting. Enough to ensure that the next time he contacted his master through the blue fire, Husk had found himself jerked into the flames and transported through tunnels of endless, searing pain, to be deposited at his master's feet.

Now he watches as Conal suffers the same fate.

Husk cannot withdraw completely. The fire requires life-force essenza to function, and it pulls with irresistible strength at his magical link with Conal. It is all Husk can do not to be drained himself.

To Husk's enhanced senses Conal is everywhere and nowhere, smeared across space between Dhauria and Andratan. The priest is in agony. Husk smiles. This is the pain he feels every day. Then a thought snares his attention . . .

Only now does Husk wake to the true danger he is in. It is not that Conal has been discovered and will soon be questioned by the Undying Man. It is that they will soon be here, in Andratan—not only the Undying Man, but also Conal and Stella. Far, far too soon for his purposes.

His breath falters. His raw, bleeding hide shivers. He has failed.

And then his unknown enemies save him. Astonishingly, beyond all hope, they intervene, pulling at the metaphysical connection between the blue fire set on the shores of Dhau Ria and the fire blazing out of control in the hearth of the Undying Man's Farsight Tower, consuming the men who served there. Godlike hands reach through twin holes in the immutable fabric separating the physical and spiritual worlds and bend the passage of the blue fire to their own purposes. Pull it towards them.

Only one question remains in Husk's mind as his avatar falls helplessly towards his unknown enemies. Better or worse than the enemies he knows, they are certainly more powerful. Can they be made allies?

FISHERMAN

CHAPTER 9

A BANQUET OF REVENGE

"SHE'S DYING, FOR ALKUON'S SAKE," Noetos snarled. "I don't care about what happens to us. Nothing else matters but her."

"She obviously doesn't think so," Duon said quietly. "Otherwise she wouldn't have injured herself trying to save you. Leave your children alone. Let them recover."

Yes, the comment made sense, as did everything else this foreigner had said since their imprisonment. Noetos chose to ignore it. Had to. He needed to know.

Anomer, he begged for the hundredth time. *Tell me. How is she?*

No answer. No answer now for hours.

Arathé had poured herself out for him, his son had told him, supplying him with unnatural strength in his bid to escape the Summer Palace. It had cost her dearly. Anomer had become more and more anxious, apparently, as she spent herself heedlessly, bolstering her father, until eventually Anomer had struck her, knocking her unconscious.

Then he had taken her place as her primary source of magical energy. Anomer had suffered hardly less than his sister.

Noetos had been unable to understand it. Why had fighting a few guards been so taxing? Surely his escape attempt had used much less of his children's power than defeating the whirlwinds?

No, Anomer had replied to his question. Wearily, Noetos thought. *The effect is cumulative. We used much of our strength against the storm. Also, Father, we are still learning. I think I may have found a way to do this more efficiently, but we do not have the strength to try it. Not yet.*

His children had nothing more to give him. They needed time to recover. Anomer might as well have told his father to go away and leave them alone. It certainly stung as much.

He'd told Duon nothing mattered but Arathé, but this didn't explain the hurt he felt at Anomer not replying to him. *Unless he also—unless he is resting. Yes, resting.*

Nor did it explain his rising fear.

Claudo had been to visit them soon after they had been thrown in here, hours ago now, trussed together and locked in. His effeminate voice spelled out the likely consequences for having slain the Neherian general and a number of his elite guards. Death would come eventually, Claudo had told them pleasantly.

"You're not showing much caution," Noetos had told him, "given that we have superhuman strength at our command. Ought we not be chained, at the least?" He was past caution. *As usual*, his son's voice had said.

"I don't care how strong you are—or were. You won't break out of this prison. You ought to know: it was your grandfather who had it built. The strength of ten men won't bring down this door."

Easy for Claudo to say, given he was currently on the far side of it.

"We'll have questions about your performance in the throne room," Claudo had continued. "You will explain to us how you accessed this wild strength, and why it is temporary."

"Could tell you now, if you like," Noetos had said. "Or show you." Bravado, but it sustained his courage.

"We don't want to know yet. Now, get some sleep. Rest up and regain your strength. We want you at your most inventive tonight. The Neherian court will be here to witness your explanations, and they require entertainment. They are notoriously difficult to please."

"The Neherian court? The court has come north? Are they insane?"

Duon had grunted. "Not as insane as leaving some of their number behind," he said. "The best way of avoiding a coup is to keep the entire court in one place."

"Oh? An expert on Neherian affairs?"

"No, but that is how it would work in Talamaq. How it did work, in fact. We lost the most powerful members of every major Alliance in the Valley of the Damned."

"Is my friend right?" Noetos asked Claudo.

"It is as he says," the man had replied, shrugging his shoulders. "What have they to fear? They have a navy and an army to protect them. Far safer here than at home. And there are special entertainments for them to look forward to. They are particularly keen to meet the surviving seed of Roudhos. Why do you think Fossa was liberated first?"

"Because it's one of the closest villages to Neherius, you feckless fool."

"You're going to torture us publicly?" Duon had said. "Barbarians."

"Torture? No. After your questioning, which is likely to be rigorous, you will be given your freedom. That is, if you are able to slay"—he paused for a moment, as though considering—"a legion of our finest soldiers. Sound fair to you?"

Noetos had spat at the door.

Claudo left them then, to endure the waiting as best they could. Noetos knew it would be a race between his children's recovery and the onset of questioning. He speculated as to what his children might be able to do to aid him, then fell to wondering what the Neherians would do to him to encourage him to talk. Hot irons; they were known for that. Pincers. The removal of body parts. He tried to think of something other than what awaited him; he knew the Neherians were leaving him time to dwell on the sordid nature of his fate in order to break down his resistance.

They didn't know, or had forgotten, that he had seen far worse than they could inflict upon him. What was his own flesh compared to the defilement and death of those nearest to him?

Noetos sighed. He wasn't fooling himself. Everyone talked under torture. After they'd finished screaming.

"Do you have any of your power left?" Duon asked him.

"None. Listen, I'm sorry you became involved in this. I didn't make you, though."

"No, let history record I came here of my own free will," Duon said dryly.

Noetos listened carefully: Duon did not sound as fearful as someone in his position ought to be.

"I saw you," Noetos said to him. "You kept up with me, which means you had power of your own."

The man grunted.

"You're a sorcerer then? Are you a true sorcerer, like my son and daughter? Or do you borrow your power, as I do?"

"As I understand it, every worker of magic borrows the power from someone else," Duon said.

"Not a true sorcerer, then." A true sorcerer would know this for certain. It had been a recent but crucial discovery, so Arathé had told them. Sorcerers died young because their magic ate them. It drew on their own energy. So the alternative, until recently known only to a few, was to absorb the essence of magic from everyone around them—and, if one was highly skilled, everything. "But you still know about magic. Who is using you?"

"I do not know. I thought I was going insane. There's a voice in my head telling me things, mocking me, but supplying me with uncanny strength. Using me. But what you've described about your children sending you power sounds very much like my experience. Except I don't know any sorcerers. Certainly I have none in my family. I don't know who it could be." Duon's voice petered out, ending on a frankly puzzled note.

"The issue for us is whether you still have that link. Can you call on your power at any time?"

"I don't know how to call on it," Duon confessed. "It just happens. It calls on me."

"Huh. Then we will have to trust your mysterious benefactor to intervene at the right moment. I don't like to plan on the basis of such an arrangement."

"He hasn't failed me yet." The man laughed, a dry sound. "Not that I know what success and failure are for him. He's told me nothing of himself or his purposes."

"And you?" Neotos asked gently. "Would you speak of yourself and your purposes?"

Duon's mouth opened, as if about to speak, then closed again, and his lips pressed together as if trapping any ill-considered words inside.

"I cannot," he said. "Not yet. I have two masters, one seen and one unseen, and I trust neither of them. My friend, I am not certain what my purpose is."

Noetos grimaced. "Unless your benefactor is strong enough to overcome our guards, I fear the only certain purpose left us is to provide entertainment for the Neherians."

Duon nodded and turned his head away.

A slitted window high above the two prisoners projected a small rectangle of sunlight on the rough walls of their cell. The rectangle moved gradually from left to right, rising higher above their heads until it turned from yellow to red and began to fade. Along with their hopes. Despite checking regularly, Noetos continued to hear nothing from his children.

The guards came for them a little while after the rectangle disappeared. A dozen strong, they arrived prepared for trouble: swords drawn, heavy chains draped over their shoulders. They all crammed themselves into the cell, their very closeness making it impossible for Noetos and Duon to fight.

Not that Noetos had the heart for it. Surely if Arathé had

survived the day, his son would have told him. He ought to have said something. The fisherman had died a hundred deaths in the course of the afternoon, starting at any strange sound, thinking it might be the beginning of Anomer's voice in his head. Eventually even his own thoughts began to sound like his son's voice. He wondered if a headache might make him unreceptive. If the thick walls of the cell were impenetrable. If he would fall asleep and make himself unreachable. If a hundred other things.

When the Neherians wrapped their chains around him, he offered no resistance. He shuffled compliantly at the point of a sword. Duon had it worse: the way they were chained together meant he had to walk backwards.

Reality gave way to a walking dream. He'd been down these corridors many times. Played in them as a child. Hidden in that alcove, stared out this window, swung on that railing. For a wonder, the pennants of the countries that had once made up Old Roudhos still decorated the southern atrium, though the lovely stained-glass windows were all smashed. The whirlwind might have done that. But the whirlwind hadn't left the pennants to moulder and slowly go grey. That had been neglect.

The ballroom, converted to an impromptu throne room earlier that day, had again been transformed. The real throne room, high above in the tower, had been broken by the storm: he had seen it lying in pieces at the foot of the cliff on which the palace was perched. But the Neherians had improvised: surely every bright and pretty thing left intact by the whirlwinds had been taken from Raceme town below and installed on the walls or hung from the ceiling. Spirals of coloured paper intertwined with strings of beads in random patterns. Paintings, many no doubt valuable, had been brought up from the vaults or moved from other corridors in the Summer Palace and scattered around the room with no thought for suitability or placement. Garlands of flowers splashed colour everywhere; the most spectacular arrangements were framed by tall, arched windows. The floor had been festooned with orchids and lilies. Servants bearing trays laden with golden goblets trod on the fragile blooms with no regard. Every kitchen and pantry, every secret store and treasure room, must have been emptied. Some of this must have come north aboard ship, or overland with the army.

Neherians, all right.

The extravagance was daunting. A table weighed down with food ran the length of the room. Buckets filled with ice—*ice! Could only have come from the Jasweyan Mountains!*—preserved seafood delicacies. Haunches of meat, placed at intervals on the table, steamed in the cool air. Air that was laden with a dizzying mix of perfume and exotic spice. Gluttony and desire.

His hearing, however, was the sense to suffer the most from this onslaught of excess. A hundred people were arranged along the far side of the table, dressed in their courtly finery, and filled the room with their talk: excited babble, raised voices as they strove to outdo each other, shouts, shrieks of laughter, nodding heads, hands slapping thighs. A parody of a banquet.

He was not the only one suffering deprivation. A score of guards stood in rows behind the empty wooden throne, four rows of five, no doubt the army's best men. Each wore a red uniform, threaded with gold, the ceremonial garb of the Valiant Protectors of the Duke of Roudhos. Five of their number had much more elaborate uniforms than the others, but appeared no less hungry. They all looked on stoically as the people they were paid to protect indulged themselves.

Noetos narrowed his eyes. The Valiant Protectors had been slaughtered, along with their Duke, seventy years ago at the behest of the Undying Man. He'd not heard of their revival, though anything that had happened in the last twenty years would have been beyond his ears. Why had the position been restored? Why had the entire court come north? No, the real question was why any of the court had come north. Surely the conquest of the Fisher Coast could be accomplished by their military might alone. What was happening here?

He knew they had not gone to this trouble purely to make sport of him. Despite the revelation that they had invaded Fossa to find him, he knew he was of little importance. Noetos of Fossa would be a small sideshow in the Neherian travelling circus. He was merely a loose end to be tied off. And he would likely go to his death in ignorance of the larger game being played here.

Trumpets blared a brazen fanfare. Liveried heralds advanced into the room from doors at either end, making two columns. Into the corridor between the columns came a man and a woman wearing simple circlets of silver on their heads, in clear defiance of the Edict of Regional Sovereignty which forbade any display of political independence in the Bhrudwan Empire. Together the man and the woman proceeded to the throne, arm in arm, where the man sat and the woman took station to his left on a stool provided by one of the Valiant Protectors. Still sounding their trumpets, the heralds left by the opposite doors to which they had come in. The fanfare ceased, leaving Noetos's ears ringing. A moment later the echo died, and silence fell.

A hundred and twenty pairs of eyes turned to the two prisoners.

Despite having known it was coming, Noetos could not help feeling intimidated by their regard. The combined disapproval of this many people had an impact, no matter how much one steeled oneself against it.

"Who are these people?" Duon whispered.

"The Neherian nobility," breathed Noetos in reply. "All of them, I think. Claudo was telling the truth, strange as it seems to me."

"They're staring at us." Duon's voice quavered on the edge of fear.

"Ignore them. Nosy lot."

Noetos had not realised how far his voice carried.

"Indeed, son of Demios, we are curious about you." The rich voice came from the man on the throne. "Why would we not be? Had your father been somewhat more politic, it would have been he—or you—sitting today atop this throne and this newborn empire."

Noetos tried to breathe normally, but found himself gasping a series of shallow breaths. "Local politics never held much interest for my father," he said, addressing the room. "Nor me."

His reward was a flash of anger across the regent's face. "Local politics, as you describe it, has swallowed up your village and your country just as easily as it swallowed your family."

"Ah, my family." Just like that his breathing relaxed as anger allowed him to put any consequences aside. "What would a Neherian know of filial devotion?"

"More than you might think," said the woman, in the

most beautiful, stately contralto. She smiled, a small thing. "Nephew."

She leaned back to assess the impact of her revelation.

Noetos's mind went grey, then white. *What?* "You claim me as a relative, woman? Who are you to me?" *Not my mother's sister; she was no Neherian, and would be older and likely larger than this woman.* Frantic searching of a memory deliberately repressed. *My father had no sisters. Who then?*

"She is my wife, and new-crowned Empress of the Southern Empire," said the man. "And I, young Noetos, am your uncle. Your father's younger brother. And, I am proud to say, his murderer, at least by proxy."

"Uncle Meranios? But he . . . you . . . were a loyal brother. You . . . I don't understand." Suppressed laughter from the long table accompanied his discomfiture.

"Why should you? Demios despaired of you, boy. According to him you never paid attention to your tutors. Had you, you would have learned enough of our 'local politics' to know your father's opposition to our patriotic expansionist policies could never be allowed to prevail. How many more generations were we going to wait before reclaiming Old Roudhos's legacy? Do you know, your father threatened to go to the Undying Man himself with evidence of our plans? This, after initially being the ringleader of our movement?"

"You seem surprised," Meranios' wife continued. "But why? Are you shocked that the entire court knows of this? Your family history has been a secret from no one for the last decade or more. Well, from no one but you, obviously. We have come north from Aneheri to establish this city once again as the seat of our Summer Palace, the vanguard of our push to reclaim Roudhos from the Undying Man's careless and gravely weakened grasp."

"So you ordered your brother and his family slain," Noetos said, his heart hammering. "Are you aware what was done to them? How they were killed?"

Now Noetos had been given time to adjust, he could make out the remnants of his uncle in this man's face. The face was jowly, the hair had receded and the voice was thinner, but it was him.

"Oh, yes," his uncle said. "All on the orders of the patriots. You see, his was not the only betrayal of our cause. There were others considering selling us to the *Maghdi Dasht*, and we had to provide an incentive for them to remain loyal. Avoiding the suffering and fate of Demios and his family is a good incentive, hmm?"

"Rape?" Noetos's voice was leaden. "Ripped apart by wild dogs? *Being made to watch?*"

"You'll shock no one in this room," said his aunt. "We were the ones who made the decision. Everyone here knew about it and approved of every detail. A number of those looking on you now volunteered for the mission. That decision kept us alive and, more importantly, kept the cause alive. If you'd read your Comus you would know why it was necessary. But of course you didn't. Let others do the work, as long as they kept the throne clean for your indolent backside to sit upon."

"So you believe you were right in what you did?" Noetos ran his eyes across the assembled court, and read their assent in their eyes. "You all deserve to die."

"Fortunately, it is you who will die, nephew," said the man who sat the throne. The self-styled Emperor, Noetos supposed. The fool who, sooner or later, would be slain at the order of the Undying Man.

He plunged in, their criticism of his political acumen notwithstanding. "Where are the places set for the Undying Man and his *Maghdi Dasht*? I assume this is all done with his assent. Or," he affected surprise, "are you doing this without his knowledge? You are, aren't you. Whatever death you subject me to tonight will be but a shadow of what he will engineer upon your bodies. What on earth are you thinking, Uncle?"

"So many questions," said his aunt, "and all that is missing is the wit to understand the answers. Truly, we would have to have killed them anyway, traitor or no. Could you imagine being ruled by someone as indigent and, frankly, stupid as this?"

Their laughter swelled in his ears. They mocked him, yes, but they mocked his family also, and that hurt.

"Really, it could not be simpler. We have spies in Andratan who tell us the Undying Man is severely incapacitated as a result of his invasion of Faltha. Foolishly, he spent almost all of his *Maghdi Dasht*, and has not replaced them with magicians of the same calibre. In this room are five men who will outmatch them in every conceivable way."

Magicians? Neherius, with its strange religious ways, had long rejected magicians. *What magicians*?

The five elaborately uniformed Valiant Protectors stepped forward and bowed, then returned to their places, matching smiles on their confident faces.

He could not formulate an answer.

The Emperor leaned forward. "There is only one question you wish to ask, but you do not ask it. You are either patient or frightened. I have never seen you exercise patience, so I assume it is the latter. Here is your question. 'Why was I spared on that day twenty years ago?' It has defined your existence ever since. And you are about to have an answer.

"I told you there were others potentially disloyal to our cause. We left you alive, young Noetos, but under watch, to see if you attracted any of these dissidents to your side. You were a lightning rod designed to draw out fellow traitors. And, do you know, it worked. Three men went looking for you, and found a noose instead. Because you lived, three traitors died, and our cause survived. A fair exchange, I believe.

"What entertained us most was the thought of you hiding in a poverty-stricken backwater, learning to fish, getting those fine hands dirty. And then sailing out amongst the Neherian fleet, thinking you were tweaking our noses, when all along you were simply making it easier for us to keep you under surveillance. The annual reports of our Fossan spy made diverting reading, I can assure you."

"Fossan spy?" Noetos repeated. But he didn't have to ask. He knew. Oh, Alkuon, he was every kind of fool.

It seemed he was to be told anyway. The depthless extent of his naivety was to be publicly plumbed.

"Halieutes, of course. Paid off with access to our fishing grounds, and finally eliminated when he became too greedy."

His uncle leaned over to his wife. "Do you know, dear, the look on our nephew's face has made the whole uncomfortable overland trek worthwhile. I swear I'll never forget it. Look at him: like a calf seeing the slaughterman's knife for the first time, and realising the green pastures of his childhood have done nothing but prepare him for this moment."

He stood and nodded to his court, who responded with applause.

"And speaking of slaughter," he said, resuming his seat, "we have after-meal entertainment, I understand. Claudo?"

"My Emperor," the effeminate man said, hurrying to the throne from where he waited beside his prisoners.

"Since you were the one who advocated Noetos be a lightning rod for our cause, my old friend, you have the honour of asking him the necessary questions. Now, I know everyone here approves of this course of action. However, for some of you, such a direct application of politics will not aid the digestion of your meal. This is understood by the throne. You have our leave to remove yourselves."

No one moved, though in Noetos's judgment a number of the women and at least two of the men wished they could. *They do not believe their Emperor's assurances. And why should they? They've just been reminded of a clever subterfuge to flush out the disloyal among them. Why would they not suspect another?*

"We have questions for you," Claudo said, approaching Noetos and Duon. Two soldiers accompanied him, each carrying one end of a long stake.

They mean to burn us? Inside this room?

Duon, his back to Noetos, began to shake. Noetos himself was certain he was shaking also. *Anomer! Arathé! Are you there? Please!*

Nothing.

The soldiers lifted the stake, then slipped it between the men, forcing them apart and scoring their backs with its rough, knotty surface. It would hold them upright when, as would no doubt happen in the next few moments, they could no longer stand unaided.

"I feel strange," said Duon.

Claudo cracked him across the mouth. "We'll hear from you later, black man."

A third soldier wheeled a brazier into the room, leaving it next to their torturer. Coals glowed redly, and in their midst sat half a dozen instruments. Claudo donned a glove, leaned over with the air of a scholar choosing a volume to read, and selected a pair of pincers.

To Noetos's mortification, his bladder let go. A few titters of laughter rippled around the room from those close enough to see.

"Now, we want to know from you how you learned the schedule of the Neherian fleet. How did you know in time to organise resistance at Makyra Bay?"

Noetos lifted his head wearily. "I know how this goes. What answer do you want me to give?" he said.

"Those with no imagination do not fear pain. At least," Claudo said, with a glance at Noetos's damp breeches, "not enough. The son of Demios has never had much imagination. At least, that is what our spy told us. Therefore we must stimulate it for him."

As the man lifted the pincer to Noetos's tunic, fastened on the material and ripped it away, the fisherman's thoughts turned, oddly, to the sound and smell of the sea, as though there was comfort to be found there. Strange that, at the end, he should return to a place he never liked.

"Ready!"

A thousand hands clasped each other. "Remember,"

they had been told, "you will experience discomfort, if not actual pain. Hold on, endure. The more of you who endure, the greater the number the effects will be spread across, and the less anyone will have to tolerate."

By no means everyone had believed it, though Anomer and Arathé had used their Voices widely. Those people had moved on, over the brow of the hill, and made camp there. The remaining volunteers braced themselves.

"These things are of little use to a man," Claudo said, playing to his audience. "It is almost as though they were invented for the purpose. Can't think of what else they're good for."

To Noetos, the man's voice was the cawing of a gull; the murmur of conversation from the table the wash of waves upon the reef.

The pincers closed over his left nipple and squeezed.

"Now."

And nothing happened. Claudo gritted his teeth and squeezed his gloved hand as hard as he could. Noetos watched in giddy bemusement. He could feel nothing.

Meranios leaned forward.

Claudo grasped the pincers with both hands, intending to apply more pressure. "Gah!" he cried, and jerked his gloveless hand off the handle.

A half-day's walk north of the Summer Palace, just under a thousand people felt a slight constriction on their own chests. One or two of the more sensitive among them gave an involuntary cry. The gentle pain lasted a few seconds, then ended suddenly.

*   *   *

Noetos's mind slowed, unable to keep up with events. He was still anticipating pain, but none came.

A few of the men at table were laughing, believing the torturer's actions to be an elaborate joke. Wine flowed freely, and the comments as to how the traitor's son ought to be tortured were becoming more explicit.

"Claudo?" said the man who sat the throne. "What are you doing?"

"Nothing, Mer— my Emperor. Attempting to frighten the prisoner."

"Get on with it, man. Use the knife."

Hold still, Father, Arathé sent.

"A finger, then," Claudo said, his face reassembling itself into what he probably thought was a torturer's leer. He drew a knife from his belt while one of his assistants grasp Noetos's right hand and held it firmly.

Teeth bared, Claudo drew it powerfully across the fisherman's first and second fingers.

The sensation was to Noetos like someone pressing a stick against his knuckles. A slight pressure, nothing more.

This time about twenty people put up their hands for assistance, indicating they had been hurt. They bled from slight cuts to their fingers. The rest felt little more than a tingling sensation.

"You are doing well!" Anomer told them. "Please, hold still. We will defeat the Neherians yet!"

"Aaah!" Claudo cried. "Raaah!" All sophistication was abruptly abandoned. He struck with the knife, trying to bury it in the man's hand. It bounced off the suddenly hard skin. A greater arc this time, with the same result. The third and last time he drove the knife at his victim's arm. It connected, and the blade shattered into a thousand pieces.

"Hold!"

All over the hillside people cried out with sudden pain, and blood was visible from where Anomer stood. But no one moved save those rushing with cloth bandages to staunch the wounds.

The comments from the table had become less mocking and more agitated. The Emperor shouted something, but Claudo could not hear it, preoccupied as he was with his own nightmare. He darted at the nearest assistant and drew the man's sword. Not the done thing, to unsheathe another man's weapon, but he didn't care. He took it in both hands—wincing at the burn—and swung at the traitor's unprotected neck. A mild thud, and nothing more.

"No! No!"

A frenzy came on the torturer. Had to be magic, had to be. He hacked and hacked, raining blows on the man until his sword arm dropped from exhaustion. The tip of the blade clicked on the stone floor.

The only sound in the room was Claudo's own panting.

Joined at once by Noetos's laughter. "Neherius is a dung-heap," he said. "Always was, always will be. Time to rid ourselves of dung." He turned his head towards the wide-eyed, white-faced soldiers. "Are you going to free me, or must I break free on my own?"

"We, my friend," said Duon from behind him. "We. Our hosts have yet to see my power."

The nearest soldier stammered something unintelligible, then pulled a key from his belt.

"No!" cried the Emperor, suddenly afraid. "Keep the prisoners secured! Guards! Valiant Protectors! Shield your Emperor! Magicians! Launch your attack!"

The more perceptive members of his court were already up from their chairs, but they had left it too late. Feeling like a god, Noetos flexed his multiply augmented muscles and the chains around him disintegrated. Behind him Duon appeared to have done the same thing.

"I have the north door," he said to Noetos, and was gone in a blur of movement. A moment later the remaining chains crashed to the ground, along with the stake.

The five magicians ignored Duon and came walking carefully towards Noetos.

"We believe this will work, particularly if they are not expecting it," Anomer said. There were a number of uncertain faces in front of him, but there was not time to explain. "If it fails, we will draw strength from all of you, but not enough to place anyone in danger. This is what we agreed to, remember. If any of you repent of the agreement, leave now."

No one moved.

Here was the test. Could they draw magical power from a powerful magician using sheer strength of numbers? Would their distance from Raceme reduce their strength? Were the five magicians stronger than the brave thousand?

Now, sister, he said.

Noetos felt Arathé reach through him towards the magicians. The pull of her magic was immense. A thousand people, she had said in his mind. A few weakly gifted, but all possessing essenza she could tap into.

The leftmost of the magicians winced. "What is that?" he asked. "Are you—is anyone?" His face went white and he fell to the floor.

"You all felt that," Noetos said. "Who else wants to be drained dry?"

The four pale faces looked uncertainly at each other. Then, as one, they took to their heels and ran for the south door. Their fellow writhed on the floor, crying in a soft, unregarded voice.

"Be strong, now," Anomer told those gathered on the hillside. "And do not flinch, no matter what is demanded of you. No matter what you sense, what you see. As they have done to your countrymen—and as they would do to you—so must be done to them, if we are ever to be safe."

Some of the people who had remained steadfast through pain and magical drain stood and walked away. Knowing even better than they did what was to come, Arathé did not blame them. But she knew her father would never accept surrender from those who had murdered his family. Her family. The grandparents, aunts and uncles she would never meet: Today she felt some of her father's rage.

She clenched her teeth and dug her feet into the turf beneath her, determined to do what needed to be done.

Noetos and Duon met in the middle of the room when the butchery was over. Some of it was fierce swordplay, but much of it had been simple execution. The fisherman knew he would regret this until his dying day. Not the defeat of the Neherians, but the manner in which it had been achieved. The human mind, he knew, was simply not resilient enough to cope with what he had just seen, with what he had just done.

But his soul, ever treacherous, sang in delight.

The room is even more colourful now, it said, and the realisation he was capable of such a thought sickened him.

The southerner, now his brother in arms, wore an obscene coat of red over his clothes. Noetos's own garments were torn and soaking wet, and he knew by looking at the man before him how he himself appeared. "Like a bloody sunset," he said. "The sunset of Neherian power."

Duon grinned fiercely, then frowned and put a hand to the back of his head. "Oh!" he said. His eyes widened, his head swung around wildly, and he rushed for one of the windows, retching as he went.

"We had better leave," Noetos said. Guards had come, alerted by the screaming, and at least one had escaped. The fisherman had no sense that his power was about to falter, but he knew he could take nothing for granted. And Duon had clearly lost his own source of strength.

"Come on." He grabbed at the man's arm.

"Give me a moment."

As Duon composed himself, Noetos began to hear the moans of the dying. Not every stroke had been clean, and there were those who would take time to die. Others, perhaps, who would live. He hoped so. This story needed to become part of history.

And it was his key to gain entrance to Andratan. Oh yes, the hero of Raceme would have unfettered access to the Undying Man.

"We must go," Noetos insisted. The sooner he left the room, the less it would engrave itself on his memory.

"Which way?"

"The north door, then over the battlements and down to the Duchess's Walk. I'll explain the rest when we get there."

Noetos had chosen wisely, he knew. The main force of soldiers in the Summer Palace were garrisoned in the Underfort, on the landward or southern side of the palace. They would come up the Flame Path and through the south door to the ballroom. No doubt were coming at this moment.

Noetos and Duon encountered two servants on their way to the Duchess's Walk. Both women wailed at the sight of them; one fell at their feet and begged to be spared, the other ran down a side corridor. The bespattered fugitives ignored them both.

They burst into the open and realised it was full night. Noetos had lost track of time in the ballroom, and wondered if what he planned was possible.

"Hoy!" someone shouted from somewhere to their left. Yes, of course, they were visible from lower levels, though were probably little more than shadows. "Have you seen them?"

"Through the north door!" Noetos called back.

The one who had shouted to them was perhaps forty paces away and one level down, separated from the fugitives by a stone wall. There were steps, however, not far from where he had hailed them.

"Been there! No sign of them! Is it true they've slaughtered—" The ensuing silence was no doubt the man figuring out that the men he was speaking to must have come from the south door.

"Stand still!" he cried; bravely, Noetos thought.

"I've had enough of killing," Duon said quietly.

"As have I. Can you swim?"

"Yes. But not with a sword at my side."

"I'm not leaving this behind," Noetos said. He fingered the hilt of the Heirsword.

"Then we must hope our benefactors can assist us," Duon said. "Where is the water?"

To their left the soldier clattered up the stairs, and would be on them in a moment.

"Down there." Noetos pointed over the battlements. "I've done this before." *Only once, and that when you were a much younger and more foolish man.* "You must leap at least three paces outwards from the wall to clear the rocks."

"Rocks? Ah. How far down?"

"Does it matter? Into the dark, that's all we need to know."

"Then let us leap." The man stood on the crenellation, bunched his legs and jumped. *Not far enough.*

Noetos sighed, and followed the southerner over the edge.

CHAPTER 10

LAKE WOE

"THIS CAN'T GO ON."

Arathé sighed, stretching her aching limbs. *Morning.* Noetos was making his way home, so there were no immediate demands on the ragged remnants of her strength. Sleep, more sleep, was the thing. Weeks since she'd had anything approaching a full night's rest. Still, as Anomer continually reminded her, there were many others suffering.

Those others hadn't lost their mothers, though. *Well*, she amended, remembering the whirlwinds, *perhaps some of them have*.

"What can't go on?" she answered in her hybrid language. "The constant drain on our essenza? Weeks without sleep? Or five thousand Racemen scavenging the barren hills of northern Saros?"

Her brother grunted, a sour acknowledgment of their troubles. "All of them. But I meant the last. Children are hungry, which makes their parents frightened and angry. There have been raids on local villages. Some of the men have organised foraging parties, but I've heard they are little more than thieving squads. Understandable, given their sons and daughters are crying. But an hour ago I heard men talking about killing. Villagers have heard of the Neherian raid, and one group of locals somewhere west of here mistook a foraging party for the vanguard of the Neherian forces. There was a pitched battle. Dozens of men killed, apparently."

"What is Captain Cohamma doing about this?"

"Cohamma? A chicken with his head cut off. Half the time he asks where Father has gone, the rest he spends lamenting the loss of the governor and his own superiors. He's lost control, Arathé."

"He never had it. It was his decision to abandon Raceme two nights ago that surrendered the city to the Neherians."

Her brother shook his head. "I don't think so. Perhaps he didn't intend it, but his actions saved these five thousand Racemen. Imagine what might have happened had there still been resistance in the city when the Neherian army arrived."

"I'm more worried about the other battle."

"There's another battle? Oh, you mean the storm. Arathé, I never got the straight of that. Mustar tried to explain it to me—"

Arathé waved her hands at him. "Be quiet, be quiet. Mustar knows nothing."

"I know he likes you," Anomer grinned.

Teasing her, as he'd always done. She'd missed him the last two years, more than her parents, in truth. He had been her closest friend, two years younger than her but willing to assist in any scheme she came up with. He stole the eggs she needed to make her biscuits on the wooden floor of their Old Fossan home; they'd both thought the sun-warmed surface would be hot enough to bake the dreadful mixture. Mother had been angry, blaming Arathé, but Anomer admitted his part in the fiasco and shared the subsequent beating. When she had taken up with what he called "her giggly girls", he hadn't hung around her, like younger brothers often do. He'd found friends of his own, but always he and his sister made time for each other when the friends went home. And when their father became important in the community and her old friends no longer came to play, he looked to cheer her. As now.

"Mustar remembers a girl he liked, one among many," she signed to him. "I am no longer that girl. Let him discover that for himself. We have too much else to consider."

"Yes," Anomer agreed. *Such as how a storm can be sentient*, he thought to himself.

Earlier Arathé had explained in detail to her brother her arrival in Raceme. Little enough else to occupy them on their way north as part of the five thousand survivors of the "Raceme Massacre", as some were calling it. She wished her father had been party to her tale, but he'd gone off on an overwrought, dangerous tangent of his own, as always. After a mislaid sword! Continuing to regard his judgment as unquestionable; not bothering to tell them of his plans. Putting himself—and therefore everyone else, as it turned out—in danger.

Her story took a long time to tell. On that day in Fossa when she returned to them, she had last seen Anomer when finding herself unable to escape Fisher House via the kitchen window. She described to him how she could not avoid the Recruiters, ending up grappling with Ataphaxus in the hallway. Her strength was already low, weakened through months of abuse, leaving her especially vulner-

able to those who had used her. The Recruiter's forceful
attack drove through her feeble defence and paltry magic.
He struck her blade away and came at her with a knife he'd
picked up from the kitchen. The last image that flashed
across her mind as he stepped inside her desperate block
was of using that very knife to slice vegetables in preparing
a meal years ago, before all this had begun.

He had slammed into her shoulder, spinning her around,
then struck her below her shoulder blades; the knife burned
as it went in, and the power behind the blow drove her to
the ground. The world flashed blue, then black.

She let go of life.

And awoke on fire.

Blue flames flickered everywhere, running along her
arms, spouting from her mouth as she screamed. There was
no pain, only an incredible heat from the back of her head.
She recognised it, though she had never seen it before: a
vast infusion of magical power directed at her own body,
healing it. She stood, newly healed, and a kitchen knife
clattered to the floor, startling her. Then she remembered
how it had felt going in.

She had not known magicians had the ability to self-heal
even when unconscious. *So much I was not taught*, she told
Anomer. *Did I really do the right thing at Andratan when I
refused the water magic?*

He had said nothing, but she suspected he desired a
greater share of the magic himself.

After making sure there were no Recruiters in the house,
she had stumbled outside into a cloudy Fossan morning.
No, not clouds. Smoke. Her feet turned towards Old Fossa,
hoping that someone there would know where her family
was. Hoping that, with her assumed death, the Recruiters

had abandoned them and left the village—but deep inside knowing they would not leave this unresolved, and that her family had paid the price for the selfishness she had shown in seeking their help. They must have been taken or killed. Otherwise her body would surely not have been abandoned.

She met Mustar in the crowd down by the burning boats. Strangely, he'd recognised her even before she had begun what she thought would be a long and difficult explanation. In the midst of everything, this had melted her fear-frozen soul. He'd held her as she sobbed, found her a thin blanket and told her what he knew of the previous day's tumultuous events. Noetos a hunted criminal; Opuntia and Anomer taken as surety of his surrender.

Those putting out the fires had been the first to see the approaching sails. Some of the villagers fled, but most remained, mesmerised by the continuation of strange happenings in their village. Not wanting to miss the next event, not really believing the sails bode them ill. So it was that nearly the entire village was rounded up and questioned by the Neherians, and Arathé witnessed the sordid torture and deaths of some she knew—or had once known. Mustar counselled her to keep her identity secret, and to use her blanket to hide herself from the prying eyes of those who might remember a Recruiter's servant. He need not have worried. The villagers were too preoccupied with the disaster unfolding before them.

Sautea had been the one to secure their escape. It had been a risky, almost foolhardy plan, conceived in desperation. He signalled one of the Neherian captains and told him they were shipmates of this Noetos they were searching for, a disliked man, and offered to show the captain the

man's house and other likely places he might have hidden.
It had been the old man's hope they would be accompanied by only one or two Neherians, but a squad of six was
dispatched with the captain and the three supposed informants.

Unarmed, Sautea and Mustar tried to ambush the squad
in the great room of Fisher House. The Neherians reacted
swiftly, apparently ready for any trick, and for a moment
Arathé thought she was about to be struck down in her own
home for the second time in a matter of hours; but her head
had flashed white and she felt herself drawing power from
everyone in the room, Neherian and Fossan alike. She had
four of them disarmed and writhing on the ground before
the Neherians had recovered from their shock. Mustar and
Sautea didn't know one end of a sword from the other, but
the remaining Neherians ran like cowards.

Sautea led Mustar and Arathé to cover near Tipper
Bridge. The three Fossans watched, guilt-ridden and sorrowful, as their fellow villagers were bound and transferred
to waiting ships. Slowly and with many gestures, Arathé
told the two men what had been done to her, and what had
happened to her family when she sought their help. Mustar vowed to help her stay free and find her family, but
Sautea asked them to consider something far more important: warning the Fisher Coast that the Neherian fleet was
coming.

They waited with increasing impatience until darkness
offered them the cover they needed, then took the smaller
and least damaged of Noetos's two boats. It was a decision
fraught with risk, but Sautea and Mustar were excellent
sailors and kept close to shore. They could not keep pace

with the fleet, but they could skip past them when the Neherians hove to in Farsala Sida's shallow harbour.

And, as they did, the storm began stalking them.

It was a small thing to start with, battering them with fresh northerlies as they tacked east and west, trying to hug the coast. At the same time, the far side of the storm gave the Neherian fleet, sailing in deeper waters, easy passage northward. Every day the three Fossans tried to gain the next village before the Neherian fleet, and every day they failed. Every night they expended more energy than they could afford to pass the fleet, only to repeat the misery the next day. And every day the storm kept pace with them.

The storm then began attacking them—or, at least, that was how it seemed. Rain clouds tracked them northward, dumping prodigious amounts of water into their boat. Thin waterspouts would drift into their path, forcing them to seek shelter. They were peppered with hail the size of eggs, and their pale grey days were illuminated only by the lightning that walked across the water as though quartering their location.

No natural storm, then. Its path was too calculated; its position designed to minimise their progress while maximising that of the fleet. On top of this, it sucked at them as though drawing from their essenza. Perhaps it was; perhaps magicians from the Neherian fleet manipulated the weather against the small boat. Why not just crush them? *It takes a much greater magic to move the wind than to strike openly at a target*, Arathé had been told during her time in Andratan. What sort of magician lacked the presence to attack them directly?

During the long, exhausting voyage they wondered what had happened to the Fossans. Had they been thrown overboard? Unlikely. Transported south to Aneheri to begin a life of slavery? Possible, but if this was replicated at every village along the Fisher Coast there would soon be no ships left in the fleet. Most likely they were piled in the vessels' holds, suffering the vicissitudes of a stormy sea journey. North or south, they were still prisoners.

But this led to the question the three Fossans debated through the cold nights. Why would the Neherians wish to depopulate the Fisher Coast? Surely even a conqueror needed subjects to work the fields and tend the machines of civilisation? Apparently not, if the fleet's behaviour at Fossa was typical of what was happening along the coast.

And one other thought exercised their minds as they struggled against the storm with failing strength. Why had the Neherians been seeking Noetos?

Well, Arathé had reflected as she finished her tale by describing their final run into Raceme, borne like a leaf on the wind of the now giant storm, *at least now I know why*. Not that she could tell Sautea and Mustar the full story. The latter would be crushed to learn his famous and respected father had been a Neherian informant.

Who could anticipate their parents' pasts? Arathé and Anomer had known their father was different from other fathers in Fossa. He knew much more than other men, and there were hints in his words of lands and experiences far from the sheltered harbour that constrained Fossan lives. The man was shrouded in a twenty-year silence, refusing to answer any direct questions about the details of his own childhood: where he had been born, what conditions had been like growing up, and what had happened to his family. The things any normal family shared; things that became part of family history. But nothing had led them to expect a history as exotic and painful as that which their father had finally, reluctantly, described to them.

How did she feel about this history? Anomer was angry, she knew that. Deeply angry that he, the rightful heir of Roudhos—the rightful heir given that Noetos was the Duke of Roudhos—had been kept ignorant. Part of his identity had been stolen: her brother had a right to be angry. What would it have cost the man to have told his family? Was he worried that loose talk would bring the Neherians down upon them? As it turned out, they had been known. The Neherians had come anyway. And the inescapable fact was, had Noetos told his family of his origins and title, Opuntia would likely still be alive.

Alive, but frustrated. Arathé was realist enough to recognise that. To have been a duchess by claim but not by right; that would have been too much to bear.

"It's not really his fault," she signed, meaning her father, and provoking a growl from Anomer. She raised her eyebrows. *If he knew how much like our father he sounds when he does that, he'd tear out his tongue.*

"Not his fault?" Anomer did not try to read her mind— they allowed each other too much respect for that—but he stared at her as though trying to intuit her thoughts. "Had he remained true to the cause, we might well now be living in luxury in Aneheri."

"Brother, there is so much wrong with those words I don't know where to begin."

He grimaced and his shoulders dropped. "I know. It was our grandfather who turned his back on the rump of Roudhos. He might well have made a moral decision, though it's hard to see how staying loyal to the Neherian cause could have cost more lives. And had Father stayed in Aneheri he

would never have met Mother. Better for them undoubtedly, but not for us."

"But you're not happy about it."

"Are you?"

"No. I'm confused. I didn't see Mother die. It feels as
though we left her in Fossa, and if we returned, she would
be there waiting for us."

"I saw her die. I helped bury her. She died as a result of
our father's flaws: impatience, selfishness and an unwill-
ingness to share his burdens with others. He never thinks to
trust anyone. He is always alone in a sea of people."

"Perhaps if we had seen what he saw, we might feel the
same."

"Dear sister, I saw our mother run through by a Recruiter's blade because our father would not surrender. How can
you think I suffer less than he does?"

"Would you carve up a room full of defenceless people
to have your revenge?"

"Not even to save Fisher Coast would I do what our
father did," Anomer said. "I would have found some other
way."

"So. How do we live with this man?"

"Live with my father? As much as I love him dearly,
there's no living with him."

"You're right," she signed, her hands drooping with fa-
tigue. *More sleep, I need more sleep.* "There is no way this
can end well, is there?"

"No," Anomer said. "None at all."

"Want to talk to you," said a voice, a woman's voice, as
someone shook Arathé's shoulder. "Wake, please. I need
to talk."

"Leave her alone." Anomer came to her rescue. "She needs to sleep."

"I need more than sleep," Arathé said, using more voice and fewer gestures than normal. "But sleep is a necessary beginning."

"Sorry," the woman said awkwardly, as though the word was even less familiar than others in the language she struggled to use. *One of the southerners, one of Duon's companions. Lenares.* "Sorry. But we must talk."

"Very well," Arathé signed to Anomer, who translated for the persistent woman. "I'll hear your words."

"You . . ." the woman searched for the word, "you crossed, met, the hole in the world."

"I don't understand," Arathé signed to her brother.

Neither do I, he responded.

"Don't use the mind language," Arathé said. "We've used the power enough recently to bring that storm down on our heads."

"Do you mean the storm that afflicted Raceme? With the whirlwinds?" Anomer asked the southerner. "Is that what you mean by the hole in the world?"

"The storm was the hole," she said. "The hands of . . ." Again she struggled for the correct term. "Power. God. Gods."

"I'm not sure whether she means that any storm is a 'hole' or that this particular storm is the hand of a god," Arathé signed to her brother. "Interesting, though, that she sees the storm as important enough to talk about. She obviously doesn't think it is natural."

Is it just me, or does she seem a little . . . simple?

"She speaks our language after a fashion. Do you speak hers? Who is the simple one?"

"That's not fair," Anomer said out loud. *No, I mean she seems . . . differently focused. Look at her. She hasn't relaxed for a moment. No small talk. I've never seen eyes so intense—not even yours, big sister.*

"We need to hear your story, Lenares," Arathé said, in her combination of speaking and signing.

To her astonishment, the southern woman signed back. "Yes. I will tell you my story."

"She's picked up your language so soon?" Anomer said. "How is that possible?"

"I am special," Lenares said. "I am special," she signed, shocking them both.

"You are," the siblings said together.

First she gave them her story, a rambling affair lasting hours. The big black man called Torve joined her an hour or so into her telling, his eyes hooded, saying nothing other than to offer them food. The girl told an outlandish tale of another land, far, far to the south, of a race of men—races of men—the brother and sister had never heard about. The story took two parts: the thread of movement, telling who went where and did what; and the underlying revelations as to her own personality and her special gift. Both threads captured Arathé's imagination.

"You see things as numbers?" Anomer asked, also clearly entranced. "What numbers am I?"

"I am watching you, and your sister, since we came here. You glow like sleepy fire. You are both made up of many numbers, but four hundred and ninety-six is your central number. This a special number because—"

"Because it is perfect," Anomer finished dreamily. "Because it is the sum of its divisors. One plus two plus four plus eight plus sixteen plus thirty-one plus sixty-two plus one hundred and twenty-four plus two hundred and forty-eight. All beautiful numbers."

"Yes! Yes!" The girl leapt to her feet and jumped up and down excitedly, her language lapsing in the moment. "How know you this? You are cosmographer?"

"When he was a child he sat on the floor and wrote out lists of numbers on parchment," Arathé signed. "He never wanted to go outside and play."

Anomer laughed. "I still love numbers, but my father made it clear I was not to waste my life on them. He said the world had enough scribes."

"Not enough cosmographers though! I am the only one left."

The girl tapped her chest. Which, Arathé noticed, was well proportioned. In fact, the girl was quite a beauty, despite her obvious travel stains and some curious burn scars on her cheeks. Anomer's cheeks turned faintly red: he had noticed too.

You blush prettily, my brother.

He ignored her, and cleared his throat. "So we have a perfect number. What does this mean?"

"All parts of you are in perfect proportion," Lenares said.

Anomer's blush deepened, and Arathé barked a strangled laugh. The girl realised she had said something inadvertent and tsked in impatience.

"Of you, the real you. Inside you. Your thinking, your strength, heart, all nine parts in balance." She frowned, and leaned closer to him. Disconcertingly close, invading his personal space as though she had every right to be there. "Or they were; but not now. The boy here is thinking and not glowing. Thinking bad—bitter?—thoughts. Such thoughts will damage his heart."

"You can see this how?"

"I cannot tell you how. There are not the words even in my tongue-speak. But you," she swung around to address Arathé alone, "have another number in your head, and it does not belong there. Like Duon. The same number. It is a palindrome, one hundred and ninety-one. The number of the worm. You and Duon both have worms in your heads."

They tried to get Lenares to expand on this revelation, but had little success. The girl seemed piqued at this, unreasonably angry, and Arathé wondered again at her brother's initial assessment of her as simple. Perhaps. But Arathé knew enough from the link between Duon and herself to realise the strange southern girl had uncanny knowledge, and she wished to explore it further. But the girl's reluctance baulked her. Perhaps when Duon returned.

Eventually they managed to get Lenares back to her story, and she described a vast army gathered by a cruel emperor for the purposes of a northern conquest. The cosmographers were part of this army, and the girl digressed again to explain their role in Elamaq society. After several tangential remarks, she told them how Captain Duon led the army north into an ambush and destruction, from which only four people escaped. These four wandered and were eventually snatched up by a hole in the world, then deposited in Raceme just as the whirlwinds ceased.

Hands of the gods. Holes in the world. Storms . . .

Arathé wondered.

She wondered about a storm that seemed to behave as if it had intelligence, or was guided by someone powerful. That herded herself, Mustar and Sautea, confining them to the coast and driving them into Raceme. That reached down to inflict whirlwinds on Raceme, targeting herself and anyone mind-speaking her.

She wondered about a hole in the world that herded a great southern army into an ambush. That drove the handful of survivors north into a place called Nomansland, then reached down a godlike hand and plucked them into its open throat.

She wondered. She wondered why, if she was as clever as her tutors had claimed, it had taken her so long to begin putting things together.

You and Duon have worms in your heads.

Worms. Planted by someone in Andratan. Drawing the attention of powerful magical beings, called the Son and the Daughter by Lenares. Undoubtedly southern inventions, labels for things the southerners did not understand, but that there was a reality behind the superstitious beliefs Arathé didn't doubt for a moment.

Worms that speak. A voice that worms its way into our heads, gaining our attention, guiding our thoughts and actions. An apt description, Lenares.

The southern woman was undoubtedly strange, but Arathé found herself liking her. More, respecting her. There was not the slightest hint of magical ability in the girl, but she had an otherworldliness about her, a level of intensity that appeared to give her insights at least as valuable as magic. She seemed to have few social skills; instead, she showed herself willing to interrupt others, to override them, to disregard their feelings as unimportant in the quest for what she considered truth. This was the unintended but clear subtext woven throughout her story: she was special, and because she was special she was disliked and laughed at. In response she behaved directly, which those around her mistook for obnoxiousness. Yet what Lenares wanted most of all was to be taken seriously.

Don't we all, Arathé thought, reflecting on her father.

Which thought reminded her. Leaving Anomer to talk with Lenares and Torve, Arathé focused on her father's thread, still burning brightly in her mind, and that of Duon, a pale star beside that of her father.

Are you making progress? she asked them.

Of a sort, came Duon's answer in his slow, gentle thoughts. *We were just about to bespeak you. I'm still limping, and your father is being driven to distraction. We have a small problem, you see.*

Oh? What is it? Can we help?

Well, yes, not help so much, but be mindful. We think we're being followed.

You ought to be a match for anyone following you. Just let me know what we can do for you.

Her father's gruff sending overrode Duon's thoughts. *No match for what appears to be the entire Neherian army, girl. They're catching us with every step.*

"It's more than a limp," Noetos growled, sparing a glance at Duon's trailing leg. "You'll be fortunate not to lose it."

"Let me try to put some weight on it . . . Ah! What ought I to have told them?"

He leaned back into Noetos's shoulder, jabbing his makeshift crutch fiercely into the ground.

"The truth. That you've smashed your leg to pieces, slowing us to such a degree our pursuers are likely to catch us before we reach the others."

"It's not smashed to pieces, friend Noetos, just broken in a couple of places."

"Of course. Though "broken" seems an inadequate word to describe *that*, friend Duon," Noetos said, indicating the grey skin of the man's shin. "Months to heal, especially if your nameless magician continues to hide himself."

"Then leave me, as I ask," Duon countered. "I'll hunker down somewhere. Someone can come back to get me later."

"Dig yourself a hole and cover yourself over with dirt. That'll save anyone returning."

What was the point in this discussion? Noetos had told Duon he would not be abandoned, and that was that. Anything further was a waste of the breath he needed to help the southerner.

The two men had discussed leaving Duon behind when they'd caught sight of Raceme from the top of a limestone ridge. A line of glittering sparks led out from the Water Gate, pointing up the north road; the reflection of sunlight on steel. Someone had taken charge of the army, after all. Noetos had hoped the decapitation of the Neherian leadership would have sent anyone remaining with aspirations home to consolidate their position, but it had been a forlorn hope.

The Neherians were more disciplined than that. And, he guessed, no one would want to be the man returning to Aneheri to answer the hard questions that might well attend this debacle. The public would demand blood, and the hanging trees would be full for weeks. So here came the army. Part of it, Neotos judged; but the longer they waited, the more he mistrusted that judgment. Eventually they turned their backs on the distant view of the city, from where soldiers still issued like ants from a damaged hill.

The army might not be following them, of course. It might well be continuing the Neherian march northward. But Noetos considered this highly unlikely.

He had found Duon lying unmoving on the rocks below the Summer Palace. His own leap had nearly foundered: he had plunged into the water with a breath-loosening smack, and a moment later scraped his elbows on the rocky seabed. How had he ever made this leap as a child? He had avoided hitting a rocky outcrop—the Thinking Seat, the local lads had called it; he'd sat on it many times—by less than an armspan. Had forgotten it was there. Duon, however, must have struck it with his trailing leg.

Should have made the leap a few paces to the right, he'd thought as he examined the whey-faced man. Duon tried to lie still, tried to keep quiet, but his injuries were serious. If it had been the man's own fault Noetos would have left him there. No question. Especially when it became clear that Duon's magician would not—or could not—offer healing.

Noetos was an excellent swimmer, unlike most fishermen he knew. Had learned in these very waters as a child. He had never tried to drag someone else though, and even finding a relatively efficient method—on his back, Duon's head on his chest—did not make it easy. The Raceme children had measured the distance to Rings Beach in minutes, but it took Noetos hours.

For every moment of those endless hours he fretted over swords and sharks. So far to come for the damnable Heirsword, and it threatened to drag him down into the black depths, along with Duon's blade. The shark-patrolled depths. The port always used to attract wideheads and big-mouths, especially in spring and autumn, but the fishing fleet was out somewhere, hopefully having dragged the sharks with them. He thought of dropping the swords, but it would be then, of course, that the sharks would come to inspect the taste of blood Duon's leg offered them. So he kept them, though they impeded his progress.

There ought to have been a detachment of Neherian soldiers waiting on the beach to take them into custody. He would have ordered it. Perhaps the absence of such a detachment spoke much for the disorganisation in the palace. Certainly they had heard intermittent shouting echoing down the cliffs. Chaos, Noetos hoped.

He hauled the waterlogged southerner onto the stony beach and inspected the leg by feel. Broken. He didn't need Duon's gasps to confirm that. An interminable time to find suitable pieces of driftwood in almost complete darkness, to splint and to use as a cane; then, just as they readied themselves for the long journey north, the moon came out from behind thick clouds.

Oh, thanks.

Noetos had tried bespeaking his children, but they were no doubt asleep, exhausted from the drain on their energies. He had not believed such power was possible: it had lasted far longer than during his original attempt to escape. None available now, however. Duon's benefactor was still not responding, probably also asleep.

Their initial progress northward was frantic, far too fast to be sustainable, but they had no choice, had to be well away from Raceme by first light. By the time they called a halt Duon was bleeding from the armpit, and Noetos was forced to remove his shirt and tear strips from it to make a pad to support the cane. More time wasted.

Noon had come and gone, and now Noetos's head was filled with calculations.

Somewhere north of Buntha, a mile or so perhaps. The army will halt for water at Buntha. An hour or so at the longest and they will be on the move again. Six, maybe seven, hours until sunset. The Racemen fugitives are . . . he thought carefully . . . *inland of Porasen, maybe as far north as Regar's farm. We can't make it ahead of the army.*

Yes, you can, came his daughter's cool voice. *We've been helping you since soon after dawn. How far have you come?*

Maybe twelve miles.

More like fifteen, we think. In seven hours, along a hilly road, with only three good legs. We can speed things up a little more, but it will cost us.

Is this a good idea? We are bringing the Neherian army down on top of you.

They were coming anyway. How could they have known which way you would travel, except they already knew roughly where we were? They expect to find you here, with us. Whether you are actually here or not is irrelevant.

So how is Cohamma preparing?

He is not. He doesn't believe us.

What?

He's not even here. Anomer's voice. *He's just left on horseback with a few of his cronies, off to "requisition supplies from Porasen" as he puts it.*

Wait. We're doing this wrong. Noetos thought a moment, his stomach sinking. *Idiot!* he told himself. Then to Anomer: *Why can't we send Seren and the others south with their donkeys?*

Oh, his children both said.

Half a day lost through his foolishness. So dependent so quickly on his children's magic, he'd forgotten he had sworn men. Seren, Tumar and Dagla from Eisarn Pit, and their donkeys. *They still have their donkeys?*

I'll ask, Anomer sent. A few minutes later he returned to Noetos's mind: *No donkeys. They were stabled behind the inn in Raceme and likely taken by the storm. But there are three perfectly good animals here with the refugees, and two of their owners are willing to lend them. Keep coming north. Seren will be with you soon.*

By mid-afternoon Duon had been secured to a travois ingeniously constructed by Seren and Noetos's two remaining sworn men, and the fisherman listened with half his mind's ear as his son berated him for continually ignoring the talents of others. Well-reasoned, with the best of intentions. *You don't understand*, Noetos wanted to say in response. *Trust leads to betrayal.*

Anomer must have been able to read the thought, but said nothing in response. Wisely, Noetos considered.

The Neherians overtook them just before dusk.

The signs of the approaching army were manifold. Thousands afoot—Noetos had no real idea how many, but that seemed as good a guess as any—attracted scavenging birds and created dust clouds on dry roads. Noetos used these signs to tell how fast the army travelled in relation to his own men, and took his group off the road and into shelter amidst thick bracken well before the Neherians caught them.

The army had scouts foraging ahead, but they seemed more interested in finding a campsite with convenient access to water than in uncovering spies.

About fifteen hundred, Noetos reported to Anomer as the last of them, the old and footsore, trailed past under the baleful eye of a sergeant obviously tasked with keeping any recalcitrant soldiers up to task. *Has Seren arrived yet?*

The canny mining foreman and he had spent a fruitful hour chatting, and as a result Seren had left the others behind and jogged back towards the Racemen camp.

He needs to get there soon, Noetos added on hearing the negative response. *Are you on the move?*

I don't like your plan, Anomer said. *It's no better than your ambush at Saros Rake.*

It's not my plan, son, and you know it. I described the location and Seren filled in the details. It is his plan. Time you overcame your bitterness, Anomer.

Noetos had wondered if non-verbal communication could come through the mind-link, and his suspicions were confirmed by the wordless anger that flooded his mind. *So the ocean calls the river wet!*

You're barely a brook, lad, much less a river. Come, suggest a viable alternative that confronts the certainty of contact with the Neherians and protects our vulnerable women and children. I'll listen.

That's just it, Father. There is no alternative to flight. Our trick works against a few. But we cannot oppose a thousand.

If all goes well, we won't have to. Just concentrate on getting the refugees moving.

Very well. And Cohamma? What if he has betrayed us?

That, Noetos admitted, *I have no plan to deal with.*

The moon had risen behind a thin wash of cloud by the time Noetos gained the relocated refugee camp. A cheer went up from around a few of the hearths as he strode past, leading the donkey, whose ears twitched at the noise. Arathé hugged him, then explained what they had done for him during his slaughter of the Neherian court, and what it had cost the Racemen.

"You drew on their essenza? A thousand and more?"

"I've never heard of it being done on such a scale," his daughter signed. "I am not experienced in magic, but I thought the principle should hold. If a magician can draw a great deal from a few, why not draw a little from a great many?"

"We did not expect such widespread symptoms," Anomer said, describing the superficial cuts and bleeding suffered by many of the refugees. "Our reading is, the more wholly someone gave of themselves, the more seriously they were affected. We think there are a few here with genuine water magic abilities, and they suffered most. One elderly woman near bled to death from a cut to her arm, and we have half-a-dozen neck wounds being tended to."

Noetos had trouble interpreting the stare that accompanied these words. His son wanted some kind of response from him . . .

"You might want to thank these people," Anomer said eventually, his voice carrying more than a hint of condemnation.

"Of course," Noetos replied, but in truth the thought hadn't occurred to him. *Why not? Have you become so fixated on your goal you've forgotten people?* That was what his children would say.

There would be plenty of time later to thank those who had suffered for him. Once they were safe. Right now he had to check on Seren's progress; the Neherians would be here soon after dawn.

A disturbance some way off drew his worried attention. *Has the camp been found by a scout?* He forced himself to relax. The Neherians would know where they were by the same signs he used to track them. Nothing to be done for it.

A moment later Captain Cohamma and a couple of his soldiers came stumbling across their cooling hearth. "What yer bin up to?" the captain asked, leaning forward. "Don't recall y' bein' here when we d'cided t' make camp back there. Cain't camp here. The lake's poison."

"I haven't got time to argue, Captain," Noetos replied. "Seren, hold him."

"Whaa?" The captain opened his toothless mouth in surprise as Noetos's sworn men secured him and his soldiers, tying ropes around their wrists and ankles. "You gunna leave us here fer the 'herians to make sport wiv?"

"No. Anomer here will explain to you what we're doing. I have more important business to attend to." He turned on his heel and walked off.

"High 'n' mighty one, isn't he," he heard the captain say. He waited for his children to contradict Cohamma, but either their reply was too quiet for him to hear or they chose not to answer. He'd heard nothing further by the time he was out of earshot and it did little to improve his mood.

A pale dawn revealed the Neherians marching through the notch in the hills surrounding the lake. Lake Woe it was known as by the locals, but marked as Turtle Lake on the maps of the Roudhos dukedom. Noetos was gambling a considerable amount on those old maps being the source of Neherian knowledge.

Lake Woe had no outlet. It was set among rocky gold-bearing hills, with the one relatively flat area, on the northern shore, occupied by the refugees. Perhaps half a mile across, the lake was fed by ten or so small streams, some of which flowed only in the rainy season of late autumn and early winter. As Noetos watched the Neherians file down towards the opposite shore, a gentle breeze stirred the thin mist draped across the surface of the water.

"Looks enticing," Anomer said, grimacing.

Noetos grunted a reply. "You sure you found all the warning signs?" he asked one of the locals they had rounded up during the night.

"Yar." The man was actually chewing on a straw, Noetos noted. A walking cliché. At least he was relaxed, which was more than could be said for most of those gathered here.

"Go," Noetos said to Cohamma. Against Noetos's better judgment the man had been restored to command over a hundred or so guardsmen and soldiers, all that had survived from the Neherian attack and subsequent whirlwinds. He had needed the captain's men, needed every man he could get, and therefore needed the captain, as nervous as he made Noetos feel.

The order made its way down the chain, and the soldiers burst out from the refugee camp in an untidy wave, making for the ridge above them. Feigning panic.

The Neherians will sound a trumpet. The excited baying of what sounded like a dozen trumpeters echoed around the basin as he finished the thought. *Predictable thus far.*

But they did not remain so. Some stupid commander barked an order audible across the lake, and the Neherian

forces split in two. Half the army set off in a westward direction around the shore, half eastward. As easily as that,
the plan foundered.

"No, no, what are they doing?" Noetos shook his head.
"Neherians never split their forces. Arathé, we're going to
need your help after all. Anomer, your sword." Brusque orders, positioning his loved ones like pieces in a game.

Around the lake the Neherians came, silent save for the
tramp of steel-shod boots on stone.

"Could they have guessed what I planned?" he wondered aloud.

"Seren," Anomer said shortly. Noetos turned to him
quizzically. "What Seren planned."

"Aye."

The creeks came down from gold claims up in the
notched and ragged hills. Noetos had been here a few times
as a child, the guest of his father's castellan, whose own
grandfather had been the first to discover gold in recover-
able quantities in these hills. Most of the profit had been
taken quickly, but some miners had stayed on, eking out an
existence of sorts from what remained. Such work required
creative extraction methods, and Noetos remembered an
intricate system at the head of one of these creeks: water
races and wooden aqueducts supplying a sluicing operation
with water. A dam had been built to hold the water until it
was required. The locals had confirmed its existence and
good repair. Late in his sleepless night, Noetos had been
escorted a mile up the wide eastern valley to see the dam,
and pronounced himself satisfied.

Seren and the Eisarn miners were up there now. Their
lookout would give them the signal when the Neherians
passed a predetermined spot.

Noetos left them to it. He had to. A wooden bridge spanned the largest of the western creeks. Deep but narrow, the creek could perhaps be leapt by a determined man, but such a man would need to divest himself of armour and sword, and would take a moment to recover. The Neherians would try the bridge, at least until Noetos and his son made them fear it.

"It's a holding action at best," Noetos told Anomer as they ran for the bridge. "I don't like our odds. What possessed them to split their forces?"

A loud boom echoed around the hills. For a minute or so the Neherians halted, both parts of their army trying to see what had caused the noise. *Come on, don't wait too long.* Noetos willed the eastern half of the army to move. The western half, of course, could remain there all day and make him happy doing so. Of course, the western army moved first.

The refugees moved towards the eastern side of the lake, as though in a panic. *They might well be in a panic.*

Noetos himself felt nauseous. There seemed so little chance of success now, and their flea-bites on the Neherian hides would serve only to anger them. The refugees would be slaughtered, and the blame would be his.

"Come on, come on," he said, willing the Neherians on the far shore to move forward, while at the same time wishing he could discourage those on his side of the lake.

The first Neherians eased themselves down into the eastern creek bed. Perhaps a hundred paces away the refugees waited.

It had been a good plan. *No*, Noetos admitted. It had *sounded* like a good plan. But no plan involving vastly inferior forces had much chance of succeeding. Not if the enemy avoided the subterfuge.

The Neherians to the east had begun clambering out of the creek. *What has happened to the flood?* At least fifty of them were already up on the flat land and advancing towards the refugees, who now backed away in terror, knowing something had gone wrong.

Damn, Cohamma, release your soldiers!

He could spare no further thought for the eastern shore. The other half of the army now approached the wooden bridge. With a sigh, Noetos stepped out from behind a rock and strode to the middle of the bridge.

Eager shouts told him he had been seen. Fearful shouts followed, indicating he'd been recognised. Good. A last glance behind: the eastern creek was finally filling up, but far too slowly. And not with the rush of water Seren had promised. A few Neherians lost their footing, but in nowhere near sufficient numbers to create the chaos he'd hoped for.

And still Cohamma held his soldiers back. An awful suspicion began to form in Noetos's mind. *Cohamma has fled, taking his soldiers with him. Or worse, he has betrayed us to the Neherians. Where did he go this afternoon?*

The soldiers on this side of the lake were behaving cautiously. Clearly the stories had circulated throughout the army; even more clearly, they had been exaggerated. Not that they needed much exaggeration. Noetos imagined the effect that ballroom would have had on anyone seeing it.

A shouted command. The front rank knelt, and archers emerged from behind them. They drew and fired in a moment.

"Anomer! Can you do anything?"

From the buzzing in Noetos's head, the boy and Arathé were already acting. Arrows began to clatter around them, but those coming too close caught fire. The arrowheads dropped to the ground short of their target. A second volley was dealt with in the same way, but Noetos noticed some untouched arrows landed extremely close. One thunked into the wood two paces from him.

"That's all we can raise, Father," Anomer said.

Someone in the western flank made a decision. Shouts rang out. The Neherians formed up—and turned on their heels. Began marching back around the lake.

Leaving Noetos and Anomer in limbo. They could not rush back to aid the refugees—if they left the bridge, the Neherians would surely return and cross it, surrounding them. They had to wait until the army was sufficiently far around the lake that they were committed to their new course.

Perhaps that was all their commander wanted to do.

The vanguard of the eastern army was now among the rapidly scattering refugees. "Father! We have to go!" Anomer cried. "Now!"

He was right. Noetos took to his heels.

The next few minutes were hell.

A gut-busting sprint back to where the refugees were already being cut down, their desperate pleas ignored. Beaten, stabbed, sliced. Noncombatants. Men, women, children. Screams. Terror—and horror as the full measure of Noetos's complacency, his misjudgment, was sheeted home.

He engaged the nearest Neherian and slew him without recourse to Arathé's magic. Automatic now. Decision: protect his daughter or go forward to drive the Neherians back?

Which would save most lives? He went forward, leaving his daughter with Anomer and the southerners, knowing on this day his every decision was likely cursed.

Just in front of him a woman raised her arm to shield her children. It was taken off above the elbow by an armoured warrior. Her screech ended as the same sword was shoved into her face. As her two boys stared wide-eyed and uncomprehending at their mother's bloodied, still-twitching corpse, the warrior set to work on them.

Indiscriminate payback for what Noetos had done to them. Blood for blood, atrocity for atrocity. On this small patch of level ground, the full fruit of his revenge fell from the vine and rotted.

He threw himself into the battle, uncaring of his own life. Unencumbered by armour, he used his speed advantage to strike at knees, necks, helms, visors. A full step back, then a surge to his right and a downward chop, taking the legs out from the warrior busy withdrawing his blade from a boy's body. Sword held high, blocking two separate strokes. Half-jab left into a visor, a quick withdraw amidst spurting blood, and two quick raps with the hilt against the helm of another. A blade scraped down his leg, taking off a strip of skin. He saw but did not feel the blow. Anomer beside him, moving incredibly quickly, using his Wordweave to slow his foes. Within moments the field cleared in front of the pair as the Neherians found easier opponents.

Dozens, no, hundreds of Racemen on the ground, wounded, dead or dying.

"Drive them back, force them into the lake!" Noetos called.

There were perhaps twenty defenders in all, most armed with swords, none armoured, trying to hold a line against a hundred or more attackers. More Neherian soldiers were crossing the flooded stream to join the battle. Others moved to outflank Noetos and his pitiful band. It was he who was being forced back. He who would soon be encircled. He who would fall.

Where is Cohamma?

The Neherian in front of him dropped to the ground without a hand laid on him. Noetos paused, and looked for the arrow or spear; but saw none. To his right, another. There, a third. And others screaming in their helms or casting them off.

What madness is this? If it is sorcery, I feel nothing. Yet his heart lifted as the Neherian line wavered.

Then collapsed.

"The water!" one soldier called. "There is something in the water! Tell them to keep out—"

Noetos ended the man's words with a swipe of his sword, then took time in the midst of everything to strip off the man's segmented leg armour, hacking at the leather straps until the metal came free. The man's legs were covered in weeping, bloody sores, as though something had corroded his skin.

Seren. He'd found something up in the hills and added it to the water.

"Forward!" Noetos roared, and as one the few Racemen charged at the Neherians. Back the attackers were driven, back, back, cowed by the stories about this man, the slaughter of the Summer Palace passed fearfully from company to company; and by the agonising pain seizing them, which naturally they connected to the man's sorcerous magic. Back until they stumbled down a short slope and into Lake Woe.

Where the accumulated acids and foul effluvia of decades of ruinous mining awaited them.

Yet not a victory. Most of the Neherian army remained unfought, and now Noetos had to worry about Cohamma and his hundred troops. When would they come down from the hills to bring death to their fellow citizens?

No, not a victory. Not with at least a third of the refugees turned from people into bloodied corpses.

Seren and his men appeared just as the last of the Neherians withdrew beyond the death-filled creek. Few of their adversaries realised it had been the acid-thick water that had done the damage, and so in ignorance had waded the creek in retreat. Howls of pain came from the doubly afflicted, a sound both horrifying and pleasant.

"It worked," the miner said, beaming.

Noetos cuffed him. He could no more have stopped the blow than the words that followed. As Seren got to his feet, stunned and shocked, Noetos said: "Go and tell that to those Racemen, fallen because we overestimated our own cleverness."

"I only see those we saved," the miner said stubbornly, not giving an inch.

"And I see the Neherian army preparing a second assault," Anomer said. "We should give them our attention now, and save recriminations for later. Father, I have a message from Arathé. She wonders if you would lay your stone carving aside for now, as it prevents her strengthening you. You had her worried half to death."

"She supplied me with nothing?" Noetos said, incredulous. "I felt as energised as I did in the Summer Palace."

Nevertheless, he drew out the huanu stone, looked left and right, then walked over to where Duon lay.

"I've never been on a battlefield before without the ability to defend myself," the southerner said to him. "But you showed strong. Your daughter has obviously recovered."

"I don't know, friend. This carving prevented her contacting me. I need to place it in the hands of someone trustworthy who is not magically talented."

The girl Lenares put out her hand. "Give it to me," she said peremptorily. "I need to study it anyway."

Noetos narrowed his eyes, but Duon nodded, so he surrendered the huanu stone into the girl's fine hands. *Trust. It always finds me out.*

The girl's pretty eyes narrowed and she lifted a hand to her temple. "Oh," she said. "It's coming back."

"What, Lenares?" Duon asked.

"The hole. It comes. Swiftly. I have a tie to it. We need to . . . I don't know what."

Duon lifted his head and stared into the sky. "How long?"

"Soon," she said. "Now."

"Can you spare your friends?" Noetos asked Duon, indicating the other two southerners. "The Neherians will return, no doubt along the western shore this time. I see no hope of final escape, but we . . ."

Beside Captain Duon, one of the southerners—the mercenary, Duon had called him—began to grunt, as though something inside was trying to get out.

The captain jabbered to the man in his own language, but the man ignored him, intent on his pain.

"Did he touch the water?" Noetos asked Duon.

"He was here with us the whole time. Said he was protecting me."

"Then what . . ."

Without warning the man stood, put his hands to his head, spat bile on the ground and began running towards the hills behind them at great speed.

"Coward," Noetos said.

"No, not him," Duon replied. "He's a mercenary, yes, but I've never seen him flinch or admit any kind of weakness."

"Then what's afflicted the man?"

"I have no idea."

But whatever it was began to affect others around the lake, Neherian and Racemen alike. Soldiers dropped to their knees, hands over their ears or held against their stomachs, some heaving. Refugees whimpered or screamed. Noetos felt it as a low rumble that tore at his stomach and bowels. Earthquake? No, the ground remained steady under his feet. Something was wrong with his eyes, though. Weird colours flickered across his field of vision as though it was raining dye. Others were similarly affected, if their sudden eye-rubbing was evidence. Around them stones started rattling. Earthquake, then. Though why were the rocks and stones flickering, lapped by blue flames as though a new, higher lake was forming? Could rocks burst into flame? Or had some flammable chemical from the gold mines caught fire?

"Get back! Get back from the water!" The warning came simultaneously from three or four hoarse throats.

Noetos threw a glance at the lake and saw the water surging around a central vortex, lifting into the misty air, extruded by some invisible hand. The surface of the water had definitely caught fire.

"The hole!" yelled a woman's voice. Lenares. "The hole in the world!"

The basin ignited.

Pale blue flame exploded out from the centre of the lake with a thump, rolling across the water in every direction. Noetos ran along with everyone else, though he knew— they must all know—it was hopeless.

The flame hit.

And passed through.

The fisherman took a series of deep, gasping breaths with lungs he'd expected to be full of fire. Fire that now swept up the slope and winked out. The chain of events had proved too much for many of the refugees, who fell to the ground in fear, clearly wondering why they still lived. A wonder Noetos shared.

"Fisher." Bregor, tugging at his arm.

Not fear. Shock. The lake was empty of water. The mist had dissipated. In its place, fire-dried bare earth—and, incongruously, a boat, half-buried in the earth, with a number of figures clambering out of it. Stumbling on the stone-dry ground, struggling forward.

No one spoke as the strangely robed figures climbed onto the flat beside where the lake used to be, and approached the first of the refugees.

"Excuse me," said one of the figures, an extraordinarily tall man with a rich voice at odds with the dirt clinging to his feet and legs. "Can anyone tell me where we are?"

CHAPTER 11

INTERSECTIONS

ARATHÉ HEARD THE ROAR OF the flames and waited to die. She wondered what death by fire would be like. Painful would be the least of it, she was sure, worse than the last time she had died. Then she saw the flames roll towards her and relaxed a little. They had the same appearance, the same feel, as those that had covered her after she was stabbed in Fisher House.

Nevertheless she tensed involuntarily as the blue fire flashed over her, leaving her and the rest of the group untouched. Yet the feeling of dread did not leave her. If anything, it settled more heavily on her as the flames departed.

Duon had seemingly not even seen the fire. "What was that?" he asked, struggling to lift himself from the sickly yellow grass.

Anomer turned from facing the hills. "Magical fire. I would say it was beyond belief, but it's merely apace with everything else that has happened since . . . well, since your people came to Raceme, I suppose."

Duon frowned in response, but said nothing.

Arathé signalled her agreement with her brother. "Magical fire and a questing mind, or more than one. Can you feel them?" she asked Anomer. "No, don't seek them out. And don't use mind-talk. At least one of them doesn't like us, remember?"

Two, maybe three, enormous presences hovered over the basin. Actually, "over" wasn't the best word for what they were doing. "Within", perhaps, as though they occupied the too-small spaces between her muscles and her veins. Confined and trying to get out. Beside her, the girl Lenares was doubled over, moaning and retching. The curly-haired black southerner leaned over her supportively, muttering in the soft-edged southern language. A few refugees huddled together, obviously suffering the effects of the weight of these manifestations. The vast majority of the crowd, though battered, scared and confused, clearly could sense nothing.

The hole in the world, Lenares had called it. She really must talk more with the strange southern girl. One hole at least, certainly more than one hole-maker. Hole-makers with a purpose; one that seemed to involve them. A purpose wider than the conflict over the Fisher Coast, as evidenced by the presence of the southerners, pulled from their homeland by some impatient power. Game pieces, just like the Neherians—and the Fossans.

As if conjured by thoughts of her home town, Bregor, the Fossan Hegeoman, bustled into the centre of their group. "What happened to Cohamma?" he demanded, as though anyone there could tell him. As though it was possible to think while being pressed from all sides by unseen powers. "What's happened to the Neherians? And who are *those* people?" This last was accompanied by a gesture towards the lake.

Or what used to be the lake. Something had happened to it. Despite the pain in her head, Arathé found her eyes drawn to the gaping hole, an empty eye socket with the liquid scooped out. Where had the water gone?

Bregor went over to where Noetos stood, blood congealing on his Roudhos sword. "Fisher," he said, directing the gaze of Arathé's father to the group of tall, bedraggled figures emerging from the lake bed.

The tallest among them spoke for a few seconds in a language unknown to Arathé.

After a pause, he spoke again, using the Bhrudwan common tongue. "Excuse me, can anyone tell me where we are."

Arathé sensed something, a great power, but not the same as the overwhelming presences; this was much sharper, more narrowly focused. Without a word, she pulled Duon to his feet. Anomer guessed her intent and brought the southerner his crutch.

"Lake Woe," her father replied guardedly, and the man nodded his head like a wading bird dipping for a fish.

"A day's hard walking north of Raceme on the Fisher Coast," the man said in the voice of an aristocrat, then added, "And a month or more south of Malayu. In Bhrudwo, at least."

Some of those with him nodded or shook their heads. He repeated his words in another language, eliciting groans from the rest.

One of their number collapsed suddenly, one moment standing, the next on his face in the dirt, insensate. The tall man kicked him, hard, in the ribs. "Witness the architect of our misfortune," he said angrily. The man on the ground groaned and stirred.

One of the figures, a woman, said something to the tall man. It sounded like she was pleading or excusing the collapsed man, but she made no move to assist him.

Another tall man, the first man's grandfather perhaps, put a restraining hand on the man's arm and shook his head as he spoke to him.

"Ah, the legendary Dhaurian energy," the first man said, more than a hint of mockery in his voice. "Always ready to ignore the obvious and preserve the status quo."

"Enough," Noetos ordered, and the bickering stopped. "You emerge in the midst of a battlefield in a burst of unnatural flame, and then spend your time arguing with each other? Declare yourselves!"

The second tall man muttered in the other language, likely translating for those who did not speak the Bhrudwan common tongue. Which begged the question of why they did not speak it.

Arathé shuddered. Her father could not know that at least two of these people likely possessed the ability to destroy him where he stood, if she sensed their power correctly. Be *easy*, she warned him in her mind-speech.

The result would have been comical had matters not been so tense. Seven heads turned in her direction, three of them from the group newly emerged from Lake Woe. And three—definitely three—hidden presences turned their crushing attention towards her.

"Don't think your strong thoughts," said Lenares into the silence. Though not strong, her voice was audible to everyone gathered there. "The holes in the world will hear you, and they will destroy us all."

"You are right," Arathé signalled her. "We must talk about this."

The girl smiled triumphantly. "You need me," she said in her improving Bhrudwan. "Everyone needs me. Only I can see what is happening."

"Well, I certainly cannot," Noetos growled. "Nor can I keep up with this confusion of languages. I want answers in the language of this soil."

He turned his attention to the newcomers. "No answers for us, friends? Are you Neherians? Neherian magicians, perhaps?"

A shorter, but still impressive, man—a soldier, surely, by his bearing—took a pace towards Arathé's father, babbling as he did so.

"Fair point, Robal," said the tall man. Then to Noetos: "Forgive him; he did not understand your request. He asks what battle you refer to. Has there been fighting?"

"Aye, behind you are those who would slay defenceless women and children," Noetos replied.

The newcomers turned as one. Arathé followed their gaze across the empty basin and beheld the Neherians in disarray. Less than half their army still stood. Bodies had nearly blocked the poisoned stream, and were strewn between there and the southern end of the lake, tracing the line of their retreat. The faint sounds of suffering drifted across the lake bed, mixing eerily with those closer by.

There was no doubt that further retreat would be called when the Neherians worked out what had happened to them.

So much agony, so much death, and Arathé had no idea why. Had not been given enough time to think it through.

Perhaps there was no answer; perhaps the puzzle was missing too many pieces.

"Neherians," the tallest newcomer said. "What are they doing so far north?"

"You continue to evade my questions," Noetos observed. "Do I have to slaughter unarmed men?"

"Yes, and no. Yes, I will continue to evade your questions, and no, you cannot harm us." This said with absolute confidence. "I can assure you, we are neither Neherians nor your enemies, even while your hand remains wrapped around the hilt of that most notable sword. Indeed, if the Neherians are this far north, they are my enemies also."

"We have no weapons to lend you should the Neherians press their attack."

Her father was nonplussed, Arathé could tell, and he was not enjoying losing control of the conversation.

"We need no weapons," the man replied.

The soldier, clearly sensing the rising tension, put a hand to his own sword hilt. Magic and steel: this new group was dangerous.

"They seem to have lost their stomach for battle since the trick Seren played on them," Anomer said. "But they are not our concern, and have never been our real problem."

Noetos bristled. "They lay about the Racemen with swords, slaying those they would have ruled; they come close to killing us all, and yet are not our real problem? You are your mother's son, no doubt of it. Only she lived in a world like yours."

"My mother's son and proud to be so," Anomer replied.

Arathé signalled him: "No time for this now."

"There's never time," Anomer said, and sighed. "You

are right, as always." He turned back to his father, indicating with a glance that the words did not include him.

During these speeches the fallen newcomer had struggled to his feet. He spoke, his voice a whine, complaining about something, waving his hands. Those of his fellows who turned to him wore unsympathetic frowns.

Conversations flying everywhere on a battlefield where the bodies had not yet cooled.

The man seemed to be addressing his comments to one of his number: the young woman who had spoken earlier. There was another woman with them, even younger, and six men, all wearing versions of the same outfit: a flowing white robe gathered at the waist, with sleeves to the wrist. Like something out of the Play of the Gods, where Alkuon pits himself against the twin betrayers. Arathé had seen it performed in Fossa a few years ago by bearded players dressed as though from the dawn of history, just as these people were.

The young woman snapped at the speaker, then changed languages. "First we have to make sure these people here, or those over there, don't swipe off our heads with their swords."

"Then we have to work out what went wrong with the fire," the tallest man said.

"And why the fire was used in the first place," said the other tall man. "Eight of us, drawn against our will from—"

"Eight of us with secrets not yet for sharing, not in the open language," interrupted the first man.

He turned his handsome, fine-featured face to Noetos. "We offer you no threat," he said, palms open. "In fact, we may be able to assist some of the wounded among you, and will stand with you should the Neherians attack again. Then we shall take our leave, obviating the need for awkward questions—on both sides, as an openly declared Heir of Roudhos is strange news in these days. You are the Heir of Roudhos?"

The question hung threateningly in the air.

Arathé could almost see the mutual suspicion solidifying between members of both groups. *All three groups*, she corrected herself. Eight newcomers, four southerners and—including Seren and her father's two sworn men—nine from the Fisher Coast, not including the refugees. Drawn together to an intersection not of their own making.

And three presences, slowly withdrawing, but palpable nonetheless.

Noetos had simply lost track. Too many people, too many threads, and no explanation for any of it. This even disregarding the Neherians, who seemed to have nothing to do with either group of supposed allies. But whoever they were, these newcomers had magical power. One queasy glance at Duon's exposed bone being eased back into place by the extraordinarily long fingers of the tall white-robed stranger was enough to assure him on that score.

But the Recruiters had possessed magical power, and it had not availed them.

"Lenares," he said, stretching out his hand to her. He took care with his words; she was not quite right in the head. "Some time ago I gave you a stone to look after. Do you still have it?"

She frowned at him, as though angered by his mistrust, but produced the huanu stone from a fold of her tunic.

"Thank you," he said with exaggerated politeness. He

found such people somewhat distasteful, unpredictable, difficult to deal with. Unsettling. Sautea once had an idiot son; the accident-prone, obnoxious boy had drowned when still young, a blessing to everyone really. Best to have as little contact with that sort as possible.

He felt much better with the stone in his grasp. Despite the stranger's assurances, he and his companions seemed dangerous. Certainly magic such as that now being demonstrated could be used offensively. *That which one can repair, one can re-break*, he told himself. *But not with this in my hand.*

Seren came forward, with his shadows Tumar and Dagla—truly more Seren's men now than his. The miner seemed to have shrugged off the rebuke Noetos had given him earlier. "Are these people on our side?" he asked. "Anything we can do?"

"I don't know yet," Neotos said, knowing he was stating the obvious. "Of more concern tactically is Cohamma and his men. Seren, did you see Cohamma?"

"I did," the miner said, his gaze flashing across the scene, clearly still trying to work out what had taken place. "He and his men took the Finder's Track, back beyond the front hills there." He waved his hands vaguely. "Round back o' the Neherians, it seemed. Did you give 'em new orders?"

"No, but someone did."

The miner grunted; no one had to explain the ramifications to him. "Wasn't us. Had our hands full bustin' the dam—the thing has bin repaired but recently 'n' proved almost impossible to crack. 'Splosives only reduced it a little. Coulda done with Omiy; none of us know much about settin' charges. Still, we made a breach big enough for a fair trickle. But you'd'a seen that, right enough. Did the Neherians like my sulphur 'n' palquat mix? Dagla here found it—got himself burned, actually. Show 'em your arm, boy."

"You did a good job," Noetos said, though he was reluctant to offer the praise. How many hundreds died because Seren hadn't been swift enough? The gruff miner certainly wouldn't let their deaths trouble his conscience; he lacked the imagination for it. Still, it wasn't young Dagla's fault. "Go take that arm to that tall man wearing the white robes and see if he'll fix it for you."

All around, the once-injured refugees flexed healing limbs or wonderingly rubbed fading puncture marks. A deep weariness settled on Noetos, as though . . . *Isn't that what Arathé said? That practitioners of magic draw from those around them?* This was why she had refused Andratan's teaching, and had been enslaved because of that refusal. For the first time he could understand her decision.

Yet I've had the stone in my hand while much of the healing has taken place. How exhausted must the others feel?

And what gives them the right to take without asking? Even to do good?

"Aye, we did a good job, though not good enough," Seren said, surprising him. "More time to plan, mebbe enough to do some reconnaissance, and we might've been able to hold the Neherians out."

"Four hundred and fifty-one bodies, as best as we c'n tell," said Tumar in his raspy voice. "All hacked up, some scattered, like. Nothin' the magickers could do about them."

"How many Neherians?" Noetos asked angrily.

Bregor answered. "A hundred or more, most scalded by the water. Some still alive, though we changed that."

The man drew a deep breath. "Well, the Racemen did. Beat them to death with sticks, mostly, or used their own weapons against them."

Bregor spoke with hardly a hint of the damage Noetos had done to the man's throat during their flight from Fossa. A throat he now cleared in obvious nervousness.

"What is it?" Noetos asked, trying but failing to keep the impatience out of his voice.

"I'm taking the refugees back to Raceme," the man said, speaking quickly as if staving off an expected interruption. "I'll be careful to avoid the Neherians, but I don't think they'll stop in Raceme after what's happened to them. I'm thinking I'll put out a call along the coast. Perhaps there are some who will come north and make their homes here."

"You mean to become the Lord of the Coast?" Noetos said, not sure whether to laugh or be angry. "You and a few thousand women and children? Don't you think you ought to ask permission of the Heir of Roudhos?"

"I certainly wouldn't expect you to condescend to help us, consumed as you are with ideas of revenge," Bregor huffed. "Go north and take your toy army with you and bash your heads against the walls of Andratan. Get yourself killed. Meanwhile these people have to live somewhere; I don't see why it shouldn't be in Raceme. I've decided, and there's nothing you can do to change my mind."

"I wouldn't dream of it." Noetos smiled. "It's a relief, actually. I had no idea what to do with all these people save leaving them in Cohamma's lap. Now the charlatan has likely sold himself to the losing side, you're the best option. He'll be your main problem, of course. The Neherians might come at you again, but now they have lost their court . . . Ah, no time for this now. I'll talk to you before you go."

"That's it? We escape from Fossa together and you let me go without an argument?"

"What do you want? You want me to oppose a good idea? Beg you to continue north with us?" He glanced around and lowered his voice. "Bregor, you admitted sleeping with my wife. If I understand it right, you *both* slept with her. No judge in the land would deny my right to redress, no matter who you are or how you phrase your defence of what you did. I hardly think a week or two together, you as my captive, with no apology for what you did, makes for an everlasting friendship in the face of *that*, does it, my friend?" He spat the last two words as though they were a curse.

"Redress? Of course. You'd seek redress for Opuntia in the same way as you'd look for compensation for any lost possession. Do you have even a glimmer of an idea how to live with real people, Fisher? You never understood just how you turned a wonderful girl into a frightened woman with your boorishness and self-centredness. And you are well on the way to doing the same with her children. Yes, I know now you had a reason, a terrible secret, and I pity you for it, but a reason is not of itself an excuse. I might step wary of you, Fisher, but I'll never respect you."

The Fossan Hegeoman stepped back as though expecting a furious reply. Even to evade a fist perhaps.

Her children?

Dumbfounded, Noetos did nothing but stare slack-jawed at the man. Arathé and Anomer looked on, along with his sworn men and a few of the newcomers. *Her* children? A question begged, which if answered in the negative would rip out his heart by the roots.

He would not ask it.

But he had to give response.

"You respect my sword arm, Bregor, and the stone I carry. Both of which you might one day need to defend Raceme from those who see it as an easy mark."

"Are you saying you will join me?" Incredulity and real hope in the man's voice.

"What I'm saying is *you* should join *me*. Come north and get the answers you want from the throne of Andratan. Then return south with me and together we'll put Raceme to rights. The Heir sword would be respected there."

"And in the meantime thousands of people are left without a protector," Bregor said.

"You? You call yourself a protector? Who will protect you? And when the next Neherian fleet comes by, what will you set fire to in order to signal your betrayal?"

"Enough!" Anomer cried. "More than enough! You two will destroy each other. People depend upon both of you, don't you understand?"

Arathé signalled something, and Anomer translated. "Have this discussion in private, my sister says. She's right."

"In the meantime we need to find a safe place for these people," said Sautea. "Get them hid and fed and you can argue all night, if that's your wish. Though nothing but bitterness will come of it, of a certainty."

Noetos sighed, then nodded. They all criticised him, but everyone looked to him for leadership. At the least they smelled something of his grandfather on him; he ought to be proud of that. But the old Duke of Roudhos would have ordered heads struck off for such talk, he was sure of it.

Ignoring the whispering, he took time to organise the camp. The Neherians had begun to move, filing out through the same notch in the hills they had come through. There were so many fewer standing now than earlier in the day, and Noetos no longer feared them. There was therefore no need—and little time—to relocate the refugees to somewhere more defendable. They would spend the night here, in the open. He assigned Bregor to supervise foraging parties, and sent Tumar to organise a firewood detail. Water they could fetch from the cleanest of the streams: at least one was relatively unpolluted. Good enough for one night, at least.

He had put an end to the Neherian threat. He was identified as the Heir of Roudhos, and had taken his revenge upon those who had slain his family. His son and his daughter lived, and remained by his side. Why then, he wondered as he issued orders to people who didn't need them, did he feel so . . . so lorn?

He'd heard the talk. Hundreds of Racemen had participated in his rescue by allowing Arathé and Anomer to draw strength from them, spreading his injuries amongst themselves. Vicariously they had sampled the violence directed at him, and had then been part of the much greater violence he had brought to bear on the Neherians. According to Anomer, very few of them had abandoned the venture even during the killing at the banquet; but afterwards the talk had started.

Excessive, many called it. Even among those who said it had to be done, there were some who felt the killings had been little more than executions. The Summer Palace

Massacre, it was being called. Someone, probably Bregor, had told the refugees the story of his family, and while some said they understood, most felt they had been duped into supporting a personal vendetta.

And now four hundred and fifty-one deaths that everyone said was retribution for the Summer Palace killings. White-faced relatives of the dead stared at him, their eyes glittering with anger or dull with grief. His fault. No matter that the Neherians had done the actual killing; no matter that he and his children had risked their lives for them. That his plan had saved them.

Even were he to abandon his plan to travel north, he could not remain with Bregor and the Racemen. He'd end up with a knife in his back before the week was out.

So be it. He would stay one more night with the refugees, then leave them in Bregor's care. He'd take his children north, and anyone else who cared to go with them. He would not give up his quest.

A young boy approached with a basket containing bread and strips of dried meat. As Noetos reached for a crust the boy leaned away from him, as though fearful of contact.

"Oh, for Alkuon's sake!" Noetos snapped.

The boy dropped the basket and burst into tears.

This has gone far enough. "Take me to your parents," he said to the boy as gently as he could, knowing his voice still had rough edges enough to frighten the lad further.

"I . . . my father, my father . . ." He could say no more.

Who had pressed this poor little fellow into bringing around the food? Was no one else willing to serve? He took the shaking boy by the hand and went in search of Bregor.

What he found was a collection of serious-looking men

standing around in a stony clearing surrounded by gorse and bramble, a worked-over prospecting site. While he had been taking his ease, it seemed Bregor had gathered what passed for the leaders of the Racemen, and now addressed them, outlining his plans. They had taken themselves off some distance from the others, though what needed to be said in private was beyond the fisherman.

The boy snatched his hand away from Noetos and ran to one of the men, burying his head against the man's hip. Trying to relax what he knew would be an angry scowl on his face, Noetos approached the man.

"Excuse me," he said quietly, "is this your lad?"

In the distance Bregor prattled on about rebuilding Raceme; the rest of the crowd remained intent on him.

"Uh-huh," the man answered without turning around. "Been in trouble, has he?"

"Quite the opposite. Someone sent him to take food to Noetos of Fossa, and the little fellow is frightened—"

"I'm not surprised! Noetos Fellhand? And this after he's lost his mother?" The man turned his tear-streaked face to Noetos. "I sent him off to find . . ." His voice petered out.

"Don't you think you ought to have provided the boy with an escort?" Noetos said blandly. "Perhaps a hundred of your best men? It was Noetos Fellhand, after all, to whom he was bringing food. You know, the man who slays innocent children." It was no use: he could not control his voice. "I'm surprised the boy returned alive."

The man tried to answer, but Noetos was not interested.

"Why bother bringing food to the embodiment of evil anyway?" he went on. "What's Fellhand done for you in the last hour? Yes, he stopped the whirlwind, he wiped out

the Neherian leadership come north to enslave you, and
he helped defeat the Neherian army, but that's all in the
past!"

Bregor had stopped talking, and people were turning,
seeking the source of the shouting, but Noetos could not
stop.

"Wouldn't you all be better off without me? Well, you'll
get your wish, friends. Go and grumble at someone else.
That man there"—he pointed at Bregor—"will do as well
as anyone."

For a moment the little boy's sobbing was the only
sound in the clearing.

"You can't stop this, Fisher," Bregor said, walking over
to him.

"Oh, yes I can." Noetos lowered his voice. "You don't
know how easily I could stop this, with a few words about
what happened at Fossa, if I thought it would do any good.
But it won't." He sighed, and raised his voice to a little less
than a shout. "You're all fools. Raceme ought to be left
for years at a minimum; generations at best. The Neherian
force is broken now, but do you think Neherius is cowed?
That there is no one left willing to seize on these events as
an opportunity to establish themselves in the absence of
the old court? The first thing an ambitious man will do is
raise a punitive army. Such a thing will cement his popu-
larity with the public and his leadership with whatever remains of their army. Thought of that, Bregor? Or was this
the subject of this meeting?" He well knew it wasn't.

The Hegeoman made to reply, but Noetos found he really wasn't concerned, and told them so.

"You'll ignore my advice anyway," he said. "You'll
have this man rule over you, despite the fact he cannot

protect you and your children. Ask him how well he protected his own village! And one day—one day soon—the
Neherians, or some other force, will appear and you won't
be able to run fast enough."

This is ridiculous, he told himself as he harangued them
with his frightening words. No, not his words; his father
the strategist's. Words Noetos thought he'd paid no attention to; indeed, had been punished for not learning. Evidently he had learned them.

But what he had not learned was to know when to keep
those words to himself. These people were determined to
rebuild; and, really, could he blame them? Could he do
anything but admire their courage? Was what they intended any more dangerous than his stated goal of marching north to beard the Undying Man in his lair?

Anomer was right. He needed to control his tongue.

"Let us hope that day never comes," he said by way of
apology. "Or, if it does, you have a plan prepared to deal
with it. In the meantime, go with my blessing."

Lame, insincere, and Bregor would know it.

Rather than thanking Noetos for his kind words, and
with no recognition of what they had cost him, the Hegeoman glowered at him. "I don't know what has possessed
you of late," he said, "but you have even less tolerance
than you once had. Rather than wishing a broken people
well, you harangue them, frightening those who need as-
surance. Did you care that some of the men standing here
have lost their wives or children today? Fisher, you are a
poison. Take that mouth of yours away and use it on the
Undying Man. Maybe after you've had your say to him
you'll be of some use to someone."

A dozen retorts filled his mouth. He hesitated a

moment, purely through a desire to select the most incisive one.

"My, your family has loud voices."

Noetos jumped: who was this? He had not heard the stranger come alongside him; the tall man who had emerged first from Lake Woe. With his white robe billowing in the rising afternoon breeze the man ought to have been visible from some distance away, but such had been Bregor's and Noetos's preoccupation, the tall figure had been able to drift, cloud-like, up to them.

"Loud voice? It's an open space, in case you hadn't noticed. How else ought one to communicate?" Noetos knew he sounded peevish, but he'd had enough of justifying himself. "Besides, if you have been observing us, as it appears you have, you will have noticed my daughter does not have a voice at all."

Appropriate rebuke selected, he turned back to Bregor, who awaited his reply with chin raised belligerently.

"I'm not referring to your physical voice," the man said, and instantly Noetos sharpened his focus on the speaker, ignoring Bregor. "A number of your people use mindvoices in ways I have never before heard. I wish to talk with you about this. And before you object, there are dangers as well as benefits to using mind-speech of any kind. You really ought to hear what I have to say, unless you truly do not value the lives of those you speak with."

A sliver of fear worked its way into Noetos's mind. A part of him had wondered whether what his children had done for him—through him—carried risks as well as rewards. What it might already have cost them. He had successfully suppressed his concern, but it was there. "Don't use what you don't understand," Cyclamere had told him once, when showing him a variety of weapons. He'd handed Noetos two sticks linked by a length of chain. "A very effective weapon, this." Noetos had grabbed hold of one of the sticks and swung the other, only to strike himself a stinging blow on the wrist. "Point demonstrated," his teacher had exclaimed with satisfaction.

"I'll hear you," Noetos said, his right hand unconsciously rubbing his left wrist. "After the evening meal. I'll bring those who might profit from your words. But your people need to do some explaining. We'll need your names at the least, and you'll need to explain what you are doing here, and that trick with the fire and the lake. There's a lot going on here that no one understands."

The tall man stared down at him. "And there you have our motivation," he said in a voice as smooth as oil. "We need to understand what is happening here as much as you do. We will meet you here at sunset."

Noetos had nodded, turned and walked a dozen paces before he realised he had been commanded and dismissed by an experienced leader. He would think about this over whatever scraps the food-gatherers had been able to find.

With the low overcast sky characteristic of northern Saros in early summer, the exact time of sunset was difficult to determine. So Noetos herded his people up the gully to the meeting place while there was still plenty of light. One or two of the southerners had not had the time to find something to eat, but this meeting, Noetos judged, was more important.

The raw, stony gully gave way to the flat-bottomed depression in which Bregor had met with the men of Raceme that afternoon. In the fading light it looked a forlorn place.

Scrubby thorn bushes obscured much of the human detritus, but enough of the gold workings remained visible for Noetos to judge it had once been an important site for the precious metal, and lucrative, at least for the few who had established themselves there first, if it was like most sites in this region. Lucrative, too, for the suppliers of food and liquor, and the moneylenders and whores. The way of things meant that most of the miners would have made little, if any, profit from all the days and months of hazardous, back-breaking work.

There had once been a town here, Seren had told him, that went by the name of Knife In The Back. Noetos remembered coming across such a town on one of the old maps he'd pored over as a child, along with other names such as Last Chance, Stony Ground and Waste O' Time. They evoked scenes of chaotic vigour in his mind: grizzled miners cheek by jowl with oily salesmen and others desiring to part the miners from their wealth.

There was plenty of evidence to show the town's existence. In the centre of the open space a lone chimney stood, but the foundations of other buildings could be discerned, overgrown as they were. Scratching in the dirt would reveal tools or other cast-offs: buckles, coins, scraps of cloth. And there were the workings themselves. The most obvious was the cliff behind where the town had stood, formed by the miners sluicing away the front half of the hill. Tailings of loose stone lay across the landscape. The effect was one of desolation.

The sort of place Noetos would have loved to play in as a child; but as an adult it unsettled him, reminding him of the impermanence of human endeavour. The failure of plans and hopes. No doubt those who had founded this place were as dedicated as Bregor and his Racemen, or as Noetos himself in his plan to go north and expose Andratan for the place of evil it was.

Well, at least I get to select the ground, he thought. Then realised he was treating the upcoming meeting as though it were a battle and he was identifying the most advantageous place for his army. Reacting to everything as though it was a threat. *In this case I may well be justified.* It was just a feeling, but it was strong. He would not ignore it.

He chose a pile of sluice tailings—large, moss-covered stones embedded in crumbling dirt—and directed Anomer and Arathé to find a comfortable place to sit. From here they could see the entrance to the basin. Moreover, there were two other piles close by, larger but not as high. Small advantages, but who knew when such things might become important?

The four southerners seated themselves on the tailings to Noetos's right. A strange group, and one about which he had a number of questions. Why, for example, did they appear so different? Dark-skinned Captain Duon, his hair long and straight, beard dark and wild, the picture of an explorer. The mercenary Dryman, hair and beard trimmed, features broad, eyes deep and widely set apart, showing no traces of the fear that had overcome him when the newcomers had arrived in their firestorm. And the ill-matched couple—obviously a couple, though by their careful gestures it appeared they sought to prevent others realising it. The cosmographer and the Omeran. The latter considered an animal in the south, apparently, though he looked human enough, despite extraordinary black skin and a powerful, thick-set body. And the former, a woman of considerable beauty, despite her lack of grooming. Certainly she was of northern stock, if her companions were anything to go by. She reminded him disconcertingly of Opuntia, actually. It was the eyes, he decided: piercingly direct, even more so than those of his wife. His former wife. But this woman's whole being was marred by an intellectual lack, as though part of her brain had not grown, or had been removed. Not a woman he wanted to be near, but one—if Arathé was right—who might be necessary in understanding what was happening to them all.

And as the third group strode into the clearing, their white robes dull now in the fading light, Noetos could sense something gathering, a faint thrumming on the connection between himself and his daughter, as though someone plucked it with a giant finger. As Noetos had planned, the newcomers seated themselves atop the third and least significant of the three tailings mounds. Five of them had elected to come: the two tall men, who looked like brothers; the young woman, her black hair and deep eyes shining; the soldier, who sat with his weight on his feet, as though ready to spring into action; and the short, stout man who had collapsed when they had emerged from the lake.

"Well we are met," the tallest of the strangers said in perfect, cultured Bhrudwan, instantly taking control of proceedings. "I will speak in the language of this land, as I know it well. Please feel free to translate my words for those who do not speak it." His clear gaze held them all. "There are stories to be told, warnings to be issued and statements to be made. Let the first statement be made now."

Noetos opened his mouth to speak—to take the initia-tive now or lose it forever—and then realised he would never have it, not in this company. Another faint plucking, and the scraggly bushes between the three mounds burst into flame.

"We will need light," the tall man said by way of explanation, as the blue flames crackled in the thorn bushes without appearing to consume them. "And, later, warmth. Should anyone wish to take over the provision of light and heat, please let me know."

He is fishing, Noetos realised. *Trying to find out if anyone else has the sorcery he does.*

"Tell us about yourselves," he asked the man, civilly enough, he thought. "Your names, your home towns, your abilities, and what brings you here."

"An excellent idea," the man responded, as though sanctioning it with his agreement. "With your permission, then?"

With or without your permission, he means, and everyone here knows it.

"I am Heredrew, an adventurer and sorcerer from Haurn, a small country in the land of Faltha. My companions are Phemanderac, a scholar of Dhauria; Bandy of Instruere; her guardsman Robal, also of Instruere; and the smaller man, who might consider himself fortunate to be alive, is Conal of Yossa, a priest of the Koinobia, also known as the Halites. Some of us are widely travelled, hence our familiarity with the language here."

No hint in his inflections as to truth and falsity, but the southern girl began shaking her head.

The man naming himself Heredrew saw the movement. "You suspect I do not tell all the truth? You are right. But we are hard pressed: there is less time available to us than you yet know, and it would not be wise for us to tell everything we know. Some of you have already sensed a gathering of power, which, whatever our stories as to how we came to this place, is the real reason we are here. Where there is power, there is a wielder of power. I would prefer that power-wielder to remain ignorant until we have determined the extent of that power and whether it is benign or malignant."

"We might say the same of you," Noetos said.

"If you were a fool, which I doubt, you might," said Heredrew. "But we were drawn here, and while we have power, as I have manifested, we were clearly subjected to a power far greater. Hear our account, then decide whether to share your own."

"I don't like lies," the girl Lenares shouted. "You lie with your words and you lie with your body. Your numbers are all lies and deceit. Tell the truth or be quiet!"

The tall man stood and stepped forward until he reached the base of his mound. "If you were held captive in a dungeon, girl, would you tell your jailer about the knife in your boot? Wouldn't you instead pool resources with all the other captives so you could overwhelm the jailer and escape?"

"Is that what you think?" Noetos asked. "That we are imprisoned?"

The man smiled, a thin affair more menacing than reassuring. "That is exactly what I think," he said.

Lenares leaned forward. "Truth is more powerful than lies," she insisted. "I have things to tell you all that will help you to understand what is happening. No one else knows them. If no one else will, at least I will tell the truth."

"You will wait for your turn to speak," Heredrew said, his voice so commanding it set everyone back. "And if what you are saying will aid our enemy, we will request you to be silent."

Somehow the word *request* sounded like *compel* in the tall man's mouth. Lenares' mouth snapped shut, but her knife-edge frown remained directed at the tall man as he continued talking.

"We are a diverse group, drawn together, I think, because the world has suddenly begun to change. Perhaps at some other time we will tell you how we all met, but suffice it to say I had prepared a method—risky, but necessary—to travel from Dhauria in Faltha to Andratan in Bhrudwo, as a number of us wished to consult with the ruler of Bhrudwo. Unfortunately, one of us interfered with the process and made us vulnerable as we travelled using the blue fire." He waved a hand at the burning bush between them, while the stout priest bowed his head.

"Someone or something took advantage of our vulnerability. We were pulled—or pushed, it is not certain—from our intended path, and ended up here, in the middle of a poisonous lake. It took a great deal of sorcery to preserve our lives—power which I drew from the closest source at hand, which turned out to be a Neherian army, I am gratified to discover. It left them somewhat worse off, which apparently worked in your interests, though only coincidentally.

"We wish to resume our journey to Andratan as soon as possible. However, I am concerned that any attempt to use the blue fire to travel will again expose us to the power that almost destroyed us today. Until we have identified and removed this threat, we are limited to non-magical ways of travelling." He pointed at his feet, shod in mud-spattered boots.

"Very well," Noetos said, trying to bring the gathering back under his control. "We have heard you. I have no doubt there are those here who have questions for you, specifically concerning the nature and extent of your power, but you will now hear our stories."

With that, he launched into an abridged account of his family's adventures. He watched the newcomers' faces as he told his tale, and noticed the tall man Heredrew's features tighten as he spoke of the unnatural storm and whirlwind. He showed no such emotion on hearing of the destruction of the Neherian court and, though Noetos was vague in the telling—he did not want to reveal the extent of his own power—the defeat of the Neherians prompted no questions.

He knows far more than he is telling. The girl Lenares is right.

And speaking of Lenares: "Captain Duon, would you tell of events in the southlands?" Noetos said.

"But, the girl . . . Certainly, Noetos," said the soldier, slightly slow on the uptake as usual.

Duon told the southerners' story simply, but it took far longer as so many of the places and characters were unfamiliar to his listeners. He explained what a cosmographer was, detailed the purposes of the Emperor as he knew them—though Noetos suspected he dissembled somewhat—and told of Lenares' encounters with what she called the "hole in the world". His description of their encounter with the hole in Nomansland, and their subsequent arrival in Raceme at the height of the storm, made for an interesting tale. The man was a natural storyteller.

Beside him Lenares fiddled with her hair, looping strands around her nose or biting on them in obvious agitation. She wanted the chance to speak, to tell them all how important she was. That she would not do, not while Noetos was in charge.

"Thank you, Captain," he said as soon as the tale was told. "Now, before we interrogate each other to no purpose, has anyone observed any patterns?"

Lenares opened her mouth to speak.

"We will come to you later, Lenares," Noetos said, cutting her off. "Let's hear from us lesser thinkers first." He gave what he supposed was an indulgent smile to the others.

"No," said a new voice. "We will hear from the cosmographer now."

The speaker was another of the southerners, the mercenary Dryman. He had said very little in the two days since Noetos had first encountered him, his typical pose being seated, head bowed, staring upwards out of heavy-lidded eyes. But now he sat erect, and his eyes were wide open as he made his demand. In fluent Bhrudwan, which he had given absolutely no previous indication of understanding. And there was something else: Noetos felt a weight pressing in on him as the man said his few words, as though some enormous being leaned close to listen.

The cosmographer stood up, scrambled down from her perch on the pile of tailings, stood where everyone could see her and opened her mouth. But what came out was not speech, but a sudden shriek.

She howled and screeched, a sound louder than a human throat ought to be able to make. Her hands were on either side of her head and she knelt, seemingly driven to her knees by whatever troubled her. By whatever internal workings had gone awry, Noetos thought, as he reluctantly stepped forward to deal with her.

The curly-haired black man was already at her side. "Lenares! Lenares!" he cried. Then followed it with an explosion of the southern language. Dryman cracked a sharp response in the same language, and the man dropped his head, but did not otherwise move. *Some sort of power struggle*, Noetos guessed as he approached the screaming girl.

She turned her face to him and stopped him cold, as though she had struck him a blow to the stomach. He had never seen such intense agony on a human face: her mouth and eyes were so distended she seemed a caricature. Blood seeped from her mouth where she had bitten her tongue.

This is no act.

Her fear-filled eyes were not focused on him, but on something else, some private reality. He turned, despite himself, and saw movement in the distance. Something was happening . . .

As the moon edged nervously above the farthest hills and began coating them in silvery light, the three assembled groups watched as the horizon . . . changed. The low clouds in the distance swirled and peeled away into some other place, vanishing like leaves in a whirlpool. Below the disappearing clouds the ground itself began to move, to shake, to swirl.

"Like Nomansland!" Captain Duon shouted.

Having listened to his story, everyone there knew what he meant. But despite having seen the whirlwind, Noetos found he didn't believe it. Whirlwinds and storms were natural phenomena given supernatural meaning by credulous humans. He could almost hear his father lecturing him. "That hillside you see, it is not really bubbling, son. It is not glowing orange with heat."

Then what am I seeing, Father?

Atop a nearby hill stood a figure, his arms raised. Too far away to recognise, but Noetos thought he knew the man anyway. *It couldn't be him. The man died in Raceme. I saw the whirlwind come for him.*

With a crack and a rumble a distant hillside soared into the air, rocks, soil, trees and bushes—and an animal or two—falling away as it rose. It made Noetos nauseous to watch the natural order of things being subverted. One or two of those watching cried out; cries that echoed across the hills as the refugees closer to the lake—and to the hillside ripped out by the roots—beheld the scene.

The figure atop the hill lowered his hands. This could not be his doing. *I swear he has no magic, or why would he have let me take the stone?*

"This will be terrible."

It was the woman from the Falthan group. Bandy of Instruere.

"Get everyone away from here," she said, tugging at Noetos's sleeve. "Whatever tore the ground up will come searching for us."

"Stell— Bandy's right," said the tall man. "You're the leader of the refugees: command them to flee. We are being hunted."

The hillside vanished into the distant vortex . . . *No*, thought Noetos, *not so distant now. They are right. It is coming for us.*

"It must be targeting someone among us," he said to them. "It might be a mistake to go down to the refugees."

But his words went unheeded: already his daughter

and son were running down to the narrow gully leading to Lake Woe.

He knew he shouldn't, sensed he was making a mistake, but he simply couldn't help himself. How could a father do otherwise? He reached into his belt, clasped the huanu stone and threw it to the ground, marking well where it landed. Then he concentrated on his children and hoped they would hear him.

Arathé! Anomer! Come back!

Something heard.

Panic filled him as he realised what he'd done, what he had brought down upon them all. He snatched up the stone. "Split up!" he cried as he ran amongst the three groups. "Run in different directions!"

"No!" Heredrew countermanded. "Combine whatever powers we have and resist what is coming!"

"But my way we will lose only one or two at most," Noetos said. *The chances are it will not be my children, please Alkuon . . .*

And now a roaring began, a thunderous sound coming from the vortex in the sky, a throat into another reality. As if some giant shouted words of defeat at them. A white spot emerged from the hole in the clouds; a white, glowing thing, trailing embers in a long tail, swinging around towards them. On the nearby hill the mysterious figure leaped up and down as though cheering it on.

"No time to run," the mercenary observed in a voice that seemed wholly unconcerned with his imminent death. Indeed, he smiled at Noetos as he added, "Let's see how strong these people really are."

Down it came: a fireball spearing towards them, thrown by a god. Some of the talented among them gathered around the tall man, but Anomer and Arathé were nowhere to be seen. Safe. The ground began to shake under his feet, sending ripples across the dirt and shaking the bushes.

Noetos consigned himself to oblivion.

"He's killed us all," Anomer panted as he tried to keep up with his surprisingly swift sister. "I heard him shout at us along our link." She really was running quickly. *She's using power, trying to draw attention away from Father and the others, he thought. Then: No, she would not put the refugees at risk.* She must only be using her natural strength, yet she drew away from him.

His foolish, thick-headed father had finally succeeded in killing them all. *We ought to have left him to the Neherians,* part of him thought. And no other part of his mind supplied a cogent argument to oppose it.

Out onto the flat area his sister ran, and he followed a moment later. The fiery object grew rapidly closer—too rapidly, they would have only moments—but it seemed it was not travelling straight for them. Rather it would hit the basin they had just left . . .

At the last moment Noetos raised his head. He would stare his death right in its flaming eye.

The last image seared itself on his mind. Crimson, orange and golden flame bursting from a black ball of half-consumed rock, seemingly covering half the sky as it smashed into—

Into some sort of shield thrown up by the magicians. The air thickened, and an enormous concussion rocked the basin. He fell to his knees, surprised he still had knees to fall to . . .

*   *   *

"Nnnnnnoo!" Arathé shrieked, and tried to fashion a hasty shield above her. Beside her Anomer did the same.

Neither of them succeeded.

The burning hillside crashed through their half-formed, flimsy defence, deflected slightly and crumped into the ground, shattering into a thousand fragments, each one raining fiery destruction on Lake Woe and those gathered around it. The largest pieces bounced towards the centre of the lake, but smaller rocks scythed through the fleeing refugees. Those who escaped losing limbs or being punched through by stones and pebbles were showered with molten dirt, which caught fire on their clothes or their flesh.

Into the midst of this horror Arathé crawled, bleeding from her ears and nose. The air itself seemed to be on fire, and though she could feel the noise of the explosion reverberating around her, she could not hear it. Every breath scorched her lungs. She would not live. She did not deserve to.

And now Noetos drank to the depths of the cup he had prepared for himself the day he vowed revenge for the death of his family. On shaking legs he walked across the place where the refugees had been—where they still were, butchered as they fled, holed, burned and twitching, some still alive, writhing, crying out for death or life, anything as long as it offered relief from the pain. As many grunts as screams. The magicians rushed to help, but for most there was little they could do.

Yes, a part of him acknowledged that he himself had not hurled the fireball at the refugees. But he had alerted the gods, had drawn them by his selfish words. He knew his children would see it this way, even if the remaining Racemen did not.

It seemed to him that evening, as he moved among the dead and dying, that he walked like a farmer through his autumn harvest.

And when his son and his daughter came to confront him, the look on their faces made him wish he had died.

COSMOGRAPHER

CHAPTER 12

THE TEA HOUSE

THE YACOPPICA CLIFFS TEA HOUSE sat high above the restless sea. The windswept clifftop was not the ideal place to grow yacoppica, but the herb was hardy and the shelter belts had grown sufficiently thick that the plant spread rapidly and the tea house gained fame throughout the district. Mainly for the views, of course, but appreciation of the tea followed, as local supplies were supplemented by increasing imports. The house had become one of the prime links in the famous Ikhnos Tea Chain, ensuring the fame and fortune of the proprietors.

The Ikhnos Tea Chain was the social lifeblood of the northernmost Fisher Coast country. Considering themselves more civilised than their southern neighbours, the Ikhnal used alcohol sparingly, choosing instead to exploit the full potential of herbal and plant-based drinks. Tea was an essential part of cultured society, their host explained to Lenares. The cosmographer noted her three companions were not listening. They never listened. How could they tell whether something was going to be important if they didn't listen?

Lenares always listened. Their host beamed at her, pleased to have a receptive audience. Lenares smiled back. Learning new things was always a pleasure.

The five of them—four from the glorious Empire of Elamaq, one from the small and self-important country of Ikhnos—waited at one of the entrances to the Yacoppica Cliffs Tea House, standing among unremarkable waist-high broad-leaved bushes. Their host, a middle-aged woman with a wide face, large bosom and friendly smile, spent a lot of time talking about these bushes. Their roots, she told them, would be dug up, scrubbed and boiled. After a time the water would be drawn off and other flavouring ingredients added, according to the guest's humour. Lenares had not heard of the ingredients the woman listed: ginger, damiana and nutmeg for stimulation, kava for congeniality, chamomile for relaxation, and aniseed, peppermint, fennel, cloves and cinnamon for taste. She rolled the words around on her tongue, enjoying the sound they made. The discarded root would be pounded into powder, making a sweet delicacy that could be chewed or made into tea, and was exported from Ikhnos to many Bhrudwan countries. A favourite of the Undying Man, their host said proudly.

She asked them to remove their footwear, invited them through the guest entrance, and escorted them across the pale wooden floor to the open-walled section of the tea house. "You will be wanting to appreciate the view, as all our visitors do," she told them. "There's a brisk breeze today, but we think the sight of the sea is worth the slight inconvenience. At any time, of course, we can move you to a screened booth, where you can enjoy your tea in privacy."

"I'm surprised the locals don't take all the best spaces," Captain Duon said.

"Oh, but they do," their host said sweetly. "For the Ikhnal, tea is a serious matter. They prefer to sit in the booths without the distraction of the sea view. You will come to appreciate this during your journey through Ikhnos, though not many tea houses have such beautiful distractions. Apart from Boiling Waters Tea House up near the Patina Padouk border, of course. I haven't been there myself, but I'm given to understand it is the first among the great houses of the chain. I'll go there one day.

"Take a seat, please." She pointed them to oddly shaped wooden seats arranged around a low table. "You kneel on the padded crosspiece—there, that's right—and sit on this part."

Lenares did as she was directed and, to her surprise, the arrangement worked well, taking the tension out of her back, which had been stiffening after weeks of walking.

"Now I will bring the yacoppica root and steep it in water."

The woman bent down and adjusted a metal grille under the table: immediately heat came roaring out of the contraption, warming their legs. A young girl, responding to some signal Lenares missed, came bearing a small stone cauldron and placed it in an inset in the table, directly above the heat source. After a few minutes the water began to steam.

Their host withdrew a fibrous root from her tunic and placed it in the water. "I will leave you for perhaps half an hour," she told them, "and then I will return with special ingredients I have selected based on what I have seen of you."

"Do you see numbers?" Lenares asked, wondering how the woman could be so confident as to select ingredients for them based on a few minutes' acquaintance.

"Numbers? What do you mean, madam?"

"I am wondering . . . no, never mind. You just guess."

The woman's eyebrows rose, but she appeared in no other way offended. "It's somewhat more than guess-work, madam. We train diligently for this, you know. From girls."

"Like cosmographers," Lenares said, deciding to nod to a fellow professional.

The woman made off to organise her ingredients, and Dryman scowled menacingly at Lenares. "I told you there was to be no unnecessary talk," he said. "I want our passage through these lands unremarked. And yet you start jabbering to everyone you meet."

Lenares looked him up and down. "*Your* talk is unnecessary," she countered. "I talk when I need to. I don't waste words, and I won't waste them with you. Now be quiet and let each of us get on with serving the Emperor as best we can."

The mercenary's face darkened at this, but she continued staring into his unpleasant features. "You're not in charge of me," she said to him. "And you don't frighten me either. Cosmographers report directly to the Emperor. You're not in charge of the captain either. You're just a bully, the same as the Emperor. I don't like you."

Torve leaned towards her. "Lenares, please, there are things you don't understand—"

"I don't understand why Captain Duon is not the leader of this expedition. I don't understand what this man is doing here, and why he has frightened you into doing what he wants. Can anyone explain that?"

Lenares began to nibble at a strand of her hair. The numbers were maddeningly incomplete where this strange man was concerned, she thought. It might be because the holes in the world had burned away some of the threads and nodes she needed to make sense of what she was experiencing, or perhaps it had to do with the unknown reason why nothing would add up in Dryman's presence. She waited for his answer, waited to test its truth.

"There is a simple reason why I command," Dryman said, as a faint smile played across his face. "Because for the last three months you have followed me. If Duon were a true leader we would be on our way back to Talamaq, about to be executed for our cowardice and disobedience."

Some of Lenares' scorn must have shown on her face, for he continued: "Yes, it is a facetious reason, I admit. The real reason, cosmographer, is that should Captain Duon return home without the many thousands of men he started out with, he will face much worse than death. He and his family will be disgraced, and his Alliance will fall. History will rank him alongside Caniole of Farbar, the man who lost the Emperor's golden fleet. There is only one way for our hero to redeem himself, and that is to bring something home of such worth the Emperor will overlook the triviality of thirty thousand deaths. Captain Duon has allied himself to me, as I have persuaded him I know of something with such value and will need his help in recovering it."

He leaned back as far as the kneeling stool would allow and folded his arms. "An accurate summary, Captain?"

"Gods help me," Duon concurred sourly. "To serve the Emperor, I follow a mercenary."

The water in the cauldron began to boil, reminding Lenares of the stories she had been told when very young: witches in the mountains brewing spells to entrap the wayward. She remembered the stories in detail, every line, every word. *Herb in the pot, herb in the pot, find out whether she's been good or not . . .*

Who had told her the stories? She couldn't remember that.

More and more, especially in the three weeks since the fireball star had landed amongst them, she found herself retreating into memories of those early times. So many nodes burned out on that day of earthquake and fire, the dark intelligence behind the hole in the world must have been laughing. The gruesome manner of the refugees' deaths had neither impressed nor frightened Lenares. Dead was dead. But she had been so angry at having been outwitted again. It was *her* world being messed with, not that of the hole's creator. She had a tie to him, and so should have had plenty of warning. Which made her think the hillside torn up and thrown at them had been a spur-of-the-moment choice.

Spur of the moment it may have been, but it had achieved its purpose, sowing confusion into the three groups who might have worked together against the god. It was no coincidence, Lenares thought, that the fireball had come just as she readied herself to tell them all she knew and guessed. The dreadful arguments following the terrible events of the evening had broken the fragile alliance before it even had a chance to form, and the three groups left Lake Woe separately amid acrimony. Lenares' words had been left unsaid. Just as the god behind the hole would have wanted it.

And there was another reason she spent much of her time in memory-land. Torve.

Her beloved Torve, genuine but false, open but keeper of secrets. Victim of a hidden compulsion, if her guess was accurate. Well, more than a guess. Something kept his mouth closed when he desperately wanted to open it. Worse, the compulsion seemed now to extend to personal matters.

He made her feel so good, and so bad. Every time he opened his mouth she hoped it would be to talk to her, to tell her private, special things. Every time he looked at her she searched for the numbers that told her, far more eloquently than his words or glances could, that he loved her. But he had not said anything beyond the normal functional things one travelling companion would say to another. She often found herself looking at him, watching the way his calf muscles moved as he walked, wishing she could run her hands over his broad shoulders or kiss those dark lips. And other things. The weight of him, the feel of him, his urgency, his catching breath. His beautiful numbers and their intriguing patterns. Oh, she was glad none of her companions could read her mind. How Rouza and Palain would have ridiculed her had they known! Of course, they were dead now, killed in the ambush in the Valley of the Damned.

It seemed that the hole in the world wanted to kill everybody. Perhaps the Son could not re-enter the world until sufficient nodes had been removed. Surely someone, somewhere, knew how he might be stopped.

Their host returned and sniffed at the cauldron. "Just a moment longer," she said, smiling as though she was about to solve every one of the mysteries bothering Lenares.

"Then the blend will mend your problems, as we say in Ikhnos."

"How does it work?" Lenares asked, curious. She ignored the stare from Dryman. *You can't touch me, you bully.*

The woman beamed at her as though she'd just been acclaimed queen of the realm. "Every person is a combination of four humours, madam. Virility, sobriety, congeniality and activity. The 'Four Teas', we call them." She paused.

In the past Lenares would not have known what the pause was for, but she had learned. The woman wanted them to laugh. Lenares could not identify any humour in her words, but she found her own unintentional pun funny so she laughed. Their host was pleased.

"The traditional method of making tea gives us the time to assess each participant," she continued. "Your companions are mysterious, with their dusky skin and strange eyes, but I think I have their measure. You, dear, are an open book to me, and I believe I have just the drink for you. It will relax your body while stimulating your mind, an organ you put much store in. Am I right?"

"You are," Lenares replied, smiling faintly. *Guesswork. The woman can tell I use my mind because I ask lots of questions.*

"Ah, you doubt me,' the woman said. "Everyone does at first. The Yacoppica Cliffs Tea House prides itself on the skill of its readers, as we are known. We offer you this test. Take a sip from the cup of each of your companions. Should you find their infusions more pleasurable than your own, we will refund your money."

Dryman looked up. "That is fair," he said. "Now, enough

of the fairground fakery. Fetch us our drinks. We would be out of here within the hour."

"Fakery? One wonders why you have availed yourself of our services if you do not believe in their efficacy." Her voice rose as she spoke and the skin around her eyes tightened.

"Just get our tea, woman," Dryman growled.

"Rude as well as a bully," Lenares said as the woman walked away, their cauldron in hand, her back ramrod-stiff.

"Oh, come, cosmographer. You can see as well as I just how foolish all this is."

"I thought I was the insensitive one," she said. "Rouza and Palain tell me all the time I can't tell a pig from shit. But you deliberately try to hurt people."

As she said the words, two heretofore separate numbers came together. *Oh, oh. Torve, oh.*

"Then I am better than you," he said, "since you only hurt people by accident. At least I can put their pain to some use."

Torve glanced up, the surprise on his face a confirmation. Dryman smiled, the expression reflecting thoughts he no doubt considered secret. Another person to underestimate her.

Now I know what you do, she thought as she observed the mercenary. *All I have to do is find out who you are.*

Their host returned, four cups on a tray, and placed one in front of each of their party without a word. She was still upset but was trying to be professional. On an impulse, Lenares put out her hand to the woman.

"Wait a moment," she said. "Would you please give us a fifth cup? Make this for someone strong and powerful who has been imprisoned most of his life. Someone who has hopes of freedom."

"Oh, yes?" The woman's brows rose. "And where is this person?"

"I have high hopes he will make an appearance before the ceremony is over," Lenares said. Her impulse felt better and better the more she reflected upon it. *Create a god-shaped hole . . .*

"Which of the four humours does he favour?" the woman asked, again pleased Lenares showed an interest.

"Virility and activity," the cosmographer replied promptly.

"Oh, my dear," said the woman, her smile broadening. "When your friend does arrive, would you advise him I would be happy to assess him more closely?"

Another double meaning. *Was conversation never free of them?* Lenares had no intention of exposing this kind woman to their potential fifth guest. Nevertheless, she nodded. Only a few months ago she would not have been able to lie, even by nodding "yes" when she meant "no".

The woman went off, and returned a minute later with a small cup, hardly larger than a thimble, from which thick fumes wafted.

"You tell your friend to drink this slowly," she said. "There's enough here to slow down the most ardent of suitors. That's if you want him slowed down." She winked at the girl, then nodded towards where Dryman and Torve sat, heads together, deep in conversation. "His fault if he hasn't been listening."

Oh. Had she misunderstood the woman? A deep fear speared through her: was her growing insight into conversation coming at the expense of her unique number-based vision?

Think about that later.

"Come and drink your tea," she said quietly, aiming her voice along the pattern of numbers she had discerned, the link into the hole in the world. "Come on, it's getting cold." Like a mother entreating a child.

And he came.

There was no compulsion, Lenares knew that. All she was doing was offering the most tenuous of invitations. Not too strong, lest she aid him in tearing the hole wider. No more solid than the wisps of steam now forming a shape, a face, a taloned hand.

The three men couldn't see him. Why should they? Would she have seen the god's face in a steaming cup of tea had she not been looking for it?

His hands, no more than a sketch in mist, were fine-boned and lovely. His face . . . his face . . .

A brow twitched, the lips pursed. *Are you surprised?* she asked Lenares.

"Yes," Lenares whispered, and she was. Her invitation had drawn the Daughter, not the Son. Something was wrong. She had made a mistake somewhere.

Both eyebrows rose, pulling the eyes open. *Disappointed?*

"No. You were so kind. You saved me in the House of— in your house. You let me sit on your seat."

A beatific smile, eyes still wide open, inviting. *I could let you have more than that.*

"Lenares? Who are you talking to?" Torve asked. The breath in his words rippled through the steam, contorting the Daughter's beautiful face, making the eyes asymmetrical and the mouth sag open as though she were a madman.

"Torve, be quiet!" Lenares snapped. Torve pulled back as though slapped.

"Come back, come back," she whispered. "Have some of the tea. Our host says you'll like it."

The face had not reassembled itself, but the clawed hand, outlined in steam, took the cup—and lifted it.

Were the others seeing this? Did they note how the steam arced downwards, creating a loop? That it raised the small cup? Did they see the liquid disappear?

Colour spread through the vapour. Pale pink, filling in cheeks and chin. Green eyes, the tips of blonde hair. Red lips, parting to speak.

"I remember," said the Daughter. "I remember the taste, the heat. How could I have turned my back on such things?"

"But you did," Lenares breathed.

Dryman, Duon and Torve stared at her as though she was crazy. No, there was something other than disdain in Dryman's eyes.

"What are you doing, cosmographer?" he asked. "What are you conjuring? I can feel it. She."

"Yes, I did," the Daughter said, ignoring or simply not hearing the mercenary. "I'm so cold, so cold. Look at me. I made a mistake. You could help me get back. Together we could stop my brother, close the hole in the world, make things right. So cold, Lenares. Everything you wanted. We could be friends. You could show me, warm me." A pause: the drink cooled. "Lenares?"

Lenares thought of the bronze map, the secrets of the world inscribed on it, visible from the three seats of the gods. She thought of the House of the Gods and the time she and Torve had spent there, and a tear of longing formed in the corner of her eye. She could not imagine a more perfect world. The Daughter could give it to her.

"What do you want me to do?"

"Just give me a place, Lenares, a small place in your flesh, a link to this world." The misty figure licked her lips. "The warmth of this world."

Dryman stood. "I asked you, cosmographer, what you were doing. Answer me!"

The mist curled away from the man, losing its shape and colour.

A final whisper. "Help me, Lenares."

No point in lying. "I tried to establish a link to the power making the hole in the world," she said. "I thought I could summon him."

Oh, but I am lying, in all the things I did not say. No mention of the link I have already forged to the hole. I said I was trying to summon a male, but didn't say I actually summoned a female. I didn't even say it worked.

Dryman strode around the table and put a hand on her shoulder, pressing harder than he ought to have. "What made you think you could call down a god?"

A sudden breeze roared in from the sea, and the steam vanished, along with the mists in her own mind.

"Don't touch me," she said, spitting the words. "Keep your hands to yourself." Protective words, routine words, words to make people keep their distance. Especially this man, now she had worked out what he did with his hands. With the hand still resting on her shoulder.

She shrugged it off. "I don't have to answer you," she said.

"No?" He stood perfectly still.

"Please," Torve said.

The air around them began to thicken, and Lenares felt a weight pressing on her chest.

"Good morning," came a halting voice from nearby. "May we have table with you?"

The pressure vanished, and at the same moment Dryman growled, an inhuman sound. Torve glanced wearily at his master's face and read the world of anger there. *Oh, Lenares, please leave this man alone. Don't get in his way.*

The hail had come from one of the Falthans; the wet nurse, his master had called the man disparagingly. The man acted as a guard to one of the women. Why, it was not certain: according to Dryman, the woman was much more powerful than her guard. Two other Falthans were with him, the tall leader and the woman he guarded.

Torve waited for Dryman to pour invective at them, to tell them to leave.

"Of course, please join us," Dryman said, his face a sudden mask. "I'm sure our hosts won't mind if you pull up another table. Are all of you still alive?"

The last delivered as sweetly as the first, the barb unmissable. Unless, of course, the man struggled with the language, as clearly he did. As Torve did, in truth, despite a month's diligent study at Dryman's command. The root of the tongue was much the same as that spoken by the Amaqi, but the differences in grammar and expression were subtle and confusing. He persevered because his master demanded it.

Torve welcomed the arrival of the Falthans. He would have welcomed anyone who stayed long enough to take his master's attention away from him. He feared he was losing his sanity, maybe had already lost it, as the cumulative weight of the occasional night expeditions settled ever more heavily on his mind. And not just the killing and the torturing; that he had become at least partly inured to years ago. It now took a particularly savage or sadistic killing to awaken pity in his breast, and when the Emperor decided to execute his work swiftly, Torve helped him with vigour. Better for everyone that way. However, his need to keep his activities secret from Lenares, and his equal and opposite need for her to find out, clove him in two. How, oh how, was his master keeping her ignorant?

The question was unanswerable because he could not ask it.

Moreover, the voice of command his master once used only when necessary seemed to have become his normal mode of conversation. The sheer weight of it, the depth of suffering and power and history and knowledge wrapped in it, threatened to overwhelm him, to strip his soul. Was overwhelming him. Plunging him into a world of unreason.

How could he sustain love in such a world?

Every day he gazed on Lenares with the memory of longing, but he was increasingly unable to hang on to it. Because there was a small and diminishing amount of him able to be called human.

His Defiance no longer offered him protection. He hadn't been able to finish it for weeks. Hadn't even attempted it for days. It seemed so polluted. His compartmentalised life had broken down, the horrors were leaching in, and all he could see in his mind's eye were struggling bodies and flailing limbs. Pleading and screams and bewildered questions filled his ears. He cursed his parents, his race, for their unwitting betrayal. None of them had been compelled to serve such a one as the Emperor had become. None had foreseen it when making their terrible bargain with the Amaqi. Better for the race to have died than this.

Torve took a deep, shuddering breath.

The two groups introduced themselves, formal, tentative. Though names had been exchanged in the aftermath of the fireball, Torve could not have given any of the Falthans their correct names. He suspected Lenares did not need the introductions. She never forgot anything.

"They serve good tea here?" the woman, Bandy, asked.

"Tea and a lecture," Captain Duon answered. "The tea is excellent, the lecture less so. But the view is, as the locals claim, stunning."

Lenares thrust her face forward. "You weren't listening to the woman: how do you know whether what she said was interesting or not?"

Everyone drew back a little, as though Lenares had spat poison onto the table. As though social niceties were of more importance than the truth. And that was the heart of Torve's troubles: he was beginning to see the world the way Lenares did. Not literally, of course: she had described her strange world of colours and smells and numbers to him, a mixture well beyond his comprehension. But her worldview was unassailable. Why, indeed, did people allow themselves to be held prisoner by such niceties, conventions designed to hide the truth? How could the truth hurt more than this continual evasion, this multiplicity of meaning so amenable to abuse by the powerful?

He was beginning to see things the way Lenares did, and her view was the complete opposite of his. *Submerge your own will to that of your master*, his upbringing told him. *His word is truth. Ask no questions.* An absolutism derived from absolute subsumption of himself. While Lenares submitted to no one, accepted no truth but her own, and asked every question with her whole being, no matter how unimportant the answer. An absolutism derived from absolute assertion of herself.

Dryman answered her. "She interested you. Signal enough to the rest of us, I would have thought." He shifted his attention to the Falthans. "Lenares has special gifts, but they come at the expense of other abilities."

He smiled, the way he smiled when taking an experimental subject to the gates of death, and Torve shuddered.

Bandy drew her chair forward so she could lean over and touch Lenares on the arm. Torve saw Lenares' lips work—*don't touch me*—but she didn't say the words.

"I've been surprised how cruel people are in this part of the world," Bandy said. "Or perhaps not; I've had some experience in the east before." A half-glance over at the tall, dignified man Heredrew, an unreadable exchange. "I have no problem with plain speaking, but I do not find cruelty for its own sake clever or endearing. Nor does it persuade me that I am dealing with a man worth listening to. Now, Dryman, would you consider taking greater care with your words? I have no desire to experience a repeat of what happened at Lake Woe."

Dryman's face remained perfectly passive, but his eyes burned, measuring her, no doubt envisioning his hands on her, inflicting pain. Torve willed the woman to be careful. He had no desire to see this one suffer.

She was a woman of power, this Bandy. When everything had begun to fall apart beside Lake Woe, she had very nearly kept the three groups together. Fluent in neither Falthan nor Bhrudwan, Torve had struggled to keep up with the arguments and recriminations as they developed. Lenares had explained events later, but he knew what she had witnessed would have been quite different from what everyone else had seen. Heredrew had demanded to know who possessed the power to repel the fireball that, according to him, ought to have killed them all. No one had admitted to it, prompting the tall man to suggest that some people there were not what they seemed.

Lenares had described to Torve the words used when the three groups had gathered in the midst of the charnel field, hurling accusations at each other. The magical ones among them had been able to sense great power, and fingers began to point. Of course, those who were singled out responded by asking how the finger-pointers knew. Lenares had laughed, telling him later. She could have pointed them all out, had anyone thought to ask her. She had tried to tell them, but they weren't listening. Heredrew had the greatest power, she had claimed; in fact, his physical semblance was a shell for something else. Bandy also had great power, like yet unlike that of the tall man. Of the Bhrudwans, the two children of Noetos possessed a deal of raw power, and Noetos himself, while having no magic of his own, had something that made him impervious to magical interference. Whatever it was, it didn't prevent Lenares from making an assessment of the man. Only Dryman had succeeded in avoiding her succinct summaries.

Accusations broadened as people questioned the motives and purposes of each group. An angry and distraught Noetos refused to answer any questions, while asking many of his own. Once the rudest of the questions had been translated for him, Bandy's guardsman, Robal, had reacted belligerently and threatened violence. This amidst a sea of dead bodies and still-glowing rocks.

Bandy had tried to make the peace. Telling her guard to stand down, she stood up to the powerful men and asked each group to consider why they had been drawn to this place. Who were they up against? How might they find out? Questions Lenares also wanted to debate, Torve knew, and she joined her voice to that of the Falthan woman. But fear and mistrust won over rationality. The Bhrudwans had withdrawn first, arguing a more important set of priorities. They were right, Lenares conceded, or not right, depending on the length of view one took: this was uncomfortable thinking for her. The few hundred surviving refugees needed to be cared for, yes, and the dead disposed of before such debates could be undertaken; yet they could be assaulted anew at any moment by their hidden opponent, and so surely a discussion designed to reveal that opponent was the safest way forward.

Bandy had been brave, but she had failed. At least the three groups did not assault each other; but the Amaqi had left in a different direction from the Bhrudwans, leaving the Falthans alone and no doubt bemused on the shores of a vanished lake amid the detritus of a battle not of their making.

And now here they were, travelling north as they had indicated they would, daring to make contact with one of the other groups. Courageous, if nothing else. Or foolish.

"You wish me to take greater care with my words?" Dryman said. "Very well. Captain Duon will do the talking."

From another man Torve would have considered it a fit of pique, but the Emperor had much to hide, and perhaps no real way of knowing how powerful these Falthans were.

"We simply wish to understand what is happening here," Bandy said carefully. "How it might be tied in to events in Faltha, and to what extent we can assist in resolving things. We are not an invading force, we do not seek riches or power, nor do we wish to destabilise any nation or regime."

Torve turned to Lenares even before she started speaking. He knew she would not wait for Captain Duon to make his cumbersome explanations.

"This is what is happening," she said, rushing her words as though she expected to be interrupted at any moment. "Thousands of years ago there were three gods: a father and his two children. The children rebelled against their father and drove him out. This damaged the—the material, I think the word is—between our world and theirs. Now one of the two children is using the damage to break through into our world. He has enlarged the damage into a hole in the world by killing people and breaking the threads connecting them to everything else. The material separating our world from theirs is woven from the things we do, you see, so any untimely killing of people near the existing hole in the world makes the hole bigger. Now he and his sister can reach through and affect things. And I think we have been brought together to oppose them."

"To oppose them? Oppose who? I've not heard of three gods before." Bandy shook her head, confused.

"The numbers all match," Lenares said. "Three gods, three empires, three groups. One group from each empire to oppose the gods."

"But who are these gods?" Bandy insisted.

"I've heard something of this," Heredrew said, his voice troubled. "From a most impeccable source. *The* most impeccable source, you understand?" He faced his own people, obviously communicating something.

"We are finally making progress because I am telling the truth," Lenares said, anger in her voice. "If you keep secrets, we will not be able to prevent the Son and the Daughter breaking through. So you must tell us what source you heard the story from."

"I *must* tell you nothing," Heredrew said. "You will have to accept that we will keep some secrets relating to our identities—as at least one of your number does, I note." He nodded to Dryman, whose expression did not change. "Besides, the truth, as you call it, would not be believed."

"Can no one else taste and smell truth?" Lenares cried. "For all your magic, why are you all so crippled?" She pointed a shaking finger at Heredrew. "You are telling the truth as you see it when you say you think people wouldn't believe you. But I would believe you, if you told the truth. So what you are saying is the truth, but it is not true. You need more than your own knowledge to decide whether something is truth. That's why you should all listen to me. I'm a cosmographer."

She awaited their reaction, but there was none.

"Don't you know what a cosmographer is?"

Three Falthan heads shook in the negative.

"You don't have cosmographers in Faltha? Well. We didn't have many in Elamaq either, and no real ones for hundreds of years, not until me. A cosmographer uses numbers to see how the world is shaped, and to explain the actions of the gods. I am the most gifted cosmographer ever, Mahudia always said. I can see things that are hidden: the actions and secrets of people are colours and smells and numbers to me. If you do two things, I can see the relationship between them. Three things and I can work out the numbers that define you. I can see your place in the world. The more I watch and listen to you, the more threads I can see, until I can tell you almost everything about your life. The same applies to any trace of the gods. I can see the holes they have made, and I have spoken to one of them. Today."

"A mixed-mind," Heredrew breathed. "I've only ever met one other."

Lenares came to full attention. "You have? Where is he?" And, after a pause: "I have a name?"

"Yes, you have a name," Heredrew said, not hesitating to look right at her. She liked that, Torve knew. She wanted people to be direct. "You belong to a rare and privileged group of people," the Falthan said. "I once knew a man who could paint music, and for whom letters had colours, but he had no facility with numbers, as I recall."

"Can I meet him?" The gods now forgotten.

"I'm sorry, Lenares, he died a long time ago."

Again his head turned to Bandy, and they exchanged a glance. Entirely unconscious, no doubt, but Lenares would not have missed it.

Her eyes widened. "You are very old," she said. "He died before I was born, didn't he."

"I am a sorcerer," the man responded blandly. "Sorcerers generally have long lives."

Lenares stood and started pacing around the table, a small giggle in her voice. Totally absorbed, totally alive. "Still not all the truth. You're afraid that we won't listen to you if we find out just how old you are. You must be a very good sorcerer, Heredrew."

Bandy choked, and recovered to cough politely. "Hear that, Heredrew? A *good* sorcerer."

But Lenares was now immersed in her own visions and did not notice the further elision. "What I don't know is who drew everyone here. The Son is not happy we are all here; he sees us as enemies brought to defeat him. The Daughter—I'm not sure about the Daughter. She wants to escape, but she is not cruel like the Son. But they both must be bad, because they drove their father away."

Her pacing increased; Torve gave up following her with his eyes as she circled the tables.

"Bad people don't have parents, Rouza said. I must have done something bad to drive my own parents away, she told me, and I don't want to believe her, but where did my parents go? The Daughter understands me and wants to be my friend. Perhaps, like me, she didn't realise what she did to make her father go away. She has spoken to me twice; once more and I can define her. Then I will have my answers."

Her thoughts followed each other in an associative rather than logical sequence, forcing Torve to listen carefully. The rest of those gathered did the same, if the silence around the table was anything to go by. *Finally, after thousands of lives lost, they listen to her.*

"The Daughter says it is cold outside the world. I feel sorry for her, but not enough to let her in. She says she could keep her brother out but I don't believe her. If I knew who brought us here I could solve the mystery. A hand comes out of the hole in the sky"—she was clearly reliving the Nomansland experience—"and snatches us up. A hand with talons. She had talons when I spoke to her today, but her hand was thinner, more elegant. I think the Son brought us here, but I don't know, not yet. If the Son did bring us here, it must be for his benefit and not ours."

She stopped pacing. Her perambulations had brought her back to her own seat, so she sat down and leaned forward. "Who brought you here?" she asked the Falthans.

Bandy answered. "We're not sure. Heredrew used powerful Fire magic to transport us to Andratan, but Conal here interfered with the spell. We think Water magic might have become mixed with the Fire as a result, making the incantation vulnerable. Whatever the reason, we were between Dhauria and Andratan, somewhere outside the world if I'm guessing correctly, when we were pulled away from our intended route. Test this for truth, Lenares: none of us knows who was responsible. But Heredrew thinks he sensed another magician pushing us, working in partnership with the strong hand that drew us here. Heredrew might well be the strongest magician alive, but he could not free us from the pull. So here we are, sampling the wares of an Ikhnal Tea House, after nearly drowning in a disappearing lake, almost being struck by a fireball and enduring three weeks of foot-wearying boredom in our struggle to catch up with you."

As though conjured, a woman appeared at Heredrew's shoulder. "Can I arrange tea for you?" she asked him. "Mimia, the host who explained to you newcomers how the tea house operates, is busy serving the rest of your party, but she has communicated to me your likely needs. May I serve you?"

Heredrew nodded graciously, sending her off with a compliment, and Torve found himself wishing this temperate, considered man was the Emperor of Elamaq. Heredrew would likely not have instigated quests in search of immortality, or derived pleasure from torture. Spending time in Lenares' company had refined his own truth-sense, Torve had no doubt of it. If only he could be rid of the torment . . .

"There is something else to consider," Heredrew added. "One of our number has an unexplained voice in his head."

"A voice?" This from Captain Duon, who appeared a little agitated, perhaps because Lenares steered the conversation despite Dryman's command. "What sort of voice?"

"Unfortunately you cannot question him directly, as he knows no Bhrudwan and refuses to learn." Heredrew indicated the young man who had fainted when they first emerged from Lake Woe. "This is Conal, priest of Yosse, who is alive and still with us only on sufferance. I make no secret of my opposition to this, but I was overruled. Others in our party consider his knowledge, and especially his revelation that he has a voice of power in his head, of potential value. I say he ought to have been sent on his way for betrayal and interference. He claims to hear from an unknown magician, who has come to his aid with guidance and, on one memorable occasion, unnatural strength."

"Oh?" Captain Duon said, further discomfited. "Unnatural strength?"

"Indeed." Heredrew went on to tell a fantastic tale of the priest rescuing Bandy by slaying a *Maghdi Dasht*, a most powerful magician and servant of the Undying Man. Robal, the guardsman, had apparently witnessed feats of most unlikely physical prowess from the otherwise cowardly and weak priest.

Torve could see that the captain was taking this news strangely. His face continued to pale, and even a refill of the tea their host brought them did nothing to restore him. His pallor had caught the attention of one or two of the Falthans.

"Is the voice—can you ask him, that is—whether the voice is arrogant and full of mocking laughter?" Captain Duon wore a look of desperation.

"I'll ask," Heredrew said, his eyes narrowing, "but I don't really need to, do I?"

A small shake of the head from the captain, his eyes downcast.

The tall Falthan translated the question anyway, and the pasty-faced priest gave a brief answer. His features did not betray any curiosity in the questioner, but his dark eyes sparkled.

"He says yes, that sounds like the voice. So. We have two people around this table influenced by an unknown person. I'm sure I am not alone in feeling uneasy about this. Is this unknown person in fact one of the Most High's children? Does he overhear us even now?"

"Or," Bandy said, "is this some other person entirely? Perhaps a renegade *Maghdi Dasht*—they have been known to betray the Undying Man's cause—has brought us together. The more we discover, the less I like any of this."

Lenares stood. "I almost know what it is," she said. "Give me a moment to follow the thread. It was something Arathé said." She began pacing around the table again, then stopped.

"No," she said, her face suddenly white. "No, I don't know anything."

What? A clear lie. So unlike Lenares, Torve felt ill even considering it. *What is she doing?*

Heredrew interrupted their musing.

"New arrivals?" He wore a worried frown. "I've just re-alised: did the serving woman say something about new arrivals? Do you suppose—"

Robal was first to react, though Torve had seen a flash of something like amusement in Dryman's eyes. "Get away from the window!" the Falthan soldier cried and, seizing Bandy by the shoulders, dragged her towards the landward end of the tea house. He knocked down a free-standing partition and there they were, the Bhrudwans, all eight of them, heads down in discussion, the steam from their beverages rising—then abruptly fluttering and flattening out as a breeze sprang from somewhere.

"Outside!" Robal shouted. "We must flee!"

Beside Torve, Lenares began to mutter. "The gods don't want us to put all the truths together. Every time we get close, they try to stop us." She turned towards the window.

Torve took her by the hand. "Leave her," Dryman commanded. The Omeran's hand spasmed, but kept hold of hers. His master's voice came again, shaped with its full weight. "Leave her."

How deep was his conditioning to obey? Clearly deeper than his love for Lenares. His hand twitched open and his arm jerked away from her. Another betrayal.

Shrieks from somewhere, a loud roar from behind them. A bone-deep thump as the ground shook. Another fireball? Torve shouldered through the half-open door and began running up the hill beyond the tea house. Ahead of him were hosts and guests, running, stumbling, turning open-mouthed.

He turned too, and saw the wave.

*   *   *

Was it possible for a mind to become worn, Duon wondered. For the edge of reason, once sharp, to be dulled? Weariness had definitely played a part: he and his fellows had received no respite for months. But if his mind was failing him, it was because of other things. The voice in his head, for example: reminder of a magician who had empowered him with strength beyond his dreams—at a cost as yet unknown. Perhaps he was the candle, his mind the wick to the magician's flame, burning brightly but about to wink out.

Or his memories of that day in the Summer Palace. Waiting for death, then facing the Neherians, believing he was about to die. A fear overwhelmed by the strange mix of exaltation and horror as the magician's strength rose in him and he began to kill.

He had begged the voice in his head to erase the memories. They had instead blurred together into a gory pastiche. Whether this was a product of his own mind or some sadistic intent of the voice, he could not tell.

Or maybe the cause of his blurriness was the constant, disconcerting alteration of the rules of reality. Nomansland had always played by its own rules, and their shepherding there had been frightening but not surprising. But storms and whirlwinds, vanishing lakes and fireballs, not to mention supernatural strength and an orgy of bloody death—all these served to separate him from the comfort of the real.

So the giant wave, towering above the cliff and the tea house, made surprisingly little impression on Duon's weary mind. He began running only because the voice in his head took over his nervous system, impelling his legs. A glance behind revealed the foaming water rearing above them like an angry stallion; he turned away and so felt rather than saw the wave crash to the ground. *Don't look*, he told himself, but the thump pulled his head around.

The bulk of the wave had come down on the tea house. The structure had vanished under a white explosion that appeared to be erupting up and out from the clifftop. Running figures covered the hillside above the coast; most well clear of the water. Like him, many of them paused to watch the spectacle. And to watch the fate of those not so fortunate, who had not taken to their heels at the first indication of trouble.

Lenares was one such. Just below him, Duon could see Torve hopping from foot to foot, clearly desperate to rescue the cosmographer, but something restrained him. Dryman, no doubt. The man held an unhealthy, uncanny sway over the Omeran and no command of Duon's had been able to break it.

The remaining power of the wave washed up towards the struggling girl. There seemed comparatively little strength left in it, but it hit her with force and took the legs out from under her. The wave ran another ten or twenty paces up the hill, then began to draw back. It withdrew from the place Lenares had been standing, but she was no longer there.

The water raced back towards the sea as though pulled by an overstretched cord. It smashed into the ruins of the tea house with as much vehemence as the original wave, and the one remaining wall succumbed, vanishing over the cliff in a flurry of foam, trees and detritus. And bodies, no doubt.

The magician lurking like an eel in the crevices of his mind began to laugh, puffing like a bellows. *Out to sea like a piece of wood in a flood*, he said, sharing his delight with Duon. *That girl could have ruined everything.*

Duon realised the next few moments would be crucial,
not only for his own survival, but also perhaps in thwarting
whatever assault the gods were perpetrating on the world.
The thought surged through his mind as an unvoiced feeling, and now he could try—*had* to try—the mental technique he'd devised during the days and weeks on the road
north; days he'd been left alone by the voice save for a few
brief checks. An answer, possibly, to the question: how
does one mislead someone residing in one's head?

He augmented the images in his head, feigning relief
as Lenares fell into the foaming water and disappeared, to
be sucked, along with beams, bushes and bodies, over the
cliff. He imagined her, fearful and already half-drowned,
tumbling down towards dark rocks. A moment of abject
terror, then pain, disintegration and darkness.

I thought you were sympathetic to her, the magician
said.

*She was a valuable asset to my Emperor, so I tolerated
her*, Duon sent earnestly. *But three months on the road
taught me that usefulness is no substitute for true humanity. She irked me beyond belief in the last few weeks. No one
here will mourn her passing.*

*Is that so? I ought to have paid more attention. Perhaps
you could have done the job for me.*

Had you but asked, Duon sent, desperately masking his
feelings.

*Ah, I see. Perhaps it is time for me to propose a more
formal alliance, and in so doing explain what I am doing
in your head.*

*Of course. But it might be wise to wait until I'm less
busy. I will be expected to at least go through the motions*

of searching for survivors. I don't imagine this will be of much interest to you.

The magician gave assent to this. *I have other things to attend to. When you have finished your task, you may summon me by speaking the word "Deorc" in the mind-voice you are using now. I will attend you as soon as I am able.*

Then came the curious "leaving" sensation as the magician withdrew, as though something moved from the front to the back of his head. The top of Duon's neck tingled and warmed. Then the parasite was gone and Duon found himself alone.

He blew out a breath. He had no way of knowing what the magician might do if he learned he had been deceived. Fry his mind perhaps, or make him throw himself off a cliff or walk into a bonfire. He dared not make a single mistake.

Now to help the others find Lenares. He had a feeling that without her they were lost.

Drawn by curiosity, an urge to see the patterns and to identify which of the holes it was, Lenares calculated the speed and size of the approaching wave. Her calculation was perfect, as always, but as a result of her curiosity she didn't have enough time to react to the information the numbers supplied her. She managed to find the trap she'd set, which told her a god had conjured the wave, but wasted precious seconds doing so, and then she was out of time. The water would reach her before she could escape.

Seeing herself as a creature of the mind, Lenares had never paid her body much attention. Some of the cosmographers had primped and pampered their bodies, while others had regarded their fleshly housing as not much more

than a nuisance, but primper and ascetic alike had perished
in agony in the Valley of the Damned. To pay too much
attention to her physical needs, Lenares had decided, was
a waste. So she had done nothing to augment her natural
fitness, nor had she learned how to run efficiently. Either
might have made the difference. Either might have saved
her.

She ran as hard as she could, arms and legs flying in all
directions, but as soon as her feet started uphill she could
feel her strength draining. Ahead of her the Falthans struggled up the slope, the oldest of them borne in Robal's arms.
Come back for me! she wanted to shout. The crash behind
her was louder and much closer than she had imagined, and
a moment later something punched her behind her knees.
She tumbled backwards, her legs shooting out from beneath her, and ended up underwater.

She knew about waves like this. She was a cosmographer: it was her job to know about every geographical phenomenon that could be affected by the gods. Such waves
were generated by vast, deep movements of the earth, and
could appear hours after such quakes. They were little
waves while out to sea, according to the few sea captains
who had seen them, but when they came ashore they grew
enormous, like a tiny mouth opening wide to swallow a
large meal.

But knowing about them did nothing to help her survive
them. Something hard cracked the back of her skull. She
immediately stopped fighting the water and wrapped her
arms around her head.

How long can I hold my breath?

Her numbers offered her no answer.

I can't die. Please! Not when everyone needs my help!

Her legs smacked against some hidden obstacle: the water threw her upwards, and she took a hasty, watery breath before plunging back into the foam. She had seen enough, however, to signal her approaching death. The obstacle had been part of the tea house: the cliff was seconds away.

Lenares screamed with frustration and her mouth filled with water.

Not enough time left even to think . . .

Then she was falling, surrounded by a circular curtain of water, tumbling towards the sea far below. Two breaths, one, all she had left.

And the water around her slowed, began to resolve into millions of shimmering droplets—a part of her mind was not happy with the imprecise idea of *millions* and set about counting them all—drifting downwards slower than dust motes. She herself had slowed.

So this is what happens in the moment before death.

Her eye was caught by a peculiar arrangement of droplets and foam directly below her. Almost in the shape of a face, a woman's face, if the shadows of the rocks below weren't playing a trick on her. Surrounding the image a curtain of water continued to sift gently towards the sea.

Lenares, the image seemed to say. *Finally we are alone.*

"Daughter?" she replied, not knowing what else to call her. Definitely the same face she'd seen earlier in the day, outlined in steam.

I have a choice to offer you, the goddess said, her voice so sweet it seemed to sparkle on Lenares' tongue.

"You offered me a choice before, in the tea house," said the cosmographer.

*So I did. In a way this choice, too, is in the tea house.
Look around you, above you.*

She looked. Dark shapes encircled her: wreckage from
the building atop the cliff, heading with her towards obliteration.

"Are you slowing time?"

Where I dwell there is no time, said the Daughter. *It is a
beautiful place.*

"You can't fool me," Lenares said. "Pelanesse said time
and space are the same thing, because space implies time
required to cross it. I've seen the mathematics. If you don't
experience time, you don't have a place."

The goddess smiled. *You would happily argue with me
even as you crashed into the rocks below. I like that about
you.*

Lenares noted the Daughter did not refute her accusation about time and space.

Here is my offer to you, said the Daughter, her face sparkling madly. *Give me a place in your flesh, so I can touch
the world directly. It's only fair; my brother already has a
host among you, and so grows stronger every day. I could
ask for so much more. I could demand that we exchange
places, that you go into the agony of darkness, where you
find yourself smeared across the stars, each point of light
a prick of anguish in a body no longer there, while I drink
the warmth of your body and learn to be you. I would do a
better job of being Lenares, too, much better than you. I'd
have Torve on me and in me, again and again; I'd unmask
the Son's host; I'd save the world from him. But I'm not
asking that of you.*

Not yet, went the unspoken words.

All I want is the chance to battle my brother on equal

terms. All I need is a place in your mind. From there we could work together to drive the Son out, to heal the rift in the walls of the world, perhaps even to call the Father back from exile and let the world find balance again.

And then the sweetest enticement of all.

You would know so much, the Daughter said, her voice caressing Lenares' ears. *The secrets of the universe are far vaster than anything your mind can imagine. I can share them with you. We can travel together in an instant and sit on the High Seat. You can ask me anything and I will give you answer.*

Or you can fall to your death.

They were noticeably closer to the rocks.

Could she time this right?

"I . . . I would like to know more," Lenares said. "More about how the numbers in my mind work, more about why I am different from others. Can you tell me more about those things?"

Of course, said the goddess, gazing up at Lenares.

Gazing up. Everything depended on how aware the Daughter was of the world around her, a world in which she was unwelcome, alien.

Of course. What do you want to know?

"Why do I think in numbers? Why doesn't everyone else? What is wrong with them?"

The Daughter's eyes flashed. Not real eyes, drops of water reflecting light. She said, *Their minds are like the rooms in a house. A person can be in only one room at a time, in a house like theirs. They're seeing or hearing or tasting or touching or smelling. But in your house there is only one room. Your mind sees and hears and tastes and touches and smells all at the same time. It's why you have*

*no real memory of your childhood: your mind took far
longer than most people's minds do to come to terms with
what the world was telling it.*

"It makes sense," Lenares breathed, and she did not have
to feign her excitement. "My room is large, while theirs
are small. I see everything, while they separate the world
into different categories." She smiled at the goddess. Soon,
soon. "I'd rather be like me."

*And because you have such a large mind, you will not
even notice sharing it with me. Your mind is so large, so
warm; you and I will be fast friends, Lenares. My name
was . . . is Umu. You can call me by my name because we
are friends. Lenares, will we be friends? Can I come into
your mind? All you have to do is say yes. Invite me in. I
won't leave you like Mahudia did, or like Martje, your real
mother. Say yes, Lenares.*

Only a moment more . . .

*Martje? Oh, goddess Umu, we could have been friends,
if you weren't such a liar.*

"Yes? Just yes?"

That's all. Anticipation thrumming through the words,
a slavering hunger.

"No!"

The goddess shrieked in anger, time returned with a jerk
and Lenares plummeted perhaps five paces to the rocks
below.

Her last thought before the blackness swallowed her
was that she'd underestimated the pain.

CHAPTER 13

NOCTURNAL REFLECTIONS

EVENING CAME AT LAST, COATING the gentle northland summer landscape in a patina of forgetfulness, blurring the outlines of hills and trees so familiar to the searchers after hours of looking. Telling them it was time to end their endeavours; they had done all they could and more, surely. Time for food, for drink, for laughter and companionship, time to put the day's tragedy behind them and let the healing process begin.

Torve had no truck with the night. All it gave him was a chance to reprise his litany of suffering. And now it conspired to steal his hope.

Lenares, his beloved, was one of three lost in the great wave. A local man from the nearest town had been found wedged among the piles of the tea house, and a mangled body, most likely that of one of the hosts, was located at the foot of the cliff. The path down to the sea had been obliterated by the wave, and it had taken an hour for a brave villager to clamber down to the body. During that hour Torve had been desolate, believing the body was that of Lenares.

He remained impassive, so his master could not read him, but stricken with grief nonetheless.

The body was too small to be hers, the villager reported when he returned, and had a distinctive birthmark under the chin. Balanced against Torve's short-term relief, a rotund woman collapsed to the debris-strewn grass, sobbing her anguish. A daughter lost.

Who will mourn the loss of Lenares?

At the least, Duon and Dryman ought to have joined him in his distress, but neither seemed troubled beyond annoyance at the loss of a useful asset. He realised he was experiencing the beginnings of anger, an emotion he'd always kept under control. If anything, the Falthans and Bhrudwans seemed more concerned. Arathé and Bandy, in particular, had not stinted in their searching.

But now, with nightfall imminent, the hands of sympathetic townspeople, themselves shocked by events, reached towards the strangers, beckoning them towards pale paths leading to lamplit homes and fire-warmed food. Torve found himself in the company of three young men, perhaps fifteen years of age, eagerly doing their part—and obviously enjoying the welcome interruption in the routine of their lives.

"Where are you from?" one of them asked him.

"Pardon me?" Torve responded. He did not have the heart to join in the conversation, nor the ill manners to ignore the question.

"Where do you come from?"

The boy asking the question had tight, curly hair, not unlike his own, reminding him of the Children of the Desert. For a moment he wished he was back there. He and Lenares should never have left.

But I had no choice.

"From Talamaq," he replied.

"Is that as far south as Raceme? I went to Raceme once." The boy turned eager eyes on him, trying to prove he was not some back-country lad.

"Further," Torve said, drawn in by the lad's enthusiasm. "Much further. With more people living in one city than all the people on the Fisher Coast combined."

"Don't bother him," one of the other boys whispered fiercely to the curly-headed lad. "He's lost his girl. Dad said not to bother him."

"Was jus' asking. Thought he might want to talk."

"Would you? Say it had been Ina swept away. Would you want to talk?"

Curly-hair grunted something unintelligible in reply.

The village lay half an hour's walk inland from the sea. By the time they arrived darkness added its own distance, making conversation much less certain: no one liked talking when the listeners' faces were hidden. Torve was thankful.

"This is Foulwater," said the quietest of the three youths. "The name was given the village by the Undying Man hundreds of years ago. But we call it The Water. Dad says you're to come straight to our place. He's asked Ma to get a bath ready for you."

A pause; no doubt Torve was supposed to be impressed. And he was. Not by the bath, but by the trouble these villagers had taken on their account. The wave wasn't their fault, but the townspeople had acted as though it was, and were not prepared to let the strangers go on their way without caring for them first.

"Foulwater," Torve repeated, his brain still slow.

"Aye. Nothing wrong with the water, but apparently not to the Undying Man's taste, so he cursed us with the name. We ignore it. Easy to do, this far south of Andratan."

"How far south?"

"Two months' walking, they say, or a month aboard."

To the right and left of them doors to small houses opened, letting yellow fingers of light into the street. One by one the strangers were shepherded into homes by earnest villagers. Torve noted where his master was taken, and the inevitable question raised itself: *Will he require me tonight?*

Of course he will. He will not be able to resist.

So the village would pay for its hospitality with a life.

He was welcomed into a tiny hut by a spectacularly wrinkled woman and a bent-backed man, who treated him like a visiting prince. He spoke politely to them in his rapidly improving Bhrudwan, but giving the conversation only as much attention as required. His mind still rested on a difficult but beautiful woman, lost in the water and the darkness. Ignoring his preoccupation they fed him, then showed him the barn where he would bathe and sleep, and the aroma of scented water brought a tear of longing to his eye, reminding him of easier days in Talamaq Palace. Days before the Emperor went mad.

As he lay in the rusty metal tub, his exhausted body fighting sleep, Torve realised that, apart from those days spent in the House of the Gods with Lenares, this would be the first night for many years he had slept in a different house from his master.

He awoke to cold water, a wrinkled body and a hand on his shoulder.

"Did you not mark where I was housed?" his master asked him, anger freighting his words. "I expected you before now. I wait for an hour or more, only to find you taking your ease rather than serving your rightful master. Get out and get dressed. We have work to do."

Torve scrambled out of the tub, and found his clothes neatly folded on a chair, courtesy, no doubt, of the wrinkle-faced woman. *And I will thank you by tormenting one of your fellow villagers.*

"Haven't you learned enough yet, master?" Torve asked. The question slipped out before he could exercise his usual caution, tiredness and heart-sickness contributing to his rash words.

"I have learned, Omeran, not to tolerate criticism from slaves."

The last word bit into Torve, as it was intended to, reminding him that he had been a gift to the young Emperor-in-waiting, had been brought up with him, partaking of all the privileges of the Palace while his fellow Omerans suffered abused, shortened lives at the hands of their masters.

But then the Emperor smiled at him, removing much of the force from his words.

"You were once a friend, Torve," he said, his voice softening a little. "We shared superior minds and insatiable curiosities. But since this cosmographer entered our lives, you have drawn away from me. You bring me little more joy now than any beast, and less value."

Dare he say it? Could he say it? Drawing the strings of his tunic closed, he opened his mouth—and the words came out.

"Might it not be, master, that you have changed more than I? I have no right to ask, but were someone of status to comment on your altered behaviour, could you deny it? I am not defending my own actions, save to say I have remained ever loyal, as my nature commands; rather, as I once did, I am acting as a mirror, reflecting your question back on yourself. Since the day Lenares appeared, *you* have changed." A final risk. "Why, my friend? Why?"

To his astonishment, his master closed his eyes and bowed his head. "Ah, Torve, you shame me. You are right: I kept many secrets from you."

A long pause. Something obviously under consideration. The eyes opened, a decision made.

"You were not privy to what happened late one night, the night following our dear cosmographer's presentation to the court at Talamaq. I was visited, Torve; visited by a god."

His eyes widened and he stared at the Omeran: they were black, rimmed with white, the pupils mere pinpricks in the darkness. Profoundly disturbing.

"A god, Torve. The Son, no less. I know I abolished the gods, but that night they taught me better. They are real, my Omeran. They speak. The Son did not require worship, he said to me; indeed, far from making me abase myself before him, he acknowledged me as an equal. He had heard what the cosmographer had to say, and asked if he could sift my thoughts and memories. I know it sounds incautious of me, but his presence was so . . . so starkly real, everything else felt false and hollow. I doubt I could have resisted even had I wished to. So I opened myself up to him."

The Emperor raised his arms, spreading them wide, and a grinding weight came down upon them both, setting the air itself to groaning. A deep rumbling and shuddering shook the barn, sending dust drifting across the lamplight. In the rear of the barn a cow lowed nervously.

"I opened myself to the Son," the Emperor continued, in a deeper and more commanding voice, "and he came. He changed me. At every stage he asked my permission and, after examining what he had done, I granted it. He enlarged my mind and changed me for the better. One of the many benefits, Torve, is that the halfwit Lenares can no longer read me. She will never associate me with the mask-wearing Emperor.

"And neither did anyone else. The court acknowledged the mask, just as they did the afternoon we played a prank on them and you wore it. But under the instruction of the Son, I shed my mask and walked through the corridors and halls of the Talamaq Palace. None marked me. Even you did not mark me.

"It was that day I conceived my plan to secure absolute control of the Empire. Titular head to a murderous group of Alliances does not offer me the security I need, nor the power I desire. I used the fool Duon as the excuse to or-ganise an expedition with a twofold purpose: to go north myself in search of the secret of immortality, and to be rid of the Alliances forever. So I contacted the Marasmians."

Torve staggered and slumped against the bath, slopping water everywhere. "You contacted the Marasmians? *You* masterminded the death of your own army?"

His master's smile was wide and self-satisfied. "Indeed, my friend. We lost many soldiers that day, but the price was worth it to be rid of so many drones. We can grow more soldiers! You see the logic of it, do you not? Many times we talked about the Alliances and what it would take to break their power over the Empire. Now they are broken, without any cost to Talamaq. Not a house burned, not a single murder on the streets. A plan breathtaking in its elegance."

"Yours or his?"

"Now, Torve, no need for bitterness. Changed though I am, I am still your master. I hope I have demonstrated this on our nocturnal forays. To tell the truth, in an attempt to convince you I am still whom I once was, I have been more vigorous in my pursuit of answers to our eternal question. Yes, it was the Son's plan, but it was my execution, and it could not have been more perfect. Even the intervention of those interesting desert children served my purpose, delivering us from the Marasmians who were about, I suspect, to double-cross us. And here we are, in the company of powerful men, none of whom suspect my real identity."

Certainly Torve had not suspected the mercenary of being his Emperor. He'd wondered about that in the weeks after Dryman had revealed himself, but he'd not seen the Emperor maskless since his tenth birthday, his Masking Day. So how was he to read his childhood companion in the soldier's bland face? The voice ought to have given him away, but it had subtly altered; deeper and huskier now than the voice he remembered. Altered just enough to confound Lenares, who had repeatedly expressed her frustration at her ignorance.

So now his master carried the Son with him.

Torve decided to make it his mission to find out what benefit the Emperor thought to derive from the arrangement, and what cost he—and, by extension, everyone— might be paying.

If only Lenares were here, he said to himself.

*   *   *

The Emperor selected their victim with patience and care. The village of Foulwater was a small one, with perhaps five hundred residents, and as a consequence the starlit roads were almost empty: few people were about after dark. Torve and his master waited for perhaps an hour and saw no more than a handful. Those who were to be found outside appeared to be fetching things for their guests inconvenienced by the destruction of the Yacoppica Cliffs Tea House: food, drink, washwater and washcloths.

As soon as Torve saw the woman, he knew his master would not be able to resist her. Her face was shadowed, but it was clearly the same woman who had hosted them in the tea house that morning.

The Emperor stepped into the street. "Excuse me, we've lost our way," he said. "Can you help us?"

"Of course." Her face was drawn, weary in appearance; the bags under her eyes were recent additions to an already unflattering appearance. *A day searching for a lost work-mate can do that to a person*, Torve considered. "You're staying at the Nevem place. If you return the way you have come—"

Her breath hissed as the Emperor placed his knife against her belly. She didn't cry out. She would later, Torve knew. *Oh, lady, you should have cried out. Perhaps someone would have heard.*

"You know what this is?" the Emperor said.

"I know." Remarkably calm. "I have no money, but the village would be happy—"

He moved until he had the knife pressed against the small of her back. "You do not yet know what we want," he whispered into her ear, and this intimacy alerted her to the likely nature of this encounter.

She took a deep breath, that was all, as Dryman forced her along the street and down a side alley, away from the houses and past a smithy on the edge of town. Her chance to call for help gone.

"You don't mean to leave me alive, do you?" she said, her eyes darting right and left. Her voice had thinned, as though forced through a constricted throat.

"That really depends on how well you answer our questions," Dryman said, in control, doubtless already moving towards the state of exultation that was his immediate reward for these excursions.

"In other words, no."

The woman shrank visibly before them. Then she stumbled, as though losing the strength in her legs. The blade must have bitten her, for she hissed again, and Torve watched a darker stain slowly spread amid the dark shadow of her back. The woman began to shake. *Early for the shakes, but she already knows what we're about.*

They walked for perhaps twenty minutes, leaving the town well behind. The Emperor found a ridgeline and surveyed the surrounding land, looking for a secluded area. In the darkness Torve could see little but wooded slopes. Perhaps the god within the Emperor had augmented the man's sight. It would certainly explain his ability to conduct this business in the dark.

What is the Son making of this? Is he shocked? Or— more likely—is this perverted appetite one of the reasons he chose the Emperor as his host?

There appeared to be no dwellings nearby. The Emperor shepherded the woman down into a bush-lined gully—a place that during the day would be of undoubted beauty—

and bade her sit down beside a tree. Nearby a stream gurgled in the darkness.

"Ropes," the Emperor murmured, and Torve pulled them from his pack. The woman saw them and hissed again, the sound this time accompanied by an involuntary exclamation. Part of Torve's role was to show her the ropes as he bound her feet, to let her know there was no escaping them. Her face sagged and silent tears began to flow. Despite this, Torve thought her brave. He'd often wondered how he would react if he became one of the Emperor's victims. Bravery and cowardice both came to the same end, however.

"Bad things happen to punish people for their wrongdoing, don't they?" the Emperor asked. It was one of his standard questions. Victims always agreed, hoping to convince him they were innocent of wrongdoing and therefore wrongly held.

But not this woman.

"Of course not," she said. "Bad things happen for a variety of reasons. In this case they will happen because bad men choose to take advantage of the goodwill of our village."

"Ah, a philosopher," the Emperor breathed. "We are fortunate."

"No, you are foolish. The poor girl with you was right in what she said this morning: you don't listen. I told you then I have been trained to interpret people's personalities. Do you not think in twenty years of tea-house service I have seen every type of behaviour known? More than long enough to reflect on good and evil. To know you for what you are. A madman."

The Emperor grunted, clearly puzzled by the woman's boldness in the face of her fear.

"So you want to question me," she continued. "You're wasting your time. If what I witnessed this morning is any guide, you'll not listen to the answers anyway."

The knife flashed towards her chin, held back at the last moment but still nicking her skin. Remarkable control by the Emperor, but it was matched by the woman's continued commentary in the face of death. She began speaking again after barely a pause.

"This is not the first time you've done this: you are far too polished and not nervous enough. So I have no doubt there is a trail of tortured bodies behind you. Ample proof that you have never listened, never learned, and have suffered repeated failures."

Was the woman trying to hasten her own death by making the Emperor angry? She could not possibly contend with him. The more likely result would be prolonging her pain. Torve wanted to counsel her, to advise her to keep quiet, but he knew his role tonight and was compelled to keep to it.

The Emperor had decided to play the chief role, and began his work on her. He took even more care than usual, playing the woman as though she was some sort of organic musical instrument. She whimpered, bit her lip until the blood flowed, then screamed, and her eyes began that darting dance with which Torve was so familiar. They all did it. *Will help come? Do I hear someone? Is anybody there?* Thoughts like these no doubt flickered through her mind as her body began to bruise and bleed and break.

Torve found himself wishing there were ways he might overcome the breeding of three thousand years. To disobey just once; to break the chains binding him to this hateful man. To pick up the pipe and bash and bash and bash him . . .

Peta Onacanthia knew she would die tonight, and the death would not be easy. On the contrary, it would be terrible, worse than she could imagine. No matter what she said or did, how clever or submissive she was, she would not see another dawn. The dawns here—aaah, a finger gave way to something the man was doing; she would not look, refused to look, but she could not hold back the scream—the dawns here were so beautiful. She always asked for the earliest shift at the tea house so she could watch the pulsing yellow sun push its way up from the sea and emerge swirling and steaming into the sky. This day had dawned in low cloud, the sunrise hardly noticed: had she known it was the last one she would ever see, she—aaah! God of the sea, another finger; she shrieked out pain, anger and bewilderment, powerless to prevent her display of vulnerability. Had she known this would be her end, she would have paid more attention to the dawn. Then, she supposed, had she known, she would have run. Let someone else be taken.

They haven't even asked my name. That she should be murdered like this, so impersonally! To these cruel men she could have been anyone, could have been that useless Belain from Northend. *No, don't wish ill on others.* Just a body to them, a body with limits to explore. To invade, to annex, to destroy.

"You are suffering," said the man with dead eyes, the one who was doing the terrible things to her. "Far beyond anything you've endured before. But there is much worse to come."

"You are wrong," she panted, trying to keep her wits together. "I've endured worse on the birthing bed. Not something you would know. And as I die I'll hold the memories of my beautiful children in my mind. I won't see you. I won't feel your touch. You won't exist."

The man nodded, as though trying to memorise her words. As though taking notes.

"Denial," he said to his silent accomplice. "They all deny something in the end."

"Is that what you are doing?" she asked him. "A study of pain?"

"You're a clever woman for a village drab. A study, indeed, but of death, not of pain. To learn from those about to die how one might avoid it. Thus, I want you to tell me: of what are you most afraid? The dying, or death itself? Pain or oblivion? What lies do you tell yourself to rationalise the nothingness to come? Everyone dies in terror: is such deep fear a necessary ingredient for death to occur?"

The man's left hand, in which hers lay with her last unbroken finger stretched out, quivered as he asked the question. *Ah*, she thought, despite her pain. *I see your secret.*

"No lies," she said. He lifted the pliers and her hand, though firmly held, contracted involuntarily, causing her fingers to erupt in a cascade of agony. A minute or so later, when she could think again, she continued. "No lies. I'm not afraid of death. Not like you; you're terrified. If you'd ever had a real friend or family you would understand the bittersweetness of passing. And its necessity in the order of things, to clear the way for the next generation. No sweetness for you, only bitterness. No next generation, only you, forever and ever. But unlike you, I will be mourned, then remembered with fondness and love."

"Oh? Within a month your family will be fighting over your possessions." The dead-eyed man smiled thinly at the thought. "I've seen it happen, even in the wealthiest houses. A year and you will be forgotten by your precious next generation. It will be as though you never existed."

"Not so, ignorant one. Those who you say will forget were born of my body. The only way it would be as though I had never existed would be . . ." She faltered, not wanting to lead him.

But he was sharp, her killer.

"I could, you know," he said, leaning closer. "I have the power. I have your thread in my hand, and I'm about to burn it out of the tapestry of the world. I could follow the threads of anyone entangled with you. Burn them out, destroy them. I could not be stopped."

She wanted to beg him, implore him not to do it, but such words would only encourage him. *Feign indifference.*

"Even if you were a god, you could not erase the past."

She hoped the desperation edging her voice was not audible to the man's ears. Better to say nothing; but anything was preferable to the sound of her own screams.

"Don't you fear oblivion?" he asked, his voice an obscene caress. He set her hand down on a stone, and held her wrist. "Hammer, Torve. Surely any kind of life, even a life filled with pain"—he struck her remaining finger a brutal blow with the hammer, shattering her top joint, and she shrieked—"is preferable to everlasting absence."

This time she blacked out for a moment. But as soon as she could talk, she did, panting out the pain. "I've had a good life. I'm not afraid of the sleep to come. I deserve a rest."

His features soured. "You do not fear because you lack the imagination."

"For what? To entangle myself trying to imagine what it's like without the ability to imagine? What sort of accursed fool are you, wasting your life enquiring of the dying? *Don't you realise the person really dying here is you?*"

She drew a shuddering breath, then fixed his horrible eyes with her most compassionate gaze.

"Why not live?" she asked, and threw her entire soul into the question.

He struck her then, his fist a god-augmented ball of anger. Her head jerked to one side. Blood mixed with spittle began to flow from her mouth, and fluid leaked from a cut below her eye.

"This experiment is flawed," he said to Torve as he waited for the woman to regain consciousness. "These subjects live such predictable, mundane lives they never spare the time to consider death."

Torve judged his words carefully, then spoke with what he hoped was the right amount of detachment. "I am beginning to suspect, master, that the question is not amenable to being answered in this fashion. I believe we may need to consider another approach."

"Perhaps," his master said, as the woman stirred. "I will think on this later. For now I have had all the debate I care for. Time to take this unfortunate to the gates of death. Perhaps she can see through the grey veil. Tell us what awaits."

He took a short pipe from his wallet. The woman—gods respect her spirit—did not flinch. At first.

*   *   *

They broke her, crudely and without mercy. Dispassionately, as though preparing her for disposal. But not as swiftly as she'd hoped. Before the end she begged and pleaded, just as he had predicted she would.

She died, not with an image of her loved ones in her mind as she'd boasted, but with one thought glowing faintly, the last to wink out.

They never asked my name.

"So. You've gone to a great deal of trouble to arrange this, southerner. Have your say and let me get back to my room. I'm supposed to be under guard, you know."

Graceless. The Falthan priest reminded Duon of Ampater, his second on his first journey through the Azrain Mountains to Lut. Whatever goodness in Ampater had come not from his natural disposition, but from the demands of his bizarre southern religion. Impersonal, forced and unpleasant. The man had perished on the return journey, victim of an avalanche. Duon had not searched the snow too diligently.

"Then let us be swift," said the Bhrudwan lad, earning a nod of agreement from his sister. Graceless as the priest was, these two were his opposite. Vibrant, passionate, unfettered. Prepared to place other people, other issues, before their own desires.

"Very well." Duon drew a deep breath: he had lived with this for months and, to tell the truth, felt a little reluctant to bring it out into the open. "It has emerged that the three of us hear a voice in our head. It seems to be the same voice, that of a male magician. Agreed thus far?"

A sullen, almost reluctant grunt from Conal; two vigorous nods from the Bhrudwan siblings.

"Arathé and I believe we were in Andratan two years and longer ago, in the autumn," Duon went on. "She is certain she was there for at least a year, which, we think, overlapped with the few weeks I spent in the fortress. So, Conal, when were you there?"

The priest jumped, almost coming off the log he sat on. "I didn't say I was there," he said evasively.

"On your calling as a priest, or however it is expressed in Faltha, can you swear to me you have never set foot in Andratan?"

Conal brushed his long fringe away from his eyes. "No," he admitted.

"Very well, then. You were there, I don't care why. Here is our dilemma. It is likely we were infected during our stay in the Undying Man's fortress. We don't know who by or what for. And we can't even discuss it for fear of being overheard."

"We can't even think it," Anomer agreed.

"So here we are, meeting at night, on the assumption that even a magician needs to sleep, hoping we can—in as brief a time as possible—make sense of what is happening to us and decide what to do about it."

"Don't forget what Lenares calls—called—the hole in the world. Our thoughts are being overheard by something desiring our deaths, it seems."

"I agree, Anomer, and you are right to mention—"

"It tried to kill us, I think, in Faltha," said Conal.

"There was a hole in Faltha?" Duon asked, surprised by the abruptness with which the priest joined the conversation.

"Must have been. It was when I first joined Stella—ah, Bandy—and her guardsman. We were on a boat in the Aleinus River and encountered a waterspout. I remember Bandy telling me later that she thought the spout was searching for something. It could have been me, couldn't it?" He licked his lips. "We might be targets of the gods. Mightn't we?"

"Undoubtedly," Anomer said. "Arathé, and anyone in mind-conversation with her, has been hunted by the hole. We are the reason the hole pursues our friends, and why thousands of people have died."

"Our choices are stark," said Duon. "Flight, keeping away from centres of population, hoping to remain hidden from the hole. Or to walk boldly towards it, hoping to destroy it, and those behind it, somehow, before it destroys us."

"Why can't we just stop talking to it?" asked Conal.

"Do you really think you can keep the voice out of your mind? Given what your companions said about you, the voice has taken you over completely at least twice: once to save your companion—Stella, was that her name? Or Bandy? Nevertheless, once to save her and once to kill her."

"They told you that? All of it? So . . . you know about her and Heredrew?"

"Know what? How can we know whether we have heard everything?" Duon leaned forward, his face close to that of the priest. The faint starlight revealed a sheen of sweat on the man's cheeks. "What do we need to know about Bandy and Heredrew, aside from the fact that Bandy goes by another name?"

The priest paused a moment, then lifted his head and

smiled at them. "If I tell you, you must promise not to do anything rash."

He's either a fool or a very clever man, Duon thought— *or possibly both*. "No promises. Just tell us."

Conal smiled slyly. "I called her Stella, a slip of the tongue, but that is her real name, a name she does not want known. Do either of you children know the name of the Falthan queen?"

Arathé exchanged a blank look with her brother.

"Ah, then perhaps you know the name of the Undying Man's one-time consort?"

Arathé made a series of hand gestures to her brother, accompanied by moaning and grunting noises, the sort a simpleton would make. Though Duon knew the woman was intelligent and articulate in her own fashion, his cultural conditioning screamed "lackwit". With difficulty he put his prejudice to one side and instead marvelled at the siblings' ability to communicate, particularly given the darkness.

"Stella Pellwen," said Anomer at once. "Well known to anyone conscripted to learn magic in Andratan."

More signals from his sister, this time frantic.

"Are you suggesting the young woman with Heredrew is the Dark Consort? Arathé says if the woman was still alive she would be ancient. Nearly a hundred years old."

"I merely asked a question," Conal said. "You understand, if I am asked whether I have kept Bandy's secret, I wish to say with honesty I have told no one."

Duon scratched his head. "So, if she is the Dark Consort, then the man Heredrew—"

Anomer chimed in. "The self-confessed powerful sorcerer—"

"Is the Undying Man himself," Duon finished. "But Heredrew looks nothing like the man I met in Andratan."

"And sorcerers are bound always to present their true appearance to the world?" Conal asked. "Did you see the Destroyer's true form in Andratan, I wonder?"

"The Destroyer?" Duon could not remember hearing the term.

"Falthan name for him," Conal said, a defensive note in his voice. "Understandable, surely, given the history, that Falthans see him as a tyrant. But I've been surprised since coming here how benign his influence appears to be." This last seemed an unwilling confession.

"Lenares did say Heredrew was hiding something," Anomer observed. Arathé signalled, and her brother nodded his head. "We wish she was still alive," he continued. "Lenares' gifts would be of great use to us now."

All of a sudden the magician's voice reverberated in Duon's head. *What are you doing? I leave you alone for a moment and you share our secrets?* Duon could feel the man's anger building: the back of his head began to warm with it.

You threaten me? he asked.

Indeed. I could burn your brain from the inside out. Make you throw yourself from somewhere high, or walk into a fire. Eat poisoned berries. Anything. I repeat: what are you doing?

By now the other three had turned to him.

"His voice is spilling over," Conal whispered, his face white. "We can hear every word."

Duon was almost certain the magician knew nothing of the proximity-induced spillover between his three tools, but it took everything he had to avoid consciously thinking of it, or to speculate on how he might use the knowledge, as he conversed with his unwanted parasite.

And if his parasite could pick the underlying thoughts from his mind, he was already doomed.

Trying to find out what your other two hosts know, he mind-voiced.

Oh, so you've worked that out? Clever.

So hard, so very hard, not to articulate the conclusions he could draw from this one statement. We three are the only ones. He knows less than we think. And he doesn't always hear what we say or even what we think. Blurs of knowledge, not proper thoughts.

We have some questions for you.

No doubt. But do you really think I will answer them? Certainly I will give no information to anyone not sworn to my allegiance.

Then you will answer some of my questions?

When I have proof of your fidelity. I have a task for you to complete. We will speak again when I give you that task, and questions and answers may follow, if you satisfy me.

And should I refuse?

Then we both will have learned something. But, in your case, the lesson will be your last.

The exchange took a bare moment, but Duon still missed Anomer's next question. The others, however, would not have missed the exchange. More explaining to do, more risk of being found out.

"What do we do with what we know?" Anomer repeated.

Clever lad. Sufficiently vague that the listening magician would be able to make little of it, but necessary to ask so the magician didn't realise he was being overheard.

"We return to our billets and think about it," Duon said, signalling them with his eyes. A waste of time: he doubted they could see the gesture. "We must not prolong the risk of discovery by remaining here. We do not want anyone else to put the three of us together, or they may come to the obvious conclusion and dispose of us."

The voice in Duon's mind hissed, and Duon wondered what he had said; but at that moment he became aware of another presence. Someone stood on the ridge above them.

Of the four of them, Conal sat in the darkest shadows; without prompting he eased himself backwards until hidden. *Clever man*, Duon thought. *Or a voice in his mind gave him instructions*. Then, a moment later, he realised such a conversation would have spilled over.

Two figures descended the ridge towards them, resolving into the Omeran slave and his master, Dryman the mercenary. The second grave complication in Duon's life.

"Couldn't sleep either?" Dryman asked.

The question rang false on many levels: overly hearty for a man who normally wouldn't enquire about anyone else's wellbeing; designed to offer an explanation for the man's own presence in a woodland path after dark.

Ask him where he's been and what he's been doing.

Oh, Duon intended to.

"Where have you been, Dryman? What business draws you out night after night? You might think you are unobserved, but I see you and your thrall creep out of the camp again and again. What do you get up to?"

The voice in Duon's mind cried for him to exercise caution, but Duon was having none of it.

Dryman gave no answer. His deep eyes were shadowed, and Duon shivered at the unseen menace. Nevertheless.

"Then what about you, Torve? You are a man of integrity. Yes, a man, no matter what we Amaqi say about Omerans. So why don't you tell us what you've been doing?"

"No," Torve said.

"No you will not, or no you cannot?" Duon pressed on, aware of the risk he was taking. The mercenary could cut him down—unless his personal magician strengthened him. Emboldened by the thought, he pressed Torve.

"Cannot? The clear implication is you are protecting your master, which means you and he are up to no good. Remind me, Torve, why this man commands you? I thought you were the Emperor's personal pet?"

"He commands me because he is the true leader of our expedition," Torve responded, his voice guarded, his eyes sorrowful. "He carries forward the will of the Emperor. As he has said, you would have led us home. Therefore I must obey him."

"Besides, we are not the only ones who have been out wandering at night," Dryman said, taking a step forward. "Here you are with as little justification as Torve and myself. But not so long ago you left everyone behind one night and returned to Raceme, consulting no one, to offer support in the slaughter of defenceless courtiers." He leaned forward. "I don't answer to hypocrites."

"You always have an answer," Duon replied. "But none of them satisfy me. I intend to make it my business to find out who you are and why you are destroying the Emperor's expedition."

His words sounded faintly ridiculous in his own ears. Destroying it? The expedition had been destroyed when the Alliances had usurped Duon's leadership and marched their army into an ambush. Nothing to do with Dryman.

The mercenary tilted back his head and laughed. Some startled animal, a squirrel or possum perhaps, fled between he and Duon. It took some time for the echoes to die away.

Once again the brave explorer crushes himself, said the sardonic voice in his mind. *Even a fool learns eventually. Will you one day learn enough to be considered merely a fool?*

Duon slunk back to his host's house, aware of the eyes on him. Why could he never give answer to Dryman? And what thoughts were forming in the other two magician-cursed minds? Thoughts reflecting on his betrayal of them? His foolishness?

How soon would someone decide his continued existence was unnecessary?

In all his previous adventures he had never failed to find at least some sleep during the night, no matter how difficult the situation. During their time in Nomansland he'd slept; he had even found rest amid the terrible cries from the Valley of the Damned. But this night he lay awake on his cot through the hours until dawn, reflecting on his failures.

Allowing the Emperor to appoint him titular head of an unmanageable expedition. Almost as though he was set up to fail.

Failing to ride the political winds of the Alliances, resulting in his removal as leader at precisely the time when it did the most damage.

Acquiescing to Dryman's leadership out of some misguided feeling of worthlessness. Allowing a man with no past and no standing to overrule his better judgment.

Losing thirty thousand people.

Near dawn his thoughts drifted into unfamiliar channels. Seditious pathways. The Emperor *expected* him to fail. The voice in his head had first appeared when he was heralded as leader of the expedition—clearly the magician was in league with the Emperor. His sovereign benefited from the loss of his army . . . how? Because it destroyed the power of the Alliances. Part of the Emperor's plan. Yet he survived, along with Torve and Lenares, because of Dryman's intervention. The Emperor's will? Yes, yes. Dryman was the Emperor's tool, a bodyguard whose task it was to keep his master's three most important assets alive. Lenares for her witchy ways—now lost. Torve for his unquestioning obedience, and Duon for his experience in the northlands. A bodyguard, nothing more. Chosen for his fighting prowess, charged not to reveal the Emperor's plan. Only a bodyguard. Not a leader.

Not a leader. Why, then, should he continue to follow the man?

For one reason. He'd succeeded in convincing Duon he knew the will of the Emperor, knew the real goal of this expedition. The admission that there was a real goal meant the Emperor had set this up to start with. The army was never intended to survive.

He would walk a way further with this mercenary. But he would demand answers as the price of his continued co-operation. And when he completed the task for which he had been chosen, whatever it was, he would watch his back.

If thirty thousand people could be dispensed with, Duon told himself as the sun rose, so could one.

Torve also did not sleep, but for a different reason from that of his fellow southerner. With a thrill of wonder over his entire body he recalled something his master had said earlier that night, during the revelation that he was god-possessed.

"The halfwit Lenares can no longer read me," he had said. "She will never associate me with the mask-wearing Emperor."

It wasn't much, but Torve knew his master. He would not have said *can* and *will* if Lenares were truly dead. How the Emperor knew, Torve could only speculate: perhaps the oversight of the god within told him what others did not know.

Lenares had to be alive.

CHAPTER 14

THE DAUGHTER'S NUMBER

A TUG ON HER MIND jerked Lenares awake.

She liked to wake to one thing at a time, but even before she opened her eyes she was assailed from every direction by sensations and their associated numbers.

Another tug.

The sound of waves crashing. A cold splash.

The heat and ache of pain; the numbness of what she feared might be a serious injury.

Cool wind brushing her face, pulling at her hair, making a hollow booming sound behind her.

An insistent tug.

The arcing cry of a seagull.

The sun beating down on her eyelids, the sting of salt in the corners of her eyes.

The tug, tug of the mathematical line she had secured to the hole in the world. One of the holes. The one exploited by the Daughter.

She opened her eyes.

She lay on rocks below a seaside cliff, but not the same rocks as yesterday. There had been no cave in the cliffs yesterday. She shuddered. The sight of any hole, any void, set her on edge.

Tug. Tug, tug.

She had been shifted since she fell. Perhaps she did it herself. Yes, that was it: an explanation for the abrasions on her body, on her hands and knees, that hadn't been there yesterday.

The annoying tugging hadn't been there either.

Something was broken in her chest. Lenares was a little hazy about anatomy, but it wasn't her heart or lungs; it felt more like the dull ache she imagined would be associated with a broken bone. One of her ribs perhaps. It hurt to breathe, but the pain wasn't unbearable.

Tug.

Stop tugging me!

She had bled on the rocks yesterday, but these rocks were clean. The tide was almost in, her numbers told her, but she was safe from the waves, though the spray spattered her with stinging drops of salty water.

One of her knees hurt, the left one. She had to sit up to see it; her leg hung down from the rocks and her foot actually trailed in the water. She hissed at the pain in her chest as she moved.

Tug.

Snarling, Lenares snatched at the link between herself and the hole, the one she had spun with her experimental numbers. The link seemed to have no solid anchor in the hole—apart from her unproven notion that the far end was held by Mahudia. Her dead Mahudia.

The link shook, then oscillated like the wave she could

make in a skipping rope if the other girls let her play. The wave reached the far end.

Ah, so you are awake, little one.

"I'm not speaking to you."

Oh yes, you are. See? You've always had trouble with numbers, little Lenares. Particularly zero. You say something isn't, when clearly it is.

"That sounds like a lie. I don't lie."

No? So when you said you weren't speaking to me, what did you mean?

The Daughter was right. "I will find out how you were able to trick me, and change my thinking. I'm not perfect."

There are more important things to consider, little one. There is a nexus coming, and you need to be there. Are you ready to travel?

"I'm not doing anything you tell me to."

Really? Breathe, Lenares.

For an instant she considered holding her breath, but that would just be childish. "I'm not breathing because you told me to," she argued. "You could say 'live' to me and the only way I could disobey you would be to die. But that doesn't make you my lord."

Your problem, Lenares, is that you don't truly understand numbers.

There are things you don't understand either, Daughter, Lenares thought; but, unlike the unwise god, she did not speak her thoughts aloud.

One of the things Lenares felt certain the Daughter didn't understand was that Lenares had tied a numerical link to the hole the Daughter used. Had the god known, she would surely have taken steps to undo it. The link allowed Lenares to sense with much more clarity not only the Daughter's numbers, but also her emotions and thoughts.

But the Daughter was right: Lenares didn't fully understand the numbers she had used. She had puzzled over the mathematical concept of "nothing" for a long time, even before she had become aware of the hole. Perhaps—she couldn't remember, but it seemed likely—her thinking about how to express "nothing" had led her to the discovery of the hole. Holes. She still wasn't certain how many.

The cosmographers had a strong tradition of recording and debating concepts, and Lenares had spent many happy days in the vaults reading complex theorems. But none of them did more than touch on the notion of "nothing" as a mathematical concept.

Then one day she had come across the notes of the madman Qarismi of Kutrubul, a small town in the Biyyamid, a fertile area well to the south of Talamaq. He was famous for getting himself arrested every market day for his outrageous and blasphemous statements. Latterly, though, the Emperor had encouraged him, employing a note-taker to record his ramblings. These notes had recently been deposited in the cosmographers' library, and no one else had seen them. Lenares was certain of that: cosmographers were taught to respect documents, but these were covered with some sort of jam. Mahudia would have lamented the state of the notes, but Lenares hadn't cared.

The madman had obviously appended new material to his lectures. "How many sons do I have?" the crazy Qarismi asked himself in frenzied jottings in the margins of a discussion about root vegetables. "None. My heart is a void, I have no sons. What number is the number of my sons? How can the number of my sons be a number when it is nothing?" The last line had been crossed out, but Lenares could still read it: "How can nothing be something? Is 'none' a quantity of something?"

Lenares had read on, fascinated. "Let x be the number of brothers I have, and y be the number of sisters. Let $x = y$. The mathematical difference between x and y is a number, but it is nothing. How can it be a number and a nothing? It must be a number—called 0. Zero after Ahmal's naming. So, $x - y = 0$. But what does that mean? Zero is here defined as brothers minus sisters. But what does that mean?"

The marginal notes continued on the next page. "Zero is defined by its context. Consider my debts: I and the moneylender Aleb know well it is possible for me to have less than no money. I buy a pastina, I have no money left. I buy another pastina, I owe Aleb. So zero is a placeholder: between the state of owning and owing, reality and its negation."

These strange words had come back to Lenares' mind as she considered the hole in the world. She had tied her strange numbers to . . . to what? Not to nothing. To a mathematical concept that was defined by being between something? Yes. The hole was in the wall of the world, the material worldwall that separated time and space from the realm of the gods. So the hole was defined by the wall, in the same way that having no money was defined by being neither the state of owning nor owing. That was what she had instinctively worked out when she had assigned her own numbers to the hole. She had defined the hole by its context. Now she could track any contact the Daughter might make with the world. It would tug at her.

As it did now.

But she was no nearer knowing whether she had imagined Mahudia's hand taking her numbers and tying them to the hole. Patience. Understanding would come.

"No, I don't truly understand what it is like not to exist," she said. "You would have to be a god to understand that." She smiled, not a nice smile. "What's it like, Daughter? Is it a wonderful thing, not existing?"

I don't understand you. Of course I exist. The Daughter's voice sounded vexed.

"Then why all this effort to return to the world?"

To help you, fool. Not that you're proving worthy of it. Get up, girl; there is someone approaching. I have worked hard to bring him here. He, also, is necessary.

"Poor cold Daughter, wrecking the world in an attempt to get back what you left behind. How much more will you destroy before you admit defeat?"

Silence, little one. Or I will dispose of you and find someone more suited.

"You can't kill me," Lenares said. Time to test another of her theories. "You don't have the strength. Especially not since you've just spent most of it on the wave that smashed the tea house, and the remainder helping me to this place."

Not all of my strength is spent, said the Daughter, her voice roughening. *I still have enough to crush you like a bug.*

"And do you want to attract your brother's attention in your weakened state?"

The big gamble, but her numbers led her to suspect it. There was a simple pattern in the interval between major attacks through the hole(s) in the world that implied a recovery period. Finite strength.

Not much of a risk, the voice hissed. *Since he helped me with the wave.*

Oh. Get up, get up, Lenares told herself. *I miscalculated.*

She grasped the rocks with abraded hands and heaved herself upwards, hissing as her chest tightened painfully. *Hurry*, she told herself, *something is coming.*

And something came from out of the sun, a dazzling blaze of light, so bright Lenares had to shield her eyes. When next she looked there were three suns, one on each side of the main sun.

"Pretty," she said, as she scrambled across the rocks and towards the cave. "But an illusion."

I've made the air colder so I can manifest myself, said the Daughter. Then: *Where are you going? Don't go in the cave, Lenares. Please.*

Lenares blinked: her eyes were still dazed by the glare of the sun. The cave mouth was disturbingly circular and, as she focused, she could see nothing within. *But it is open to the sun: light should be illuminating the rear of the cave.*

Not a cave, then.

She found herself between gods.

A cold mist emerged from the cave, the barest emanation, but flowing against the onshore breeze. It flailed in the air, writhed, then began to shape itself into a hand. Cruelly sharp talons raked the air above Lenares, searching.

He has awoken, the Daughter said. *You must flee.*

"I'm already fleeing you!" Lenares yelled. The talons might be made of mist, but she had no doubt they could hurt her.

Flee. I will keep him at bay.

"Why should I care? He's no worse than you."

You are wrong, Lenares; of all the things you have ever

claimed, that is the most wrong. The Son must never be let loose in the world. He will lay waste to it.

A hand of shimmering rainbow light came from out of the sea, a sun-shaped amalgam of sparkle on the waves and reflection from the clouds. It was the most beautiful, fragile thing Lenares had ever seen, and she said so, even as she scrambled for her life.

It is all I can do, the Daughter admitted, *in my weakened state. Manipulate sunlight and cloud crystals through temperature. Behold the battle of the exhausted gods, fought with weapons without substance.* A bitter laugh rippled across the shore.

The two hands came together, the grey hand of the Son and the shimmering rainbow-hued hand of the Daughter. Clashed, drew apart, and clashed again, looking for a grip. Lenares reached the sand and began to run in earnest. Her rib flamed in agony, but she forced herself to ignore it.

Out of my way, sister, rumbled a voice so deep it shook the earth. Small rocks were shaken loose from the cliff above and clattered down onto the beach. Lenares had to wait until they stopped falling.

She is mine. I found her, I raised her. Find yourself another tool.

I don't want her. I need no tool. I simply want to deprive you of her.

The fingers locked together with a ghostly sound. Ethereal digits squirmed above the rocks as the two gods traded spiteful insults.

She's mine.

I should have killed you before our ascension.

Then you would not have been chosen, you fool.

It would have been worth it. This whole effort to

become corporeal again is so I can get my hands around your throat. I want to feel your arteries pumping in vain against my fingers.

So you've said, many times. I still don't believe you. I loved you once, brother, and I know you loved me.

Stop lying. There is no moral high ground to be claimed between you and me. The girl believes you are no better than I am. She is right.

The beach was nearly at an end. Ahead lay a small promontory. If she could just get around the point, she might be able to scale the cliff, or find shelter somewhere. To avoid their gaze long enough to devise some strategy. Eventually to find the others.

To find Torve.

She turned to see the two giant hands wrestling on the beach, scoring deep marks on the sand, knocking rocks from the cliff-face, occasionally splashing in the surf. The Son appeared to be getting the better of his sister. His hand was larger, his talons longer, while hers struggled under his, pale knuckles scraping on the rocks. The rainbow colours had dimmed.

Just then the sun went behind a cloud.

The Daughter's hand disappeared and the Son roared in triumph. Lenares leapt forward onto the rocks of the headland, spurred on by the bellows behind her, bellows drawing nearer to the accompaniment of crashing and thumping, as though the god dragged the cave along with him.

She did not want to get caught up in that grey hand.

She had underestimated them both. Her numbers were correct, but only in a relative sense. All her calculations of the strength of the gods had to be increased by some constant below which they did not fall. It made sense: they had to have some baseline strength or they would not survive beyond the walls of the world. The strength might come from beyond the world, in which case it could not be enumerated.

Could that be a way to defeat them? Cause them to draw more and more of their strength until they no longer had enough to sustain themselves?

A thought for another day.

Could a misty hand cast a shadow? Something loomed over her. She kept her head down, she did not want to look; her fear was finally getting the better of her, it was harder and harder to take steps forward; so cruel, she had almost escaped . . .

"Ahoy, the shore!" a cheery voice cried. It came from somewhere to her right, out to sea.

Above her a deep growl shook the headland, and the shadow vanished.

"Hoy!" There was a man in a boat, and he was waving to her with a small, pale hand. A human, welcoming hand. "Can you tell me how far it is to Foulwater Mouth? Oh my, I'm lost, oh yes indeed."

The man brought his boat to shore on the next beach. Lenares helped him to drag it the last few yards, though the effort bit into her chest.

She watched the man carefully. *Something must be special about him, else why did the gods flee?* She didn't think it was because they had fought themselves to exhaustion. The Son had seemed on the point of killing her and vanquishing the Daughter.

"I thank you, oh yes, you've been most kind," said the funny little man. He was old, over thirty at least, with thin, wispy hair and a pate burned red by the sun. His features were generous to a fault: too much mouth, a large nose and wide, staring eyes. He looked harmless, but she would soon know.

"My name is Lenares," she said.

"Oh my, yes. Mine is Olifa, late of Eisarn," he said in a breathless rush. "A long way south of here. Inland Not much of a sailor really, but this boat and I have gotten along just fine, oh yes. Are you local? Do you know the way to Foulwater Mouth?"

"I am Lenares of Talamaq," she said, then corrected herself. "I mean, Lenares the Cosmographer. No, I am not local. You are more local than me."

"You look like a local, yes you do. So you don't know how to find Foulwater Mouth?"

"No, but I can help row a boat," she said, wincing at the thought of the damage she might do her rib. He saw her wince, she was certain of it, but he passed no comment, pausing in silence for a while, obviously thinking.

"Well, it would be pleasant to have an attractive companion on my journey north, oh yes," he said eventually.

"Is that why you want to go to Foulwater Mouth? To find an attractive companion?"

The man laughed. "Oh my, young lady, how funny you are!" He licked his lips. "I will not have to look very far for attractive companionship, no indeed. Not far at all."

"That's good," Lenares said. "I want to travel Fatherward, I mean north, as quickly as I can. I am trying to find someone, and I think he will be walking north. So I hope your search doesn't take long."

This occasioned another laugh from the man.

His numbers were ambiguous. A teller of truth who had

recently taken up lying; a killer of men who had aided an important quest. A man with more than one name; a man who had endured mockery. He intended, according to the numbers, to enjoy her companionship to the full.

She could see no real threat in that.

They launched the little boat on the outgoing tide. It had bench seats in the front and the back—the bow and the stern, she told the man, having read a scroll about sailing some years ago—and a place in the middle that held the mast and sail. The mast was down at the moment, the man explained, because he didn't know how to use it. He seemed ineffectual, for all the history she could read in him, and Lenares wondered if she had made a mistake taking up with him. Who would travel by boat while not knowing how to operate it?

She became thoroughly soaked during the launching process, and the saltwater stung her wounds. She sucked at the more accessible cuts, but this didn't help.

"You ought to use some ointment on those," said Olifa. "Keep them free of infection. I've seen what can happen to a dirty wound. Oh my, yes."

"I would if I had any."

"I'm something of an expert on mixtures and the like," the man said. "I'll see if I can find you something in the next town."

"I don't have any money," Lenares said anxiously. "And I haven't eaten or drunk since yesterday."

"My, you are in a bad way," the man said. "Never mind, I have plenty of money, and food and drink enough to share, if you don't mind your bread stale and your cheese hard, oh yes. And as for repayment, there are many ways you can make yourself useful on our journey north, however long it lasts, oh yes indeed."

Lenares knew the words he spoke had more than one meaning, but she put them aside. The man seemed friendly, and would hardly attack her now she had made it clear she had no money. She had just been in the presence of two gods powerful enough to reshape the world, and the harmlessness of this man encouraged her to relax. To lower her guard.

They let down the sail and soon it filled with the breeze. Once they had mastered the skill of jibbing, the boat propelled them northward more quickly and certainly with far less effort than rowing, though they both suffered the occasional knock when the boat didn't behave as they expected.

She told him her story as the beautiful green waters rolled under the hull and the wild coast passed them by. A new world revealed itself to Lenares as she watched fish darting about in large groups, weaving their way between strange multicoloured trees. He seemed very interested in what she had to say, so she continued, even though she really wanted silence in which to contemplate the wonderful underwater panorama passing below. She did spread herself across the bow seat, with her head over the gunwale, watching the amazing antics of the fish as she talked and nibbled on a hard heel of bread.

Olifa did not believe all the parts about the gods and the holes in the world, though he was too polite to say so. He was fascinated, though, by her tales of Raceme and the Bhrudwans she had fallen in with.

"A red-haired man and his two children? Two? Oh my, a girl as well as a boy? Do tell!"

And he clapped his hands as she told of the fireball and then of the wave sent to smash the tea house.

"You have a wonderful imagination, Lenares," he said. "Such description; I can well believe what it must have been like. But I am a scientist, my girl, and I know such things don't happen without a natural explanation. I don't hold with all this intervention of the gods."

"How else do you think I ended up on the beach?" Lenares said. "You interrupted a battle between the gods: surely you saw the great hands?"

"Oh dear, oh my, no hands did I see," he replied, and she knew he told the truth, hard as it was to accept: he had been right there in his boat.

Surely it was not all in my head. Of course not: people saw the other manifestations of the gods. She wanted to know why the gods had been invisible to this man, but he had already moved on. She hoped it had not taken place entirely within her head, and, at the thought, part of her wanted to go back to the beach and check the sand for marks.

"Whatever the explanation, I'm glad you are with me," Olifa said, smiling toothily. "Oh my, yes."

Lenares smiled back. "No one says that to me. Not even Torve lately."

"Torve is your lover?" A casual question.

Lenares could feel herself blushing. "No. I thought he might be, but his master won't let him."

"Ah, an oft-repeated tale. Well, I have no master to tell me what to do."

His glance at her was intended to be meaningful, but

Lenares could not interpret it. Did he want to be her lover? Surely not; he was so old.

She thought again of Torve. He would have wanted to search for her, but she doubted Dryman would let him. She could ask Olifa to take her back to the beach. She could maybe scale the cliff, and hope the gods weren't still there, waiting for her. But when she got to the top, there would be no one there. And she would then have to hurry through an unfamiliar country to catch them up. No, this was the better way.

The morning blended into afternoon as Olifa talked about himself while Lenares watched the parade of the sea. He was an alchemist, he said, a man of wealth and great talent (all true, the numbers said, or, at least, he believed it to be true, though he had not said the wealth was recent) who had worked for years in an enormous mine. He made the occupation sound important and mysterious. His tales of seeking for precious metals hidden under the ground appealed to Lenares and her love of puzzles, and she told him so.

"You are a lovely girl, oh yes, so I will tell you our secret," he said. "We dig for many metals, yes, but our real purpose is to search for a special stone. It is found in the heart of our richest lodes, in such small quantities it is almost impossible to identify, but I am an expert, oh yes. The expert, really. The only one."

She smiled again at the man. He was practically bald, his teeth were crooked and his breath smelled bad, but Lenares found him interesting. Almost a kindred mind.

"I, too, am the only expert left," she said. "The last cosmographer. Do they listen to you? They don't listen to me."

"Oh, they listen to me all right, yes indeed. They don't listen, they end up smeared all over the mine. They've learned to listen, oh yes."

"They don't listen to me," Lenares repeated. "And many people have already died because of it."

"I'll listen to you, yes, I'll listen," Olifa said. "I always listen. There is so much to learn."

A kindred mind indeed. He didn't always agree with her, but he listened. More than Dryman or Captain Duon did.

"So let me tell you about the special stone," Olifa said, pleased by her interest. "It is very rare, oh my, and there are many theories as to what makes it form. My own personal belief is that it needs extreme heat and pressure to be created, so, despite the ridicule of my peers, I suggested the stone was born of meteorites, yes indeed I did."

"Meteorites? Fireballs?"

"Indeed," he said, his eyebrows raised.

"You didn't think I'd know what a fireball was, did you. I told you, I saw one."

"You did, Lenares, and I apologise, yes I do. It was not your seeing the fireball I doubted, for, as I am about to tell you, I saw it too. No, it is the method of creation. Oh my, meteorites are falling stars, and they come from beyond the walls of the world—"

"No, they do not," Lenares said. "Nothing gets through the worldwall—well, almost nothing, and certainly not meteorites."

"I'm not going to argue with you, girl, oh no, because it doesn't matter. I investigated the site of the fireball north of Raceme just after it fell, yes I did, I spent a week and a day digging where I calculated the stone would be, and I found the special stone." He smiled, and drew a small glass vial out of a pocket in his tunic. "Oh my. There it is, genuine huanu stone, oh yes. Olifa was right."

"It's very small," Lenares said.

"I told you it was. But powerful all the same. With it—"

"I know what it does," she said, and watched as his eyes opened wide in surprise—though not as surprised as she had expected. "It stops magic. *Absorbs* magic. But I've seen a much bigger huanu stone. I've held a piece"—she looked closely at the stone—"four hundred and twenty-six times the volume of the one in your glass container."

He nodded, not at all surprised by this.

"You knew," she said. "You know Noetos and his huanu stone, don't you?"

"Noetos? Oh yes, indeed. Oh my. Famous, he is. Famous, but an angry man. I'm surprised he let you hold the stone, my dear, oh yes. But with *this* stone I will also be famous," he crowed. "Oh my, the most famous alchemist in the world. And the richest. No more to be stuck down filthy mines with filthy miners."

"So where are you taking it?"

"Why, to its rightful owner, oh yes," the mad alchemist replied. "The Undying Man of Bhrudwo, our rightful Emperor. And if he is prepared to pay what it is worth, he can have it."

"And if not?"

"Well, there's not much he can do, is there, no indeed, since the huanu stone negates magic while in my possession."

"I am going north also," she confessed, "but I will not travel all the way with you. I would like to rejoin my companions."

"Of course," he said grandly. "Any time you want to leave, all you have to do is step off the boat. Now, Lenares, you're tired and sore, so you are. Why don't you take some rest? I'll keep this boat going north, oh yes I will."

Even as Lenares lay back in the bow of the boat, her head still above the gunwale, her numbers showed hidden plans in the man. Unseen dangers. Treachery against Noetos, against the Undying Man. She would keep a careful eye on him when next she woke.

She awoke in a panic. The boat was being tossed about and something dark and heavy had landed on top of her, crushing her already painful rib. A cloth had been pressed against her eyes and there was a fumbling at her tunic.

"What?" she cried, and received a sharp blow in the mouth. Something was attacking her. She went to cry out and tasted blood. The boat continued its frenzied rocking.

"Olifa! Something—"

The cloth slipped enough for her to see. The weight on her chest was Olifa himself, his naked torso pinning hers to the hull. It was his hand fumbling with her tunic. Her shocked brain took a moment longer to assemble the obvious explanation.

"No! Don't touch me!" she screamed, and began to twist and jerk underneath him, trying to fetch him a blow with her knees.

"Stop fighting," he said, already panting. "You have to pay me for passage, oh yes, and pay me you will, in coin of my choosing."

"Nobody touches me," she snarled, struggling to free herself. "Not without my permission." But though he was a small man, and very old, he was tough and wiry. A *miner*, she thought. *Miners are strong and I am weak.*

"You boarded my boat," the man said. "That's permission enough in my book, oh yes."

His breath was hot and foul on her neck. With one hand he unfastened his breeches, letting them slide down his scrawny legs, exposing his worm.

Lenares closed her eyes and twisted her head away. He was too strong for her; she didn't want to see what he was about to do. She had wanted Torve to do this to her, she still did, but it was Torve she wanted, not the act alone, and this man was stealing and hurting. His horrible worm touched her leg and she screamed, involuntarily opening her eyes as the scream ended.

And looked straight into the eye of an enormous fish.

Take hold of the boat, little Lenares, came the Daughter's voice, though weakly, as though from a great distance, and full of pain.

Lenares clamped her arm under the bow seat, and the massive eye vanished.

"You'll enjoy it," Olifa said, fondling her. "Women always enjoy it—"

A great weight crashed into the bottom and side of the boat, lifting it up and out of the water. Lenares held fast, managing to wedge one of her feet under the stern seat, but Olifa was not so lucky. He grabbed at something, anything, which turned out to be Lenares, but she shook him off. The boat thumped back down into the water with a splash, and the man was no longer in it.

Lenares got to her knees and looked for a weapon. Under the stern seat was a pack, with a knife strapped to the back: she snatched at it and missed, then grabbed it on the second attempt. She stood, making the boat rock from side to side, and searched the water for Olifa.

Nothing.

She wasn't letting go of the knife in her right hand, so she began to do up her tunic with her left, but couldn't manage it, so unnerved and fumble-fingered his attack had left her. Why? What right did he have? And what good was cleverness if it could be defeated by mere strength? She was angry at Olifa for betraying her, at herself for being so weak, and at the Daughter for saving her.

Where was the big fish?

A splash beside the boat made her scream. A hand reached out of the water and grabbed the gunwale, tipping the boat alarmingly. She sat down with a squeal. A head followed the hand.

"Lenares, Lenares," the miner said, spitting out water, "pull me back into the boat."

No please, no sorry, no promises not to do it again.

"Why should I? You frightened me. You were going to hurt me."

"I can't get my boots off, no," he said. "They are miner's boots with steel toecaps, and they will pull me down, yes, down to drown. You don't want me to drown, oh no. Who will guide you back to your friends? Who will help with the boat? Only Olifa, oh yes."

"Yes, I do. I do want you to drown. Drown, mister."

"It's my boat."

The worst thing he could have said.

"It was my body!" Lenares screamed, and brandished the knife.

Behind Olifa the big fish raised its head out of the water and opened its mouth, revealing two rows of saw-sharp teeth. *Run your knife along his knuckles*, the Daughter said. *It will make him let go. The cut doesn't have to be deep. If you don't, he'll climb back in and do worse things to you.*

Lenares nodded to the fish, took her knife, looked Olifa in the eye—more than he'd done to her, with his cloth over her face—and ran the blade briskly across the tops of his fingers.

"Aaah, girl, what are you doing?"

"Making you let go. So let go, or I'll chop your fingers right off."

"You can't do this to me. I have the huanu stone!"

"I'm not magical," she said. "Not strong either, only clever. So your stone avails you nothing. Let go."

She ran the knife across his fingers again, more forcefully this time, raising blood. Still he clung to the boat.

"There's something in the water," the man said, his voice shaking.

The fish had lowered its head under the surface, but it wouldn't be far away. In fact, there was a long black shadow nearby. He could probably see it.

"Swim to shore, you can make it," Lenares said.

He made no move to obey her.

"I warned you."

She stabbed the knife towards his hand. He let go of the boat just in time and she missed his fingers. The blade thunked into the gunwale. Immediately the man began to drift backwards—only relative to the boat, Lenares told herself.

"Swim!" she shouted to him.

He dog-paddled furiously, trying to stay above water, all the while calling her vile names.

The fish raised its head directly behind him.

Don't look, little Lenares.

Olifa noticed she was looking beyond him, turned his head, saw the fish and shrieked in a high-pitched voice.

We wait until beyond range of the magic-killer in your boat, the Daughter said. *Then we strike.*

"No, Lenares! Come back, I beg of you!"

Who could resist such a plea? She didn't want him eaten by the Daughter-fish. Now she had the knife, what could he do? She put a hand to the tiller.

The water around the miner erupted. Six fish, each as big as the first, formed a circle—a hole—around the frantic man, who uttered one last cry before the creatures lunged. A frenzy of thrashing, water bubbling and boiling, then turning red. One or two things bobbed to the surface. Bits of meat. A boot with no toe.

And now I really do have to recuperate, said the Daughter. *And digest everything that has happened today.* Laughter, then silence.

QUEEN

CHAPTER 15

CONAL GREATHEART

THE DHAURIAN ATTIRE HAD BEEN a good idea in Dhauria, but a fortnight of warm summer rain had rendered Stella's robes practically unusable. She sighed and rubbed her clammy hands on the wet fabric. The garment had been practical and comfortable in the hot westerly winds that swept over Ikhnos, but then the humid southerlies rolled in, bringing low cloud and persistent drizzle that no clothes, let alone a flimsy robe, could keep out for long.

Surprisingly, it was Robal who called the halt and sought the nearest town. His salt-and-pepper whiskers, now a proper beard, dripped rainwater onto his sodden robe: he looked ridiculous and he knew it.

"We're practically begging to be robbed," he said, explaining his choice of road. "Not to mention the chafing. At least my trousers were waterproof. And," he added grimly, "I want to be rid of this red stain."

"Might be horses here," said Stella. "And they might even be willing to sell them."

"We are hardly going to be set upon by thieves," Heredrew

said, ignoring Stella's jibe. His mood, never bright, had descended into barely controlled fury at their enforced walk. He couldn't even use the blue fire to communicate with Andratan, he said, for fear it would be wrested from him by the gods. Robal had laughed at that, pointing out the fable in which men steal fire from the gods, but Heredrew had not shared the humour. He'd wondered aloud how much longer his *Maghdi Dasht* castellan would wait without communication before annexing the keep and kingdom both, assuming his master had somehow perished. Stella had privately wished the castellan good fortune, but had been prudent enough not to mention this sentiment to Heredrew.

The Undying Man's hands twitched as he spoke. Probably wishing someone would set upon them.

"Perhaps in this town we'll find someone who acknowledges Andratan's authority sufficiently to give us horses," Conal said brightly, an innocent smile playing on his lips.

Heredrew's other sore point neatly targeted. He had admitted to his companions that the level of submission to his authority was far lower than he had imagined; certainly far lower than he'd been led to believe by the Ikhnos factors. He had invoked the Seal of Andratan in every town and village they had passed through, and at only one place had the locals been obliging enough to sell—sell, not give!—them a weary pony and wearier dray, to allow Phemanderac an easier passage. The sorcerer had very nearly decided to reveal his identity in one small town, a few days north of Foulwater, where his seal was met with scorn and outright hostility. Stella had been able to persuade him to stay his hand, though she herself had been incensed that night when catching the cook urinating in their stew. She had not objected to the beating Robal had given the man, and had held a drawn sword when Heredrew ordered the villagers assemble and told them their days of disrespect and ease were over. They would respect the Seal of Andratan, or someone would be sent to teach them respect.

Heredrew turned his head slightly towards the priest. "Perhaps in this town we'll find someone sufficiently desperate to take you off our hands. A stablemaster, perhaps?" He raised an eyebrow to Stella. "How much do you think we would have to pay to have him taken on as an apprentice?"

"We might get the forequarters of a horse in exchange," said Robal, deliberately loud enough for the priest to hear.

"Hindquarters," Heredrew corrected, drawing a snort of laughter from the guardsman.

Men make easy friends and even easier enemies, Stella reflected as she followed. Heredrew and Robal, her self-appointed guardians, in their approach to the town gate. Behind her Kilfor and his father led the dray. Phemanderac and Moralye rode inside it. *Women are much more careful with their trust*.

The rain doubled in intensity as the Falthans sheltered under the stone arch. Farmer's Flat, the carved words on the keystone told them. Stella caught a whiff of sulphur as they waited for Robal to negotiate their entrance. Towns, just like people, had their unique odours; this was less pleasant than most. She wondered what they manufactured here that required such a foul chemical.

"Farmer's Flat? Not what I called it last time I was here," Heredrew said.

"Oh?" Conal turned to face him. "Stinkpit, perhaps? Smelltown? Dungheap? Did you curse it because some peasant forgot to tug his forelock? Or perhaps because the women were less than accommodating?"

Heredrew tilted his head towards Stella, but she was a little too slow in realising he was requesting her permission. A moment later his hand flicked out and he fetched Conal a brutal slap across the cheek. *Struck*, Stella thought, *by a hand that is not there*.

"And so the mighty Undying Man answers his critics," the priest said, spitting out blood and phlegm.

"No, I would normally bring in experts to give you answer," Heredrew said equably. "And, believe me, they are expert. Autocracy depends on the enforcement of discipline, as I'm sure your Archpriest has demonstrated."

"He has you there." Stella carefully kept any sympathy out of her voice: for a priest, Conal had been remarkably unrepentant about his actions in Dhauria. She had fought hard to prevent Heredrew slaying the man; had bargained her cooperation in the Undying Man's attempt to save the world—if indeed that was what he was doing, and his altruism was not a front for something more nefarious—to win Conal's life. Bitterness and gall had been her reward. Conal now seemed to despise her as much as he had once been infatuated with her, convinced she had been collaborating with the Enemy of Faltha from the start. A natural reaction, she supposed, but one a priest ought to be above, or at least recognise for what it was.

Not this fellow. He was stamped with the same mark as his master, the Archpriest, who had tried to capture and interrogate her for the crime of having been captured by the Undying Man during the Falthan War.

And this Conal was the Archpriest in miniature. Best to remember that. There was only so far this man could

be pushed before he pushed back; and, despite his lack of
magical power, he had already proved—twice—that he
was capable of extraordinary feats. Once to save her; once
to kill her. The man bore close watching.

The Falthans were admitted to the town of Farmer's
Flat, the odd smell commented on by no one, out of politeness. Once inside the walls Moralye took the lead. She
had proved time and again her useful talent for identifying
the friendliest people in town, the most pleasant and least
expensive lodgings. If anyone could secure horseflesh, she
was that one. It was a little late in the afternoon for a visit
to the stables, so she led them down a street she had never
previously seen, in a land she had never been in before,
trusting some obscure instinct to reveal a place to eat and
stay the night.

Stella admired the woman immensely. Moralye had
been jerked out of her world by forces she had read about
but never expected to experience; had been confronted with
the legendary bogeyman of her culture, yet had set to with
vigour to understand what had happened; and, even more
commendable, to make herself useful. Phemanderac pro-
fessed himself delighted with her, and Stella had to agree.

Within minutes Moralye had engaged a group of young
women in conversation. Less than two months in a strange
land and she could converse like a native: the sharpest mind
of them all, no question. Her intelligence was frightening.
But the formidable analytical mind was hidden now as
she laughed and giggled with the local women, words and
gestures describing cloth and shape and colour, a whirling
exchange too fast for Stella to follow. *The body does not
age*, she acknowledged, *but the mind still atrophies*. What

would she be like in a thousand years? How had Kannwar kept his mind lively?

The young Dhaurian scholar beckoned them over, and within minutes an impromptu market stall had opened on the side of the road. Women from all over the town brought cloth, and in some cases complete garments, for the strangers to cast their eyes over. The prices asked were high, but no one complained. Heredrew's supply of Bhrudwan coin seemed inexhaustible, and the fabric was good quality. Each Falthan accepted a complete outfit—some of the garments were mismatched but even the worst of the clothes was more suitable than the filthy and frayed robes they wore. Heredrew and Phemanderac were the only exceptions: Phemanderac because his robes had been protected by travelling in the dray; Heredrew due to the fact that no garments came anywhere near fitting him.

New clothes would be made overnight, the women promised, in addition to the garments they had purchased. Stella shuddered, picturing the women working by dim candlelight into the small hours, but none of the seamstresses looked displeased at the prospect. They bade the visitors farewell and hurried to their homes.

The town, though substantial, apparently had only one public eating place: the aptly named Boiling Waters Tea House. Steam rose from behind the low thatched-roof buildings of the tea house, borne away on the wet wind, but despite the wind and rain the buildings seemed to give off an even more concentrated unpleasant smell, as though rotten eggs were stored inside. Apparently the tea house kept a small cottage where travellers could stay overnight, but, despite the rain, none of the party appeared keen.

"Perhaps we could try our luck in the next village,"

Robal said, a hand over his face. "I wouldn't want to dine in a place that smells like this."

"The next village," Heredrew said, "is a long way north of here and a great deal less civilised. Besides, you have resplendent new robes waiting for you here. Who wouldn't want to be seen in that orange tunic?" He paused, then added thoughtfully: "It seems this place has improved since last I was here."

Stella gave Conal a sidelong glance, but the chastened priest did not rise to the bait. *Good boy*, she thought; and the thought must have been reflected on her face because Conal turned away, his own face twisted.

He loves me and he hates me. Not good news. He could do anything and justify it.

As they entered the tea house, two or three of the closest groups beckoned them further in, broad smiles on their faces. Many wore no tunics, not surprising in the sudden, oppressive heat of the room. "Cummin 'n shut the hole behind yer!" one young man cried. "Man could freeze his stones orf out there!" His companions laughed at his wit.

The interior of the Boiling Waters Tea House took their breath away.

Rather than a standard wooden floor, a series of boardwalks wound around open grey earth, brown pits of mud and pools of steaming water. What had looked from the outside to be a series of buildings was revealed to be one vast structure with many roofs, interspersed with gaps open to the sky, and no interior walls. Groups of Bhrudwans sat around talking, laughing and singing; a surprising contrast to the way the more solemn Yacoppica Tea House far to the south had been. Here and there tall, thick poles of pale wood supported the roof, and around them were hung dozens of labelled bags filled with herbs.

They were approached by a smiling woman wearing a garland of flowers around her neck. "Welcome," she said. "For one fena each you can have your own cauldron and choice of herbs, or for—"

Smiling even wider than the woman, Heredrew took her arm. "We'll have your premier service, in the seats closest to the Matron."

"Ah!" she said, not at all discomfited by his interruption. "Are you a regular visitor to the Tea Chain?"

He laughed. "Regular, yes. But my visits, though regular, are spaced out longer than I'd like. Last time I was here this was open ground. I remember the Matron though. I trust she is as timely as ever?"

"But . . . but sir, the Boiling Waters Tea House has been up for thirty years or more."

"I'm older than I look. Now, our seats, please?"

"Payment?" she responded.

Heredrew pulled out his Seal of Andratan. The woman paled visibly, then nodded and beckoned them forward.

"Finally some respect," he said as they followed the woman along a narrow boardwalk between two mud pools.

"Fear, more like," Conal muttered, but Stella didn't think the Undying Man heard. He couldn't have: he was not the sort of man to ignore an insult—accurate, as this one was, or otherwise.

Her fellow Falthans were clearly uncomfortable in the presence of the Destroyer, though not as uncomfortable as she. But the discomfort went both ways. Stella suspected that if not for their company, Kannwar would have punished many of those who had dealt with them with such insolence. He was trying to act even-handedly, presumably because he needed her cooperation to fulfil the task he had accepted. He had been forced to lay aside his pride. Stella smiled to herself. She could not conceive of a more fitting punishment for the man.

The pale young woman indicated their seats. Unlike other seating in the tea house, these were fixed to the floor, and arranged in a semicircle around a small pool. The rear seats were raised somewhat, as though to afford people a view of the pool. A few people, better dressed than the average patron, had congregated there, sitting, talking and generating an air of expectancy. Above them the roof was open to the darkening sky: rain hissed into the steaming pool by their feet.

"The Matron will be along shortly," their host said.

"Thank you." Stella smiled reassuringly at her. She was unsure why they needed a matron, or why they had to be seated here, in a very public part of the tea house, in order to be served by her.

Phemanderac and Moralye sat closer to the pool, engaged in a conversation in a language Stella did not know. The native language of Dhauria, she supposed. Probably debating some esoteric philosophy. The *dominie* did not seem to be getting the best of it either.

Kilfor and his father were quiet. The older man had been experiencing pain in his joints, brought on by the damp weather, he said. His son kept a close and loving eye on him, fussing terribly over the old reprobate whenever he thought people weren't watching. He was doing it now, adjusting Sauxa's collar.

The woman who had guided them here remained standing nearby. Stella had just begun to wonder why when the woman gathered herself and knelt in front of Heredrew. "Please, sir," she said, "you have the seal. Our family has lived here for generations, and we understand the power Andratan wields. You are undoubtedly close to the Undying Man, an adviser perhaps. Thus I would ask a boon, sir, an answer to a simple question."

The Undying Man's eyebrows rose. "Ask your question."

"My brother was recruited fifteen years ago and taken to Andratan to serve the Undying Man. His name is Porcaro Nobe. He had long black hair and was a well-favoured man, powerful in magic and loved by all who knew him. Have you any news of him?"

Stella watched Heredrew carefully. He was not able entirely to mask his reaction: his eyebrows twitched when the woman gave her brother's name, and he focused an intense stare on her. She noticed it too, Stella was sure.

"Woman, I am but one of many in that vast fortress. There are a thousand servants, a hundred jailers, dozens of tutors and recruiters, and more students than I have ever bothered to count. Andratan is more like a city than a castle. Surely the chances of me knowing your brother must be slim?"

The woman bowed her head, and for a moment Stella thought she would accept his words. Then she looked up, and the intensity of her gaze almost seemed to burn the air.

"Sir, forgive me for speaking, but I must. The sum of your words is nothing, yet your eyes tell me something else. You know him, or at least what happened to him. Please, sir, if you have even a mite of compassion, and wish to honour the noble name of Andratan, tell me of my brother."

A squawk of derisive laughter from Conal, quickly disguised as a cough. *That one still treads close to the cliff*, Stella thought.

The girl's eyes were wells of misplaced hope. *Courageous, undoubtedly magically gifted at least to a small degree, and about to be cruelly rejected.*

"I'm prepared to do better than that," Heredrew said. "I can take you to see him."

"No, Drew!" Stella cried. "Don't be so cruel!"

Her words were almost obscured by the shouts of pleasure from the woman, who began jumping on the spot and clapping her hands. Then moisture sprang up around her eyes. "You wouldn't be teasing me, sir?"

"Trying to ensure good service, more like," Conal muttered, in a voice more distinct than he no doubt intended.

Heredrew fixed Stella with his grey eyes—grey today, they might be any colour tomorrow—clearly asking her to take responsibility for her companion. She nodded, took Conal by the arm, and led him a few paces down the boardwalk.

"Conal, you are alive only on his sufferance and by my sacrifice," she said to him, reverting to the Falthan common tongue. "For someone who has expressed such a strong wish for everlasting life, you do take the most extraordinary risks. Don't you understand he could erase you from existence? Or entrap you in an eternal agony of torment? Why do you do it? Why do you bait him so?"

"Perhaps my death would bring you to your senses," he replied, his chin jutting in defiance, an altogether ridiculous sight.

"It is not I who needs to find good sense," Stella said. "Yes, you have an excuse for your actions, but being over-powered by the magician in your head is starting to wear thin. Do you not yet understand? The latter gods are about to burst back into the world, to its ruin, and the man you and I despise may be our only hope. So, priest, you face the age-old dilemma about means and ends. Would you prefer the world to end in fire over acknowledging the Destroyer as our saviour?"

"Those aren't the only choices," Conal said stubbornly. "The Most High will have many plans. Did He not say to Leith, your husband"—he hissed the word—"that he was but one of many called to walk the path? Do I have to re-mind you of the Castle of Fealty and the prophetic paint-ing there, which showed Leith as one of many potential saviours? And, when ultimately he failed, did Hal not step in and take his place?" His eyes flashed. "So it was then, so it will be now."

"Oh, Conal, so many of the Most High's plans have been opposed by those believing themselves right. I remember a young girl running to the arms of the charming Tanghin rather than remain obedient to her village headman, only to discover Tanghin was in reality Deorc, the Destroyer's henchman. How many of the Most High's plans did I turn over that night?"

"Your argument makes my point," Conal said. "You trusted a man in disguise and were enslaved by him. Well, I will make no such mistake. I do not see Drew, the suave charmer who apparently fills your eyes and your heart, but rather the Destroyer, the torturer of innocents like Arathe of the Bhrudwans."

He turned on his heel and found a place to sit behind

the group, on the highest level of seating. Stella stared after him, forcing her hands into rigid fists at her sides, reminding herself that even he was not the true enemy.

The woman who had dared ask Heredrew her question had vanished, no doubt to make preparations for a journey from hope to bitterness. As much as Stella opposed Conal's rejection of the Undying Man, she was not blind to his essential wickedness. Conal was right, in a way. "Drew" did fill her heart, but with fear, not love. She had not forgotten, would never forget, what he had done to her.

How he had allowed her to escape him, how she had fought for a week through the cold and privation of the Bhirinj highlands in winter, barely surviving, believing she was free; only to find a cottage with smoke rising from the chimney. She had thrust open the door to see him standing by the fire, laughing, as he revealed he had engineered her escape for his amusement and her education.

How he had demonstrated his ruthlessness to her and to his entire army by commanding his most loyal and upright general to put a defiant village to the flames. The man—she could not remember his name, only that he had been known as the Red Duke—refused, and he had been staked and burned, along with his staff. Their cries had been horrible.

How he had then put the entire village to death as a demonstration of his power, nailing the men to the doors of their houses so they could watch his soldiers cut the hands and feet from their children, and rape their wives and daughters. "I have something to show you!" he had cried before the slaughter had begun.

These and other memories cascaded through her head as she returned to the seats around the pool to await the arrival of the mysterious matron. No, she would not forget what sort of monster lurked underneath the so-attractive skin of the man Heredrew. Conal was right, in a way, but could not have been more wrong.

Yet she had seen little of the Destroyer's evil since Heredrew had joined them north of the Great Desert. Nor had her companions, Conal's complaints notwithstanding. For example, when they emerged from the blue fire into the caustic lake, Sauxa had been ready to take to the sorcerer with his knife, despite the fact it had only been the Undying Man's magic that had saved them. But now the old man talked with him as with any other companion.

It is very difficult when a legend is revealed as simply a man, Stella reflected. *No, strike that. This man is anything but simple.*

Even Phemanderac had come to some understanding with the man. Stella would not have believed it possible that a Dhaurian, the mortal enemies of Andratan, could have found a place of commonality, yet she had listened to them talking about the times of the First Men as though they were lifelong companions. She recalled one scene: Phemanderac laughing in his reedy way as Heredrew mercilessly dissected Dhaurian theories about the Vale of Youth.

Kilfor, younger and perhaps more self-reliant, seemed less enamoured of the sorcerer, no doubt confident that the edge of a sword rather than foul-tainted magic would bring them victory. His friend Robal shared his view. Yet even they made no overt protest at his continued presence with them. Why?

Expediency was the answer. Whatever else this man was, he was powerful. All the legends agreed on that. There was likely no one more powerful on three continents. "He might be evil," Robal had remarked to her late one afternoon a day or two north of Foulwater, "but at least he's strong. And while he's working with us, he's not working against us."

They all saw him as a tool, then, to be used and discarded. Perhaps even the Most High saw him like that. But not Stella. She viewed him differently: after all, she was cursed, eternally cursed, because of his juxtaposition of cruelty and love; destined to live forever with his godcursed blood in her veins. He would not prove a tool comfortable to the hand, nor would he be easy to discard.

While she had been brooding, cauldrons had been brought and placed in small pools off to one side. Heredrew asked her which herb she favoured, and she sent him to fetch her a relaxant of some potency. It wasn't until she caught herself watching his upright back disappearing into the crowd that she began to wonder just how strong his influence over her remained.

He'd loved her in his own fashion. Her capture was serendipitous, he'd claimed: she had been pulled through the blue fire a few hours earlier, an accident caused when his attempt to speak through flame had burned out of control. The Destroyer had known her for one of the enemy, one close to Leith, and so ransacked her mind, wresting from her everything she knew about the Falthan War effort, which wasn't much. Instead he found there something he admired and coveted—and evidence of his lieutenant's treachery. Evidence Stella had planted deep in her own mind. The Destroyer's subsequent drawing of Deorc was no accident. Enraged, he gave his lieutenant no chance to explain himself. Stella had watched in open-mouthed horror as the Undying Man destroyed Deorc, burning his body until it was unrecognisable, then binding him in cords of agony and preservation to endure as a pain-raddled husk for all time.

His regard for her had been cemented when he'd saved her life by giving her a transfusion of his own blood. She had become his unwilling queen-to-be.

After letting the herb steep for the recommended time, Stella drew out a cupful of the flavoured water and sipped at it. Chamomile and thyme blended nicely on her tongue, with a smooth ginger aftertaste. She shrugged her shoulders, letting her cares go for a moment. A little time for herself.

Others in the tea house began gathering around the pool, either finding a seat or standing on the far side, ignoring signs in the local language. Stella supposed them to be warning signs—certainly the pool looked dangerous, bubbling and steaming the way it did—although they could equally be telling the locals where to stand in safety.

A rotund woman, clad in an unflatteringly short dress and wearing the garland of flowers that seemed to symbolise employment at the tea house, came forward and stood by the pool. The matron, at last. But no; she took up a long stick with a container on the end and emptied the contents onto a small prominence poking above the waters of the pool. She then withdrew.

"Matron needs soap in order to erupt," said a man next to Stella, leaning over to speak to her, one hand extended. "They say it was discovered by a woman who came here many centuries ago to wash her clothes in the hot water." He grinned. "Yours could do with washing, eh, after all that dirt and rain out there. I'll wash 'em for you later, if you want to slither out of 'em."

An invitation of some sort. The man was handsome enough, but not her type; a little rough, a little dangerous. Not her type? A small part of her mind laughed. Just how dangerous was the man she'd taken up with?

But oh, a chance to be human again. If only she could take it.

"No, thanks," she said, smiling at him. "You wouldn't like what I'd give you."

The man snatched his hand back and turned to his fellows.

And so it goes.

A mystery solved, though. This pool was the Matron, and was about to erupt.

The small part of her mind that had just finished mocking her began to murmur worriedly at that. Stella really couldn't be bothered listening to it. Taking another cup of the drowse-inducing brew, she leaned back against the leg of the person behind her and watched the show.

The pool continued bubbling, then stopped as though suddenly snap-frozen in a northern frost. At the same moment a rumbling shook the seating, and a spout of scalding water and steam leapt from the throat of the protuberance in the pool. Up and up it went, higher and higher, and the reason for the opening in the roof became clear. It was an awe-inspiring spectacle, for all it had been primed by something as prosaic as soap.

As a thin watery mist—no longer scalding, but still hot—began drifting over those standing on the far side of the pool, she wondered whether the eruption was always the same size. And what would happen if . . .

No. The tea house has been here for years.
Just like the tea house át Yacoppica.

She considered whether she should shout out a warning, but the geyser began to subside and the shuddering stopped. All around her the locals applauded, heralding the end of the show. *Overcautious fool*, she chided herself.

Now others gathered, many of whom were locals who had no doubt seen the geyser erupt often enough to no longer be impressed, laughing and joking as they stood ten deep or more around the pool. No doubting what sort of herbs had been enjoyed by the majority: stimulants that would bear their own fruit of excitement and love later in the evening. Little wonder that Boiling Waters was considered the premier tea house in the entire Ikhnos Tea Chain.

The woman who had asked Heredrew her question entered the thronging circle and immediately the ribaldry ceased. She carried a musical instrument over her shoulder—*oh, Phemanderac, a harp*. His chosen instrument, one he had not been able to play for many years, since age twisted his hands. Stella glanced behind her to where the old scholar sat. He leaned forward, excitement on his face.

Was she the only one bitter about the ravages of time? She, who was not subject to it.

The woman sat directly in front of Heredrew, a shy smile on her young face. "There are foreigners here tonight," she said. "Before we eat, I will play in their honour a song I learned from Arotapa, the great travelling minstrel; a song of foreign lands. It is known as the Lay of Conal Greatheart."

This announcement occasioned varied reactions. Heredrew smiled widely at the girl, a crocodile preparing to eat a helpless, unsuspecting victim. At the rear of the gathering, Conal the priest hissed in surprise. The majority of the crowd applauded, though none gave any hint they recognised the title.

The most unusual reaction, though, came from Phemanderac. He had frozen in place, his long face a sculpture, the only movement coming from his lips, which repeatedly mouthed one word. To Stella it seemed like "Arotapa".

The woman pulled up her dress, exposing a generous amount of leg and occasioning a murmur of approval from the men present. She sat on the boardwalk and positioned the harp between her legs, then ran her fingers across the strings.

The clear liquid notes drew Stella back to the day she had finally returned to Instruere, free at last from the Destroyer's grasp, on the very day Leith had been crowned King of Faltha. She had pushed open the huge wooden doors to the Hall of Meeting and entered just as Leith ascended the throne to the stirring sounds of Phemanderac's harp.

The girl began to sing in a husky contralto:

Born in a bitter house,
Last of a line of sons,
Conal Greatheart lived his life amid the curséd ones.
Trained to wait on tables,
To serve the Lord of lies,
Conal Greatheart forged a fate beyond the greatest prize.

The words were simple, written not by a poet but by a musician, intended to be memorised easily both by travelling players and their audiences. But the tune, by contrast, was memorable. Stella knew she would be humming it tomorrow.

The lay continued, describing Conal's disgust at the habits of his family's oppressor, the Usurper of Instruere. Stella knew the story well—it was a staple all over Faltha— but, oddly, had not thought of it since Conal of Yosse had entered her orbit. The Usurper of Instruere, she reminded herself, was none other than the Destroyer, who had taken Instruere by force for the first time a thousand years ago, until driven out by Conal Greatheart and the Knights of Fealty.

Oh, it was all suddenly so clear. She cursed herself for being so obtuse. How could she not have seen it? The priest, curse his foolish mind, saw himself as a modern-day Greatheart.

How did it go? She racked her memory. Conal Greatheart had found his mother dead, killed by one of the Destroyer's henchmen, and vowed revenge. Uncanny, that, given what they themselves had found just after leaving Foulwater.

The three groups—Falthan, Bhrudwan and Elamaq— had met briefly early on the morning following the cataclysm that destroyed the Yacoppica Tea House. They agreed to separate, to journey northward independently of each other, to avoid drawing the concentrated attention of the gods, as seemed to have happened both at Yacoppica and Lake Woe. Enough people had died. Each group would try to solve their problems as they saw them. Perhaps one or more of the groups would find a solution they could all use, or at least assist in.

The three remaining Amaqi had actually gone southward, along with a few of the villagers, to continue searching the ruins for Lenares' body. The Bhrudwans went north on a minor road, vowing to reach Malayu before the end of summer. And the Falthans, the largest group, went east, back to the road by the sea.

About half an hour's walk from the town, they came across a gruesome scene: a myriad of carrion birds fighting over something in a gully beside the road.

Robal had slithered down the muddy slope, staining his Dhaurian robes, and driven the birds away, revealing a body. It had been cut, bruised, beaten and bled to death. Robal said he recognised her from the tea house. One of the hosts, he said.

They had taken the woman's body back to the town, and Stella was reminded of other times of sorrow when she had borne bad news. This news, however, was received with anger rather than sorrow, given the condition of the body. And then someone in the village remembered seeing one of the Amaqi with similar red mud stains on his breeches. The black, curly-haired fellow.

A swift exodus had followed, the men of the village arming themselves and leaving in search of the three Amaqi. There was no doubt an explanation for what they had found, but Stella had wondered if the Amaqi would be given an opportunity to offer it.

The girl's sweet voice continued the song. She told how Conal escaped his master, fleeing the servants quarters and living wild in the forest, gathering disaffected men to him, the beginnings of an army. Fierce and fanatical, Conal Greatheart demanded and received total loyalty.

Stella laughed inside: the song made virtue out of bit-terness and anger. Conal Greatheart had been a necessary man, a great man, but not a good one. He had put to death dozens of his followers with his own hand—those who showed signs of questioning his leadership, even some he accused of harbouring rebellious thoughts. Quite the madman, Conal Greatheart, according to the records in Instruere's Hall of Meeting. Not that you'd know it from the song; the sweet voice of the singer made him sound holy.

Funny how the best leaders were hard-edged. Leith had never been a great leader, for all his admirable qualities. Too soft, too ready to see all sides of a dispute, never willing to make an example of anyone. She'd loved him for it, but under his rule the continent had not prospered as it might have done, and latterly the individual kingdoms and the Koinobia had been given latitude to strengthen their own power bases.

The Undying Man had been a great leader by any external measurement. Bhrudwo had not had more than a handful of rebellions in the two thousand years he had ruled them, and Stella had seen no abject poverty of the sort many Falthans experienced. But external measurement could sometimes be misleading, and never told the whole story. Fear might keep citizens in line, but surely it affected their quality of life. Look at this woman singing for them: she had been in terror of the man from Andratan, and would no doubt have soiled her drawers had she known whom she had been speaking to.

Like his historical namesake, Conal of Yosse was not cowed, however. Conal Greatheart had openly questioned the Bhrudwan overlord's right to rule, and Conal of Yosse had challenged Heredrew's right to lead the Falthan group. It had been a fierce discussion, and all around them water fled before the sorcerer's magic. But nothing Heredrew said or threatened could bend the stubborn priest, and Conal offered no apology or explanation at the time. Later he told them about the voice in his head, and openly admitted that its advice had been in line with his own wishes.

The Lay of Conal Greatheart moved to its intense climax. He and his band of heroes returned to the city under the cover of darkness and set about sabotaging the Bhrudwan chain of command, ruthlessly slaying any Falthan who worked for the Undying Man. Of course the song did not mention that Conal had ordered his own brothers killed, and that his eldest brother died on Conal's own sword point.

Ah, Stella thought, as the final stanza began. *This version has omitted the gratuitous and wholly imaginary swordfight between Conal Greatheart and the Destroyer*. In fact, most scholars of Falthan history believed Conal and the Destroyer never actually met.

Nevertheless, Conal Greatheart had driven the Destroyer from Instruere by making his rule untenable. The cost had been in thousands of lives, almost all of them Falthan. After a year of the campaign no Falthan would work for the Destroyer, and his own army began deserting him. Five bitter years the so-called War of Tears lasted, until, as the last line of the song so eloquently put it, the Instruians awoke one morn to an empty throne.

Polite applause rippled around the tea house as the patrons wondered how they ought to receive a song with such a blatant anti-Andratan message.

Did Conal of Yosse have something similar planned? Would he work to undermine Heredrew's leadership? She had better warn him . . .

Listen to yourself, woman. Anyone would think you were his protector. That you wished him well in whatever scheme he was running to increase his power at the expense of Faltha. That you loved him and wanted him to succeed.

"I asked the girl to sing that song," Heredrew said quietly beside Stella's ear.

"Trying to measure the level of sedition in your backwater provinces?"

"Not at all. I'm trying to bring the thoughts of our friend the priest out into the open. I need to learn what is behind his actions, whether, as he says, there is a magician in his head. And if there is, who, and what he intends."

"Why don't you ask?"

Heredrew laughed. "Have you ever received a straight answer from the man? If it weren't for our agreement I'd strip his mind, such as it is, and expose this magician. I'm concerned he could do us great harm."

"Our agreement stands. You touch his mind, you lose my support."

"As you say. But be aware that this is folly. The man is a murderer. He needs to be drained and slain, not cosseted."

"Oh?" Stella turned and nearly brushed his face with her lips. *His illusory face*. "Is that the standard punishment for all murderers? Are you prepared to apply it to yourself?"

"Your question has no meaning. I cannot be slain—and neither can you. And that, Stella, is something we need to talk about. You told me you journeyed east to seek answers from the Undying Man. You have been travelling with him for a month or more and there have been no questions. Did you lie, or are you afraid?"

"I told you that because I believed you were Heredrew," she whispered.

"Afraid then. Yet it must be faced, Immortal One, because it is at the heart of what we need to do. Of what the Most High wants of us." He paused, then pinned her with a penetrating stare. "You loathe me. I understand that. Yet we must talk."

They sat together in a small alcove, away from the revellers. They would not be overheard: the nearest customer, a blonde-haired girl, was bent over her drink, paying them no attention. The other Falthans sat some distance away, heads together, intent on some discussion or other. Or perhaps debating the merits of the pit-cooked meal, which had been the best food Stella had tasted since leaving Instruere.

She forced her mind to return to Heredrew's comments.

"I refuse to believe it," she said. "You are playing us all. It's a clever plan to seize control of Faltha and Elamaq all in one go."

He spread his elongated hands wide. "No plan," he said.

"So you expect me to believe you are a reformed character. The evil Emperor has seen his flaws, and now he does the bidding of the one he hates the most, the one who cursed him and drove him out of paradise."

"No." Simple answers, almost hypnotic in their repetition. "I am not reformed."

"Then why, Heredrew? Or should that be Kannwar? Why are you risking everything to do what the Most High told you to do?"

"What risk is there? Compared to the certainty of failure should we do nothing, how can this be considered a risk?"

"Doesn't answer my question. You're good at not answering my questions."

"Because I'm trying to let you do the talking. The more

I say, the more you will feel I have steered you. And how likely are you to do my bidding?"

"As likely as you are to follow the Most High."

"And yet, here we are. I lead your group. Who, Stella, leads me?"

"No, curse you, no. You are not a willing game piece of the Most High."

He sighed and leaned back in his chair. "No, you are right, I am not. I will never be his counter. I am many of the things you say. I have killed and do not regret it. I have tortured and maimed people, always for a purpose, but have come to enjoy it. I lie whenever it suits me. But I have amassed two thousand years of wisdom, the kind earned through two thousand years of mistakes. I have learned, Stella, to listen to the truth, no matter whose lips it comes from.

"Let me summarise. The Most High told me his two rebellious children were going to destroy the world. Yet we get a slightly different story from the people of the Fisher Coast and the Amaqi. Lenares—such an intriguing girl, such a loss—told us of the Elamaq legends. The Son and Daughter drove out the Father, Stella. The Most High never told us that his glorious journey north from beyond Jangela, as described in the ancient scrolls, was in fact a rout, a remnant fleeing a rebellion. You and I, Stella, we are descendants of those the Amaqi defeated.

"Worse, our God, our mighty Most High, was overpowered by his own children. How does that work? Is he not as powerful as our theologians tell us? Or has he chosen weakness in some vast balancing act, so that by his weakness we might have freedom of will? I know well that the stronger the leader, the fewer choices are afforded his followers. Or perhaps his children have become stronger? Not just the Son and Daughter, but . . . his other immortals?"

He reached out for her, and she let him take her hand. The touch of his skin made her nauseous, despite knowing he had no real hand.

"And you?" she said. "Have you become stronger?"

"You know the answer, Queen of Faltha," he breathed. "For seventy years we have been connected. You could sense me, and I you. I actively cultivated that sense, using my arts to magnify the connection, so I could feel what you felt. I suffered your pain along with my own, and rejoiced as the agony gradually faded. So much more quickly than did mine."

"Then you are a fool," she snarled. "Nobody should have to experience pain like that, and no one in their right mind would embrace it voluntarily."

"I learned that you never gave your heart in love," Heredrew said.

Stella jerked back her hand.

"You were grateful, you sought to please him, you admired and respected him, but you never loved him."

Tears spilled down her cheeks. "You spied on me. I could feel you there, but I didn't try to find out what you thought or felt, even though the knowledge might have served Faltha. What right did you have to invade my heart?"

"Your mind, you mean."

"I tried to love him. But because of you, your filth and torture and taunting and your curséd tainted blood, I could not—could not share with him. For fear of infecting him." She broke into sobs and put her hands to her stinging eyes. "You know this."

"And so you wrestled with guilt for seventy years," he said softly. "As did I."

She wanted to kill him. To pick him up by the neck and sink him into the ground, into some abyss of fire. She imagined him shrieking in some lake of lava, while all around the red walls of his prison shook with the violence of the earth.

"Stella. Stella! Are you doing this?"

She pulled her hands away from her eyes. Blurry movement resolved into people running along walkways. Her seat jerked. The plate and mug on a nearby table rattled. People shouted and shrieked as the earth rumbled.

All at once she remembered her fear: that the gods would somehow exploit the thermal features to destroy them.

"You are putting out enormous power," Heredrew said, clasping her arm. "What are you doing?"

"Nothing. Nothing!"

The pool nearest them started to bubble furiously and a deep red glow spread across its surface. With a hiss, steam began escaping from a crack in the earth. Other fractures began to appear.

"This is not me."

"It's not her," said a new voice, a familiar voice. The blonde-haired girl unfolded herself from her seat and stood up. "It's the Son. But the Daughter and I, we are holding him off."

She was gaunt, dishevelled, and grim of face, but Stella recognised her. The girl held a shaking hand out in front of her, the muscles in her bare arm straining as though she pulled hard on something, yet Stella could see nothing.

"Tug, tug, tug," Lenares said. "Back to your cage, Umu. Your brother has gone."

The shaking slowed, then ceased, and the sound of rattling china and frenzied boiling water faded away.

"You have . . . you have captured the Daughter? She does your will?" Heredrew stood before the thin Amaqi, amazement in his voice

"Yes," the girl said, her voice strained. "But I am running out of strength. Would you please help me?"

CHAPTER 16

MERLA OF SAYONAE

"SO WE KILLED HIM," LENARES said.

"He deserved it," Kilfor remarked. "If anyone deserves to die, it's a man who forces himself on a woman."

"We didn't kill Olifa because he deserved it. We killed him to stop him coming after me. The Daughter can't always be here, and I must sometimes sleep. No matter where I ran to, he would have come for his stone. So we had to kill him."

"Yes, the stone," Heredrew said, a little too keenly. "You say the Daughter herself could not come close to you with the stone in the boat. I've heard of stones like that."

If he asks to see the stone, or even wants to know any more about it, I will forbid her to answer, Stella thought. She waited patiently as the strange southerner prepared her response.

"It's not much to look at," Lenares said finally. "But he wanted it anyway." She pressed her lips together. "He wanted many things."

"How did he die?" An inane question, but Stella wanted the subject to move on from the stone.

"The Daughter sent a fish to bump the boat and he fell in. I cut his fingers to make him let go, and then the Daughter brought other fish. Hungry fish."

"Oh, I see."

"I didn't want him to die, but if he had been nice it wouldn't have happened."

"Quite," Stella agreed. *This woman is innocent—and deadly.*

"This is the woman for you, son," Sauxa said loudly, cuffing Kilfor on the back of his head. "Not one of those soft Falthan city women you mooned after. Someone who deals in life and death. Well, why do you wait? Ask her to marry you!"

Kilfor rounded on his father. "You ask her. She's about the age you like them, old man."

Protracted coughing from inside the dray interrupted the mock quarrel.

"We have to find a physic," Robal said. "Phemanderac does not sound well."

"Indeed, he is very unwell," Moralye said. "What sort of horse would shy at an eel and tip the dray into the water? Surely in this land they train animals to cross rivers?"

The peevish outburst was unlike her, but she was clearly worried about the old scholar. As was Stella.

They had left behind the Boiling Waters Tea House three days earlier, having stayed in the cottage a night and a day; and now they drew close to the northern borders of the Fisher Coast. The country had become progressively wilder, looking to Stella like the more remote parts of the Wodranian Mountains in central Faltha. Not as majestic as the mountains of Firanes, her homeland, but dramatic all the same. To the west, bush-draped hills towered over the party, while to the east a complex series of tree-lined ridges separated the road from the sea. The occasional farm had been carved out of the wilderness, mostly on the seaward side of the road; extensive paddocks mostly empty of live-stock.

"This was deep forest once," Heredrew had told them. "Two centuries ago the Red Duke tried to extend his rule into Patina Padouk by settling some of his more enter-prising burghers here, but most left or died within a gen-eration. The foresters and farmers are almost all gone now. They suffered too many deaths at the hands of the forest people."

He'd laughed, and Stella was reminded of the De-stroyer hiding under Heredrew's exterior. *That's all it is, an exterior.*

"Turns out the soil here is too poor to support anything but sheep and goats," he'd said.

A day north of the tea house Phemanderac's dray had tipped into a swollen stream. They had discussed return-ing to the town, but no one had considered it a serious op-tion: with the latest evidence of the Son's willingness to interfere, the Falthans wanted to stay as far from inhabited areas as possible. So, after somewhat ineffectually drying Phemanderac and his wagon—the rain made it all but im-possible for any of them to remain dry—they pressed on.

Within hours the scholar developed a hacking cough. Phemanderac had been part of Stella's life for seventy years; it was easy to see him as an immovable fixture. But he was old: over ninety years of age. Too old, perhaps, to be engaging in what looked like being a long overland jour-ney. Certainly too old to survive pneumonia. And not yet desperate enough to ask for Heredrew's healing.

Stella sought answers regarding the duration and difficulty of their road, but no one, not even Heredrew, could
give a satisfactory answer. The journey between the Fisher
Coast and Malayu—the nearest port to Andratan and the
only place from which a regular service to the fortress op-
erated—was normally undertaken by ship. Heredrew had
never travelled overland through Patina Padouk.

Stella had asked, quite reasonably, she thought, why
they were attempting it.

Because the risk was likely to be less journeying by foot
than by ship, Heredrew had argued. He did not want to be
out there on the open sea, exposed to the machinations of
the gods.

Stella had to agree; she had no way of knowing what
faced them on the overland journey, but did not want to
drown in a sinking ship. If she could drown. A hideous
picture of herself standing on the sea floor, her leg snared
by the anchor chain of some great boat, flashed before her
eyes. Awaiting the changing of the earth to be freed.

How could anyone think immortality was to be
desired?

She would gladly have donated some of her remaining
time in the world to Phemanderac. He was such a great-
souled man. Never angry or impatient, always prepared to
consider any point of view, slow to speak yet with so much
to say, if only people paid attention to him.

They arrived at an innocuous road junction. A narrow
road, little more than a track, went west, disappearing into
the mountains, while a much broader road arrowed down a
narrow valley towards the sea. Directly ahead of the travellers stood a dark wall of trees: not the orderly trees of
Faltha, row after row of noble, tall pines, firs and birches,

but a many-tentacled explosion of growth, a hundred shades of verdancy, every level from forest floor to canopy filled with something twisted or spiked. *Less of a forest*, Stella thought, *and more of a fight*.

"We going that way?" Kilfor asked. No trail ran from the crossroads towards the forest edge.

"Not if I can help it," Heredrew replied. "The choices are stark: either we take a ship or travel through the jungle. I have already explained why we will not be sailing to Malayu. But there are paths, or at least there were. And, I think," he said, glancing at Lenares, "it might be useful if we were to be hidden for a while."

"There's nowhere you can hide," the girl said in a monotone.

In the lead, Robal halted and turned. "Then you may have to free your prisoner. If holding her captive allows the Son to track us, how have we gained an advantage?"

"A question that begs many others, guardsman," Heredrew said gruffly. "It's time, I think, for some plain talk from our cosmographer."

"Then we halt here for our midday meal," Robal said. "And while we eat, Moralye can tend Phemanderac and we will listen to Lenares tell us how she came to capture a god."

"I trapped her," Lenares said simply. Stella shuddered at the smugness in the girl's voice. How could one be so self-satisfied at having a bear by the tail?

"How, Lenares? How did you trap her?" the guardsman asked patiently, nibbling at an apple.

"I told you how Umu and I stopped Olifa from attacking me. After the Daughter-fishes ate him up, we sailed north, me in the boat, making it sail straight, and the Daughter surrounding me with a circle of dolphins. You shouldn't have done that, should you, Umu? Tug, tug." Lenares giggled like an excited child.

"Why do you call her Umu?"

"Because that's her name. She was given it so long ago that sometimes she doesn't remember it herself. She doesn't remember her mother or father, or the names of her brothers and sisters. She's very silly."

"So she doesn't know the name of the Son?"

"I asked her that," Lenares said. "But the Son is not her brother, not her real brother. The Father took one child from each side and drew life from them, making them gods."

"Drew life?" Heredrew asked, a covetous gleam in his eye. He sat in the middle of the crossroads, a little way apart from the others, but shifted a pace closer at these words. Stella thought no one else had heard his question. Was *that* what he wanted? Hadn't he enough of life?

"A child from each side?" Robal pressed. "What sides?"

"There was a war," Lenares explained. "The Time of Quarrels. The children of the Father broke into two groups, one to the north, one to the south. They lived apart for a time, but the world was not large enough to contain their quarrels, and so they fought." She closed her eyes.

"*The people fought,*" she said in a voice not entirely her own. "*Under the weeping eye of their god some ran and some chased, some became predators, others prey. Some made traps and others became snared in them.*" She shuddered, and the deep tones in her voice faded. "The god tried to stop the fighting, but the children would not listen, except for two: a man of the south and a woman of the north."

"The Son and the Daughter," Robal said. The guardsman scratched his rapidly growing beard. Stella thought it made him look like a wild man, but said nothing. He was prideful, and anything she said to him these days tended to be taken the wrong way.

"Yes. He made them into gods. To become gods they had to give up so much, Umu says, so much they didn't realise they owned. The breath of life is something we all have. Umu says it is like a warm, wet wind with the promise of rain, that it flows through every part of us all. You can't know what it is like to lose it, she says. It's like spending an eternity in the baking desert, watching sweet rain fall on the horizon."

"So why did they do it, if it cost them so much?" Sauxa asked, laying aside a piece of bread to ask the question.

"Because they didn't know!" Lenares cried, and her voice changed again. *"Because the Father deceived us!"* Her mouth snapped shut and she looked around wildly, as though she didn't remember where she was. Or who she was.

"Who has captured whom?" Kilfor whispered to his father.

Lenares shook her head like a dog after a drink, then resumed her tale. "They agreed to godhood, to sacrifice themselves to stop the fighting. Yes, the Most High explained what they would lose. But no explanation, Umu says, can match the reality of consciousness without life.

"The Son and the Daughter stopped the fighting. But, being new to godhood and desirous of all its secrets, they refused to make the sacrifice complete. The Most High wanted them to fade into the nothingness, but they hung on and hardened there, in the void beyond the world-wall. Now they are trapped. Tug, tug."

"A fascinating story," Heredrew said. "But you still haven't told us how you captured the Daughter."

"No, I haven't. Because none of you would understand."

"None of us?" Heredrew rumbled.

"Certainly not you," Lenares replied, straightening her shoulders. "Torve might understand, if he were here. Maybe Moralye or Phemanderac. But not you."

"Try me," he snapped. "Of course, you may not be sufficiently clever to make your explanation simple enough for us to follow."

"I might not be," Lenares replied, and Stella could see it was the simple truth: she really believed she would struggle to explain what she'd done.

"I've discovered some new numbers," she said. "They are complex, not simple like counting numbers. When I lived in Talamaq, in my little world, all I needed were counting numbers, the ones that make sense to everyone." She looked from face to face, her expression clearly frustrated, worried she'd already surpassed them.

"One, two, three and so on," Stella said.

"Yes. But when I lost my centre, when I left Talamaq behind and lost count of how many steps I'd taken, I needed something else to base my numbers on. I had no centre, nothing. That's when I realised 'nothing' could be a number, like Qarismi of Kutrubul said. Nothing can be something. It took me a long time to believe it, but I do now, particularly since I trapped the Daughter with nothing." She laughed.

"Now you are leaving us behind," Stella said.

"I knew I would. Qarismi called 'nothing' the zero number. It helps us subtract everything. Say you have three loyal Amaqi citizens, and then the cruel Emperor puts them to death. How many are left?"

"None, of course."

"Of course, but in numbers we call that zero. What say you owe the Emperor a great debt, and he takes your three children in part payment. He says the debt will not be forgiven until he has four of your children. How many children do you have?"

"None," Stella repeated.

"No," Heredrew said. "You have one fewer than no children; that's right, isn't it, Lenares."

The girl smiled, and for a moment it was as though the sun had peeked out from behind dark clouds. "Yes," she said. "Because if you bear another child, you lose that one too. You count into loss. So, let's count down. Five, four, three, two, one, zero, less one, less two, less three and so on. It's like looking at numbers in the mirror: profit on your side, loss on the other side. And, right at the centre, surrounded by numbers stretching away forever, is zero."

She waited until comprehension began to show on a few of the faces around her. Stella almost had it . . .

A voice came from behind them. "So, if you position your numbers carefully, the hole in the world is at the centre? It is zero?" Moralye sounded uncertain.

"Yes, that's what I did. But I went much further. If zero is something, then some very strange things begin to happen to numbers. I read a note scribbled in the margin of Qarismi's papers: 'Don't divide by zero, or, if you do, be prepared to deal with what happens.' I wondered what he meant. Any number can be divided, because numbers stand for things, and things can be divided. So we return to the question: is zero something or nothing? I have shown it can be a number, it can be something, the central something. If it can be something, it can be divided. And if zero can be divided, so can the hole in the world. I might be able to halve it, and halve it again, until I trap the Daughter within it. Until the hole is so small she can't move."

She giggled. "I was right, totally right. Zero can be divided. Not only that, zero is a divisor." She bit her lip, casting around for an example, and grabbed a slice of bread from the cloth laid between them. "This bread is one thing. The more times I divide it, the more pieces I have. But something strange happens if I divide it by less than one but more than zero—a fraction of one, if you understand me. I know this will hurt your head, but what I'm saying follows the rules of numbers. One thing divided by a half grows to twice the size; divided by a quarter it quadruples. The smaller the number the thing is divided by, the larger it gets, until if it is divided by the tiniest fraction it is as big as the world. And if it is divided by zero, it goes on forever."

She snatched up a stick and began drawing in the sand. "Look here. Let me show you in mathematical language. I graph quotients,"—she drew a "Q" by one axis—"against divisors,"—and added a "D" by the other—"so that as the divisor approaches zero, the quotient gets larger and larger until it has no limit. Like I said, strange things begin to happen to the numbers."

Heredrew turned to her angrily. "Very well, you've proved you know more about mathematics than I do. What of it?"

"When I first arrived at Raceme I was drawn by the Daughter through a hole in the world. I assigned a number—zero—to the hole, and made it my centre. It therefore became defined. It was as though I had tied a string

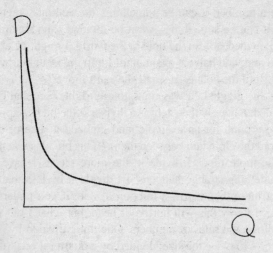

to it, tug, tug. All I had to do was start dividing it using more strings—dividing zero by zero—until I trapped the Daughter in a piece too small for her to escape. So she is trapped.

"I thought about it all night before I did it. In the morning I watched her dolphins circling me, until I could work out which one was her. Then I divided zero again and again with my string, which is itself zero, always dividing the part of the hole she swam in. It took her a while to work out what I was doing, didn't it, Umu? By then she was trapped. I let her swim along beside me for a week or so, and found I could control everything about her.

"I have her still. She is here, near us, sometimes a bird and sometimes a fox. I could bring her down to this blanket if I wanted. I could let you kill her. We could spit her and eat her for our dinner. Or I could put the stone on her.

It hurts her so much she doesn't want to get too close to me. When she saved me from Olifa it cost her a lot of her strength. So now she is totally in my power."

"Why don't we kill her then?" Robal asked. "If she's responsible for what happened at Lake Woe and at the tea house, she ought to pay for it with her life."

"Oh, but that wasn't her. That was the Son, he's the more powerful of the two. He controls the entire continent of Elamaq, while the Daughter has few assets to call upon. I think we can make the Daughter work for us, and help us to get rid of the Son. Then we can talk about what we do with her. Tug, tug, tug."

Somewhere in the distance a bird, probably a hawk, screeched in anger.

"I have never been so impressed," Heredrew said. "You did all this with your mind. I'll await further proof of this, of course, but what we saw at the Boiling Waters Tea House seems to support your claim."

Lenares giggled again. "I am special," she said. "Mahudia always said so. The first real cosmographer in hundreds of years, she said." She lowered her voice. "I think I had help," she said. "The Daughter killed Mahudia, my Talamaq mother, by becoming a lion and eating her up. Torve saw her do it. So something of Mahudia is now in the Daughter. When I first tried to assign my zero to the hole in the world, to make it something so it could be divided, I couldn't tie it to anything. Then I felt Mahudia's hand take the string from mine." She blinked huge tears out of her eyes. "I think she holds the other end of the string."

Stella shook her head. *Fanciful.* The girl was a savant, extraordinarily capable in one area at the expense of many others. Her explanation—zeroes, strings, dolphins, dead mothers—meant nothing, surely. Nevertheless, somehow she had tied it all together. Out of nothing she had captured the Daughter. Still, Stella was not entirely convinced.

"When we met you in the Boiling Waters Tea House, you said that you were nearly out of strength. I don't understand. How can numbers get weaker? Does your trap depend on something other than numbers?"

"Yes, I think so. Mahudia is strengthening the trap with something she gets from the void. But it felt as though she was slipping away. Heredrew has been lending his strength to me."

Stella smiled. This sounded far more likely than zeroes and strings made of numbers. Or perhaps it was some strange combination of magic and logic.

"You miss Mahudia, don't you?"

Perhaps that was the real magic: that Lenares had been able to tap into something stronger than magic. *Ah, it sounds like a bard's tale. Love conquers all.*

"Yes," Lenares replied. "She shouldn't have died. The Daughter will have to explain to me why she ate my mother. Unless she can come up with a very good reason, I think I might end up eating her."

The meal finished, the members of the group went in separate directions to attend to personal matters. Stella found Heredrew sitting on a stump, picking at his teeth.

"Thought you would have some magical system to keep your teeth clean," she said.

He shook his head.

"No? You certainly manage to keep your robes in good condition."

"Ah, well, I spare a little sorcery for that," he said. "Do

you think an evil lord would be credible with food on his robes?"

She snorted. "You're not doing a very good impression of an evil lord at the moment. Serving the Most High, allowing annoying mortals like Conal to oppose you and live, even talking civilly to your enemies the Falthans. Why, you haven't needlessly slaughtered anyone in days."

"Weeks, actually," he said blandly. "Don't be fooled. You might be immortal, but you're new at it. There are many things you simply don't perceive. For example, do you know where I get the magic from to keep my robe clean?"

She shook her head.

"From you, of course, and the others."

She froze. "What? You hurt us just to keep yourself looking good?"

"Relax," he said, smiling. "It takes an infinitesimal amount of power to maintain my clothes. My physical shell, on the other hand, requires enormous strength. I get that from myself, largely, now that I am prohibited the blue fire."

"Largely?"

He shrugged. "Yes, well."

"What did you think of Lenares' explanation?" she asked him.

"I followed it easily enough," he said, "though I decided it is best to deal with her by pretending she knows more than everyone else. I followed it, yes, but I can't say I would have thought to try it. She really is an interesting woman."

"I wouldn't have thought you were interested in women," she said carelessly, then instantly regretted the words.

"Oh? Tell me, Stella, when did you stop being interested in men? And remember, I've been in your head, so no lying."

"I'm sorry, Heredrew. I didn't have the right to ask."

"But you want to know, don't you. I'm interested in women, but I stop short of fathering children. Why would I wish potential rivals upon myself?"

"You never thought . . . that you would infect them?"

"With the curse? No. It would take—is that why? All those years, you never touched him?" He turned his head away. "You are a better person than I."

Stella stood and angrily brushed dirt from her breeches. "Was there ever any doubt, Kannwar? Has there ever been a person in the history of the world who couldn't claim to be a better person than you?"

He shrugged his shoulders. "I showed you my interpretation of the *Domaz Skreud*. When assessing a man's life, I don't think you can rely totally on history written by his enemies."

She handed him a water bottle. "There's another reason you want us to travel overland, isn't there?"

"And what would that be?"

"I think you're afraid of what you will find in Malayu. You're anxious about how long you've been away from your dungeons and battlements. You think that in your absence one of the other snakes has slithered onto your throne. A snake powerful enough to prevent you from using your magic to take us directly to Andratan. And you think this snake might well be talking into the minds of the three voice-possessed."

The sorcerer said nothing for a moment, then grunted. "Clever girl."

"Cleverer than you think," she retorted to his condescension. "I know why you are here. Why you've put your entire empire at risk."

"Because we were drawn off course by the power of the gods."

"No. Well, yes, that's why we're here in southern Bhrudwo. But I know why you agreed to follow the Most High. Why you were in Dhauria. Why you joined us."

"Oh?" He stared into her eyes, his own hypnotisingly deep pools of pain and desire. "Oh?" He lifted his finger to her face and placed it gently on her lips, jolting her entire body. "You do, don't you. You'd best keep the thought unvoiced, Stella, lest our enemies overhear."

She could not draw her gaze away from his. He had her in thrall, was expending his magic to keep her docile, but nothing in her desired to struggle. Instead, every part of her wished to . . . surrender.

"It's not our enemies you wish to keep secrets from," she murmured, her lips moving against his elegant, illusionary finger. "It's the Most High."

He sighed then, an exhalation of longing, and drew his finger away; then reached for her and took her in his arms, enveloping her in darkness. "Yes," he whispered in her ear, his voice the merest breath. "Clever girl."

They took the east road, and walked all that day and most of the next, until they crested a ridge and came to the sea. Huddled against the coast was a port, small when compared to some in Faltha, but unexpected all the same in such a sparsely inhabited region. And standing in the road was the woman from the tea house that Heredrew had agreed to take north with him.

"I assumed she'd decided against the trip," Robal said quietly to Stella.

"Sadly for her, she has not," Stella replied.

So their party grew by one, now numbering ten; though Stella, listening to the persistent coughing coming from the dray, and observing the concern on Moralye's face, worried that the number might yet decline.

The girl's name was Pernessa, a pretty, fussy name, entirely suitable for its owner, it seemed. She carried a small harp, wrapped in oiled skins, over one shoulder, and far too much baggage over the other.

"Put that on the dray," Heredrew told her.

All very well, but who would carry the baggage once they took the forest path? Stella doubted they would be taking the pony and wagon north. For that matter, what would they do with Phemanderac?

A half-hour's pleasant walk brought them to the seaport. Sayonae, Heredrew named it, and for once he didn't have a bad word to say about the place. The travellers had six inns to choose from—no tea houses, sadly; Stella had come to enjoy the brewed herbs—and each seemed clean and well-run, at least from the outside. *Quite a feat for a port town*, Stella considered.

Heredrew chose the Silver Tankard, the best of the six inns, and they filed in. Two dozen men sat around a low central table, clearly the site of communal drinking, while others filled tables around the walls. The main room was smoky and somewhat odorous with salt and sweat but otherwise pleasant, rushes rather than sawdust lining the floor, and even sporting three faded tapestries on the walls. One, Stella was sure, depicted the Undying Man on his throne.

The sorcerer spoke with the proprietor, a youngish woman

with hard features, and with her permission arranged three tables together to provide enough seating for the party.

It wasn't until the meal was served that the trouble began. Broiled fish and baked potatoes arrived on large platters, each carried by two women. One of them dropped her end of the platter on the table, stared with narrowed eyes at the party, then had a whispered word in the proprietor's ear.

"I'm going to have to ask you to leave," the hard-faced woman said to them in a voice loud enough to carry throughout the room. "Cylene's been in enough trouble recently without taking up with you men. You assured me you were respectable, but my customers won't be having goings-on like this. The girl's antics are well known. Now, out with you."

Heredrew drew himself up. "I'm sure—"

"You're about to go on about a misunderstanding," the proprietor said. "Don't waste your breath. Your only misunderstanding is mistaking the Silver Tankard for a brothel. Out, before I set my men on you."

Two men with cudgels approached the group.

"I don't want to have to call Gul and Haff onto you, but call them I will. Move."

Stella nudged the Undying Man in the ribs. "Don't make any fuss," she said. "Let's sort this out by talking, not by magic. We'll speak to Pernessa and uncover her deception."

"Very well," Heredrew grated. "But she'll not be travelling a step further with us."

"Of course," Stella murmured. "Can't have someone pretending to be someone they're not, can we?"

As they reached the door, having passed through a gauntlet of dark mutterings from the townsfolk, the proprietor called out: "Not you, Cylene. I'll be taking you home to your family. The rest of you can leave."

"And our coin for the meal and accommodation?"

"Is forfeit, tall man. Read the sign." She pointed to a small metal square on which words had been scribed. Stella certainly hadn't noticed it. "Those who don't abide by the rules don't get refunds."

Heredrew snorted, then muttered, "The first place on the Fisher Coast I've ever seen my rules properly enforced, and it had to be here and now."

"I said stay, Cylene!" the hard-featured woman cried. Stella went to put a hand on Pernessa's arm, but it wasn't her the woman strode towards, a soup ladle brandished menacingly.

It was Lenares.

Stella tried reason one last time. "But she's been with us for weeks. Why would we deceive you? We are already disgraced in the town; what do we have to gain from furthering a deception? We're telling you the truth!"

A crowd had gathered in the town square. A misnomer: the space was circular, with a scaffold in the centre, noose swaying slightly in the late afternoon sea breeze. It was as though the buildings had drawn away equidistant from the scaffold. Stella had seen nothing like this in any other Bhrudwan town, but this was the northern extremity of the Fisher Coast. Perhaps justice was more brutal here.

The townspeople weren't quite ready to hang anyone, but they clearly could not understand why these strangers wanted to claim one of their own.

For one of their own Lenares clearly was. Person after person talked of how Cylene had been a permanent fixture in the town, growing up in a famously large family, and, with the death of her father, had learned to fend for herself from a young age. Lenares denied it all, of course, with an entirely credible look of puzzlement on her face. Stella would have believed her without question—except how could she say with certainty where Lenares had come from? By her own admission she had been deposited in Raceme by a hole in the world. Now, in the light of the townspeople's claims, the story sounded dubious at best. Was the Daughter really held captive by this woman? Had there been, was there still, a hole in the world? Only now did Stella realise just how much of their understanding of this crisis depended on Lenares' word.

She decided to risk open conversation. "Don't you think it might be time to ask Umu for help?" she called to the cosmographer.

"I told her not to, not just yet," Heredrew said from close behind Stella. "I wish to let this play out for a while."

One of the young men holding the cosmographer's shoulders spoke up. "Cylene's been gone for months. I should know, I saw her the night before she left. No, I can't explain how she left aboard ship and then turns up with these strangers, clearly having come overland. But that's Cylene. No doubt about it."

"Here they are!" a boy cried.

Everyone looked towards the landward gates, through which, amid a cloud of dust, rode at least a dozen people; the first mounted travellers Stella could remember seeing on the Fisher Coast.

Horse after horse drew up in the town square. The crowd waited patiently as the riders dismounted, tied their mounts to a hitching rail, dusted themselves off and presented themselves. A thin, pinched-looking woman in a florid pink dress came forward, unfurled a lime green parasol, which she held over her eyes to shade out the low sun, and peered at the people gathered there. Behind her, a few of the figures fingered large cudgels in their belts.

"What is the meaning of this?" she snapped out. "Why have we been summoned?"

In answer, the proprietor of the Silver Tankard pushed Lenares forward.

"So you have come home," the woman said to her, her voice nasal and haughty in tone. "What have you done to your hair?"

"That's not Cylene, Mother," said one of the smaller boys standing behind the haughty woman.

"Of course it is. Well, girl? What do you wish to say in your defence? I hear you left on a smugglers' ship, serving as the captain's whore. How do you justify our continued shame in Sayonae?"

Lenares stared at the woman, her face pale. "I don't know what a whore is," she said, "and I don't know who you are."

"We brought you up to speak better than that, Cylene. Is this how your smuggler captain has corrupted you, even to the extent of coarsening your tongue? And those clothes!" The woman turned to the riders behind her. "Boon, take your sister home. The rest of you, remain with me. I'll have a word with these strangers, to see if thanks are in order."

"The girl goes nowhere," Heredrew said. He took six swift strides to where the townspeople stood and put a possessive arm on Lenares' shoulder.

"Boys," the woman said, quietly enough.

"You don't want to oppose the Umertas," one of the townspeople said, his voice breathless.

"I thank you for the advice," Heredrew replied, "which was no doubt well meaning. But the Umertas, whoever they are, would do well not to oppose me."

"I offer you a last chance," said the woman. "Let my daughter go, or my boys will be forced to take measures."

The crowd edged back. Clearly they expected the woman's threat to be made good.

"Don't hurt anyone," Stella said.

"Very well." Heredrew leaned back against the scaffold, his hand still grasping Lenares' shoulder.

Eight young men, all with sandy hair and narrow noses, made for Heredrew, cudgels drawn. The sorcerer pushed Lenares behind him and stepped forward a pace, no expression on his face.

"We require you to move," said the oldest of the young men. Mid-to-late twenties, Stella reckoned.

"No."

With no further negotiation, the man drew his cudgel and aimed a blow at Heredrew's forehead. It struck, there was no doubt of it: the crack echoed around the square. One of the younger boys grunted and fell to the ground, while Heredrew remained unmoved.

"Take a look at your brother," the sorcerer said, "and try to figure out what just happened."

The man hissed, then ran his hand through his hair, tilted his head and struck again, this time at Heredrew's arm.

The youngest boy, a lad no more than ten years of age, shrieked and clutched at his upper arm. The man wielding the cudgel turned at the sound.

"Nasty break the boy has," Heredrew said. "It will take

weeks to heal, and all that time it means someone not helping with the horses. "Three, counting the first lad you struck and the person who will have to look after them both. I don't think your mother will be pleased."

The young man backed away, returning to the line of his brothers.

"Greenstick fracture," said a girl, looking up from the young boy's kneeling form. The first boy remained stretched out on the ground, unmoving. One of the other boys knelt beside him.

"What did you do?" the woman asked Heredrew, her voice thinner now, a mask of fear on her face. "Are you some sort of sorcerer? You'll be reported to Andratan for this."

"I'll save you the trouble," Heredrew said, pulling out his seal and lifting it high. "Hear this," he said, his voice amplified somehow so everyone in the square could hear it clearly. "I've travelled through this ignorant and backward country for the last few weeks and have seen nothing but contempt for Andratan and the servants of the Undying Man. I have been treated with disrespect. Because I have chosen to travel with guests of the empire, I have tempered my response to this. And now I have finally heard the name of Andratan invoked—as a threat."

He took a step forward, then another, and as he did so his body seemed to grow taller: ten, twenty, thirty feet tall. The crowd cried out and pushed each other to get away from the sorcerer.

"You are wondering who I am," the giant figure said, and buildings shook as his voice roared. "I am neither Recruiter nor *Maghdi Dasht*, fatal as that would have been should you have shown them lack of respect. So who could I be? I am the Undying Man himself come amongst you, surveying the empire I built—and I am displeased!"

Stella wanted to cry out, but a deep dread had seized her heart and she could not move. *So . . . much . . . power!*

The figure crooked his arm and the oldest Umerta boy rose into the air, his cudgel still in his hand. "The honour of Andratan has been impugned, son. You struck your ruler's person and you must pay the price. I will have the respect I deserve."

Higher and higher the boy rose, whimpering as he did, and the acrid smell of urine wafted around the square. The helpless boy was not the only source.

The sorcerer made a fist. The young man arched backwards, going into convulsions, and strangled cries issued from his open mouth. The fist opened and the youth fell thirty feet to the ground. A small cloud of dust rose, then dispersed.

Stella watched for any signs of life, but there were none.

"May I approach?" the woman asked, her voice shaking. The parasol lay discarded on the ground behind her.

"You may," said the sorcerer.

He held me in his arms a few hours ago, Stella found herself thinking.

The woman knelt before the giant figure, her face working, betraying the great effort she made to keep her composure. "I make plea neither for myself nor for my son, whom you have . . ." she licked her lips, "whom you have rightly punished. Instead, following protocol, I invite the guests of the Bhrudwan Empire to sup with us this evening, and stay the night should they wish."

The giant vanished and Heredrew stood in its place.

"We accept. And there we will solve the mystery of our

travelling companion whom you claim as your daughter. Perhaps reasoned discussion will achieve what violence could not."

The Umerta steading lay half an hour's ride north of the port, a little inland of the golden beaches ribboning the coast, surrounded by forbidding forest. The land they worked was extensive, with a significant live-in workforce in addition to the matriarch's many sons—their number now reduced by one.

Their homestead was enormous, and palatial in almost every respect. A stone exterior, in contrast to the wooden houses of Sayonae. How far had the stone been brought, and at what cost, Conal wondered. He had not imagined Bhrudwo, which he'd envisaged as a poor place, sucked dry by the Destroyer, would contain places such as this.

The entire steading gathered to receive their unwelcome guests, and to pay respect to the body of the Umerta heir. *They have an awkward task*, Conal thought. *To lie with everything they have in order to convince the monster they are pleased to entertain him on the night they should be mourning the loss of the eldest son.* There stood the matriarch, head high, a smile pasted on her face, which had sagged noticeably since this afternoon. Either side of her stood her sons and daughters, bowing and curtseying as the Destroyer led the Falthans into the large reception room.

"So the bear reveals his claws," Conal hissed as he approached Stella.

"Tonight is not about your feelings," came the reply.

"But some night must be. The monster must die for the sake of the world."

"My hand will be on the knife that separates him into

a thousand pieces," his queen said, and his heart rose. "As soon as he has served his purpose."

Conal found himself presented to the stony-faced matriarch. He kissed her hand, as seemed to be tradition in this barbaric land, then looked up into her dead eyes and whispered: "I will kill him."

"You are a fool to think such things," the woman said, but her eyes sparkled as she spoke. "And an even greater fool for saying them. Perhaps, if it lies within the grace of our lord of Andratan, you could give me some time to correct your thinking."

Conal nodded, wondering what the woman could mean, and allowed himself to be led into the dining room.

The Falthans were accorded privileged positions directly opposite the hostess, yet their number, including the obviously bedazzled Pernessa, filled less than half one side of the enormous table. Conal was seated next to Robal; Stella had clearly manoeuvred things to ensure he was close to the guard. To his left were a pale Phemanderac and, next to him, Moralye, who patted at his mouth with a cloth and appeared ready to spoon-feed him. On the far side of Robal sat Stella, then Kilfor, Sauxa and Pernessa. The remainder of the table was filled by the Umerta family.

Eight exquisite courses served on the finest porcelain, and yet no one but Heredrew ate more than the smallest portion of food. Surely the monster must notice? If so, he did not acknowledge it. *So much sorrow and fear resting on this place, and all he can do is stuff his cheeks full of his victim's food.*

A side door opened and a woman entered, tiptoed across the room and stood at the matriarch's left; a place away from the Destroyer, who of course had been given the honoured place at her right hand.

"My lord, this woman was to have been my daughter-in-law," the woman said, her voice level. "She was betrothed to my son."

The monster looked up from his feast. "Plenty more brothers," he said, and turned back to his meal.

"Providing any of them are alive by morning," Conal breathed. The pretty but wan-faced girl beside him—Sena, she'd named herself—drew in a sharp breath.

"I don't doubt some of your brothers will try to revenge themselves tonight," he said to her. "If they try, they will die. Tell them that, will you? And you can also tell them," he added, lowering his voice, "that there are others, more capable, working to rid the world of this man. Let them take heart from that."

"Why do you travel with him?"

Sena really did have the most intense blue eyes, which bored into his as she asked the question. She had a pretty face too, and—he was a priest. These thoughts were distracting him.

He smiled at her, shaping his face in what he imagined was a ruthless look. "I travel with him for a chance to see him dead."

"Now, it is time to talk of Lenares," the Destroyer said to the woman whose son he'd killed. "I would have this mystery solved without further bloodshed. You may speak without fear, as long as you speak the truth. But first, I would have you speak of yourself."

"My name is Martje," she said without hesitation. "I am

not from the Fisher Coast, and have not been raised in its ways."

"No," the Destroyer agreed. "You have the look of one from Astralagus."

"The Hanseia Hills, actually, near the Nordalagus border."

"Ah, the Hanseia Hills, from which come at least half the rebellions in Bhrudwo—and half the *Maghdi Dasht*. I am beginning to understand. Now, for one foreign to the Fisher Coast, you seem well versed in its etiquette, no matter what you say. A pity your son did not have your natural caution."

"You forget it was I who ordered him to strike," she said, raising her chin.

"I needed someone to punish, in the interests of preserving public order."

"You should have chosen me," she said.

"I still could, Martje."

She blanched at this, but did not pull away.

"Now, Lenares," he said, turning to her, "please oblige me by standing against the far wall." He waved his hand at a wall covered in portraits of men and women.

"Any questions?" he asked those still at the table as the girl stood amid the well-trimmed beards and elaborate frocks. "Just to make it even clearer, would the Umerta family members stand either side of Lenares, please?"

There could be no doubt, even for one as sceptical as Conal knew himself to be. He wanted the Destroyer to be wrong, wanted to see him humiliated. But he was clever, two thousand years clever. The faces gathered against the gold-leafed wall were all of the same stock. Lenares, whatever her protestations, was one of them.

The Destroyer stood, brushing away the remnants of his meal. "Lenares, you're from the south, are you not?"

"Yes," she answered, her face pale. She had said little since arriving here, obsessed, no doubt, by trying to work this out using her system of numbers. If that wasn't also a sham. Perhaps the girl was afraid of being exposed as an opportunist.

"Yes," she repeated. "Lenares the Cosmographer, of Talamaq. I am an Amaqi."

"And are Duon and the man who calls himself Dryman also Amaqi?"

"Yes, but they are from southern areas."

"You are trying to steer me away from the inevitable conclusion to these questions," the Destroyer said. "That is not like you, Lenares. Are there others in Talamaq with pale hair and skin?"

"No," Lenares replied. "Mahudia, my mother, said I was special."

"She's not your real mother though, is she?"

"She was the only real mother I ever had."

"But not your birth mother."

Lenares hung her head. "No. I cannot remember my birth mother."

"A serious admission for one such as yourself, who remembers everything. Now, can you explain why you look almost exactly like the portrait just above your head?"

It was a small picture, insignificant enough amongst a wall as grand as this was to escape attention, of a girl with the same eyes, mouth, jaw, complexion—the same everything as Lenares bar the hair, and that was only a matter of style, not colour.

The Destroyer turned to Martje. "I assume the girl in the portrait is Cylene?"

"No," the woman said serenely. "That is a picture of me at her age."

"And do you have a portrait of your errant daughter?" asked the Destroyer undeterred. "One, perhaps, that might recently have been taken down from the wall because of the shame she has brought this house?"

"Mikal, go and fetch your sister's painting," Martje said. "You'll find it in my room."

"Sitting beside your bed, no doubt much wept over." Seeing her surprised look, he went on: "You'd be surprised how many similar cases one comes across if one lives long enough. While your son fetches the final piece of compelling evidence, let me see if I can fill in the remaining blank spaces. You were married to a Fisher Coast man who disgraced himself in some way. Usually in these situations he is a drunkard, a gambler or a philanderer, but not always. Whatever the reason, he runs down the family fortune. Then one or more of the children go missing, their loss usually attributed by the father to an accident, but in reality they are sold as slaves to fund whatever vile habit that has cost the man his soul. I assume your husband is no longer with you?"

"He is not," she said. "And it was for none of those reasons I parted with him. Had he been merely a drunkard or those other things you mentioned, I would have remained with him." Her face pinched in even more tightly than usual.

"I am sorry to hear this," the Destroyer said, with a catch in his voice as if he genuinely cared for the people he was destroying. "There is a fourth common reason, but I did not mention it for reasons of shame and honour."

· The woman's head bowed. "That is the reason," she said.

This brought a grunt from him. "Did you kill him?"

The answer, when it came, was barely audible. "Yes. With the help of my daughters."

The admission occasioned whispering from daughters and sons alike.

"But I am right in guessing that about twelve years ago, give or take a year or two, one of your daughters went missing?"

"Died. She died. Cylene's twin."

"Put it together," the Destroyer said quietly. "You did not see your daughter's body after she died, did you?"

"She was taken by the sea; she walked too close to the crumbling cliffs." A tear leaked from her left eye.

"And your husband came home overflowing with grief, claiming he saw her fall, blaming himself. They always do. He tried to rescue her, which explained the scratches on his arms, yes?"

"He said she fell." Martje looked from face to face. "My daughter, she fell. An accident. We could not find the body."

"You know there was no accident. There never is. Your husband rid himself of someone about to reveal his dark secret, and made a profit into the bargain. No accident, Martje. What was her name?"

"Merla." The words came out between deep gasps. "We called her Merla after her grandmother, who was also a twin."

The boy sent on the errand returned and placed the picture in the Destroyer's hand. He looked at it a moment, then walked over to a white-faced Lenares.

"Here, Merla," he said. "Here's a picture of your twin sister."

He smiled at her, one corner of his mouth curling up in a most cruel fashion.

"I can guarantee your numbers never told you this was coming," he said.

"The only thing left to determine is whether the wife aided the husband."

"Surely not," Stella said.

"In significantly more than half the cases reported by my factors, the mother and father colluded in the death or sale of the child. The mother agrees to cover the shame that would otherwise accrue. And in most of these cases, one or the other spouse meets with an unfortunate accident in the months or years following, to ensure the secret is kept."

"I don't know why I'm listening to you."

Stella drew even further away from the man, as though afraid of being burned by his evil. For a while the chirp of crickets was the only sound that crossed the courtyard. The bench upon which the two immortals sat creaked a little as Heredrew changed position.

"They all think they are being so clever, that their stories will be believed because they've truly thought it through. Oh, Stella, in order to truly see the black places in the abyss of human depravity all one has to do is to live long enough."

He sighed. "I know that this afternoon's events have convinced you I am every bit as evil as you thought I was. I'll not gloss over what I did, nor will I pretend to be sorry or

say I won't do it again. But I did it in the light, in order
to prevent lawlessness. These people do it in the darkness,
and kill each other to prevent light being shone on their
actions."

"Finding a darker shade of black doesn't make you
white."

He nodded. "True. I lost my innocence the day the Most
High convinced me to accept the Fire of Life before I felt
I was ready. I was three years of age. When did you lose
yours, Stella? When you fled your village, leaving your
mother and father to care for your drunkard brother and believing you dead? When you ran from your company and
delivered yourself into Deorc's hands? Or when you tried to
trick me into believing he had betrayed me? Ah, that was a
marvellous piece of deception, worthy of a dark lord. When
I saw you holding those images in your head, all lies, in
order to convince me Deorc had used you, I knew I had
found a soul mate. Pure, sweet Stella. You should have seen
your face as I punished him. Do you remember begging me
to stop? Do you still suffer guilt?"

He leaned closer, until his nose almost touched her
stricken face.

"You should," he said. "I do."

Robal tried to sleep but could not. Lying in a large, expen-
sively furnished room on his own, he found himself unsettled, missing the small noises made by sleeping companions
on the road. More importantly, he could not hear her; could
not ascertain beyond doubt that she was safe, that she had
not yet succumbed.

So now he walked the marble halls of this place in the
dim light of turned-down lamps, idly examining tapestries

and sculptures, his mind wandering. *Where did the builders get the marble from? Why does she continue to allow the Destroyer to remain among us? Who would have thought there was so much money in horses? Has he had her yet?*

Robal knew himself to be a man of action not of vision. He'd had his moment: he could have drunk an immortal's blood, but had passed on it, content to remain a small man, a servant, a protector. All he wanted was one heart.

But how could he rival an immortal?

No, he had to continue his patient wait, hoping the Destroyer would demonstrate his unworthiness sufficiently clearly to Stella.

Or he could find something to bring the Destroyer down. That way he'd be doing everyone a favour.

He wandered out into the rose garden, closing an exquisite stained-glass door quietly behind him. A faint light spread from the door, enough to show him he was not the only one out late at night.

There was Lenares, or perhaps he should call her Merla, sitting on a small bench, her back against a stone wall, her head in her hands. Another person broken by the Destroyer. They could all have walked away from the confrontation in Sayonae. A boy would still be alive, and this girl could have remained ignorant of her bitter past.

He sat down next to her. She shivered in the cold, and he put a burly arm around her. Her dress had been torn in places, as though she had blundered through thorny bushes, and blood stained one bare arm.

"Don't touch me," she whispered, but he didn't let her go and she said nothing further.

Another life destroyed.

Gradually he became aware she was mumbling to

herself. He knew he should leave her, that she wouldn't want anyone to overhear, that she was likely not even aware of his presence, but he stayed. The honest truth was it did him good to comfort someone. It reminded him that he could still be of use.

"Mahudia," she said. "Mahudia, she is nothing. Nothing. I have seen her numbers. Slavery. Sold into slavery. One mother sells, the other buys. One eaten by a lion, the other by guilt."

The words plucked at Robal's soul. "Merla, don't."

"Don't call me that!' she said, lifting her head and fixing him with bleary eyes. "And don't touch me."

"I'm sorry, Lenares."

He let her go, and she promptly plunged back into his arms.

"Why me and not my sister?" she cried, then burst into tears.

"I don't know," he said, racking his brains for something to say. He was not much for giving words of comfort. "Perhaps it was necessary. Maybe you wouldn't have developed your skill with numbers had you stayed here."

He cupped her pale face in his hands. "Don't you think you have had a lucky escape? What sort of life would you have had here?"

She looked up at him, blinking furiously. "What? I was poor all my life. Mahudia found me in an alley, eating scraps from the midden heaps. The cosmographers gave me a home, but we always lived with nothing. What sort of life would I have had here? I could have had anything I wanted, you silly man."

"Except love, seemingly," Robal replied. "Don't forget that."

Her face crumpled. "You are right. My father slept with all his daughters. I would not have wanted that. I have no memory . . . no memory of anything—of this place, of parents, brothers or sisters."

"But you are certain the story is true?"

"Oh yes. I knew even before Heredrew told me. I listened carefully to Martje and checked her numbers. She has built this place on lies. Every brick of it was earned through deception. She sold horses doctored to hide their infirmities, shipped them off to far away places where they could not be traced back to her. She held her sons here with false claims about her health, when they would rather have left to seek their fortunes. Her daughters she kept home with threats. Only Cylene has escaped her. I know so much about my mother, and everything I know makes me hate her even more. I wish Heredrew had killed her. I wish it wasn't true." She swallowed. "I wish I had never found out."

He pulled her forehead to his lips and kissed her gently. "Not all truth is good," he whispered.

A noise behind them. He turned to find Stella staring at him. She said nothing, but she didn't need to: he could read the message written there. He wanted to cry out, to explain himself, but for some reason he held back.

Why should I bother? Why so desperate to appear virtuous in her eyes?

"What's wrong?" he said. "Isn't a man allowed to offer comfort to a travelling companion? Or were you waiting for me to claim that this isn't what it looks like?"

She smiled weakly. "Not what it looks like? It looks like you care for someone who needs caring for. Of course you can offer her comfort. But please be careful; she's vulnerable."

Robal laughed. "I've never met anyone less vulnerable in my life," he said. "Except, perhaps, the man you offer comfort to."

Stella pursed her lips together. "Do you really expect me to stand here and answer such accusations? Or have I misjudged you? Robal, you are my guard. You've been close by me ever since we left Instruere. Even if I'd had a mind to, I could not have shared intimacy with the man."

"But you love him all the same," he told her, as if revealing a truth of which she was unaware. Which perhaps she was. Many people denied things they shouldn't feel.

"If you know my feelings as well as you claim, you know it's much more complicated than that," she said. "I cared for him at the end of the Falthan War, nursed him back from the brink of madness. And he and I are two of a kind. That makes for bonding, Robal. It doesn't necessarily lead to love."

"Fair enough," he said. "He's the kind of man best loved from a safe distance; if any distance is safe enough, that is. My first wife was like that."

Turning his head, he sneaked a sidelong glance at Lenares, the truthfinder. She wasn't wearing the disgusted expression she adopted when in the presence of lies, so maybe Stella was telling the truth. Of course, the girl's mind may have been somewhere else, but Robal doubted it. This one was sharp.

"So tell me, guardsman," Stella said, sitting on the bench next to him. "What do you think is really going on?"

"What do you mean?" He swallowed.

"I mean, do you really believe this is coincidence? Lenares just happening to find out she is some long-lost child of a wealthy family? A secret twin sold into slavery? Robal, it doesn't feel right."

He nodded at the girl in his arms, her eyes closed as if asleep. "Don't you think she would know if there was some sort of confidence trick being run? Anyway, who benefits from this?"

"Many parties, if Lenares remains behind, as her mother is suggesting. Particularly the Daughter, who will undoubtedly break free if Heredrew withdraws his support for her."

"I am growing stronger," Lenares said, her voice muffled by Robal's tunic. "I don't need his help."

"Lenares, Robal, please consider this. The hole in the world interferes with the proper running of the earth. Earthquakes, fireballs, storms, whirlwinds. We've seen this. What if it—if the gods acting through it—can interfere with time as well as space? What if they can mess with our memories? What if they can change what has happened? Could they not have engineered this?"

"No, Stella, no," he said gently. "If we start doubting our memories, we can never know anything for certain. I won't live in a world like that. Besides, do you think your immortal friend would be fooled?"

Stella sighed. "Right now, Robal, my belief in the Undying Man is the only thing keeping me sane," she said. "That, and the earthy good sense of a certain guardsman."

She smiled as she rose to her feet, and his poor heart turned over, just as it always did.

Earthy good sense? He watched her walk away, her body silhouetted in the light from the stained-glass door. Good sense was exactly what he lacked, he thought, when it came to earthy things. For, as he traced the outline of her with his eyes, he knew he'd do anything to make her his own.

CHAPTER 17

NIGHT OF DESIRE

CONAL HAD BARELY DRIFTED OFF to sleep when the knock came. Soft, gentle, on the edge of hearing, the tapping was a sound he would undoubtedly not have heard had he been more deeply asleep. A woman's knock.

It could be her.

He remembered Stella's fierce avowal earlier in the evening: she would see the task completed, then see the Destroyer dead. He now saw her complicity for what it was: a sham designed to encourage the Destroyer to lower his guard, to let her slip under it. *Courageous woman!*

He felt his manhood stiffen at the mere thought of her. She had obviously kept her true feelings well hidden, so she might well feel for him what he felt for her. Certainly he had no real rival for her affection. Not the boorish, ignorant guard, nor the lout from the prairies. And certainly not the suave charlatan who specialised in destroying lives.

He imagined her at the door, begging admittance. Once inside his room, she would outline a bold and dangerous plan to put an end to the Undying Man, then seal it with another offer . . .

"Are you awake?"

His heart sank. Not Stella. Some other voice, some other woman, but something to which he had to give reply. Awkward, given he was still embarrassingly tumescent.

"Just give me a moment, please," he answered, gritting his teeth, willing things to soften. As always, thinking of his mother did the trick. Eventually Conal was composed enough to crack the door open.

"Yes?"

It was Martje, and someone else, hidden behind her.

"Oh, please come in."

He opened the door and the matriarch and one of her daughters walked in, both wrapped in woollen rugs. The daughters had all looked much the same, but this was surely the one who sat beside him during the meal. Sena.

"I understand you are a priest," Martje said as soon as the door clicked shut behind them. "Tell me, what kind of priest are you?"

"Please, take a seat," Conal said, indicating a long couch. He found himself a seat on the edge of his bed. "I don't understand the question. What kinds of priest are there?"

"There have been no priests in the Fisher Coast for a long time now, not since the Undying Man tightened his grip on these lands with the aid of Deorc of Jasweyah," she replied.

Her daughter said nothing, just stared at him with those intense blue eyes. His hand went involuntarily to his crotch, but things there were under control for the moment.

The mother continued: "But once there were dark priests, familiar with sacrifice and blood and invocation. Are you a dark priest? Do you have such knowledge? Do you require a sacrifice?"

His heart chilled in his chest. Sacrifice? Was that why the woman had brought her daughter?

"No," he replied carefully, "I am not that kind of priest. Falthan priests do not make human sacrifices. But we are not without power, though it is of a different kind. Please, tell me what you require."

A familiar flaming in the back of his head alerted him to his sorcerous passenger. *Ah*, the magician said. *I have been hoping for something like this.*

Like what?

Proof that the old powers are still known, still practised. We have need of them.

"I have a thirst for revenge," Martje said. "My eldest son and heir lies dead on a cold stone bier, while his murderer lies in my most opulent room, sleeping off the excesses of my forced largesse. Perhaps those of the Fisher Coast or of your own milk-livered land would let such a grievous insult pass, but not I. Not someone from the Hanseia Hills."

"He's immortal, you know. You can't kill him."

"No, but there are other things I can do. I can incapacitate him, weaken him. I can bind him to a place, any place, so that he cannot leave it. The cost will be high, but I—but *we*—are prepared to pay it. Are you?"

There was no mistaking the look she gave him. Conal cleared his throat.

"What makes you think I have the power you require?"

"I can sense you, priest. You have great power, buried deep. Though young and inexperienced, you are very strong indeed. Not as strong as he who sullies my honour by sleeping in my house tonight, but as powerful as any *Maghdi Dasht* I have met. Perhaps even as powerful as my own great uncle, lost many years ago in your land in the vanguard of a futile war. Old magic runs in my family," she said. "So I can see yours. Well, priest? I heard you wish him dead. Will you help me?"

His manhood had risen again, but this time he made no move to halt it. Both his visitors had their eye on him. They knew.

"I need to pray," he said. "To ascertain the will of my god."

"No doubt you do," Martje said, a one-sided smile on her face. "My daughter Sena is very good at praying. Together I am sure you can gain the ear of your god. I will leave you, and return in one hour. We will then discuss what to do about our mutual enemy."

"One . . . one hour," he croaked. "I will be ready."

She cast an eye over him, her gaze coming to rest on his groin. "No doubt," she said.

Sena had risen from the couch, her eyes flashing, fingers working the buttons of her shift, and was upon him even before the door had clicked shut.

Eventually Lenares fell asleep in Robal's arms. He had been patient, solicitous of her need to talk, a listening ear, but her shock and sorrow had sapped her youthful strength to the point of exhaustion. Fortunately she had not been reading him closely. He had been as genuine as he could; indeed, he truly cared about her sorrows, and wished to do something about them. And he could, now she was drowsing.

Robal eased himself out from beside her, gently guiding her head to the rough wooden bench. He flicked off his blanket and laid it under her hair, then checked her breathing. Steady, rhythmical. *Now, where would she keep it?* He didn't want to have to search her thoroughly. Though as a guard, he knew how to search a prisoner, normally they were awake when he did it, and he'd never been known as a gentle man.

He found it in the third pocket.

The thing about these great people, he reflected as he pocketed the huanu stone, these immortals, these sorcerers, scholars and savants, was they eventually ceased paying attention to those without their gifts. They assumed that normal people were just part of the landscape, not able to influence events in the manner of the great. He would make one of them regret this lack of attention.

It was a risk, he acknowledged to himself as he eased closed the stained-glass door and padded quietly down the hall past sculptures that would have graced the Hall of Meeting in Instruere. But if he had read everything right, if he understood correctly the power of the stone in his hand, the threat posed by the Destroyer would end tonight.

A short detour to his room to change. A younger Robal would not have hesitated: with such an advantage in his hand, he would have charged into battle, and not taken the time to slip on his leather tunic and strap his sword around his waist. The small knife against his hip would have been enough. But there had been times when the younger Robal had nearly not become any older, and he was a more cautious man now.

He ran his fingers over the hilt of his sword, visualising the next few minutes. The only risk involved his interpretation of what his companions had said about the stone. This Noetos of Bhrudwo had such a stone, apparently, a large one, though Robal had not once talked to the man directly: their paths had crossed only twice, at Lake Woe and at the Yacoppica Tea House. There had been some hints as to what the stone meant, but he'd not paid much attention to it. He wished he had now.

Lenares, on the other hand, had been much more forthcoming about her stone. It was precious, clearly, as the alchemist's desire for it had cost him his life. It was powerful, as it had kept the Daughter from destroying Lenares. She had then been able to capture the Daughter, to make the god obey her. Robal had no esoteric way of capturing the Destroyer and bending him to obedience. He would have to make do with a more direct plan.

This was the door. He'd noted it earlier in the evening: one of Martje's sons had been told to fetch a portrait from the lady's bedroom. Robal had been sitting at the corner of the table closest to the door of the dining room, and had seen the son stride along the hall and enter the room at the far end. Later, Martje had offered the Destroyer her own accommodation, an offer that had been accepted. So this had to be the door.

A faint blue glow leaked out from underneath. Some sort of night light? Or the magical blue fire?

He put his hand to the door handle. Tell the truth, he didn't expect the door to open. He expected to be thwarted here, forcing him to enter through the fancy windows at the far end of the room, the ones he'd seen as he walked through the rose garden. There would be noise, no doubt, and after he'd done the deed Robal fully expected to have to fight for his life. As yet, he was unsure whether he'd bother.

The handle gave way, the blue glow winked out and the door opened in silence.

Clutching the stone in his left hand and the sword in his right, Robal stepped into the room.

It was large, and shrouded in almost complete darkness save for a small candle burning on a dresser by the bed and the light coming from the hallway behind him. The candle would give enough light, he decided, so he closed the door and waited a few moments for his eyes to adjust to the darkness.

A strange rhythmic noise came from his right, from the far corner of the room nearest the window, away from the candle. Some arcane device to generate magic? An animal grunting, about to be sacrificed? Every one of Robal's senses tingled, heightened by his awareness of what he was about to do. Robal Anders, slayer of an immortal.

He flicked his eyes to the enormous four-poster bed, partly obscured by a large wardrobe. There ought to be a lump, the outline of his quarry's body, but he could not see it. He stole across the room, eyes down, noting the luxurious rugs he walked upon, checking each step carefully so as not to make any untoward sound.

There was no one in the bed. The covers had not even been turned back.

Was he mistaken? Did the Destroyer not need sleep? Or was he even now engaged in some other tryst, his mouth on hers? Was that the source of the noise? His head snapped up.

"I am over here, Robal."

It wasn't magic that froze him, but simple surprise. One of the side effects of carefully planning an attack was that it took a few seconds to adjust to changing circumstances. In those seconds the Destroyer spoke.

"I know why you're here, Robal; I know what you have in your hand. I can feel it. Should you come at me with your sword, I will have no magical defence. But I hope you might speak to me, and let me talk to you, so we can resolve—"

Don't let him wrap his words around your mind, Robal told himself. He launched himself at the Destroyer, his sword coming around in a vicious sweep aimed at the man's neck.

The hour was nearly over. Sena had proved herself skilled indeed, bringing Conal twice back to life after their intense, almost agonising, first coupling.

"I practise with my brothers," she'd said as they caught their breath the first time. She had smiled wryly and he'd assumed she was joking. Hoped. But then she had inflamed him again and he'd put the comment to the back of his mind.

Where a magician sat like a toad on a lily pad, watching the activity through inscrutable eyes. There seemed to be no voyeuristic intent in the presence, just patience, a quiet waiting for the preliminaries to be dispensed with.

It brought to mind his first time, in a brothel in Remenoir, a morning's ride north of Yosse. He'd been persuaded there by a friend, his name now forgotten. The friend had insisted on hiring two women and the largest room in the house. There had been two beds, but instead of getting down to business himself, his friend had first watched Conal's clumsy attempts at ridding himself of his virginity. The priest flushed at the memory.

"Oh," Sena said. "Are you ready?" She cocked her head. "I don't think we have time."

The door opened, and for a terrible moment Conal imagined Stella stepping into the room. He had been so consumed by the lovemaking he'd not considered barring the door. In an instant fear cycled to guilt, and the priest realised anew what he'd always known: he was not worthy of her. Nor of his calling.

"So," said Martje, "you have kept yourselves occupied while I have been away, yes?" Her eye ran over them both, their naked bodies, the rumpled bed. "Good. Plenty of energy here for a witch to harness. Sena, your arm."

Ah, I think she knows the Rite of Entrapment, said the toad in the back of Conal's head. *Excellent. She requires a woman's invigorated blood, which she will take from her daughter's arm with the aid of a tapknife. And she requires something from you.*

What does she want from me? When were you going to explain all this?

The girl gave a cry as her mother slid the point of a narrow blade into her arm, just above the elbow. Instantly blood began to flow.

You fool, said the magician. *You ought to have asked her—not that she would have told you the truth. The Rite of Entrapment has serious consequences for those who enact it. The subject of the incantation is paralysed, yes, for as long as the enchanter wishes; but so are the others involved in the ritual. When the fluids are mixed Sena will be rendered immobile, as will you, as your energy is stolen for use in the spell. Martje will utter the incantation—it is long and complex and so will take her a while—and then will herself become paralysed. She can then have one of her sons kill the subject while she looks on. When the subject dies, she is released, along with Sena and yourself. Of course, the Undying Man cannot die. She will content herself with watching as he is tortured over the long years, while you moulder in some dark room, no doubt. Perhaps she might even practise her technique on you. Cruel to her daughter, but the thirst for vengeance clearly runs deep in this family. Martje believes you do not know this ritual, because you told her you were not that kind of priest. Fortunately for you, I am.*

What does she want from me? Conal shrieked in his mind. He began to struggle: maybe he could stop this! But his muscles were suddenly not his own, and he could not move.

Stay still, the magician said. *This witch may yet solve one of my problems.*

Please, tell me! What does she want?

She already has it, the magician answered.

It took Conal a moment longer to understand, but what Martje was doing to her daughter made it clear. In moments the matriarch had two vials of liquid in her hands.

A sudden thump sounded from somewhere in the house.

Martje's head snapped in the direction of the noise. "Ssss," she said. "He knows what I'm doing."

How does my being paralysed and tortured help you? Conal screamed.

If my goal was purely to see the Undying Man endure the sort of pain and suffering I have endured, I would cast you aside without a moment's thought, came the reply. *But I need more than that. Martje cannot kill him, and I need to see him dead. So I will prevent you from suffering the full effects of the spell, and this will mean the hold she will have over the Undying Man will be only a temporary one.*

After a glance at the door Martje lifted both vials. With a guttural cry she cast them on the floor, where they shattered.

What do you mean, full effects?

The matriarch began intoning something in a strange language seemingly made up of cacophonous cries, clicks and whistles. A screech like the forceful bending of a thousand metal hinges filled the air. Conal leapt to his feet, intent on flight. A blinding flash turned everything white, and he fell to the floor beside Sena, unable to move anything apart from his eyes.

Filling his field of vision was the girl's frozen face, wearing a mocking grin. Filling his ears was the grating sound of the incantation. And filling his mind was the sound of the magician's laughter.

The Destroyer took Robal's initial blow on the left forearm. The blade bit at an angle, deep enough to strike the bone. *He has bone, at least.* Robal had half-expected the man to be made of smoke.

He bore the sorcerer down, crashing with him into a tall wardrobe. He had to disengage, make space to take advantage of his sword. *Mistake. Should have had the knife in my hand. Hah, should have had three hands.* The sword spun from his grasp.

Something clubbed him in the face, taking him on the left cheek, knocking him onto the bed. For a moment he lost his footing, and the Destroyer was on him, face against his neck, teeth poised either side of his artery.

He blinked.

Hah. He doesn't even have one *hand.*

Robal jerked his head right, and the man's teeth scored his neck. He bucked the Undying Man's body off and pushed himself to his feet.

He faced an apparition from his deepest nightmares.

Lenares' stone had done its work, there could be no doubt. The Undying Man had no hands: it had been a handless stump that had taken him under the eye. The urbane Heredrew had gone and in his place stood a hairless, misshapen horror. Its orange skin appeared as though it had been slowly melted over an open fire. One eye hung half out of its cracked and weeping face, as though held there by a cord. Sinews taut as bowstrings seemed barely to be holding in blood and bone.

For a long moment Robal stared at the man.

"Has Stella seen you like this?" he asked eventually.

The figure spat. "Once," he rasped.

"What did she say?"

A pause, filled with heavy breathing. "I did not ask her."

"The water of life did this?"

The Destroyer pushed himself to his feet. His forearm bled freely. "Kill me," he said, "but don't pity me."

Robal drew his knife. "You're the immortal enemy of our civilisation," he said. "Reason enough to kill you."

"Yes. But I am your civilisation's only hope, so your god believes, as does your queen. Reason enough to keep me alive."

"Stella Pellwen is in love with you, to her ruination. Why should I let you live?"

"I could have slain you the moment you entered my room, before you brought the stone too close. Why did I let you live?"

"Slain me how?" He knew the man wasn't lying.

"Frozen your blood or warmed it. Boiled your brain in its pan. I'm extremely familiar with the inner workings of fragile bodies, Robal. Perhaps I'm about to receive a brief glimpse of the inner workings of my own." He smiled, a hideous grimace. "Come then, friend. Show me your knife."

"Why didn't you kill me?"

"Because I wanted to talk with you. And because I was . . . distracted."

"Was that you making the noise?" Robal thought carefully about what he'd heard. "Sobbing?"

"I have already said I don't want your pity," growled the Destroyer. "If you wish to end my life, do it now. I am defenceless. If not, leave me to think; or, better yet, stay with me and help me plan. There are a great many things brewing tonight."

Robal gripped his knife more firmly. Whatever might be brewing, whatever Stella wanted the Destroyer to do, the world would be a better place without this man. He took a pace forward.

The Undying Man threw himself backwards with complete recklessness, landing on the bed, then tumbling onto the floor behind it. Robal made to follow, but it was too late. His opponent was now outside the stone's influence, at least enough to resume his illusory body. And undoubtedly regain access to his magic.

More noises out in the hall. The guardsman ran for the door, his thoughts now on escape. The Undying Man leapt onto the bed, trying to keep his distance. The door handle rattled. Robal drew back into the shadows, and the Destroyer lay down as if asleep.

The door opened, letting in light and a shadowed figure, then closed again.

*   *   *

Conal felt their hands on him. Though he had lost all movement he retained every sense. They lifted and dragged him
across the room and out into the corridor. His elbow struck
the door frame; the pain blurred his eyes.

She is skilled, this witch, said the toad. *Such a waste.*

What's going to happen to me? Conal asked. He'd be
begging for an answer soon, he had no doubt.

*I'm very interested to find out. Will they do anything to
you? Will they take you to the room in which they hold the
Undying Man? I'm hoping for both, to be honest.*

You want me to suffer?

Make a better man of you, said the magician. *It did for
me. Of course, I don't wish on you the suffering I've endured. At least, not until I've finished with you.*

*What have I done to deserve this? I've never been a bad
person!*

But you've been a fool, and that's all it takes.

Was that Stella emerging from a bedroom back down
the hall? He thought he'd glimpsed her face. He sincerely
hoped she had not glimpsed his.

Into another room, this one bare of furnishing save a
single long bench. His porters dropped him gracelessly to
the floor. Again the pain coupled with deep humiliation and
fearful helplessness. Sena, however, they propped up on
the wooden bench. Then they dragged him over and placed
him in front of the bench, so that those come to see the
spectacle could use him for a footstool.

Had his tear ducts been working, he would have wept at
the indignity of it.

"Heredrew! Are you there?" Stella's voice.

Robal willed himself to complete stillness.

"Kannwar!"

"Over here, dear one."

She approached the bed. "There's some sort of commotion in the hall. I heard a screeching noise, then there were sons and daughters everywhere, along with servants. I wondered what was happening."

"I am expecting a move against me tonight," the Destroyer replied casually. "This may signal it."

"Perhaps I should come back later, then," she said quietly. "To tend the bodies broken by your cruelty. Or remain here and watch. If we are lucky, we might see them succeed."

The guardsman, his own plan ruined, lifted his head at Stella's words.

"No," the Destroyer said, and Robal could hear a note of anxiety in his voice. "Speak to me now."

"I've been thinking," she said, taking a seat on the edge of the bed. "After your display this afternoon, I'm no longer certain we should continue following you north. Go back to Andratan, by all means, but we will not follow. I do not believe the Most High has entrusted his plan to the likes of you."

Robal let his breath out slowly. *This would be every bit as good as his death. Better, because the rejection comes from her.*

"Have you discussed this with your fellows?" came the Destroyer's tempered response.

"No," she admitted. "But I doubt they feel any different than I. Killing that boy was entirely gratuitous."

"Was it now? Let me tell you something, monarch." The last word was clipped, the only concession to the man's temper. "You respect Lenares of Talamaq almost to the point of veneration because of her skill with numbers. If that is so, you should pay attention to me. I employ statisticians on Andratan, people who collect and analyse numbers relating to a large number of things. They estimate that the judicious culling of criminals and the disobedient actually saves hundreds and thousands of lives every year. If it is not done, they argue, rebellion rises and wars claim families, towns, cities and even countries. What I did this afternoon, Stella, ought—according to those in my employ—to be considered humane."

She snorted. "Death and misery can't be dealt with in the aggregate. Leith and I often debated this, though no matter what conclusion we came to we would never have slaughtered people in order to make them an example to others. We preferred to invest in education and wealth rather than in soldiers and hangmen."

"Just so. And I understand that investment is currently funding rebellions in Piskasia and Favony."

"The situation is somewhat more complicated than that," she said, her voice rising.

"Indeed. But Bhrudwo has a long history of structure and obedience. Any lessening of control will promote anarchy."

"And so you govern by fear."

He shrugged his shoulders.

"There's something you should know about the death this afternoon," he said.

"There's nothing more I wish to know. I will withdraw now, and bid you goodbye. Perhaps we will offer a final farewell tomorrow morning."

She went to rise but, as Robal watched, struggled to move. "What have you done to me?"

"I extended the courtesy of allowing you to remain in my room uninvited, and listened as you gave your message. Now you will listen to mine.

"The boy is not dead. Simple magic cushioned his fall; infinitely more complex magic sank him into the deepest unconsciousness. He breathes but seldom now. Should I wish it, however, he will arise within minutes of my releasing the spell. No death, no injury, no harm done."

Stella's objections seemed to tumble over each other in her keenness to express them. "No injury? But—what of the family's grief? The blow to their honour? How can you say 'no harm done'?"

In the shadows Robal nodded his agreement—though the Destroyer's revelation had shocked him.

"For the sake of everyone in the district, this family needed reducing. You were in Sayonae yesterday: did it strike you as a particularly wealthy town? Why is the wealth concentrated here at the Umerta steading? Who has suffered as a consequence? Judging by yesterday's behaviour, every time this family believes itself wronged the members ride into town and deliver their own brand of correction. I have diminished them in the public eye, and made things a little better for everyone. Maybe, if I read it right, even for some members of this family.

"And yes, before you raise it, there will be a cost. The boy can't remain here after he returns to consciousness. I'll command him to leave the Fisher Coast. In fact, I suspect he has relatives in the Hanseia Hills who would take him in."

The figure raised itself onto one stump—arm, Robal corrected.

"That is how Bhrudwo is governed," the Destroyer said,

his voice tightly controlled. "The ignorant, not in possession of all the facts, judge my decisions and call them evil. Harsh, yes, I'll concede that, but not evil."

"So you torture and kill and call it good."

"If the arithmetic works, yes."

Stella had begun to cry. "There was a village in Bhirinj." She sniffed. "You remember it, on the long march westward. What happened there—how could you ever justify it?"

"Stella, I have lived two thousand years. Must I now recall and discuss every motive, every reason, for every action? Listen, my dear. I had an army comprised of factions who were still technically at war with each other. My actions at that village, coupled with the burning of the Red Duke, brought unity to my army and prevented the same thing being perpetrated in every Falthan village. It saved thousands of lives."

But it smeared the souls of all who took part, Robal wanted to shout. *A hundred, a thousand, a million people ought to die to prevent such a thing happening again!*

"A justification can be found for every action," Stella said. "But what frightened me most of all was how you seemed to enjoy it. You did, didn't you. You enjoyed watching the children bleed from the stumps of their handless arms. You enjoyed the screams of the women as your men—as they . . . Don't lie to me. Tell me you enjoyed it."

The man took two deep breaths. In the silence Robal found himself tempted to lob the stone towards him, to make his false skin vanish to reveal the corruption underneath. Perhaps the magic would do the same for his arguments, which, Robal feared, were halfway to deceiving his queen.

"I won't lie," said the Undying Man. "Part of me re-
joices in my continued life whenever I behold suffering and
death. Have you never breathed a sigh of relief at a funeral,
happy it is not you on the bier?"

"No," Stella said. A long silence followed. The only
sound, apart from Stella's distressed breathing, was a
crackling sound from somewhere within the room.

"No," she repeated, in a small voice. "Never. I've seen
hundreds of funerals, and at every one bar the very first I
wished it was me embracing the flames."

"You want to die? Why? You have the gift the rest of the
world desires!"

"You know why. Purity so potent it acts like corruption
pouring through your veins, every muscle screaming with
pain—"

"A pain that reduces over the years."

"— your loved ones growing older around you, partici-
pating in a cycle of life and death forever barred to you, and
strangers rise to take their place—"

"New companions! New friends! New loves!"

"Any love I have now will not last. If I take a lover, he
will fade and die in bitterness and fear, knowing I will never
share his fate. And so it will go on until, at the end, only I
and the one I despise the most remain, standing at opposite
ends of a charred and lifeless world, watching the cold sun
die and the moon crash to earth."

Robal's heart seemed to stop beating as hope and fear
seized him in equal measure. The sun could die and the
moon crash for all he cared. He just wanted her to say
clearly whom she meant. To say his name and the word
"lover" in the same sentence.

"You despise me?" the Undying Man said, leaning

towards her. "You lie. You desire me as much as I desire you."

"I . . ." She licked her lips. "I cannot deny it. But I despise you all the more for it."

A dreadful screech rang through the dwelling, provoking a gasp from the man lying on the bed, his arm outstretched towards Stella. He appeared to freeze in place, then toppled off the bed with agonising slowness, cracking his arm on the dresser beside the bed.

"Heredrew! What has happened?" Stella cried.

They were under attack of some kind. Robal could no more control his action than control the wild hope flooding his heart, filling him with energy. He hefted his knife and rushed into the centre of the room. He could see very little. The lord of Bhrudwo lay on the floor, one arm still extended, as though carved from stone. His eyes rolled left and right, the whites visible, but otherwise he appeared unable to move. Stella bent over the Destroyer, then looked up and saw Robal. Her eyes widened.

From behind them came a whoosh, as though someone had opened a window in a strong breeze. A curtain had somehow caught fire. As Robal tried to take this in another curtain caught alight, and flames began to lick the blankets. A crash of breaking glass came from behind the first curtain, and the flames roared.

An ugly possibility seized the guardsman. The fire was clearly magical. It moved too swiftly for a natural blaze. What if the Destroyer, angered by Stella's rejection, had started the fire himself? And even now fuelled the flames while lying there pretending to be paralysed in order to hold Stella in the room?

"Robal! Help me with—"

"He is evil!" Robal roared. "He must die!" Still roaring, he swung his sword at the frozen figure.

"No!" Stella cried, and put her arm up in the Undying Man's defence. His blade took her arm off at the elbow. The tip thumped uselessly into the Destroyer's shoulder.

She screamed, her eyes wide with fear and confusion, as her bright blood began to spurt.

He threw down his blade, taken by terror at what he'd done, and shoved the stone in the pocket of his tunic. "Stella, Stella," he said, as if the repetition of her name was a spell capable of repairing the damage. "Stella, your poor arm. I'm sorry, so sorry!"

"Get help," she said to him, her face pale, lips barely moving. "Fetch the mistress of the house. And fetch Lenares. Get Moralye to bring Phemanderac. Someone must have a cure for what ails him."

"Him? What ails *him*? What of you?"

What sort of madness had taken hold of her? And why wasn't the Destroyer's real body visible, given he had the—It wasn't in his pocket. He must have dropped it. He scurried back for the precious stone, soon finding it.

"You seek the mistress of the house?" said a voice. "She is here."

Conal's self-pitying inward gaze was arrested by movement seen from the corner of his eye. The far door opened and in staggered two men bearing the body of the Destroyer. They carried it into the centre of the room and laid it on the floor, then moved away, leaving it there, rocking slightly, frozen in an attitude of entreaty. The man had been begging when the spell took him.

The same two men reappeared with an obviously paralysed Martje in their grasp. Her they placed carefully on the bench above Conal, her back resting against the wall. No doubt she would enjoy a clear view of the proceedings.

The magician in Conal's mind gave a long sigh of pleasure and settled back to watch.

More movement, this time accompanied by thumping and raised voices. Stella and the thug Robal were dragged into the room and forced to sit on the floor some distance away. There was something wrong with one of Stella's hands: she had been injured in some way, her arm ended short of where it ought to, in a red blur. As he watched, unable to decipher what his eyes were seeing, someone—a servant, he thought—tightened a strap around her arm, then smeared something on the redness. Stella screamed at its touch.

"Did you see to the fire?" someone asked the servant. "Mother will be displeased if her bedroom is ruined."

"Aye, it was under control last I looked, if it please you, sir. I will check again for you." The servant vanished.

You set this in motion, the magician said to him. *Everything that happens tonight is on your head.*

"My mother doubted this would work," someone said, just out of Conal's restricted field of vision. One of the sons, no doubt, the words addressed to the Undying Man. "But we had to try anyway. We are surprised at how little resistance you offered. I doubt any of us could have escaped the spell once the incantation was complete, but any one of us, even young Tomana, would have put up more of a fight than you did. Disappointing, really. The great Undying Man exposed as a charlatan. How many real magicians did your bidding, I wonder, and with what bribes or promises did you bind them?"

A foot came into view: it landed a vicious kick on the Destroyer's exposed arm.

"This is what we shall do. Each of your companions will be tortured before your eyes, and you will watch them die, one by one. Then you will be tortured in your turn, but we will not attempt to kill you. Instead, we will summon the factors of the realm—they will come; our good name will see to that, as well as the evidences we will send them— and, after assembling them here to see your humiliation, we shall lift the spell."

The voice paused, no doubt allowing the message to sink in.

"You will never rule again. Everyone who has ever suffered at your cruel hand will seek revenge against you. The rest of your days will be a misery, and you will never forget what you did to offend the Umerta family. The name we carve on every inch of your skin will assist your memory.

"Now, let our vengeance begin."

Rough hands seized Stella and dragged her into the open space, dropping her beside the Destroyer. Knives appeared in those hands, and their wielders bent over her bound body and began cutting away her clothes.

This should be interesting, said the voice in Conal's head. Not for the first time, he wished he could silence it.

When the knives had finished and the screaming died away, they dragged the body across the floor, leaving trails of bright red blood. A soft thump told him they had cast it aside. Conal's heart shrieked in his chest, as though it had its own voice independent of his terrified mind.

"Now for the so-called priest," the voice said, and hands stretched out for him.

Don't worry, I won't let them kill you, said the magician, a chuckle in his voice.

But the pain! I don't want to bleed.

As long as they preserve your life, your hearing and your sight, I don't care what else happens. In fact, it should be interesting.

Please! Please! But the magician had retreated to some dark place. Conal was left with no one to plead with.

One of the knife-wielders leaned close to him and brought his blade up to Conal's eye. "You saw our dear sister Sena naked," the man hissed. "You thought yourself worthy to lie with her. There is a price to pay for such temerity."

The blade pricked the corner of Conal's right eye and entered the skin at the edge of his eye socket. The pressure increased—he knew what was about to happen, but was helpless to resist—and sudden, indescribable pain tore through his head. His vision went white, then red, then black.

He wished to faint, cried out for release, but it would not come. The tip of the blade rooted around in his socket a moment longer.

"Look, brothers and sisters, what I have in my hand," said the man. "Look, Mother. One of the eyes of the man who looked upon Sena. Shall I fetch you the other?"

Please! Help me! Conal begged the magician. He could not believe it, yet he knew what they had done, and that his protector had allowed it. *Please! Get them to put it back in. Fix it for me! I will serve you well!*

Nothing but faint laughter answered his pleas.

"Show him his eye," said a girl's voice. Not Sena, one of the other daughters.

He blinked, his head roared with pain, but the vision in his left eye cleared—and immediately he wished it had not. A hand hovered in front of his face, and on it lay a red and white mess, a jelly-like shape with a cord dangling from it.

"Leave him his other eye," the female voice said. "For now."

Robal could not bear the horror. He had watched them slice and stab his already wounded Stella, and then take the obnoxious, foolish but ultimately blameless Conal and carve out one of his eyes. The priest had been unnaturally still, paralysed in the same way as the Undying Man. Perhaps he had offered some resistance then, to be treated in this fashion; if so, losing an eye was a cruel reward for such bravery. Now the men with the knives turned towards the guardsman, and he steeled himself for his own suffering and death.

There was one chance . . .

The huanu stone lay in a pocket in his tunic, stuffed there at the first sign of trouble, and was now their only hope. Since the moment they had overpowered him and bound his hands and feet with rope, he had been trying to work his fingers into the pocket without being noticed. He'd been feverish with desperation as he'd heard Stella scream, but the cursed seamstresses at Farmer's Flat had done their work far too well. Even when he finally managed to grasp the pocket, he could neither reach the stone with the tips of his fingers nor rip the pocket from his tunic. He'd even tried arching his back so the stone would fall out. That had been noticed: a man wielding a sword now hovered over him.

The door crashed open. A servant rushed over to one of the sons and whispered urgently in his ear.

How is Stella? Robal wondered frantically. *Did they kill her? Can they?*

The man the servant had spoken to screamed in anger. "What? Employ every man to put it out! Find more men! As for these, slay the rest. We must leave this place."

They seized Robal and threw him across the room like a sack of pumpkins. He landed close to the body of the Destroyer. Close enough. Despite being winded, he tilted his torso towards the man, just to be sure, and hoped he had guessed right.

With a tremendous cry of rage the Undying Man rose to his feet, all sinew and skin, face cracked and ruined. The Umertas shrieked, then hurled themselves at him, knives raised, swords whistling from their scabbards.

Even as he threw himself to one side, giving the sorcerer the necessary distance from the stone, Robal knew he was saving the man he'd tried to kill. But that attempt had cost his beloved her arm. What might another attempt cost? He rolled and rolled until he fetched up against the wall, as far from the Destroyer as possible.

When he looked back, the Undying Man had resumed his disguise and the blades did him no damage. There was only one way the fight could end now, so he eased himself onto his knees and sought her. There she was, a series of red and white streaks, lying discarded on the floor like the husk of a midsummer firework.

"Oh, Stella, forgive me," he said, squirming towards her as swiftly as his bonds allowed. "I didn't mean to do it."

Her eyes flicked open. They were occluded with pain. "Fetch my hand, Robal," she whispered.

Thumps on the floor behind him: someone approached. He spun around, in time to see a knife, but he could not move swiftly enough . . . No need: it was Kilfor, and the knife sawed through the ropes binding him.

"What happened here?" his friend asked, horror in his voice. "Have you seen the priest?"

"Later," Robal breathed. "See to Stella. Water, cloths, salve, anything you can find. I need to fetch something."

A great roar masked the plainsman's reply. The far door collapsed in flames and heat washed over everyone in the room.

"Out, now!" the Destroyer cried.

The survivors gathered in two groups and watched the homestead burn to its bones of stone. The Falthans surrounded the remaining Umertas and their servants, their hosts' weapons in their hands, wary of trouble even though the captives were securely bound. A necessary precaution in Robal's view. Though why the Umertas hadn't been thrown to the flames, he did not know.

They had barely made it out before the roof had come down. Robal's skin had been singed by the great gouts of flame blown out by the collapse. He had no doubt a few of the servants had been trapped in the blaze.

He had been the last of the Falthans to escape. Would still be in there, had it been up to him. She'd sent him to recover the arm he'd severed, but the fire had already swept through that part of the house. He had found bone and melted flesh, and with the discovery came his realisation that he could not face her. So he'd walked back into the hall and awaited his end.

He had been rescued by the Undying Man. He appeared,

walking through the flames, with the girl Lenares next to him. He had returned, he said, to search for Lenares and him both. The girl had been held in a small room by one of the servants, and had barely avoided the flames. Umu had promised to save her, but was either cutting it fine or intent on betraying the girl, so the Undying Man had intervened.

Lenares had held out her hand. Robal knew what she wanted. He placed the stone in the small palm, and her pale fingers wrapped themselves around it.

"Don't steal," she'd said.

The flames roared, and the Destroyer carried him out into the open air despite his struggling and pleading. "She wants you," was all he would say.

So he returned empty-handed, in the arms of the man he had tried to kill; arms that deposited him on the ground at her feet. That she stood was a miracle; but he had witnessed this miracle before. He knew she was already healing with unnatural swiftness. But she would never have a right arm again.

The priest made the most pathetic sight, crawling unheeded on the grass, free of the spell and in hideous pain, his ruined face and dreadful hollowed pit washed with light from the flickering flames. "Stella," he croaked. "Stella." Everyone there turned their faces away from him.

Heredrew had forced Martje to tell him what she had done. Conal's part in the disaster had been revealed. Robal felt as revulsed as Stella had looked. Something, some perverse honesty, had compelled him to say to her, "He was a dupe."

She had stared at him, brushed a stray lock from in front of her eyes, and had never looked as unattainable as the moment she said, "So were you."

Later, the Undying Man had explained to them all how his deception had attempted to preserve the life of the Umerta heir.

"My efforts have all now, of course, been undone," he said. "Somewhere in there, consumed by the flames, is the bier and the body on it." He raised his voice for the benefit of the woman lying bound a few paces distant, now separated from her surviving children. "Had you not moved against me, Martje, he would be alive now. We would be taking our leave of you. A lesson would have been learned. As it is, my mercy has cost my companions and I dearly, and your desire for revenge has cost you and your family even more."

His solemn gaze turned to Stella standing beside him, her arm now ending at the elbow. "I should have chosen justice."

He strode closer to the Umertas. "This cannot go unpunished," he said. "I now restore your paralysis, Martje, and anchor you to the ground." He closed his illusory fist and it was so. "You cannot move, nor can others move you. Here you will die. But I have freed your mouth and throat. You will find this a mixed blessing at best." With that he turned away.

"Let her see the ruination of her life," he said to Sauxa and Kilfor. "The rest of the family will remain tied up until someone finds them. They may invent any story they wish in order to explain what happened here, but I do not expect them to let the truth be known; nor, I daresay, would it be believed. Now, let us take our leave."

The last sound they heard as they made their way from the steading, walking slowly behind Phemanderac's horse-drawn dray, was Martje's screams.

INTERLUDE

HUSK IS THE MOST CONTENT he has been in seventy years.

Other men, he knows, would be at their wits' end, stretched beyond their abilities as they tried to weave the various strands of the plan into something that might achieve the intended goal. But he is not like other men; he has proved that yet again, and wishes only for an appreciative audience to marvel at his skill, intelligence and patience. He will have the audience he wants soon. Three months at the most. By the middle of winter Stella will be begging him for mercy over the Destroyer's dead body.

Not like other men, no. Not a man at all, in fact. The first of a new breed. The first god to dwell among men. And, despite having no eyes, the most far-sighted of them all.

Well has he learned that obsession makes one blind. The Son has no thought other than to recover his place in the world, and so focuses his thoughts so narrowly he does not see what Husk is doing to him, clever, clever Husk, drawing off power through the link he has made with the obsessed god.

And what does he do with the power? He has made for himself a new skin, a glossy thing, a beautiful thing, with restored nerves and feeling, and with the capacity for something akin to sight. Better by far than the original. Yes, it means an increase in pain, but that is the price of being alive. New lungs, purged of decades-old blood; lungs that can sustain him without magic. He has not yet been able to grow proper appendages, but that will come. The delay will give him time to decide what he wants to become. Not merely human again. No, he must be greater than that. His new body must reflect the greatness of his soul, forged in the fires of suffering.

He has a tongue now, a voice, a mouth, rather than a ragged hole. But why stop with one? He plans a second and a third, all designed to suck every available sensation from the world around him; to consume everything, then to expel it all, blessed, sanctified, that others might live on his leavings.

All due to the gamble he took, the bargain he struck with the Son and the Daughter. They are his allies now, uneasy and duplicitous though the relationship is, and have been since they offered their assistance to him. Together they intercepted the Undying Man as he pulled his companions eastward to Andratan through the blue fire. It would not have suited Husk to have the Undying Man arrive back in his fortress with Stella in tow, oh no. Nor would it have suited him to destroy them mid-journey, though he had considered it. There was a possibility he could have ended them, almost a certainty had the gods agreed to help him, but his great soul demands far more than their deaths. They must suffer, and he must watch.

The agreement was struck in an instant, and the power

the gods loosed through him was like nothing in his experience. His own power had strength, he knew, greater than that of almost anyone who had ever lived, but he had been easily surpassed by that of the Undying Man, who burned with a white-hot flame. But the gods, ah, the gods seemed to compress the power of all the worlds into his veins as they pulled through him: the lasting impression was not of strength, or fire, but incalculable *weight*. Of something so heavy that to be overwhelmed by it would pull one down, down through the world, through the universe and out into the nothingness of the void, to fall forever. Such power!

Patience over long, long years, and an instant of boldness, won him his prize. He snatched at the ragged edge of their concentrated might, drawing off the merest filament and attaching it to himself. A conduit of raw energy from beyond the wall of the world, threaded through the hole the gods have made.

For the first time, Husk thinks, the ledger is balanced, is more than balanced. He would have endured all the suffering, ten times the suffering, for a chance such as this. No longer does he have to battle for every breath; no longer is he forced to steal life from those around him. Oh yes, Husk is happy.

But there are important implications for his new state. He cannot allow the gods to achieve their goals. Once they have left the void and returned to the world, his source of power will vanish. They must be kept alive and on the far side of the great rent in the world-wall. Husk is realistic enough to know that this state of affairs cannot continue forever, but there is a critical moment ahead, some incalculable time in the future, when he will no longer need the power of the gods. The energy he is absorbing will become self-sustaining. He will be able to make his own hole in the worldwall and draw directly from the void beyond.

He has regrets, if a new god can be said to have regrets. If only he had risked more, he laments. Had he grabbed a larger filament the process would be swifter. He was afraid at the time, unknowing of the power and sensitivity of the gods, frightened that even the tiny filament he took would be noticed. But it was not. How large a piece of their power could he have stolen? Might he already be independent of them? Caution and courage are not bedfellows: he did well even to think of stealing fire from the gods. No use berating himself. After all, the only thing required now is patience.

So, ought he to continue with his plan? Are the Stone, the Blood and the Emperor's hate necessary any longer? No, they are not. But he will cultivate them anyway. The gods would rightly suspect any deviation from his plan. They know what he wants, and are interested in how he will achieve it. He has revealed as little as possible, but the Daughter—by far the smarter of the two—seems to grasp what he intends to do. Certainly both gods now know why three groups of people, one from Faltha, one from Bhrudwo and one from Elamaq, are approaching Andratan.

But there is a problem. His spikes are interfering with the gods' own plans. The spikes are slivers of pure magic, and interact in unpredictable ways with the movement of the gods through the ever-enlarging holes in the world. In fact, they have in some strange manner been drawing the attention of the gods. The Son wants all the spikes destroyed, while the Daughter is content to let them survive as long as they do not coalesce. She wants the three groups kept ignorant of the gods' real intentions, but the Son does not believe this possible.

The humans do not comprehend the mechanism by which the gods intend to break into the world. Lenares has a dim understanding, but they will keep her apart from the others—at least, Husk and the Daughter intend this. The Son seeks to kill her. Husk will prevent this, for a time at least. Lenares, after all, is his main threat, for she also has a filament connected to a god. Of course, unlike him, she does not realise what she has in her hand. Nor, he hopes, does she have the magic to exploit it. He was certain of this until recently, but events at the Umerta house have cast doubt on this. Lenares, a daughter of a practitioner of the old magic. Who could have known? From the Hanseia Hills, no less. Perhaps this Lenares is an unconscious practitioner herself. That would explain a great deal.

None of his spikes, nor any of those travelling with them, even Lenares with her numbers, truly understands what is happening. The worldwall is comprised of the lives—the thoughts, actions and, above all, the intersections—of all those in the world. Remove the worldwall, everybody dies and the world is open to the void. In order to penetrate the worldwall, lives must be destroyed before their time, their threads burned away, their nodes torn out. When the holes are made large enough, the gods will come through and live again.

Their plan is simple: to reach through the holes and kill as many people as possible, thus enlarging the holes. Up until now they have used the natural world against those they wished to destroy. While they continue to do this, and natural disasters follow wherever the gods go, Husk suspects they intend to use other means in future. He is almost certain he has already seen one of these means in action.

The gods will kill as many people as it takes. But they

will keep a connection to the void beyond, so maintaining their godhood, and will, they believe, be the first gods to live in the world. Well, each believes they will destroy the other and be the only god to live on earth.

They are both wrong.

Husk smiles to himself at the surprise in store for them.

FISHERMAN

CHAPTER 18

ON THE OCEAN

WHEN IT HAD COME TO it, the choice had been easy. They would travel by sea.

It was, after all, what they knew. None of them had been as far north as Sayonae, on whose docks they now stood, and everyone they had asked had told them the same thing: there was no way through the formidable jungles of Patina Padouk. Arathe hadn't wanted to board a ship; her experience coming north from Fossa to Raceme had cured her of any desire for sea travel. But none of the others had objected to Noetos's plan.

Sautea had money enough to cover their passage, but only in steerage class. Staggeringly, his life savings, which he always kept in a small bag on a string around his neck, could not get them better passage, no matter how aggressively he and Noetos bargained. The autumn waters were dangerous, Noetos knew that, but he had anticipated that fares would therefore be reduced during this period. On the contrary, the ship's captain explained. Since no one else was prepared to make the run, he could charge whatever he liked. It was only his generosity, he said, that saw rates this affordable. The fisherman had watched Sautea's money disappear into the captain's pocket with real regret. Noetos offered the older man his thanks, but he brushed it off.

"At the rates you paid, I couldn't have afforded the widow Nellas until I was ninety anyway."

"I saw the way she looked at you," Noetos countered. "I'm sure she would have given you a discount."

The captain leered at them. "If you're looking for that sort of service, bring some money aboard ship."

"Thanks," said Noetos, "but you have already taken practically everything we have."

The man grunted, then left them, called away by his first mate. Something to do with repairs to one of the sails.

Noetos didn't know what to make of the ship's captain. The surprisingly sophisticated man was also the ship's owner, a conjunction uncommon on the Fisher Coast, but apparently more common in the prosperous north, especially in Malayu and around the Northern Roads. He was a Raceman, so he said, though Noetos had not heard of his family, the Kidsons. "Named after the son of a goat who first bought a boat," the captain had joked.

The joking ceased when Noetos told him that the city had suffered a calamity. He did not elaborate, save to mention the whirlwinds, though he did not indicate they were anything other than a natural phenomenon. For a time Captain Kidson talked of sailing south to see what could be done, but he eventually admitted his schedule would not allow it, and his family had not lived there for several generations.

The trip north at this time of year, Kidson told them, would likely be unpleasant even for the experienced sailors, due to the autumn storms. Noetos knew that for his

children and the miners it would be terrible, especially if
they were followed by one of the so-called holes in the
world. But he also knew there was no other way. They had
to go north. Someone had to give answer for what had happened to them.

The first mate beckoned them up the gangplank. Seren
and Tumar carried their gear, most of which had been accumulated on the road north in exchange for work. The others
followed, Dagla at their head, his eyes darting left and right
excitedly, taking in everything about this new experience.
Noetos admired the lad's attitude. *If I was planning to continue fishing, this is a man I'd seek to hire*. Noetos scratched
his red beard as he followed his children on board: he'd not
thought of life after Andratan in quite some time.

"Look, Noetos," Dagla said happily. "Always wanted to
go on a boat. M'father promised me he'd take me one day,
but the tunnel collapsed an' he never did."

The young miner constantly came out with such things.
If he'd done one good thing on this path he'd taken, rescuing Dagla was it.

Their accommodation was neither as poor as he'd feared
or as good as he'd hoped. Bunks were stacked three high,
built into the hull of the ship, but thick curtains provided
a degree of modesty. Steerage passengers were supposed
to spend most of their time aboard in the thirty-foot space
between the two rows of bunks: here they would eat, on
trestle tables set up for the purpose, anchored to the floor
by leather straps; in the evenings the tables were cleared
away and games, dances and other pursuits were encouraged. Food—the most important part of any shipboard journey—promised to be monotonous, consisting of preserved
meat, oatmeal and ship's biscuit. Noetos had noticed live

animals on board, but no meat or produce seemed likely to make it past cabin class.

The ship was called the MF *Conch*. Kidson had explained his family tradition of naming their Malayu Factor ships after seashells: the *Periwinkle* and the *Clam* plied the route between Malayu and the northern Astralagus ports; and the pride of his fleet, the galleon *Nautilus*, ran the dangerous but profitable route from Malayu to Andratan and return, under a charter from the Undying Man himself. Four ships, yet he chose to make this one his own, Noetos thought, and wondered why. The *Conch* was nothing exceptional: a three-master clearly designed for cargo, with two large holds packed with goods and two smaller holds adapted for paying passengers. About two hundred tons excluding cargo, Noetos estimated, and a hundred passengers, seventy of them in steerage. He'd seen ships in better condition, having spent much of his childhood playing around the Raceme wharves, but he'd seen far worse. As a rule passenger ships were kept in better shape than cargo ships, and this was a fairly good example of the latter. The *Conch* would perform well on the open sea.

Depending, of course, on the crew. Noetos would take a close interest in the performance of the hired hands. On the days his father and his tutors had demanded too much, or had been too stuffy for words, he'd imagined himself running away to sea. To tell the truth he had never liked the sea, but during those days it had seemed infinitely preferable to studying in overhot rooms, trying to stay awake amid the drone of irrelevant voices.

As the days passed he began to look with fondness on his stuffy childhood studies. Below decks was oven-like, an unbearable cauldron of smells, noise and sweat. Crying children and grunting adults, both seemingly unaware of travelling in company, kept his nights virtually sleepless. Days were punctuated by hunger and sudden fights: there appeared to be two families aboard determined to revenge themselves on each other for some past wrong, and nothing Noetos said to either group would dissuade them. Altogether unsatisfactory; and the crew would do nothing about it. Considered, indeed, the voyage to be rather a tame one.

"Wait till you bin attacked by freeboarders, or had ta deal with an outbreak of pox," said the first mate when Noetos asked for some intervention. "Let 'lone the storms."

He asked if he could help the crew. He'd be willing to do anything to escape the boredom weighing him down, he told them, anything to keep him above decks. They turned him down, claiming there was nothing for an unskilled hand to do. "I'm not tellin' one of my men to look after you while y'do a job he could do in half the time," the first mate explained. "Now, you've had yer time on deck. Back down you go."

On the fifth day out from port Noetos found himself staring at one of the ship's slatterns. There were three of them, girls hired by the captain to entertain the single men who could afford them. Noetos was familiar with the concept, but this was the first time he'd come across it as an adult: he'd been too young in Raceme to notice them, and Fossa had strict laws about such things. The girls generally kept to cabin class, where there was sufficient coin, but were occasionally hired by men—and once, to everyone's scandal, a woman—in steerage. Over the first few days of the voyage families swapped places with the single men, until, when one descended the narrow ladder, families occupied the bunks on the left, single men the right. The curtains kept out the sights—thankfully, Noetos told himself—but not the sounds. Vigorous and seemingly never-ending, they served as a pointed reminder of what he had lost; and, to be honest, what he had never had.

The youngest girl sat on one of the long benches at the table on which dinner would soon be served, rearranging herself after her latest encounter. Oddly, she reminded him of the cosmographer girl—an improbable comparison. Lenares had surely never made noises such as had recently issued from a nearby bunk, nor had she worn such a world-weary expression as this girl, Sai, now displayed on her fraying face.

So what was it? There was something about the eyes, the way they looked right through a person, penetrating to an unwelcome depth, as though she knew all one's secrets. The hair colour was different: this girl wore her hair red and frizzled, but both were so plainly artificial her hair might well be similar to the cosmographer's long pale locks. There—she took an end of her hair and stuck it firmly between nose and mouth, the exact comfort-habit he'd noticed Lenares do. And there were other mannerisms. And her smile. Uncanny.

Anyone would think you've developed a fondness for young foreign halfwits, he told himself angrily. Given the activity he'd just listened to, no wonder his thoughts drifted in such ways.

He rose from his bunk and made to leave. He could see Anomer and Arathé playing cards down the far end of the room; he'd join them. Though he had a mild distaste for cards, for gambling of any sort, it would lead his mind away from uncomfortable roads.

"Ho, fisherman," the girl said cheerfully. Noetos was

not sure how he'd earned the nickname; no doubt one of the others had been telling stories. "What've you been doing? Casting your net on your own? I could help you with that."

"I haven't heard it called that," he said genially, brushing past her.

"I doubt you've heard it called anything for a long time," she said, her eyes narrowing. "I'm right, aren't I?"

He stopped and gave her an angry look, but did not deter her.

"I've seen you staring at me, eyes all over me. Make an honest man of yourself and take me to your bunk."

"I've been staring at you, Miss Sai, because you remind me of someone."

He wanted to end the conversation, to move on, especially when he knew others were listening from behind their curtains; but, paradoxically, he could not find it in him to be rude to her. Such a direct, desperate occupation: how could he brush her off?

She laughed. Genuine, unaffected. So much like Lenares, for a moment he was sure he could not be imagining it. "They all say that, fisherman. It's part of the art. We learn to be whoever you want us to be: mothers, daughters, absent lovers."

"It's an art? You are trained?" Drawn in despite himself, Noetos sat on the bench opposite her.

"Ooooh, yes," she said, batting her eyelids and wiggling her hips, so obviously coquettish they both laughed. "Training on the job mostly, and most of it ain't fun," she said, all seriousness for a moment. "So your pole don't need greasing?"

"No, Miss Sai, it doesn't. I can't deny I'd appreciate

release, but that's all it would be. And you don't even get that, for all your acting to the contrary. I've seen you abovedecks: as much mopping and cleaning for your employer as bedwork, it seems to me."

"Look at the bright side," she said. "I get to make the beds and to lie in them." Another laugh, but this one was definitely forced.

"Ah well, fisherman, take that pole o' yours off with you; I believe there's a gentleman in cabin class who needs his little doggie taken for a walk. I'll see you again, I'm sure." She smiled at him.

"And I'll hear you about, Miss Sai," he responded.

Her smile fell, but she nodded politely and made her way up the ladder to the hatch. His last glimpse of her was panties and petticoats. He sighed, and went to find his children.

His relationship with Anomer and Arathé had improved markedly aboard the *Conch*. He supposed it to be because he was no longer leading; the ship took them to a predetermined destination and there were no decisions to be made, hence no conflict. *Problems deferred, not solved*, he was honest enough to acknowledge, but he made the most of their willingness to talk with him.

On the seventh day from Sayonae, Arathé sought him out. He had learned enough of her peculiar language that he no longer needed her brother to interpret; conversation was still slow—though not as slow as that awful first day in Fossa. She sat down on the side of the bunk, pulled the curtain closed and began to talk.

As she told him what was on her mind, he found himself looking at her, really looking at her, for the first time in a month or more. His memories of her as a willowy, fair-skinned child would never leave him, he knew, but more recent images of a dumpy, hollow-eyed wreck were gradually being replaced. She had lost weight, her eyes had lost that dark, unhealthy colour, and she again began to approximate the girl he knew, albeit with a maturity not entirely flattering. Not surprising, given how she'd achieved it.

"I'm sorry, Arathé, forgive me, but I wasn't listening," he said. "I was thinking about you, and how you've coped with what happened to you in Andratan."

"I think about that too," she signalled. "My"—the next word was difficult, but he interpreted it as "remember-ings"—"my rememberings hurt me, but not as much as they once did. I want to talk about one remembering with you, but now is not the time."

"Your mother?"

She grimaced, and he knew he'd guessed right.

"Why not now?"

"Because the voice in my head has started speaking again," she signed.

A feeling of revulsion swept over him. Andratan had stolen his daughter's innocence, and would have taken her life but for her courage. And now it lurked in her mind, not only as awful memories but as an actual voice, trying to steer her to destruction. A voice most probably linked to the gods who were trying to kill her.

It was so unfair. How could his beautiful daughter, his firstborn, have attracted such a curse?

"What is it saying?" he asked with a heavy heart.

"It talks about Miss Sai," she said.

This simple statement took many minutes to communicate: the symbols she used to indicate the slattern's name

were impenetrable at first, and then for a while Noetos
thought the voice was suggesting some sort of unnatural
congress. It took him some time to overcome his outrage.

"Why, Arathé? Why would the voice talk about the slattern? What is it saying?"

"I do not know yet. It wants me to observe her. Father,
do you have any idea why the voice might make this
request?"

"Why haven't you spoken to Anomer? You're closer to
him than to me."

She did not deny the point. "Because I think Anomer
desires her," she signalled.

"What man aboard this vessel does not?" Noetos replied. "We are a captive audience, treated daily to a display
designed to inflame us. I know of married men who have
tried to manoeuvre their families away from their bunks so
they can conduct a liaison with Miss Sai. Just last night two
men fought over her." He smiled grimly. "She's good at her
job, it seems."

"That's what the voice says too. It seems very curious
about her. It asks me much the same questions it asked
about Lenares."

Noetos grunted in surprise. "That's odd. I talked with
her a while ago, and was struck by the resemblance."

"I don't see it."

"Well, there's clearly no connection. Lenares is from
another continent. Besides, she has, shall we say, difficul-
ties getting on with people. I don't see any evidence of that
with Miss Sai."

Arathé laughed, a strange, gurgling sound, but it did him
good to hear it. *She's getting better, I know she is.*

Now there was only the matter of Opuntia to deal with,

and, once he had sorted it out, he would have his children's hearts once again.

The storm came during the second week at sea. It began as mare's tails high in the sky, followed by a vast radial pattern of cloud emanating from the north. Noetos didn't need the redoubled activity from the crew to tell him what was coming. In the afternoon of the next day he saw a purple bruise on the horizon, one that grew rapidly and spread its mouth widely, dragging the darkness behind it.

"Arathé says it's not a god-made storm," Anomer said to Noetos.

"Doesn't have to be," the fisherman replied. "Autumn storms from the north are fearful things. Perhaps that is why our passage cost so much. Not every captain would risk a journey in this season."

Privately he wondered whether the storm was entirely natural. Maybe the gods had become cleverer, and had learned the trick of disguising themselves, now they knew that people were aware of their machinations. Their journey had taken a predictable turn, sounding like every fireside tale of adventures at sea. The fugitive went out on the ocean, and the wind came, and the storm battered the boat until the ship's crew cried out, "What are we to do?" And the sea god Alkuon said: "Throw me the man among you, the man who seeks to escape from me; throw only him and I will let the rest of you live." So they took the man up and consigned him to the deep; and immediately his head sank below the waves, all was calm and the storm vanished. As the storm bore down upon them now, their election to journey by sea did not seem so sensible an idea.

The storm blew for two full days and into the third. Noetos and Captain Kidson were the only two aboard not to be taken ill: many of the duties done by the crew fell to them. The fisherman found himself out in the worst of the weather, tying down the longboat after it came loose, reefing in the sails on the mizzenmast, attending to a cracked bowsprit, and, most often, wrestling with a recalcitrant wheel. It sometimes took their combined strength to head the *Conch* into the waves, and one of them had always to be on hand in case the ship should be turned broadside to the tremendous swells.

On the afternoon of the third day the two men slapped each other on the back with relief. The sea still heaved, the rain still fell, but the troughs were not as deep and the rain came at an angle, not horizontally. The worst was over.

Kidson was a sight. His hair was matted with grime and salt, his face red and briny, his clothes soaked, even his oilskin sodden, stuck to his wiry frame. Noetos expected he appeared exactly the same. The man beckoned Noetos to follow him. After a slow and careful transit of the deck, they ended up in the captain's cabin.

"Go rouse the first mate," Kidson told the cabin boy. "It's his ship for a watch. Fisherman 'n' me are going to get ourselves drunk. And fetch Miss Sai. Tell her to clean up first."

The boy rushed off.

"Wish that old son of a goat had stuck to collectin' shells, not boats," the captain said, smiling, and Noetos nodded. "You're some sailor. I know you say you've never been aboard a deep-drawing ship before, but you made yourself useful while those miserable sons o' besoms spent their time decoratin' their rooms with yesterday's swill. I'm grateful, sir, grateful. Here, have a drink."

Kidson drew a mug from a cupboard and poured a full measure into it. "Stout stuff, this. Too good for a smuggler like me. You might like it, though."

Noetos took a sip, partly out of in-bred politeness, but mostly to hide the surprise on his face.

Kidson raised his eyebrows. "You knew about the smuggling, right? I'm sure you did. No one goes out in the autumn unless the stakes are high. And they're high, all right. Silks from southern Jasweyah, sewn into the most exquisite garments, so I'm told." He stopped and looked at Noetos's bemused face. "You didn't know? You came up on deck and risked your life with no expectation of reward?"

The fisherman found himself able to talk. "The reward I wanted was to see my son and daughter again. I needed no greater incentive, Captain Kidson."

The captain nodded. "As you say. Yet I have an offer for you. I've been watching you these past two days, racking my brain, trying to figure out where I've seen you before. I thought it must have been Raceme, on the few times I came to call at that port, but why would a lowly fisherman have come to my attention? Then I pegged it. The Summer Palace. You're as near as spit the image of the old governor. You're his son, aren't you? The sole survivor of the infamous massacre." He sat back, waiting for a reaction.

"You claim to recognise someone from a brief meeting with his father more than twenty years ago?"

"No. Actually, the face is familiar to me, and more than familiar. My grandfather expanded the family business, doing so with capital borrowed from this man." His finger stabbed in the direction of the wall to their left. On the wall hung a small painting. The Red Duke of Roudhos.

"Grandfather would never have funded smuggling!"

"Oh ho! You admit your relationship to him, then! And yes he would have, especially if his part of the profits funded resistance to Andratan and Neherius." Kidson smiled. "Now you can work it out. Half the capital of this fleet is owed to the descendants of the Red Duke, so half this ship is rightly yours. Except, of course, no court would recognise your claim. So neither do I. You may be angry about it now, but you'll recognise the justice of it later."

"Had I wanted to be rich," Noetos countered, "I could have been. Nor do I seek wealth now. I want what I said I wanted: for my family to arrive safely at our destination."

A gentle knock sounded at the door.

"Wait a moment, Sai," Kidson called. Then he leaned closer to Noetos.

"Very well," he said. "Here's my offer. If you desire revenge against Neherius, I will put whatever resources I have at your disposal, even to helping you set up a rebellion. I have little love for Andratan, and less for the Neherian fleet, which has on occasion hounded me even further north than here, if you could credit it."

"I could credit it well," Noetos said with a smile. "But I have good news for you on that score. The Neherian fleet is severely reduced. I witnessed it, and played a small part in it. And the Neherian court is decimated, and in that I played a large part."

"The news gets better and better," Kidson said. "And it is clearly a story I must hear. However, my doxy and my cabin boy are standing out in the rain." He raised his voice. "Miss Sai, please enter!"

The girl that followed the cabin boy in looked little like the girl Noetos had talked with only a week or so ago. Her cheeks had been hollowed out by the storm and her hair lay lank on her face. Nevertheless she took her place at the table. The captain passed her a mug, which she upended in swift order.

"You wanted me, Captain?" she asked wearily, her voice carrying no traces of beguilement.

"Aye. Our friend the fisherman has helped us keep afloat over the last few days. You spoke to me of him last week, of how he fascinated you. I will place one gold coin, Malayu standard, in your purse if you spend the night with this man."

Noetos expelled his breath noisily. He could feel his heart racing at the thought. In the brief silence that followed the pronouncement, Noetos examined his options. He knew he should refuse, but he couldn't refuse the captain without offending him. And if he refused, Miss Sai would not get her gold coin.

Miss Sai came to his rescue. "His children are in steerage," she said to the captain. "I am sure our fisherman would have trouble with his rod should his son and daughter form the audience."

"True," said the captain. He thought a moment. "Then the first mate must make room for him." He signalled the cabin boy. "Go tell Sepa I want to see him, will you?"

He smiled at them both. "Not often I can give everyone what they want," he said.

"Thank you, Captain," Noetos made himself say.

"The room will be yours at dusk, and you must leave by dawn. I trust that will be long enough." He laughed at the double meaning, then slapped Noetos on the back.

Noetos spent an hour with the captain; long enough to further blur his consciousness, already affected by two nights of little sleep. Then, as the sky darkened towards evening, he made his way down to steerage.

Conditions were dreadful. Two of the tables and one of the benches had overturned, having broken their strapping; a man lay on the floor moaning, a leg badly bent beneath him; and every surface was covered in stale vomit. Noetos barely held his own bile in check.

I'd take a few willing hands to help clean this up rather than the "reward" Kidson has offered me. He would refuse, of course; it was a grand gesture, a buy-off of someone he thought might have taken this voyage to confront one who owed him a great deal of money.

He called out for assistance, and a few pale faces pulled aside their curtains. His children were not among them: probably asleep. He secured the reluctant assistance of three helpers, their work with water and cloth partly undone when one of them threw up over the portion of floor they had cleaned. Noetos helped for what seemed an age, then sighed and left them to it.

The first mate's cabin was tucked in behind the mizzenmast, right at the stern of the ship. Not the ideal place, it was subject to a great deal of roll, but the seaway had settled down and, as Noetos closed the door, it certainly had a charm not offered by steerage in its current state. Including that of the girl waiting for him.

He took a breath of surprise and his resolve wavered for a moment. She had used the time he'd spent cleaning steerage to further tidy herself, and now appeared absolutely lovely. Her red hair, set high on her head, hung in ringlets framing her pale face and red lips. She had dressed in finery, her gown of lace and low neckline made from materials far beyond her purse, no doubt supplied by the captain when she entertained him. *My doxy*, he'd said.

Noetos sat down on a wooden bench some distance from her. She wrinkled her nose at him, but her eyes were alight and her lips curved in a smile. No one had ever smiled like that for him. Not Opuntia, not even in the early days; her smile had always been part calculation. How did this girl manage to seem so genuine? He hated those who played games. Unwittingly, perhaps, she had found the secret key to him.

"You need a bath," she said. "I have had a tub heated for you. Come, disrobe, take your bath while I search for clothes fit for our evening together."

"Don't your, ah, men dispense with clothes?"

"There are no other men here tonight," she said. "I don't want to talk of them."

He nodded, then stripped off his foul garments. She took them and dropped them outside the door, then stood back and appraised him.

"For an old man, you look good," she said, her eyes crinkling as she spoke. "Pole's about what I expected."

He stepped into the tub and lowered himself into the gloriously warm water. "You understand you and I will not be coupling tonight, do you not?" He stared at her, eyebrows raised.

"I thought not," she said. "Part of why—" She bit her lip.

"Part of why you find me fascinating?" he finished for her. She nodded, her lip still between her teeth, staining them red.

"Miss Sai, I spoke to you with civility, that's all. I treated you as a person when others treat you—well, as the

Recruiters treated my own daughter. I'm very sorry you have come to such a poor pass that merely being treated as human fascinates you."

He expected her to become angry, or perhaps break down and cry at his words. She did neither, simply taking the sponge and setting to work on his naked back.

"What happened to your daughter?" she asked. "She has the look of one who has suffered."

All of a sudden his chest and stomach turned hot. Tears broke from his eyes and coursed down his face. *She has the key to me.* He tried to hold his emotion in check, but within moments he was shaking with sobs, her arms around his neck.

"It's good to cry," she whispered. "I know, I know."

Oh, Alkuon, he had not realised how locked up his feelings had become. An image surfaced in his mind: of Arathé in the dungeon of the Undying Man, mouth held open, pliers coming for her tongue. He told Miss Sai the story. They shared tears before it had finished.

He rose from the now-cool water and dried himself. She looked at him, wiping her eyes. "I was going to find you fitting clothes," she said.

"A sheet will do," he replied, and took one from the bed.

She raised an eyebrow. "You look ridiculous."

"Not as ridiculous as the puffing men must look," he said, thoughtlessly.

She reached over and placed a finger on his lips. "No other men, I told you," she said.

"Sorry, Miss Sai."

"You've spoken of a daughter," she said, "but not of her

mother. There is greater sorrow yet, fisherman. How wide must I cast my net to encompass it all?"

"Why? Why do you care?" he whispered.

"Because I can save you," she replied in a small voice. "Because I could not save another."

So he told her, told it all, the noble and the sordid, and her young face displayed nothing but understanding. *This is a miracle*, he told himself. Candles burned down, flickering into darkness as knots decades old began to loosen within him. He spoke for hours, spoke until his throat was raw.

"Ai, I was right," she said, rubbing her fingers across his forehead. "I could see it. I have a gift, you know. I can tell things about people."

"Before this journey I would not have believed it," he said, his mouth against her soft hair. "But I have seen so much I cannot explain. I believe in your gift. I am grateful for it."

"You fascinated me, fisherman, because I have never seen a man so strong, yet so burdened, so close to breaking. Had we slept together tonight, it would have broken you. You would have seen your daughter under you; you would never have lived with it. I know, I know, I've seen it. My own father, I've seen it."

"What did he do to you?" Noetos asked, staggered at her confidence in him, her openness, and in the new sensitivity unfurling in his breast. Her story would have held no compulsion for him a week ago, so filled with his own hurt he had become.

"Are you sure? My story is not full of bravery like yours."

"I would not refuse you, Sai," he said.

"Cylene," she corrected. "Cylene is my proper name."

I knew it, said a voice in the back of his head.

What? What? he shouted at it, staggered and shocked at her invasion. *Have you been listening?*

Father, I . . . let me explain, but not now. This is what the voice told me: her name is Cylene, she is from Sayonae, and she helped kill her twin sister in order to save her father, who had become her lover. Listen to her story, Father, and keep acting sympathetic as you have done until now. It is important!

Acting? I'm not acting! But his daughter had gone.

"Fisherman? Are you all right?"

"Yes, sorry, I haven't had much sleep. Tell me your story, Cylene." *No, I don't want this wonderful girl drawn into our troubles!*

"I am the thirteenth child and sixth daughter of the Umertas, horse-breeders and too-proud residents of Sayonae," she said, her eyes swimming with tears, her whole body an open entreaty to him, begging him to understand. "Six minutes older than the seventh daughter of the family. My tragedy is I killed my sister as a rival to the love of my father." She took a deep breath and her eyes steadied. "I am dead inside, fisherman, completely dead; so I chose a profession where life is not required, where acting is everything. Do you pity me yet?"

"I have seen dead men," he whispered to her. "I have seen their faces. I have looked into their eyes. You are not dead, Cylene."

"I have tried to die," she said. "I should be dead. My father, he was a great man, but he had needs, strange needs for which he used his daughters."

"I have heard of such things," Noetos said carefully, determined not to be shocked, to keep a straight face, for her sake.

"My older sisters hated it, hated him, but were trapped. I didn't hate him. I loved him. I begged him to put the others aside, to love only me, but he delighted in my sister." Her tears were hot; he collected them in a calloused hand. "I hated her. So I told him she was set to betray him, to tell the authorities, the men of the town.

"He took her on a walk one afternoon, not long after our eighth birthday. They went to the cliffs to pick wildflowers. He came back alone." She could hardly speak; his heart felt it was about to rip apart. "She fell, he said, but he winked at me. That night, after all the searching was over, when he came to me, he told me he'd pushed her. He'd watched her body break on the rocks, then seen the waves bear her away." She licked her salty lips. "I tried to scratch his eyes out. He never came to me again."

She burst into great heaving sobs, a deepest agony of spirit. For many minutes she simply could not speak, so intense her pain.

"I play dead," she said eventually. "It's the only way to stop the hurting. Oh, fisherman, I am going to split in two. What can I do? What can I do?"

We have to tell her.

Arathé, please leave me alone. This is important.

Yes, Father. Take another look at this poor creature. Tell me, who does she remind you of?

And he saw it. He held her at arm's length and he saw it, saw it for true. Had been seeing it for a week or more, but his mind had denied it.

"You are certain your sister is dead? That your father killed her?"

"He said so," Cylene replied. "He taunted me with it. It must have been so."

I will not tell her, Noetos said. *She would not credit the source of our knowledge. I'm not sure I do.*

It's complicated, Father. Lenares has joined the Falthans, and they passed through Sayonae a week or so ago. Do you see where this is going?

Cylene's family mistook Lenares for her sister? Was the reconciliation a happy one?

Arathé sighed: the sound was like a cold wind through his mind. *No, Father, it was not.*

They held each other throughout the night, two needy souls entwined by desperation. And, when morning came, they parted; he to steerage, her to the captain's cabin, his secret knowledge of her unspoken.

CHAPTER 19

MISS SAI

"HOW LONG AGO WAS IT?" Anomer asked insistently. "Less than three months, according to what I can remember. How long, Arathé?"

"Three months or so, as you say." Her fingers moved desultorily in the exhausting heat.

"He has no business doing this," he said. "Less than three months since Mother died. He should still be in mourning. Three years would still be too soon."

"Anomer, I'm trying to sleep."

"You always have an excuse to avoid this discussion. Are you on his side? Is this not important enough to you? Are you becoming like him?"

She propped herself up on one elbow, which slowed her speaking but established eye contact. Anomer had always been slightly in awe of his sister, and many times had not been able to look her in the eye. Now they were again eye to eye, she on her bunk, he kneeling beside it, and it would not be he who backed down.

"Anomer, it is you, not me, who is becoming like him. Four months ago I was in the hands of the Recruiters, who used me however they wanted. Everything I had was at their disposal. They helped themselves to my body, to my magic, to my strength. As a result I become easily tired, brother; hadn't you noticed? Even Father doesn't overtax me. So who is the thoughtless one now?"

The first of many rebukes. Anomer steeled himself.

"We're all tired, sister." He used the same inflexion she had. "We've been in this steam-room for two weeks now. No one on board is in better condition, I promise you. So, if not now, when can we talk?"

"Very well," she said. "You say he feels no remorse for what he did to Mother."

"Exactly."

She held up two fingers and waggled the first. "Point one: what happened to Mother was not his doing. She made her own choices, and you were there. You told us she ran to the Hegeoman's house, which is where the Recruiters captured you. Had she not invested herself so heavily in Bregor and his wife, she and you might have escaped the Recruiters."

"Circumstances. And who drove her to make that investment? You know what he's like. I cannot find it in myself to blame her."

"Yet women are not helpless, Anomer. We can still make choices. What happened to Mother was at least partially the result of her own choices."

"Was it her choice that saw Saros Rake come down on top of her? That led to a sword through her belly? Father's plan was flawed from the start."

"The flaw was in trusting the alchemist and the traitorous miners," Arathé signalled. Her fingers had slowed even since the start of their discussion. Perhaps the heat really was affecting her as she claimed.

"He didn't even grieve at her graveside," Anomer said.

"That, I'll admit, counts against him. I don't understand why he didn't."

A flicker of guilt smouldered in Anomer's chest: it had been Bregor and himself who had driven his father away from the site of her burial. He repressed it. If it helped Arathé understand what sort of father she had, if it dimmed him in her eyes, he would allow her to continue believing it.

Anomer leaned forward, not quite meeting his sister's gaze. "So yesterday he came and tried to apologise. Claimed he'd decided to let his guilt go. I told him I'd seen no evidence of his ever having picked it up in the first place. Oh, he became angry at that. Give him credit, he kept his temper, but it was an effort."

"Progress, then."

Anomer sighed audibly. *Always she sees the good in him.*

"Of a sort, Arathé, or perhaps he's feeling a little more vulnerable now you're not making your magical strength available to him. I admire you, by the way, it was a courageous decision. He could have fallen at any time during that storm, could have been lost overboard."

"I was ready to help him had he needed it," she said. "Besides, it was your idea. It took cowardice, not courage, to agree to it. I should have stood up to you."

"Nonsense. Once he realises he's not invulnerable, he'll begin to put more trust in those around him."

"I thought we agreed that's what caused the debacle at Saros Rake."

She was doing it again. He was accounted a quick thinker, but he had never bested his sister in an argument. She could twist anything he said and use it against him.

"You said that," he said. "I didn't agree."

"You didn't argue the point. Oh, Anomer, why do we so often end up fighting about Father?"

"Both strong-willed, I suppose; another legacy of our dear father."

"Did you accept his apology?"

"Of course not! How many lives have his actions cost? Why, it may only be his guilt that prevents him making further mistakes."

"You're harsher than he is," Arathé said, as her eyes began to droop. She summoned the energy from somewhere. "He rescued miners from execution; how is that an action that cost lives? You could argue that his wiping out of the Neherian court, and his defeat of their army, saved many more lives than were lost. What if he'd walked away, minding his own business? Would the Neherians now be besieging Sayonae, or Malayu itself?"

"There must have been a better way to do it," Anomer said sullenly. She was winning again. "A way that didn't involve the slaughter of the defenceless. I know they weren't blameless, but the images we saw from the ballroom of the Summer Palace were inexcusable."

"No different from the havoc you caused among the miners who tried to take the huanu stone."

"I've made my decision. When we land at Malayu, I'm leaving him and returning south. Bregor asked me to join him, you know, to help him in re-establishing Raceme. I think I'll take up his offer. More productive than the misguided revenge Father is bent on seeking."

"Very well," she signalled, her fingers stiffly making the symbols. "But should he come to me, I'll listen to him."

"I'd like you to come south with me," Anomer added.

"And I'd like you to reconcile yourself with our father," she countered. "We do not always get what we want, even Father has realised that. Still, he should understand that he cannot take our support for granted. I'll speak to him soon."

"As you like. I've done speaking."

He stood, stretched the tension from the muscles in his legs, and turned towards the interminable card game at the stern end of the room, presided over as always by Tumar. Behind him the curtain closed, leaving him feeling yet again as though he'd lost something more than a mere argument.

The only time Arathé felt at ease was on her infrequent excursions above decks. The steerage deck had become quite unbearable: sleeping there actually deprived her of energy. A combination of constant noise, oppressive heat and noisome fumes had ground her down until she found herself more and more sustaining her strength by borrowing—stealing, really—from those around her.

Walking the open deck, or standing at the rail, watching the water break on the ship's bow or churn behind its stern, gulls crying, clouds parading their ever-changing shapes, the wind whipping at her hair, was as life was to death. Steerage passengers were allowed two hours on deck if weather permitted, one hour in the morning, the other before dusk. Those hours rushed by, the pleasure she derived from them seeming to make the interminable time

below decks even less bearable than it otherwise might
have been.

She stood quietly, one hand on the foremast, and
watched her fellow steerage passengers take the air. Six
families made up over half those in steerage; of those, two
families had ten members each. Sadly, the Fallows had lost
their youngest daughter last week. No one had even known
she was ill. She had come down with a fever, apparently,
nothing exceptional, but she had insisted the light hurt her
eyes and that her neck was sore. A few bewildering hours
later her little body had been cooling on the deck, shrouded
in sailcloth in preparation for a sea burial. Her parents had
wanted to take the body home, but the captain had refused.
Two weeks out of port, he said, in this weather, would cor-
rupt the body beyond what anyone could stand. Besides,
there was the risk of disease. No one knew what the girl had
died of: there were no lumps of pustules, and her sputum
had been clear. The only sign of her illness had been a rash
on her chest and back. Truth, half those aboard had rashes.
The captain decided not to impose disease measures, but
the other passengers drew away from the family until it was
clear none of them had caught the fever.

Her mother's eyes were still hollow, circled in black;
Arathé doubted she was sleeping. The rest of the family,
though, frolicked about on the deck: the father played loop-
toss with his three youngest sons, all beautiful dark-haired
children. There had been a death, yes, but life continued; a
lesson her brother Anomer had yet to learn, it seemed.

Life not only continued, it burgeoned, even in this awful
autumn heat. One of the single men—one who might have
been of interest to Arathé before her time in Andratan—
waited for his girl beside the main mast. She was the old-

est of eight children in what was now the largest family aboard, and it was clear from Arathé's repeated observation that her parents did not know of the liaison.

Arathé smiled. Here she came now, a young thing indeed, probably no older than sixteen years of age, measured against the man's midtwenties. She looked around, eyes wide, and located her parents walking back towards the hatch. Time almost over for another day. As soon as the mother's sunhat disappeared, the pair were in each other's arms. Arathé doubted the couple would keep knowledge of their liaison private much longer. There were few secrets on a ship.

Her attention turned to her father. He stood amidships, leaning against the port railing, staring towards the setting sun. His preoccupation was not a secret.

Ah, there she is. Miss Sai emerged from the hatch and walked slowly across the main deck towards the broad ladder—really a stairway—leading to the upper deck and the captain's cabin. She took an age to make the journey; a deliberate action to keep her on view as long as possible. Most of the men's eyes followed her, hunger in many of them, while the women pointedly looked away or stared malevolently. She ignored them all.

But one pair of eyes contained a hunger beyond mere bodily desire. He had turned from his contemplation of the sea and now watched her as she reached the ladder. And there, as she had done every day for the past nine, she turned and smiled her heartbreaking smile at him. Just a momentary contact, all they could reasonably obtain without raising the captain's suspicions.

The trouble was, he already knew.

Miss Sai turned her head back and ascended the stairs,

her carriage and gait belying the notion of a slattern—yet that was what she was. A woman employed to have sex with as many men as possible in order to make a profit for the captain. And should anything distract her from that task, the captain would remove it.

So he'd said to Arathé the day before yesterday. He had called her into his cabin, his face set in a grimace as he'd explained the situation.

"I have made a mistake," he said. "I gave Miss Sai to your father as a reward; he'd been extremely valuable, even heroic, during the storm. But he has formed an unwholesome attachment to her. I've seen him mooning after her as she advertises herself around the ship. So has the first mate. I doubt he realises how ridiculous he looks, or what comment he is attracting. I am not yet certain what to do about it."

He'd sucked on his teeth a moment, then leaned forward. "I see and hear more than the passengers think. Have to. It's the secret of running a good ship. And there are reasons I need to keep everything above board, as they say. I've approached you instead of your brother because, from what I hear, your father is more likely to listen to you than to him. So convey my message well, or I'll have to tell your brother."

Arathé had put her answer down on paper for him. *If mooning was a sign of attachment*, she'd written, *half the men on the boat are guilty. Your slattern does her job too well*.

"My slattern is half in love with your father," the captain said. "If this attachment interferes with her duties I will put your father in the brig. I want you to tell him so."

A fine reward for all he has done to assist you, she wrote.

He shrugged. "This is a friendly warning. It's not about fairness, it's about business. Sai is the best I've ever had, and I don't want to lose her. You tell your father to stay away from Miss Sai. Is that clear, Arathé of Fossa?"

She had agreed without making a fuss. Her father was not the fickle man Anomer painted him to be. Nothing had happened that night with Cylene—fortunately, given the complication of her heritage. Her father had known that, which was why he acted responsibly. Besides, she could hardly defy the captain. Their swords were deep in the cargo hold, and would be returned only when they stood on the Malayu docks. Out here on the ocean the captain was the only authority. So she had nodded, written a brief thanks to the captain for his forbearance, and promised to deliver the message.

Two days had passed, in which she'd hoped to behold proof that the attachment was temporary. Unfortunately, the evidence pointed in quite the opposite direction. Her father's eyes remained on Miss Sai until she disappeared behind the mizzenmast. Two women whispered together directly below Arathé, Noetos's behaviour clearly the topic of their conversation.

To make matters worse, the captain emerged from the hatch just as Miss Sai vanished from view, but not before he took in the scene. He turned about, scanning the deck until he saw Arathé, then came up beside her.

"Remember our agreement, Arathé of Fossa?" he asked. She nodded to him, embarrassed.

He walked to the upper deck ladder, then waited, clearly expecting her to do something immediately. She sighed, descended the steps and walked over to her father, who had resumed his unthinking contemplation of the ocean.

"Father, we must talk," she signalled.

"What? Is it time to go below?"

She glanced over her shoulder to where the captain waited. "We've been given a few minutes longer," she mimed, slow enough, she hoped, for him to understand.

"We have? Have they finally realised how unwell you have become down in steerage?"

"No. Of course not. They see only life and death. Life is conducted in steerage; death means being wrapped in a cloth and thrown overboard."

He waited until she'd finished signalling this; it took some time. "My, you are disturbed, daughter. Something you want to tell me?"

"Yes. We can begin here, and later, down in steerage, I will use mind-voice to speak further."

"Has someone done something to you? Tried to take advantage? Made a threat?"

She seized on his words. "Yes, that is exactly what has happened."

"Who? Tell me, Arathé!"

Her father might be many things, she thought, but he did not stint in his love for her. She smiled a moment, then smoothed her face.

"Captain Kidson wants you to stay away from Miss Sai," she explained. "He says you are putting her off doing her job. He says—" She stopped. "What is wrong?"

Her father had begun to chuckle.

"Nothing is wrong, Arathé, absolutely nothing. He said that, did he? The best news I've had in days."

"What? Father, what do you mean?"

"I've been watching her go about her work. Listening to her. Arathé, you might consider me foolish, but it has been akin to torture. Now I hear her behaviour has changed. Kidson says she's been put off her job. Of course I'm happy."

"And will you leave her alone?"

"I've done nothing, daughter. We shared a night, as the captain asked me to, but nothing happened of a physical nature. Both Cylene and myself recognised that for me to have slept with her would have been a disaster. Arathé, you were privy to my thoughts; I can't deceive you and I'm not trying to. It's not her body I'm after, it's her conversation. I've never encountered someone so perceptive. I so much want to talk with her again."

"But you cannot," she said. "The captain will put you in the brig as soon as he sees or hears of it."

"Aye," he said, his head down. "He owns her while she is aboard. Well, then, I can be patient."

"Father," Arathe signed uneasily, "what are you thinking?"

"Oh, nothing," he said, and smiled. "Time we went down."

"He escorted his daughter down the ladder as though she were a queen, smiling all the while. And as he left her to find his own bunk, she heard him say; "Put off her job!"

It took no magical powers for Arathe to sense trouble coming.

Northward progress was slow. No wind was worse than a slight head wind, and Noetos had every reason to want a swift passage to Malayu. But the smuggler's ship stayed well out to sea, avoiding coastal patrols and certainly not docking at any ports. Nearer the coast, sea breezes would

see the ship make progress, but the captain valued secrecy
more highly than speed.

After a week in which the *Conch* made very little head-
way, whispers of food shortages began to circulate. The
rumours translated into reality for the steerage class on the
fourth week of the journey. Water was rationed, as they had
received no rain since the third night of the storm, and they
were fed nothing but weevil-infested ship's biscuit. The
first mate appeared at what was laughably called the "evening meal" to explain the situation.

"You've heard we're short on rations," he said, scratching his bald head as he spoke. "Tis true. Captain is thinking
of putting in on the coast, perhaps at Long Pike Mouth, to
bring on supplies. He'll only do this if we make no progress in the next few days."

"Will he put off passengers?" one of the single men
wanted to know.

"There'll be no forced disembarkments, but if someone
wants to leave, I guess that's two problems solved."

"How long until we get to Malayu?" asked an older
woman.

"Look, ma'am, this ain't like riding in a coach. Arrival
times can't be predicted. Were we to get a following wind,
we could get to Malayu in a week. But at the current rate o'
progress we're more likely to end up back in Sayonae."

"But I've got a sick mother in Malayu," the woman
said angrily. "I paid as much money for my single berth
as I paid five years ago for my whole family to sail north.
Surely something can be done?"

"No, ma'am, it can't," Noetos said. "We are at the mercy
of the elements. The crew no doubt know some tricks to get

a little extra from the ship, but beyond that we must all be patient."

The woman continued to complain as the first mate took his leave.

As he reached the base of the ladder, he beckoned Noetos over.

"Listen, friend," he said into Noetos's ear. "Not all of us approve of what the captain's doing with regard t' Miss Sai and yourself. Some of us think that if she wants to talk to you, well, she should be allowed to. So, if you're prepared to help ease the passengers' concerns regarding ship's progress, I won't say anything if I see you and she talking in the upper cargo hold in the hour after dusk tonight. And neither will none of my men. We ain't for gotten what you done for us, fisherman. Fair enough?"

Noetos kept his face straight and his voice level, though he wanted to shout and leap with happiness. "It's fair," he said. "But how do I know Miss Sai will be there?"

"Cos I've already arranged it," the first mate said, scratching away at his ear. "She'll be there. She looked about as excited as you do, and she fooled me about as well as you are."

"Aye, well, since I heard the captain's view I've been careful," Noetos said. "And thank you, friend. If we are discovered I will not mention you."

The man nodded. "Go to the smaller hatch a few minutes after dusk. Knock once and give my name. Tell them Rate sent you. Old Three-tooth will let you in." He winked at Noetos. "An hour ought to be long enough."

Noetos wanted to protest, to explain that it wasn't like

that, he and Cylene were not going to . . . but he held his tongue. The man wouldn't have understood.

Miss Sai made her circuit of the ship, and Noetos heard her footfalls as she passed close by. He forced himself to face out to sea, focusing on the glowering sun setting in a cloudless sky. The bell rang, and the steerage passengers made their reluctant way below decks. Noetos went too, but slowly, ensuring he was the last to approach the hatch. He cut left, finding the small door that led to the upper cargo hold: the two sailors watching both smiled widely at him. The first mate had no doubt hand-picked those on duty this evening.

He knocked on the smaller door, and it swung open at his call of "Rafe". The old sailor smiled at him, a sight to frighten small children. He let Noetos in, then climbed out of the hatch and closed it behind him.

"Hello, fisherman," she said.

He couldn't help it: his heart surged at her voice, and he hurried over to where she sat as though he was a boy about to begin his first courting. So foolish. He was sure he cut a ridiculous figure.

"Hello yourself, Cylene," he said, and was astonished at how shy his voice sounded. "May I sit?"

In answer she patted the blanket beside her. As he sat, Noetos took a look around them. By the light of a lamp he saw boxes of silk, but also mountains of other goods: tools, elegant furniture, machinery of some kind, including a lathe, and various other things he could not identify in the poor light. All things that attracted a high duty.

He took a steadying breath and brought his mind back to

the girl beside him. "I'm sorry I've been ignoring you," he said, "but the captain warned me off."

"He warned me off too," she said. "And I've been worried my continued employment would offend you."

"How could it? What other choice do you have?"

"None," she said, "but since that night, I have come back to life. And it hurts, fisherman, it hurts. Every time now I'm with a man, I'm with *him*, and I can't stand it."

"Your father?"

"Yes," she said fiercely. "It felt so right as a child, but so wrong now. Noetos, I'm breaking into pieces and it's your fault. Can you fix me?"

He looked into her troubled eyes, so like those of the cosmographer who had made him so uncomfortable, yet with a subtle difference. These eyes were equally intense, equally perceptive, but they saw a different kind of truth: hearts, not numbers. She shared her twin sister's rare gift of seeing things as they really were, but used it differently.

"No, Cylene, I cannot fix you," he said, hoping the words he chose were the right ones. "But I might be able to help you fix yourself."

She bowed her head. "So it must be," she said softly. "No short paths. One of the things I most like about you, fisherman, is you coat nothing with sugar."

"Wouldn't know how," he said.

She smiled. "Answer me a question. I've told you what I did. You know what I am. Why would you wish to help?"

Because I know what you do not, he wished to tell her. *I know your father did not kill your sister, but sold her into slavery. I know she became a crucial part of a great empire. I know, Cylene, she is still alive. And I know that if I have anything to do with it you and she will meet, will be reconciled, and all the happiness stolen from you by a selfish man will be returned to you. And, Cylene, I want to be there to see the smile on your face and the happiness in your eyes.*

He said none of these things. Instead, as he composed his reply, his eyes wandered over the cargo. He saw a stack of boxes with food labels on them: roe, saffron, Agakoussa cheese, burnt toffee. He'd heard of the cheese—Agakoussa was only a day's walk inland of Fossa—but none of the other foods. They had to be expensive in order to be worth a smuggler's while. With the rationing as it was, though, he couldn't help taking a moment to wonder whether the captain could supplement the low food stocks with one or two of these boxes.

Her eyes were on him, and he had no doubt she knew he held thoughts back from her. He hoped she would take note of his good intentions and the depth of his regard for her.

He took a calming breath. "Let me answer this way. I was much older than you when my own sister was murdered before my eyes, along with the rest of my family. I believed I was responsible for it somehow: why, otherwise, would my family's killers have let me go? I carried that burden for many years, more years than you have been alive, until a day when a woman unlocked my heart. That woman allowed me to see I bore the blame for something not of my doing. Is that same woman now asking that man to return the favour?"

She sat very still, her eyes wide. "I know," she said, and her lip trembled. "I know, logic is so easy. I was only a child; how could I have been responsible for the unnatural lusts of my father? But some horrible thing in me wants me to die, fisherman, to balance what happened to my sister. The only option I can see is to give in to it."

"I could supply you with another reason to live," he said, his voice husky with emotion.

"Ah," she said, smiling wanly. "You are going to declare your love for me. It's not enough, fisherman."

"No, it's not," he agreed. "And I wasn't going to say those words, Cylene, because they are not true."

She drew back from him, her face shocked into woodenness. "You do not?" she asked, and it was as if death hovered over her heart like a knife.

"No, I do not," he said gently. "Not yet. But I think I soon will, dear one. Forgive me, but I do not want to burden you with lies. My dead wife was only a few years older than you when I first met her, and we rushed into an arrangement that satisfied neither of us. But what I can say, Cylene, is that I have only ever met one person remotely like you. She, like you, is a precious gift to the world, an exquisite crystal glass fashioned to hold the rarest of wines, but used by unthinking men to quaff stale beer." He reached out and took her chin in his hand. "Even that is not enough. You were not made for others to use: my own daughter has suffered that. You exist for your own sake, and you must find your value independently of what other people want of you, even of those who might soon fall in love with you."

He was so close to her now he could see twin reflections of his own earnest face in her eyes.

"Cylene, I want to spend every moment of every day talking with you, learning everything there is to know about you, and telling you everything about myself, the good and the bad. You know, I am sure, there are many things I have not yet told you about myself and my friends. But I cannot open my heart to a dead woman. I lived like that for years, and fear it more than anything. I am afraid, deeply afraid, that you will choose to go back to your living death, and I will lose you before I even find you."

"But it hurts, fisherman," she whispered, her lips barely moving.

"So does every birth," he replied. "All you need is someone to help you through the pain." He took her in his arms and met her lips with his.

The knock sounded all too soon. "Miss Sai," came the voice of the toothless old sailor. "Miss Sai, hour's up. Come out."

Noetos released her from his embrace with a sigh. She'd offered, as she would, and he'd refused, as he must. It was the right decision, though it had been so difficult to make. But that kind of comfort was not, he judged, what she required.

"Goodbye, Cylene," he said. "I hope to speak to you again before voyage's end."

She smiled at him. "I will try to live a little longer," she said. "I want to see if this man I know will fall in love."

"Fair enough," he said, and helped her to her feet.

The sun hung in the sky like a circle of brass. Day after day it leached away the strength of those aboard the *Conch*, until Captain Kidson made his decision. "We head to shore," he announced, and the passengers and crew breathed a collective sigh of relief.

But an announcement from the captain of a ship does not of itself enable that ship to move, and passengers and crew alike had to endure three more days of hunger, heat and boredom before finding an easterly breeze. It was a scant thing, this breeze, but enough to bring them closer to shore, where they picked up a cool northerly wind that promised to deliver them to Long Pike Mouth three weeks late and two hundred miles from their destination.

When the first mate announced the ship was a day out from Long Pike Mouth, Noetos sought out the captain. They sat on boxes directly beneath the main mast, with two crewmen keeping other passengers away.

"You have five minutes," Kidson said. He'd positioned himself so the mast partly obscured his face. Noetos had to lean to the left to get a good sight of him.

"Five minutes are all I need," he replied. "I did what you asked and stayed away from Miss Sai. If her work was less than satisfactory, it is not I who is to blame."

"I'll save you the trouble of coming to the point," Kidson said. "You want to make an offer for her. The answer is no."

"No? You refuse before you hear what the offer is?"

"Of course I do. You think having Miss Sai on board is all about business?"

"No, I think it is about status. By holding on to her you continue your reputation as the premier shipping line on the Inland Sea, and you cock a snook at the descendant of the man your family humbled itself to in order to start this venture. What is mere money compared to that?"

"We understand each other then," Kidson said, and made to leave.

"Two things," Noetos said quietly.

"And they are?"

"First, my offer was going to be the exclusive right to ship cargo from Aneheri. You never heard my tale, Captain

Kidson, and you do not understand that should I claim Neherius, there is no one who can stand against me. A fortune for the ages, Captain, and you have turned it down."

The man's neck went red. "You are certain your claim will be entertained?"

"A hundred or more of the Neherian court died under my sword," Noetos said, leaning forward and fixing the captain with his most intense stare. "There is no one left to oppose me."

"So why are you not there now?"

"Because I wish first to speak with the Undying Man. I have every reason to believe he will support my claim."

The captain rubbed at his chin. "I do not believe you," he said, though Noetos could hear the doubt in his voice. "Were you the natural inheritor of the Neherian rulership you would be in Aneheri now, consolidating your position. I think you would be slain if you showed your face there, fisherman."

His gambit had failed. Even the most despotic ruler would not be able to allocate such rights without consultation with the merchants and traders of the land. And Kidson was right. After slaughtering the Neherian court he'd receive a knife in the back should he ever try to claim the southern power for his own. He'd failed, but he'd needed to try.

"The second thing," Noetos continued, "is that you are sitting on a box of dried meat. Why did we suffer such short rations when you had ample food in your cargo holds?"

"It's not just dried meat," Kidson replied, "but venison from the Saysch Valley high in the Weyan Massif. I expect to sell this to the Malayu consortium that supplies Andratan. It's not for distributing amongst passengers."

"I thought as much," Noetos said. "One box, man, that's all we needed. Three children are sick down below, and one is unlikely to survive the night. Better food might have made the difference. How do you sleep with such a cruel heart?"

Kidson smiled, though Noetos could tell he'd made him furious. A mistake. He'd thought merely to unsettle the man, but he could see the captain closing to him.

"I sleep with the help of the woman you cannot afford," Kidson said, biting off each word. "Now, unless you care to offer me the official customs position at Aneheri, along with the kingship of Jasweyah and the throne of Andratan, our conversation is at an end."

He stood and made a two-handed gesture, flicking his fingers forward. Immediately the two sailors came and stood either side of the fisherman, a cudgel in their left hands, a dagger in their right.

"What is this?" Noetos said.

"Exactly what it looks like. I have something you want and, if you are to be believed, you are a dangerous killer. Why should I leave you at liberty to plot against me?"

"You're going to put us off at Long Pike Mouth?"

"Of course," Kidson said. "But don't worry: I'll refund you a portion of your fare. You ought to be pleased, as you'll be solving both shipboard problems at once. Miss Sai will be able to concentrate on what she does best, and the other passengers will have more food to go around. An elegant solution."

"Elegant for you—"

Noetos had been watching for a signal from Kidson, but if there was one, the fisherman never saw it. He glimpsed movement from his left and swung around to face it, providing a clear target for the man to his right. The blow blossomed red and he went down in an unknowing heap.

Noetos awoke in a dark, foetid world. He groaned in pain: his eyes felt as though they were about to explode in his head. There was something on his face, a cloth . . . no, a sack on his head, stinking of sheep dung. He tried to take it off, but his hands were bound behind his back.

"He's awake," someone said.

He tried to turn his head towards the sound. His stomach suddenly rebelled and he vomited into the cloth. Someone said something, but all sound faded.

Father, wake up. Wake up. An insistent voice picked at him. *Wake up, wake up, Father.*

I am awake, he replied, then realised the conversation was taking place in his head.

You weren't breathing. We thought you'd choked on your vomit.

That's me I smell, isn't it.

Not just you. Dagla is badly hurt, and has messed himself. He's making noises but doesn't seem able to talk.

Where are we, Arathé?

We think we're in the brig.

How many?

She knew what he meant. *All of us.*

This is my fault, Arathé. I thought I could persuade Kidson to let Miss Sai go.

That's what Anomer thought. He's awake, in case you wondered.

You're angry I mentioned her name before his?

He would be.

Noetos cleared his throat and spat something foul out of his mouth. "Anomer, are you all right?"

Arathé smiled in his mind.

"Yes, Father." His voice was muffled and faint. "And you? You're fine?"

"Not exactly, but I'll mend. Are we all wearing sacks?"

"Why has this been done to us, Father?" Anomer's voice was sharp.

"You think this is my fault?" Noetos could not help it: he found himself instantly on the defensive.

"I know this is your fault. Every time we get into trouble, you are to blame."

Noetos decided to speak plainly. Or as plainly as he could with a sack over his head. This was not the place for it, nor was it the audience, but the boy was becoming insufferable.

"I am often to blame, my son, because I seem to be the only one prepared to do anything about injustice. We got into trouble at Saros Rake because I came after you. I suppose I could have stayed at home—like you would have, perhaps. I faced down the whirlwinds at Raceme to protect you and your sister. Are you saying I should have left Arathé to face the Fingers of God alone? I make mistakes because I do things. Until you've made your own mistakes, I don't want to hear any more talk of blame from you.

"We're here because I tried to bargain with the captain for Miss Sai's freedom. Is there anyone here who thinks I ought not to have tried?"

His son had courage, if not sense. "Less than three months after my mother died, you are chasing a slattern. Who could possibly agree that a sad old man thinking of his own selfish needs deserves anyone's support? Father, she's Arathé's age. I'm embarrassed for you."

In the long silence that followed this, Noetos could hear someone—Dagla, if Arathé was right—struggling for breath. A muffled murmuring came from one direction: two voices that sounded like Seren and Tumar, discussing the boy's injury.

Arathé, have you spoken to Anomer about Miss Sai?

I'm speaking to him now.

Tell him—no, ask him—to think before he speaks, would you? He's a gifted lad, but no one will follow him if all he does is criticise others. I want to reconcile with him, Arathé, and I'd appreciate your help.

Very well, I will tell him.

The sound of booted feet brought Noetos out of the semi-daze he'd fallen into.

"Is there going to be any trouble?" came a voice. *The first mate's*, Noetos thought. *In the end, he's the captain's creature.*

"We'll not make it," Noetos said.

"Good man. This is what is going t' happen. We're going t' loop a rope through all your bindings and lead you from the ship. All your possessions will be placed in a pile. You'll get most o' your coin back, but some goes to one of our agents who will guard you until we're wellclear and on our way back to sea. Then your blindfolds will come off and you'll be set free. Is that all clear?"

"It is." They were trapped.

No, we're not. Arathé's voice in his mind. *Father, Anomer says he's sorry, and wonders whether you require the strength of his children. You could overpower the guards—*

No, Arathè. We don't know how many of the crew are out

there. And even were I somehow to prevail over them, the whole ship would be against us. Passengers and crew.

But we should try! Anomer's voice.

We know where she is, Noetos told his children. *If we allow the inevitable now, we can rebuild our resources later. I know I normally rush in, but this is not the time for action.*

"Stand up, the lot of you."

"One of us can't stand," Seren growled. "If you've done him permanent harm, be assured I'll find who did it and—aaah!" A thump accompanied the shout of pain.

"Enough!" Noetos cried. "We're doing what you want. Please, just do as you said you would and let this be ended."

If Noetos had been on his own, of course he would have tried something. But his children and his sworn men were his responsibility. It hurt him deeply to leave Miss Sai in the hands of such a blackguard, but he truly saw no choice.

They were to be transferred to the longboat, which was lowered and launched with a great deal of shouting and swearing from the crew. The first mate informed his captives of what was happening all the while.

As they shuffled across the deck, Noetos became aware that what sounded like the entire passenger list had been assembled to see them leave. Mutters and mumbles distinguished them from the crew, whose exertions told on their breathing. No doubt this assembly was Kidson's final attempt to humiliate them. He listened with everything he had as he walked past the watching passengers, their lighter breathing marking them out. Could he tell?

He didn't need to. "Goodbye, fisherman," she said.

"I'll return." It was all he had time to say. So much he wished to tell

Cylene; a deep unease at his decision to keep the truth about herself from her. Too late for regrets now.

Slowly down the rope ladder, gently easing themselves into the longboat, the slap of choppy water on the sides. Then slow strokes and the sounds of the ship fading into the distance.

"Do we really need these sacks on our heads?" Seren asked.

"Captain's orders," said the first mate.

"And do you always follow captain's orders?" Noetos countered.

"When the captain's nearby, he does," Kidson said.

There was no more conversation. Eventually the boat came to a halt, and ropes were secured. By then Noetos was nauseous, the heat working on his fouled head covering. He wondered how the others fared, but would not give Kidson the satisfaction of enquiring. He could check on his children, of course, who told him they were uncomfortable but well. Anomer expressed real concern for Dagla, who was barely breathing.

Up another ladder they were guided, and they found themselves on rough wooden planking, a wharf of some kind. People were watching. Noetos could hear their laughter clearly. A final thump—probably Dagla—and then silence.

"Untie us," Noetos said. "We need to see to our man."

"You'll wait until I say," a voice growled.

Noetos wriggled his way over to where he'd heard the thump. Someone lay there, someone who wasn't breathing.

"Please! He's dying!"

"I said wait."

Anomer! Arathè! Lend me your strength now! Dagla—
Shh. Anomer will do it.

The next minute was among the most frustrating Noetos had ever endured. A great pull in the back of his mind, then a shout, followed by further shouting, scuffling sounds and a thump, then a splash. Someone—it must be Anomer—went to work on Dagla. Heavy breathing, then muttering, and a cry of anguish.

"What, Anomer? What? Is he all right?"

Hands at his neck, pulling the sack from his head. Anomer's sweatstreaked face hovering above his own.

"Dagla is dead," his son said to him.

The survivors stood on the dock, free of their bonds and surrounded by inquisitive locals. Noetos swept the sea with his eyes: the longboat had already drawn some distance away. He wanted to scream at the retreating cowards, but he held his tongue.

The boy was dead, and the blame rested firmly on the uncaring shoulders of that thug in the longboat. Noetos walked over to the body and bent bown beside the pale, dirt-streaked face.

"He never had a chance," Tumar said, joining him. "Even if we'd bin allowed t' help him, he woulda died. Head wound was too bad." The man had tears in his eyes. "He was a luv'ly boy. Never woulda hurt anyone. No need to hit him so hard. My knife an' I want to hear that captain do some explaining."

"So do I," said Noetos, "but explanations will have to wait a while."

Anomer approached. "Everyone else is well. What shall we do with Dagla?"

"That depends," said Noetos, looking at the young man's body, "on what the captain left us."

"No swords, no coin, no luggage," Seren reported. Was the miner weeping? Without doubt. "Though the ship's agent has a weapon 'n' a purse. I've secured 'em both."

Noetos grunted an acknowledgment. No luggage. On the first day of the voyage he'd taken the huanu stone and sewn it into the lining of his pack. He had reasoned that the danger of accidental contact with his children outweighed the need to have the stone on his person. Now the stone was lost; and, surprisingly, he felt more relief than disappointment.

"Not a man of his word, then," he said. "I cannot say I am surprised. Then neither will we keep ours."

He took a step forward, and another, carefully stretching cramped legs, until he reached the seaward end of the wharf. The *Conch* came into view, more than half a mile distant, slowly rounding the headland that defined the bay.

"We will return, Cylene," he whispered, though the words were as much for Kidson as for her. "I promise."

COSMOGRAPHER

CHAPTER 20

THE LAKE OF FIRE

WHAT DID CAPIXABA REALLY KNOW?

Torve sent a series of paired spiral kicks into the air directly above him, one-two, one-two, one-two, as fast as he could count. He wondered if he could lift himself completely off the ground with his own effort so he hovered unsupported in the air. Capixaba had said such a thing was not possible.

But the ancient progenitor of the Omeran Defiance had said a great many things, passed down from generation to generation without question, and Torve now knew some of them were not true. What had been his biggest lie? That the Defiance could only be used for self-expression? Or that it was a necessary part of what made him Omeran?

Both were untrue; he realised that now.

It was Capixaba he duelled with today, the most proficient exponent of Defiance ever to have lived. Or so said the lore. Was this also a lie?

The man was good, Torve would grant him that. He knew exactly how much to move in order to fake Torve out, a ripple of a shoulder or twitch of a thigh enough to trick him into moving precipitately. For the first few minutes of their encounter the imaginary master had entirely dominated him. Torve had found himself fully occupied with responding to Capixaba's movement.

And really, that was the problem. By accepting this man's teachings as heart and law, the Omerans had locked themselves into an ever-repeating pattern of subservience. Three thousand years of it, father and son, mother and daughter, bound by the ritual designed to set them free.

Yes, it had prevented them from being destroyed by the fierce Amaqi. But Torve had begun to harbour doubts about even that truth. Could this also be a lie? *Tell me, Capixaba, is there any truth in you?* He scissored his ramrod-straight legs left and right while supporting himself on the ground with splayed hands. The old master was there to meet his move, and flowed with it, always a step ahead. *As he always will be if I continue to use only the prescribed movements, the ones he invented.*

Do something new, he told himself.

Could he? Was it possible to escape millennia of restrictive practices? To lead rather than follow?

He would try.

Torve pushed back with his hands, landing on the balls of his feet. He tensed his strong leg muscles, then leaped forward, tumbling through the air, and landed on his hands, sending waves of pain through his wrists. But his illusory opponent had not tracked the move. A flick of the knee, an extension of the ankle, and his foot stopped a finger-width short of the master's head, which had still not turned to follow him.

The wave of pure ecstasy that swept through Torve at that moment was the single most powerful emotion he had ever experienced. It undid all the fear and loathing that had built up after the terrible events at Foulwater.

Had he become something other than Omeran? Would the Desert Children, whom he saw as his pure ancestors, approve of what he had done, or would they reject him?

Had they been watching from some spirit world as he killed those defenceless villagers?

He let go of his meticulous training, his pattern of Defiance comprised of endlessly repeated prescribed movements, and moved his body at random. Capixaba stood motionless, unable to oppose him.

His freed mind went back to that morning, weeks ago, when the villagers of Foulwater came to confront the Amaqi. Dryman had led them south of the village, back to the wreckage of the Yacoppica Tea House, to search for any sign of Lenares.

"She's disappeared," he said, encouraging Torve and Duon to search for any sign of her.

"We saw her swept away," Duon replied patiently. "No one could have survived such force of water. Of course she disappeared." He spoke as though to a child. Torve also could not understand what his master meant.

"No, it's not just that she's missing," the mercenary said testily. "I can't sense her any more. It's as though she no longer exists. Even if she died, even if her body is buried under rubble or crushed and broken into pieces, I ought to be able to sense her still."

Duon looked up from the wreckage he was searching through. "What are you talking about? How do you 'sense' her?"

"You are remarkably obtuse, even for a human," Dryman said. "Have you not yet worked it out?"

Duon looked at Torve. "Worked out what? What is the man talking about?"

Torve could not answer, of course, for fear that he might betray his master's secret; though it appeared his master was on the point of doing so himself. At that moment the first villagers, angry and out of breath, burst through the shelter belt and out into the open.

"What did you do to her?" one of them shouted in between deep gasps for breath. "What did you do?"

He had a flimsy stick in his hand, clearly broken from some bush. The others with him were similarly equipped.

"We know what they did," said a youngster. It was the curly-haired boy at whose parents' house Torve had stayed last night. "Foul murderers. I want to know why!"

"What is going on here?" Duon cried, as a line of twenty villagers, sticks and farm implements in their hands, advanced on them. "What did we do to whom?"

Dryman stepped forward. "We killed her," he said, and the villagers roared, an ugly sound.

Duon spun to face him. "I killed no one! What are you talking about? I don't understand."

"Those words will be on your lips when you die," Dryman said. "You'll never understand. Now get out of the way."

The message must have made its way back through the forest, as the next group of villagers to emerge—older men, well-armed with axes and swords—asked no questions.

"Get them!" a burly man cried, and the crowd surged forward.

Duon and Dryman had weapons, but Torve was unarmed. As an Omeran, he'd never been taught their use, so even if he could disarm the men rushing towards him, he could do nothing to oppose them. Nor could he protect his master, except by interposing himself between him and the mob. And that would slow them down only for a moment. Nevertheless, he took a step forward.

I'll be with you soon, Lenares.

Such anxiety, such helplessness, had settled upon him that he automatically thought of his Defiance. To think was to act; and, before he could check himself, he'd assumed the opening stance.

A single thought flashed through his mind, one of the five basic tenets of the discipline: *The Defiance can only be used for self-expression. It is not a weapon.* Then the mob was upon him.

He convinced himself they were imaginary and began throwing moves at his attackers. But for the first hectic seconds he could not make contact with them; his blows, learned from thousands of sessions on his own, stopped short. *It is not enough to dominate them, he told himself. I must strike.*

The first blow, delivered by the rigid outer edge of his right foot, took a man in the throat. The feel of his foot crashing into the man's neck, of the complex and delicate membranes of the throat tearing, crushed beyond repair, almost paralysed him with self-loathing. But the Defiance had him now, and he could no more stop than he could disobey his master, who was shouting: "Kill them! Kill them all!"

To his eternal shame, he felt a sort of glory come over him. *This is what all these movements are for; this is the real purpose of the Defiance.* Chops, thrusts, rapid blows, closed fists, open palms, patterns interwoven in the classic combinations he'd trained himself in his whole life, but taken to their logical conclusions. That the recipients of these blows didn't deserve to die barely touched his consciousness.

He danced, as the Children of the Desert had danced, and found his true self amidst death.

"Torve! Torve! They are fleeing!"

Duon's shout brought him back to himself. His real opponents had melted away and he'd carried on defying imaginary foes. He forced himself to stillness—it took an effort, even though his muscles screamed with agony—and bowed to the retreating backs of the villagers as they disappeared into the trees.

"Count them, Torve," his master said.

"What?"

"Your victims. Look around you."

Ten bodies lay still, scattered in a circle around him. Ten lives ended. No sign of the curly-headed boy; perhaps he'd run rather than fought. Three more people groaned with their injuries, two faintly stirring where they lay. The third—a woman—crawled slowly towards the trees.

Ten. He'd just killed ten people. Or, more correctly, his Omeran heritage had slain them. He bent over the first of the injured, to see what he could do for them.

"Greedy Torve," said his master cheerfully. "Leave them for me, would you?" He came over to the young man Torve was examining, who had suffered a broken back, and pulled out his research knife.

"Master!"

Duon walked over. "What is he doing?" he asked, as the man set to work on the villager.

A roar sounded from the trees. The villagers had returned, bringing reinforcements, including those who had been slower to arrive in the first place.

Dryman growled in frustration, pushing the villager aside with his boot. "You have angered them, Omeran," he said, in a mock-chiding voice. "They will keep coming until we wipe them all out. Those lying injured here will keep until we are through with this."

The villagers advanced, exercising much more caution. Dryman strode forward, raised his arms and, with an ear-popping *whoosh*, the vegetation around the villagers erupted into flame. Screams rose from the trees ahead as stragglers were suddenly surrounded by fire. The villagers who had already entered the tea house clearing were trapped between the three Amaqi and the flames.

"Take care of these fools," his master bade Torve. "I will subdue the village. Duon, stand where you are and do not interfere. Instead, reflect on your uselessness."

It was one thing for Torve to use his Defiance to defend himself against assault, however justified; entirely another to pursue and attack people who had lost the stomach for fighting. Yet his master had commanded him and Torve was compelled to obey.

Wasn't he?

The memories of that morning were already an inextricable part of who he had become. Revealed as a killer, gifted with the deadly legacy of his heritage. He had stepped—no, he had been *pushed*—over a line forbidden to his race, and was now a dangerous weapon in the service of his ruthless master.

But, his mind whispered, he had crossed one line. Could he not cross another? Could he not disobey his master? Could he not . . . could he not break free?

That morning he had tried. A dozen villagers had been trapped between himself and the burning trees and, from their faces, it was clear none of them wished to engage him. His master had gone in pursuit of the rest, striding into the flames as though they weren't there, leaving Torve alone to fulfil the man's wishes. Which were what exactly? *Take care of these fools.* How much room did those instructions give him? Could he literally take care of them? Succour them, ensure their continued good health?

No. Even as he formed the thought an immobilising burst of fear took hold of him, the paralysis that claimed him whenever he entertained any thought of disobedience. It was such a basic part of his nature that Torve had never questioned it until recently: were he to think of doing something forbidden, his muscles locked tight; while a decision not to do something he had been commanded led to a burst of energy blossoming within him, forcing him to act.

This attempt at disobedience was complicated: he'd intended doing the opposite of what he'd been bidden, using the ambiguity in the command he'd been issued. His master had been careless. His body tried to respond in two contradictory ways, by both paralysing and energising him. He screamed with the shock of it, and the villagers, taking heart from what must have appeared like an injury to them, scurried towards him.

His equal and opposite imperatives remained so only for a moment, until paralysis gave way to the immediate need for energy. This, he understood in that moment, must be what the Emperor had trained him for: to generate and use in his service the energy released by thoughts of disobedience. He'd always known he was a tool, but had not realised just how cynically he had been manipulated. By someone who called him "friend".

He moved with a precision and swiftness even greater than that which he had seen in the Children. Not a single inch of wasted momentum. It was almost as though he could predict where the villagers' slow, untrained bodies would be. Again the glory of his body's efficiency overwhelmed him and he ceased to consider the deadly consequences of his actions.

This time Duon did not recall him to himself. In fact, when he regained his normal thought patterns—rather, when his mind slowed to normality—the explorer was nowhere to be seen. The only things moving in the clearing were himself and half a dozen severely wounded villagers.

Very well, Torve told himself. *I have taken care of them. Now I will see what my master has done to subdue the village.*

Torve's thoughts returned momentarily to the present. A total of seventeen villagers slain by one Omeran: an unheard-of number for a member of a pacifist race. But the guilt associated with such behaviour gave way before the abhorrence he felt towards what had happened next. For what his master had done to the village.

Disoriented by smoke, Torve had stumbled through the smouldering trees for an age before finding the small village of Foulwater. The Emperor, or whoever the Emperor had now become, had already surrounded the village with a ring of fire. Deep red flames with bright orange cores rose in sheets from the ground itself, as though a chasm had opened into the molten underworld, a chasm that bent around until joining with itself at the far side of the town. Dryman himself stood in the middle of the main street, surrounded by the men and women of Foulwater, some begging him to put out the flames, others demanding to know what had happened to their brothers, sisters, husbands, wives, fathers and mothers. Their voices mixed with the crackle and roar of the flames to create a discordant sound that ground on Torve's already abraded nerves.

The ground shook, and through the shimmering heat Torve could see the Emperor raise his arms, an expression on his face like a mad prophet. At first he could not tell what was happening, but then he saw the ground within the fiery circle jerk and settle a foot lower. His master lifted his head and began to howl like a rabid wolf. The very air around Torve crackled as something essential was drawn from it and sucked towards the centre of the village. A great weight settled on the scene, pressing on everything inside the circle. Houses began groaning, and a roof gave way, collapsing with a sigh. The flames barely flickered with the wind it created. Another house crumbled, and another. Villagers put their hands to their heads; blood began to run from noses and ears. A small boy fell to his knees, vomiting blood. People struggled to move, and even standing was almost impossible. Steam and smoke made it difficult to see what was happening within the circle, but occasional glimpses more than sufficed. And still Torve's master howled, still the air crackled, and the encircled village continued to sink further below the land around it.

Something hot and red began to flood into the circle. For a moment Torve thought it was blood, but it was too thick for that. The chasm surrounding the village now spat molten lava, gouts of it being flung into the air and spattering back to earth. The villagers saw it too, and those that retained the ability to move dragged themselves closer to where the Emperor stood. One mother would not leave her two children, stricken and probably already dead from the weight. The lava found them first, flaring briefly into yellow flame as it consumed them, then her. Her cries were borne on the superheated air to Torve, whose tears evaporated before they could flow down his cheeks.

Houses burst into flame and sunk into the viscous lake forming where the disintegrating village had once stood. Some villagers, surrendering hope, threw themselves into the lake, their bodies briefly flaring yellow before being destroyed. A few climbed the remaining structures, only to have the houses collapse under them; they shrieked as they fell into the lake of fire. Others ran ever inward, surrounding the Emperor, no doubt reasoning that as he would not destroy himself they would be safe.

The smoke and superheated air made it difficult for Torve to see what happened next. The lava surged towards the Emperor—who began somehow to rise against the crushing weight, levitating into the air as though made of ash. A man grasped at his heel, hoping to escape, but his hand seemed to pass right through. A moment later the lava reached the remaining villagers, washing against their feet, and the final shriek these people gave as their bodies caught fire was a truly horrific sound.

A moment later the fires vanished and the lava ceased pouring out of the trench. The depression where the village of Foulwater had once stood slowly filled with liquid fire. The great heat reignited some of the surrounding trees. Torve's eyes stung; he could not see what had become of his master.

Who suddenly stood beside him, and spoke a single word.

The air around them changed subtly, and a cool wind
came from somewhere far above them. Within moments it
began to rain, rapidly increasing to a torrential downpour.
The rain was icy, stinging as it fell like needles from the
sky, and Torve had to shelter his face with his hand. Hail
began to fall, hissing like a thousand snakes as it drove into
the unnatural red lake. Colder still it became, as though
balancing out the heat of a few minutes ago, and it was all
ice now. When next Torve could raise his gaze to the site of
the village, the lake had lost its red glow and was coloured
a bluish-purple, an enormous bruise on the landscape.

"Who are you?" Duon said in a cracked voice. "What
have you done?" Amid the destruction Torve had not noticed the captain arrive.

"I am your Emperor," his master said to Duon, and the
weight returned. "You knew I was not merely a mercenary,
so do not act surprised. Bow before your Emperor, Captain
Duon."

The explorer doubled over under the weight, his face
striking the ground in a parody of the triple obeisance.

"Good. I do like worshipful servants," said the
Emperor.

Torve wanted answers to the captain's questions. "You
are not my master," he said.

"I am as much your Emperor as ever I was," the man had
replied, but his words, which were all he would say, left
much unanswered. Far too much.

Having relived the horror of that morning Torve continued his Defiance, but now his opponent was as elusive as
ash borne on a rising heat. The Omeran poured everything
of himself into his effort, but could not so much as touch
his insubstantial opponent. His master—but much more

than that—avoided every blow, no matter how skilled, how swift, how random. A mercenary, a master, an emperor—and a god. Unable to be defied.

The events of three weeks ago had not faded in Duon's memory either. He had not witnessed the obliteration of the village, having been trapped by opposing walls of flame as he ran through the forest, but that the man calling himself Dryman had somehow engineered the death and destruction of Foulwater could not be disputed. It seemed that none of the Amaqi were what they appeared: Torve, the butcher, possessed of the ability to kill people with his hands and feet; Lenares, the woman who could see truth, now lost; and Dryman, finally revealed as the Emperor of Elamaq and a magician of extraordinary abilities.

And himself, with a voice in his head.

All of which begged a number of questions, which the voice did not stint in asking. Who was this man who called himself Dryman? Had they even now learned all there was to know about him? What could Duon remember of him? When did he join the army, and who hired him? And why, if he was the Emperor and so powerful a sorcerer, had he not come to the aid of his own army in the Valley of the Damned?

This last question haunted Duon also. If the Dryman-magician-Emperor had possessed these powers back then, might he not have saved both the army and Duon's reputation? And if he had not, how had he come by them since? To the voice's chagrin, Duon had not actually seen the full extent of the man's magical powers with his own eyes, though Torve's garbled story had been harrowing enough. But to return to the point, why had the man not come to the aid of those who paid his wage? And what had prompted the great Emperor of all Elamaq to disguise himself—surely at enormous risk—then to endure deprivation as a part of his own army, only to see them fall to their enemies the Marasmians?

The Omeran had his suspicions, that was clear, but refused to talk about it. More than ever Duon wished Lenares was here. She would have had an interesting perspective on the horrors they had witnessed. She would have the insight he so keenly wished for.

And she would have asked more questions. She would have wanted to know what had been done to attract the anger of the villagers. Dryman—he had to stop calling him by that name—the Emperor had said something about having "killed her". Killed whom? Lenares? Or was this linked to something else Duon had noticed: a worrying pattern of death that followed them?

It had started immediately after the lions had attacked the army not far north of Talamaq. About the same time Dryman had first come to his attention, now he thought about it. Over the next few days Duon's outriders had found clawed and eviscerated corpses, one each morning, and it had been thought that the lions had trailed the army looking for more easy meat, picking off anyone who wandered too far from their fellows. But he'd not quite been convinced. The marks were not the same as those they had found on the remnants of Mahudia's corpse: there had been slashes, but not the crushing caused by those powerful jaws. It looked as though someone had carefully simulated injuries from the attack of a large animal.

Then there had been the incident in the camp of the Children of the Desert, as Torve had called them. One of their young had been found dead, cut and slashed to pieces. No attempt had been made to make it look accidental: it had to have been inflicted by humans. And it had been about that time that Duon had noticed the mercenary regularly disappearing at night, often taking the Omeran with him. Unfortunately he could not remember if he'd noticed them missing on that particular night.

On the flight north from Raceme Duon had tried to keep a close eye on Dryman, but the man had escaped his attention. A small boy had been found dead the next morning, but there were few marks on his body and it was supposed the boy had suffered some misadventure, a fall perhaps. Now Duon wondered. And there had been other deaths, some likely to be no more suspicious than the usual mishaps that befell a large, mobile population whose members found themselves in unfamiliar circumstances. True, there were more than he would have expected from an army of similar size, but these were untrained townspeople in the main. They were accidents.

Or perhaps the killer had become more wary.

And then there had been the moment when Dryman pulled out a knife and began to slice at one of the injured Foulwater villagers. Why? Torture to reveal the origin of the attack, or something even more sinister?

The voice in Duon's head asked numerous questions about the deaths, few of which the explorer could answer. Nor did he wish to engage the voice in extensive conversation. Not when he was refused answers to his own questions. Why should he share information with a voice that would not reveal who he was?

He knew he played a dangerous game. His thoughts had always been orderly, his mind disciplined, but now he needed to shield as much information from his parasitical passenger as possible. Whenever he needed to suppress his thoughts, he allowed himself to recall the images of horror in the ballroom of Raceme's Summer Palace: screams, smells, colours coalescing into red. The voice could retrieve nothing from him while those memories paraded across his mind. But all it would take was one slip, one revelation of knowledge previously kept from the voice, and he did not doubt he would discover the damage his possessor could do to him.

His conversations became rapid and concise. Tell the Emperor the minimum necessary to satisfy him, be obedient at all times, stay out of his way; but listen carefully to everything said, watch everything done, and ask gentle, probing questions whenever he was sure the voice was not listening. What he needed was someone to share this with. He wished the cosmographer had not died, and wondered if the Emperor had not somehow rid himself of her. And all the while Duon wondered about the effect on his sanity of this speculation, and of the voice and the deadly game he played with it.

Three blessed weeks without any research ended abruptly not far north of a small port town, the name of which Torve did not know. They set a fire not far from the edge of what looked like a deep forest, and lay silently, as they always did, waiting for sleep to take them. Duon's breathing evened out as the unhappy man finally relaxed.

"I thought he would never fall asleep," his master eventually said. "Rise, Torve; I have found a candidate upon which to continue my studies."

He rose. How could he refuse? But first he put out a

hand and touched the man on the arm. "I want you to tell me why you are doing the research," he said.

His master peered at him, puzzled. "For the same reason as always, friend," he said. "So we can uncover the secrets of immortality. It has been our lifelong task, and we are nearer to achieving our goal than ever."

Torve willed himself to stillness. Nearer their goal? Nonsense. Their last conversation had established the uselessness of continuing the research.

"I know why the Emperor wished to torture and kill," he said. "But I don't know why the Son wishes to continue his work."

The pause before his master spoke was just a little too long. "The Son? What have the gods to do with anything?"

"You admitted you gained access to his memories. You gave him far more, it seems: a disguise to protect his identity from Lenares and the others around him, and great powers to destroy those who oppose him. Master, I think you are no longer entirely human. Don't you realise the Son possesses you? What did you think was happening when you stood in the centre of Foulwater while fire bloomed in a circle around you? Was that the natural behaviour of the Emperor who just a few months ago had forbidden even the mention of the gods? I know what Lenares would have said. She would have recognised the hole in the world, centred on you. She would have said, 'You are the Son.'"

No pause this time. "I am more than I was, it's true," he said. "Just by having been within me, the Son has left me certain gifts. How could it have been otherwise? The gods are so much greater than us, greater by far even than an emperor, and they do not leave us unchanged. I have gained powers, Torve, but I am still mortal."

The hunger in his voice, on his face, was genuine, even though his words were not. Just sounds designed to keep his pet docile.

"Mortal for now," Torve said, making docile sounds of his own. Pretending to be pacified. "You'll win the secret one day."

"Perhaps today," said the being claiming to be his master, as it took up a stick from the fire to use as a torch. "But not if we stay here talking."

Torve nodded, his thoughts swirling around his head. If the man ordering him about wasn't his master, then did he need to be obeyed? Or, if as was more likely, the man was partly his master and partly something else, how much loyalty was he owed?

As the two men left the campsite, Duon allowed his breathing to resume its normal rate.

The questions repeated themselves in various permutations as the man—the best description Torve could give him—walked a purposeful path through scrub towards an open space. It was time to put his theory to the test, time to systematically attempt to disobey his master. Just one act, he was sure, would be enough to break his conditioning. He tried to stop walking, but that was too blatant an action. His legs resisted him: he did not even break stride. Something more subtle, then.

His flickering torch revealed the strangest scene. A woman lay on the ground, elbow, hip and foot touching the earth, body facing what was obviously the shell of a burned building. Not a house, surely; the ruin was far too large for that. But there was something strange about the woman. She seemed to be lying unnaturally, her body held rigid, with far less of it in contact with the ground than looked normal.

The Emperor approached. A small shelter had been built to one side of her, as though protecting her from the weather. The woman could see them as they moved in front of her: her eyes were open, and they moved backwards and forwards between her two visitors. Not a statue, then. But her face was curiously immobile, and she made no reaction to their nearness. The remnants of a meal lay in front of her: mashed food of the sort fed to babies, and a half-full pitcher of water.

Something was very wrong.

"This must be the Daughter's work," his master said. "Look, Torve; she has been anchored here by someone of subtle power." He touched her skin; the woman did not flinch. "See, she cannot move."

So saying, he drew his knife.

The woman's eyes darted left and right in the familiar panicstricken dance of those about to die.

"I'm going to carve a piece out of you," the man said conversationally.

Her eyes widened, circled with fear. But the man did not make good his threat. Instead, he bent down and angled his head until he could see what she saw.

"She's been placed here so she cannot avoid the sight of this ruin," his master said, musing. "Something happened here that she was responsible for, I think, and her punishment is to lie in this place and contemplate what she has done. Someone she valued has perished here as a result of her actions. I am right, Torve," he added, looking into her eyes and reading assent there. "A cruel punishment: she's already half insane."

He licked his lips. "Perfect for our purposes. I wonder if I can make her talk?"

He soon found out he could make her scream. As soon as he cut into her she cried out, and he took a step backwards.

"The woman is a magician," he told Torve. "I felt it through the knife. And magician though she is, she's bound by a spell I have never seen."

"Something the Emperor has never seen, or something new even to the Son?"

"Both, Torve. Don't you understand? I am both."

Curiosity consumed the man. He would walk her to the gates of death in good time, but first he sought to discover what had happened to her, and who had done it. She held back as much as she could, showing a bravery Torve had never before seen, but her immobility made her so uniquely vulnerable something had to give eventually.

"Martje!" she screamed. "My name is Martje!"

"Good," his master crooned. He turned to Torve. "There is no spell known in the world or beyond it that can force a person to tell what they wish to keep secret. Persuasion and threat are our only weapons, and neither are magical. But I do have a simple incantation to ensure that what is said is the truth."

He bent over and whispered something in the woman's ear, then sat back and watched her for a moment.

"Who paralysed you?" he asked.

"I paralysed myself."

"See? Cooperation is the easiest way forward. Every

truth you tell wins a reward. Your first reward is a change of researcher." He handed his bloodied knife to Torve.

"Why did you paralyse yourself?" Torve asked her.

"I sought to cast a spell on my guests. One of them had harmed my son and heir."

"What spell?"

"The Rite of Entrapment."

The Emperor hissed. "Powerful magic. But the spell that binds you now is not the Rite of Entrapment. Where are the others involved in the incantation? The woman, the magician and the victim?"

Torve knew nothing about such rites; nor, he was sure, did his Emperor. This was entirely from the Son.

"The victim broke the spell," the woman said. "He set the others free but re-bound me, I do not know how."

"And who is this powerful victim foolish enough to be snared, yet strong enough to escape?"

The woman refused to answer.

His master scowled. "I see. More afraid of him than of us."

He sought and held Torve's gaze. "I want there to be no misunderstanding, my friend. You are to press this woman hard, using every technique I have taught you, in the attempt to discover who this man was. If there is someone this powerful loose in this part of the world, I want to know all about him."

Torve considered his master's careful phrasing of the command, and wondered whether the man had read his mind, whether he had sensed his servant's earlier attempts at disobedience. He felt the familiar surge of energy associated with an effort to turn the command aside. Even an attempt to evade such a direct command, to prevaricate, proved futile.

You might have my body, Torve thought as he set to work, *but you do not have my will*. But even as he said it he despised himself anew.

To confound the situation still further, the woman provided real proof of one of Torve's own theories. "Death does not arrive so much as life leaves," he'd claimed years ago. His master had rejected the idea. He'd believed—wanted, Torve thought—death to be a tangible thing, a presence that could be fought or denied. But the cryptic words uttered by the paralysed magician in the moments before her death suggested an even more fundamental truth.

"What do you see?" Torve asked.

"A membrane," she whispered. She knew what awaited her, but all resistance to the will of her tormentor had long been excised. She was almost cooperative, very nearly curious, so skilled had Torve and his master become. "A thin wall."

"What is beyond it?"

She did not answer for perhaps three breaths, then said: "I do not know."

"I will take you there and bring you back," Torve said, his stomach churning at the terrifying things he was forced to do. He took a deep breath and stopped her heart for the first time.

Only the many years of experience they had spent together enabled the two researchers to keep their subject alive. Torve pushed air into her lungs, blowing directly down her throat, while his master pumped her chest. It was far more difficult than usual, due at least in part to the magic fixing her in place, but eventually they brought her back.

They had done this many times before, but had never received anything but the vaguest of reports from those they retrieved from death. This time, however, the woman returned to them with a clear answer.

"I saw a void," she said, her eyes wide. "And in the void were bright lights, a myriad of bright lights. Each one . . ." She paused for breath.

"Yes?" the Emperor said eagerly.

"Each one is a soul. I will be a star. Let me go there. Please."

"There is something lacking in her explanation," said the Emperor, though his hands shook with excitement. He spoke again, in another voice: "I have been in the void, I have seen the stars, but I have never been able to reach them. The stars have immense power. I will return there now and observe. Take her through again."

And, in that moment, Torve seized his chance.

"No," he said.

CHAPTER 21

PATINA PADOUK

THE STORM BROKE DURING THEIR second week in the jungle. It had been building for days. The humidity grew dire, an enervating dampness in the air that set them sweating and chafing. Layer upon layer of clouds built on the eastern horizon, always closer, always darker, whenever the endless treescape relented enough to give the Amaqi travellers a glimpse of the wider world. The forest itself seemed in no need of a dousing, such was its verdancy. Jungle giants of grey and green, their broad trunks swathed in vines and creepers, let little light into the understoreys below their vast canopies, but myriad plants grew there nonetheless, many directly from the trees themselves, adopting gaudy colours to attract inquisitive insects to their pollen and seeds—and sometimes their mouth-like traps. On the forest floor brightly coloured fungi, in every shape imaginable, compered with ferns and young trees for the remaining space. An environment more unlike that in which he had grown up was hard for Duon to imagine.

And now the rains had arrived, making the journey north surreal, almost dream-like. Though the forest was dense to the point of being impenetrable, the rain still found a way through, casting a grey haze over everything more than a few paces away. The travellers' view of more distant vistas was completely obscured, which made route-finding extraordinarily difficult.

Or it would have, had they been travelling as three ordinary men and their hired porters.

Duon had no doubt that the mercenary—he persisted in granting him that epithet despite recent revelations—could find his way through the forest in absolute darkness. Since the destruction of Foulwater even a fool would have known Dryman was not what he seemed, and Duon was no fool. He'd suspected the man as soon as he'd first seen him, since he'd first heard his glib explanations. But now he had learned the mercenary was no ordinary man. Duon knew he wasn't even anything as simple as a magician. No, he journeyed with a mad, blood-lusty god-Emperor and his servant.

The words spoken between master and servant had confirmed beyond doubt that Dryman was the Emperor of Elamaq. Though Torve had spoken of his master in the third person, it seemed clear that he was speaking of Dryman, the Emperor—or, at least, the Emperor's body, possessed by the Son.

Duon had been shocked beyond belief at what he'd learned. No wonder the mercenary could speak with confidence of the Emperor's will; no wonder he could command the Omeran's obedience. The magic was explained by the presence of the Son, a second great shock; and the third was the confirmation of his two companions' nocturnal activities. "Research" into immortality, involving torturing innocents to death. The burden of shame that fell on him at this knowledge was impossible to bear. He felt broken inside. That the truth could have been kept from him for so long! That the Emperor had deliberately engineered the deaths of his own subjects! That he had given himself to the dark heart of a god intent on breaking the world! Together with that god, he and his servant were taking lives in the most gruesome manner imaginable. It could not be borne. It could not continue.

But it did continue, despite his resolution—and despite his attempts to break free. After the night of revelation, as Duon thought of it, Dryman had led them to the coast and the port of Sayonae. After a protracted and futile attempt to hire porters for the long journey north through the jungle, Duon had tried to convince the man to take ship, but he refused even to consider it. Duon then tried to find a ship that might take him alone. However, none would risk the autumn *mausum*, the time of unpredictable sea storms.

The voice cornered him. *I wish you to remain with this man*, it said. *Should you attempt to leave, I will compel you to return.* After this there had seemed no point in considering flight.

A group of six men, who turned out to be brothers, approached Dryman just north of the city and offered themselves as porters. "We could not approach you in the city," they said, "for we are not well liked there. But we know the jungle well, and can guide you through the skirts of the deep forest." Dryman accepted their offer without question.

One of the brothers had died on their second night in the jungle, torn apart by a wild animal; except, of course, he hadn't been killed by an animal, unless that name could be applied to the . . . the *thing* that now led them through the rain. As much as anything, it appeared, Dryman saw the porters as a ready source for his research.

Duon's true sympathies lay with the Omeran. The night of revelation had seen a most dreadful fight between Torve and the Emperor. Duon had not caught the gist of it, but he believed Torve had tried to defy his master, perhaps when his master had taken the guise of the Son, but the disobedience had been unsuccessful. Duon had always believed that it was simply physically impossible for Omerans to disobey their masters, but it appeared the truth was more complicated. It must be; what else would explain how Torve was able to mount an attack? He attacked his master in the same way he'd gone for those poor villagers, but hadn't landed a single blow. It almost seemed as though the mercenary had ordered the Omeran to attack him—surely a difficult concept for one brought up to do his master no harm. The mercenary had given his servant a fearful beating, necessitating a two-day delay beside a stream at the border of the great forest to allow the Omeran to recover.

"We'll camp here," said the oldest of the brothers, breaking in on Duon's thoughts. "As good a place as any, in this rain."

He had found a dead banyan tree, the trunk gone and only the roots remaining, shaped like a cage. It would keep away any animals foolish enough to be out in this weather, and, when the oiled tarpaulin was draped over it, would offer at least partial shelter from the curséd rain.

Two nights and a day of rain, and already all previous hardships had faded into dim memories. How could the Had Hills or even Nomansland have been as bad as this constant heat, this incessant chafing, and the smack smack

smack of drops gathered by branches far above and flung at them?

The sinister voice in his head had largely been absent in the last fortnight; surprising given what Duon had witnessed. Perhaps the magician knew it already, or maybe he had other matters to attend to. Duon wondered what had happened to the other two who could hear the man's voice: that quietly spoken girl with the haunted eyes and the bookish Falthan priest. If what kept the voice away from Duon was a preoccupation with their affairs, they must indeed be suffering. Perhaps they suffered for the same reason he did.

Did each group travel with a god? Was it as simple as that?

He tossed the question around in his mind as the porters prepared the meal. Was there a simple symmetry about the three groups—Falthan, Bhrudwan, Amaqi—that no one seemed to have noticed? Had the Father, long believed to have passed out of time after his banishment by his children, returned, now to journey with the Falthans? And did the Daughter accompany the Bhrudwans? Three groups, three magician-afflicted messengers, three gods.

Not for the first time, not for the last, he wished the cosmographer were here. She would know.

Torve stirred in his sleep, then rose to reluctant wakefulness. No doubt, he reflected with deep bitterness, he slept poorly because he was accustomed to being woken during the night. The Emperor-god had shaken him awake but once on this latest leg of their journey, believing he could risk killing one of the porters, but he'd not chanced a second. Torve had no doubt that as soon as they discovered another town, village or even isolated family, he would be called to witness—no, to take part in—more deaths. A brief respite, then, in the endless killing, but he couldn't sleep through the night.

His bruises had almost faded to match his dark skin, though he was some way from a full recovery. The deepest bruising, though, could not be seen. His master had known, he had *known*, what Torve had been planning; had been clever enough to goad him into an act of disobedience. Torve had defied the god, hoping it would be easier than defying the Emperor. But as soon as he had said the word he'd realised it simply didn't work that way: the one he defied was not the one who commanded him. The god could not compel him with the force of his breeding, but the god didn't need to. He had other ways of ensuring obedience. So Torve's cry of "no" had been punished as if it had been disobedience, and he'd submitted, as he had to, to the beating in the knowledge his Defiance had not benefited him.

And as for his Defiance, he would never use it again. He'd made the resolution even as the blows crashed down upon him, and that, at least, was something he had control over.

He could not flee. The Emperor had instructed him to remain by his side. Even if the Son were to explicitly countermand this, it would not have the force necessary. He must remain with his master.

Was there any hope? He could see none. He had nothing but memories. His eyes filled with tears whenever he recalled those days of discovery with Lenares in the House of the Gods, and he wished with his whole heart he could go back to that place, with her, even for one day.

*   *   *

"Up, explorer. A wet day awaits. Onward to the heart of the jungle!"

Duon hated the man's false cheeriness. Everything about him was false. He would almost have preferred the man to reveal himself and control the expedition by force rather than subterfuge. He could not decide whether it was worse to have been gulled unknowingly, or to play along with it now.

"Very well," he said, and stowed his damp bedroll in his pack.

Speech seldom passed between the men as they made their way through the forest. Even the porters said little, which was unusual. Duon had a fair degree of experience with such men, and they generally kept themselves and their clients amused with stories, songs and chatter. This group, however, despite being brothers, walked with their heads down, hoods up and mouths closed. Perhaps it was the weather; but Duon could not remember much, if any, conversation around the campfires or on the trail even before the rains had come.

To his surprise, someone broke the silence.

"There, off to the left, on the far side of the stream."

The words came from behind him, where the younger brothers walked. An answering grunt floated back from ahead. Duon turned his head, but could see nothing.

"Again."

This time he caught a flash of movement. Some animal. He found himself unconcerned. What animal had the faintest chance of harming them when they journeyed with a god?

There were no more announcements of sightings that morning, but gradually Duon realised they were being tracked—even herded—by people carrying spears and dressed in rags.

He had been to Andratan, but had travelled much of the way by ship. This forest and its inhabitants were new to him. But not to the porters, who began to talk in worried whispers.

"Pay the creatures no heed," Dryman said, as the brothers whispered amongst themselves. "We will press on."

"But we must pay them heed," said the oldest brother. "This is their land, and they do not allow strangers to traverse it save on the approved routes."

"Their land? I wandered here before their ancestors rose from the swamps. I am home; why should I give way to latecomers?"

Duon had no idea what the brothers made of this speech, but it told him something. At the very least the man walking with them had lived here for a time, thousands of years ago. Perhaps these trees hid the birthplace of a god.

They came to another innocuous stream, swollen by the persistent rain but otherwise indistinguishable from hundreds of others they had crossed. On the far side the ground rose, and here the trees seemed taller, darker and more tormented, as though the creepers and vines not only grew in competition with the forest giants but also sought to strangle them. His eyes were drawn up: the canopy seemed impossibly high, hundreds of feet above them, lost in the mist. And he could see movement up there. Small animals, monkeys perhaps, running to and fro along vines seemingly strung for the purpose.

"Far enough," came a voice.

The travellers halted. People had materialised on the stream's far bank, spears and blades in their hands. There were six of them, all tall, brown-skinned and black-haired, their clothing scant but serviceable. Barefoot; an odd lack. How could they walk barefoot on ground littered with the detritus of the forest, Duon wondered. There were reptiles and insects here that would fasten on exposed skin, injecting poison, or would paralyse, secrete muscle-eating venom or even drink the blood of unwary travellers. Or so said the porters. The blood-drinkers, at least, were true: fat slug-like slimers that expanded as they drew blood from their host. Duon found himself constantly brushing them from his neck and hands. He could not imagine how the people on the far bank of the stream survived the forest in near-nakedness.

He laughed at himself. He was making the mistake explorers always made: assuming the inhabitants of an area were more primitive than he simply because they were differently adapted to their environment.

"You may go no further." No trace of an accent: pure Fisher Coast Bhrudwan, at least to Duon's ears. "No discussion. You turn around now." The spears were raised.

Duon had been in situations like this before, had even lost men, but had never faced them with the singular lack of fear he experienced now. *This is not my concern*, he told himself. He did not expect the mercenary to ask his advice.

"Why do you bar our way?" Dryman asked.

His answer was an arrow from the trees. It hissed through the air and embedded itself in his chest with a thunk like an axe into wood.

The man didn't even blink, he simply smiled. A moment later he turned to the porters. "Do not move. I am not about to die. If you try to flee I will kill you."

"This is our land," the spokesman, the shortest among the six on the bank, said eventually. His voice retained most of its poise; an admirable effort, Duon thought.

"I'm not disputing that," Dryman said quietly, and the fletching of the arrow moved as he talked. It had to be deep in his lung. "But we need to travel north. Why would you prevent us making our journey?"

Two arrows this time. Perhaps from a distance it appeared that the first arrow had lodged in hidden armour, although the sound had clearly been stone point on flesh. The same sound—thwack, thwack—rang out clearly as the arrows took the mercenary in the stomach.

No sound from beyond the stream, but two of the porters moaned in fear.

"We will walk around your sacred heart if you wish it," Dryman offered. "We have no desire to learn your secrets or steal your land."

Twenty arrows at least. Most found their target, but a few flew past the mercenary into the jungle behind them, and one took a porter just above the knee. The boy shrieked, and his brothers cried out in consternation. They gathered around him, calling instructions to each other, and one of them threw off his pack and began rummaging through it. Duon was puzzled for a moment at their urgency, then the boy took a fit, his limbs spasming.

Poison-tipped. Perhaps he ought to fear, after all.

A sudden question: why was the mercenary concerned with immortality if he could survive such an assault? The man looked like a hedgehog, yet was clearly unaffected by a dozen and a half arrows.

"We will make our way along the stream, keeping to this side," said Dryman. "If you wish to waste any more arrows, make sure you hit me. Otherwise you'll lose them in the forest."

No arrows this time, at least. The mercenary stepped forward, one foot in the stream, then turned and addressed the porters.

"Leave him. He's already dead, though it will take some time for his body to stop twitching. You know about the foresters' use of poison, but you clearly do not know enough. Andali poison has no antidote. Line up behind me and say nothing."

"If you stray we will kill your servants," said the tribe's spokesman.

"I understand."

Which was more than could be said for the porters.

"We're not leaving our brother," the oldest said in a thick voice. "We will return home with his body."

"You will not," said Dryman heavily. "This is what will happen if you do not do as I say. As soon as I leave this place without you, you will die under their arrows. And even if they stay their hand, you will die from any serious attempt to carry your brother back through the forest. Andali is fatal in minute quantities. In fact, I suspect at least one of you will perish as a result of the ministration you've already offered your dead brother."

The remaining brothers cowered away from Dryman, as afraid of the pin-cushioned figure as of the bowmen hidden on the far side of the stream. One of them began to cough, and put a shaking hand to his mouth.

"I'm not a heartless man," Dryman continued, in the face of all the evidence. "Take a few moments to assess your options. But don't touch your brother."

*　　*　　*

As they walked, the stream grew before their eyes, swollen by rain that had increased markedly in intensity in the hours since they had begun their guided trek. They were being led by the inhabitants of the forest, it seemed. Though Torve had heard the conversation between his master and the spokesman for the natives, he had not understood it: the language used was one he had never heard. Dryman had seemed to acquiesce to something. Surprising they would make a request of him, given the fearful veneration they now displayed towards him.

Torve was soaked through to his skin, but that did not account for his constant shivering. That was due entirely to the appearance of the man directly in front of him.

"I'm not immortal, Torve," the Emperor-god had said. "The Son has blessed me with unnatural power, that is true, and it grows within me every day. But I can still be slain, and I will eventually die of old age, if nothing else. You must believe your old friend the Emperor exists, and cares for you still."

Torve had not replied. It was not the Emperor talking. The weight pressed down on all of them—the surviving porters could feel it—and the man's voice had taken on the deep timbre of the Son. There was nothing left of his so-called friend in that arrow-pierced shell. Torve put his head down and concentrated on not stumbling in this world of insanity.

The travellers were escorted across the stream, which, under the influence of the rain, had become a deep, muddy brown torrent stretching a full hundred paces from bank to bank. The three remaining porters stumbled over rocks, then waded into the deeper water, each grasping a rope

strung there to aid the crossing. Duon winced at their blank
expressions. They were just the latest to wear what he had
come to consider the "mercenary face": the look of shock
and loss one experienced after having been in the man's
presence for any length of time.

As he grappled with the rope, knowing the swift stream
would take him if he lost his grip, something buzzed in
his head: . . . aai ninn see hou. Uee whirr aah see . . . followed by silence. Not the usual voice. It had sounded like
the tongueless language Arathé used, but he'd not heard
enough to be sure.

A genuine path wound up the bank on the far side of the
stream. The forest people's spokesman invited the mercenary to walk with them, and Duon heard one of the porters
breathe a relieved sigh as the man moved well ahead of
them. *Yes, son, we're all frightened of him.*

They walked for perhaps half an hour, in what direction
Duon couldn't tell. His well-trained spatial senses were
of no use here: the rain. hid any evidence of sunlight, and
the path had twists and turns enough to defeat him. Running now would ensure either a swift—though not swift
enough—death at arrow-point, or a slower death lost in the
forest. Of course, he would not be permitted to run.

No such stricture bound the porters, though they must
have made the same assessment as he. There seemed no
other reason for them to keep shuffling in the mercenary's
wake.

A wall of darkness emerged from the gloom. Some sort
of meteorological effect? Another manifestation of the hole
in the world? It said everything about his mental state that
he suspected a magical before a natural cause. The wall

gained solidity as they drew closer, finally resolving into a cliff stretching up out of sight.

By invitation of the forest people, they camped that night at the base of the cliff, their chosen site partially sheltered from the rain. It was only when a bonfire was lit that the rest of the people came out from the trees, at least fifty of them, half with bows and what were likely poisoned arrows in quivers on their backs. Each of them walked up to where the mercenary sat, peered at the arrows lodged in his torso, and then returned to the other side of the fire and found somewhere to sit. The whole process took nearly an hour. Dryman said nothing during this time, impassively accepting their scrutiny.

Eventually the spokesman came forward and nodded to the mercenary. "My people are satisfied," he said. "We will take you further in, as you request, but you are not to remain there to dwell. We are our own masters."

Dryman laughed, drawing every eye. "You've chosen to do as I request? Ah, you always were a stubborn people. Request? Choice?" He laughed again. "Of course I will not dwell here. I imagine the jungle has destroyed every trace of my former home."

"It is as you suppose," the man said carefully. His speech remained cultured, smooth, his manners as one treating with a dangerous beast. *Wise man*, Duon thought.

"Last time my home was not at the top of a cliff," said Dryman.

"The land has changed. Warriors regularly approach the site, seeking to test their courage, but none have profaned it. The stories tell of many earthquakes, of the rumbling of the ground, of the creeping movement of the earth over the generations. Nothing remains the same, Keppia."

The mercenary raised his gaze to the spokesman, who did not flinch. "Some things do," he said softly. "My name, for instance. No one else in the world remembers that name.

"We will arise at dawn," he continued. "We will travel whether it rains or not."

"The *mausum* will afflict us for weeks yet. Do you not remember the late summer winds from the sea?"

"I remember many things, and, as you say, things I remember may have changed. The forest once received rain all year."

"Not now, Keppia. The *mausum* pushes west from the warm sea across the cooling autumn land, and our forest prospers."

"Yet the fishermen and the farmers eat at it from the south, and I have no doubt those living north of Patina Padouk gnaw the forest edge also."

The spokesman spat. "You speak true. We cannot hold them back. I lived in their lands a long time, and returned to tell my brothers why their trees are being taken."

The mercenary smiled. "Did they understand?"

"No. And two of them, entranced by my story of cities and powdered women, left the forest. I will not go back there."

"No, you will not." The comment sounded more like a prediction than an observation.

"My warriors wonder if they might retrieve their arrows," the spokesman offered.

"Oh? So they can mount them above their hearths as a boast to their grandchildren? Tell your warriors to wait. I will wear them as a reminder to you of my forbearance.

Inform them I will return their arrows on the day I leave your lands. May that day be soon."

"May that day be soon," the spokesman echoed, in what sounded like a ritual.

The forest people contented themselves with their own company, remaining on the far side of the fire, directly under the cliff. The three porters took themselves off, faces raw with weeping, no doubt to observe some sad memorial for their lost brothers. The mercenary sat perfectly still: in the time it took for sleep to settle on Duon, two arrows worked their way out of the man's chest and clattered to the ground. The last sounds Duon heard were those of the forest, the chittering, cawing night animals and the patter of the unrelenting rain.

He awoke twice during the night. The first was a brief, half-conscious stirring at the sound of a voice in his mind: . . . *Don't touch them. They'll kill you without even piercing the skin. I told you coming this way was foolish; far better if we had taken ship* . . . The voice of the Falthan priest faded away to nothing, merging with his own anxious, unfathomable dreams.

The second was to see Torve rise at the bidding of a dark figure. So the mercenary would carry on his so-called research even among people who seemed to treat him as a god. The idea was shocking even in light of the man's behaviour.

A light touch woke Torve from a shallow sleep. He had been expecting it, of course. New people, same experiments. As he opened his eyes he wondered whether his master would try to replicate his success with the woman near Sayonae.

"Torve? Shh, don't say anything."

He froze. "Lenares?"

She put a hand to his lips. "Please, please, be quiet. Get up and follow me."

He rose, trying to convince himself this was a dream, but he knew he was awake. He wanted Lenares alive, of course he did, more than anything, but he could not bear any more disintegration of the order of things. The world had become an unfamiliar place, where torrents of water fell from the sky, emperors went about in disguise, Omerans slew people with the Defiance, and people came back from the dead. So his mind tried to reject it. But she was no dream. He put his hand on her bare, cool forearm and allowed her to guide him away from the camp.

"Lenares? How can it be you? You are dead, drowned, lost."

"No, Torve. The Daughter rescued me. Now please, do what I tell you. Don't you say anything more. The Daughter says this is the tricky bit. We have to avoid the Patouk sentries. Hold your breath and put your feet in the same places I do."

A hundred paces from the campfire the forest was completely black. He wondered how she would find her way, but she seemed to step with confidence through the foliage.

They came to a path and began to ascend. After a few minutes of this they both began to breathe heavily, and Lenares tugged his arm, indicating he should stop.

"I am alive," she whispered in his ear, rather unnecessarily, he thought. Her warm breath made him tingle.

"How?"

"I told you, the Daughter saved me. I was swept away but the Daughter kept me from falling. She wanted my body to live in, but I knew she would steal it from me, so I tricked her. Then I caught her in my trap, and now she has to do what I tell her to."

"Lenares, I still think I'm going to wake up and realise you are dead, and discover I was dreaming this." He took her upper arms in his hands. Her eyes glowed, perhaps giving off their own illumination or capturing the faintest of forest lights, but he could see nothing of her features. "I don't want to wake up."

"If I was a dream, would I do this?" she said, and kissed him.

"Yes," Torve said, after a moment. "That is exactly what you would do."

"The Daughter wants us to go on. She says we need to be at the house before dawn."

"The house? Where are we going?"

"To the House of the Gods. The Daughter says there is an entrance nearby."

"Can you trust her?"

"No. But I must go. I must sit on the seat and look into the bronze map. We could live there, Torve! Just you and I!"

"You would let the world be ripped apart?"

"Well, no. We still have to defeat the gods. But that will be easy now I have one of them under my control. It won't be long, Torve, until we can live together."

The deep longing in her voice stirred his own desire, and he found himself weeping as they resumed their climb. She told him her story, and he praised her cleverness, the more so because he very nearly understood what she'd done with her numbers. His responses to her detailing of the capture pleased her immensely; it seemed no one else had followed the numerate description of her feat.

"Lenares, defeating the Son will not be as easy as you seem to think," he said when her story ended. "Do you know where he is?"

"The Daughter seems to think he is nearby, but can't pinpoint him exactly. Captain Duon is in your camp, and so two of the three who hear voices in their heads are close together: the priest is with the Falthans, who are nearby. They brought me here."

He wanted to hear how she had joined the Falthans, and also how the Falthans had made it past the boundary of the forest people's lands, but more immediate questions raised themselves. "We must hope the Bhrudwans are far away, then, or we will bring the gods down on us."

"But they are already here," Lenares said reasonably.

"Yes, they are. The Son is in our camp. Lenares, he is in Dryman, the man we travelled north with. You know you could never read him."

"He had some way of keeping himself hidden from me?"

"It's even more complicated. Dryman is the Emperor."

He'd said it without thinking, and marvelled that he'd been able to disobey a command. But a moment's thought found the reason: his master had already given the truth away. He'd been commanded to keep all his master's secrets, but his identity was no longer a secret, so he had not been disobedient.

But he'd *thought* he had at the moment he'd spoken.

"That's what you've been unable to tell me all along, isn't it," she said. "He could hide himself from me because I've never seen his Emperor face, just his Dryman face."

"It is part of what I could not tell you. Forgive me, Lenares, but there are still things I cannot say. I am trying so hard to be disobedient, but the compulsion is very hard to break."

She said nothing, but he could sense her disappointment. Far better that than what she would think were he to reveal the rest of the truth.

They climbed for at least two hours, perhaps much more, until they found themselves above the clouds and under a starlit sky. He persuaded her to rest, though he could sense she wanted to continue. The tentative beginnings of a new day could be seen off to their right.

"We're nearly there," Lenares said, and led him on.

She stopped him with slight pressure to his hand. "I learned who my true mother is," she told him in her typical abrupt manner, without preamble. "I am from a farm near Sayonae, but it burned down," she said, and his heart sank. "My mother—"

"No." *No, it could not be; such cruelty would not be permitted. The Father in his mercy, in his mercy, in his mercy . . . .* "Lenares, I do not want to hear this story."

"Torve, the truth cannot hurt us." He could see her eager smile in the growing light, and it squeezed his heart.

"Yes, Lenares," he said. "It can."

"My mother . . . my birth mother . . . is not a nice person. When we went—"

"Please, no more, not now. I want to be happy with you for a while."

She frowned at him, but did not continue her telling. They walked in silence for a time, and Torve wondered if he could possibly keep the truth from her. Was everything a circle?

"We're here," she said.

The sun's bright disc rose above the tree-lined horizon and threw their surroundings into relief. They stood in the centre of a wide plateau a thousand paces above the surrounding jungle. The ground was relatively flat and almost completely treeless; small shrubs were the dominant species, the larger specimens bending away from the sun in the still morning as though sculptured by an invisible wind.

"We're late," Lenares said, and led him to the only two trees on the plateau.

The sun had already caught their upper branches, colouring the broad leaves a virile green. They stood either side of a faint path, a portal into an ancient house. She led him between the trees, and the sun disappeared. Bark turned to rock walls and leaves to sand. Within moments they were descending a stone staircase into a narrow, lake-floored fissure.

"She was telling the truth," Lenares said, and turned to him, the most beautiful smile on her wide open face.

They kissed there, in the morning room, and stayed to watch the sun illuminate the walls and listen to the solar choir, as they had done months ago on their first visit to this house.

"There are doors all over the world," Lenares said. "We can come here whenever we like."

He wanted to stay, but she led him on to find the room with the three chairs. It was much further away than he remembered, and she told him that, according to the Daughter, the rooms didn't stay in the same place. They walked through one room he didn't remember. It was filled with geometric shapes—enormous cubes and pyramids and spheres, and shapes even stranger—but none of them were in focus. No matter how he squinted, the edges of each shape remained blurred. The room troubled him, though it excited Lenares, but she did not linger. The Daughter, apparently, called them on.

He did not trust this Daughter. Lenares was very clever, but so trusting. Why would a captive lead her captor to such a place unless it contained a way for her to escape? He said this to Lenares as they scrambled through the Wave Room, but she shook her head.

"I'm forcing her to tell me. I've been asking her how to get to the House of the Gods ever since I captured her."

Her answer heartened him, but did not entirely deal with his unease.

Finally they arrived.

"Oh," Lenares said. Torve's breath caught in his throat.

The circular room had been destroyed. There was no sign of the three chairs, and the lake had vanished. A small sandy depression was all that remained of the site of the map of bronze.

"The whirlwind did this," Torve said, as he watched her face crumple with the realisation. "When it took us up out of Nomansland. The chairs and the map must have fallen with us into Raceme."

"We need to go back there," Lenares said, her voice strained. "Hire men to find the chairs and the map, and to bring the pieces back. I must see."

"No, Lenares. The Daughter is trying to sidetrack you."

I am not, a voice whispered. *Yes, you can recreate this place. But because it was destroyed, you can remake it to suit yourselves. In fashioning your own chairs, you will fashion yourselves as gods.*

"And you and the Son will take our place in the world. Lenares, why can't you see what she's doing?"

"I can," she said. "But I can keep her from doing it."

She had already moved away from him, searching for rocks with which to begin building her chair.

He took hold of her. "Please," he said. "We can come back here when the gods are vanquished. You said yourself that there are doors everywhere. Put it aside for a moment."

She looked into his eyes with such longing. He seized on it. "Can't we take some time for ourselves?"

"Yes," she said. She slipped an arm around his head and drew him close.

He had thought about this in the days before he lost her. If the chance ever came, he would fill his mind with only her. He would not see her as an experimental subject; would block the sights and sounds of his research from his memory and do his best to see beauty and not terror. Even if he struggled to succeed, he would give everything good of himself to her.

On the day she had been lost he'd thought their chance gone forever. But here she was again, and here was their chance, on the sandy floor of the House of the Gods.

And there it was that Dryman found them.

CHAPTER 22

DARK HEART

STELLA SWORE TO HERSELF. AT a word from Conal—the first words he'd spoken for days—the Falthans had abandoned their largely coastal path and plunged into the heart of the forest. His voice had told him Arathé and the Bhrudwans were in trouble. He'd not been especially convincing, but why else did they keep him with them, given his recent betrayals, if not to keep track of the others through his voice? Either disregard his warning and be rid of him, Heredrew had argued, or listen to him. After a protracted argument they had decided on the latter.

It soon became clear that Arathé was not in any particular difficulty. Indeed, she was also rushing into the forest, along with her fellow Bhrudwans, having fallen for the same ruse as the Falthans. They had made contact the previous afternoon, on the border of the inner lands of Patina Padouk, the place known, so Heredrew said, as Dark Heart. Each group had thought the other in trouble. Conal and Arathé compared notes and together tried to engage their mysterious magician in conversation, but they could not raise the treacherous voice. It therefore became a matter of urgency that they locate Captain Duon, the third of the voice-infested people. Heredrew was, rightly, not prepared to continue if it meant the three of them came together and attracted more activity of the gods.

After searching their immediate surroundings and finding no sign of the Amaqi party, the two groups had camped together last night. Their tales of the last few weeks had kept them up late into the evening.

The Falthan party had gratefully accepted the rest. Stella huddled next to the fire, body bent over her missing arm, one ear on the conversation. Heredrew had performed a combination of magical and field surgery on her stump, but, without the rest of the forearm and hand, had not been able to recreate it. Instead, he'd taught her how to produce an illusory hand. "One thing I am competent at," he'd said with a wry smile. She appreciated his trouble, but it seemed poor compensation for the loss. The pain was still severe, greater because of the shedding of immortal blood, but more significant than the pain was the knowledge she was marked in the same way he was.

"Perhaps an immortal can die," she had said to him. "Chop me up into sufficiently small pieces and burn them. You'll be rid of me, and it will be no great loss."

He ignored her self-pity. It would take her months if not years of practice before her illusory arm became even partially corporeal, he warned her. Just because she could see it did not mean she could use it for anything.

"Illusion works on the mind of the beholder," he had said. "Others, even those who know of your loss, will see a normal hand and arm, but you will not. It requires intense practice to convince yourself it is real, which is what is required for corporeality to be effective. I never thought to try it until I lost my second hand," he admitted.

Heredrew had also privately confided that he could have healed Conal's sight. "We had the ruins of his eye. Had it been you, Stella, I would have repaired the damage. But I thought it best that the priest not recover his full vision. If his eyes have served as windows for this unknown magician, better that they are shut. I confess I am tempted to give the man the symmetry he craves, but not in the way he wishes."

The priest suffered, and Stella was glad of it. His physical pain was underscored by his knowledge that his actions had endangered them all. He had expected to be put to death, and was surprised when Stella overruled an informal vote. She had been the only one to support him. But even she had run out of patience. He would serve them in one narrow area, the reporting of anything the voice said, and otherwise suffer himself to be led by the wishes of the party.

Sauxa had been the most vocal in his efforts to have the priest pay with his life. "He's played us all for fools," the old man said. "In Chardzou we'd string up anyone who gave away secrets to the Straux officials. It's about trust. Stupidity can be forgiven, which is why my son remains with us, but betrayal brings death."

Moralye had agreed. "We cannot allow one self-obsessed priest to jeopardise everything we are trying to do. He must die." She had glanced around the camp as she spoke, the look in her eyes that of the morally righteous. None of the doubt that curled around Stella like vines on a tree. "Give me your sharpest knife. I will do it."

Conal had begged and cried pardon with words fit to

break the hardest heart. He had given them his story, crying out all the time for the loss of his eye, emphasising his oppressed background, his confused feelings and his potential usefulness—each component designed to appeal to one or more of those judging him. In the end Stella could not condemn him; not when another like him, who had pleaded for understanding albeit in a rather more sophisticated fashion, remained unpunished in their midst. She merely pointed to Conal's usefulness as a pretext; a sop to her own conscience.

Robal said very little, seeming badly affected by the events at the Umerta steading. Even Kilfor could coax next to nothing from him. Stella worried for him. She found herself longing to take him aside, to see if she could help him in any way, but such things would only make matters more complicated still. And were Heredrew to find out . . .

They had decided to leave Phemanderac in Sayonae, with Moralye to nurse him, but the old *dominie* rallied himself and joined them. Stella had grave concerns about the sense of this, but she'd also doubted his ability to survive unaided in a strange town. *Better where I can see him*, she had decided. Privately she wondered if Heredrew lent him strength. Goodness knew, she would give him some of hers if only she knew how to do it. Another thing to ask Heredrew; another debt to add to the list.

If I'm going to live forever, she acknowledged, *perhaps I need to learn how to harness the magic loose in me*.

At first light—some indeterminate time after dawn—they rose, breakfasted, then crossed a river, using a rope tied there for the purpose, and set off warily into the jungle heartland.

*   *   *

"I warned you what would happen if you pursued this girl," said Dryman.

His hand was still buried in Torve's tunic where he had grabbed it to haul the Omeran up from the ground. The echoes of his voice rippled around the strange enclosure, and the onlookers, including Duon, found themselves momentarily distracted by the odd, whispery mutterings the sound seemed to call from the walls.

"But you didn't forbid it."

Duon found new admiration for the Omeran. He would have lost his water before this point, fearing what was to come, but Torve kept his gaze steady. His breeches were open and his manhood dangled free, but nonetheless he had an odd dignity about him.

The mercenary turned to his three porters. "Fetch me the largest stone you can carry. Don't go beyond this enclosure: you can't bring anything in here from the other rooms. Take your time. Chisel it from the wall if you have to. I want my servant to reflect on what is about to happen to him."

Lenares put a hand out, as though reaching for some invisible rope. Her drawers were around her knees and her tunic undone, but she seemed neither to notice nor care. "Tug, tug, tug!" she cried, or something similar. "Put a stop to this!"

"She won't listen to you, little halfwit," Dryman said, smiling. "Not while I stand unveiled in this room. She is trapped beyond the worldwall, rendered ineffective courtesy of your misguided animal cunning, while I am here by invitation of this man I possess. While this remains the case, I can dampen what little power she can exercise in this place. She won't dare challenge me."

"You called me friend," Torve said.

"And you, friend, went and rutted with a halfwit, one I thought we were rid of. Look at you. Omerans mate only when their masters tell them. You know this. Not only did you wriggle through the net I placed about you to keep you pliant and obedient, you took up with another animal!"

"Why is that worse than if he'd fornicated with a human?" Duon heard himself ask. His voice sounded angry, but in his heart he was frightened of the man with arrow-shafts in his chest. There were things worse than death . . .

"It is worse because I say it is!" the man snapped, not even turning his head. "Because I established the laws three thousand years ago to keep the races pure! Their behaviour threatens everything!" He turned and sought the porters. "Where is that stone?"

"You said not to hurry," one of them said, very unwisely.

"HURRY NOW!"

The words pressed in on Duon's ears. Guiltily he realised he'd escaped the god-Emperor's wrath. He watched it descend on the unfortunate porter.

"Please!"

"Let my brother live!"

The shouts were ignored. The speaker fell to the ground, hands on his ears, but the blood seeped through his fingers regardless and leaked onto the pale sand.

The reason for the mercenary's sudden anxiety revealed itself when a near-dozen people filed into the enclosure. Duon recognised the Falthans, the tall man at their head.

"It would be wise to leave the boy alone," the tall man said. Heredrew, Duon thought, recalling the name.

Duon was unsure which boy was meant: the one dying on the sand or the one in Dryman's grasp.

"He is mine and beyond your power," the mercenary said.

"He is that," Heredrew agreed. "I'm asking you. Appealing to you."

Dryman released the Omeran, who fell to the ground as though boneless.

"No," he said. "I'm doing something I ought to have had done some time ago. Take your people and leave this place, unless you are prepared to see their blood join his on the sand."

"And this is how you would live in the world? How you would deal with the weak and vulnerable? Are you trying to raise up an opposition to yourself and your sister, or is it merely a by-product of your towering arrogance? If you would have a place among us, you cannot behave like this."

"Leave," Dryman said, his word hard as rock, heavy as a building, sharp as the edge of a blade. The Falthans had no choice but to back away and file out of the canyon.

Duon had hoped Heredrew possessed the strength to intervene, but either he did not or he chose not to use it. The latter, possibly. Why, after all, should the fate of an Amaqi servant concern a Falthan?

Why should it concern you? Duon barely noticed the voice's arrival, and did not acknowledge it.

The last two brothers fought with a stone half-embedded in the rock wall, but it would clearly be some time before they broke it free. Dryman beckoned with one hand and the wall exploded in a shower of rock and sand. The stone flew through the air, fetching one of the brothers a clip on the side of his head, and landed at the mercenary's feet.

The two porters scrambled over the debris and made their way to Dryman's side. Pasty-faced and dull-eyed, they seemed more automaton than alive.

"Hold him," commanded the mercenary. "You on the shoulders, you on the legs. Force his legs apart."

Torve began to struggle, but Dryman put a hand on his servant's forehead and the fight seemed to drain from him.

"In the absence of a surgeon this will have to do," he said. "You are lucky, my pet. Anyone else attempting this would kill you. However, with me you will lose exactly what I want you to lose."

"No!" cried Lenares, throwing herself on the mercenary. He swatted her away: her body flew impossibly high, landed in a heap and flopped limply beside the small depression in the ground. She moaned once and went still.

He drew a small knife and held it up to the light, then breathed on the blade. Duon recognised it as the man's "research" knife. At a command the porters lowered Torve until his rear lay astride the stone, then pulled down his breeches. Dryman grasped the Omeran's member and pulled it taut, then raised the knife and sliced it free, along with the balls. Torve shrieked, then fainted. Blood spurted in a great flow, but the mercenary passed a hand over the wound. Duon saw the hand glow briefly white, and heard the hiss as the wound was cauterised, then blanched at the stench of cooked meat.

He'd seen this done once in the desert, an attempt to save a soldier from cock-rot, but it had not been successful. Of course, the surgeon had not been a god.

"No!" cried a cracked voice. "Umu, I set you free! Heal him!"

Lenares' hand twitched, as though letting go of a string, and in answer a manic laugh rang out across the enclosure.

"You wish me to contend with my brother for your lover's manhood?" the voice shrieked, pressed full with glee. "What will haunt you forever, little Lenares, is the knowledge I could have helped him—but I chose not to! And now I take my freedom!"

The voice came from a shadowed part of the room. Duon could make out a misty form, feminine and curved, with long hair unbound and head tilted back, as though taken with uncontrollable laughter.

"Brother," the voice said in acknowledgment, and the head dipped. "You make progress, I see. Yet you remain soft-hearted. Why keep the Omeran alive?"

Dryman raised his eyes from the damage he had done. "Because he is an anomaly. I remain curious about him. And he may yet hold the key to my research."

The Daughter laughed. "You continue to tinker with the gates of death. I, on the other hand, am well prepared to step through them at the end of a long and triumphant life. That makes me more powerful than you."

"And more ruthless," her brother replied, seemingly unconcerned by her boast. "What do you intend to do with your erstwhile captor?"

"Oh, she will suffer before she dies. And I do not have to raise a finger to achieve it; you have seen to that. You cannot imagine how profoundly her lover's loss will affect her. Far more than it will affect him, in fact."

Her voice grew stronger by the moment, her form more

substantial. "May I ask you a favour?" she said to her brother.

"Anything within reason," he replied.

"The trophy in your hand," she said. "I would like to have it. I have the perfect setting for it."

He nodded, as though the request was a reasonable one. "As you wish," he said. "But do not allow yourself to be deceived. You and I will face each other some time soon. One of us will rule as the Father once did, will be made whole again, dwelling completely within the world yet anchored in the void beyond the wall. Until that day we will continue to cooperate, as we have done."

"Why not end it now?" asked the Daughter. "Two-thirds of them are here, with the other third close by. Why not destroy them? They are strong, but even the strongest could not stand against our combined might. Recall how we dealt with the Crynon Magickers. They used the power of Ilix against us, but it did not avail them."

"These people are not as they appear to you. Sister, you are ever a fool. In your haste to inflict death and destruction you never consider the long game. I have already given you my reason for keeping the Omeran alive; rest assured I have equally valid reasons to see the others keep drawing breath, for now. Little Umu, if you wish to kill someone, why not try your strength against me?"

He flicked a finger and instantly he was encased in a bubble of what looked like water. Immediately it began to grow, forcing those nearby away from him.

"Come, sister, our power is enhanced in this place. Raise your hand against mine. Let us see if cunning and desperation can defeat strength and wisdom."

The Daughter's figure wavered as the bubble drew

slowly nearer. Some distance short of where Duon stood it stopped and held firm. The membrane looked as though it could be pierced with a pin, but Duon was not prepared to touch it.

Neither was the Daughter, it seemed, even though the Son's goading had angered her.

The god smiled. "You will leave now," he said pleasantly. "We will discuss this further elsewhere. This is my place and my time. Pleasant as a discussion with you always is, this one is at an end. Go and recover your strength."

"You do not command me, brother. Yet I shall leave you to your doctoring and your research. And when you travel through the gates of death for yourself, I will be there to watch you. Perhaps you will be good enough to tell me of what you see there, so I might avoid your failure."

He took a step towards her and raised a hand, but did not attack. Instead, he threw a small, bloody object in her direction. Duon watched it arc through the air, spattering drops as it went, until it was swallowed in the shadows.

"It will make a suitable trophy," she said. "I will think of little Lenares whenever I see it." Her fragile form wavered, then dissolved.

Dryman picked up his servant, who remained unconscious, legs akimbo, wearing a great red scar where his manhood had once rested. "My servant and I will now leave," the mercenary announced. "You will not try to interfere with our passing. And you will not attempt to track us with any of the devices you employ."

He turned his head to where Lenares had fallen: the girl had hauled herself to a sitting position. "To you I offer a special caution. You are alive only because the Daughter wishes to exact a full measure of retribution for her imprisonment—and, I confess, because I wish you to escape her grasp; a reward you deserve for providing me with the entertainment of watching her enslaved. But if you attempt your number-working on me, it will cost you your life and the lives of all those you consider precious. And remember, I hold what remains of your lover in my hands. Your word is all that stands between him and death. Do you give it? Do you promise you will not interfere? Or must I commence slicing away other parts of this animal?"

"No, don't hurt him," Lenares said, sobbing where she sat. "Please. I give you a promise that I will do nothing to harm you. Just let him live."

"Good. You are a truth-sayer and a truth-keeper. You will not break your word, just as he cannot disobey me. You are both now trapped, and my Father's plan is stymied."

He laid the Omeran down on the sand and drew himself up to his full height. As he spoke he seemed to tower over everyone else in the enclosure.

"Do you hear me, Father? I have taken your weapons and blunted them! Did you think I wouldn't recognise your finger's print on these foolish dupes? You are defeated, old man. I SAID, DO YOU HEAR ME?"

The words were not shouted, but they carried incredible weight, impacting on their hearers' ears as though they were the tolling of a bell.

"What is happening? What is he doing? What was that scream?" Sauxa plied Stella with questions enough for everyone in the party.

She waved her hand behind her back, not wanting to turn around. "Hush," she said. "The mercenary has done something to his servant. Cut something. I hope it was not—oh, Most High, it was."

"What? Tell us!" The old man had no taste for suspense, and a lack of patience to boot.

"He's castrated poor Torve."

"His servant," Sauxa said dismissively. "But he'll not survive without a sawbones to patch him up. I've gelded many a colt; I could help."

"It was more than a gelding, Sauxa," Stella said. "The blade took everything. I doubt there is much you could do for him. Nor do I think the mercenary would let you."

Heredrew eased his way into the narrow passageway, his shoulder pressed hard against hers. "Dryman is much more than he appears to be," he said. "Even the name is ironic. I fear he has been deceiving everyone. The power he used to drive us out of the room was immense."

"Your equivalent, then?" Phemanderac questioned. "The overlord of Elamaq?"

"Perhaps," Heredrew replied. "If he is not, I do not want to meet his master."

"What is happening now?" the man from Chardzou wanted to know. "My eyes aren't so good any more. Tell me."

"Hush. Someone else has entered the enclosure. Someone very powerful." Heredrew shook his head in denial or disgust.

"No one went past us," Stella said wryly.

"I believe both the Son and the Daughter are manifested in front of us. No wonder I cannot force my way back in."

Conal cleared his throat, then spoke. But the voice that came from his mouth was not his. "We are very nearly defeated," it said.

Both Stella and Heredrew snapped their heads around in shock; instantly Stella knew who spoke to them. As did Heredrew, by the look of hatred on his face. The others drew back.

"Is this the voice in Conal's head?" Phemanderac asked. "The hidden magician?"

"No," said Stella.

"Who then?"

"I don't . . . want to say." *I'm frightened.*

Conal's mouth spoke again. "I have a request to make of Stella and of Kannwar. I have no right to expect more of two who have suffered so much, but only you can accomplish my deception."

A pause, punctuated by the priest's heavy breathing, as though he tried to fight the possession of his throat.

"He's served as a conduit for that voice before," Heredrew said. "It was not welcome then, and clearly it is not welcome now."

"I wish to trick my son," the voice said. "Will you assist me? Will both of you lend me yourselves for just a while?"

"You've asked this of me before," said Heredrew, "when I was far too young to know what it would cost. Yet I knew enough to refuse you. What makes you think I will answer differently this time?"

"I don't think," said the voice candidly. "I only ask. Remember, I always have other plans. But I choose the plan that offers most benefit to all who participate in it."

"Benefit?" Heredrew cried bitterly. "Your plan was for me to become a freak, a boy despised by his peers. And it happened, even though I tried to resist. Where is the choice, Most High?"

"Must we always have this conversation, Kannwar? You have exacted your revenge on me and on those I love many times over my precipitate action. But for some people, chosen by birth or circumstance to be pivots on which the world turns, choice is subsumed by need."

"Your need."

The voice did not deny it.

"I will assist you," Stella said.

"No, Stella!" Heredrew said. "Not like this. You have no idea what it will cost you!"

She turned to face him, face twitching, then struck him a ringing blow across the cheek with her open hand. "What it will cost? How could it cost as much as the price I'm paying for your assistance all those years ago?" Her voice softened. "Drew, how can you talk of selfishness and need, when everything you do serves your own purposes?"

He stared at her strangely, then down at the hand she'd used to strike him. "Look at your hand," he said.

"Oh, I did, didn't I. With my illusory hand." She smiled. "I must have wanted to hurt you so much the desire to strike you overcame my doubt."

"Good," he said, smiling back at her. "I will endeavour to engineer many more such occasions then."

"Serving him together could be such an occasion," she said.

They both smiled.

A reply came to the god-Emperor's challenge.

"We hear you, Keppia. And we are reminded why we must oppose you, of why our long efforts over thousands of years must succeed."

Movement at the entrance to the enclosure, then someone walked in. The young woman Stella, followed by Heredrew. There was no sign of the other Falthans. Neither of the two was the source of the voice, Duon realised, yet it seemed they both spoke, and the sound the voice made was a combination of her cool, pleasant tone and his well-spoken, clipped one. A sound of compelling authority.

The mercenary acted with incredible swiftness. The bubble around him, which had shrunk to little more than the size of his body, sprang out again to encompass at least half the enclosure.

"Have you come to do battle, ancient one?"

"No," was the reply. The hybrid voice sent chills of fear down Duon's spine. He could hear age in it, and responsibility, and a desperate weariness.

And, inside his head, the magician listened.

"No, we have not come to challenge you, not yet. But you must know we are involved, and we have planned longer and with more care for these days than you can imagine. The very fact we awaited you here indicates we foresaw your actions. Keppia, it is not too late to return to the void. Or, if you desire it, we can give you release, the freedom you crave."

The mercenary's eyes bulged. "Do not patronise me! Release, indeed! Freedom for you to pursue your own goal of subjugating everyone under your smothering hand of benevolence. You are vulnerable here, Father, and I mean to make you pay for your mistake!"

He flung out an arm and drew up sand from the ground, then breathed on it with a breath of fire, fashioning six long spears of what looked to Duon like glass. *Just like they manufacture glass back in Talamaq*, he thought, somewhat irrelevantly. The spears' tips were sharp, their centres hollow.

"Seek!" the mercenary shouted, and the slivers of glass arrowed from him towards where the two Falthans stood, hand in hand. As the spears approached the edge of his bubble it vanished.

The Falthans did not move.

"We always have a plan, Son," said the voice, and the two bodies changed, becoming something else: shapes of fire, with water for veins. The spears passed through without so much as a sound, then vanished into the wall of the enclosure. The two Falthans resumed their true shapes. Or had Duon just witnessed their true form?

"No!" Dryman shouted.

"Have you forgotten the way this enclosure works?" the gentle voice asked the mercenary. "I remember it. I remember playing here with you, Keppia, when you were a child, before you went out into the world. Tossing stones against the wall, seeing who could throw the highest. Remember what happened to those stones, Keppia?"

Duon saw the spears materialise on the far side of the enclosure. He saw them continue their journey as though nothing had interrupted them. Heading straight for the unwitting Dryman.

"I do not want to remember!" the mercenary shouted, as the glass needles pierced him. "I choose to remember my hatred of you! I REJECT YOUR LOVE!"

The needles slipped through his body as if through water, emerging from his torso, his neck and his mouth, to fall spent at his feet.

"Aaah!" the mercenary cried. "You have killed him!"

The body changed before Duon's horrified eyes, its

features altering subtly. This was a man he'd never seen before, wholly the Emperor of Elamaq, exposed without his golden mask. The Son had left him, gone back to the void on the far side of the hole.

"No," said the Emperor in his own voice, thick with blood. "No."

That was all: two puzzled exclamations of defiance against the black tide rolling through him. And then he fell to the ground, dead.

Stella and Heredrew walked slowly towards the body, but Torve was there before them, having crawled across the sand from where he had fallen.

"What do you see?" he shouted, his mouth pressed down against his master's ear. "What do you see? Are there gates, great one?" He shook the body. "Do those you killed await you there? Tell me! Is death the end? TELL ME WHAT YOU SEE!"

He collapsed on the body, crying like a child.

extras

orbit

meet the author

Russell Kirkpatrick's love of literature and a chance encounter with fantasy novels as a teenager opened up a vast number of possibilities to him. The idea that he could marry storytelling and mapmaking (his other passion) into one project grabbed him and wouldn't let go. He lives in New Zealand with his wife and two children. Find out more about Russell Kirkpatrick at www.russell kirkpatrick.com.

introducing

If you enjoyed DARK HEART,
look out for

BEYOND THE WALL OF TIME

Book Three of the Broken Man Trilogy
by Russell Kirkpatrick

PROLOGUE

HUSK CANNOT REMEMBER what it is like to think with any kind of clarity. Seven decades of unrelenting pain have created a permanent cloud in his mind. He constantly has to fight off a desire to go to sleep and never wake up, continually resisting the creeping lassitude that threatens to engulf him. Even now, despite his link to the unlimited power beyond the wall around the world and the freedom from pain it brings, he struggles to focus on the important things happening in a remote valley a few hundred leagues away.

Part of Husk's trouble is he does not know the location of the House of the Gods. Normally this would not matter: his magical contact with his three spikes does not depend on his knowing where they are. But designing a strategy certainly does. The place on which his attention is focused, in which his hosts now contend with the gods, is to be found at perhaps half a dozen locations in the world at once, and yet fully in none of them: a paradox of the kind of which the gods are distressingly fond. Part of the perplexing nature of the House of the Gods.

So he preoccupies himself with questions. Will the travellers—his spikes and his enemies—emerge into Patina

Padouk, the land from which they entered this version of the House of the Gods? Or will they appear somewhere else? Husk cannot lay his plans until he knows. Trouble is, with all the fog in his head he fears he may well have missed some essential clue.

Husk hates not knowing things.

He needs to know where everyone is because he must decide whether to confront his enemies here, in the Undying Man's fortress of Andratan, or there, wherever *there* might be. He wishes to destroy them in a way that pays them back for his years of suffering, while of course risking himself as little as possible. Best of all would be a public triumph, perhaps at Andratan itself. Himself in the Tower of Farsight, the Destroyer and his curséd consort writhing out their agony in ways that reduce the memories of his own pain to inconsequentiality. It is no longer enough for him merely to remain alive. Not even enough to be immortal, the rich prize now almost in his grasp. To truly live he must destroy them both. No, more accurately they must be destroyed again and again. He must be able to return whenever the mood takes him, to watch them suffer. A private gallery in which the destruction of Stella and Kannwar is the main installation, that is what he needs.

He wonders just how many centuries it will take to cancel out his own hurt. If his hurting will ever end.

Events in the House of the Gods are seriously limiting his own supply of power from beyond the Wall around the world. The three gods all draw deeply from the hole in the world, that blessed opening first made when the Son and Daughter drove their Father out, and their combined power is squeezing his small, unnoticed conduit until it is now almost shut off. Nevertheless, his small link continues to restore him. Husk no longer feels mortal pain, but he remembers it. He has grown new limbs to replace those seared away by the Destroyer's magic, but their fragility means he cannot yet walk on them. He now breathes air unmixed with his own blood. But his great plans, his transformation to godhood, the elimination of all who might possibly hurt him and the subjugation of everyone else, await a respite in the hostilities between the gods.

In the meantime Lenares is the great danger. She seeks to close the hole in the world, despite having forged her own conduit of power through it. Ironic, this, given how desperately she is trying to close the hole. She managed to ensnare the Daughter by tying something—Husk is not exactly sure what it is she tied—to someone beyond the Wall. Husk does not know who, though Lenares herself thinks it is her dead foster mother. Her use of mathematics was flawed, but it worked nonetheless. Lenares has tapped into her own source of power. She has drawn on it unwittingly, helping her to capture the Daughter for a time; and, worryingly, may draw on it again, interfering with his plans. It is unlikely she will learn how to harness her power, especially given the logical, mathematical cast to her mind, and its associated limits. However unlikely, Husk cannot risk her interference. He must find some way to kill her. No elaborate revenge, no desire to inflict pain; Husk just wants an end to her.

Another question nags at him. Has he any further need for his spikes? Arathé, Conal and Duon have served him well but, unless his new-found power is totally severed, he no longer needs them. In fact, he expends energy keeping hold of them that he could better use in strengthening himself. And it is not as though they are of much use to him. Conal is blinded in one eye and in all his opinions, and his recent possession by the Father has rendered him untrustworthy. Imagine if the Father seized the lad's mind when Husk was in possession of it! Arathé is becoming increasingly wary of the voice in her head, and is devising ever-cleverer ways of keeping him out. And Duon is trying to deceive him. A futile attempt—Husk can read the minds of those he has spiked—but it makes the Amaqi captain, of whom he had high hopes, less dependable.

Husk had supposed the huanu stone would aid him in defeating the Destroyer, but now wonders even at this. The stone is now as much a risk to himself as it is to the Destroyer, and it is not yet in his hands. The ignorant fisherman Noetos carries it, not a man known for listening to anyone and therefore not easy to deceive, even by Arathé his daughter.

The same logic can be applied to the immortal's blood he had planned to drain from Stella. Not yet in his possession, and just as likely could be used to promote someone else to the ranks of the deathless. With his own conduit to the raw power beyond the Wall, Husk need not risk the problematic—and painful—immortality offered by the blood. Maybe he needs to keep the blood and the stone away from Andratan. The only difficulty with this line of thought is his inability to prevent them being brought north regardless. He has put all this in motion, and now it appears he is powerless to stop it.

Husk frowns with newly-restored facial muscles. Now there are two alternate ways to become immortal his options have increased, so he ought not to be feeling the anxiety as strongly as he does. Thump, thump, thump goes his heart. His blood hisses through his veins and threatens to erupt from the tips of his fingers. The bubble and fizz of fearful thoughts must be resisted or they will overman him. But it is so hard, despite the fact he is familiar with despair. Desperation has shaped him over the foggy decades of pain, yet is so much sharper now he has real hope.

But he is no longer tempted to give up, to crawl away to some dark corner of the Destroyer's dungeon and die. He reminds himself that, due to his new power, he is Husk no longer. He will put his self-imposed name aside and take his old name back. Deorc of Jasweyah. No, Deorc the Great. Far more suitable.

Husk laughs at himself, at the caricature of evil he seems about to become. All he needs is the cackle and he'd be the legendary Jasweyan Witch-Hag reborn. No matter: they will make fireside tales about him, and he will be around to hear them. He'll make them forget about their folk-villains, the Witch-Hag and the Undying Man both. They'll have no need to fear anything but him. And oh, he will work hard to ensure they fear him.

He licks his lips, tasting the victory about to be his; and, though he knows it to be a cliché, cannot resist the laughter bubbling up from within him. The thick walls of Andratan ring with the sound, and the denizens of the fortress pause in sudden fright.

Their fear is balm to Husk's scarred soul.

CHAPTER 1

BLOOD ON THE SAND

THERE IS A SILENCE FAR DEEPER than the mere absence of sound. It can settle on a scene despite, say, the thin wail of a woman weeping. Even the laboured breathing of someone in severe pain does little to disturb such stillness. This silence is a calm, black pool of quiet. It is the sound of shock.

Noetos remembered all too well what such silence sounded like. He had experienced it in the aftermath of his slaughter of the Neherian gentry. It was a stunned disbelief at what had happened coupled with an expectation that one would soon wake up to find nothing of the sort had happened. But, of course, it had.

He watched from a distance as his travelling companions stared at each other, saying nothing. They moved in slow motion, hands twitching with the need to do something but not knowing what. The fisherman had been nothing but an observer to the events leading to one man's castration and the death of the one who wielded the knife, but he could help with restoring calm. Guidance, order, leadership were what was needed. He made his way towards the tight knot of people.

"He is gone." The one-eyed priest's voice was a ripple of sound breaking the deep silence as though a pebble had been dropped in a pool.

"Yes," said Duon, looking up, his hand on Dryman's unmoving chest. "He's gone, all praise to the gods." This was followed by a grimace, no doubt as he realised anew just whom he was praising.

Noetos strode across the sandy floor of the enclosure, and his two children followed him. Three piles made up of enormous slabs of rock were the only interruption to the smooth floor, apart from the figures gathered around the dead, the injured and the maimed. And a smaller rock soaked in blood.

The thought came to him that, of the three groups drawn together in the contention of the gods, his had fared the worst. Gawl and Dagla were dead. Of the miners, only Tumar and Seren remained. Sautea and Mustar were still with him, but they had come north because of Arathé, not him, and might well leave at any moment. Omiy the alchemist had betrayed him, Bregor had left him and Noetos had not succeeded in getting Cylene to join them. True, the Amaqi had just been reduced from four to three with the death of Dryman, but that had been their only loss. *If you don't count the loss of thirty thousand soldiers,* he reminded himself. *Even I haven't failed that spectacularly.*

The Falthans had done best. All eight remained alive, though Stella had apparently lost an arm—she used some form of magic to disguise this, but it was only intermittently effective—and the priest an eye. *She hasn't had whirlwinds and Neherians to cope with.* He frowned. *But now we have all to deal with angry gods and mysterious voices in people's heads, as well as blood and death at human hands.*